新制多益
NEW TOEIC

閱讀

Reading

滿分奪金演練
1000 題練出黃金應試力

作者 PAGODA Academy　譯者 劉嘉珮／蘇裕承／關亭薇

嚴選完整 10 回精華全真考題，一次掌握多益閱讀必考題型和常見陷阱。

收錄多元文章類型，有效提升臨場反應、培養直覺作答力。

附試題中譯，幫助釐清考點，累積奪金硬實力！

目錄

何謂多益？

TOEIC 為 Test of English for International Communication 的縮寫，針對英語非母語人士所設計，測驗其在日常生活或國際業務上所具備的英語應用能力。

該測驗的評量重點在於「與他人溝通的能力」（communication ability），著重英語的運用與其功能層面，測驗「運用英語的能力」，而非單純針對「英語知識」出題。

1979 年美國 ETS（Educational Testing Service）研發出 TOEIC，而後在全世界 160 個國家中獲得超過 14,000 個機構採用，作為升遷、外派、人才招募之依據，全球每年超過 700 萬人次報考。

›› 多益測驗題型

	Part	測驗題型		題數	時間	分數
聽力 Listening Comprehension	1	照片描述		6	45 分鐘	495 分
	2	應答問題		25		
	3	簡短對話		39		
	4	簡短獨白		30		
閱讀 Reading Comprehension	5	句子填空		30	75 分鐘	495 分
	6	段落填空		16		
	7	閱測	單篇閱讀	29		
			多篇閱讀	25		
總計				200	約 150 分鐘 ✻	990 分

✻ 含基本資料及問卷填寫

多益各大題簡介

PART 5　INCOMPLETE SENTENCE 句子填空

Part 5 的考題會在一句話中挖一個空格，要求從四個選項中選出一個最適當的詞彙或片語填入，總共 30 題。

題數	共 30 題（第 101 至第 130 題）
考題類型	〔詞類變化題〕先確認該空格置於句中的位置，再從四個選項中選出一個最適當的詞性或形態填入。詞類變化題約會出現 10 題，只要具備判斷詞性的基礎，就能順利解題，因此屬於難度稍低的考題。
	〔詞彙題〕此類考題考的是詞彙的正確使用方式。選項會出現四個詞性相同的相異詞彙，在 Part 5 中屬於難度偏高的考題。30 題中至少會出現一半以上的詞彙題，出題比例逐年增加。
	〔文法題〕考題包含「掌握句型結構」、「判斷片語或子句的差別」、「分辨介系詞、連接詞與副詞的差異」、「空格應填入連接詞時，判斷應填入名詞子句、形容詞子句或副詞子句的連接詞」等。一般會出現 6 至 7 題，除了難度偏低的考題之外，也會出現高難度考題。

詞類變化題
»

101. If our request for new computer equipment receives -------, we are going to purchase 10 extra monitors.

    (A) approval　　　　　(B) approved

    (C) approve　　　　　(D) approves

詞彙題
»

102. After being employed at a Tokyo-based technology firm for two decades, Ms. Mayne ------- to Vancouver to start her own IT company.

    (A) visited　　　　　(B) returned

    (C) happened　　　　　(D) compared

文法題
»

103. ------- the demand for the PFS-2x smartphone, production will be tripled next quarter.

    (A) Even if　　　　　(B) Just as

    (C) As a result of　　　　　(D) Moreover

答案 101. (A) 102. (B) 103. (C)

PART 6 TEXT COMPLETION 段落填空

Part 6 有四篇文章，每篇文章有四道題目，總共 16 題。考題要求填入最適當的詞彙、片語或句子，近似於 Part 5 和 Part 7 的考題類型。

題數	**四篇文章，共 16 題（第 131 至第 146 題）**
文章類型	說明書、信件、電子郵件、報導、公告、引導文、廣告、備忘錄等
考題類型	〔**詞類變化題**〕先確認該空格置於句中的位置，再從四個選項中選出一個最適當的詞性或形態填入。與 Part 5 的考題類型相同。16 道題中約莫出現 3 至 4 題。 〔**詞彙題**〕要求從四個選項中選出意思最為適當的詞彙。需先掌握上下文意，才能順利解題，因此難度略高於 Part 5 的詞彙題。一般會出現 5 至 6 題。 〔**文法題**〕考的是對於句子結構的掌握程度。該類考題在 Part 6 中的出題頻率較低，但是難度遠高於 Part 5。16 道題中約會出現 1 至 2 題。 〔**句子插入題**〕與 Part 7 的考題相同，需掌握整篇文章的脈絡。根據上下文，從四個選項中選出最適合填入空格的句子，為難度最高的考題。每篇文章出 1 題，一共為 4 題。

Questions 131-134 refer to the following e-mail.

To: sford@etnnet.com
From: customersupport@interhostptimes.ca
Date: July 1
Subject: Re: Your Subscription

Congratulations on becoming a reader of *International Hospitality Times*. __131.__ the plan you have subscribed to, you will not only have unlimited access to our online content, but you will also receive our hard copy edition each month. If you wish to __132.__ your subscription preferences, contact our Customer Support Center at +28 07896 325422. Most __133.__ may also make updates to their accounts on our Web site at www.interhosptimes.ca. Please note that due to compatibility issues, it may not be possible for customers in certain countries to access their accounts online. __134.__ Your business is greatly appreciated.

International Hospitality Times

文法題
>>

131. (A) Besides
(B) As if
(C) Under
(D) Prior to

詞彙題
>>

132. (A) purchase
(B) modify
(C) collect
(D) inform

詞類變化題
>>

133. (A) subscribe (B) subscriptions
(C) subscribers (D) subscribing

句子插入題
>>

134. (A) We have branches in over 30 countries around the globe.
(B) We provide online content that includes Web extras and archives.
(C) We are working to make this service available to all readers soon.
(D) We would like to remind you that your contract expires this month.

答案 131. (C) 132. (B) 133. (C) 134. (C)

5

PART 7 READING COMPREHENSION
閱讀理解

Part 7 考的是閱讀文章後，針對該文章對應的題目（2 至 5 題），選出適當的答案。當中涵蓋各式各樣的文章類型，並分成單篇閱讀、雙篇閱讀與多篇閱讀題。

題數	共 54 題（第 147 至第 200 題）➡	單篇閱讀：10 篇文章，共 19 題 雙篇閱讀：2 篇文章，共 10 題 多篇閱讀：3 篇文章，共 15 題
文章類型	信件、電子郵件、廣告、公告、備忘錄、報導、導覽、網頁（公司或產品介紹、活動簡介、客戶使用評論）、請款單據、收據、簡訊、線上聊天文等。	
考題類型	• 詢問主旨或目的　　　• 相關細節題　　　• 暗示或推論題 • 確認事實與否題　　　• 同義詞考題　　　• 掌握說話者意圖題 • 句子插入題	

Questions 151-152 refer to the following text message chain.

Naijia Kuti

My bus to Ibadan was canceled due to engine problems, and all other buses to that city are full. I don't know if I can give my presentation at the history conference. What should I do?　12:02 P.M.

12:04 P.M.　Not to worry. I'll come pick you up in my car.　**Adebiyi Achebe**

Naijia Kuti

I appreciate it! My seminar starts at 5 P.M. As long as we depart from Lagos by 1:30, I'll be able to make it on time.　12:05 P.M.

Naijia Kuti

12:07 P.M.　Where should I go?　**Adebiyi Achebe**

Naijia Kuti

In front of La Pointe Restaurant, near Terminal Rodoviario. Call me when you're getting close.　12:08 P.M.

掌握說話者意圖題 ≫

151. At 12:04 P.M., what does Mr. Achebe most likely mean when he writes, "Not to worry"?
(A) He has a solution to Ms. Kuti's problem.
(B) He can reschedule a presentation.
(C) He knows another bus will arrive soon.
(D) He is happy to cover Ms. Kuti's shift.

相關細節題 ≫

152. What is implied about Ms. Kuti?
(A) She has a meeting at a restaurant.
(B) She is going to be late for a seminar.
(C) She plans to pick up a client at 1:30 P.M.
(D) She is within driving distance of a conference.

Questions 158-160 refer to the following Web page.

http://www.sdayrealestate.com/listing18293

Looking for a new home for your family? This house, located on 18293 Winding Grove, was remodeled last month. It features 2,500 square feet of floor space, with 5,000 square feet devoted to a gorgeous backyard. Also included is a 625 square feet garage that can comfortably fit two mid-sized vehicles —[1]—. Located just a five-minute drive from the Fairweather Metro Station, this property allows for easy access to the downtown area, while providing plenty of room for you and your family. —[2]—. A serene lake is just 100–feet walk away from the house. —[3]—. A 15 percent down payment is required to secure the property. —[4]—. For more detailed information or to arrange a showing, please email Jerry@sdayrealestate.com.

相關細節題
»

158. How large is the parking space?
(A) 100 square feet
(B) 625 square feet
(C) 2,500 square feet
(D) 5,000 square feet

確認事實與否題
»

159. What is NOT stated as an advantage of the property?
(A) It has a spacious design.
(B) It has been recently renovated.
(C) It is in a quiet neighborhood.
(D) It is near public transportation.

句子插入題
»

160. In which of the positions marked [1], [2], [3], and [4] does the following sentence best belong?
"A smaller amount may be accepted, depending on the buyer's financial situation."
(A) [1]
(B) [2]
(C) [3]
(D) [4]

答案 158. (B) 159. (C) 160. (D)

學習計畫表

雙週計畫表

DAY 1	DAY 2	DAY 3	DAY 4	DAY 5
TEST 01 設定時間作答 計算分數並參閱詳解	**TEST 02** 設定時間作答 計算分數並參閱詳解	**TEST 03** 設定時間作答 計算分數並參閱詳解	**TEST 04** 設定時間作答 計算分數並參閱詳解	**TEST 05** 設定時間作答 計算分數並參閱詳解

DAY 6	DAY 7	DAY 8	DAY 9	DAY 10
TEST 06 設定時間作答 計算分數並參閱詳解	**TEST 07** 設定時間作答 計算分數並參閱詳解	**TEST 08** 設定時間作答 計算分數並參閱詳解	**TEST 09** 設定時間作答 計算分數並參閱詳解	**TEST 10** 設定時間作答 計算分數並參閱詳解

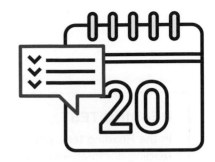

四週計畫表

DAY 1	DAY 2	DAY 3	DAY 4	DAY 5
TEST 01 設定時間作答 計算分數並參閱 詳解	**複習** TEST 01	**TEST 02** 設定時間作答 計算分數並參閱 詳解	**複習** TEST 02	**TEST 03** 設定時間作答 計算分數並參閱 詳解

DAY 6	DAY 7	DAY 8	DAY 9	DAY 10
複習 TEST 03	**TEST 04** 設定時間作答 計算分數並參閱 詳解	**複習** TEST 04	**TEST 05** 設定時間作答 計算分數並參閱 詳解	**複習** TEST 05

DAY 11	DAY 12	DAY 13	DAY 14	DAY 15
TEST 06 設定時間作答 計算分數並參閱 詳解	**複習** TEST 06	**TEST 07** 設定時間作答 計算分數並參閱 詳解	**複習** TEST 07	**TEST 08** 設定時間作答 計算分數並參閱 詳解

DAY 16	DAY 17	DAY 18	DAY 19	DAY 20
複習 TEST 08	**TEST 09** 設定時間作答 計算分數並參閱 詳解	**複習** TEST 09	**TEST 10** 設定時間作答 計算分數並參閱 詳解	**複習** TEST 10

READING TEST

In the Reading test, you will read a variety of texts and answer several different types of reading comprehension questions. The entire Reading test will last 75 minutes. There are three parts, and directions are given for each part. You are encouraged to answer as many questions as possible within the time allowed.

You must mark your answers on the separate answer sheet. Do not write your answers in your test book.

PART 5

Directions: A word or phrase is missing in each of the sentences below. Four answer choices are given below each sentence. Select the best answer to complete the sentence. Then mark the letter (A), (B), (C), or (D) on your answer sheet.

101. Thirty percent of Packerville businesses operate ------- Broadway Avenue.

(A) efficiently
(B) along
(C) sideways
(D) apart

102. Most responders to the internet survey are familiar with Freezey Yogurt, and 65 percent of ------- have purchased it at least once.

(A) them
(B) theirs
(C) themselves
(D) they

103. Companies expanding into new ------- frequently encounter difficulty because they do not understand the local culture.

(A) market
(B) markets
(C) marketed
(D) marketable

104. The Purchasing Department ------- to relocate to a larger office next month.

(A) predicts
(B) reports
(C) plans
(D) thinks

105. The construction supervisor expects Crestview Library to be open to the public no ------- than next Thursday.

(A) lately
(B) latest
(C) late
(D) later

106. The water filtration experts will submit the results of their ------- to the panel.

(A) resolution
(B) qualification
(C) perception
(D) investigation

107. Emilia Aeronautics acquired an ------- young engineering expert last week.

(A) extreme
(B) accurate
(C) overall
(D) exceptional

108. After ------- the processor of Mr. Kraven's computer, the technician recommended he replace it.

(A) examine
(B) examining
(C) examined
(D) examination

109. The number of personnel needed to prepare all the required items ------- on order size.

(A) depending
(B) to depend
(C) depends
(D) depend

110. The Ridgeline Park hike will be postponed if the weather is ------- hot on Sunday.

(A) uncomfortably
(B) essentially
(C) cautiously
(D) nearly

111. To work as a master electrician, Mr. Ranganathan is obligated to renew his professional certification ------- five years.

(A) still
(B) fewer
(C) every
(D) wherever

112. In response to student -------, Xavier College will host a series of professional development lectures.

(A) permit
(B) balance
(C) entry
(D) demand

113. After the seminar, the attendees were allowed a ------- amount of time to ask about the presentations.

(A) generous
(B) generousness
(C) generously
(D) generosity

114. The Bruder demonstration at the Kitchen Equipment Exhibition garnered much -------.

(A) interests
(B) interest
(C) interesting
(D) interested

115. The Vice President met French investors ------- a brunch yesterday in Nice.

(A) like
(B) when
(C) at
(D) had

116. The deadline for the monthly budget report was postponed to ------- comment from the board of directors.

(A) turn into
(B) use up
(C) allow for
(D) count on

117. Passengers must arrive at the airport ------- 1 hour prior to their flight's departure.

(A) by then
(B) so that
(C) as little
(D) at least

118. A team of chemical engineers is experimenting with panel coatings ------- can survive extreme conditions.

(A) then
(B) what
(C) into
(D) that

119. Argent Auto Parts Company manufactures higher-quality oil filters ------- its rivals do.

(A) such
(B) than
(C) where
(D) these

120. Buena Vista Outdoor is holding a big ------- sale since the store is moving to a new location.

(A) clearable
(B) clearance
(C) clearing
(D) cleared

GO ON TO THE NEXT PAGE

121. The Business Channel will broadcast a new program ------- to product development and innovative designs.

(A) introduced
(B) permitted
(C) arranged
(D) dedicated

122. Ms. Ming courteously ------- the position offered by Verrazano Imports Ltd.

(A) converted
(B) declined
(C) lessened
(D) restricted

123. ------- it is fairly difficult, the climbing wall at Masters Gym is very popular with members.

(A) Basically
(B) Although
(C) Overall
(D) Reasoning

124. Ms. Armor worked on the sales floor for three days before she was ------- introduced to the branch manager.

(A) presently
(B) formally
(C) considerably
(D) primarily

125. The bank's new policy allows you to refinance your mortgage according to a ------- 10-year plan.

(A) manages
(B) managing
(C) manageable
(D) manageably

126. Mr. Lee has requested a maintenance worker, ------- within two hours.

(A) preference
(B) preferable
(C) preferably
(D) prefer

127. Hexel Industries lowered operating costs, but even more significant for its future, it has strengthened its ------- advantage.

(A) diverse
(B) competitive
(C) sharp
(D) careful

128. Ms. Fitzpatrick regards dependability as a vital ------- for all her employees to possess.

(A) version
(B) trait
(C) instrument
(D) action

129. This shipment cannot ------- until we have obtained final approval.

(A) being processed
(B) to process
(C) has processed
(D) be processed

130. The cost of providing training instructors has been factored ------- the system installation fee.

(A) into
(B) from
(C) with
(D) onto

PART 6

Directions: Read the texts that follow. A word, phrase, or sentence is missing in parts of each text. Four answer choices for each question are given below the text. Select the best answer to complete the text. Then mark the letter (A), (B), (C), or (D) on your answer sheet.

Questions 131-134 refer to the following notice.

On Friday, June 22, the Department of Public Works (DPW) will perform maintenance on the main road that passes through the City College campus. This is the stretch of Palm Avenue ------- Maron Boulevard and Hoover Street. Crews will work to complete all
131.
needed repairs by August 1. -------. This is the time when student traffic on Palm Avenue
132.
is at its minimum. DPW will also have one lane available at all times so that the road stays ------- during the work. Despite this, drivers ------- alternate routes.
133.   **134.**

131. (A) between
(B) from
(C) above
(D) among

132. (A) Subway service will still be available.
(B) This project will take place during the college's summer vacation.
(C) They had initially hoped to finish six months earlier.
(D) An exact timeline is still being discussed.

133. (A) opens
(B) opening
(C) open
(D) opener

134. (A) to be considering
(B) will have considered
(C) have considered
(D) should consider

GO ON TO THE NEXT PAGE

Questions 135-138 refer to the following notice.

Protecting the environment is an important part ------- ErnieMart's values. We care about
135.
creating a healthy world for future generations. With this in mind, we will be launching

our Green November campaign. During the entire month of November, one quarter of

profits from select purchases ------- to organizations promoting clean air and water.
136.

ErnieMart produce, bakery items, and most packaged food are all considered eligible

purchases. Candy, personal care products, and beverages do not qualify. Other -------
137.
products will be listed on the ErnieMart home page for your reference.

The Green November campaign raised almost one million dollars last year for a variety of

environmental causes. -------. To learn more, please visit www.erniemart.com/erniecares
138.
or pick up a brochure at any of our stores.

---

135. (A) across
(B) as
(C) of
(D) through

136. (A) will contribute
(B) are contributing
(C) was contributed
(D) will be contributed

137. (A) unopened
(B) damaged
(C) excluded
(D) discontinued

138. (A) This time, we expect to triple that
amount.
(B) It has been a difficult time for our
association.
(C) Every participating company will be
charged for admission.
(D) This will be our last year of running
the campaign.

Questions 139-142 refer to the following e-mail.

From: Londi Fumarolo
To: All Trek Fitness Center (TFC) members
Date: April 25
Subject: GymDirect

Dear TFC Members,

You ------- a message from our new billing agency, GymDirect. Included in it was a link to
       139.
our member Web site for all bill payment services. -------. Starting next month, all of your
                                                          140.
billing will be processed through this Web site. You will not receive further messages

regarding your billing issues.

Furthermore, the message from GymDirect should contain a temporary login ID and

password. These should be used to access the site, and you should do ------- by the
                                                                        141.
end of this week. -------, your temporary login information will expire.
                   142.

Please give me a call at 1-800-555-1212 if you need assistance with this process.

Best regards,

Londi Fumarolo
TFC Member Services Manager

139. (A) might get
(B) have been getting
(C) should have gotten
(D) will be getting

140. (A) Save this address for your
convenience.
(B) This page is not currently available.
(C) We have several new facilities you
can use.
(D) Unfortunately, your account was
billed incorrectly.

141. (A) other
(B) so
(C) again
(D) both

142. (A) Meanwhile
(B) However
(C) At any time
(D) After that

GO ON TO THE NEXT PAGE

March 15

Jarvis McMahon
1211 E. California Rd.
Fort Wayne, IN 46806

Dear Mr. McMahon,

This letter is in response to your ------- visit to our investor service center. At that time,
143.
we discussed the possibility of moving your retirement savings to Kamberis Financial.

We would be very happy to assist you with this. ------- is a brochure explaining our
144.
services and investment options, per your request. -------.
145.

Our investor service representatives are available at any time should you require
additional information or assistance. When you are ready, we will also handle the process
of moving your ------- from your present institution to Kamberis Financial.
146.

Once again, thank you for your interest in Kamberis Financial. We look forward to
working with you in the future.

Best regards,

James Cleary
Investor Services Associate

Kamberis Financial
219-555-1212

---

143. (A) further
(B) recent
(C) next
(D) delayed

144. (A) Enclose
(B) Enclosed
(C) Enclosing
(D) Enclosure

145. (A) We will waive your maintenance fee
for the first year.
(B) Your feedback will help us better
serve you in the future.
(C) Your investments have all been
selected and purchased.
(D) I think you will find that we have a
variety of excellent choices.

146. (A) suggestion
(B) edition
(C) account
(D) preference

PART 7

Directions: In this part you will read a selection of texts, such as magazine and newspaper articles, emails, and instant messages. Each text or set of texts is followed by several questions. Select the best answer for each question and mark the letter (A), (B), (C), or (D) on your answer sheet.

Questions 147-148 refer to the following instructions.

Directions

1. Insert cash.

2. Open the door to insert garments. Do not overload the machine.

3. Insert soap and select appropriate temperature.

4. Close the door and press the start button to begin the wash.

5. In the event an alarm sounds, rearrange the contents of the machine so that they are balanced.

6. When finished, transfer items to the dryer within five minutes so that others can use the machine.

147. Where would the instructions most likely appear?

(A) At a car wash business
(B) At a laundry facility
(C) At a home appliance store
(D) At a clothing store

148. According to the instructions, which step is NOT always required?

(A) Step 2
(B) Step 4
(C) Step 5
(D) Step 6

GO ON TO THE NEXT PAGE

Arc IT Infrastructure

Installation Request Form

Client: Rosewood Medical Clinic

Contact: linda.richards@rosewoodmc.com

Address: 35 Ash Ct., Fairfax VA 22030

Date: July 26

Technician: Roberta Coe

Order #: 8233

Equipment: 700m, Cat 5 cable

Labor Estimate: 4.5 hours

Work Location: East Wing

Work Description: Connect all computers and printers in all staff areas to network outlets, and test the connections. No access when surgeries are in progress. Finish during non-business hours (8:00 P.M. to 4:30 A.M.). Contact security at extension 457 in the lobby.

149. What is indicated about the job at Rosewood Medical Clinic?

(A) It will be done at night.
(B) It was paid for on July 26.
(C) It will need several workers.
(D) It is the first phase of a project.

150. What is implied about the Rosewood Medical Clinic?

(A) It is located near Arc IT Infrastructure's office.
(B) It has extended its operating hours.
(C) It is hiring new security staff.
(D) It has multiple building sections.

Questions 151-152 refer to the following advertisement.

Jefferson Apartment Company (JAC):

Our New Francis Street Apartments

JAC is opening a new apartment complex this fall. These great units are exclusively open to Madwell University students who don't want to live in dormitories but would still like to be a part of on-campus life. The complex is conveniently situated three blocks from Barrett Hall with great access to public transportation, all within a five-minute walk of the lovely nature trails in San Andreas Park. Enjoy our state-of-the-art fitness center, where you can engage in various recreational activities. All units include private kitchens and living room areas. The building also features a 24-hour laundry facility equipped with brand-new washers and dryers. Each tenant is provided with one parking spot in our large parking lot. Act quickly before all units fill up.

---

151. What does the advertisement promote?

(A) A university seminar series
(B) The opening of a new business
(C) Housing for a particular population
(D) Newly added hiking trails

152. What is NOT mentioned in the advertisement?

(A) Pricing
(B) Location
(C) Activities
(D) Parking

GO ON TO THE NEXT PAGE

Questions 153-154 refer to the following text message chain.

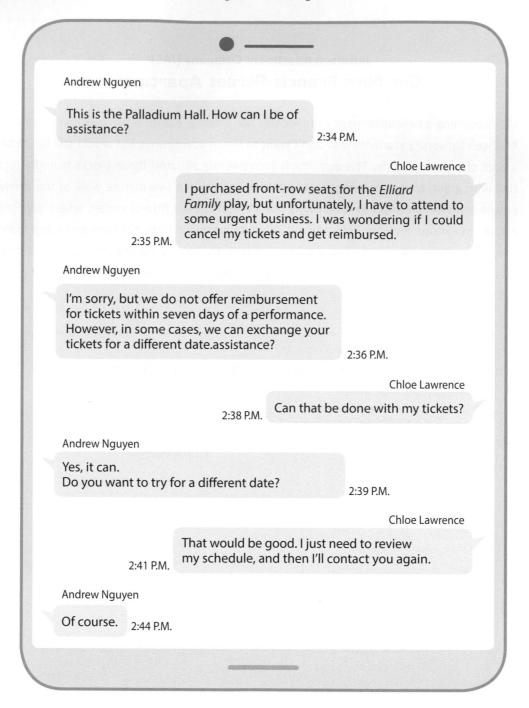

Andrew Nguyen

This is the Palladium Hall. How can I be of assistance?
2:34 P.M.

Chloe Lawrence

I purchased front-row seats for the *Elliard Family* play, but unfortunately, I have to attend to some urgent business. I was wondering if I could cancel my tickets and get reimbursed.
2:35 P.M.

Andrew Nguyen

I'm sorry, but we do not offer reimbursement for tickets within seven days of a performance. However, in some cases, we can exchange your tickets for a different date.assistance?
2:36 P.M.

Chloe Lawrence

Can that be done with my tickets?
2:38 P.M.

Andrew Nguyen

Yes, it can.
Do you want to try for a different date?
2:39 P.M.

Chloe Lawrence

That would be good. I just need to review my schedule, and then I'll contact you again.
2:41 P.M.

Andrew Nguyen

Of course. 2:44 P.M.

153. Why does Ms. Lawrence contact the Palladium Hall?

(A) To offer some feedback
(B) To upgrade some seats
(C) To inquire about an artist
(D) To request a refund

154. At 2:41 P.M. what does Ms. Lawrence most likely mean when she writes, "That would be good"?

(A) She can buy new tickets immediately.
(B) She will do as Mr. Nguyen suggests.
(C) She can go to a show next week.
(D) She will watch a performance online.

Questions 155-157 refer to the following notice.

To All Barrett Coffee House (BCH) Customers:

This is a notice regarding the proper use of our bulletin board.

Due to limited space, any flyers posted will remain on the board for a period of 14 days. To facilitate this, we require that all materials include a date sticker from BCH indicating when they were posted. (Please note: any materials that do not have this label will be removed.) Additionally, we do not allow any oversized flyers or multiple postings for the same event.

If you are interested in placing a flyer on our board, please schedule an appointment with us so that we can discuss the materials together. You will need to show us your materials at least five days before your desired post date. We will let you know by phone once your flyer has been approved.

Best,

TJ Jenson, Manager

155. What is the main purpose of the notice?

(A) To describe a policy
(B) To notify customers of an expansion project
(C) To explain why some materials were removed
(D) To advertise a new business

156. What kind of materials will be taken off the bulletin board?

(A) Materials promoting a social event
(B) Materials posted for more than seven days
(C) Materials without a date sticker
(D) Materials including a company logo

157. What is mentioned about materials posted at BCH?

(A) They cannot promote products.
(B) They should be presented five days in advance.
(C) They need to be paid for beforehand.
(D) They must be emailed to the BCH office.

GO ON TO THE NEXT PAGE

CityBeat.com/local

By Ekon Diallo
May 30

It has been 15 years since Tabatha Lin started out at Twain and Roth as a records clerk. Inspired by the firm's commitment to the local community, she enrolled in law school. These days, she is not only one of the prominent firm's partners, but also the leader of their effort to open a new law office dedicated to property law on Main Avenue.

Nowadays, Ms. Lin is often the first to arrive at the office and the last to leave. Even when she's out of the office, she's conducting research or meeting with new clients. However, she says she's happy to put in long hours. "We're building something special, and I'm honored to take part," she explains.

Ms. Lin says that her experience at every level of the firm informs the way she works today. She is approachable and thoughtful, taking time to listen to everyone, from the top litigators to the newest interns. "Everyone's perspective and experience are important," she says, "and no one can do their best work without help from others."

Ms. Lin believes that the firm has benefited from the opportunity to hire graduates from the top law schools in the country, but "teamwork and communication are always the biggest keys to success."

158. What is the main purpose of the article?

(A) To profile an attorney
(B) To publicize a vacant legal assistant position
(C) To discuss a recent trial
(D) To explain a law school's new policy

159. The word "informs" in paragraph 3, line 2, is closest in meaning to

(A) instructs
(B) invests
(C) influences
(D) interacts

160. What is mentioned about Twain and Roth?

(A) It recruits from prestigious universities.
(B) It recently relocated to a new office.
(C) It has won several big property cases.
(D) It has hired a number of new interns.

Questions 161-163 refer to the following letter.

Kamala Williams
Ames Industries
32 Redwood Way
Salt Lake City, UT 84104

Dear Ms. Williams,

Two weeks ago, your final copy of *Micasa Magazine* was delivered, but we haven't received your renewal request. —[1]—. Over the past decade, *Micasa Magazine* has identified trends in flooring patterns, lighting, and effective management of indoor space. —[2]—. This informative resource for your business is worth much more than the $55 annual subscription fee. —[3]—. However, included with this notice is a renewal offer marked down 30 percent from the usual yearly subscription rate. Send it back before April 30 to take advantage of this special deal. —[4]—. Don't lose out on this valuable business resource. Act now!

Best regards,

Miles Stanford
Customer Services

ENCLOSURE

161. Who most likely is Ms. Williams?

(A) A broadcasting executive
(B) A magazine editor
(C) A corporate accountant
(D) An interior designer

162. What is offered to Ms. Williams?

(A) A discounted subscription
(B) Free advertising space
(C) An individual consultation
(D) Some product samples

163. In which of positions marked [1], [2], [3], and [4] does the following sentence best belong?

"This is a reminder in case you had not intended for this situation to occur."

(A) [1]
(B) [2]
(C) [3]
(D) [4]

GO ON TO THE NEXT PAGE

Questions 164-167 refer to the following online chat discussion.

Sharon West [1:02 P.M.]
Hope everyone had a good lunch. The company is planning to hold an info session regarding our upcoming merger next Tuesday or Wednesday. I want to find out which day is best for each team. Participation is mandatory for all employees.

Gloria Fukuzaki [1:04 P.M.]
Well, Personnel will be unavailable all day on Tuesday because of job interviews. However, our schedule's pretty flexible on Wednesday. When will they be held?

Sharon West [1:06 P.M.]
We haven't set the exact times yet. All of the managers need to let us know their preferences first. Oliver, when would be good for you?

Oliver Ferguson [1:08 P.M.]
IT employees are usually busy during the afternoon, so Tuesday morning would be ideal.

Sharon West [1:09 P.M.]
We could probably hold two separate sessions if the event hall is open on those days. Gloria, do you mind seeing if the event hall is available?

Gloria Fukuzaki [1:12 P.M.]
According to the system, the event hall will be in use on Tuesday morning and Wednesday afternoon.

Sharon West [1:14 P.M.]
Would you please get in touch with the department that booked the event hall for Tuesday morning? Please check if they'd be willing to move their event. If they're OK with it, book the hall from 10:00 A.M. to 11:00 A.M. for both days.

Gloria Fukuzaki [1:18 P.M.]
Done. I just got off the phone with Ms. Cartman. We can use the event hall on both days now. I'll have my team attend on Wednesday morning.

Oliver Ferguson [1:19 P.M.]
We'll stick with Tuesday morning.

SEND

164. What is the main topic of the discussion?

(A) Meeting potential clients
(B) Updating a computer system
(C) Analyzing some survey results
(D) Scheduling an information session

165. What is indicated about Ms. Fukuzaki?

(A) She will not be available this week.
(B) She is a Personnel employee.
(C) She will postpone her appointment.
(D) She is Ms. Cartman's manager.

166. At 1:18 P.M., what does Ms. Fukuzaki imply when she writes, "Done"?

(A) She submitted an application form.
(B) She managed to reserve a venue.
(C) She completed a project early.
(D) She revised a document.

167. When will the IT team attend the session?

(A) On Tuesday morning
(B) On Tuesday afternoon
(C) On Wednesday morning
(D) On Wednesday afternoon

Questions 168-171 refer to the following information.

ACTUAL TEST 01

PART 7

Midwest Interior Design Fair (MIDF), Dayton, Ohio

Terms of Use

A. Contracts: All approved exhibitors must complete and sign all related documents no later than two weeks before the event. Participants who fail to meet MIDF's strict guidelines for appropriate exhibit content will be denied booth space.

B. Costs: Booth spaces in the convention hall are made available to exhibitors from 9:00 A.M. to 7:00 P.M., which includes one hour before and after the hall is publicly accessible. Booths cost $435 per day or $800 for both days. There may be additional costs related to usage (refer to terms C and D).

C. Booths: Spaces provided to exhibitors in the convention hall are 14 feet by 14 feet. One floor outlet contains 4 sockets (120V). For furnishings, internet connectivity, or sign-printing services, please contact vendor_info@midf.org. Note that these services will incur additional fees. In addition, any booth that holds raffles, contests, or other events that might cause a crowd to gather must obtain MIDF's prior approval to ensure that the event does not create an excessive burden on fellow exhibitors. For all exhibitors offering refreshments, a $10 surcharge will be collected to cover the cost of waste removal.

D. Distribution of Materials: Exhibitors are permitted to give away informational materials, product samples, and promotional items. However, due to security restrictions, attendees are only permitted to carry bags issued by the convention hall. Therefore, we highly recommend that any distributed items be able to fit into a 5 inch by 15 inch opening.

168. According to the information, why might a booth request be rejected?

(A) An exhibitor's products are unsuitable for the event.
(B) A company did not make a payment on time.
(C) Company contact information was not provided.
(D) An exhibitor requires a larger booth size.

169. What is suggested about the Midwest Interior Design Fair?

(A) It lasts for two days.
(B) It offers attendees free internet access.
(C) It takes place annually in Dayton.
(D) It has a $10 entry fee.

170. According to the information, what is most likely an objective of MIDF employees?

(A) Drawing a large number of participants
(B) Ensuring that all exhibitors use available space fairly
(C) Making transportation arrangements for international attendees
(D) Grouping companies with similar products together

171. What is true about the MIDF exhibitors?

(A) They can have only a certain amount of employees.
(B) They must wear their ID badges at all times.
(C) Their booths will be inspected one hour before the fair begins.
(D) Their promotional items should not exceed a certain size.

GO ON TO THE NEXT PAGE

25

Questions 172-175 refer to the following Web page.

LONDON (8 August) – ElliptiCorp, the creators of the popular mobile application, Insider, announced a new round of investments Tuesday night. The investments bring the company's valuation to $50 million. —[1]—. The investment was spurred by growing use of the app, which solicits dining recommendations from registered locals, rather than anonymous users.

"Our idea is pretty straightforward," said ElliptiCorp CEO Angela Moss. "We aim to guide people and their food preferences to the right place. The app allows users to read in-depth reviews about a restaurant's menu, location, and environment. Insider makes it easy to choose the best place to get a bite."—[2]—.

Although the application was designed with customers in mind, its popularity has certainly not been limited to its original target users. —[3]—. Daniel Miller, who runs one of London's oldest bistros, believes that Insider has helped improve declining sales. —[4]—. "We didn't know what was wrong at first since everyone said our food was great," said Miller. "However, after going through some reviews, we realized that we didn't have enough workers to provide timely service. We were able to remedy this situation within a month."

Insider is available for download in all major app stores or at <u>ElliptiCorp.com/insider</u>.

172. What is indicated about Insider?

(A) It appointed a new CEO.
(B) It was launched six months ago.
(C) Its posts come from area residents.
(D) Its users are unidentified.

173. According to the Web page, what is one function of the Insider application?

(A) Arranging food delivery
(B) Finding suitable eateries
(C) Reserving a table
(D) Purchasing kitchen supplies

174. What did Mr. Miller likely change?

(A) The prices of some products
(B) The number of employees
(C) The date of a training session
(D) The hours of a store

175. In which of the positions marked [1], [2], [3], and [4] does the following sentence best belong?

"Business owners are also making use of the application."

(A) [1]
(B) [2]
(C) [3]
(D) [4]

GO ON TO THE NEXT PAGE

Questions 176-180 refer to the following article and e-mail.

The Carverton Republic
Business Spotlight

Beirut Café, owned and managed by Jean Christophe Ayoub, opened its doors a decade ago, and they remain open today thanks to his business knowledge. He had already worked in the food service industry for many years and understood that every restaurant takes time to build a reliable clientele and earn a profit. However, even Mr. Ayoub didn't expect the local economic downturn to last so long.

Mr. Ayoub spoke to the Carverton Chamber of Commerce last Tuesday, offering some advice to new restaurant owners. He emphasized that the long-term viability of a business depends on the surrounding community. "A lot of customers will go out to eat only a few times a month," he said. "So you need something unique to pull them to your restaurant."

"Carverton is a diverse community, and a lot of people are familiar with Lebanese cuisine," he explained, "that was a big help in the early years. There are also several specialty markets that provide excellent fresh ingredients."

Mr. Ayoub devoted much of his talk to the importance of being prepared for major expenses early on, especially for advertising. "Estimate how much you think effective ads will cost," he said, "and then triple it." That early investment in radio and newspaper promotions helped Beirut Café stay open and survive four hard years before the business became truly profitable.

Now that Mr. Ayoub's restaurant has a loyal following, his advice for retaining those customers is simple. "We try to keep our clientele eager to come back by creating weekly specials and offering discounts for regulars. Also, if there's a special request, my chefs will do their best to complete the order," he said. "After all, making customers happy is what it's all about."

To	Mina Salazar <msalazar@dfu.edu>
From	Reza Kosch <rezak@carvertoncc.org>
Date	November 18
Subject	News

Dear Mina,

I was happy to hear that you graduated from culinary school. I'm sure that you've started looking for jobs, and so I'm writing to let you know of an opening in Carverton. The position is for a morning kitchen assistant who helps prepare ingredients, bake, and manage deliveries. The job posting can be found at www.beirutcafe.com/recruit. The owner was my classmate at Sullivan University. Don't forget to mention your experience cooking at the Mayer Summer Camp.

All the best,

Reza

176. In the article, the word "pull" in paragraph 2, line 4, is closest in meaning to

(A) stretch
(B) draw
(C) remove
(D) tear

177. How did Mr. Ayoub help his restaurant survive the economic downturn?

(A) He got a loan from the Carverton Chamber of Commerce.
(B) He only did business with local farms.
(C) He moved into a smaller building.
(D) He anticipated high initial costs.

178. What has contributed to Beirut Café's recent success?

(A) Its selection of organic ingredients.
(B) Its famous head chef.
(C) Its large selection of menu items.
(D) Its commitment to regular clientele.

179. Why did Mr. Kosch write the e-mail?

(A) To request that a Web site be changed
(B) To promote a new restaurant location
(C) To explain how to prepare a dish
(D) To announce an open position

180. What is suggested about Mr. Kosch?

(A) He went to school with Mr. Ayoub.
(B) He is hiring staff for his new restaurant.
(C) The Beirut Café sells a menu item designed by him.
(D) Ms. Salazar was his student at the culinary school.

GO ON TO THE NEXT PAGE

Eduline Lecture on Overseas Digital Marketing

Have you been considering ways to boost international sales? Are you thinking of advertising on foreign Web sites? If you are, create an account on www.eduline.org to sign up for a series of interactive panels on Internet Marketing, which are provided to audiences abroad. Methods to attract business in markets across the world using simple computer tools will be discussed by a panel of marketing veterans. The lectures will be aired live on Thursday, October 17, from 3:20 P.M. to 6:30 P.M. (Hawaii Standard Time)

There will be a total of three presentations:
"Sell It with a Photo: Viral Image Sharing in China" - Mari Polk
"Taking Advantage of Automatic Translations" - Sora Han
"Utilizing Social Network Services in Vietnam" - Rene Torres

If you are having difficulty signing up online, contact Lars Orloff at 1-800-555-3627 anytime before October 15.

Busy at the time of the live event? Check out the Streams section on our Web site. Every event is available for viewing within 12 hours of the live broadcast.

---

www.eduline.org/feedback_survey/1017

Dear Josh Cortez,

Thank you for being a part of the Eduline Lectures on Overseas Digital Marketing. We invite you to provide some feedback in order to improve future sessions.

Please rate the lectures (1 = not helpful to 5 = very helpful)

Usefulness of the lecture's subject	5
Presenter's information and clarity	5
Relevant examples to lecture topics	5

What did you like the most?

Mr. Torres' presentation helped me get a much better idea of how I can market my products more effectively. It was delivered with real depth and passion. I appreciated that he allowed more time to answer all the participants' questions.

What would you like to be improved in future lecture events?

I currently live in London, and I had to wait until 1:20 A.M. to join the live broadcast. I'm sure many participants would appreciate it if there were more options for lecture times.

181. What is suggested about the lectures?

(A) They are only open to Hawaiian business owners.
(B) They will be offered throughout the month.
(C) They are intended for graduate students.
(D) They will be delivered online.

182. According to the advertisement, why should readers contact Mr. Orloff?

(A) To get access to the lectures
(B) To ask for a video file
(C) To propose new event topics
(D) To ask a speaker some questions

183. What is implied about the panelists?

(A) They are conference organizers.
(B) They are marketing professors.
(C) They have all been previously employed at Eduline.
(D) They have extensive experience in advertising abroad.

184. What is suggested about Mr. Cortez?

(A) He will move to London at the end of October.
(B) He plans to promote his merchandise in Vietnam.
(C) He often works extra hours.
(D) He participates in professional seminars often.

185. What aspect of the lectures does Mr. Cortez recommend changing?

(A) The venue
(B) The sign-up procedure
(C) The pricing
(D) The scheduling

GO ON TO THE NEXT PAGE

To: akatrakis@ecodress.org
From: bmunoz@texcycle.com
Date: February 12
Subject: March Itinerary

Dear Ms. Katrakis,

This message serves as confirmation that a Textiling Recycling truck will arrive at your business the afternoon of March 26. We would greatly appreciate it if the donated clothing was already sorted to speed up our collection process. Please note that your signature will be required before payment can be made.

Textile Recycling offers market rates, which fluctuate daily, for used clothing and fabrics. Currently, the value for linens is slightly down from last month. Chiffon and leather are at an all-time low due to their decreasing usage. However, as winter comes to an end, be on the lookout for polyester, which has tripled in value since last November. A company located in Vietnam is buying as much as we can offer them in the next several months.

Thank you for your business.

Regards,

Bonnie Munoz
Textile Recycling, Customer Relations

Eco-Dress

Serving the metro area since 1986, we are your number one used clothing and apparel shop. Donations are always welcome! Items should be placed in the following locations:

Basket A: Coats, jackets, and sweaters
Basket B: Pants, shirts, and shorts
Shelves: Gloves, shawls, and other accessories

The demand for certain types of insulating textiles is quite high. So, for the time being, we are also welcoming donations of thermal protectors, such as cooler carriers, winter bedding, and shoe liners through March 25.

Eco-Dress keeps our planet green through its clothing recycling program. If you need anything, just ask at the checkout counter.

HAI PHONG (October 3) — Bocat has announced a new line of specialized hiking boots, the Ultrawalk DX. This new line of footwear is ideal for extreme weather conditions, including high altitude trekking where temperatures can plunge below -55°C (-67°F). The protection these shoes provide is made possible by a newly-developed custom weave of synthetic insulation. The Ultrawalk DX is also the first high-performance footwear made of more than 70 percent recycled materials, most of which are taken from cast-off clothing. The Ultrawalk DX will be sold, starting next week, exclusively at the Bocat head store in Hanoi. While international sales will begin on October 31, Bocat will begin delivering the new shoes to retailers throughout Vietnam by October 15.

186. What does Ms. Katrakis most likely do?

(A) Design women's apparel
(B) Write for a fashion magazine
(C) Run a used clothing store
(D) Operate a textile factory

187. According to the notice, where should an item like a scarf be placed?

(A) In Basket A
(B) In Basket B
(C) At the checkout counter
(D) On the shelves

188. Why did Eco-Dress ask that thermal protectors be dropped off by March 25?

(A) Because a buyer will arrive the next day
(B) Because winter will end soon
(C) Because a sale will begin
(D) Because new inventory will be coming in

189. What is Bocat most likely using in its new hiking boots?

(A) Linen
(B) Chiffon
(C) Leather
(D) Polyester

190. When will the new footwear be available outside of Vietnam?

(A) October 3
(B) October 10
(C) October 15
(D) October 31

GO ON TO THE NEXT PAGE

Knoxville Commercial Development Commission
Special Courses for Recent Graduates

A series of seminars designed for recent graduates who are interested in raising funds to establish their own Internet startup companies will be held by the Knoxville Commercial Development Commission (KCDC) from January 4 to 7 in the Knoxville Riverside Conference Center.

David Michaels, an independent consultant who works with dozens of new companies every year, will speak to participants about the basics of writing a summary of a proposed business strategy. Chris O'Caroll will discuss ways to get investors' attention through online advertising. Olivia Arietta will explain how crowd-funding, or getting small amounts of money from online donations, can help get your business off to a good start. Finally, the last day will be devoted to helping participants prepare to explain their visions and goals to actual investors.

Most courses are free, but a $25 materials fee is required for the investor presentation session. Sign up by emailing courses@kcdc.org.

KCDC PROGRAM AGENDA

Special Courses for Recent Graduates

Day, Date, Title	Place	Time
Wednesday, January 4		
• Crafting a Sales Pitch	Conference Room B	9:30 A.M.
• Business Plan Fundamentals	Conference Room C	10:30 A.M.
• Individual Consultation	Room 714	11:30 A.M.
Thursday, January 5		
• Online Promotions	Conference Room B	10:30 A.M.
• Individual Consultation	Room 714	11:30 A.M.
Friday, January 6		
• Getting Public Funding	Conference Room B	10:30 A.M.
• Individual Consultation	Room 714	11:30 A.M.
Saturday, January 7		
• Investor Presentation Practice	Meeting Hall A	10:30 A.M.

KCDC Seminars a Great Success

Knoxville (January 10) — Hopeful business owners participated in four days of seminars and lectures created to help them get their own startup companies operating, all thanks to the Knoxville Commercial Development Commission (KCDC).

"The seminars provided a wealth of information related to promoting my business through the internet," explained David Weisner, who plans to start a restaurant review Web site.

Also in attendance was Mary Kim, who hopes to open a digital education company. She especially enjoyed the opportunity to practice her investor presentation, during which the main selling points of her business were assessed. "I will be able to talk to investors much more effectively thanks to the information that was provided," she explained.

Sanduk Tabin, President of the KCDC, plans to host this sort of event again in July, based on the positive feedback and high turnout.

191. According to the brochure, what is a stated purpose of the program?

(A) To hire instructors for a series of lectures
(B) To boost the reputation of KCDC
(C) To instruct graduates on getting money to launch a company
(D) To help business professionals expand their networks

192. What is suggested about Mr. Michaels?

(A) He gave a talk on Wednesday.
(B) He is knowledgeable about internet promotions.
(C) He manages an accounting team at KCDC.
(D) He analyzes feedback provided by participants.

193. What does the program schedule indicate?

(A) All events take place in the same conference room.
(B) The presentation practice begins earlier than other sessions.
(C) Attendees will get several chances to have private consultations.
(D) Each day only features one class.

194. What is implied about Ms. Kim?

(A) She gave advice about making short speeches.
(B) She wanted to hear Mr. Tabin speak.
(C) She appreciated Ms. Arietta's feedback.
(D) She paid a fee to the KCDC.

195. What is mentioned in the article about KCDC?

(A) It has been run by Mr. Tabin for many years.
(B) It provided investment funds for Mr. Weisner.
(C) It is not well-known in Knoxville.
(D) It will offer similar courses in the summer.

GO ON TO THE NEXT PAGE

From: e.hassan@typeflow.com
To: m.lim@kare.edu
Date: June 30
Subject: Accounting Courses

Dear Ms. Lim,

I have just enrolled in your Accounting Professional Training Certification Program and will be starting my first classes this fall. On your Web site's Frequently Asked Questions page, it says that AC113: Accounting Compliance is a required class for certification, but I have already taken a similar class through Oklahoma State University with Professor Carolyn Smith. I would therefore appreciate it if this requirement could be waived. In addition, I'm unsure of the best order in which to take the classes. I would appreciate it if you could provide a recommendation.

Sincerely,

Elliot Hassan

From: m.lim@kare.edu
To: e.hassan@typeflow.com
Date: July 1
Subject: Re: Accounting Courses

Dear Mr. Hassan,

Let me begin by congratulating you on your decision to earn an accounting certificate. Unfortunately, waiving AC113 is not possible. The class provides grounding in the very latest applicable financial reporting laws and will be referenced frequently in other classes.

During the fall semester, you are required to take AC102: Accounting Fundamentals, which will be held in one of the computer labs.

As a new student, you can find a more thorough explanation of our institute's requirements and policies in the program guide. The following sections are relevant to your course:

Accounting Professional Training Certification Overview: pp. 1-5
Mandatory Accounting Classes: pp. 6-10
Optional Accounting Classes: pp. 11-12
Recommended Sequence of Classes: pp. 22-23

A copy of the guide should arrive in the mail this week. After reviewing it, please contact me with any further questions you may have.

Regards,

May Lim
Kare Institute

Kare Institute Computer Labs

Kare faculty and students are provided with computer labs (more information below) fully equipped to meet their needs.

General Use Lab: Room 200
50 computers with accounting and word-processing software; may be accessed by anyone with a Kare staff or student ID.

Accounting Lab: Room 210
15 computers with currently-used software for general accounting purposes; may only be accessed by those enrolled in first-year classes.

Professional Lab: Room 212
21 computers with payroll and tax accounting software, as well as banking simulation programs, available for AC203: Corporate Tax Filings and AC215: Staff Disbursement or with faculty approval.

Testing Lab: Room 315
Certification testing computers with software for various accounting scenarios; available only during certification testing.

Notices in every lab give the hours they are in use for classes and when they are available for personal use. Other computers for class and public use can be found in the lounge area on the first floor and are available 24/7.

196. Why does Mr. Hassan mention the Accounting Compliance class?

(A) To check if he must take it
(B) To ask for information about the professor
(C) To see if it can be done online
(D) To inquire about the price of textbooks

197. What is indicated about the guide?

(A) It offers faculty contact information.
(B) It includes an audio CD.
(C) Mr. Hassan will soon receive it.
(D) Ms. Lim helped edit it.

198. What page numbers in the guide most likely contain the answer to Mr. Hassan's inquiry?

(A) pp. 1-5
(B) pp. 6-10
(C) pp. 11-12
(D) pp. 22-23

199. Where will the Accounting Compliance class most likely take place?

(A) The General Use Lab
(B) The Accounting Lab
(C) The Professional Lab
(D) The Testing Lab

200. What is true about the computer labs?

(A) They all offer software for accounting.
(B) They all have reservation schedules.
(C) They all offer technical support staff.
(D) They all have 24-hour access.

Stop! This is the end of the test. If you finish before time is called, you may go back to Parts 5, 6, and 7 and check your work.

READING TEST

In the Reading test, you will read a variety of texts and answer several different types of reading comprehension questions. The entire Reading test will last 75 minutes. There are three parts, and directions are given for each part. You are encouraged to answer as many questions as possible within the time allowed.

You must mark your answers on the separate answer sheet. Do not write your answers in your test book.

PART 5

Directions: A word or phrase is missing in each of the sentences below. Four answer choices are given below each sentence. Select the best answer to complete the sentence. Then mark the letter (A), (B), (C), or (D) on your answer sheet.

101. Monitor Shipping now has ------- with 32 major clothing retailers.

(A) contracts
(B) contract
(C) contractor
(D) contracting

102. Official authorization must ------- prior to utilizing Sunian Inc.'s trademark.

(A) obtain
(B) be obtained
(C) obtaining
(D) be obtaining

103. The Customer Service Department should employ more personnel ------- client accounts have increased by 45 percent.

(A) therefore
(B) because of
(C) even though
(D) since

104. Frateri Inc. lost the ------- percentage of its clients to Planter Corporation.

(A) farthest
(B) deepest
(C) greatest
(D) lightest

105. Ms. Kajima's ------- duties consist of organizing and calculating assets of recently acquired clients.

(A) accountable
(B) accounting
(C) accounted
(D) account

106. Doctors recommend putting ice over the swollen area for twenty ------- thirty minutes a day.

(A) by
(B) as
(C) to
(D) on

107. The HR Department at Brenn Inc. offers bonuses ------- staff productivity.

(A) stimulating
(B) stimulate
(C) to stimulate
(D) will stimulate

108. I have included a sample portfolio of my designs for your -------.

(A) consideration
(B) anticipation
(C) explanation
(D) participation

109. Even though the task took ------- five hours to finish, the employees will be compensated for a full day's work.

(A) before
(B) for
(C) only
(D) right

110. Before the televisions are packaged, they are ------- thoroughly to ensure they function properly.

(A) assigned
(B) selected
(C) managed
(D) inspected

111. ------- on the organizing committee contributed to the great success of the workshop.

(A) Whoever
(B) Everyone
(C) Each other
(D) One another

112. Kraven Financial has ------- an agreement to lease a larger office space.

(A) signed
(B) defined
(C) engaged
(D) involved

113. Scantron personal finance software can help ------- track accounts, create budgets, and process payments.

(A) yourself
(B) yours
(C) your
(D) you

114. Providing custom glassware to a ------- array of companies, Prezis Glazier just celebrated 150 years of doing business in Bern.

(A) widen
(B) wide
(C) width
(D) widely

115. All announcements must receive approval from the PR Manager before they can be released -------.

(A) largely
(B) utterly
(C) absolutely
(D) externally

116. The International Binders Confederation ------- the interests of book publishers worldwide.

(A) recreates
(B) represents
(C) functions
(D) contributes

117. Prior to your upcoming interview, please complete the ------- applicant information form.

(A) enclosing
(B) enclose
(C) enclosed
(D) enclosure

118. The memo concerning the proposed ------- of Heath Landscaping by Manchester Builders Ltd. has been distributed.

(A) compliance
(B) acquisition
(C) attachment
(D) document

119. While many financial apps transfer money only to local banks, MoneyTime can send to international ones -------.

(A) before then
(B) so far
(C) throughout
(D) as well

120. The Vice President has ------- the importance of gaining new clients next year.

(A) administered
(B) ordered
(C) emphasized
(D) requested

GO ON TO THE NEXT PAGE

121. Ms. Park has proven ------- to be a loyal and innovative member of the R&D team.

(A) herself
(B) itself
(C) it
(D) she

122. Ms. Talia Ghulal, representative of Quartermain Solutions, stressed her company's ------- for stricter quality standards.

(A) consciousness
(B) placement
(C) fairness
(D) support

123. The shop had a ------- display of the latest novel from the popular science-fiction writer.

(A) gifted
(B) default
(C) massive
(D) thankful

124. Demeter Technologies is attempting to upgrade the portable unit ------- next month's Renewable Energy Expo.

(A) opposite from
(B) in spite of
(C) in addition to
(D) ahead of

125. Both strong and secure, the storage units from Bulldog Boxing are also large ------- to be used for holding vehicles.

(A) well
(B) fully
(C) closely
(D) enough

126. According to Mr. Kim's -------, 300 square meters of marble tiles are required to finish the lobby floor.

(A) calculations
(B) calculated
(C) calculates
(D) calculate

127. Get a 40 percent discount on any chair ------- you buy an office desk at Franklin's Furniture.

(A) whenever
(B) although
(C) after all
(D) such as

128. Patients have been truly ------- of our efforts to lower the amount of time they have to spend waiting.

(A) appreciative
(B) appreciation
(C) appreciate
(D) appreciating

129. The scratches on the lobby floor are ------- visible now that the polishing work has been done.

(A) falsely
(B) barely
(C) correctly
(D) precisely

130. The shareholders have requested that Mr. Tran ------- all possible ways to lower overhead expenses at the Bangkok facility.

(A) examine
(B) is examining
(C) to examine
(D) has examined

PART 6

Directions: Read the texts that follow. A word, phrase, or sentence is missing in parts of each text. Four answer choices for each question are given below the text. Select the best answer to complete the text. Then mark the letter (A), (B), (C), or (D) on your answer sheet.

Questions 131-134 refer to the following article.

The Kansai Park Authority this morning ------- its decision on whether or not to create
131.
additional hiking trails in Kansai National Forest. In a press conference today, Park
Director Lisa Hasegawa stated that more research on the environment is required -------
132.
the Park Authority can move forward with the project. -------. Yet, the forest has been
133.
attracting far more visitors since the opening of the Kansai Forest Resort. Analysts
attribute the ------- in hiking activities to the resort. According to Ms. Hasegawa, the Park
134.
Authority will discuss the matter again after four months.

131. (A) questioned
(B) confirmed
(C) approved
(D) delayed

132. (A) once
(B) after
(C) before
(D) during

133. (A) Ms. Hasegawa advises that all hikers bring protective gear.
(B) The Park Authority is looking to hire experienced tour guides.
(C) There are currently only three trails available to guests.
(D) Kansai recently introduced new environmental laws.

134. (A) increase
(B) advertisement
(C) disappointment
(D) plateau

GO ON TO THE NEXT PAGE

Questions 135-138 refer to the following e-mail.

From: Shirley Watanabe
To: All Employees
Date: August 12
Subject: System update

Today, all employee computers will be upgraded to the latest version of our security software. -------. You will still be able to access your programs while the installation is
135.
being performed, but you might ------- that your system is not running as fast as it
136.
should. Once the installation is done, you will have to reboot your computer. -------, if
137.
you are working on something, you can complete the process at a more convenient time.

We apologize in advance for any -------.
138.

---

135. (A) We are working towards revising our security guidelines.
(B) Our security office is open until 8 P.M. today.
(C) The upgrade will automatically start at 1 P.M.
(D) This upgrade will only work on certain computer models.

136. (A) remember
(B) notice
(C) persuade
(D) criticize

137. (A) In fact
(B) In particular
(C) Consequently
(D) However

138. (A) interruptive
(B) interrupt
(C) interruptions
(D) interrupted

Questions 139-142 refer to the following article.

For the last four decades, Ernest Fong has been designing and selling tables and cabinets in Hertzfield. At the end of this month, he will ------- bid farewell to his loyal
139.
customers and start a new position at the local community college. -------. "I've spent
140.
years perfecting my craft, and now, I'd like to share my passion and skills with my younger colleagues," he commented. Before Mr. Fong permanently closes his shop, he is planning to hold a sale for his remaining merchandise. Several unique ------- items will
141.
be sold at reduced prices. Some previously-owned tables and cabinets will ------- be
142.
available for purchase. The event will take place next Saturday at 2 P.M.

139. (A) finalize
(B) finally
(C) final
(D) finale

140. (A) Mr. Fong will be teaching classes as well as mentoring a successor.
(B) Mr. Fong worked part-time at a home décor company in Asia during college.
(C) His products are displayed at conventions every year.
(D) His store offers the most affordable prices in the city.

141. (A) painting
(B) electronics
(C) clothing
(D) furniture

142. (A) instead
(B) rarely
(C) also
(D) simply

GO ON TO THE NEXT PAGE

From: Calvin Newton, President of TW Electronics
To: All TW Electronics employees
Date: March 12
Subject: Acquisition update

As you are probably aware, on May 2 our acquisition of Wasserman Tech will be finalized. From that date ------- , we will be called TWW Electronics Corporation. This
143.
purchase will make us the biggest ------- of consumer electronics in the country.
144.

You are probably wondering how this acquisition will impact you. Fortunately, your job title, duties, and salary will all remain as specified in your current employee agreement with TW Electronics. ------- .
145.

Nevertheless, you will see many changes in the coming months. ------- will be discussed
146.
at our next quarterly meeting on April 3 at 9:00 A.M. in the Main Auditorium. We will make sure to address all of your questions at that time.

---

143. (A) aside
(B) later
(C) until
(D) forward

144. (A) supplier
(B) supplies
(C) supplying
(D) supplied

145. (A) We will begin looking for a suitable candidate to replace the current president.
(B) Your specific job duties may vary to some extent.
(C) New agreements will be sent to you confirming the changes.
(D) Actually, the company is considering creating more positions.

146. (A) We
(B) Either
(C) These
(D) It

PART 7

Directions: In this part you will read a selection of texts, such as magazine and newspaper articles, emails, and instant messages. Each text or set of texts is followed by several questions. Select the best answer for each question and mark the letter (A), (B), (C), or (D) on your answer sheet.

Questions 147-148 refer to the following job advertisement.

Aspengrove

Aspengrove is hiring clerks, housekeepers, concierge agents, and maintenance staff for its newest location, which opens its doors on May 31 across from the Lennox Convention Center. Clerks should have more than two years' experience in customer relations, while concierge agents should have a year or more of experience. For housekeepers and maintenance staff, prior experience is a plus, but we will train entry-level staff. Interviews are being held next week on May 22 and 23. Candidates should bring a résumé and other relevant documentation. To find out more, visit www.aspengrove.com.

147. What type of business is Aspengrove?

(A) A hotel chain
(B) A manufacturing plant
(C) A landscaping company
(D) A conference facility

148. What is suggested about the advertised positions?

(A) Prior experience is required for most of them.
(B) All of them must be filled by May 23.
(C) Candidates can apply for them at any company location.
(D) They all provide paid training.

GO ON TO THE NEXT PAGE

Questions 149-150 refer to the following text message chain.

Mitchell Song

Hi, I saw a flyer on campus seeking students interested in volunteering for the Wildlife Conservation Society's membership fundraising campaign. It said to text this number to learn ways to help.

2:07 P.M.

Erin Mendoza

Thank you for getting in touch! Currently, we are preparing to hold an art auction to raise money. We need help contacting artists and arranging for them to donate work. We rely on this auction to fund our activities for the year, so we need their support.

2:08 P.M.

Mitchell Song

Sure! I would be happy to help with that. Can you tell me where you are located and when I should come by? I finish teaching at 5:00 P.M.

2:11 P.M.

Erin Mendoza

Well, could you give me your phone number? Once I receive responses from a few more people, we can finalize a schedule. I will send further information then.

2:13 P.M.

Mitchell Song

Of course. It's 555-9423. I'm so glad I can help out.

2:14 P.M.

149. Why did Mr. Song contact Ms. Mendoza?

(A) To donate some money
(B) To give feedback on a class
(C) To inquire about a volunteer position
(D) To reserve an exhibition booth

150. At 2:11 P.M., what does Mr. Song most likely mean when he writes, "I finish teaching at 5:00 P.M."?

(A) He worries he will be late for a meeting.
(B) He plans to call Ms. Mendoza later.
(C) He has time to help out in the evenings.
(D) He would like a ride from Ms. Mendoza.

Questions 151-153 refer to the following information.

National Association of Museum Curators
August 15-17, Cornell University
Ithaca, New York
10th Annual Conference

Dining Options

Welcome to the National Association of Museum Curators' 10th annual conference. Attendees are encouraged to purchase prepaid meal cards upon check-in at the registration tables in Olive Tjaden Hall. Meal cards cover breakfast, lunch, and dinner, and are $20 and $55 for one and three days, respectively. Conference passes will be issued at the same time and should be worn at all times. Meal cards are optional, but without one, conference participants will be required to pay the full price of $10 per meal. Please be aware that meal cards are only valid on the university campus.

On-campus cafeterias open at 6 A.M. and close at 9 P.M. Buffet-style meals are available in Risley Hall and Appel Commons, which also has a coffee house. Global selections, including Asian, Middle Eastern, and Latin American dishes, are offered in Willard Straight Hall. Please refer to the campus map included in the conference program to locate an eatery that matches your tastes.

There are many off-campus dining options near the conference venues as well, including the Jersey Mac Grill, Crispin's Bistro, and Empire State Pizza.

151. What is suggested about the National Association of Museum Curators?

(A) Its participants registered online.
(B) It is hosting a special dinner for guests.
(C) Its first professional gathering was held a decade ago.
(D) It is attended by international curators.

152. Where will conference attendees NOT be served lunch?

(A) In Olive Tjaden Hall
(B) In Risley Hall
(C) In Willard Straight Hall
(D) In Appel Commons

153. What is true about places to eat outside the conference site?

(A) They will not accept conference-issued meal cards.
(B) They charge $10 for lunch.
(C) They are shown on the map included in the conference program.
(D) They all close at 9 P.M.

GO ON TO THE NEXT PAGE

Lockhead Laboratories

2 April

Dear Mr. Reddington,

We have read your e-mail dated 31 March regarding the research assistant position here at Lockhead Labs. As stated in our job advertisement, we cannot accept applications after 14 March. There were many qualified candidates, and we have offered the position to one of them. However, your qualifications are impressive, and I will keep your information on file. I am especially interested in your current position as a research assistant at Hanborough Scientifics, as their work is similar to ours.

Thank you for expressing an interest in Lockhead Labs. I will contact you if we have another research assistant opening at the company.

Kind regards,

Elizabeth Van Horrens
Elizabeth Van Horrens
Laboratory Manager

---

154. Why was the letter written?

(A) To confirm an interview date
(B) To provide details about the duties of a job
(C) To request a work sample
(D) To explain that a job vacancy has been filled

155. What is indicated about Mr. Reddington?

(A) He is currently employed.
(B) His application was submitted before the deadline.
(C) He is applying for a lab manager position.
(D) He has limited work experience.

Questions 156-157 refer to the following e-mail.

To: m.luciano@californiacatering.com
From: r.hall@fshie.org
Date: June 27
Subject: Food Services and Hospitality Expo

Dear Ms. Luciano,

We were delighted that you attended the Food Services and Hospitality Expo last year. However, to date, we have yet to receive your registration for this year's event. Early registration for a reduced fee of €225 is only available until the end of the month. After June 30, the price will increase to €300.

Included in the conference fee are the following:

- Reserved seating at the welcome buffet on Tuesday, October 7
- Access to all expo events
- A ticket to the closing ceremony on Thursday, October 9

The following is not included in the registration fee:

- Association Members' dinner on Wednesday, October 8. (Transportation to the event's location will be provided. A separate payment must be made directly via the Food Industry Association Web site, if you would like to participate.)

We look forward to seeing you again this year.

Sincerely,

Roberta Hall

156. Why did Mr. Hall send the e-mail to Ms. Luciano?

(A) To advise her of an upcoming deadline
(B) To encourage her to speak at an exposition
(C) To request that she revise a schedule
(D) To acknowledge that a payment was received

157. What is indicated about the event on October 8?

(A) It will feature some important guests.
(B) It can be attended at an additional cost.
(C) It will take place in the expo's facilities.
(D) It does not have many spots left.

GO ON TO THE NEXT PAGE

http://www.parliamentarylibrary.co.uk/archivesdatabase

Parliamentary Library Archives Database

This database is designed to help you find historical Parliamentary records. It includes hundreds of thousands of legislative documents dating back to the 1600s, many of which are not available anywhere else. —[1]—. Listings are searchable by author or by the date of the document's creation. Each includes a synopsis of its contents. A new version, allowing for searches by location, will be available this spring. Materials marked "offline" may, in some cases, be viewed at the Archives Office. To gain access to these, you must receive approval from one of our employees. —[2]—.

[SAMPLE ENTRY]

Rowlandson-Lloyd Letters

A collection of letters exchanged over a hundred years ago between Peter Rowlandson and Paul George. —[3]—. Seven of the eight letters referred to have been preserved. They include discussions of proposed tax rates and Rowlandson's personal reflections. Also, they contain a partial draft of George's 29 April House of Commons address, with a number of handwritten revisions. —[4]—.

158. What is indicated about materials in the Parliamentary Library Archives Database?

(A) They are organized alphabetically.
(B) They are all available electronically.
(C) Some of them require approval to access.
(D) Some of them can be taken home.

159. What is true about the Rowlandson-Lloyd letters?

(A) They were written more than a century ago.
(B) They include images of old tax documents.
(C) They were restored by library employees.
(D) They will be uploaded to a Web site.

160. In which of the positions marked [1], [2], [3], and [4] does the following sentence best belong?

"Because of their age, many of these documents are quite fragile and may only be viewed online."

(A) [1]
(B) [2]
(C) [3]
(D) [4]

Questions 161-164 refer to the following letter.

McAllister High School
3455 S. 18th Terrace
Miami, FL 33125
786-555-6623

October 10

Ms. Jeri Cooper
Cooper's
1452 Hardaway Dr.
Mirada, CA 90638

Dear Ms. Cooper,

I wanted to let you know how much the Music Department at McAllister High School appreciates your generosity. The twenty brass instruments your organization donated, as well as the sheet music and recordings, have helped us a great deal. —[1]—. Our school now has enough instruments to instruct 32 pupils at a time. When we last spoke, you were curious about how the students would share the equipment. We currently allow three students to use each instrument during the course of the school day. For students requiring their own mouthpieces, they pay just $25. At the beginning of the school year, a sign-up sheet is provided for everyone to choose an instrument. —[2]—.

Also, the funds you donated made it possible to hire two part-time teachers for after-school music activities. The music room is open for practice until 6:00 P.M., Monday to Friday, which has increased participation among students whose parents work. —[3]—. Some students have even started a band with one of the new teachers. If you have time, please come to one of our events and hear them play! —[4]—.

In the future, we hope to add an orchestra section to the McAllister auditorium so that we can feature live music in our theater productions. If this initiative is of interest to you, we would certainly appreciate the support. I will keep you informed about our plans for this.

Once again, thank you for supporting McAllister's aspiring musicians.

Sincerely,

Daniel O'Malley

Daniel O'Malley
McAllister High School, Principal

161. Why was the letter written?

(A) To invite Ms. Cooper to a music audition
(B) To thank Ms. Cooper for a contribution
(C) To profile a new teacher
(D) To request help with a performance

162. What is suggested about McAllister High School?

(A) It has recruited more staff.
(B) It is considering adding a concert hall.
(C) It will be raising class fees.
(D) It is going to open a new theater.

163. What is mentioned about the instruments at McAllister High School?

(A) They were ordered by Mr. O'Malley.
(B) They have to be repaired.
(C) They are shared by several students.
(D) They are for after-school activities only.

164. In which of the positions marked [1], [2], [3], and [4] does the following sentence best belong?

"Also, for those who cannot take a music class during the school day, this provides a chance to do so despite a full schedule."

(A) [1]
(B) [2]
(C) [3]
(D) [4]

Questions 165-168 refer to the following text message chain.

Allie Nguyen [8:43 A.M.]
Good morning, Hector and Chris. I can't make it into my shift on Wednesday. I know that both of you had asked about working extra hours. Would either of you be interested?

Hector Ramirez [8:44 A.M.]
Sure, although it depends on the time. When do you work?

Allie Nguyen [8:46 A.M.]
6:00 A.M. to 2:00 P.M.

Chris Trautschold [8:47 A.M.]
I'm scheduled from 2:00 P.M. to 10:00 P.M., but I can come in early for your shift, Allie.

Hector Ramirez [8:48 A.M.]
I have a dentist appointment until 10:00 A.M. and the drive there is 40 minutes, so I'm afraid I can't make it at that time

Allie Nguyen [8:52 A.M.]
Ah, I see. That's understandable. So, Chris, are you certain you can do it?

Chris Trautschold [8:53 A.M.]
Definitely. I will tell Ms. Kim that I'll be arriving early on Wednesday.

Allie Nguyen [8:55 A.M.]
OK. I'll send her a message to confirm. I'll see you at work on Sunday, Chris. Thank you so much!

SEND

---

165. Why did Ms. Nguyen contact her coworkers?

(A) To check the status of their assignments
(B) To instruct them to log their extra hours
(C) To instruct them to submit vacation requests
(D) To check if they can work in her place

166. What is suggested about Mr. Trautschold?

(A) He recently trained Ms. Nguyen on some tasks.
(B) He is scheduled to work with Ms. Nguyen on the weekend.
(C) He typically works overtime.
(D) He often comes to work early for his shift.

167. At 8:52 A.M., what does Ms. Nguyen most likely mean when she writes, "That's understandable"?

(A) She accepts Mr. Ramirez's explanation.
(B) She believes that Mr. Trautschold is dependable.
(C) She heard about Mr. Ramirez's appointment beforehand.
(D) She is familiar with a traffic situation.

168. What is most likely true about Ms. Kim?

(A) She drives to the office.
(B) She is trying to work extra hours.
(C) She is scheduled to work on Sunday.
(D) She manages the employees' schedules.

Questions 169-171 refer to the following letter.

The Alberta News

Dear Ms. Shen,

Thank you for continuing to support *The Alberta News*. You'll be pleased to know that we will now be offering a weekend edition, which will include an event calendar with listings of upcoming festivals and performances in the province, and a section for film and theater reviews. It will also contain discount coupons for entertainment venues, restaurants, and other local businesses.

As a special courtesy to our long-time customers, we offer this edition to you at no cost for one month. Your free trial will start on Monday, September 1, and will end on Tuesday, September 30. If you wish to continue receiving the edition after that time, you will only have to pay $7.50 more each month.

We also invite you to try using our referral program by introducing our newspaper to family members and friends. If any of your family members or friends subscribe to *The Alberta News*, you will receive our newspaper for free for one whole month!

Please send any questions or concerns to customerservice@albertanews.com.

Sincerely,

Sasha Ringwald
Customer Service Representative

---

169. What is the purpose of the letter?

(A) To request a customer to make a payment
(B) To offer discounts to entertainment venues
(C) To promote newspaper advertising to local businesses
(D) To explain a new service to an existing customer

170. What will NOT be included in the weekend edition of *The Alberta News*?

(A) Recipes for traditional dishes
(B) Listings of future events
(C) Reviews of movies and plays
(D) Discounts to local restaurants

171. What will happen if Ms. Shen chooses to continue receiving the weekend edition after September?

(A) The fees for advertising will be lowered.
(B) Her family and friends will be eligible for a discount.
(C) The cost of the edition will be added to her monthly bill.
(D) She will be given free tickets to performances.

GO ON TO THE NEXT PAGE

White Owl Industries

Attention All Staff

We're making progress with our Corporate Environmental Program! Here are some of the latest details:

Our board has voted to boost funding to reduce the amount of waste our office produces.

Management is pleased that many of you have decided to participate in the Bike to Work initiative. More than half of our employees ride their bicycles at least three times a week.

We have achieved great results by switching to energy-efficient office lighting. We now use 45 percent less electricity, but employees are still reminded to power down appliances, lights, and computers when not in use.

Bins for materials you plan to discard are located in each department's office area:

• Regular garbage should be put in the blue trash cans.
• Materials that can be recycled should be placed in the correct trash can according to their material type. Deposit metal items in the red trash cans. (This includes cans of any size, paper clips, and foil wrap.) Put paper into the green trash cans. Please ensure that all sensitive documents are shredded before being discarded.
• The blue trash cans are emptied every day. All other trash cans are taken out every other evening.

A recent company poll indicated that employees would like to recycle plastic products as well. We are looking into this and will let you know more at Friday's meeting.

Together we can make a difference!

Sincerely,

Anwar al Falasi
Director of Maintenance

172. Why did Mr. al Falasi write the notice?

(A) To give an update about a program
(B) To announce an upcoming inspection
(C) To discuss responses to a poll
(D) To ask for a bigger budget

173. What is suggested as an additional way to save resources?

(A) Riding a bicycle twice a week
(B) Turning unused electronics off
(C) Ensuring that discarded paper is shredded
(D) Bringing recyclable products to the office

174. How often are recyclable materials removed?

(A) Every day
(B) Every other day
(C) Once a week
(D) Once a month

175. What is NOT currently being recycled at the company?

(A) Plastic bottles
(B) Paper
(C) Paper clips
(D) Small cans

GO ON TO THE NEXT PAGE

Questions 176-180 refer to the following Web page and e-mail.

www.adoradocc.org_location_contact

| About Us | Our Services | Location & Contact | Programs & Outreach |

Business Marketing Seminars
Sponsored by Benton Advertising and the Adorado Chamber of Commerce

Benton Advertising and the Adorado Chamber of Commerce (ACC) are pleased to offer a new series of marketing seminars. These sessions are presented at no cost to our members by professionals in the field of marketing who will provide instruction on a range of issues. Please note that registration for each seminar is limited to 100 attendees and must be completed at the ACC's downtown location on Broadhurst Ave. Participants will receive travel mugs with the ACC logo.

Topic	Time	Date	Location	Instructor
The Value of Social Media Ads	1:00 P.M. - 5:00 P.M.	June 3	ACC Auditorium	Alyssa Vazquez
The Right Way to Advertise Your New Business	10:00 A.M. - 1:00 P.M.	June 8	ACC Auditorium	Enrique Perez
Big Data for Small Business	3:30 P.M. - 6:00 P.M.	June 15	ACC Auditorium	Andrea Fernandez
Billboards Are Out, Pop-ups Are In	6:00 P.M. - 7:30 P.M.	June 29	ACC Auditorium	Jose Martin

---

From: info@adoradocc.org
To: ajohns@ihat.com
Date: June 2
Subject: Seminar registration
Attachment: Johns.rtf

Dear Ms. Johns,

We applaud your decision to join us for our business marketing seminar. We are sure that you will gain valuable knowledge about how to promote the opening of your store. You will be able to apply everything you learn immediately.

Attached with this e-mail is acknowledgement of your seminar registration. Visit our Web site to view a map to the event facility. Be sure to sign in at the front desk to get a visitor's badge. From there, signs will guide you to the auditorium.

Thank you for your contribution as a member of the Adorado Chamber of Commerce.

Alejandro de las Torres
Adorado Chamber of Commerce

176. According to the Web page, what is being offered?

(A) Private face-to-face meetings with professionals
(B) A computer program to help analyze information
(C) A chance to increase marketing knowledge
(D) Teaching opportunities at a local business school

177. What is NOT indicated about the seminars?

(A) They are hosted by Benton Advertising and the ACC.
(B) They are held in a different location every year.
(C) They are offered to ACC members.
(D) They can fit only up to a certain number of guests.

178. Who will lead the event Ms. Johns is planning to attend?

(A) Ms. Vazquez
(B) Mr. Perez
(C) Ms. Fernandez
(D) Mr. Martin

179. In the e-mail, the word "apply" in paragraph 1, line 2, is closest in meaning to

(A) inquire
(B) use
(C) spread
(D) place

180. What file is attached to the e-mail?

(A) An attendee's confirmation
(B) A certificate of completion
(C) A list of seminar topics
(D) Directions to a venue

GO ON TO THE NEXT PAGE

Questions 181-185 refer to the following memo and e-mail.

To: All Staff
From: HR Department
Date: February 3
Subject: Announcement

At the beginning of the year, Sinor Tech added a new policy, Rule 31-4. It introduces dress code guidelines in the office. Please refrain from wearing exercise-related attire (e.g. hooded track jackets or tight leggings) and clothing with graphic elements (e.g. large logos or images) while at work. Also, please avoid wearing hats or sneakers.

We appreciate your attention to the updated policy. Rule 31-4 will help us maintain a professional office environment.

From: HR Department
To: Staff List
Date: February 12
Subject: Poll: Appropriate Office Attire

Attention Staff:

On Friday, Glassoffice researcher Stan Johnson will pay a visit to Sinor Tech to talk with volunteers about their opinions and experiences with casual office attire and the rules in place prohibiting it. He will present research showing that casual dress standards reduce morale as staff complaints to HR occur more frequently.

Mr. Johnson will also be adding to his research by giving an online questionnaire to our staff. The questionnaire should only require five minutes to complete and is optional. Sinor Tech staff who choose to participate won't be asked for any information that could be used to identify them, and all names will be removed from any published results.

You can fill out the questionnaire by visiting https://www.glassoffice.com/questionnaire.

We value everyone's input.

181. Why was the memo sent?

(A) To give an update on an upcoming product launch
(B) To explain a revised benefits package
(C) To remind staff of a company regulation
(D) To announce a new corporate logo

182. What is the purpose of Mr. Johnson's visit?

(A) To discuss marketing techniques
(B) To demonstrate a device
(C) To introduce a new type of fabric
(D) To share research on dress codes

183. According to Mr. Johnson's research, what will Rule 31-4 most likely reduce?

(A) Staff absences
(B) Employee complaints
(C) Shipping errors
(D) Clothing sales

184. What is indicated about the questionnaire?

(A) It can be accessed through Sinor Tech's Web site.
(B) It has only five questions.
(C) It will be led by the Sinor Tech advertising team.
(D) Participants will not be identified.

185. In the e-mail, the word "value" in paragraph 4, line 1, is closest in meaning to

(A) appreciate
(B) assess
(C) profit
(D) charge

GO ON TO THE NEXT PAGE

To: wjenkins@photoshoot.biz
From: esmythe@aspentree.com
Date: May 3
Subject: Aspentree Country Club's Community Appreciation Day

Dear Mr. Jenkins,

As a long-time member of Aspentree Country Club, it would be a pleasure to see you at our Community Appreciation Day on Sunday, May 31. We are excited to welcome you, as we are planning to host many different activities to promote the benefits of participating in sports. If you reply to this e-mail message before May 10, we will mail you a voucher to receive a special gift.

Eric Smythe
Outreach Director, Aspentree Country Club

Aspentree Country Club's Community Appreciation Day, May 31

Roles and Tasks

• Outreach coordinator: Eric Smythe

• Sponsorship liaison: Lena Goldstein

• Speakers: Ji-hye Lee (Swimming), Scott McAllister (Tennis)

• Children's Badminton Contest: Antonio de Velazquez

• Sports and Arts Instruction / Trainers: Hillary von Teesdale, Mitchell Yorke, Shirley Thorncleft

Appreciation Bash at Aspentree Country Club

by Erin Keelstone, June 2

Last Sunday, Aspentree Country Club held an exciting Community Appreciation Day. In addition to celebrating 35 years in operation, the occasion was a way to thank the community for its support. The facility opened its doors to members and the public alike during this well-attended event.

Participants were able to listen to top athletes give talks, and T-shirts, notebooks, and pens were handed out by business sponsors. Attendees with a special voucher were able to play a complimentary round of golf with our professional instructors.

Throughout the day, a significant number of people gathered for Mitchell Yorke's presentations. "I had intended to find out more about the tennis and swimming classes, but I did not expect to be so entertained by Mr. Yorke's demonstration on how to step to the rhythm of Latin music," said Wally Jenkins.

Without a doubt, the presentation that gathered the biggest crowd was Olympic champion Ji-hye Lee's talk on taking lessons at the club's pool when she was growing up. The audience, which included more than 70 students, was clearly fascinated by the stories of her swimming career. She stayed much longer than scheduled, answering questions and signing autographs.

The badminton competition featuring both singles and doubles matches made all the young attendees very happy. There were treats and ribbons presented by the staff member supervising the games. Aspentree Country Club was so pleased with the turnout that they may make the event a yearly one.

186. What is Mr. Jenkins encouraged to do?

(A) Attend an event
(B) Fill out a questionnaire
(C) Meet with Mr. Smythe
(D) Plan an event

187. How did some attendees likely get a free golf lesson?

(A) By replying to Mr. Smythe's e-mail
(B) By entering a contest
(C) By listening to Ms. Thorncleft's talk
(D) By showing up early to an event

188. What does Mr. Yorke most likely specialize in?

(A) Tennis
(B) Dance
(C) Swimming
(D) Badminton

189. What is indicated about the presentation on swimming?

(A) It drew a lot of interest.
(B) It was canceled.
(C) It was shown on television.
(D) It was given by a country club director.

190. Who most likely distributed ribbons?

(A) Eric Smythe
(B) Hillary von Teesdale
(C) Antonio de Velazquez
(D) Scott McAllister

GO ON TO THE NEXT PAGE

Questions 191-195 refer to the following Web page, e-mail, and notice.

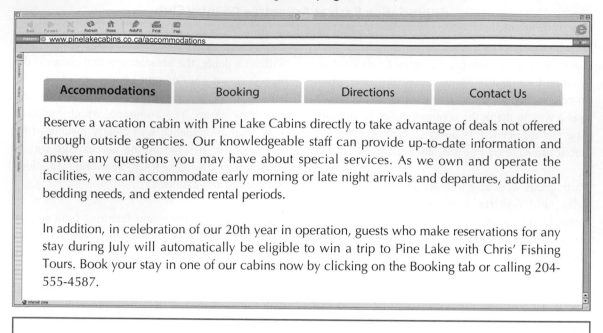

| Accommodations | Booking | Directions | Contact Us |

Reserve a vacation cabin with Pine Lake Cabins directly to take advantage of deals not offered through outside agencies. Our knowledgeable staff can provide up-to-date information and answer any questions you may have about special services. As we own and operate the facilities, we can accommodate early morning or late night arrivals and departures, additional bedding needs, and extended rental periods.

In addition, in celebration of our 20th year in operation, guests who make reservations for any stay during July will automatically be eligible to win a trip to Pine Lake with Chris' Fishing Tours. Book your stay in one of our cabins now by clicking on the Booking tab or calling 204-555-4587.

To: Marcia_Weissblum@friendlymail.com
From: cabins@pinelakecabins.co.ca
Date: 12 June
Subject: Reservation Successful

Dear Ms. Weissblum,

We appreciate your reservation of a cabin through Pine Lake Cabins' Web site. Information regarding your stay is listed below.

Pine Lake Cabins
Pine Lake, BC V0L1C0
Canada

Cabin	Pink Chalet
Rate/Night	$215.00
Additional Charges	3 inflatable kayaks ($30/day each)
Check-in	Thursday, 20 July
Check-out	Saturday, 22 July
Confirmation Code	#759J34

A valid form of identification must be presented upon check-in, along with a 20 percent security deposit. The remainder of your total will be due upon check-out. For recommendations on local activities or tickets to events, please contact the manager on duty.

We hope you enjoy your stay at Pine Lake Cabins.

Sincerely,

Anna Hooper
Pine Lake Cabins

Attention Guests

During your stay, please note the following:

• Jemore Bistro, our on-site facility, is undergoing maintenance and will be closed July 20 through July 24. Please ask one of our receptionists for other great options in town.

• Due to damage from recent storms, our dock is being rebuilt during the week of July 23. Our neighbors, Pine Lake Condos, will provide a place to keep your boat. The usual $25 daily fee applies.

We apologize in advance for any inconvenience that this may cause.

Pine Lake Cabins Rental Management

191. According to the Web page, what is true about Pine Lake Cabins?

(A) Residents are offered reduced rates.
(B) It is frequently booked by travel agencies.
(C) Customers can make special arrangements.
(D) It is currently hiring additional employees.

192. According to the e-mail, what must Ms. Weissblum do on July 20?

(A) Respond to an email
(B) Make a deposit
(C) Bring a coupon
(D) Return some equipment

193. What is implied about Pine Lake Cabins?

(A) It has no vacancy in July.
(B) It is mainly used by families.
(C) It processed Ms. Weissblum's reservation over the phone.
(D) It has entered Ms. Weissblum in a contest.

194. According to the notice, what information can guests obtain from a receptionist?

(A) What eateries are nearby
(B) How to contact cleaning staff
(C) When community events will be held
(D) Where tourist attractions are located

195. What is indicated about Ms. Weissblum?

(A) She will not be able to reserve additional kayaks.
(B) She would prefer to check in earlier in the day.
(C) She would prefer to upgrade her cabin.
(D) She cannot dine at a restaurant on the cabin premises.

GO ON TO THE NEXT PAGE

Questions 196-200 refer to the following letter and e-mails.

October 6

Desiree Sinor
Valiant Manufacturing Ltd.
Marketing Division
Wickham Building

Ms. Sinor,

On November 11, you are invited to attend the safety training session. Company policies and procedures for workplace health and safety will be covered, and a contact list of local emergency services will also be distributed.

Be aware that all full-time staff members are required to attend the event. It will be held in the Northrup Building's event hall from 9 A.M. to 12 P.M. Afterward, a catered meal will be provided across the street in the Camlan Building's dining hall.

To prepare for the training, please read the company manual that was given to you, as it covers some of the content that will be discussed during the session. In the event that you are unable to participate, you will need to alert your team leader and your department's designated personnel associate, David Symonds, right away. Mr. Symonds can be contacted at dsymonds@valiantltd.co.uk or by dialing #432 on your office phone.

We hope to see you at the session.

Sincerely,

Brian Arthur
Head of Personnel
Valiant Manufacturing Ltd.

From: Desiree Sinor
To: David Symonds
Date: November 12
Subject: Safety training

Mr. Symonds,

I was scheduled to participate in the safety training session on November 11. Unfortunately, I had a severe cold in the early morning and went to the hospital that day. I have a confirmation note written by my doctor and can provide it if required. Please advise if there are any additional actions I should take to resolve the situation.

Regards,

Desiree Sinor

From	David Symonds
To	Desiree Sinor
Date	November 12
Subject	RE: Safety training

Hello Ms. Sinor,

I'm sorry to hear you didn't feel well. Please bring me a copy of the doctor's note, and I will add it to your records. I work in the Personnel Department, in suite 407 of the Shalott Building. You are also welcome to send it to me via company e-mail. This is all that we require, as your supervisor has told us that he is aware of the situation.

An additional training event has been scheduled for December 2. It will take place from 3 P.M. to 6 P.M. due to other meetings being held earlier in the day. No meal will be provided, but coffee and light snacks will be available. Refer to the original invitation you received if you need more details.

Sincerely,

David Symonds
Personnel Associate
Valiant Manufacturing Ltd.

196. According to the letter, what is true about the training session?

(A) It is held every two weeks.
(B) It is only open to Personnel employees.
(C) Full-time staff will not be asked to participate.
(D) Staff should review some materials beforehand.

197. Where is Mr. Arthur's office located?

(A) In the Wickham Building
(B) In the Northrup Building
(C) In the Camlan Building
(D) In the Shalott Building

198. Why did Ms. Sinor send the e-mail to Mr. Symonds?

(A) To request a detailed timetable of a workshop
(B) To find out how to make up for a missed event
(C) To suggest a revision to some safety guidelines
(D) To get directions to the Personnel Department's office

199. What will Ms. Sinor probably do next?

(A) Provide a document to the Personnel Department
(B) Ask for a new invitation letter
(C) Complete and upload a file to the company Web site
(D) Speak to a supervisor about her problem

200. What is indicated about the session on December 2?

(A) Attendees will receive a meal voucher.
(B) It will be led by Mr. Symonds.
(C) Some emergency contact information will be given.
(D) It will take place during the morning.

Stop! This is the end of the test. If you finish before time is called, you may go back to Parts 5, 6, and 7 and check your work.

READING TEST

In the Reading test, you will read a variety of texts and answer several different types of reading comprehension questions. The entire Reading test will last 75 minutes. There are three parts, and directions are given for each part. You are encouraged to answer as many questions as possible within the time allowed.

You must mark your answers on the separate answer sheet. Do not write your answers in your test book.

PART 5

Directions: A word or phrase is missing in each of the sentences below. Four answer choices are given below each sentence. Select the best answer to complete the sentence. Then mark the letter (A), (B), (C), or (D) on your answer sheet.

101. They have not ------- reserved a room for the monthly meeting.

(A) soon
(B) much
(C) yet
(D) less

102. In order to file an auto insurance claim, the policy holder must provide ------- from at least two repair shops.

(A) reservations
(B) associations
(C) comprises
(D) estimates

103. Since ------- combined with NW Catch, our market share of the North American salmon industry has expanded.

(A) it　　　　(B) we
(C) its　　　 (D) us

104. The MacGregor Oil Field, which produced ------- 400,000 barrels of oil per day last month, has been purchased by a Norwegian company.

(A) toward
(B) across
(C) nearby
(D) over

105. For the last six months, the Rader Company ------- on an ad campaign for its newly designed model, the R40 motorbike.

(A) has focused　(B) are focused
(C) focusing　　 (D) focuses

106. In spite of a production ------- in the third quarter, unit numbers are still under the monthly target projected in the schedule.

(A) increased　　(B) increase
(C) to increasing　(D) increasing

107. Blackbriar NGO's representatives are ------- to the board of directors.

(A) accounting
(B) account
(C) accountable
(D) accountability

108. Since the parking garage is currently being repaired, guests may reach Prentiss Business Center more ------- by riding the bus.

(A) apparently
(B) accurately
(C) extensively
(D) conveniently

109. Ms. Zhang in the HR Department will call ------- applicants to schedule appointments.

(A) selected
(B) selects
(C) selecting
(D) selection

110. The recent merger means that ------- of SW Corporation's and DC, Inc.'s departments will combine to cut costs.

(A) several
(B) which
(C) range
(D) another

111. The 1.5 million square meter Greun Botanical Garden was ------- the largest park in Barterton.

(A) neither
(B) once
(C) apart
(D) that

112. The responsibility for running GMS Ltd.'s Web site has been ------- to Mr. Reece.

(A) updated
(B) provided
(C) delegated
(D) responded

113. Ten books, five of ------- were over 100 years old, were recently found on the property.

(A) what
(B) which
(C) them
(D) these

114. Less than one year after it ------- bankruptcy, Colby Kitchen Supplies' stock is trading well.

(A) faced
(B) face
(C) facing
(D) faces

115. *Practical Investment Strategies* contains helpful ------- for inexperienced stock traders.

(A) advisable
(B) advisor
(C) advises
(D) advice

116. Despite performing ------- analysis, the engineers were unable to determine the cause of the problem with the new solar panel.

(A) exhaust
(B) exhausted
(C) exhaustedly
(D) exhaustive

117. The study's organizers will consult with universities ------- across the nation.

(A) at
(B) from
(C) in
(D) then

118. Textbooks are ------- shipped to the campus by an assistant in our main warehouse.

(A) greatly
(B) timely
(C) harshly
(D) typically

119. As of this morning, all finalists ------- of their results both by e-mail and by text message.

(A) notified
(B) have been notified
(C) will notify
(D) are notifying

120. ------- the head receptionist is on leave, her assistant will be temporarily promoted to fill her position.

(A) Rather
(B) Instead
(C) While
(D) Yet

GO ON TO THE NEXT PAGE

121. Review Fashion accepts ------- clothes, which are repurposed and donated to local charities.

(A) willing
(B) careless
(C) announced
(D) unwanted

122. Welmarch National Park guests who opt to go on the self-guided walking tour can explore the trails at their own -------.

(A) stability
(B) style
(C) action
(D) pace

123. The publishing company is seeking to hire an editorial assistant capable of ------- various tasks at once.

(A) manage
(B) manager
(C) manages
(D) managing

124. The Ballins Supermarket manager instructed that all display stands be arranged by Friday night in ------- for the weekend sale.

(A) return
(B) preparation
(C) result
(D) compensation

125. To allow enough time to edit, we ------- that articles be emailed at least a week before the publication date.

(A) transmit
(B) recognize
(C) recommend
(D) assure

126. ------- the Morriston City Council, house purchases in the city increased by 20 percent over the previous year.

(A) Regarding
(B) Rather than
(C) While
(D) According to

127. The records archive was reorganized ------- to enable clerks to locate customer data without difficulty.

(A) commonly
(B) considerably
(C) carelessly
(D) consecutively

128. Because of the ------- of car rental agencies in Huntsville, taxi drivers have been making huge profits during the expo.

(A) shortest
(B) shortage
(C) short
(D) shortening

129. Newly released guides often contain glossaries of ------- terms for those unfamiliar with the topic.

(A) relevant
(B) damaged
(C) eventual
(D) constant

130. Ms. Tran will ------- train tickets for all employees taking part in the seminar.

(A) book
(B) accept
(C) authorize
(D) vend

PART 6

Directions: Read the texts that follow. A word, phrase, or sentence is missing in parts of each text. Four answer choices for each question are given below the text. Select the best answer to complete the text. Then mark the letter (A), (B), (C), or (D) on your answer sheet.

Questions 131-134 refer to the following article.

Housing Sales Increasing

The Housing Authority anticipates that by the end of this year new home purchases will exceed 2,000 transactions. This number is 20 percent higher than the ------- year's figure
                                                                                                    131.
and exceeds the all-time record set two years ago. The Housing Authority believes that this increase has occurred for various reasons, ------- the availability of special loans to
                                                                        132.
first-time buyers. Contrary to the demand for residential properties, the commercial real estate market has shown almost no ------- during the past decade despite the city's
                                                              133.
effort to attract new businesses to the area. -------.
                                             134.

131. (A) previous
(B) present
(C) following
(D) overall

132. (A) particular
(B) particularly
(C) particulars
(D) particularity

133. (A) competition
(B) advantage
(C) cost
(D) improvement

134. (A) Some office complexes will actually be demolished in the coming year.
(B) Another reason is the reputation of the local school district.
(C) This effort has been successful thanks to support from the community.
(D) Companies are drawn to the city by low taxes and excellent infrastructure.

GO ON TO THE NEXT PAGE

Questions 135-138 refer to the following information.

Your Denizli beverage dispenser will be an important addition to your business. -------,
135.
making sure that the dispenser is working properly will be an essential part of your daily
operations. Here are several important things to remember to keep your machine in good
condition. First, use Denizli-certified -------, especially Denizli water filters. Second, be
136.
cautious when changing tanks and hoses. Reviewing the user guide will help you to
avoid leaks and spills. Third, stick to the recommended cleaning schedule. -------. Last
137.
of all, if your dispenser requires maintenance, we recommend that you choose a -------
138.
repair specialist. If you keep these four things in mind, your beverage dispenser should
last you a long time.

135. (A) Therefore
(B) Despite this
(C) Basically
(D) In that case

136. (A) connection
(B) power
(C) workers
(D) parts

137. (A) The beverage dispenser can be
operated continuously.
(B) Make sure to use only sterilized
equipment and cleaning solutions
approved by Denizli.
(C) If urgent repairs are required, call the
number on the back of the machine.
(D) Certain drinks are served in much
larger volumes than others.

138. (A) qualify
(B) qualified
(C) qualifying
(D) qualification

Questions 139-142 refer to the following memo.

From: S. Pers, Zoo Superintendent
To: All Staff
Date: 15 August
Subject: Animal Show Policy

This memo is to let all employees know about an update to the ------- policy for our
139.
animal shows, which goes into effect today. We have received a number of same-day
requests from ticket holders who ask to sit next to the aisle due to the extra space.
Effective immediately, we will allow such changes ------- on the day the reservations are
140.
made. Going forward, attendees ------- more leg room are encouraged to sit in the back
141.
rows, as they often have spots available. -------. This change should reduce distractions
142.
while the shows are being held.

139. (A) seating
(B) parking
(C) camera
(D) payment

140. (A) more
(B) only
(C) late
(D) well

141. (A) they require
(B) required
(C) having required
(D) who require

142. (A) The view is not that great, but it is
much more comfortable there.
(B) The dolphin show is currently one of
the most popular attractions.
(C) Weekends are an especially busy
time for us.
(D) Visitors are reminded not to touch or
feed the animals at any time.

GO ON TO THE NEXT PAGE

Coscia Manufacturing, a plastic production company in Lenexa, KS, has received funding from the Kansas Conservation Organization (KCO). The funding was granted based on development plans reviewed by the KCO. These plans call for redesigning Coscia's main plant as an environmentally-friendly facility.

-------. In addition, funding will be used for plant upgrades ------- air filtration and waste
   143.   **144.**
recycling systems. Following these -------, any leftover funds will be invested in research
                              145.
to develop more bio-degradable products.

Don Stecher, Vice President of Manufacturing, ------- this project in partnership with
                                                   146.
Kathleen Valentine of the KCO.

143. (A) Environmental concerns have received much attention in the plastics industry.
    (B) Mr. Stecher is reported to have conducted a similar project at his former company.
    (C) One major inclusion will be solar panels to generate power for machines.
    (D) Finding alternative material sources is a common goal for manufacturers.

144. (A) such as
    (B) whereas
    (C) despite
    (D) so that

145. (A) appointments
    (B) corrections
    (C) advances
    (D) improvements

146. (A) to supervise
    (B) supervising
    (C) will supervise
    (D) were supervising

PART 7

Directions: In this part you will read a selection of texts, such as magazine and newspaper articles, emails, and instant messages. Each text or set of texts is followed by several questions. Select the best answer for each question and mark the letter (A), (B), (C), or (D) on your answer sheet.

Questions 147-148 refer to the following notice.

Details for Classified Advertising

The deadline for placing a classified ad in the *Gilliam Weekly* is Thursday morning at 11:30, for publication on Friday. No changes will be accepted after you submit your text. Only Gilliam reserves the right to edit the text.

Ads are paid for in advance. Advertisements that have already been paid for to run for a month can be canceled after one week for advertising credit in the future. Send the text for your ad to adv@gilliamweekly.com. Discounts are offered for multiple ads.

Call 413-9598 for pricing.

147. What will happen if an advertiser submits an ad on a Friday morning?

(A) The ad will be more expensive for the advertiser.
(B) The ad will be rejected by the newspaper.
(C) The ad will be posted on the following Friday.
(D) The ad will be published on that afternoon.

148. According to the notice, when do advertisers receive credit?

(A) When the newspaper edits the text
(B) When they place a half-page ad
(C) When the newspaper misprints the text
(D) When they cancel an ad

GO ON TO THE NEXT PAGE

Questions 149-150 refer to the following online chat discussion.

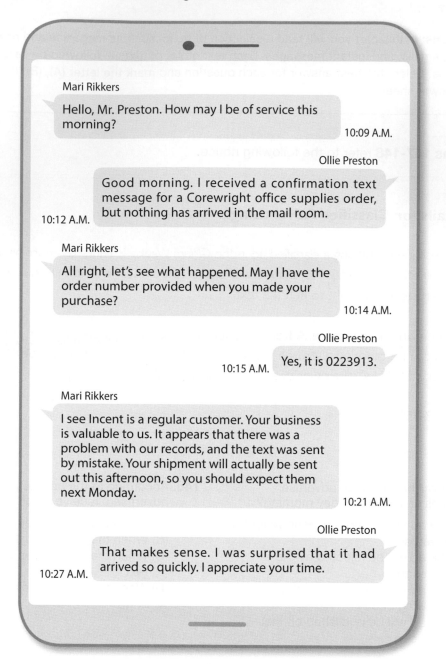

Mari Rikkers

Hello, Mr. Preston. How may I be of service this morning?

10:09 A.M.

Ollie Preston

Good morning. I received a confirmation text message for a Corewright office supplies order, but nothing has arrived in the mail room.

10:12 A.M.

Mari Rikkers

All right, let's see what happened. May I have the order number provided when you made your purchase?

10:14 A.M.

Ollie Preston

10:15 A.M.   Yes, it is 0223913.

Mari Rikkers

I see Incent is a regular customer. Your business is valuable to us. It appears that there was a problem with our records, and the text was sent by mistake. Your shipment will actually be sent out this afternoon, so you should expect them next Monday.

10:21 A.M.

Ollie Preston

That makes sense. I was surprised that it had arrived so quickly. I appreciate your time.

10:27 A.M.

149. What is suggested about Incent?

(A) It is interviewing Mr. Preston next week.
(B) It is a major shipping firm.
(C) It has just updated some customer records.
(D) It has bought from Corewright before.

150. At 10:27 A.M., what does Mr. Preston most likely mean when he writes, "That makes sense"?

(A) He understands why a delivery did not arrive.
(B) He forgot to respond to a text message.
(C) He discovered that a payment was not processed.
(D) He did not go to the right mail room.

Questions 151-152 refer to the following advertisement.

North American Loggers Conference (NALC)

For more than a decade, the NALC has attracted the biggest industry names and thousands of attendees. This year promises to be another big event. It begins with a keynote speech by Alan Luciano, CEO of Westfalls Logging, and continues throughout the week with workshops, seminars, and lectures given by business leaders in the industry. This year's main topic is on the sustainable future of responsible forestry and how paperless offices will affect future growth.

Participating in the NALC guarantees you insider knowledge in today's competitive market. Sign up before April 15 to receive a promotional discount at www.nalc.org.

151. What is indicated about the NALC?

(A) It features talks by business leaders.
(B) It is sponsored by international companies.
(C) It includes product demonstrations.
(D) It is hosted by Westfalls Logging.

152. What event detail is NOT included in the advertisement?

(A) The main topic
(B) A promotion deadline
(C) The location
(D) A guest speaker's job title

GO ON TO THE NEXT PAGE

Questions 153-154 refer to the following Web page.

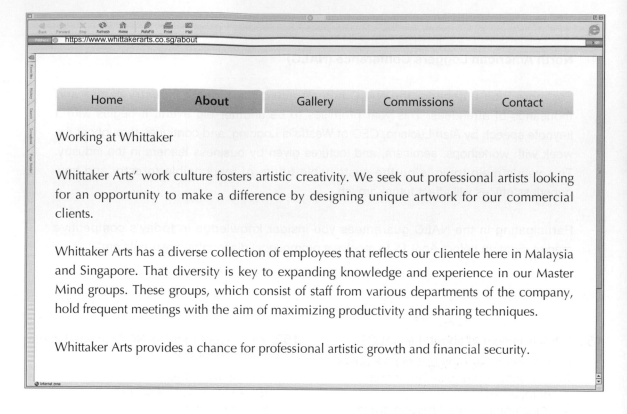

Home   About   Gallery   Commissions   Contact

Working at Whittaker

Whittaker Arts' work culture fosters artistic creativity. We seek out professional artists looking for an opportunity to make a difference by designing unique artwork for our commercial clients.

Whittaker Arts has a diverse collection of employees that reflects our clientele here in Malaysia and Singapore. That diversity is key to expanding knowledge and experience in our Master Mind groups. These groups, which consist of staff from various departments of the company, hold frequent meetings with the aim of maximizing productivity and sharing techniques.

Whittaker Arts provides a chance for professional artistic growth and financial security.

153. What is mentioned about Whittaker Arts' staff?

(A) They are hired by a job placement firm.
(B) They like collaborating with other artists.
(C) They worked for multiple companies.
(D) They are from various backgrounds.

154. What is a purpose of Whittaker Arts' Master Mind groups?

(A) Discussing potential solutions
(B) Recruiting new workers
(C) Contacting potential clients
(D) Providing financial advice

Questions 155-157 refer to the following e-mail.

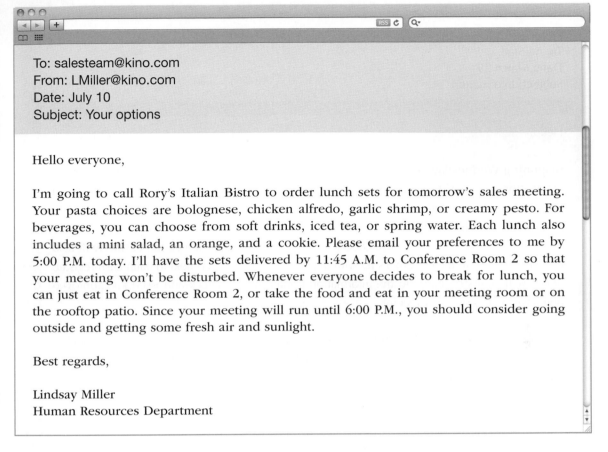

To: salesteam@kino.com
From: LMiller@kino.com
Date: July 10
Subject: Your options

Hello everyone,

I'm going to call Rory's Italian Bistro to order lunch sets for tomorrow's sales meeting. Your pasta choices are bolognese, chicken alfredo, garlic shrimp, or creamy pesto. For beverages, you can choose from soft drinks, iced tea, or spring water. Each lunch also includes a mini salad, an orange, and a cookie. Please email your preferences to me by 5:00 P.M. today. I'll have the sets delivered by 11:45 A.M. to Conference Room 2 so that your meeting won't be disturbed. Whenever everyone decides to break for lunch, you can just eat in Conference Room 2, or take the food and eat in your meeting room or on the rooftop patio. Since your meeting will run until 6:00 P.M., you should consider going outside and getting some fresh air and sunlight.

Best regards,

Lindsay Miller
Human Resources Department

155. What is the purpose of the e-mail?

(A) To inform staff members of a meeting location
(B) To organize the details of a meal
(C) To announce the opening of a new restaurant
(D) To request reimbursement for food expenses

156. What is indicated about the lunch sets?

(A) They include a piece of fruit.
(B) They are offered at a discounted price.
(C) They will be delivered on July 10.
(D) They will be served outdoors.

157. What is suggested about the meeting?

(A) It is held once a year.
(B) It will not stop for lunch at a set time.
(C) It will discuss food and drink sales.
(D) It will take place in Conference Room 2.

GO ON TO THE NEXT PAGE

Questions 158-160 refer to the following e-mail.

From: Erin Sui
To: All Staff
Date: March 29
Subject: Information

Hello,

Beginning Wednesday, Sencomp Electronics will begin requiring the use of a new ID verification system. Customers paying in cash or by credit card will not notice a change upon checkout, but the procedure for customers paying with checks will be different.

Customers will still be able to use checks for their purchases. However, the cashier will also be required to scan the customer's ID with the new scanner located next to each cash register, which will compare the ID to the information printed on the check and issue an "approved purchase" stamp on every receipt.

These new precautions will be instituted in every store nationwide. Customers using voucher slips issued by domestic banks are exempt from this requirement. Please refer to chapter 10 in the employee handbook if you have any questions.

Sincerely,

Erin Sui
CFO
Sencomp Electronics

158. Why was the e-mail written?

(A) To explain the results of a survey
(B) To follow up on a recent order
(C) To suggest a plan to increase sales
(D) To describe a new process

159. What does Ms. Sui indicate about Sencomp Electronics?

(A) It will require identification for some purchases.
(B) It is selling a new line of scanners.
(C) It plans to update its employee handbook.
(D) It will close early on Wednesdays.

160. Who will receive an approval stamp when paying?

(A) Customers paying with cash
(B) Customers paying with a credit card
(C) Customers paying with a check
(D) Customers paying with a voucher slip

Questions 161-164 refer to the following article.

Chao and Tzao Advertising plans on expanding their staff. Company representative George Chao confirmed that at least 150 more workers will be hired to keep up with the changing industry.

"Broadcast advertising has been steadily declining, while digital advertising has been growing at a rapid pace," commented Chao. —[1]—. "Therefore, there has been a growing need for qualified professionals who possess not only creative and editorial skills, but also technical knowledge." —[2]—.

In order to expand its pool of applicants, Chao and Tzao Advertising will be participating in local career fairs. The next fairs in Hong Kong are scheduled on November 28 at the Waterfront Convention Center and on December 9 at City University of Hong Kong. —[3]—. Those seeking employment but unable to attend these job fairs can email Yunna Kim at YKim@chaotzaoad.com for more information. —[4]—.

161. What does Mr. Chao indicate about digital advertising?

(A) It is cheaper than traditional advertising methods.
(B) It requires companies to seek employees with multiple skills.
(C) It is a popular subject for university study.
(D) It will replace conventional forms of advertising.

162. According to the article, what is Chao and Tzao Advertising planning to do?

(A) Raise the salaries of its workers
(B) Open a new location
(C) Take part in events held in Hong Kong
(D) Modify its training procedure

163. Who most likely is Ms. Kim?

(A) A Human Resources specialist
(B) A company sales representative
(C) A university professor
(D) A building manager

164. In which of the positions marked [1], [2], [3], and [4] does the following sentence best belong?

"In particular, the agency is looking for graphic designers, copy editors, technical advisors, and salespeople."

(A) [1]
(B) [2]
(C) [3]
(D) [4]

GO ON TO THE NEXT PAGE

Questions 165-167 refer to the following Web page.

Sierra Theater

A Theater for Performing Arts Showcasing Local and National Productions
We are pleased to present the play, *The Frontier's Cry*

Performances of this musical production will begin on September 15 as part of the theater's *American Greats* series. Theater members may reserve tickets in advance of the show. It features classic and modern songs about life on the frontier.

Allison Lindy, the director of the show, brings more than two decades of experience to the production, which is to run for seven weeks. Before joining the theater's management staff in January of this year, Ms. Lindy was the director of productions at SRO Theater in Boston for seven years; she also spent four years teaching Performing Arts at the Franklin School of the Arts, located in Chicago.

The Frontier's Cry uses state-of-the-art lighting, special effects, and pyrotechnics, as well as historical clothing, hairstyles, and props from America's pioneer days. The performers will hold acting seminars on several dates in October. The price for the workshop is $20 in addition to the normal ticket price and includes free costume rental.

165. What is indicated about *The Frontier's Cry*?

(A) It plays both old and new music.
(B) It will be shown through the end of September.
(C) It is based on recent events.
(D) It is the first performance in the *American Greats* series.

166. Who is Ms. Lindy?

(A) A theater employee
(B) A famous performer
(C) An arts critic
(D) A history professor

167. According to the Web page, what can theater visitors do for an extra fee?

(A) Receive a souvenir
(B) Join an acting workshop
(C) Tour a facility
(D) Watch an exclusive show

Questions 168-171 refer to the following online chat discussion.

Woojung Bae [1:09 P.M.]
I hope you all had a good lunch. I wanted to see where we are on the marketing presentation for our client meeting on Thursday.

Connie Julius [1:10 P.M.]
It's almost completed, but we still need to add the company introduction video.

Woojung Bae [1:11 P.M.]
I believe Jay is in charge of making the video.

Jay Perkins [1:12 P.M.]
Well, I finished filming all of the content. However, I'm having some issues with the video editing software. I can't seem to save my work.

Woojung Bae [1:14 P.M.]
That's not good. Have you tried talking to someone from the IT team?

Jay Perkins [1:15 P.M.]
Yes, I talked to Tim Stowe yesterday, but he wasn't familiar with the program.

Connie Julius [1:17 P.M.]
Have you tried talking to the software's manufacturer? They may be able to provide you with a solution.

Jay Perkins [1:18 P.M.]
Why didn't I think of that? OK, I'll do that right now.

Woojung Bae [1:20 P.M.]
Jay, please let me know once you get that resolved. By the way, Connie, did you make sure we have the conference room for this Thursday?

Jay Perkins [1:21 P.M.]
Of course.

Connie Julius [1:22 P.M.]
I'll contact the HR Manager and check with him.

SEND

168. What is indicated about the presentation?

(A) Its deadline has been extended.
(B) It is missing some materials.
(C) Its content needs to be revised.
(D) It will include a product demonstration.

169. What department does Mr. Stowe most likely work in?

(A) Marketing
(B) Information Technology
(C) Editorial
(D) Human Resources

170. At 1:18 P.M., what does Mr. Perkins mean when he writes, "Why didn't I think of that"?

(A) He did not know about a technical issue.
(B) He wished he provided a better solution.
(C) He should have contacted a business.
(D) He will consider meeting Mr. Stowe.

171. What is Ms. Julius asked to do next?

(A) Confirm a reservation
(B) Interview a candidate
(C) Submit an application
(D) Review a document

GO ON TO THE NEXT PAGE

COGISTICS OPENS LARGE FACILITY

Porto Velho [10 October] — Cogistics Agricorp, the Brazilian coffee producer headquartered in our city, has begun construction of a new processing facility located in Mixco, Guatemala, which is due to open on 7 January. This plant, to be one of the largest in the country, will be managed exclusively by local employees.

The plant will help the company make greater inroads into North American markets. "Roasting our farmers' coffee in Mixco will help us produce fresher, better products. —[1]—. "This should make us one of the top players in a competitive industry," explained Cogistics CEO Marcela Sousa. Ms. Sousa and the rest of the board will lead the inaugural ceremony of the Mixco facility.

Cogistics began offering its products to North American vendors three years ago. —[2]—. This was also where its newest blends of coffee were first introduced. —[3]—. However, regional sales figures have faltered, slumping from a high of $5.1 million in its first year to $3.4 million this year. The company believes that the facility's closer proximity to markets will improve product quality and lead to increased sales.

Cogistics' three other roasting facilities are located in the Brazilian cities of Jaru and Sorocaba and in Cochabamba, Bolivia. —[4]—. Ms. Sousa has also stated that negotiations for a plant located in the Mexican state of Chiapas are underway with government officials there. She believes that a deal will be reached soon.

172. What is mentioned about Cogistics Agricorp?

(A) It plans to increase its business in North America.
(B) It will merge with a competing North American company.
(C) It plans to relocate its headquarters.
(D) It began its operations three years ago.

173. What is suggested about Ms. Sousa?

(A) She will visit Guatemala in January.
(B) She travels to North America frequently.
(C) She will become Mixco's first plant manager.
(D) She is satisfied with the profits from the newest coffee blends.

174. Where will Cogistics Agricorp most likely build its next roasting facility?

(A) In Brazil
(B) In Guatemala
(C) In Mexico
(D) In Bolivia

175. In which of the positions marked [1], [2], [3], and [4] does the following sentence best belong?

"At 9,000 tons of coffee annually, its production goal for this facility is ambitious."

(A) [1]
(B) [2]
(C) [3]
(D) [4]

GO ON TO THE NEXT PAGE

The Pine Oak Hiking Club
What's on the September Agenda?

• **September 9** – Red Deer Trail

   Guide: Nora Bryson
   Difficulty: Easy
   Total length: 5 kilometers
   Trail conditions: Few obstacles; you may encounter strong winds in open areas.

   Meet in front of the Pine Oak Center at 11:00 A.M. Bring water and snacks, and make sure to dress warmly.

• **September 16** – Sequoia Nature Trail

   Guide: Zachary Quinn
   Difficulty: Moderate
   Total length: 7.5 kilometers
   Trail conditions: Some uneven and rocky paths

   Bring water and snacks. We recommend walking sticks.

• **September 23** – No hikes scheduled

• **September 30** – Appalachian Blaze Trail

   Guide: Cooper Hayden
   Difficulty: Moderate to Difficult
   Total length: 11 kilometers
   Trail conditions: Trail grade is steep initially. The rest of the paths are moderate. Two streams must be crossed.

   Pack lunch and water. A camera is recommended to capture some of the breathtaking views. Wear waterproof shoes.

Unless otherwise stated, all hikes will start in front of the Pine Oak Center at 9 A.M. To register or for more information, contact Sydney Brennan at sbrennan@pineoakhike.com.

If you have any questions or want to volunteer to lead a hike, let Sydney know.

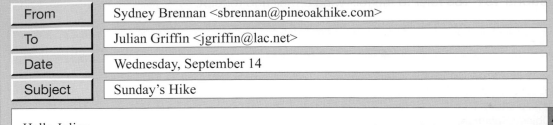

From	Sydney Brennan <sbrennan@pineoakhike.com>
To	Julian Griffin <jgriffin@lac.net>
Date	Wednesday, September 14
Subject	Sunday's Hike

Hello Julian,

You signed up for the hike that Zachary Quinn was scheduled to lead. Unfortunately, Zachary has been suddenly called away on a business trip, so he will not be able to lead that hike. Therefore, we will reschedule the hike for mid-October and also replace the trail with the Plateau View Trail, which is always popular. Its length and difficulty level are similar to that of the Sequoia Nature Trail. I will be personally leading this one. We will meet in the main parking lot of the Fair Creek Hotel and walk to the trailhead together. If you would like to join this hike, please email me by 8 A.M. tomorrow.

Regards,

Sydney

176. What is the purpose of the notice?

(A) To announce changes to club policies
(B) To compare similar types of trails
(C) To request assistance with upcoming club activities
(D) To inform people about hiking opportunities

177. Who most likely is Mr. Quinn?

(A) A club volunteer
(B) A hotel receptionist
(C) A club president
(D) A professional photographer

178. What trail is probably most challenging?

(A) Red Deer Trail
(B) Sequoia Nature Trail
(C) Appalachian Blaze Trail
(D) Plateau View Trail

179. What is true about the hike on September 16?

(A) It requires waterproof shoes.
(B) It has been postponed.
(C) It was originally supposed to be led by Ms. Brennan.
(D) It is perfect for beginners.

180. What is indicated about the Plateau View Trail?

(A) The trail crosses several streams.
(B) The trail is exposed to strong winds.
(C) It has not been hiked by the group.
(D) It is about 7.5 kilometers long.

GO ON TO THE NEXT PAGE

Questions 181-185 refer to the following e-mail and receipt.

From: lfernandes@musemarketers.com
To: customersupport@officepoint.com
Date: January 11
Subject: Shipment
Attachment: Invoice

To Whom It May Concern:

I bought a variety of products from OfficePoint, which arrived yesterday. While the online catalog said the order would take 7 to 10 days to ship, it arrived in just four. However, I was surprised by the low quality of the items. The binders don't close properly; the misalignment of the three inside rings causes the plastic sleeves to fall out. The electric staplers are difficult to turn on. I used the glossy paper to print some brochures, but the coating wasn't as bright as I expected. And although I did not open the box of the matte printer paper, I'll just go for another brand.

I plan to return items 1, 2, 4, and 5 as listed on the attached invoice. I would appreciate it if you could send a package label at your earliest convenience. Our company had no issues with our last purchase through your catalog and left a positive comment on the Web site. Unfortunately, based on our experience this time, we are quite dissatisfied.

Sincerely,

Lionel Fernandes

OfficePoint
www.officepoint.com
The Professional's Choice in Office Supplies

Item	Amount	Price
1. Glossy printer paper (box of 5 reams)	2 @ $40.25	$80.50
2. Matte printer paper (box of 5 reams)	3 @ $29.50	$88.50
3. Paperclips (box of 100)	50 @ $2.99	$149.50
4. Binder with clear sleeves (3 pack)	25 @ $1.99	$49.75
5. Stapler (electric)	5 @ $14.99	$74.95

Subtotal: $443.20

Promo Code: OFFICE10 − $15.00

Tax (7.5%): $32.12

Shipping and Handling:
(standard 7-10 business days) $20.00

Total: $480.32

Returns: Most unopened or unused products can be returned within three months of delivery with credit to your account for the amount of the purchase. Products that have been opened or used are not covered by this policy and may not be returned under any circumstances. A product of equal value may be ordered in situations where a product is deemed defective.

181. What is indicated about Mr. Fernandes' order?

(A) It was delivered earlier than anticipated.
(B) It contained ten electric staplers.
(C) It included damaged merchandise.
(D) It had an extra item.

182. What does Mr. Fernandes mention in the e-mail?

(A) His company has done a marketing campaign for OfficePoint.
(B) He has called OfficePoint's Customer Support.
(C) He received a package label from OfficePoint.
(D) His company has ordered from OfficePoint before.

183. In the e-mail, the phrase "go for" in paragraph 1, line 6, is closest in meaning to

(A) move
(B) rush
(C) reach
(D) choose

184. Which item will Mr. Fernandes most likely have to keep?

(A) The glossy printer paper
(B) The matte printer paper
(C) The binders
(D) The staplers

185. What does OfficePoint offer to its customers?

(A) Credit for items that have been returned
(B) Discounts for large orders
(C) IT support for office equipment
(D) Complimentary shipping for defective items

GO ON TO THE NEXT PAGE

Questions 186-190 refer to the following e-mails and press release.

From	Sean Kim
To	Danica Tomasi
Date	Friday, 7 June, 10:48 A.M.
Subject	Advertisement

Dear Ms. Tomasi,

Good morning from headquarters!

Our Marketing Manager in Beijing, Gwan-yun Yu, has said that the Mandarin translation of our Engage to Exercise Program advertisement can be done by Tuesday, as scheduled, in order for it to be sent out to Mandarin-speaking regions where we conduct business.

However, Mr. Yu recommended that the descriptions accompanying the images be reduced in length. He said most Chinese news agencies request that ads do not contain more than 200 words. He added that the ad will have a higher chance of being published if it's shorter. (I will send you his text message in a moment.) As such, it may be a good idea to make some changes. Please respond when you and your team have decided what to do.

Regards,

Sean Kim
Community Outreach Supervisor
Spectranova, Inc.

From: Danica Tomasi
To: Sean Kim
Date: Friday, 7 June, 3:25 P.M.
Subject: RE: Advertisement
Attachment: New_program.doc

Good afternoon Sean,

It is good to hear from you. I have applied Mr. Yu's suggestion. Please send it to him for translation and distribution after looking it over to ensure that it is error-free. In addition to our media contacts, please remind him that a number of advertisements should be printed and provided to program participants.

Sincerely,

Danica Tomasi
Media Relations Manager
Spectranova, Inc.

Spectranova Reaches Out with New Program

Spectranova, Inc. moves forward with its Engage to Exercise Program. The company is committed to putting $40 million towards athletic clothing and equipment for schools in countries where it conducts business in order to get more children involved in sports, playing a role in promoting healthy activities among the youth. By partnering with school districts and educational outreach organizations, a variety of fitness techniques will be taught to professional educators and academic administrators. Educational institutions will use their facilities to host events, and teachers will coach individual teams to create a greater sense of pride and accomplishment in students' lives. More information about the program can be found online at www.spectranova.co.au/eep.

Spectranova, Inc. is an athletic sporting goods company based in Sydney, with branches in Singapore, Beijing, Taipei, and Los Angeles.

186. What is most likely true about Mr. Yu?

(A) He knows much about news formats in China.
(B) He used to live in Los Angeles.
(C) He is in charge of the Engage to Exercise Program.
(D) He is meeting with Mr. Kim next week.

187. What did Ms. Tomasi do recently?

(A) She went on a business trip to Sydney.
(B) She visited several schools.
(C) She updated some content.
(D) She translated an advertisement.

188. What is one reason for the program?

(A) To invest in factories producing athletic products
(B) To train teachers on fitness activities
(C) To open new educational institutions
(D) To help students learn about national sports teams

189. What is mentioned in the press release?

(A) The type of sports events held at Spectranova
(B) The annual profit that Spectranova generates
(C) The application requirements for Spectranova's program
(D) The market in which Spectranova specializes

190. Where does Mr. Kim most likely work?

(A) In Sydney
(B) In Singapore
(C) In Taipei
(D) In Los Angeles

GO ON TO THE NEXT PAGE

Worldwide Butterfly Forum Rules

• Discussions should relate to butterfly identification only. While there is no limit to the length of a post, off-topic posts such as those related to collecting and breeding butterflies, or equipment sales will be removed.

• Topic lines should be written in the following format: "location, butterfly appearance." Please keep in mind that because posts are made by members from around the world, this information is critical. For example, an acceptable topic line would be: "Gagauzia, Orange, tan, black spots." "I require some assistance" on the other hand is unacceptable.

• Please include high-resolution images of the butterfly as well as information related to the date, time, and temperature of your sighting. The less information you provide, the harder it is to make an accurate identification.

• Because of this Web site's popularity, administrators take around three to five days to comment on a post. Therefore, we ask that members limit themselves to one post per day.

Worldwide Butterfly Forum
Sign up to Become a Member!

Full name: William Hermann

E-mail address: whermann@openmail.net

* Background in insect-related fields: Master's Degree in Botany, research focus on flowering bushes

* Most recent employer: Merricut College

* not required but helps our members identify expert sources of information in posted comments.

Would you like to subscribe to our monthly publication delivered to your inbox?
Yes ☑   No ☐

Member consent agreement:
I agree that the Worldwide Butterfly Forum may use content posted by its users for promotional or advertising purposes. Members' private information will never be sold to other parties.
I agree ☑   I don't agree ☐

New Topic Post

Member: William Hermann
Topic line: Need help with ID
Time: 07/24 2:35 P.M.

I'm on a year-long research trip in Romania where I have encountered this copper and blue butterfly in the field near my worksite. I believe that it is a long-tailed blue butterfly, but want to double-check. A former research assistant of mine said that it is quite destructive to broom plants, which I am here to study. Before I attempt to remove them, I'd like a positive identification. Attached is a photo I took yesterday.

copper_blue_0723.jpg

191. What does the Web page indicate about the forum?

(A) It requires a membership fee to view.
(B) It removes a post after 24 hours.
(C) It allows users to promote their merchandise.
(D) It is used by international participants.

192. What does the Worldwide Butterfly Forum promise its members?

(A) It offers a weekly online newsletter.
(B) It checks work references of new members.
(C) It keeps private information secure.
(D) It will respond to a post within one day.

193. Why did Mr. Hermann post on the forum?

(A) To provide professional advice on a topic
(B) To confirm an assumption
(C) To reply to a post made by another member
(D) To ask for butterfly breeding assistance

194. How did Mr. Hermann break the forum rules?

(A) His topic line is not detailed.
(B) His post does not contain an image.
(C) He advertised an item for sale.
(D) He wrote a post that is too long.

195. What is most likely true about Mr. Hermann?

(A) He is a Web site administrator.
(B) He is applying for a research grant.
(C) He recently published an article in a scientific journal.
(D) He used to do research at a college.

GO ON TO THE NEXT PAGE

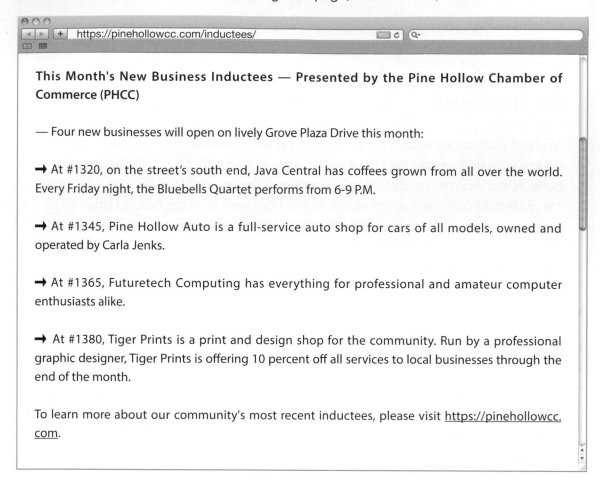

This Month's New Business Inductees — Presented by the Pine Hollow Chamber of Commerce (PHCC)

— Four new businesses will open on lively Grove Plaza Drive this month:

→ At #1320, on the street's south end, Java Central has coffees grown from all over the world. Every Friday night, the Bluebells Quartet performs from 6-9 P.M.

→ At #1345, Pine Hollow Auto is a full-service auto shop for cars of all models, owned and operated by Carla Jenks.

→ At #1365, Futuretech Computing has everything for professional and amateur computer enthusiasts alike.

→ At #1380, Tiger Prints is a print and design shop for the community. Run by a professional graphic designer, Tiger Prints is offering 10 percent off all services to local businesses through the end of the month.

To learn more about our community's most recent inductees, please visit https://pinehollowcc.com.

Pine Hollow Online Gazette—Business Section

Java Central Opens Doors to Sleepy Town

By Tammy Smith

Java Central's doors opened yesterday to wake the sleepy residents of Pine Hollow. Owner Gary Jeffers served more than half the town's population in just hours after opening. The highlight of the day was when Mr. Jeffers began handing out free cappuccinos to every customer in the store. For those not familiar with coffee drinks, like the Cinnamon Mocha Twirl, colorful pictures of each drink are framed on the walls. Next month, Mr. Jeffers will also be adding a small bakery, right next to Java Central, to complement his coffee shop.

Java Central would like to thank Ed Brown for making the beautiful pictures of their different beverages. His store is located at #1380 Grove Plaza Drive.

To	Ed Brown <edbrown@sendanemail.com>
From	Carla Jenks <c.jenks@phauto.com>
Date	Wednesday, April 13
Subject	Request

Hi Ed,

This is Carla from over at Pine Hollow Auto. We met briefly at the Chamber of Commerce ceremony about two weeks ago. I read the *Pine Hollow Online Gazette*'s article about Java Central and saw the beautiful pictures. I was wondering if you could help me make 500 posters. Let me know how long it will take you to complete my order. If possible, I'd like them to arrive at my shop by next Friday. I need my order by this date because I am preparing for an upcoming trade show at Berkenshire. The event will last from April 25 to April 27. Oh, and I'd like to know if I'm able to take advantage of your promotion.

Thank you so much,
Carla

196. What is suggested about Grove Plaza Drive?

(A) Its rental costs have gone up.
(B) Its businesses will provide discounts to local residents.
(C) A new store will open near its southern end.
(D) The PHCC's main office is located there.

197. In the review, the word "highlight" in paragraph 1, line 2, is closest in meaning to

(A) spot
(B) feature
(C) peak
(D) point

198. What is most likely true about Ms. Jenks?

(A) She is a member of the Pine Hollow City Council.
(B) She will sell her office space to Mr. Jeffers next month.
(C) She plans to meet Mr. Brown at an opening ceremony.
(D) She wants Tiger Prints to design some promotional material.

199. Where would Ms. Jenks like her order to be delivered to next Friday?

(A) At 1320 Grove Plaza Drive
(B) At 1345 Grove Plaza Drive
(C) At 1365 Grove Plaza Drive
(D) At 1380 Grove Plaza Drive

200. According to the e-mail, what will happen on April 25?

(A) Mr. Brown will hold a special sale.
(B) Ms. Jenks will relocate her shop.
(C) A convention will begin at Berkenshire.
(D) A new bakery will open on Grove Plaza Drive.

Stop! This is the end of the test. If you finish before time is called, you may go back to Parts 5, 6, and 7 and check your work.

04

READING TEST

In the Reading test, you will read a variety of texts and answer several different types of reading comprehension questions. The entire Reading test will last 75 minutes. There are three parts, and directions are given for each part. You are encouraged to answer as many questions as possible within the time allowed.

You must mark your answers on the separate answer sheet. Do not write your answers in your test book.

PART 5

Directions: A word or phrase is missing in each of the sentences below. Four answer choices are given below each sentence. Select the best answer to complete the sentence. Then mark the letter (A), (B), (C), or (D) on your answer sheet.

101. Vienna Bakery ------- certified organic ingredients to elevate the quality of its pastries.

(A) uses
(B) sets
(C) spends
(D) allows

102. Your responsibilities as a market researcher are essentially the same as -------.

(A) his
(B) himself
(C) he
(D) him

103. All guests will experience outstanding service at our ------- renovated resort on Crystal Cay.

(A) readily
(B) widely
(C) newly
(D) yearly

104. Aberdeen Footwear offers a complete ------- of boots tailored for a variety of indoor and outdoor conditions.

(A) kind
(B) range
(C) fashion
(D) method

105. Please inform the guests that ------- business suites are fully furnished and have wireless internet.

(A) each
(B) all
(C) every
(D) whole

106. Please send ------- for the amount on the utility bill by next Friday.

(A) paid
(B) pays
(C) paying
(D) payment

107. ------- you are unable to locate the information you require, feel free to email us at notfaqs@dgmail.com.

(A) If
(B) As
(C) So
(D) Or

108. The Samson Architects Awards Board introduced a new ------- for designs constructed with eco-friendly materials.

(A) superiority
(B) recruitment
(C) category
(D) engagement

109. A confident presenter is more likely to move around the stage or remain ------- the stand rather than behind it.

(A) against
(B) after
(C) beside
(D) into

110. Ms. Martinez figured that the orientation session ------- three hours, but the talks ran longer than expected.

(A) to last
(B) would last
(C) is lasting
(D) has lasted

111. The receptionist should ------- you with the list of documents you need to enroll in the course.

(A) provide
(B) suggest
(C) explain
(D) outline

112. Providing images of athletes wearing the clothing makes any sportswear campaign more -------.

(A) effectiveness
(B) effectively
(C) effective
(D) effect

113. The science fiction graphic novel *Season of the Trickster* is being transformed into a miniseries ------- Rachel Stonewall and Selena Vasquez.

(A) stars
(B) star
(C) starred
(D) starring

114. After a lengthy debate, the proposal to construct a second bridge across Mohican River was ------- declined.

(A) formerly
(B) finally
(C) densely
(D) hardly

115. The merger cannot be ratified ------- next month because the contract will not be delivered over the public holiday.

(A) among
(B) notwithstanding
(C) following
(D) until

116. Stockbroker Cali Dufresne acknowledges her ability to make ------- trades to skills she learned from her mother.

(A) profited
(B) profiting
(C) profitable
(D) profits

117. Ms. Hwang, the new HR Director, has just ------- the scheduling conflicts that had led to many complications last quarter.

(A) resolved
(B) reminded
(C) finished
(D) offered

118. Mr. Park has been a dependable member of Holcroft & Associates ------- interning during university.

(A) while
(B) since
(C) on
(D) were

119. Ms. Katagara found presenting at the Osaka Tech Convention ------- easy.

(A) comparatively
(B) comparing
(C) comparable
(D) compared

120. Direton businesses are being requested to strictly limit their electricity ------- during the heat wave.

(A) usable
(B) usage
(C) user
(D) useful

GO ON TO THE NEXT PAGE

121. The budget for the technology conference is firmly ------, leaving no possibility for discussion.

(A) establishing
(B) have established
(C) establish
(D) established

122. Holiday donations ------ by the Hartford City Council will be distributed to charities throughout the city.

(A) collect
(B) collected
(C) have collected
(D) are collecting

123. The cabins on the newest cruise ship in the Moonlight Tour fleet have been ------ designed for comfort on long voyages and stormy seas.

(A) instantly
(B) extremely
(C) approximately
(D) intentionally

124. ------ its attractive membership package, Accusure Tax Preparers sees little client turnover.

(A) In support of
(B) Inside
(C) Due to
(D) Regarding

125. Notebook manufacturer Portability confirmed this morning that its ZPC-2050 is already in ------ and will be available in stores by the end of the year.

(A) recession
(B) perception
(C) production
(D) management

126. The Accounting Department requires all staff members ------ payment slips by Thursday at 6 P.M.

(A) submitting
(B) had submitted
(C) to submit
(D) submitted

127. Hermes & Associates' lawyers are ------ permitted to speak to the media during a trial.

(A) hard
(B) high
(C) distant
(D) seldom

128. ------ Mr. Tartus can do to improve the mobile application would be welcomed.

(A) Much
(B) That
(C) Anything
(D) Almost

129. Periodic updates made to member files by Curtis Medical Group are completely ------ and ensures patients' safety and confidentiality.

(A) secure
(B) authentic
(C) definite
(D) dedicated

130. Over the last decade, the maintenance of facilities in the park ------ by the New Jersey Recreation Department.

(A) was managed
(B) has been managed
(C) had managed
(D) would have managed

PART 6

Directions: Read the texts that follow. A word, phrase, or sentence is missing in parts of each text. Four answer choices for each question are given below the text. Select the best answer to complete the text. Then mark the letter (A), (B), (C), or (D) on your answer sheet.

Questions 131-134 refer to the following press release.

Market Tracker, hosted by Tony Calabrese and Josephine Gargano, is a local television show offering the latest updates on the economy ------- investment-related news. *Market*
131.
Tracker was first broadcast a decade ago, with Calabrese giving the updates.

It became one of the most highly-regarded programs in New England after Calabrese

------- Gargano five years later. Over time, the partners ------- to broaden the range of
132. **133.**
program topics to include advice about investment-related matters. -------.
134.

Market Tracker is on once a week, after the stock market closes on Friday afternoon.

131. (A) therefore
(B) along with
(C) additionally
(D) in regard

132. (A) referred
(B) transferred
(C) joined
(D) hired

133. (A) agreeing
(B) agreement
(C) agreed
(D) agreeable

134. (A) The shows often feature talks by successful money managers.
(B) Financial journalism has become a very competitive field over the decade.
(C) Investors can do research on their own by using the internet.
(D) Most advisors recommend owning a wide variety of investments to reduce risk.

GO ON TO THE NEXT PAGE

GreenPlus Hotel

Frequently Asked Questions

How can I confirm that my hotel reservation has been processed?

-------. If you do not receive this notification, contact your financial institution. If no
135.
payment has been made to our resort, it is ------- that your transaction was not
136.
completed.

-------, please call us at 800-555-1212 so that we may assist you with the problem. This
137.
number is toll-free if you are calling from inside the country, but ------- that you may be
138.
charged for calls made from foreign locations.

---

135. (A) Please note that we will never contact you about payments via e-mail.
(B) We offer several convenient online booking options for overseas guests.
(C) Visitors who arrive without reservations are accommodated when possible.
(D) You should receive your room information via e-mail within 24 hours.

136. (A) likely
(B) simple
(C) necessary
(D) appropriate

137. (A) However
(B) Furthermore
(C) In this event
(D) In conclusion

138. (A) remember
(B) remembers
(C) remembered
(D) remembering

Questions 139-142 refer to the following memo.

To: All Marley Supplements staff
From: Edgar Marley
Date: December 3
Subject: Survey Findings

At today's board meeting, a decision was made that will increase company profits and also improve our firm's reputation.

The Strategy Department ------- findings from their survey at the meeting. They also
139.
showed how purchasing locally-raised agricultural products to support the area's economy would reduce our shipping expenses.

The survey revealed that customers prefer to buy from companies that invest in the local economy. Accordingly, ------- will replace our present overseas partners with nearby
140.
producers.

Furthermore, the Shipping Department will begin working with several companies here in town for storage and delivery services that create jobs for the people of this community. Our drivers, warehouse workers, and other valued employees will be hired from the immediate vicinity.

-------. In the long run, these changes should have a ------- impact on both our
141.   142.
profitability and our image in the community.

139. (A) will have shared
(B) will share
(C) shared
(D) is sharing

140. (A) we
(B) it
(C) your
(D) her

141. (A) This is because there simply are too few qualified candidates in this area.
(B) Current employees should be given the opportunity to apply first for any such opening.
(C) An announcement will be posted on our Web site to inform the public about these exciting plans.
(D) Some board members were unable to attend because of prior commitments.

142. (A) supplementary
(B) reduced
(C) favorable
(D) foreign

GO ON TO THE NEXT PAGE

Josephine Lucchese
Trujillo Systems
9822 W. 95 St.
Overland Park, KS 66212

Dear Ms. Lucchese,

-------. Trujillo Systems' product sorting machine has been extremely helpful to us in the
143.
six months since we installed it. Our factory ------- reliable and accurate methods of
144.
inspecting and sorting large shipments of agricultural materials. Now that we are using

Trujillo Systems' product, we can evaluate the quality of materials better and quickly

organize them in our plant. Due to its customizable features, workers are able to

configure the machine to their ------- settings. Since the machine has allowed us to
145.
reduce time spent on projects, we have achieved major ------- in efficiency. We continue
146.
to be very impressed with your product, and we fully expect to attain even better results

thanks to Trujillo Systems as time goes on.

Best regards,

David Benavides

David Benavides
Vice President, AgroSur Industries

---

143. (A) We thank you for considering a
career at AgroSur Industries.
(B) Your business has been a loyal client
of AgroSur Industries.
(C) AgroSur Industries needs to
purchase a new product sorting
machine soon.
(D) I am happy to provide input as a
representative of AgroSur Industries.

144. (A) will lack
(B) are lacking
(C) lack
(D) used to lack

145. (A) final
(B) desired
(C) extra
(D) useful

146. (A) instructions
(B) separations
(C) improvements
(D) answers

PART 7

Directions: In this part you will read a selection of texts, such as magazine and newspaper articles, emails, and instant messages. Each text or set of texts is followed by several questions. Select the best answer for each question and mark the letter (A), (B), (C), or (D) on your answer sheet.

Questions 147-148 refer to the following information.

Take Citywide Info

Don't have time to go to the post office? We guarantee that our bike messengers can complete urgent deliveries anywhere in town in under an hour, at any time of day or night.

Just log on to our Web site to find out how much you have to pay for delivery. Your quote will be based on how much your package weighs.

After our messenger takes your parcel, you will be provided with a special code that allows you to track its progress in real time, with a constantly-updated arrival time.

147. What is included in the information?

(A) Short distance deliveries are discounted.
(B) Large parcels must be sent out by regular mail.
(C) Customers can calculate a price online.
(D) Bike messengers will call recipients before departing.

148. What is the purpose of the special code?

(A) To change an order's destination
(B) To view a delivery's progress
(C) To receive a cost estimate
(D) To estimate a package's size

GO ON TO THE NEXT PAGE

Questions 149-150 refer to the following e-mail.

To: Liam Daniels
From: Eilana Guedes
Date: May 29
Subject: Remerton branch

Dear Mr. Daniels,

Last November, your application to relocate to the Remerton branch was not approved because there was no availability there during that time. The Remerton branch director contacted me today, however, and said that he's looking for an experienced assistant store manager. In addition, he is considering internal applicants first, so I wanted to give you priority. If you are still interested in this opportunity, please inform me by this Thursday. If you would like to just stay at your current branch, I'll go ahead and post the opening on our company's announcement board. I await your response.

Sincerely,
Eilana Guedes

149. Why was the e-mail written?
(A) To request feedback on a computer program
(B) To introduce a new assistant store manager
(C) To forward directions to an office
(D) To announce an open position

150. What will Ms. Guedes wait to do?
(A) Speak with a branch director
(B) Hold a training session
(C) Respond to an e-mail
(D) Publish an ad

Questions 151-152 refer to the following text message chain.

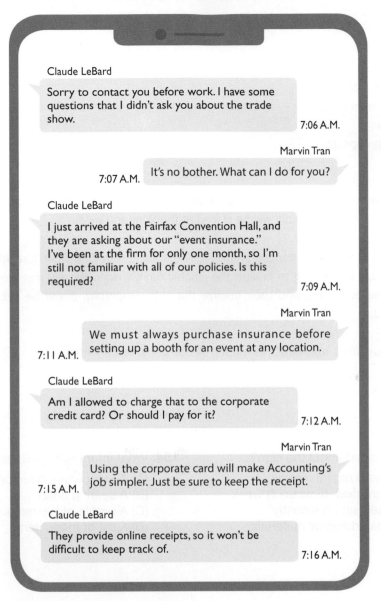

Claude LeBard
Sorry to contact you before work. I have some questions that I didn't ask you about the trade show.
7:06 A.M.

Marvin Tran
7:07 A.M.
It's no bother. What can I do for you?

Claude LeBard
I just arrived at the Fairfax Convention Hall, and they are asking about our "event insurance." I've been at the firm for only one month, so I'm still not familiar with all of our policies. Is this required?
7:09 A.M.

Marvin Tran
We must always purchase insurance before setting up a booth for an event at any location.
7:11 A.M.

Claude LeBard
Am I allowed to charge that to the corporate credit card? Or should I pay for it?
7:12 A.M.

Marvin Tran
Using the corporate card will make Accounting's job simpler. Just be sure to keep the receipt.
7:15 A.M.

Claude LeBard
They provide online receipts, so it won't be difficult to keep track of.
7:16 A.M.

151. At 7:07 A.M., what does Mr. Tran mean when he writes, "It's no bother"?

(A) He thinks that Mr. LeBard should not purchase additional insurance.
(B) He welcomes Mr. LeBard's inquiries.
(C) Mr. LeBard is able to submit an online receipt.
(D) Mr. LeBard can easily find information about booth setup.

152. What is indicated about Mr. LeBard?

(A) He requires reimbursement for his meals.
(B) He has signed up for a new credit card.
(C) He needs help preparing for a presentation.
(D) He has recently joined a new company.

GO ON TO THE NEXT PAGE

MEMO

FROM: Garett Jacotey
TO: Ciao Down Employees
DATE: June 3
SUBJECT: Sign update

This is to provide further information about our recently purchased electronic display which our restaurant's owner has said will be placed at the front entrance.

The new screen will feature images of daily specials along with Ciao Down's regular options, although we are still waiting to finalize the graphic design work. We will make our decision in the next several days, and then finalize the sign. Hopefully, it will be set up by the beginning of July.

If you have questions regarding this matter, please get in touch with me.

Garett Jacotey

153. What is indicated about the sign?

(A) It will have a digital display.
(B) It will show new items each week.
(C) It has been set up recently.
(D) It requires additional materials.

154. What information will the sign include?

(A) An employee directory
(B) A seating chart
(C) A profile of the restaurant's owner
(D) A list of menu items

Questions 155-157 refer to the following article.

June 5—The Delaney Bay Cultural Association (DBCA) announced yesterday that Janice Sullivan won the Eighth Annual Amateur Photography Contest. Her award-winning entry, titled *Peace*, along with the entries of the other twelve finalists, will be shown from August 1 to August 10 at the DBCA Arts Center. On August 11, there will be an award ceremony where Ms. Sullivan will be presented with a $2,000 cash prize in honor of her achievement by DBCA President Phillip Gonzales. While admission to the exhibition is free, any financial contributions are welcome to support the DBCA's work.

This will be the first time that the DBCA will be featuring the works of this year's competitors on its Web site. "The online gallery will allow more people to view and enjoy selected works by some of our city's most talented photographers," said Mr. Gonzales.

It is important to note that the arts center won't be open from August 12 to August 31 due to its yearly summer break. The center will reopen for its fall season on Monday, September 1, with a special lecture on different types of jazz music presented by local musicologist Dr. Miriam Katano.

155. What is NOT indicated about exhibition?

(A) It will end on August 10.
(B) It is only open to professional photographers.
(C) It does not charge an entrance fee.
(D) It will feature Ms. Sullivan's work.

156. What is indicated about Ms. Sullivan?

(A) She will judge a photography competition in June.
(B) She is a member of a cultural organization.
(C) She is a music professor at a university.
(D) She will be attending an event on August 11.

157. What does the article imply about the arts center?

(A) It offers art courses to the public.
(B) It has recently attracted more visitors.
(C) The winning entry from last year is available online.
(D) The photography exhibit will be the last show of the season.

GO ON TO THE NEXT PAGE

Questions 158-160 refer to the following advertisement.

Doiron Financial

Doiron Financial provides excellent investing and wealth management services. It was started 25 years ago by Allan Doiron, who came to New Haven after working as a successful banker for many years in Hartford.

Originally focused on individuals wishing to prepare for retirement or invest in stocks, the company built up a sound reputation locally. That helped it to get small- and medium-sized business clients that needed services beyond just basic investments. Allan's daughter became the company's CEO six years ago and began working with many high-profile corporations across the state, including Delta-U Pharmaceuticals and Avytech Electronics, and opened new offices in Hartford and Bridgeport.

While the markets have had their ups and downs, and competition is fierce, the company has a reputation for providing long-term strategies that stand the test of time and help corporate and individual clients meet their objectives.

For financial assistance you can rely on, look no further than Doiron Financial. Information and services are provided on our Web site at www.doironfinancial.com.

---

158. Where would the advertisement most likely appear?

(A) At an electronics convention
(B) In a city newspaper
(C) At a job fair
(D) In a travel magazine

159. What is most likely true about Doiron Financial?

(A) It is planning to purchase a rival firm.
(B) It is a family-run company.
(C) Its clients are mostly retirees.
(D) Its main office is in Hartford.

160. What is NOT stated as a change Doiron Financial has experienced?

(A) An update to its security policies
(B) An appointment of a new executive
(C) An expansion into other cities
(D) An increase to its customer base

Questions 161-164 refer to the following online chat discussion.

Julia Cassel [2:09 P.M.]
Good afternoon, Sora and Kevin. I'm wondering if a package was dropped off. Some documents are supposed to be delivered to me today, but I'm concerned they may have been sent to another building. They're from Ortlieb Marketing and should have a label that says "priority."

Sora Johnson [2:10 P.M.]
We haven't received anything at the reception desk. I think you should go to the Security Office in the main lobby.

Kevin Lee [2:12 P.M.]
I see a large envelope from Ortlieb Marketing, here in the HR office, but I can't find the recipient's name.

Julia Cassel [2:13 P.M.]
That is probably mine. Do you mind checking the package's label again?

Kevin Lee [2:14 P.M.]
I apologize. I see your name now. It was written underneath the address.

Julia Cassel [2:16 P.M.]
Wonderful. I need that package sent over to my office right away, please.

Kevin Lee [2:17 P.M.]
Sure. I was about to go to the 3rd floor anyway.

Julia Cassel [2:20 P.M.]
Thank you so much.

SEND

---

161. Why did Ms. Cassel start the online chat discussion?

(A) She is preparing a sales report.
(B) She is waiting for some important documents.
(C) She sent a package to the wrong address.
(D) She is expecting some clients to arrive soon.

162. What does Ms. Johnson recommend doing?

(A) Contacting Ortlieb Marketing
(B) Visiting another area
(C) Checking the receptionist desk
(D) Moving a meeting location

163. At 2:14 P.M., what does Mr. Lee most likely mean when he writes, "I apologize"?

(A) He did not read a label correctly.
(B) He needs Ms. Cassel to provide clearer directions.
(C) He is unable to arrive at the office on time.
(D) He cannot find a shipping invoice.

164. What will Mr. Lee probably do with the package?

(A) Review its contents
(B) Give it a receptionist
(C) Take it to the post office
(D) Bring it to Ms. Cassel

GO ON TO THE NEXT PAGE

ANDREA SARCHET'S RETURN

The Operations Oversight Division is pleased to welcome back senior corporate counsel Andrea Sarchet. —[1]—. For six weeks, Andrea has been in New York City participating in a professional workshop on Corporate Legal Requirements. Legal policy training enables companies to ensure that they obey the latest regulations. Andrea is a part of an increasing number of executives who have finished this challenging program. —[2]—. As a member of the National Committee of Corporate Legal Counselors (NCCLC), Andrea was recognized for playing a role in writing a set of guidelines to help companies avoid lawsuits. —[3]—. Fantastic job, Andrea! —[4]—.

165. What is suggested about Andrea Sarchet?

(A) She was recently promoted.
(B) She works as a lawyer.
(C) She often goes on business trips.
(D) She lives in New York City.

166. What is NOT indicated about the workshop?

(A) It lasted for six weeks.
(B) It provided training on corporate regulations.
(C) It was organized by the NCCLC.
(D) It has been attracting more executives.

167. In which of the positions marked [1], [2], [3], and [4] does the following sentence best belong?

"Several participants are CEOs from well-known corporations."

(A) [1]
(B) [2]
(C) [3]
(D) [4]

Work Continues at Local Parks

MIDDLETON (September 6) – The town of Middleton is currently expanding and renovating 15 of its 30 parks. These improvements so far have cost the town €4.1 million, which is equivalent to the annual amount spent by the Middleton Parks Department (MPD) on operating and maintaining the park's facilities. An extra €1.5 million will also be spent before all the renovation work is finished next month, which brings the total cost to approximately €5.6 million.

However, this renovation project will not burden the town's budget, as it is funded by the MPD. Over the last few years, the local parks have drawn more and more visitors from outside of town.

This has helped lead to a strong growth in profits, which come from parking fees, equipment rental fees, sales at snack shops, and events held at the parks. In fact, last year's figures show that the MPD generated €6.6 million in profit, making it one of the few Parks Departments in the country that can be considered financially independent.

The renovation project is the result of extensive research done last June by the MPD that mainly focused on the conditions of the town's parks. As part of the research, a survey was administered to 2,000 local residents who regularly frequent the town's parks. One of the main things the participants were asked to do was to evaluate the quality of the facilities and to make any suggestions. The compiled data and project proposal were then submitted to the Town Council. After careful review, the council decided to approve the MPD's renovation project.

168. How much does it cost the Middleton Parks Department each year to manage the town's parks?

(A) €1.5 million
(B) €4.1 million
(C) €5.6 million
(D) €6.6 million

169. What is expected to happen in October?

(A) Renovations will be completed.
(B) A park will be closed.
(C) Survey forms will be distributed.
(D) A new town official will be appointed.

170. How is the Middleton Parks Department different from other similar agencies?

(A) It provides a wide variety of activities.
(B) It operates the largest park system in the country.
(C) It mostly relies upon donations.
(D) It supports itself from the revenue it generates.

171. Who was consulted for suggestions before the current project began?

(A) Middleton residents
(B) International tourists
(C) Economics professors
(D) Landscape architects

GO ON TO THE NEXT PAGE

From:	Lupe Cantu
To:	Dylan Amano; Stephan Mendoza; Kira Goldstein; Melissa Ahn
Date:	September 19
Subject:	Company program
Attachments:	Class_Goals;
	Policies_Code_of_Conduct;
	Press_Release_Template

Hello everyone,

Thank you all for agreeing to create a new hire training program in anticipation of opening our second office in Calgary on December 3. —[1]—. Like we discussed during last week's planning session, five classes will need to be designed. —[2]—. I am assigning the following responsibilities to each of you; please note the dates by which each task should be completed. —[3]—.

Dylan Amano: Make detailed summaries about what will be covered for each class by October 21. (Refer to the attached class goals.)

Stephan Mendoza: Create presentation slides with the guidelines and policies to be taught. (See attached HR document.)

Dylan Amano: Upload training materials to the employee Web page. (Send this information to Seth Adalja in IT.)

Kira Goldstein: Contact all new hires about the training class schedule. (A list of names will be emailed next month.)

Melissa Ahn: Create a press release announcing our second office's opening and the new training courses. (Complete the attached press document and send it to Wren Torea in Marketing by November 19.)

—[4]—. Our next planning session will be held on October 18 to review our progress. Until that time, if you have any problems or questions, please let me know.

Lupe Cantu
Personnel Manager

172. When are the class descriptions due?

(A) On October 18
(B) On October 21
(C) On November 19
(D) On December 3

173. Who does NOT need to use one of the e-mail attachments?

(A) Mr. Amano
(B) Mr. Mendoza
(C) Ms. Goldstein
(D) Ms. Ahn

174. What does Mr. Cantu ask the recipients to do before the next meeting?

(A) Inspect a new workplace
(B) Submit their assignments to him
(C) Work in pairs on all tasks
(D) Inform him of any issues

175. In which of the positions marked [1], [2], [3], and [4] does the following sentence best belong?

"There are plenty of things to do until then."

(A) [1]
(B) [2]
(C) [3]
(D) [4]

GO ON TO THE NEXT PAGE

Questions 176-180 refer to the following Web page and e-mail.

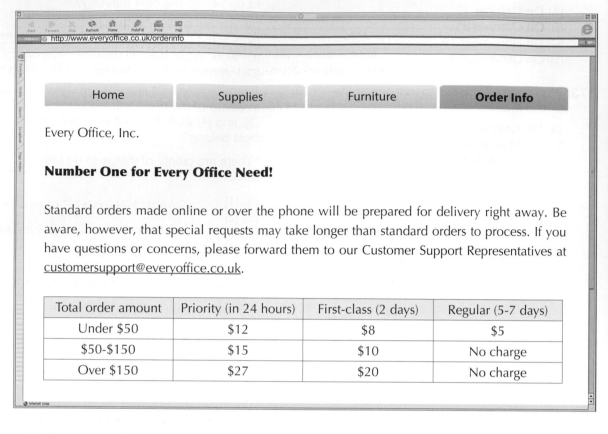

| | Home | Supplies | Furniture | **Order Info** |

Every Office, Inc.

Number One for Every Office Need!

Standard orders made online or over the phone will be prepared for delivery right away. Be aware, however, that special requests may take longer than standard orders to process. If you have questions or concerns, please forward them to our Customer Support Representatives at customersupport@everyoffice.co.uk.

Total order amount	Priority (in 24 hours)	First-class (2 days)	Regular (5-7 days)
Under $50	$12	$8	$5
$50-$150	$15	$10	No charge
Over $150	$27	$20	No charge

To	customersupport@everyoffice.co.uk
From	mkline@supermail.co.uk
Date	September 6
Subject	Delivery #4508-1E

My company ordered name badges and lanyards for $165 for a conference that begins Friday. Based on the e-mail that was sent upon receipt of my order, they should have arrived yesterday. As I am still waiting for them to arrive, despite having paid an additional fee for first-class delivery, I would ask that our account be refunded that amount. If the items do not arrive by tomorrow morning, I would appreciate it if you could cancel our order since we will need to purchase the products at a local store.

Thank you,

Mark Kline

176. In the Web page, what is indicated about Every Office, Inc.'s shipping?

(A) Regular shipping for orders less than $50 is complimentary.
(B) Shipping fees are based on the weight of the items.
(C) Local orders may receive a discount.
(D) Some orders may take seven days to be delivered.

177. On the Web page, the word "forward" in paragraph 1, line 3, is closest in meaning to

(A) ship
(B) push
(C) expedite
(D) submit

178. What is the purpose of the e-mail?

(A) To report some damaged merchandise
(B) To indicate a delivery issue
(C) To inquire about a custom order
(D) To obtain directions to a local supplier

179. How much did Mr. Kline pay for shipping?

(A) $5
(B) $12
(C) $20
(D) $27

180. According to the e-mail, why might Mr. Kline decide to visit a local store?

(A) He must have his items before a specific date.
(B) He wants to choose from a wider selection of products.
(C) He prefers to do business with local retailers.
(D) He hopes to buy the items at a cheaper price.

GO ON TO THE NEXT PAGE

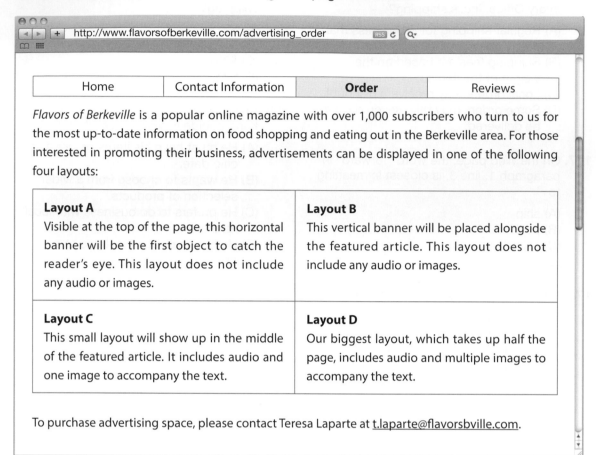

| Home | Contact Information | **Order** | Reviews |

Flavors of Berkeville is a popular online magazine with over 1,000 subscribers who turn to us for the most up-to-date information on food shopping and eating out in the Berkeville area. For those interested in promoting their business, advertisements can be displayed in one of the following four layouts:

Layout A
Visible at the top of the page, this horizontal banner will be the first object to catch the reader's eye. This layout does not include any audio or images.

Layout B
This vertical banner will be placed alongside the featured article. This layout does not include any audio or images.

Layout C
This small layout will show up in the middle of the featured article. It includes audio and one image to accompany the text.

Layout D
Our biggest layout, which takes up half the page, includes audio and multiple images to accompany the text.

To purchase advertising space, please contact Teresa Laparte at t.laparte@flavorsbville.com.

From	Benjamin Kane <b.kane@bruebistro.com>
To	Teresa Laparte <t.laparte@flavorsbville.com>
Date	October 24
Subject	Advertisement for Brue Bristo

Dear Ms. Laparte,

I was hoping to post another advertisement with *Flavors of Berkeville*. I'd like to go with the large advertisement layout again. Please go ahead and use the same audio and text as before, but this time I will give you three new photos of my recently remodeled restaurant. I'll leave it up to your design artists to decide where to place the photos in the advertisement. Could you tell me the size requirements for submitting images?

Sincerely,

Benjamin Kane
Owner,
Brue Bistro

181. Where does Ms. Laparte work?

    (A) At a local restaurant
    (B) At a food-related publisher
    (C) At a Web design firm
    (D) At a food manufacturing company

182. What is stated about Layout A?

    (A) It is easily noticed.
    (B) It is affordable.
    (C) It can be made very quickly.
    (D) It includes the most text.

183. In what advertisement layout is Mr. Kane most likely interested?

    (A) Layout A
    (B) Layout B
    (C) Layout C
    (D) Layout D

184. What is suggested about Brue Bistro?

    (A) It will be closed during renovations.
    (B) It is being remodeled by a famous design artist.
    (C) It has been advertised in *Flavors of Berkeville* before.
    (D) It was recently nominated for an award.

185. What does Mr. Kane ask about the photos?

    (A) How much does it cost to print them
    (B) How big they should be
    (C) Where they should be sent
    (D) How many are allowed

GO ON TO THE NEXT PAGE

Toronto (November 23) — Starting next week, Wayne McAllister, award-winning reporter and founder of the decade-old Ontario Online, will give a series of seminars on issues currently facing journalism.

Mr. McAllister will speak at Vancouver's Main Street Auditorium on December 1 and 2. He will speak at Quebec City's Oiseau Convention Hall on December 4. On December 6, he will give a talk in Winnipeg's Downtown Auditorium. On December 8, he will head to Toronto's Metro Conference Center. And on December 9, he will wrap up with a talk at Montreal's Commons Library.

Seats are selling out fast. For more information and to purchase tickets, visit www.ontarioonline.co.ca.

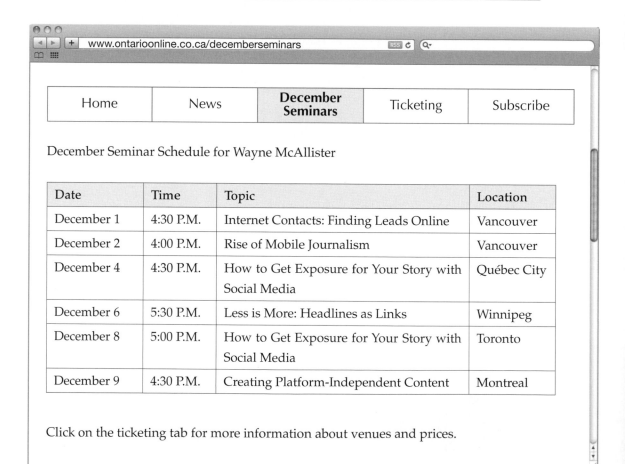

www.ontarioonline.co.ca/decemberseminars

| Home | News | **December Seminars** | Ticketing | Subscribe |

December Seminar Schedule for Wayne McAllister

Date	Time	Topic	Location
December 1	4:30 P.M.	Internet Contacts: Finding Leads Online	Vancouver
December 2	4:00 P.M.	Rise of Mobile Journalism	Vancouver
December 4	4:30 P.M.	How to Get Exposure for Your Story with Social Media	Québec City
December 6	5:30 P.M.	Less is More: Headlines as Links	Winnipeg
December 8	5:00 P.M.	How to Get Exposure for Your Story with Social Media	Toronto
December 9	4:30 P.M.	Creating Platform-Independent Content	Montreal

Click on the ticketing tab for more information about venues and prices.

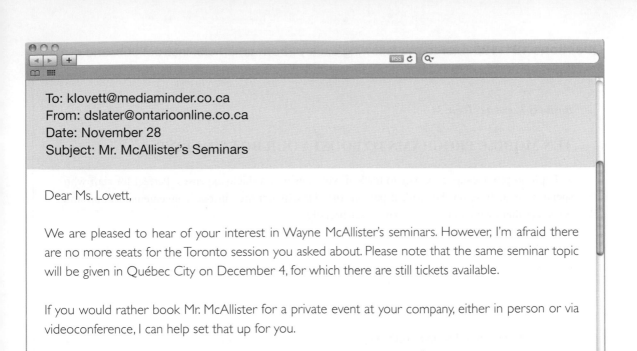

To: klovett@mediaminder.co.ca
From: dslater@ontarioonline.co.ca
Date: November 28
Subject: Mr. McAllister's Seminars

Dear Ms. Lovett,

We are pleased to hear of your interest in Wayne McAllister's seminars. However, I'm afraid there are no more seats for the Toronto session you asked about. Please note that the same seminar topic will be given in Québec City on December 4, for which there are still tickets available.

If you would rather book Mr. McAllister for a private event at your company, either in person or via videoconference, I can help set that up for you.

Sincerely,

Daniel Slater
Ontario Online

186. What is indicated about Mr. McAllister?

(A) He opened a business 10 years ago.
(B) He lives in Québec City.
(C) He regularly gives free seminars at convention halls.
(D) He tours Canada every December.

187. Where will the talk regarding headlines be given?

(A) The Main Street Auditorium
(B) The Downtown Auditorium
(C) The Oiseau Convention Hall
(D) The Commons Library

188. What is the purpose of the e-mail?

(A) To announce a scheduling delay
(B) To accept an invitation
(C) To book a private speaking engagement
(D) To reply to an inquiry

189. What event date was Ms. Lovett originally interested in?

(A) December 2
(B) December 4
(C) December 6
(D) December 8

190. What most likely is Mr. Slater's occupation?

(A) Company CEO
(B) Web site developer
(C) Administrative specialist
(D) News reporter

GO ON TO THE NEXT PAGE

Business Partners: Issue 34

TEN MOBILE PROGRAMS TO BOOST YOUR BOTTOM LINE

1. Tripfolio provides an easy way to track all your business vehicle expenses. Perfect for staff who spend a lot of time on the road, it puts all of your expenditures in one convenient location and organizes them with an interface that is user-friendly.

When you get behind the wheel with your mobile device running Tripfolio, it will track where you go with the device's navigation function and upload it. Each trip is put in a virtual log, creating an exact record of your route. Access the log to add trip details like fuel expenses or to comment on traffic conditions.

You can access new features to display traffic conditions, parking availability, or time-saving shortcuts. One popular use of this is to optimize trips that happen regularly, like deliveries, weekly client meetings, and airport shuttling.

Every route is backed up on the application's server. The app's price covers usage, storage, and ongoing development costs. A Personal plan is priced at $5 per month and comes with 20 virtual logs for the month. More expensive plans come with a larger number of virtual logs.

Thank you for downloading the Tripfolio mobile app!

To get started, please fill out the information below. Once completed, you can start your first virtual log. Don't forget that subscription upgrades are available. If you need more logs, visit www.tripfolioapp.com/accounts. Drive safely!

User Details:
Name: William Burke
E-mail: williamb@sunkitsales.com
Mobile number: 702-555-6813
How frequently do you travel? 11-14 times weekly
Do you ever visit other cities: Yes
Frequent destinations: Los Angeles, Phoenix, Santa Fe, Albuquerque

Select a Plan:
Personal: $5.00/month ☐
Small Business: $15.00/month ☐
Medium Business: $30.00/month ☑
Large Business: $50.00/month ☐

To:	williamb@sunkitsales.com
From:	support@tripfolioapp.com
Date:	November 27
Subject:	User notice

Greetings Tripfolio user,

A change will be made to our subscription package prices beginning next year. This will enable us to provide valuable updates to our service, like including more expense recording features and providing two additional language options. Also, Medium and Large Business subscribers will be able to purchase new special packages, which include printed log records and route maps when phone service is unavailable. Revised pricing, which will be effective January 1, is as follows:

Plan	Monthly Price	Virtual Log Capacity
Personal	$5	30 logs
Small Business	$15	50 logs
Medium Business	$30	100 logs
Large Business	$60	300 logs

Medium and Large Business subscribers will be given a complimentary travel bag. Get in touch if you have any questions!
support@tripfolioapp.com

191. According to the article excerpt, what does the Tripfolio mobile app allow users to do?

(A) Record customer purchases
(B) Book international flights
(C) Reserve rental vehicles
(D) Store route details

192. What is implied about the Tripfolio mobile app?

(A) It has won several awards for its design.
(B) It requires access to a device's functions.
(C) It is only compatible with the latest smart devices.
(D) It is more expensive than competing applications.

193. Why is Mr. Burke eligible to receive a travel bag?

(A) He purchased a Tripfolio subscription as a gift.
(B) He entered a community contest.
(C) He has been to many local attractions.
(D) He is a Medium Business plan subscriber.

194. What is NOT mentioned in the e-mail as a reason for the change in price?

(A) Offering new special packages
(B) Providing more ways to record expenses
(C) Allowing more countries to access the app
(D) Adding new language options

195. What specific change is being made to the Personal plan?

(A) Driving directions are being updated.
(B) Payment methods are being improved.
(C) Some unnecessary security features are being removed.
(D) The virtual log capacity will increase.

GO ON TO THE NEXT PAGE

Looking for Full-time Web Programmer

MediaMark, an award-winning IT company, has served Chicago businesses since 1992. We are looking for a Web programmer to design select aspects of our online payment programs, under the guidance of the head software developer. Qualified candidates should have either a Master's Degree in Computer Science or one year of programming experience. Applicants will need to display proven ability to create high-tech Web sites and keep them secure.

Visit www.mediamark.com/jobs to apply.

---

www.mediamark.com/jobs/web_programmer/

Name: Danica Kovac
Phone Number: 650-555-7835
E-mail: dkovac@lightningmail.com

Education: Bachelor's Degree in Computer Science from Westport University

Current Employer: Datalock Security
Position: Web programmer
Time Worked: 3 months

Past Employer: Lancet Coders
Position: Programmer
Time Worked: 12 months

Past Employer: iNet Connect
Position: Junior Software Developer
Time Worked: 2 months

Attached Documents:
CV
references

Cover Letter: I would like to apply for the full-time Web programmer position at MediaMark. I have been working as a Web programmer for a security company that maintains protected databases. As the company is a startup, I am responsible for programming work on nearly all projects. I was formerly employed at an international software firm, Lancet Coders, working under the world-renowned Dave Moss. Also, my instructor and advisor, Gina Romano, will confirm that I can design Web sites using the latest technology. As a matter of fact, while studying in university, I received a $200 cash prize for my project to make an online store, and it is currently used as an example for other university students.

Submit Form

WESTPORT UNIVERSITY
School of Computer Science

Liam Appleton
MediaMark
2992 Berkeley Ave.
Menlo Park, CA 94025

Dear Mr. Appleton,

This letter is in regard to Danica Kovac's job application. As Ms. Romano is out on leave for the remainder of the term, she requested that I write this letter in her place. Ms. Kovac's strong programming skills and an ability to quickly solve difficult problems earned her a place at the top of her class. She was given an opportunity to continue working part-time by her supervisor and notable industry leader, Philip Zhou, after a two-month internship. I am certain Ms. Kovac will be a valuable addition to your staff.

Regards,

Joshua Rhodes

Joshua Rhodes
Dean of Westport College of Engineering

---

196. What is indicated about the Web programmer position?

(A) It includes traveling to different countries.
(B) It will only be for one year.
(C) It involves designing a limited number of application features.
(D) It requires working during weekends.

197. What is true about Ms. Kovac?

(A) She has the same mentor as Mr. Moss.
(B) She works in a retail store.
(C) She has sent applications to several companies.
(D) She is qualified to fill a job opening.

198. Who is Ms. Romano?

(A) A business software developer
(B) A computer science instructor
(C) A university administrator
(D) An engineering student

199. What is implied about Westport University?

(A) It invites industry leaders to give lectures.
(B) It provides software demonstrations.
(C) It offers monetary awards.
(D) It is looking to hire a new professor.

200. Where does Mr. Zhou most likely work?

(A) MediaMark
(B) Datalock Security
(C) Lancet Coders
(D) iNet Connect

Stop! This is the end of the test. If you finish before time is called, you may go back to Parts 5, 6, and 7 and check your work.

READING TEST

In the Reading test, you will read a variety of texts and answer several different types of reading comprehension questions. The entire Reading test will last 75 minutes. There are three parts, and directions are given for each part. You are encouraged to answer as many questions as possible within the time allowed.

You must mark your answers on the separate answer sheet. Do not write your answers in your test book.

PART 5

Directions: A word or phrase is missing in each of the sentences below. Four answer choices are given below each sentence. Select the best answer to complete the sentence. Then mark the letter (A), (B), (C), or (D) on your answer sheet.

101. To be entered into the contest, your ------- must be received by June 10.

(A) submission (B) submit
(C) submitted (D) submitter

102. New tenants ------- get their apartment keys after they pay their security deposit.

(A) usually
(B) previously
(C) constantly
(D) annually

103. Nordic Angler hires sales clerks that are ------- about fishing so that they can get customers excited about purchasing items.

(A) pleasant
(B) courteous
(C) enthusiastic
(D) logical

104. In recognition of our continued business, the Berkford Office Supplies sent our company a ----- for $100.

(A) balance
(B) certificate
(C) way
(D) receipt

105. Thorndon Café invites customers to sample its array of beverages ------- locally sourced ingredients.

(A) contain (B) contains
(C) contained (D) containing

106. Should your plans change, you may ------- reschedule your reservation dates or request a partial refund.

(A) whether
(B) either
(C) except
(D) during

107. We have printed enough information packets to distribute ------- of how many guests attend.

(A) instead
(B) much
(C) regardless
(D) within

108. T&G Associates is happy to ------- that Lee's Fitness is relocating to a larger facility on Blair Street.

(A) assemble
(B) promote
(C) report
(D) supervise

109. After just two months as Department Manager, Mr. Kim has attended ------- a dozen conferences.

(A) nearer
(B) near
(C) nearing
(D) nearly

110. The CEO gave his ------- for the merger with the Tar-Spec Corporation.

(A) aspect
(B) authorization
(C) pleasure
(D) influence

111. ------- open only to enrolled students, the Deacon University Legal Library can now be accessed by members of the public.

(A) Extensively
(B) Abruptly
(C) Previously
(D) Shortly

112. This afternoon, theater guests should be aware that the *Serene Lake* performance will be ------- by repair work on the auditorium.

(A) booked
(B) composed
(C) delayed
(D) expected

113. Mr. Martini will oversee the training program for new technicians since ------- became the new department head.

(A) himself
(B) his
(C) he
(D) him

114. ------- she missed her connecting flight, Ms. Carter arrived at the Technology Expo as scheduled.

(A) Now that
(B) Although
(C) Since
(D) As soon as

115. Ms. Thompson ----- her speech when the video projector stopped working during her product presentation.

(A) improvised
(B) authorized
(C) officiated
(D) reached

116. Due to the rain, the workers are not finished ------- the roof of the house.

(A) of
(B) from
(C) in
(D) with

117. Shoppers should use the bathrooms near the rear entrance of the mall while ------- by the front entrance are being repainted.

(A) each
(B) the ones
(C) that
(D) the other

118. This year, HD Department Store is ranked second ------- in national sales.

(A) overall
(B) jointly
(C) broadly
(D) consecutively

119. For exceptional quality at ------- prices, be sure to shop at the Cherry Creek Outlets in Welmington.

(A) afforded
(B) affordable
(C) afford
(D) affording

120. Director Chieko Mori was pleased to learn several reviewers made a ------- between her film and Kintaro Igeta's beloved *A Day in Yokohama*.

(A) difference
(B) comparison
(C) request
(D) relationship

GO ON TO THE NEXT PAGE

121. The new package tracking application indicates the current location ------- the estimated delivery date and time of the parcel.

(A) when
(B) as well as
(C) in order to
(D) in addition

122. Clarkson Ltd. is searching for an experienced ------- capable of managing its Southeast Asian branch.

(A) administrating
(B) administrative
(C) administrator
(D) administer

123. The advanced tread technology of Firelake tires provides the ------- grip possible on snowy or icy roads.

(A) firmly
(B) firmest
(C) firm
(D) firmer

124. Including client testimonials on the homepage will give the firm increased ------- with the public.

(A) anticipation
(B) permission
(C) objectives
(D) credibility

125. The opening ceremony was relocated to Geordie Stadium to ensure ------- seating for all spectators.

(A) persistent
(B) adequate
(C) whole
(D) modern

126. Residents ------- Haylee Carter's decades of service to the community next week at Tieri Banquet Hall.

(A) honored
(B) have honored
(C) will have been honoring
(D) will be honoring

127. PDL Biotech requires personnel to call the Security Office ------- if they detect any leaks or malfunctions in the lab.

(A) rather
(B) right away
(C) as
(D) not many

128. It is the duty of ------- leaves the office last to turn off the lights.

(A) whoever
(B) anybody
(C) all
(D) someone

129. WHAL, Inc. and Davidson Corp. recently ------- on an environmental campaign to clean up the city streets.

(A) collaborated
(B) instituted
(C) subsided
(D) designated

130. This summer, the Children's Museum of Science attracted 20 percent more visitors than it ------- during the same time last year.

(A) did
(B) does
(C) will do
(D) has done

Directions: Read the texts that follow. A word, phrase, or sentence is missing in parts of each text. Four answer choices for each question are given below the text. Select the best answer to complete the text. Then mark the letter (A), (B), (C), or (D) on your answer sheet.

Questions 131-134 refer to the following advertisement.

With CityGolf's two-week trial membership, you'll have a chance to sample our golf facilities, lessons, and other amenities. -------. No commitment is required. To get
131.
started, you just need a credit card and a valid form of identification, but we will not charge your account unless you keep the membership for ------- 15 days. During this
132.
period, if you feel that CityGolf is not for you, ------- call our customer support center at
133.
1-800-555-1212. When you connect with a representative, ask to ------- your
134.
membership after confirming your identity. So, what are you waiting for?

131. (A) Private golf classes are not offered at this time.
(B) Our customer support specialists are always available to assist you.
(C) During the trial, you don't need to make a payment or sign a contract.
(D) You must make a small deposit when you register for a membership

132. (A) over
(B) less than
(C) nearly
(D) not quite

133. (A) simply
(B) rightly
(C) constantly
(D) normally

134. (A) activate
(B) renew
(C) extend
(D) cancel

GO ON TO THE NEXT PAGE

Like all Farisys employees, you are allowed a limited number of sick days on which you may take paid leave for medical -------. To receive full payment for the day off, you -------
135. **136.**
submit an official doctor's letter confirming that there was a health issue. ------- must
137.
clearly indicate the date you sought medical attention, the fact that you are advised not to work, and the date on which you will be able to resume your duties. This information will be kept by the branch manager in your personnel file. -------. Staff medical files are
138.
available only to your direct supervisor and the HR Department, and will not be shared with other individuals, departments, or outside organizations.

135. (A) qualifications
(B) insurance
(C) equipment
(D) reasons

136. (A) asks
(B) are asking
(C) were asking
(D) are asked to

137. (A) It
(B) I
(C) These
(D) They

138. (A) The length of your absence could depend on a variety of circumstances.
(B) Your personal information is kept strictly confidential by Farisys.
(C) You will receive a yearly review from the Human Resources Department.
(D) You should speak to your branch manager if your job is negatively affecting your health.

To: ericnakagawa@xrmail.com
From: JohnKim@hartleylaboratories.com
Date: 2 October
Subject: Starting work at Hartley Labs

Dear Mr. Nakagawa,

Welcome to Hartley Laboratories. We would like to thank you for ------- the full-time
139.
position of assistant researcher. We are excited for your first day at the Redlands,

California facility on October 9. Please come to the main laboratory and inform the

receptionist that you are looking for Karen Bautista. She ------- you to your work station.
140.
There, you will find your laboratory coat ------- all of the equipment you will need for your
141.
job here. As you know, due to the variety of hazardous materials we work with, there are

quite a lot of safety rules to follow. Reviewing the procedures manual will help make you

aware of the handling requirements of the different substances. -------.
142.

Please let me know anytime if you have questions on any of this.

Thanks,

John Kim
Facility Manager

---

139. (A) applying
(B) considering
(C) posting
(D) accepting

140. (A) directs
(B) will direct
(C) did direct
(D) direct

141. (A) along with
(B) additionally
(C) also
(D) as well

142. (A) The requirements will change later
this year.
(B) You should have received a copy via
e-mail.
(C) If a material seems hazardous, you
should contact a supervisor.
(D) You must inspect all equipment daily.

GO ON TO THE NEXT PAGE

Questions 143-146 refer to the following article.

July 21 – ARF Controls, Inc., the nation's largest supplier of thermostats, expects its incoming orders to increase dramatically in the coming year. This ------- is based on the
143.
news that additional thermostat requirements will be implemented due to stricter power plant regulations. CEO Bart Pearson predicts that ARF will sell a staggering 750,000 units this quarter. -------.
144.
ARF purchases many of its products from smaller companies and customizes them ------- plants of all sizes. "The need for increased amounts of ------- in the industry is
145. **146.**
allowing ARF to expand its business quickly," Mr. Pearson said. "We think that the future potential is enormous."

143. (A) cancellation
(B) forecast
(C) price
(D) choice

144. (A) Mr. Pearson has over 35 years of experience in the industry.
(B) ARF's five largest clients are major power plant manufacturers.
(C) This is the first time in the company's history it has reached such a figure.
(D) Nowadays, factory thermostats are very advanced.

145. (A) while
(B) for
(C) as
(D) on

146. (A) manufacture
(B) manufacturer
(C) manufactured
(D) manufacturing

PART 7

Directions: In this part you will read a selection of texts, such as magazine and newspaper articles, emails, and instant messages. Each text or set of texts is followed by several questions. Select the best answer for each question and mark the letter (A), (B), (C), or (D) on your answer sheet.

Questions 147-148 refer to the following notice.

Welcome to Gelson Inn

We will try to make sure that your stay here is an enjoyable experience. If for any reason, you are not satisfied with your stay, please call extension 200 for housekeeping.

Breakfast is served every morning from 7:00 A.M. – 11:00 A.M. in our restaurant located to the right of the reception hall on the first floor. Please present your room card to the host when you enter the restaurant.

We are always trying to improve our services, so please call me at extension 202 if you have any suggestions or comments.

Sincerely yours,

Alex Cominta
Manager
Gelson Inn

147. What is the purpose of the notice?

(A) To communicate with hotel guests
(B) To welcome a new staff member
(C) To promote a menu
(D) To hire a housekeeping worker

148. How should feedback be provided?

(A) By writing an e-mail
(B) By speaking with the hotel manager
(C) By calling the front desk
(D) By filling out a questionnaire

GO ON TO THE NEXT PAGE

Corky's Emporium

Everything must go from our beachside shop!

Corky's Emporium is clearing everything out from last season's inventory! Everything from brand name goggles to sandals has been marked down below warehouse prices. It's all available for 40-75% off!

This sale lasts from September 25 to October 3. Don't miss out!

Hours of operation: 9:30 A.M. to 8:00 P.M., open 7 days a week. Find us on the northeast corner of Main Street and Highrise Drive, or shop online at www.corkysemporium.co.ca.

149. Who most likely posted this notice?

(A) A shoe designer
(B) A warehouse supervisor
(C) A marketing director
(D) A business owner

150. What is implied about Corky's Emporium?

(A) It was recently opened.
(B) It provides coupons frequently.
(C) It is located near a body of water.
(D) It holds weekly promotional events.

Questions 151-152 refer to the following text message chain.

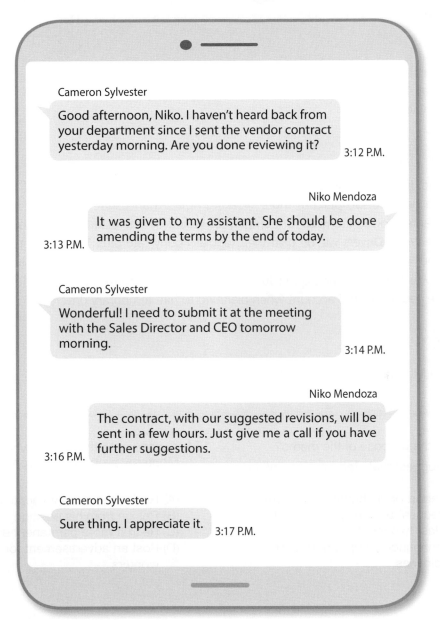

Cameron Sylvester

Good afternoon, Niko. I haven't heard back from your department since I sent the vendor contract yesterday morning. Are you done reviewing it?
3:12 P.M.

Niko Mendoza

It was given to my assistant. She should be done amending the terms by the end of today.
3:13 P.M.

Cameron Sylvester

Wonderful! I need to submit it at the meeting with the Sales Director and CEO tomorrow morning.
3:14 P.M.

Niko Mendoza

The contract, with our suggested revisions, will be sent in a few hours. Just give me a call if you have further suggestions.
3:16 P.M.

Cameron Sylvester

Sure thing. I appreciate it.
3:17 P.M.

151. For which department does Ms. Mendoza most likely work?

(A) Finance
(B) Legal
(C) Sales
(D) Personnel

152. At 3:17 P.M., what does Mr. Sylvester most likely mean when he says, "Sure thing"?

(A) He will take notes over the phone.
(B) He will email a finalized contract to a vendor.
(C) He will deliver some documents to the CEO.
(D) He will let Ms. Mendoza know about any changes.

GO ON TO THE NEXT PAGE

To: All staff
From: Stephen Monteroy
Date: May 17
Subject: Overtime work

Good morning,

June and July are traditionally the busiest months for taxi drivers. Therefore, we expect a need for 30 percent more working hours than usual. Before posting job ads, I wanted to see if any current employees would be interested in taking on some overtime work. Drivers will be paid their regular hourly rate plus 10 percent for each extra hour worked. If this interests you, please inform me by 4:00 P.M. on May 17. Also, if you are taking days off in June and July, please inform me by that date, so I can take your leave into account when planning to hire temporary drivers.

Sincerely,

Stephen Monteroy

153. What is the purpose of the memo?
(A) To suggest that staff take time off in July
(B) To report on a change in cab fares
(C) To request business expenses from the last two months
(D) To announce an opportunity for employees

154. According to the memo, what will Mr. Monteroy probably do soon after May 17?
(A) Revise the current vacation policy
(B) Resign from his position
(C) Recruit more permanent employees
(D) Post an advertisement for seasonal workers

Contributions Are Welcomed

Willow Falls Museum's (WFM) mission is to provide the public with access to our exhibits at no cost. WFM is heavily dependent on financial contributions to create and maintain the exhibitions you now see on display. Please consider contributing by filling out a form at the front desk or on our Web site at www.willowfallsmuseum.org/support.

If you are interested in becoming a WFM Friends' Club member, please stop by the information booth or sign up online at www.willowfallsmuseum.org/sponsor. Sponsors will receive our museum's collector's guide, detailing our most notable history exhibits to date, a monthly e-mail with information about all the events at our museum, and a stylish WFM T-shirt to show your support for our museum. Sponsors are asked to give at least $180 in support annually.

155. Where would the flyer most likely be distributed?

(A) In a history museum
(B) In a school office
(C) In a bookstore
(D) In a government building

156. What is stated about the museum displays?

(A) They change once a month.
(B) They are managed by a well-known curator.
(C) They do not require an admission fee.
(D) They have been recently restored.

157. What is NOT mentioned as a benefit of sponsors?

(A) Sponsors receive a clothing item.
(B) Sponsors are sent a calendar of events.
(C) Sponsors' names are posted online.
(D) Sponsors get a book showcasing certain works.

GO ON TO THE NEXT PAGE

Questions 158-160 refer to the following e-mail.

From: Lance Pratt
To: Nathan Forester
Date: Monday, October 4
Subject: Rush Hills Resort

Dear Mr. Forester,

According to our records, you and your family will be arriving at Rush Hills Resort the weekend after next. —[1]—. I'm pleased that you chose us as your vacation destination.

We should mention that the Waterford Cycling Championship will be held here in two weeks' time. It's a two-day bicycle race from Waterford to Brentshire. It's fun to watch, but please note that several tourists attractions, including the Waterford Museum, will be closed during the race. —[2]—.

The highway through town will remain open, so arriving at our facility will not be a problem. —[3]—. Do expect significant delays if you plan to head into town, due to spectators here to watch the event, especially since we are so close to the starting line of the race. It may be difficult to make reservations in Waterford's restaurants due to the increased number of visitors. —[4]—.

I didn't want this event to come as a surprise upon your arrival, so I thought I should inform you of it well in advance. If you would like more information, please give us a call.

Sincerely,

Lance Pratt
General Manager, Rush Hills Resort

---

158. Why did Mr. Pratt send the e-mail to Mr. Forester?

(A) To offer his apologies for a reservation mistake
(B) To respond to an inquiry about the resort's services
(C) To explain the process of receiving a family discount
(D) To provide information about a scheduled event

159. What is implied about the Rush Hills Resort?

(A) It is not accessible from the highway.
(B) It is located in the city of Waterford.
(C) It arranges bicycle tours for its guests.
(D) It will be closed during the race.

160. In which of the positions marked [1], [2], [3], and [4] does the following sentence best belong?

"As you have booked to stay with us for five nights, you will have other opportunities to visit them."

(A) [1]
(B) [2]
(C) [3]
(D) [4]

Henry Labasse
Rue de la Louthe 911
5451 Bordeaux
France

Dear Mr. Labasse,

Due to the current global business environment being greatly interdependent and interconnected, developing professional relationships with colleagues from all over the world is becoming more crucial than ever. That is why Medic United has created a comprehensive list with details on over 50,000 medical lab researchers located in 60 countries. Join Medic United today to expand your peer network.

If you subscribe to our Silver Business Listing, you can access the name and contact information of every individual listed in our database, as well as information on other medical professionals, such as nurses, physicians, and MRI technicians. If you decide to subscribe to our Gold Business Listing, you can access all the information mentioned above along with detailed data on current medical projects and advancements.

To give you a chance to explore this service, we will offer you a free one-month trial. To sign up for this complimentary service or to become a regular subscriber, please go to our Web site, www. mcunited.com.bg/subscription.

Sincerely,

Eleanor Renard
Eleanor Renard
Director of Marketing

161. What is the purpose of the letter?

(A) To attract a new customer
(B) To request more information
(C) To schedule a check-up
(D) To recommend medical experts

162. Who most likely is Mr. Labasse?

(A) A laboratory researcher
(B) A physician
(C) A nurse
(D) An MRI technician

163. What service does Medic United offer?

(A) Recovering lost data
(B) Facilitating professional
    communications
(C) Providing healthcare classes
(D) Developing Web sites

GO ON TO THE NEXT PAGE

Questions 164-167 refer to the following text message chain.

Amy Fischer [10:09 A.M.]
Good morning, everyone. I'm looking for Kimberly.

Jose Navarro [10:11 A.M.]
I just saw her a few minutes ago. Is everything OK?

Amy Fischer [10:12 A.M.]
Unfortunately, the projector doesn't seem to be operational, and I've tried everything.

Jose Navarro [10:13 A.M.]
That's awful! When does today's training session begin?

Amy Fischer [10:15 A.M.]
At 10:30 sharp. About 20 people have already shown up, and we're expecting 44.

Kimberly Min [10:16 A.M.]
I was in the storage room looking for an extra one, but I didn't have any luck. Amy and I still need to set up the speakers and arrange the information packets, and we've only got a few minutes left.

Jose Navarro [10:17 A.M.]
There isn't enough time to go to another branch and borrow a projector. I am going to go to Max Tech to buy a new one. It's just down the street.

SEND

164. Where most likely is Ms. Fischer?

(A) At a concert hall
(B) In a conference room
(C) In a storage facility
(D) At an electronics store

165. At 10:13 A.M., why does Mr. Navarro most likely say, "That's awful"?

(A) A machine is not working.
(B) A speaker will arrive late.
(C) A staff member is too busy.
(D) A meeting has been postponed.

166. What is implied about Ms. Min?

(A) She takes initiative.
(B) She is Mr. Navarro's supervisor.
(C) She designed a training program.
(D) She is a new employee.

167. What will Mr. Navarro most likely do next?

(A) Join Ms. Fischer and Ms. Min
(B) Call another branch
(C) Speak to a manager
(D) Purchase an item

Questions 168-171 refer to the following e-mail.

From	Martha Riva <mriva@employprospects.com>
To	Samantha Price <sprice@tmail.com>
Date	March 17
Subject	Next step

Dear Samantha,

Thank you for sending me your résumé and college transcript. I have added your information to Employ Prospects' database.

We have found several short-term positions that match your qualifications and experience. These include two administrative positions, an office assistant position in a law firm, and a front-desk position in a dental office. In addition, we have a permanent, full-time position available. This job will start as a three-month internship, but afterwards will lead to a permanent position as a production assistant in a broadcasting company. As you have a degree in Media and Communications, this would be an ideal match for you. However, your résumé states that you currently live in Stella Falls, which is quite far from the broadcasting company's office in Baltimore. Please let me know if you are willing to make the commute. The other openings are located within your area, but we can offer you more opportunities if you are flexible with long distances.

Before contacting any employer, we require two references from you. They must be professional references from either your former employers or university professors. Please email me their names and phone numbers by tomorrow. Once you have done this, we will set up an interview between you and one of our professional recruiting consultants. Please contact my office to schedule a convenient time.

Sincerely,

Martha Riva
Employ Prospects

168. What is the purpose of the e-mail?

(A) To confirm a reservation
(B) To request further information
(C) To announce an interview result
(D) To give driving directions

169. What is indicated about Ms. Price?

(A) She works for Employ Prospects.
(B) She has sent some documents to Ms. Riva.
(C) She is an experienced producer.
(D) She recently received her degree.

170. What is true about the front-desk position?

(A) It has a flexible work schedule.
(B) It is for a law firm.
(C) It is a permanent position.
(D) It is located near Stella Falls.

171. What has Ms. Riva NOT asked Ms. Price to do?

(A) Complete and return a form
(B) Confirm her willingness to travel
(C) Provide references
(D) Arrange a meeting

GO ON TO THE NEXT PAGE

Questions 172-175 refer to the following schedule of events.

Mexico City Global Marketing Convention
November 15-18 ★ Necaxa Business Center ★ Mexico City, Mexico

Program of Events
Monday, November 15

Search Engine Toolkit
7:45 A.M. to 8:30 A.M. Lecture Hall C

Elizabeth Lee, columnist for *Marketing Today*, is here to talk about industry changes, answer questions, and promote her new book, *Search Engine Toolkit*.

Web Design Introduction
8:45 A.M. to 9:30 A.M. Anahuac Pavilion

Web designers Mary Ellen Torres and Rick Garcia guide participants through several easy, hands-on lessons on creating effective Web pages.

Online Advertising Seminar
9:45 A.M. to 10:30 A.M. Jacaranda Theater

Marketing to clients on the internet.
Presenters: Jose Hernandez, i-Promote's Advertising Director, and Susan Karre, Manager of Social Media Campaigns for MarketTrue. Study materials for the session will be on sale by the entrance to the theater on the day of the seminar.

Consumers in the 21st Century
10:45 A.M. to 11:30 A.M. Conference Room 403

Panelists Roy Sinor and Bernard Diaz lead a discussion on what current patterns tell us about future marketing trends.
• Accommodations near the business center can be booked though our Web site, www.gmconf.mx. Meals are available at the center's food court or at any of the many nearby restaurants.
• A one-day ticket valid for these or any other convention events can be purchased for 1,100 pesos online or in-person.
• To ensure you have a seat, please show up early as no reservations can be made ahead of time. Please be aware that while photos are permitted, video and audio recordings of any kind are prohibited.

172. What is suggested about the opening day of the Mexico City Global Marketing Convention?

(A) Attendance is anticipated to be lower on that day.
(B) Ms. Lee will discuss ideas for a new book.
(C) No events are scheduled in the afternoon.
(D) It has been planned by a marketing publication.

173. Where will marketing convention attendees be able to participate in interactive activities?

(A) In Lecture Hall C
(B) In the Anahuac Pavilion
(C) In the Jacaranda Theater
(D) In Conference Room 403

174. What is mentioned about the seminar's study materials?

(A) They should be ordered on the last day.
(B) They must be requested from the speaker.
(C) They can be bought at the venue.
(D) They are included in the ticket price.

175. What are marketing convention attendees encouraged to do?

(A) Contact organizers with questions
(B) Take a shuttle to the business center
(C) Arrive early for the events
(D) Take photos after a session ends

GO ON TO THE NEXT PAGE

One-A Corporation

Morning Seminar at Rosedale Community Center
8:30 A.M. to 12:15 P.M., Friday, 30 June

Schedule

8:15 A.M. One-A staff arrive to check in and receive name tags

8:30 A.M. Session: My First Year as a Manager in the Accounting Department

9:15 A.M. Session: How to Manage Customer Support Employees That Need Assistance

10:00 A.M. Session: Inspiring Sales Staff for Top Performance

10:30 A.M. Meet and greet with the speakers; refreshments

11:00 A.M. Session: Taking a Career in IT Management to the Next Level

11:30 A.M. Closing address

---

14 July

Mr. David Sheppard
Clay Enterprises
88 Sidney Street
Cambridge CB2 3ND
UK

Dear Mr. Sheppard,

You may remember that we met two weeks ago during the seminar I attended with my colleagues from One-A. The sessions that you and your co-presenters gave were informative and helpful. I appreciated Ella Larsson's discussion on supervising customer support employees and Andrew Giano's talk on how to motivate team members to produce better results.

Your session was particularly interesting, however, as I will soon take on an executive role at my company. Listening to your experience on managing a large team of specialists, I learned a lot about a path I hope to follow. I am hoping that you could share more information about the techniques and resources that you have found effective in your role as Chief Technology Officer. I would be very grateful of any guidance you could provide that would help me realize my future goals.

I sincerely thank you for your time and feedback. I look forward to speaking with you again soon, at a time convenient for you.

Sincerely,

Lisa Takeda
Lisa Takeda

176. Why was the seminar organized?

(A) To invite employees to volunteer at a community center
(B) To teach staff management skills
(C) To encourage workers to obtain a marketing degree
(D) To train new personnel on security policies

177. In what department does Mr. Sheppard most likely work?

(A) Accounting
(B) Marketing
(C) Customer Service
(D) Information Technology

178. When did Mr. Giano most likely give his presentation?

(A) At 8:30 A.M.
(B) At 9:15 A.M.
(C) At 10:00 A.M.
(D) At 11:00 A.M.

179. In the letter, the word "realize" in paragraph 2, line 6, is closest in meaning to

(A) earn
(B) appreciate
(C) distinguish
(D) achieve

180. What did Ms. Takeda do in her letter to Mr. Sheppard?

(A) Requested a recommendation letter
(B) Thanked him for his input
(C) Made changes to an agenda
(D) Asked for a new contract

GO ON TO THE NEXT PAGE

From: victoriaf@brightpecan.com
To: all-employees@brightpecan.com
Date: January 27
Subject: System upgrade

Hello all,

We will be upgrading the systems on all office computers on Friday, January 31. Every company-owned machine will be updated. In particular, members of the Personnel, Accounting, and Customer Support Divisions should make sure they are ready for this, as the work might adversely affect some of the programs they are currently using.

It is very important that you save and make backups of all your important files, since we will be rebooting the computers once the upgrade is done. Users with software that runs processes continuously are cautioned that the upgrade might accidentally delete some files. So we strongly suggest that routine tasks on the date of the changeover be performed ahead of time or postponed. Any employee out of the office on vacation or business on Friday will need to make sure that their files are safely backed up before then.

Victoria Fleury

From	mjarvi@brightpecan.com
To	klao@brightpecan.com
Date	January 28
Subject	Payments

Ms. Lao,

This e-mail is in regard to a potential issue processing employee paychecks. Currently, my computer program is set up to transmit that information to the bank on Friday afternoon. However, considering Ms. Fleury's e-mail yesterday, the pay date for this month may need to be adjusted to accommodate the change. I will be participating in a seminar on Accounting Regulations tomorrow and Thursday. I could perform the process this afternoon, but that means we may need to postpone payments to some of our suppliers until next week. Or we could push payday forward to next Monday, February 3. That may be unacceptable for some employees, especially if they have payments to make on Saturday, February 1. I will need your permission one way or the other, and will then take the appropriate course of action.

Sincerely,
Martin Jarvi

181. What is the purpose of the first e-mail?

(A) To prepare staff for potential software issues
(B) To describe the process of installing a new program
(C) To request that advance notice be given for business trips
(D) To give a possible resolution to a payment problem

182. In what division does Ms. Fleury most likely work?

(A) Information Technology
(B) Accounting
(C) Personnel
(D) Customer Support

183. Why most likely does Mr. Jarvi need to reschedule a task?

(A) His computer is broken.
(B) A project deadline has changed.
(C) He wants to avoid losing data.
(D) He has not paid his credit card bill.

184. According to Mr. Jarvi, what is a possible date for the task to be rescheduled?

(A) January 27
(B) January 28
(C) January 31
(D) February 1

185. What is Mr. Jarvi planning to do on January 29?

(A) Deposit some extra paychecks
(B) Go on a holiday
(C) Meet with a supervisor
(D) Participate in a professional meeting

GO ON TO THE NEXT PAGE →

Transform Your Restaurant into a Successful Business

Does your restaurant offer high-quality food and service, but still struggle to turn a profit? Join the Restaurant Management Resource Association (RMRA) and get comprehensive training on monitoring and managing the financial side of your business! The bottom line is that the professional help is a must in this age. We have helped restaurant owners all over the country achieve their financial goals for over a decade. Here is a brief summary of what the RMRA offers.

Access to Informative Resources – An extensive collection of articles, reviews, and reports written by industry experts that focus on helping restaurant proprietors achieve sustained profitability. These resources are updated each week to provide our members with the most up-to-date information.

Customized Templates – A wide selection of free downloadable forms, worksheets, and report templates that can be modified to meet your business' specific requirements.

Connect with the Community – Join the RMRA Network, our online discussion forum, and share insights and ideas with thousands of network members who know the challenges and demands of the industry.

Specialized Lectures – Participate in various online courses covering strategies ranging from controlling food costs and pricing menus to managing overall expenses.
Note: This feature is only available with a gold membership.

Get access to the RMRA now with a one-time registration fee of $80 plus a membership fee of $100 (basic) or $150 (gold) per year.

RMRA Inductee Information

First Name: Gary
Last Name: Hansen
Name of Business: Hansen's Pizzeria
Telephone Number: 206-318-4336
Street: 18744 Garden Ln.
City: Seattle
State: Washington
Postal Code: 98102
Email Address: ghansen@hansenpizzeria.com
Create Username: ghansen99
Create Password: *******
Verify Password: *******
Choose Membership Type: √ Basic   ☐ Gold

The RMRA promises to provide the skills and knowledge necessary to attain long-term financial success. If your business' finances have not improved after one year as an RMRA member, we will reimburse half of your RMRA membership fee.
Note: This feature is only available with a gold membership.

Gary Hansen
Hansen's Pizzeria
18744 Garden Lane
Seattle, WA 98102

Dear Mr. Hansen,

We are sorry to hear that your business has not taken off, even after enrolling in our service. Unfortunately, we cannot issue you a refund.

Our policy clearly states that the refund is only available for gold members. And as you have enrolled in basic service, you do not qualify for the refund. However, what I can do for you is provide you with six more months of our service, free of charge. Please let me know if you are interested.

Best regards,

Benjamin Kim
Manager of Customer Service at RMRA

186. In the advertisement, the word "sustained" in paragraph 2, line 3, is closest in meaning to

(A) credited
(B) supported
(C) consistent
(D) saved

187. What is suggested about Mr. Hansen?

(A) He is not interested in taking online classes.
(B) He plans on expanding his business to another city.
(C) He recently renovated his store.
(D) He has replied to a letter from Mr. Kim before.

188. How much did Mr. Hansen pay for his RMRA membership?

(A) $100
(B) $150
(C) $180
(D) $230

189. When does the RMRA provide a refund?

(A) When businesses receive a damaged product
(B) When a lecture is canceled
(C) When a client is unhappy with the quality of a lecture
(D) When a service fails to create a positive outcome

190. What does Mr. Kim offer to do?

(A) Track a delivery
(B) Extend a service
(C) Mail a product catalog
(D) Review an order

GO ON TO THE NEXT PAGE

Safety Audits to Increase

SAN DIEGO [FEBRUARY 27] – The city council has passed new regulations related to safety audits for all schools. Effective right away, private schools must be audited bimonthly rather than once a quarter, and public schools must be audited monthly rather than once a year when school is in session. Audits will cover emergency preparedness and security procedures. Council member Dean Yoo, who was elected last year, is responsible for creating the Be Alert initiative. "Ensuring the well-being of our children is important to all of us," said Mr. Yoo. The city will contact school administrators directly to explain the updated rules and to schedule audits. The public can contact Ben Michaels of the Department of Public Safety at (858) 555-9823.

March 21

Carolyn Kilday

Xavier Preparatory School

Dear Ms. Kilday,

Private schools will be audited more often due to updated city regulations. A check of our office records indicates that your school's most recent safety audit was passed on November 10. It is now overdue under the new rules. We have scheduled an auditor to arrive at your institution on March 28 at 9 A.M. Should you need to change this appointment for any reason, we request that you contact Mr. Ben Michaels of the Department of Public Safety either by e-mail at b.michaels@ sandiego-dps.gov or by calling (858) 555-9823.

Yvonne Grimm

Department of Public Safety

To: Ben Michaels <b.michaels@sandiego-dps.gov>
From: Carolyn Kilday <c.kilday@xavierprep.edu>
Date: March 23
Subject: Safety audit

Dear Mr. Michaels,

This is in regard to a letter I received alerting me to a pending safety audit here at Xavier Preparatory School. This needs to be delayed. The school has purchased new smoke detectors to replace older ones that have become defective with age. The installation specialist responsible for the upgrades has said that this will take approximately five days to complete, and an additional day to fully test. I would like to reschedule the audit for the week following the one that was originally scheduled. I look forward to hearing back from you.

Sincerely,

Carolyn Kilday
Headmaster, Xavier Preparatory School

191. Who is Mr. Yoo?

(A) A local journalist
(B) A school administrator
(C) A repair technician
(D) A town official

192. How often will Xavier Preparatory School be inspected in the future?

(A) Every month
(B) Every other month
(C) Once a quarter
(D) Once a year

193. In the letter, the word "check" in paragraph 1, line 1, is closest in meaning to

(A) mark
(B) control
(C) review
(D) stop

194. Why did Ms. Kilday send the e-mail?

(A) To file a complaint about a new regulation
(B) To postpone a city employee's visit
(C) To confirm a service appointment
(D) To request an invoice for a renovation project

195. What is implied about Xavier Preparatory School's smoke detectors?

(A) They were purchased at an affordable rate.
(B) They began malfunctioning after November 10.
(C) They are in the wrong locations.
(D) They were installed by Ms. Kilday.

GO ON TO THE NEXT PAGE

From: Lawrence McGill <lmcgill@createadate.com>
To: Wendy Song <wsong@minnesota.edu>
Date: Thursday, June 2
Subject: Venue quote
Attachment: quote.rtf

Dear Ms. Song,

I appreciated your call in regard to the Minnesota State Educators Awards Brunch here in Minneapolis. I have included the details for a variety of venues that suit your needs.

As per your request, an Italian restaurant has been included. While we have never hosted an event there, it comes strongly recommended by a colleague.

To lock in the rates quoted, your full payment must be submitted by Friday, June 10. I look forward to working further with you in preparation for your event.

Regards,
Lawrence McGill

Quotes for Dining Venues

Client: Minnesota State Educators
Guest count: 36
Meal type: Brunch buffet
Set date: August 8

Restaurant	Cuisine	Extra Features	Price per Guest*	Total Cost
Riverbend	Mexican	Live music entertainment available on request	$25	$900
Gemelli Bistro	Italian	Courtyard area available	$30	$1080
Wishing Tree	Vietnamese	Personalized menus available for catering	$35	$1260
Chez Neuf	Cajun	3-minute walk to nearest subway stop	$40	$1440
Oyster Platter	Seafood	Seating for groups of up to 50	$45	$1620

*Prices are all-inclusive, parking off-site, however, may incur additional fees.

From	Wendy Song <wsong@minnesota.edu>
To	Lawrence McGill <lmcgill@createadate.com>
Date	Tuesday, June 7
Subject	Deposit

Dear Mr. McGill,

I appreciate all the work you've done on the brunch arrangements. The full payment has been made through your online payment system. The option to have musical entertainment was tempting, but the highest priority for our members is a venue with access to public transportation.

Since the event location has been chosen, what I need now is a recommendation for a shop from which to order the award plaques. I would also like to present a brief slideshow during the event, but let's discuss that when we get together on June 23. Additionally, at that meeting, I will require your assistance in finalizing the design of the invitations and selecting a print shop.

Sincerely,
Wendy Song

196. What is indicated about Mr. McGill?

(A) He is a restaurant critic.
(B) He owns a catering company.
(C) He works near an Italian restaurant.
(D) He is planning a meal.

197. What restaurant did Mr. McGill include based on Ms. Song's request?

(A) Riverbend
(B) Gemelli Bistro
(C) Wishing Tree
(D) Chez Neuf

198. What is suggested about Wishing Tree?

(A) It is the cheapest option available.
(B) It provides outdoor seating.
(C) Changes can be made to its menu.
(D) Parking is complimentary in the evening.

199. How much did Ms. Song most likely pay?

(A) $1080
(B) $1260
(C) $1440
(D) $1620

200. According to the second e-mail, what will Ms. Song do next?

(A) Mail some invitations
(B) Order award plaques
(C) Rehearse a presentation
(D) Book a meeting room

Stop! This is the end of the test. If you finish before time is called, you may go back to Parts 5, 6, and 7 and check your work.

READING TEST

In the Reading test, you will read a variety of texts and answer several different types of reading comprehension questions. The entire Reading test will last 75 minutes. There are three parts, and directions are given for each part. You are encouraged to answer as many questions as possible within the time allowed.

You must mark your answers on the separate answer sheet. Do not write your answers in your test book.

PART 5

Directions: A word or phrase is missing in each of the sentences below. Four answer choices are given below each sentence. Select the best answer to complete the sentence. Then mark the letter (A), (B), (C), or (D) on your answer sheet.

101. The ability to speak multiple languages is a crucial skill in today's rapidly ------- global economy.

(A) evolver   (B) evolve
(C) evolving   (D) evolves

102. All of the speakers will have finished their talks at the seminar ------- we arrive at the conference center.

(A) in a similar way
(B) only when
(C) by the time
(D) as early as

103. At Nemo International, the maximum ------- for shipping containers is 30 metric tons.

(A) weighing
(B) weight
(C) weigh
(D) weighted

104. While Ms. Lim is on vacation, please contact Mr. Moreau regarding any ------- matters that occur.

(A) urgent
(B) correct
(C) substitute
(D) deleted

105. The trainers at Nine Muses Academy helped Carolyn McMurphy improve ------- singing voice noticeably.

(A) hers   (B) herself
(C) she   (D) her

106. Due to seasonal demand, processing orders may take a day ------- than usual.

(A) longer
(B) longest
(C) length
(D) long

107. When sending blueprints to a company client, keep such documents ------- by using this courier service.

(A) securely
(B) securing
(C) secure
(D) security

108. CPS Motors asserts that its newest electric car runs quieter and more ------- than any other vehicle on the market.

(A) currently
(B) mainly
(C) abruptly
(D) efficiently

109. Despite the distributor's ------- that the shipment would be located, Ms. Park is thinking about ending their contract.

(A) assuredly
(B) assurance
(C) assure
(D) assured

110. A ------- briefcase is an essential item for sales representatives who travel frequently to visit clients.

(A) vigorous
(B) comparable
(C) meticulous
(D) durable

111. Gryphon Security will reply within one day to all customer complaints ------- through the company Web site.

(A) filed
(B) file
(C) files
(D) filing

112. Mr. Ramirez carefully measured the dimensions of the office ------- determining how many desks could fit in the room.

(A) but also
(B) before
(C) in fact
(D) instead

113. Both Mr. Mason's credit history and the amount ------- on his mortgage will be factors in approving his request for refinancing.

(A) occupied
(B) rented
(C) involved
(D) owed

114. Industry ------- stipulate that all employees must wear appropriate protective gear while on the factory floor.

(A) expenditures
(B) topics
(C) opinions
(D) regulations

115. The security deposit for the rental car will be returned ------- the vehicle is inspected upon being returned.

(A) only
(B) once
(C) neither
(D) although

116. To guarantee fairness, Mr. Palmer will ------- choose an employee to use the parking spot in front of the building.

(A) greatly
(B) randomly
(C) entirely
(D) proportionately

117. Matsuda Kitchen Appliances ------- as a leader in the Asian market.

(A) were to continue being seen
(B) will continue seeing
(C) to continue to see
(D) continues to be seen

118. Starting June 6, Jean Renault will ------- all questions regarding current projects at Alterman Laboratories.

(A) dedicate
(B) comply
(C) reply
(D) handle

119. Mr. Nguyen is a ------- team member with an impressive ability to design attractive advertisements.

(A) resourced
(B) resourceful
(C) resourcefully
(D) resourcefulness

120. Computer programming is among the highest-paying ------- in the South Asian region.

(A) devices
(B) industries
(C) sources
(D) situations

GO ON TO THE NEXT PAGE

121. The shuttle buses will not be running while routine maintenance ------- place.

(A) has taken
(B) taking
(C) is taking
(D) took

122. The historian has verified that this piece is a ------- Renaissance painting from the 1400s.

(A) genuine
(B) descriptive
(C) correct
(D) temporary

123. The Vice President is satisfied with how smooth the ------- of the two departments has been after restructuring.

(A) consolidates
(B) consolidate
(C) consolidation
(D) consolidated

124. The critically-acclaimed documentary *Deep Deception* advocates awareness ------- environmental issues related to water and energy conservation.

(A) at
(B) of
(C) by
(D) to

125. Kimduk Tech was ------- purchased for approximately $400 million.

(A) reporting
(B) reportedly
(C) reports
(D) reporter

126. The quarterly schedule for the R&D Department lists six ------- to be accomplished over the next three months.

(A) competitors
(B) objectives
(C) conclusions
(D) clients

127. -------, management allows employees to wear casual clothing in the office for a special occasion.

(A) Once in a while
(B) At this point
(C) By this time
(D) In a moment

128. The full title of the manual is *Revised Regulations for Laboratory Experiments*, but it is usually ------- as *The Regulations*.

(A) assembled
(B) referred to
(C) expanded on
(D) compared

129. Even though most restaurants in the area offer catering services, ------- provide the extensive list of menu items that we do.

(A) any
(B) all
(C) neither
(D) few

130. Adding more flight routes would probably have a ------- impact on travel bookings.

(A) substantial
(B) multiple
(C) biggest
(D) cooperative

PART 6

Directions: Read the texts that follow. A word, phrase, or sentence is missing in parts of each text. Four answer choices for each question are given below the text. Select the best answer to complete the text. Then mark the letter (A), (B), (C), or (D) on your answer sheet.

Questions 131-134 refer to the following e-mail.

From: service@campersdepot.co.uk
To: hendricks1577@mugremail.co.uk
Date: April 22
Subject: Re: Campers Depot Login Information

Dear Valued Customer,

This message was sent because you ------- a password reset for your Campers' Depot
                                      131.
account. Accordingly, we have updated your account, and you have been issued a

temporary password: I23bon18. Keep in mind that it will be ------- until midnight on April
                                                            132.
23. Before that, use the password to log in to the members-only section on our Web site.

To finalize the reset procedure, enter the necessary information ------- prompted.
                                                                 133.

We at Campers' Depot are committed to protecting your personal information. -------.
                                                                           134.

Best regards,

Campers' Depot Online Services

---

131. (A) would request
(B) requesting
(C) requested
(D) request

132. (A) secured
(B) accessible
(C) open
(D) valid

133. (A) from
(B) over
(C) when
(D) upon

134. (A) Customers who register for our online service will receive 10 percent off their purchases in the first year.
(B) You will find a number of upgrades to the members-only section of our Web site.
(C) If you were not the one to initiate the reset process, please call Tech Support right away.
(D) We offer top-quality camping supplies and safety equipment for all of your outdoor adventures.

GO ON TO THE NEXT PAGE

Now Accepting Tenants

Campus Towers Apartment Complex is hosting its annual Pool Party and Open House event on July 15-16. This comfortable lifestyle can be -------! Our apartments -------
135.   **136.**
convenient access to Glenfield University's campus. You'll love our fully-furnished rooms, with state-of-the-art kitchens. Every renter also has access to our fitness center and reading room. -------, you might not want to stay home too often!
137.

Campus Towers Apartment Complex is right in the heart of the city, and you have various dining and entertainment options, right outside your door. Our rental consultants are available seven days a week, from 9 A.M. to 6 P.M. -------. Give us a call to arrange a
138.
tour of our units now!

Karl Niemann (858) 555-5512

---

135. (A) most
(B) theirs
(C) yours
(D) mine

136. (A) offer
(B) offering
(C) have offered
(D) offered

137. (A) Likewise
(B) Accordingly
(C) Apparently
(D) However

138. (A) After-hours appointments can be scheduled with prior notice.
(B) We will extend these hours during the summer season.
(C) We are considering hiring more maintenance workers for this project.
(D) Several commercial units will be available for rent next month.

Questions 139-142 refer to the following comment card.

I am very happy with the Ekmekci 500. It bakes delicious food quickly and evenly. And it's much ------- than a conventional oven. It is able to cook a pizza in just three minutes.
139.
The Ekmekci 500 features a variety of helpful functions that are simple to -------. For
140.
instance, you can bake up to three different items at one time, just by pushing a few buttons on top of the machine. -------. Better yet, the ingenious space-saving design
141.
makes it easy to store ------- use.
142.

139. (A) cheaper
(B) faster
(C) stronger
(D) neater

140. (A) operate
(B) copy
(C) extend
(D) install

141. (A) I bake desserts almost every day now.
(B) A special sensor prevents overcooked or burned food.
(C) I did not find it easier to cook with this device.
(D) The Ekmekci Company also makes special bread-making appliances.

142. (A) after
(B) while
(C) once
(D) with

GO ON TO THE NEXT PAGE

The number of businesses in the Rancho Penasquitos district has risen dramatically in the last year. Results from a recent survey show that the number ------- 20 percent—

143.

more than four times the rate of adjacent neighborhoods. The area currently lacks office space to accommodate this growth. As a -------, proposals have been accepted to build

144.

three new business parks. -------. At the moment, Rancho Penasquitos only has one—

145.

the North County Office Complex. The new business parks will create a ------- 1,500

146.

offices.

143. (A) climbs
    (B) is climbing
    (C) climbed
    (D) will climb

144. (A) promotion
    (B) result
    (C) requirement
    (D) condition

145. (A) Local companies have requested several additional large conference facilities.
    (B) It is important to ensure that all safety and environmental regulations have been followed.
    (C) Surveys will be conducted regularly to ensure that local business owners are satisfied.
    (D) The necessary permits have already been acquired to begin construction.

146. (A) preliminary
    (B) temporary
    (C) further
    (D) disposable

PART 7

Directions: In this part you will read a selection of texts, such as magazine and newspaper articles, emails, and instant messages. Each text or set of texts is followed by several questions. Select the best answer for each question and mark the letter (A), (B), (C), or (D) on your answer sheet.

Questions 147-148 refer to the following letter.

September 30

Dear Mr. Moser,

Congratulations! Your Travel Rewards account has accumulated enough points for a free plane ticket. Instructions on how to use these points along with a special code to use during booking are included with this letter. Also included is a schedule of flights on participating airlines. This offer is valid until December 31.

Account holders get a free flight for every 3,000 points earned. Whenever you make a purchase at a Travel Rewards agency, you accumulate points.

Keep track of your points by logging on to your account at www.travelrewards.co.nz.

Regards,

Travel Rewards
Enclosures

147. What did Mr. Moser receive?

(A) A list of flight times
(B) A rewards card
(C) A meal ticket
(D) A voucher for travel accessories

148. What can Mr. Moser do online?

(A) Renew an account subscription
(B) Submit feedback on a Web site
(C) Find a Travel Rewards location near his neighborhood
(D) Check the number of points he has accumulated

GO ON TO THE NEXT PAGE

Questions 149-150 refer to the following text message chain.

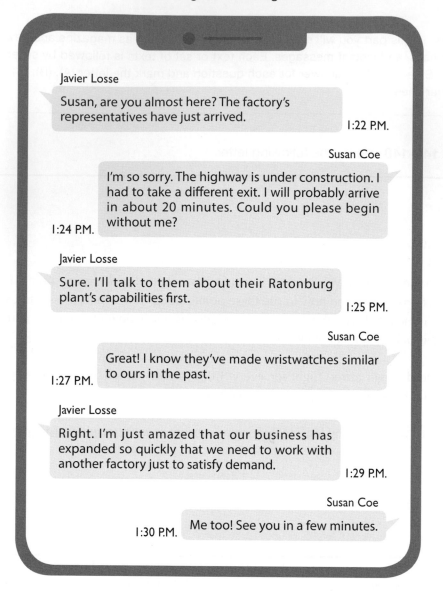

Javier Losse

Susan, are you almost here? The factory's representatives have just arrived.

1:22 P.M.

Susan Coe

I'm so sorry. The highway is under construction. I had to take a different exit. I will probably arrive in about 20 minutes. Could you please begin without me?

1:24 P.M.

Javier Losse

Sure. I'll talk to them about their Ratonburg plant's capabilities first.

1:25 P.M.

Susan Coe

Great! I know they've made wristwatches similar to ours in the past.

1:27 P.M.

Javier Losse

Right. I'm just amazed that our business has expanded so quickly that we need to work with another factory just to satisfy demand.

1:29 P.M.

Susan Coe

1:30 P.M.   Me too! See you in a few minutes.

149. What does Ms. Coe want Mr. Losse to do?

(A) Distribute product samples
(B) Meet some company representatives
(C) Finalize a manufacturing contract
(D) Postpone an appointment

150. At 1:30 P.M., what does Ms. Coe mean when she writes, "Me too"?

(A) She has traveled to Ratonburg before.
(B) She is also impressed by the expansion of the business.
(C) She thinks a factory should be renovated.
(D) She believes a highway exit will reopen in 20 minutes.

Questions 151-152 refer to the following invitation.

Tess University Hospital

204 Burlington Road
Dublin 4C6 9FD

13 July

Dr. Yoshino Fujioka
403 Orchard Street
Dublin 22G 6NM

Dear Dr. Fujioka,

I would like to cordially invite you to join us in celebrating Dr. Wayne Bradley's 30 years of service at the Tess University Hospital. On top of the quality care he has provided for his patients, Dr. Bradley has put in a significant amount of effort to raise funds for Improved Living, a local charity foundation that promotes health awareness.

As the founder of the charity, Dr. Bradley will be a member of the board after his retirement. We hope that you can attend the banquet we will be holding in his honor at the Beauford Hotel. The banquet is scheduled to take place on 10 September at 6:00 P.M.in the hotel's Grand Ballroom. Please email my assistant Jessica Steele at jsteele@tessunihospital.ie by 30 August to confirm your attendance.

All the best,

Katie Hawkins

Katie Hawkins
Director, Tess University Hospital

---

151. What type of event is being held?

(A) A corporate anniversary
(B) A retirement dinner
(C) A hospital opening
(D) A charity event

152. What are recipients of the invitation recommended to do?

(A) Reply by a specific date
(B) Arrive 30 minutes early
(C) Book a room at a hotel
(D) Make a financial donation

GO ON TO THE NEXT PAGE

Questions 153-154 refer to the following e-mail.

From: Karl Boucheron
To: Susie Bao
Date: 29 October
Subject: Request

Hello Susie,

My teaching schedule has a few changes that I'd like you to make to the online class listings. Not enough students signed up for my Monday afternoon class, so it has been closed. However, I'm busy this week teaching four other classes, so let's reserve that time for office hours.

Also, Laura Howard had to cancel her presentation at the Omaha Education Conference next month (November 18 – 20), and I agreed to take her place. I will need a flight to Omaha on November 17, ideally leaving after 8:00 P.M., and a return ticket in the afternoon of November 20. If you have questions, just call me.

Karl

153. Why did Mr. Boucheron send the e-mail?

(A) To request information about a class
(B) To organize a faculty party
(C) To arrange a pick-up service
(D) To update a Web site

154. What is Ms. Bao asked to do?

(A) Reserve a conference room
(B) Arrange a trip
(C) Make an office appointment
(D) Email Ms. Howard

Questions 155-157 refer to the following information.

Thank you for your purchase of the Speedspin, the most powerful portable air purifier on the market. In order to ensure lasting performance, clean the filter daily with a damp cloth and warm water. Once a week, disassemble the machine and wipe all surfaces with sanitizing fluid, as shown in the owner's guide. Also, note that the filter should be replaced every year.

The Speedspin is powered by a nickel-cadmium battery, which will last for several years. The battery will automatically charge when the machine is plugged in; it is not necessary to turn the machine off to recharge the battery. Please only use the connector cable that came with this product. Use of other cables can damage the machine. Check our Web site at http://www.speedspin.co.uk to learn more.

Speedspin: Fresh air follows!

155. Where most likely is this information located?

(A) In a product box
(B) In an appliance catalog
(C) In a newspaper advertisement
(D) In a community newsletter

156. What is stated about the Speedspin?

(A) It should be cleaned yearly.
(B) It includes a warranty
(C) It is made of eco-friendly materials.
(D) It can be taken apart.

157. What is indicated about the battery?

(A) It is heavy.
(B) It is durable.
(C) It is compact.
(D) It is affordable.

GO ON TO THE NEXT PAGE

Questions 158-160 refer to the following e-mail.

From:	Cecilia Johnson <c.johnson@caicorp.co.uk>
To:	Hannah Wall <h.wall@caicorp.co.uk>
Date:	December 9
Subject:	Notification
Attachment:	Logistics info

Dear Ms. Wall,

From all of us at Caicorp, I am pleased to congratulate you on your promotion to Senior Manager. The London branch is the main hub for all IT-related support, making it one of the most important facilities in the Caicorp international network.

On January 3, at 8 A.M., you will start your training with Mitch Lee from the Personnel Department. At that time, Mr. Lee will provide information about department policies, future development plans, and the specifics of your position. Also, as we are currently updating our security system, you'll have to check in at the facilities office. Therefore, please aim to get here by at least 7:50 A.M.

Attached is a document containing details about relocating from Dublin. It explains how to order supplies and get your company laptop and phone set up. If I can provide any additional assistance before January 3, please call or send me an e-mail.

Sincerely,

Cecilia Johnson
Human Resources
Caicorp Head Office

158. Why did Ms. Johnson contact Ms. Wall?
(A) To confirm some travel arrangements
(B) To discuss information related to a new role
(C) To ask about a lost ID card
(D) To announce an upcoming business merger

159. What is suggested about Caicorp?
(A) It will hire more IT employees.
(B) It has recently updated its network.
(C) It will move its headquarters to London.
(D) It has more than one office.

160. What is Ms. Wall instructed to do?
(A) Sign an apartment lease
(B) Meet Mr. Lee at a security gate
(C) Purchase supplies for a department
(D) Arrive early for a training session

Questions 161-164 refer to the newspaper article.

<UPSTATE NEW YORK SUCCESS STORY>

February 16 - Thanks to the success of his first restaurant, The Greek Tower, restaurateur George Pappas will expand his operation into different parts of the state. "I've been to many other cities in the state," Pappas explains, "and I have found some wonderful locations for my restaurant. —[1]—. It also helps when people already have a good opinion of my menu."

—[2]—. His first store opened 15 years ago and has been serving the Utica area successfully ever since. With two restaurants planned for the Albany and Genesee areas, Mr. Pappas will have his hands full. "I want our new restaurants to have the same atmosphere of the original one. Many of my customers are like family, and that is what I want to establish at my new restaurants. Family and good Greek food."

Mr. Pappas started off doing all the cooking himself. —[3]—. These days, he spends most of his time promoting and managing his restaurant to ensure the quality is consistent and his customers feel at home. "You know my mother would always tell me, 'If you feed a person well, he will be your friend for a lifetime.' I instill that same attitude into all of our cooking staff. We want to feed people well and have many lifetime friends who come back to enjoy the food and hospitality."

The Greek Tower was voted Utica's best restaurant, and Mr. Pappas hopes to earn the same title in Albany and Genesee. —[4]—. He plans on spending most of his time at the Albany and Genesee locations until they are strong enough to stand on their own. He will have his younger brother manage the Albany restaurant while his cousin will do the same at the Genesee location.

Both restaurants are scheduled to open in six months. The new locations will offer the same menu as the original location and will also feature a few new dishes. "I think the new places will give me a chance to experiment with recipes while still providing the favorites that have made The Greek Tower so popular."

Sabrina Lowenstein

---

161. What is the purpose of the article?

(A) To describe an entrepreneur's new businesses
(B) To discuss a planned merger between companies
(C) To provide information about a new culinary school
(D) To summarize the performance of a new business

162. The word "earn" in paragraph 4, line 2, is closest in meaning to

(A) lose
(B) increase
(C) praise
(D) acquire

163. What is indicated about Mr. Pappas' brother?

(A) He took cooking lessons 15 years ago.
(B) He will manage one of the restaurants.
(C) He will help renovate the restaurants.
(D) He borrowed money from a bank.

164. In which of the positions marked [1], [2], [3], and [4] does the following sentence best belong?

"He was never formally taught but learned how to cook from his mother and grandmother."

(A) [1]
(B) [2]
(C) [3]
(D) [4]

GO ON TO THE NEXT PAGE

Dashy Corporate Providers
1881 N. 17th Avenue • Las Vegas 89101
www.dashycorproviders.com 702-555-6374

We are here to help get your company settled into its new space, hassle-free. We do this through specialized planning that takes into account your specific requirements. These are just a few of the services we provide.

- Office relocation: packing, shipping, and unpacking services
- Short- and long-term storage options
- Special handling of fragile items: custom packing and climate-controlled storage
- Secure disposal of unwanted company property
- Cleanup of old and new office spaces

Complimentary evaluation: A specialist will come to your workplace to survey your business' space and logistics needs, and provide you with an estimate for the services you require within 24 hours. After that, we can begin as soon as you're ready. This first visit is free of charge, and there is no further obligation should you choose not to proceed. To make an appointment, send an e-mail to info@dashycorproviders.com.

Trend-setting business practices: Dashy Corporate Providers combines outstanding service with responsible practices. From our reusable packing materials to electric transport systems, we are committed to having minimal environmental impact while offering the same competitive rates as our rivals.

To learn more about our company and its services, call 702-555-6374 or visit www. dashycorproviders.com.

165. What type of business is Dashy?

(A) A cleaning company
(B) A packaging factory
(C) An office supply store
(D) A moving service

166. How can potential customers receive a cost estimate?

(A) By contacting Customer Support
(B) By visiting Dashy's Web site
(C) By filling out a form
(D) By scheduling a visit from Dashy

167. How do Dashy's services differ from those of its rivals?

(A) They are more affordable.
(B) They are specialized for small businesses.
(C) They are backed by a security guarantee.
(D) They are better for the environment.

Questions 168-171 refer to the following online chat discussion.

Ella Iverson [10:03 A.M.]
Hello. I'd like to hear any concerns your department members have about the office relocation to Overland Corporate Park that was announced at June's meeting.

Jirou Mazuka [10:04 A.M.]
It came as a surprise to everyone. But my staff seems excited about the move.

Mishka Petrov [10:05 A.M.]
A couple of employees are wondering how much of the current equipment will be brought over. When will more information be available?

Hannah Lim [10:07 A.M.]
Most of the employees here are asking me how this will affect their schedules. But at this point, I have no idea what to tell them.

Ella Iverson [10:10 A.M.]
Everything is still being worked out. The executive team will have more to share within the month. I'll give you the complete details during our management conference in July.

Mishka Petrov [10:11 A.M.]
I heard a rumor that the new place is going to have open-plan seating, with no individual offices. Is that true?

Ella Iverson [10:13 A.M.]
I suppose it's possible. At the start of August, the logistics team will plan where each department will be located and how to position the work stations to make the best use of the new space.

SEND

---

168. Why did Ms. Iverson write to the department heads?

(A) To explain a new procedure
(B) To receive staff input
(C) To provide policy details
(D) To give a finalized moving date

169. At 10:10 A.M., what does Ms. Iverson most likely mean when she writes, "Everything is still being worked out"?

(A) Decisions will soon be made.
(B) A floor plan needs to be revised.
(C) The building's construction is ongoing.
(D) Projects are being reassigned.

170. When will the department heads receive an update?

(A) In June
(B) In July
(C) In August
(D) In September

171. What is the logistics team expected to do?

(A) Manage employee schedules
(B) Order new equipment
(C) Maintain incoming deliveries
(D) Design an office layout

GO ON TO THE NEXT PAGE

Custom Carrots?

[January 22] — Carrots have been a key cooking ingredient for many years. —[1]—. Geographically widespread locations including Turkey, South Africa, the U.S., and Russia export millions of pounds of the vegetable. Recent agricultural innovations have allowed farmers to increase the harvesting season to 11 months while also making carrots larger, crunchier, and more colorful.

—[2]—. The way they taste, however, is a quality that has not really been given sufficient attention. That bothers American researcher Sebastian Kang, who thinks that today's larger, more uniformly-shaped carrots would have disappointed consumers just a few decades ago. "When I was a kid, we all ate carrots that tasted much better than anything available in markets these days," he said.

—[3]—. Every modification that produced a new carrot variety resulted in slightly less-flavorful vegetables, Mr. Kang explained, which is why consumers failed to notice much of a difference from year to year. The result is that many simply do not remember the mild, sweet flavor that originally made us like carrots so much.

Getting that lost taste back into carrots, while maintaining enhanced qualities such as texture and appearance, is Mr. Kang's primary goal. —[4]—. "But I think most consumers are fine with smaller vegetables, if the flavor is superior," he adds. Mr. Kang and his colleagues are confident that the desired qualities can be brought out through standard breeding methods, and their initial results have been promising.

172. What aspect of the carrots is the focus of the article?

(A) Their weight
(B) Their flavor
(C) Their color
(D) Their texture

173. How has the production of carrots changed?

(A) Carrots are all harvested the same way.
(B) Carrots can be harvested year-round.
(C) Carrots are now grown using less water.
(D) Carrots can now be grown in laboratories.

174. What is suggested about Mr. Kang?

(A) He has been doing plant-breeding experiments.
(B) He was recognized for his innovative vegetarian dishes.
(C) He was raised in a farming community.
(D) He has done research in several countries.

175. In which of the positions marked [1], [2], [3], and [4] does the following sentence best belong?

"The change didn't happen all at once."

(A) [1]
(B) [2]
(C) [3]
(D) [4]

GO ON TO THE NEXT PAGE

Australia Vacation Homes

- **Property 6735: Greenfield**

  - Cozy 2-bedroom condo

  - Minimum stay 2 nights

  Click here more details

- **Property 2500: Kanwal**

  - Stay 4 nights straight and get a complimentary 5th night stay

  - Perfect for those who need to get away and enjoy a relaxing vacation

  - Lake view

  Click here more details

- **Property 3038: Melbourne**

  - 3-bedroom apartment

  - Close to downtown and great for those who enjoy the bustling city life

  Click here more details

- **Property 8220: Hamilton Island**

  - A private beach $1,000 per week179

  Click here more details

To	Lorraine Caluso <lcaluso@auvacationrentals.co.au>
From	Whitney Johnson <wjohnson@bermaninc.co.au>
Date	June 25
Subject	Re: Vacation Plans

Hello Lorraine,

You helped arrange my family's accommodation for our summer vacation in Melbourne last year, and I was pleased with the rental home and your level of customer service. That being said, I was not fond of the surrounding area. The hectic city life was too much for me. This time, I want to stay in a place that's more relaxing, which has at least three bedrooms with lake or beach access. I cannot afford to spend more than $750-800 for one week. The one that seems most appealing to me is Property 2500. Could you let me know what the dates of availability are for this? It seems to be the most suitable for my needs.

I hope to hear from you soon.

Sincerely,

Whitney Johnson

176. What property offers a free night's stay?

(A) Property 6735
(B) Property 2500
(C) Property 3038
(D) Property 8220

177. Why did Ms. Johnson send the e-mail?

(A) To confirm a payment
(B) To ask for instructions
(C) To change a reservation
(D) To request information

178. What aspect of her previous vacation did Ms. Johnson find unsatisfactory?

(A) The pace of life in the region nearby
(B) The distance between the rental property and her home
(C) The customer service provided by a worker
(D) The condition of the place where she stayed

179. Why is Property 8220 probably unsuitable for Ms. Johnson?

(A) She would prefer to rent a condo.
(B) She does not enjoy the beach.
(C) She is looking for something less expensive.
(D) She does not need more than two bedrooms.

180. What location is Ms. Johnson interested in?

(A) Greenfield
(B) Kanwal
(C) Melbourne
(D) Hamilton Island

GO ON TO THE NEXT PAGE

Council on International Relief Aid (CIRA)

"The Role of Social Media in Aid Work"
Sienna College of Bern, June 5-8

• **Proposed Itinerary for June 5, Monday**

7:00 A.M. to 8:30 A.M.	**Convention Participants Sign in**
8:45 A.M. to 9:00 A.M.	**Welcoming Address:** Ella Paula, Convention President
9:00 A.M. to 9:30 A.M.	**Keynote Speech:** Luca Borer, CIRA Director
9:45 A.M. to 11:00 A.M.	**Get the Audience You Need:** Martin Caspari, e-Hoy Marketing Research Institute, Spain
11:10 A.M. to 12:05 P.M.	**A Look at Online Fundraising by Charities:** speaker: to be announced, European Fundraising Association, France
12:05 P.M. to 1:30 P.M.	**Lunch:** Laurel Dining Hall
1:40 P.M. to 2:45 P.M.	**Securing Visibility with Sponsorships:** Marko Litija, Virusno Studios, Slovenia
3:00 P.M. to 4:15 P.M.	**Presentation title pending:** speaker: to be announced, Brighton Association of Emergency Care Professionals, UK
4:20 P.M. to 5:30 P.M.	**Likes: Boost Your Page Views:** Miraile Wasson, NetMetrix, Inc., USA

To	Ella Paula <epaula@aidfirst.org>
From	Luca Borer <lborer@cira.or.it>
Date	April 11
Subject	RE: Proposed Monday Itinerary

Good morning Ella,

Based on your feedback from last Thursday's online discussion, I filled the spaces that were still available on Monday's proposed itinerary. Anja Lehner in France is preparing her talk about online fundraising as they are organized by charities in her country. I also called a contact in Brighton who told me that Dr. Michael Robinson would be delighted to represent his local medical community.

I'm sorry to report that Marko Litija has withdrawn from the convention. His colleague, Sara Kos, will take his place and send us her presentation topic soon.

By the way, my train from Vienna arrives at 5:40 A.M. on Monday. I bought that ticket so that I would have plenty of time to get ready for that morning's speech.

Sincerely,
Luca Borer

181. What is indicated about Mr. Borer?

(A) He will work at the information booth.
(B) He will deliver a speech after lunch.
(C) He recently took over CIRA.
(D) He will present on the first day of the convention.

182. When will an expert on marketing research be presenting?

(A) At 9:00 A.M.
(B) At 9:45 A.M.
(C) At 1:40 P.M.
(D) At 4:20 P.M.

183. In the e-mail, in paragraph 1, line 1, the word "spaces" is closest in meaning to

(A) openings
(B) locations
(C) distances
(D) capacities

184. Which session will have to be canceled?

(A) Get the Audience You Need
(B) A Look at Online Fundraising by Charities
(C) Securing Visibility with Sponsorships
(D) Likes: Boost Your Page Views

185. According to the e-mail, what information is Mr. Borer waiting to receive?

(A) The biography of a speaker
(B) The topic of a talk
(C) The convention schedule for Tuesday
(D) The telephone number of Mr. Robinson

GO ON TO THE NEXT PAGE

Norfolk Convention Center Rental Contract

262 Maplestone Ave.
Norfolk, VA 23504

Conditions

This contract is valid for one week, from June 4 to June 11, at the rate of $3,500 per day, to be fully paid on the final day. A penalty of $700 per day will be charged for late payment. Early termination of the lease will result in a $350 penalty. Electricity, water, and concessions are provided free of charge. Meals are not provided and must be negotiated with area businesses. Optional insurance is available for $500 per day. The convention center can accommodate up to 800 vehicles. Additional parking is available in the Norfolk Baseball Stadium's parking area right down the street.

Obligations

On April 12, a security deposit of $2,000 was received and will be returned within 15 days of completion of payment. Norfolk Convention Center staff will inspect the facilities both before and after the event is held. Maintenance required before the event will be addressed by the Facility Management. The security deposit will provide for any damage done to the property after the term of the lease.

Norfolk Convention Center Facilities Inspection Form

Inspector: Alan Flint
Date: May 31

Inspector Notes:
The loading docks, convention hall, and concessions area are in excellent condition. In need of some repairs is the carpet in the front lobby. In addition, the East Wing heating unit needs to be fixed. Norfolk Convention Center maintenance staff will complete this work by June 2.

Andrea Lamont	Nasef Ahmed
Norfolk Facilities Management	Company Representative, Nexo, Inc.

From:	alamont@nccenter.com
To:	nasefa@nexo.com
Date:	June 10
Subject:	Deposit
Attachment:	inspection_form

Dear Ms. Lamont,

My company, Nexo, Inc., held an event at the Norfolk Convention Center this week and received a part of the security deposit back. I am writing in regard to the $900 deduction made. While we expected to pay a $350 fine, the $550 charge is unacceptable. The invoice lists the charge as carpeting replacement, however the carpet was damaged before our event was held (please refer to the attached document). You stated that the carpet would be replaced by your maintenance staff, however there was not enough time to do the work before our event began. Please refund the $550 charge, accordingly.

Sincerely,

Nasef Ahmed

186. What is indicated in the rental contract?

(A) The convention center offers a free shuttle service.
(B) The renter must arrange for meals separately.
(C) The convention center is undergoing electrical repairs.
(D) The renter is allowed to revise the contract terms at any time.

187. What is true about the Norfolk Convention Center?

(A) It has a private dining area.
(B) It offers technical support for presenters.
(C) It is building an additional exhibition hall.
(D) It is close to a sports venue.

188. In the rental contract, the phrase "provide for" in paragraph 2, line 4, is closest in meaning to

(A) contribute
(B) offer
(C) cover
(D) arrange

189. Why must Nexo pay a $350 fine?

(A) It did not decide to purchase insurance.
(B) It used a different parking area.
(C) It canceled its lease early.
(D) It made a payment late.

190. What argument does Mr. Ahmed make?

(A) The carpet was delivered late.
(B) The venue was not heated properly.
(C) The heating unit did not have to be fixed.
(D) The damage in the lobby was not Nexo's fault.

GO ON TO THE NEXT PAGE

http://www.localpages.org

COMING UP THIS MONTH

Summer Craze Surf Contest
Location: Capi Beach, Fiji
Dates: July 20-21
Amateurs and professionals welcome!
Contact: Laura van Dijk <lvd@wavesurfer.com>

The yearly Summer Craze Surf Contest draws top surfers, their sponsors, and talented amateurs from all over the world. They hope to make a name for themselves, as well as win cash prizes. Every year, attendance has reached nearly 8,000 visitors, making it the single biggest visitor event on any of Fiji's islands. Capi Beach, one of the most renowned surf spots in the world, frequently gets 8-meter waves. In addition to the surfing contest, sponsors have booths with games and activities for all ages set up along the beach. There is no admission fee, but be sure to bring $7 for parking.

The Winners of the Summer Craze Surf Contest

International Category

Place	Country	Name	Sponsor
1st	Brazil	Silvio De Souza	Cambera
2nd	Japan	Kanoa Arai	Zelus
3rd	USA	Simon Cole	Nika
4th	Australia	Guy Jacobs	Alala
5th	France	Mathieu Defay	Phonoi

Surf's Up at Capi!

By Frank Ganilau

This year's Summer Craze Surf Contest marked a great start to the tourist season. In part due to the unusually good weather, the event attracted easily twice as many spectators as usual.

Globally recognized surfers and amateurs alike faced the challenge of Capi's famously rough surfing conditions throughout the two-day competition. Riding on waves that approached 10 meters, they made surfing through the water look fun and easy. Several truly enormous waves worried lifeguards, but competitors conquered the mountains of water with no injuries reported.

Silvio De Souza took first place, beating fan-favorite Kanoa Arai, who had won the last three Summer Craze Surf Contests. Although it was a close call right to the end, Arai fell during the last wave of the evening. While there were a number of spectacular performances, I was particularly amazed by that of Australia's representative this year. I have watched surfers all over North and South America, but I have never seen moves quite like those.

Visitors had a great time, too. In addition to meeting famous surfers, there was plenty of food, shopping, and activities. As the sun set, everyone left knowing a good summer lay ahead.

---

191. What is mentioned about the surfers?

(A) All of them are professional surfers.
(B) They have met Ms. van Dijk previously.
(C) They come from different countries.
(D) Some of them will bring their own equipment.

192. In the article, the word "faced" in paragraph 2, line 2, is closest in meaning to

(A) confronted
(B) looked
(C) crossed
(D) risked

193. What is indicated about this year's event?

(A) It took place on Capi Beach for the first time.
(B) It had more than 8,000 spectators.
(C) It charged a $7 admission fee.
(D) It was shorter than last years' event.

194. What is indicated about Mr. Arai?

(A) He lives in Australia.
(B) He almost fell during the competition.
(C) He taught surfing lessons.
(D) He has competed in the contest before.

195. Which athlete impressed Mr. Ganilau the most?

(A) Silvio De Souza
(B) Kanoa Arai
(C) Simon Cole
(D) Guy Jacobs

GO ON TO THE NEXT PAGE

Questions 196-200 refer to the following e-mails and text message.

To	Felicia Harker <fharker@gateways.com>
From	Barry Isaacson <bisaacson@havenvh.com>
Date	May 18
Subject	Your reservation

Dear Ms. Harker,

Your online request for a three-bedroom condo was received on May 2. A Haven representative has reviewed your reservation request and confirmed availability from June 5 to June 11.

In accordance with Haven's room rate list, you will be charged $1,694.88. Please note that bookings are final once payment has been received and that we do not issue refunds for cancellations. We have sent you another e-mail with specific arrival and departure guidelines. Please call us at (310) 555-8221 or email us if you have any questions. Make sure to reference your four-digit reservation number when you contact us. We will be looking forward to your arrival at Haven!

Sincerely,

Barry Isaacson
Manager of Guest Services
Haven Vacation Homes

To	Barry Isaacson <bisaacson@havenvh.com>
From	Felicia Harker <fharker@gateways.com>
Date	June 2
Subject	RE: Your reservation

Dear Mr. Isaacson,

I am writing in regard to my reservation (#4502) at Haven Vacation Homes from June 5 to June 11. You mentioned in your e-mail that you would send additional information to me by the end of May. However, I have not received another e-mail from you yet. As I would like to receive this information before leaving for my vacation, please email it to me as soon as possible. I have tried calling you on several occasions, but the line was busy. If you are not able to contact me, I will visit your office when I arrive at the property.

I hope to hear from you soon.

Sincerely,

Felicia Harker

(562) 555-4839

To: Felicia Harker, 562-555-4839

Sent: June 5, 3:00 P.M.

Hello Felicia,

It's Zack Issacson from Haven Vacation Homes. I'm sending you this message because you aren't picking up your phone. It's one hour past your check-in time, so I wanted to know if you were on your way. Please give me a call back once you get this message. Thank you.

196. What is Ms. Harker told to provide when contacting Haven Vacation Homes?

(A) Her room number
(B) Her contact information
(C) Her reservation number
(D) Her credit card information

197. In the second e-mail, the word "property" in paragraph 1, line 6, is closest in meaning to

(A) location
(B) communication
(C) possession
(D) characteristic

198. What information is NOT included in Mr. Issacson's e-mail?

(A) The policy for cancellations
(B) The directions to a place
(C) The accommodation cost
(D) The reservation dates

199. What does Ms. Harker request from Mr. Issacson?

(A) Details about check-in and check-out
(B) Rates for room services
(C) A guide for the local area
(D) A statement of credit card charges

200. According to the text message, what is suggested about Ms. Harker?

(A) She was supposed to arrive at 2 P.M.
(B) She wants to upgrade her room.
(C) She has not made a payment.
(D) She will depart on June 12.

Stop! This is the end of the test. If you finish before time is called, you may go back to Parts 5, 6, and 7 and check your work.

READING TEST

In the Reading test, you will read a variety of texts and answer several different types of reading comprehension questions. The entire Reading test will last 75 minutes. There are three parts, and directions are given for each part. You are encouraged to answer as many questions as possible within the time allowed.

You must mark your answers on the separate answer sheet. Do not write your answers in your test book.

PART 5

Directions: A word or phrase is missing in each of the sentences below. Four answer choices are given below each sentence. Select the best answer to complete the sentence. Then mark the letter (A), (B), (C), or (D) on your answer sheet.

101. Pathfinder Vacations is looking for qualified individuals with ------- working overseas.

(A) have experienced
(B) experienced
(C) experience
(D) experiencing

102. Having culinary certification ------- a candidate's chances of gaining employment at the New Caledonian Resort.

(A) improves   (B) functions
(C) achieves   (D) finalizes

103. Mr. Rader's innovative renovation of Vaduz Fine Arts Museum is -------.

(A) commends
(B) commendable
(C) commend
(D) commending

104. Ms. Vanleuven asked to have the sign that was broken ------- the flood fixed.

(A) as well as
(B) much like
(C) containing
(D) during

105. Due to security concerns, access to the server room is ------- limited.

(A) strictly   (B) barely
(C) slightly   (D) casually

106. All staff members are expected to maintain an appropriate level of ------- when interacting with clients.

(A) professionally
(B) professionalism
(C) professional
(D) profession

107. The Director of Human Resources, Ms. Conty, will ------- the applicants into two categories.

(A) offer
(B) separate
(C) consider
(D) advise

108. Because dairy products are ------- perishable, they must be kept refrigerated as much as possible while they are in transit.

(A) higher
(B) highest
(C) highly
(D) high

109. According to the Accounting Department, ------- profits increase in the next quarter, the company will be forced to close some locations.

(A) unless
(B) instead
(C) but
(D) that

110. Over the ------- nine months, the Trent Corporation has focused its resources on constructing additional factories.

(A) lasting
(B) lasted
(C) last
(D) lastly

111. The market test results indicate that the Cooler X100 does not ------- regulate the temperature of commercial refrigeration systems.

(A) preciseness
(B) precisely
(C) precision
(D) precise

112. Emilia Caporetto accepted a management position from a firm offering a benefits package that ------- her expectations.

(A) took
(B) lost
(C) met
(D) gave

113. Vertical Interior was picked to renovate the main lobby given that it can complete the job at a ------- price.

(A) severe
(B) promoted
(C) condensed
(D) reasonable

114. Maler Surfacing was late with its estimate ------- many due date postponements.

(A) actually
(B) despite
(C) although
(D) still

115. The airport's shuttle service is provided to ------- all of the hotels and resorts on the island.

(A) inside
(B) farther
(C) almost
(D) properly

116. The latest consumer survey results show that the ------- of RW's new automobile outweigh its benefits.

(A) compliments
(B) disturbances
(C) accomplishments
(D) shortcomings

117. During the annual event, Dr. Connor ------- an award for her contribution in the field of applied science.

(A) praised
(B) accepted
(C) wished
(D) nominated

118. During her three decades working at the Shimmer Auto Plant, Ms. O'Driscoll ------- various kinds of machinery on the factory floor.

(A) operate
(B) operating
(C) operated
(D) operation

119. Alterations to the reservation cannot be made less than 48 hours ------- arrival time.

(A) rather
(B) prior to
(C) owing to
(D) apart from

120. Since offline customers are our main source of income, sales training is ------- for all store employees.

(A) exceptional
(B) liable
(C) mandatory
(D) vague

GO ON TO THE NEXT PAGE

121. The IT Department was pleased that Jin Ho Park, ------- experience was quite outstanding, was selected as manager.

(A) where
(B) whose
(C) what
(D) why

122. Since Ms. Phan will transfer to the Tokyo branch in April, Mr. Sirivithan has already begun the process of ------- her.

(A) interacting
(B) identifying
(C) advancing
(D) replacing

123. By cooperating with companies in various sectors and locations, P.L. Howard Ltd. ------- its market share in Central Asia.

(A) was expanded
(B) to be expanding
(C) has been expanded
(D) will be expanding

124. Primer Fashion designed an ------- clothing line that has helped increase product sales.

(A) attentive
(B) assorted
(C) innovative
(D) urgent

125. As soon as the Marketing Department received authorization, the director ------- assigning interns.

(A) began
(B) were beginning
(C) begin
(D) has begun

126. Please make sure your seminar allows ------- time at the end to take questions from the audience.

(A) sufficient
(B) difficult
(C) accurate
(D) dependable

127. Mr. Kimble ------- tried to contact Murata, Inc.'s PR team but was unable to receive a response.

(A) repeating
(B) repeatedly
(C) repeated
(D) repetition

128. Ms. Edgerton will receive an award for lifetime ------- in medical research.

(A) achieving
(B) achieves
(C) achievable
(D) achievement

129. If market trends persist, Portos Programming may ------- recover fully but become a leading competitor in the software industry.

(A) in addition
(B) as well
(C) as such
(D) not only

130. The cheaper cleanser proved to be an effective ------- to the popular brand.

(A) possibility
(B) alternative
(C) choice
(D) option

PART 6

Directions: Read the texts that follow. A word, phrase, or sentence is missing in parts of each text. Four answer choices for each question are given below the text. Select the best answer to complete the text. Then mark the letter (A), (B), (C), or (D) on your answer sheet.

Questions 131-134 refer to the following information.

Quarterly Performance Reviews

The oral and written review is the last ------- of the employee appraisal process. It is an
131.
official evaluation of work performance over a three-month period. An overall grade is
given based on the criteria decided by the department head. -------. This also helps
132.
------- goals for the following quarter. The quarterly review is never a replacement for
133.
regular discussions concerning job performance, which are considered ------- for a
134.
productive work day.

131. (A) version
(B) condition
(C) edit
(D) step

132. (A) Lately, a lot of firms have been
implementing monthly reviews.
(B) The main reason for the review is to
provide employees with meaningful
feedback.
(C) As per company policy, we will
always keep employee evaluations
on file.
(D) Supervisors are allowed to set their
department's work hours.

133. (A) launch
(B) attempt
(C) determine
(D) appreciate

134. (A) necessary
(B) necessity
(C) necessarily
(D) necessitating

GO ON TO THE NEXT PAGE

Questions 135-138 refer to the following letter.

February 22

Erica Marsh
Regency Court
1423 E. California Rd.
Fort Wayne, IN 46805

Dear Ms. Marsh,

This letter is regarding my lease agreement for 1822 Clinton Avenue, ------- due to end

                                                        135.

on February 28. I wish to ------- a renewal of the contract. ------- new house will not be

                         136.   **137.**

available by March. For this reason, I hope to stay in my current apartment through

March 31. -------.

        138.

If you are free, let's plan on speaking by phone some time tomorrow morning. I'm also

open to meet face-to-face if you prefer.

Best regards,

Derek Lagerman

135. (A) what will
(B) that being
(C) which is
(D) one of

136. (A) request
(B) deny
(C) purchase
(D) invest

137. (A) Their
(B) Any
(C) My
(D) Its

138. (A) I have nearly finished moving out.
(B) Please advise on what can be arranged.
(C) I would like to see apartments that match these requirements.
(D) I am currently living in Fort Wayne.

Questions 139-142 refer to the following e-mail.

From: renaldpark87@mycos.net
To: info@sleekformalwear.com
Date: April 24
Subject: Invoice number 89827

Hello,

Two months ago, I bought a jacket on Sleek Formal Wear's Web site. To make sure it fit properly, I tried it on as soon as I received my order. -------, when I wore it for the first
139.
time this morning, I realized there was a small tear in the inside of the jacket. I am aware that all ------- products should be exchanged or returned within one week and that my
140.
item does not fall within this stated time frame.

-------. If it ------- out, I do not mind selecting another garment of similar value.
141.   **142.**

Please advise me on what to do.

Thank you,

Renald Park

---

139. (A) Otherwise
(B) However
(C) Thus
(D) Furthermore

140. (A) defective
(B) false
(C) ill-fitting
(D) confirmed

141. (A) I returned the item three weeks after it was delivered.
(B) Please wire the money to the bank account I provided.
(C) Nonetheless, I am hoping that you can make an exception this time.
(D) Fortunately, the application period was extended until next month.

142. (A) be selling
(B) has sold
(C) having been sold
(D) will sell

GO ON TO THE NEXT PAGE

Questions 143-146 refer to the following e-mail.

To: Jan Long <jlong@pwc.co.jp>
From: Robert Ferguson <ferg@gspec.co.jp>
Date: 5 March
Subject: Product issue

Dear Ms. Long,

We are grateful for your recent ------- of a G-spec Slim-X laptop. We are informing all
143.
customers who have recently bought this device from us that a limited number of models

require repair.

In some of our laptops, the touchpad, which acts as a pointing device, occasionally

malfunctions. -------. Please ------- whether yours is one of the affected models by
144. **145.**
checking the product's serial number, which is located on the bottom of your laptop. If

this code starts with the letters "SXRE," a repair must be performed. We will cover all

expenses related to sending back your Slim-X. Additionally, G-spec will fix ------- free of
146.
charge.

143. (A) testimonial
(B) purchase
(C) test
(D) donation

144. (A) This defect will continually interfere
with the navigation of your computer.
(B) We are confident that you will enjoy
the laptop.
(C) This model is considered one of the
most reliable of its kind.
(D) For more information, refer to our
Frequently Asked Questions page.

145. (A) confirm
(B) confirmed
(C) confirmation
(D) confirms

146. (A) theirs
(B) mine
(C) these
(D) it

PART 7

Directions: In this part you will read a selection of texts, such as magazine and newspaper articles, emails, and instant messages. Each text or set of texts is followed by several questions. Select the best answer for each question and mark the letter (A), (B), (C), or (D) on your answer sheet.

Questions 147-148 refer to the following text message.

Frank Ricci [1:45 P.M.]

Hello, Carol. My conference call with the city council members just ended, and they liked our design proposal for the town garden. Councilmember Jason Hicks requested additional client references, but I don't have those files with me. I am on my way to a worksite, so could you call a delivery service to send a copy of the Sawvale Square portfolio to him? Please include one of our brochures, too. Thank you.

147. Where does Mr. Ricci most likely work?

(A) At a government agency
(B) At a post office
(C) At an insurance firm
(D) At a landscaping company

148. What is Frank asked to do?

(A) Send some client references
(B) Respond to a message
(C) Create an e-mail list
(D) Schedule an appointment

GO ON TO THE NEXT PAGE

Questions 149-150 refer to the following e-mail.

From: Pat Merrick
To: Carter Hotel staff
Date: 21 February
Subject: Notice

Effective March 1, Carter Hotel will only provide full refunds for room cancellations when the request is made at least one week in advance.

We will post this information on our Web site and at the front desk before the end of the week. An e-mail explaining the new rule will also be sent to all currently registered guests. If a guest needs to cancel their stay with less than a week's notice, please ask the appropriate manager for help. We appreciate your cooperation.

Pat Merrick
Carter Hotel General Manager

149. What is the purpose of the e-mail?

(A) To announce some staff training
(B) To describe an updated hotel facility
(C) To introduce a new policy
(D) To report on recent sales figures

150. According to the e-mail, what will managers do?

(A) Select which workers can make schedule changes
(B) Teach guests how to make online reservations
(C) Decide how to arrange new furniture
(D) Assist guests with specific requests

Questions 151-152 refer to the following text message chain.

Nicole Meyers

Have you left the Martin Ballroom yet? 12:52

Hugo Vessly

12:55 No. The final presenter just got on stage.

Nicole Meyers

Do you plan on attending BR Tech's virtual reality demonstration? It's in Hall A. 12:56

Hugo Vessly

I'll definitely be there. They always put on a fun show.
12:57

Nicole Meyers

For sure. And it's educational, as well. 12:58

Hugo Vessly

I'm going to sit close to the stage. Should I save you a seat?
12:59

Nicole Meyers

Yes, please! 13:01

151. At 12:58, what does Ms. Meyers most likely mean when she writes, "For sure"?

(A) The lecturers in the Martin Ballroom were entertaining.
(B) She agrees with Mr. Vessly's view on BR Tech's demonstrators.
(C) She knows that Mr. Vessly will go to a demonstration.
(D) She plans to have an interview with BR Tech.

152. What is most likely true about Mr. Vessly?

(A) He wants Ms. Meyers to give a demonstration.
(B) He is a developer of virtual reality software.
(C) He will be the last speaker in the Martin Ballroom.
(D) He will get to Hall A before Ms. Meyers.

GO ON TO THE NEXT PAGE

Questions 153-154 refer to the following memo.

From: Mark Glover
To: Chuck's Restaurant Employees
Date: July 21
Subject: Requirements

Recently, we have had a high number of requests to work different shifts. Chuck's Restaurant management would like to remind everyone that requests should be made as early as possible and that 12 employees are required for each shift.

Submit a request through the company system at least two weeks in advance to ensure you get your desired shift. Unfortunately, not everyone can be accommodated. In order to maintain our citywide reputation for outstanding service, we need to keep the business fully staffed, and this requires all of your cooperation.

Should you have any questions, please bring them up with your manager.

153. What is the purpose of the memo?

(A) To request feedback on new menu options
(B) To highlight an issue with an ordering system
(C) To describe a new process
(D) To remind employees about scheduling work hours

154. What should employees do if they have a concern?

(A) Speak to their manager
(B) Email Mr. Glover
(C) Review a handbook
(D) Complete a questionnaire

Economics Monthly
Business Bulletin

Soleridge, 20 November – Developer Kenny Ritter has started work on what is going to become the Falcon Central Complex. The building, at 7863 Sears Avenue, used to be the location of the Soleridge Furniture Company. Mr. Ritter's company, the Falcon Investment Corporation, purchased it in June. Construction of the former factory will result in 400 apartments and approximately 8,000 square meters of commercial space.

There will be two stages in the development of the €200 million project. Stage one is estimated to take one and a half years and will have 300 apartments completed. The remaining apartments along with a three-story department store will be constructed during stage two, which will take about seven months. The Falcon Investment Corporation has also recently bought the Leno Building on Lakeview Street. Although development plans for it have not yet been announced, a Falcon Investment spokesperson stated that more information would be released sometime next month.

155. What is the main purpose of the article?

(A) To announce the completion of an apartment building
(B) To profile a renowned building developer
(C) To advertise a recently renovated store
(D) To discuss details of a construction project

156. What is indicated about the Falcon Central Complex buildings?

(A) It will contain both apartments and retail stores.
(B) It will be completed in seven months.
(C) It is located near a lake.
(D) It is the first building that Mr. Ritter developed.

157. What is mentioned about Mr. Ritter's company?

(A) It will relocate next month.
(B) It has purchased more than one property.
(C) Its offices are close to the Soleridge Furniture Company.
(D) It specializes in remodeling old buildings.

GO ON TO THE NEXT PAGE

Questions 158-161 refer to the following e-mail.

From	Sabrina San Luciano
To	Department supervisors
Date	July 5
Subject	Boosting employee productivity

Greetings supervisors,

—[1]—. In the coming weeks, the personnel team will be holding a series of meetings with the heads of each department to discuss employee work habits and productivity.

Open office workspaces, where employee desks are positioned next to each other, without walls in between, is a design that an increasing number of companies use because it makes it easier for employees to communicate and collaborate with each other on assignments. —[2]—. As the office reconfiguration is set for late December, we are considering whether an open office workspace design would be a better fit for our business. We will make a decision regarding this proposal after reviewing the advantages and disadvantages.

I have written this e-mail to request your input. —[3]—. At this stage, the Personnel Department is still collecting data. Please fill out the open office workspace questionnaire, located on the company's internal Web page. —[4]—. The link is on the right side of your login page.

I appreciate your help. If you have any questions, please send me an e-mail.

Sabrina San Luciano
Personnel Director
Audio Sonic Technologies

158. Why was the e-mail written?

(A) To announce a conference schedule
(B) To promote an annual company gathering
(C) To provide notice of a policy change
(D) To request completion of a questionnaire

159. What is mentioned as a benefit of open office workspaces?

(A) They allow the company to hire more employees.
(B) They help staff work well together on projects.
(C) They reduce business costs.
(D) They improve air quality in the office.

160. What is the company planning to do at the end of the year?

(A) Organize a managers' retreat
(B) Change the design of an office
(C) Launch a Web site
(D) Find a new Personnel Director

161. In which of the positions marked [1], [2], [3], and [4] does the following sentence best belong?

"Please keep in mind that we have not yet decided if an open office workspace is right for us."

(A) [1]
(B) [2]
(C) [3]
(D) [4]

Questions 162-164 refer to the following instructions.

Congratulations on your purchase of the new Estefan Deep Sleep mattress.

To make the best use of your mattress, please follow these simple guidelines.

- In order to keep the mattress clean, always use a mattress cover. Most covers can be washed by machine.

- Never fold the mattress for transport or storage.

- To remove stains, use a water-free upholstery cleaner. If water must be used on the mattress, use it sparingly, as too much water can cause mold to grow. Make sure the mattress is completely dry before using it.

- To avoid wearing out your mattress unevenly, flip the mattress several times a year (so that the topside is facing down and vice versa).

- Replace your mattress every seven to nine years or if it becomes uncomfortable.

- Do not remove the information tag from the mattress. It will serve as identification if you need to make a warranty claim.

162. In the instructions, what is suggested as possibly damaging to the mattress?

(A) A non-machine washable cover
(B) Excessive moisture
(C) Using cleaning products
(D) Transporting outdoors

163. What are mattress owners told to do regularly?

(A) Iron the mattress
(B) Air out the mattress
(C) Replace the mattress cover
(D) Turn the mattress over

164. According to the instructions, why should mattress owners retain the tag?

(A) It is required in order to file a warranty claim.
(B) It provides guidelines on using the product safely.
(C) It describes the type of materials in the mattress.
(D) It contains information about store locations.

GO ON TO THE NEXT PAGE

Questions 165-168 refer to the following online chat discussion.

Roger Zhu [10:27 A.M.]
This is Roger over in Human Resources. Ms. Kim and Ms. Ikagami, you're both scheduled to go on the executive retreat next month, correct?

Laura Kim [10:29 A.M.]
That's right. We've got flights booked for July 24 at 6:35 P.M. Why?

Roger Zhu [10:30 A.M.]
It turns out that Arborita Resort's online system lost our reservations. So, we're going to have to move the retreat to the second week of July.

April Ikagami [10:32 A.M.]
Really? I've already paid for my kids to attend summer camp that week. I won't be able to attend if my children are around.

Roger Zhu [10:33 A.M.]
Well, that's why I wanted to get in touch — to find out about any special needs you might have. We won't be using Arborita again, of course. So the team is going to be looking for alternative places to hold the retreat.

Laura Kim [10:35 A.M.]
April, could you come if they choose a resort with a child care center?

April Ikagami [10:36 A.M.]
Well... That should be OK. But I want to read about their services before I give a definite answer.

Roger Zhu [10:37 A.M.]
What about you, Ms. Kim? Is there anything you need to make this scheduling change easier?

Laura Kim [10:39 A.M.]
Nothing on my end. I'll have my assistant work it out.

April Ikagami [10:40 A.M.]
Thanks for letting us know, Mr. Zhu. Please send us brochures of the new place once it's been decided.

Roger Zhu [10:42 A.M.]
I will, Ms. Ikagami. Thanks.

SEND

165. What is the purpose of the discussion?

    (A) To apologize for a mistake
    (B) To explain a change of schedule
    (C) To ask for flight information
    (D) To promote an upcoming event

166. What is suggested about the executive retreat?

    (A) It provides child care services.
    (B) It is held once a month.
    (C) It takes place on the same week as the summer camp.
    (D) It always uses Arborita Resort as its location.

167. What does Ms. Ikagami ask Mr. Zhu to do?

    (A) Provide information about a venue
    (B) Send details about an event calendar
    (C) Increase the budget of a project
    (D) Explain a payment procedure

168. At 10:39 A.M., what does Ms. Kim mean when she writes, "Nothing on my end"?

    (A) She did not submit a report yet.
    (B) She has not received a document.
    (C) She does not need further assistance.
    (D) She will not be attending the retreat.

GO ON TO THE NEXT PAGE

Questions 169-171 refer to the following e-mail.

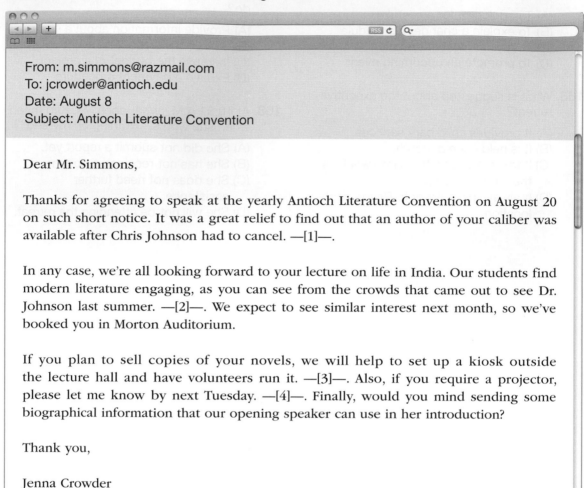

From: m.simmons@razmail.com
To: jcrowder@antioch.edu
Date: August 8
Subject: Antioch Literature Convention

Dear Mr. Simmons,

Thanks for agreeing to speak at the yearly Antioch Literature Convention on August 20 on such short notice. It was a great relief to find out that an author of your caliber was available after Chris Johnson had to cancel. —[1]—.

In any case, we're all looking forward to your lecture on life in India. Our students find modern literature engaging, as you can see from the crowds that came out to see Dr. Johnson last summer. —[2]—. We expect to see similar interest next month, so we've booked you in Morton Auditorium.

If you plan to sell copies of your novels, we will help to set up a kiosk outside the lecture hall and have volunteers run it. —[3]—. Also, if you require a projector, please let me know by next Tuesday. —[4]—. Finally, would you mind sending some biographical information that our opening speaker can use in her introduction?

Thank you,

Jenna Crowder
Event Coordinator

169. Why did Ms. Crowder write this e-mail?

(A) To announce the publication of a book
(B) To change the time of a lecture
(C) To confirm Mr. Simmons' participation in an event
(D) To discuss Mr. Simmons' volunteer duties in detail

170. What is suggested about Chris Johnson?

(A) He wrote a popular novel about India.
(B) He gave a presentation last year.
(C) He used to work with Mr. Simmons.
(D) He teaches at a university in Antioch.

171. In which of the following positions marked [1], [2], [3], and [4] does the following sentence best belong?

"I can have audiovisual equipment set up at your request."

(A) [1]
(B) [2]
(C) [3]
(D) [4]

Preparing for Your Store's Opening

The first few days of business are a great opportunity to spark interest and gain the attention of potential customers, but you'll need to do considerable planning to make it a success. The following are some important questions to ask yourself before your store's opening:

• What signs or posters will you set up? Decorations are very effective when they showcase a wide range of different products.

• How long will your decorations stay up? If you only put up decorations on the first day, there is a good chance that many customers who work that day won't get to see them.

• What kind of advertising will you use? According to some research, people usually remember what they read better than what they hear. Keep that in mind when debating whether to use print media, TV, or radio advertisements.

• How will you motivate your employees? Your employees play a key role in making customers happy, so consider giving prizes to the best workers.

172. For whom is the article intended?

(A) Entrepreneurs who are planning to start a business
(B) Store owners who are planning to expand their operations overseas
(C) Employees who want to take on supervisory roles
(D) Consumers who are looking for new types of products

173. The word "gain" in paragraph 1, line 2, is closest in meaning to

(A) build
(B) improve
(C) acquire
(D) grow

174. According to the article, what are people less likely to do on days that they work?

(A) Listen to the radio
(B) View job listings
(C) Compare different products
(D) Check out a store

175. According to the article, what is a benefit of print media ads?

(A) They are more likely to be read by local residents.
(B) They are cheaper than other forms of advertising.
(C) They are able to provide more information in a single space.
(D) They are forgotten less quickly than other forms of advertising.

GO ON TO THE NEXT PAGE

MEMO

Date: May 25
To: Rasta Motors Employees
From: Sarah Clovis, Administrative Department
Subject: GMNS Partnership

As part of the company's employee appreciation program, Rasta Motors has partnered with Global Mobile Network Systems (GMNS) to offer staff members discounted rates on mobile phone service plans. Employees who decide to sign up for a family or individual service plan with GMNS will save 20 percent and 15 percent, respectively, on the first two months of their subscription. In addition, the activation fee will be waived, saving you an extra $25. All subscriptions are for 12 months and will be automatically canceled at the end of this period unless the service is renewed.

Employees who want to take advantage of this deal should call GMNS Customer Support at 914-555-4029. Applications may also be sent electronically at www.gmns.com/promotion. When applying, staff should be ready to provide their employee number and a work email address. Also, a credit card number must be submitted along with a valid form of photo identification such as a driver's license or passport.

GMNS Customer Complaint Form

Customer Details

Name: Shay Ryans
Account Number: 85948310
Date: July 30
E-mail Address: sryans@rastamotors.com

Complaint Details

In June, I opened a mobile phone account with GMNS after reading about the special deal for Rasta Motors' employees. Based on the promotional material handed out by my company, I do not have to pay an activation fee to begin my service. Also, the GMNS representative that I spoke to on the phone confirmed this when I signed up. Yet, I have been charged an activation fee on my first month's billing statement, dated July 28. Please remove this fee from my bill and mail me an amended version. Just to be sure, the 15 percent discount for the phone charge should still be applied to the updated bill. Thank you.

176. Why was the memo issued?

(A) To remind employees not to use company phones for personal calls
(B) To announce a special benefit for employees
(C) To encourage employees to renew their current phone subscription
(D) To notify employees that signing up with GMNS is mandatory

177. What is indicated about the activation fee?

(A) It costs $25.
(B) It may be paid in installments.
(C) It will be refunded after one year.
(D) It will be added to the first two bills.

178. What is NOT required for the GMNS application?

(A) A promotional code
(B) An employee number
(C) An e-mail address
(D) A credit card number

179. What is most likely true about Ms. Ryans?

(A) She applied for an account through Rasta Motor's Web site.
(B) She has used GMNS' services before.
(C) She has subscribed to the individual service plan.
(D) She works in Ms. Clovis' department.

180. What does Ms. Ryans request that GMNS do?

(A) Send her a corrected billing statement
(B) Cancel her yearly plan
(C) Provide a discount for two more months
(D) Change the company's renewal policies

GO ON TO THE NEXT PAGE

Welcome to the Jeanneret Library of Engineering

The Jeanneret Library of Engineering at Sulgen University is open to students and guests wishing to visit our Public Access areas on the first and second floors, and our Old Archives area, found in the climate-controlled basement. We house texts, films, and photographs, as well as an enormous collection of original building designs and sketches.

Visitors and students should be aware of the following library rules in place to protect the collections:

• All guests need to present valid ID and complete the required form to become library members before they are allowed entry.
• Members may freely utilize the contents in the Public Access areas. To ensure that all materials are properly organized, please return items no longer needed to one of the Return areas located throughout the library; members are requested not to shelve items themselves.
• Members found to have caused damage to materials including, but not limited to, markings, scratches, rips, and stains will be fined.
• Two large-format scanners are available on the second floor, by the computer workstations.
• The Jeanneret Library closes at 6:00 P.M. All materials must be returned by 5:45 P.M.

The Old Archives area requires attention to these extra rules:

• No personal belongings are permitted in the Old Archives area. Please use the temporary storage service at the library's front desk. Should you need to take notes or make sketches, staff will provide you with pens or pencils.
• Materials must be requested in writing at the Old Archives counter.
• Old Archives' materials may not be taken to other library areas, and only three items may be viewed at one time. Additional items will be held at the counter.
• Old Archives items will be collected at 5:15 P.M. without exception.

Jeanneret Library of Engineering
Request Form for Old Archives Materials

Membership Number: 84323-45
Full Name: James Hayes
Date: October 15
Reason for Request: Research

Please enter information into both columns to help our staff locate your materials.

	Title	Catalog code
Item 1	The Comprehensive History of Theo van Thorne's Home Designs	720.22VF
Item 2	The 1929 Chicago Blueprints of Theo van Thorne	728JJ
Item 3	The Personal Journal of Theo van Thorne	720.9AR
Item 4	Urban Engineering Weekly (12/08/1946)	PP325-A
Item 5		

181. What is mentioned about the Jeanneret Library?

(A) It requires that visitors sign up for a membership.
(B) It provides discounts to local residents.
(C) It has a special section for university students.
(D) It closes early on the weekends.

182. According to the rules, what are visitors prohibited from doing?

(A) Reading sensitive documents
(B) Bringing in beverages
(C) Reserving items ahead of time
(D) Reshelving used items

183. How can visitors in the Old Archives area record their research?

(A) By having a specialist conduct the recording
(B) By renting a laptop from the library
(C) By asking library staff for writing materials
(D) By using a personal digital camera

184. What most likely is the topic of Mr. Hayes' research?

(A) The work of a certain architect
(B) A history of engineering publications
(C) The restoration of old manuscripts
(D) Famous engineering schools in Europe

185. What does Mr. Hayes' request for materials suggest?

(A) He will not be able to view all of his requested items at once.
(B) He is an engineering student at Sulgen University.
(C) He will give his items back by 5:45 P.M.
(D) He will need to pay a fee to request additional materials.

GO ON TO THE NEXT PAGE

Questions 186-190 refer to the following brochure and e-mails.

Gerhart Window Frames

Gerhart Window Frames has been supplying building professionals and contractors with all-weather window frames for over 30 years. Listed below are our top-selling products.

Sunray Super: Energy saving, long-lasting, and come in over 20 different colors.

Multiblock Anchor: Only available in white, rosewood, and black, but most other aspects are similar to that of Sunray Super. However, the frames are thicker, providing extra insulation.

Sunstopper Plus: For homes that get a lot of direct sun, these frames are angled to block harsh glare and keep interior temperatures comfortable.

Cinchfit Extra: Use for buildings and homes that experience extreme temperatures. Contact a certified professional for installation due to the level of precision required for this product.

For prices and exact specifications, please refer to our catalog. Questions and requests can be emailed to info@gerhartwindowframes.co.uk or call 020-7946-0924.

When choosing window frames, be sure to consider various factors. To find out the dimensions of the frames you need, use our online calculator at www.gerhartwindowframes.co.uk/calc. Just input the height and width of your window.

From: m.sheppard@rightbuild.co.uk
To: info@gerhartwindowframes.co.uk
Date: 7 April
Subject: Recent order

Gerhart Window Frames Customer Service,

I am writing concerning order #55-234A for eggplant purple window frames. My client is concerned that the color of the frames might cause his house to get too hot. I explained that the frames were unlikely to have any effect on the interior temperature, but I would like to hear if this is indeed a problem. The color is a particular favorite of his, and if possible, he would prefer not to change the order.

The last time I ordered from your company, installation videos were available to view on your Web site. I would like to watch those videos again as I have not used this particular product recently. From what I recall, it requires some special care in installation. Could you please send me a link to that page?

Sincerely,
Maria Sheppard

From	freede@gerhartwindowframes.co.uk
To	m.sheppard@rightbuild.co.uk
Date	7 April
Subject	Re: Recent order

Dear Ms. Sheppard,

Thank you for contacting Gerhart Window Frames. The frames are made of a material that does not absorb sunlight. Furthermore, based on the address in your order, no other buildings in that area have reported problems with dark colored frames, including ones that are dark blue and charcoal. Should your client wish to revise their order, let me know before the end of the day.

Regarding our Web site, we now refer our customers to the specific manufacturer's home page as they have the latest information about specific frames. We appreciate your business.

Sincerely,
Francis Reede

186. According to the brochure, how can customers determine what size frames to purchase?

(A) By consulting a specialist
(B) By using an online service
(C) By ordering product samples
(D) By downloading some graphics

187. What aspect of the frames does Ms. Sheppard need more information about?

(A) Their ability to resist humidity
(B) Their tendency to fade quickly
(C) Their thickness compared to similar products
(D) Their likeliness to trap heat

188. What type of frames did Ms. Sheppard most likely order for her client?

(A) Sunray Super
(B) Multiblock Anchor
(C) Sunstopper Plus
(D) Cinchfit Extra

189. According to Mr. Reede, why would Ms. Sheppard need to contact him again on April 7?

(A) To receive a reimbursement
(B) To request an invoice
(C) To track a delivery
(D) To revise an order

190. What is suggested about the installation videos?

(A) Ms. Sheppard accidentally deleted the files.
(B) They are not available on Gerhart Window Frames' Web site.
(C) Gerhart Window Frames will email them to Ms. Sheppard.
(D) They feature local contracting companies.

GO ON TO THE NEXT PAGE

Questions 191-195 refer to the following brochure, review, and e-mail.

LEARN JOURNALISM IN PARIS

Located in the center of Paris, the Parisian Journalism Institute (PJI) provides a range of courses for students planning to further their academic careers in graduate programs. With field offices of most global media companies nearby, it's a good place to make valuable contacts while studying. Our classes cover audio and video recording, data mining, and of course, writing for features and articles. Our classes also prepare students applying to graduate schools by providing tips on writing personal statements, crafting résumés, and compiling portfolios. Hundreds of our students have gone on to attend prestigious schools worldwide. One way we ensure their success is by employing instructors who are highly respected in the field, like Dylan Andersson, Editor-in-Chief of *International Nightly*, and Bethany Kilpatrick, of *London News Bureau*. To apply, to learn more about our school and courses, or to arrange a consultation with an academic counselor, visit our Web site at www.pji.ed.fr.

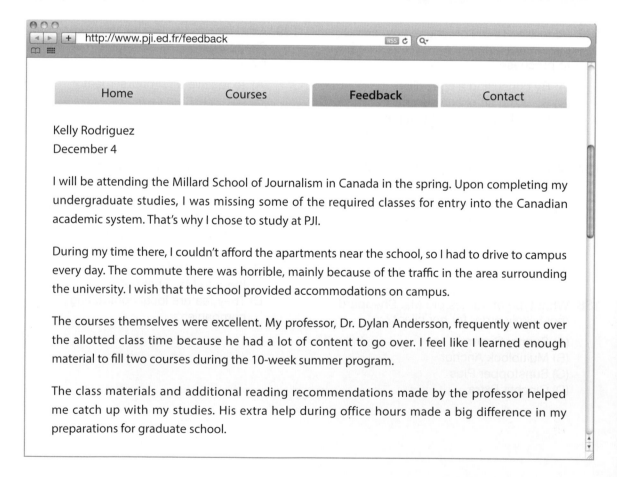

http://www.pji.ed.fr/feedback

| Home | Courses | **Feedback** | Contact |

Kelly Rodriguez
December 4

I will be attending the Millard School of Journalism in Canada in the spring. Upon completing my undergraduate studies, I was missing some of the required classes for entry into the Canadian academic system. That's why I chose to study at PJI.

During my time there, I couldn't afford the apartments near the school, so I had to drive to campus every day. The commute there was horrible, mainly because of the traffic in the area surrounding the university. I wish that the school provided accommodations on campus.

The courses themselves were excellent. My professor, Dr. Dylan Andersson, frequently went over the allotted class time because he had a lot of content to go over. I feel like I learned enough material to fill two courses during the 10-week summer program.

The class materials and additional reading recommendations made by the professor helped me catch up with my studies. His extra help during office hours made a big difference in my preparations for graduate school.

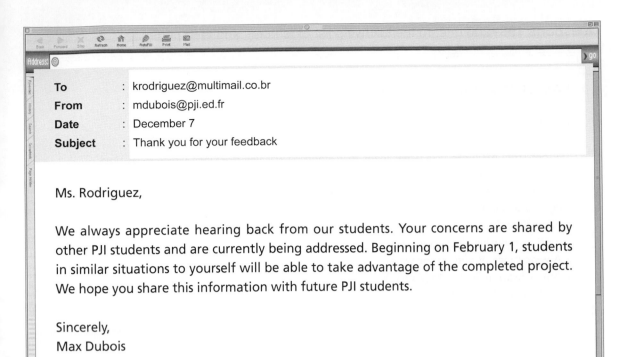

To : krodriguez@multimail.co.br
From : mdubois@pji.ed.fr
Date : December 7
Subject : Thank you for your feedback

Ms. Rodriguez,

We always appreciate hearing back from our students. Your concerns are shared by other PJI students and are currently being addressed. Beginning on February 1, students in similar situations to yourself will be able to take advantage of the completed project. We hope you share this information with future PJI students.

Sincerely,
Max Dubois

191. Who is the brochure intended for?

(A) Potential graduate students
(B) Television producers
(C) Professors looking for a job
(D) Business journalists

192. What is indicated about PJI?

(A) It provides university scholarships.
(B) It helps students find employment.
(C) It has a program for interns.
(D) It is in a crowded location.

193. What does Ms. Rodriguez mention about her professor?

(A) He required students to engage in many interactive activities.
(B) He was rarely available for office visits.
(C) He took extra time to cover class materials.
(D) He assigned projects on a weekly basis.

194. Where does Ms. Rodriguez's instructor work when he is not teaching?

(A) At PJI
(B) At *International Nightly*
(C) At *London News Bureau*
(D) At a Parisian news agency

195. How will PJI be addressing Ms. Rodriguez's complaint?

(A) By expanding classroom space
(B) By offering student housing
(C) By increasing public transportation choices
(D) By shortening the lengths of courses

GO ON TO THE NEXT PAGE

SWIRLER 12kg Jet-Stream Washing Machine Model JS-4425

FEATURES

- Super-sized basin can take larger loads than standard washing machines, which saves time.
- Stainless steel interior prevents odor and rust buildup.
- A signal lets you know if you have left an item in the machine after the end of a cycle. LED display lights also show the status of your wash cycle.
- New Blue Shift Technology assesses the amount of laundry and sets the proper amount of motion, reducing electricity use.
- A wide range of options for water, temperature, wash cycles, and different kinds of fabric.
- Anti-vibration Technology enables your machine to operate more quietly than the average washing machine, allowing you to wash your clothes at any time.

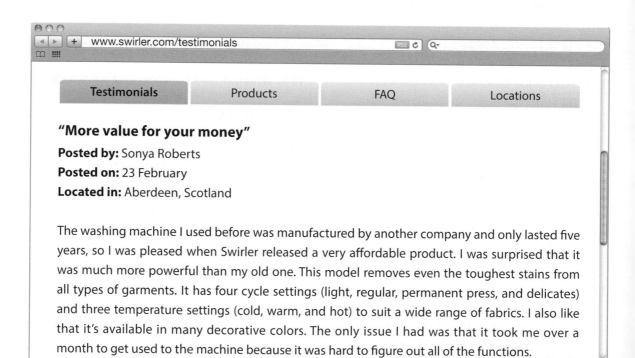

www.swirler.com/testimonials

| Testimonials | Products | FAQ | Locations |

"More value for your money"

Posted by: Sonya Roberts
Posted on: 23 February
Located in: Aberdeen, Scotland

The washing machine I used before was manufactured by another company and only lasted five years, so I was pleased when Swirler released a very affordable product. I was surprised that it was much more powerful than my old one. This model removes even the toughest stains from all types of garments. It has four cycle settings (light, regular, permanent press, and delicates) and three temperature settings (cold, warm, and hot) to suit a wide range of fabrics. I also like that it's available in many decorative colors. The only issue I had was that it took me over a month to get used to the machine because it was hard to figure out all of the functions.

196. Where would the list of features most likely be found?

(A) Printed in a clothing catalog
(B) Shown on the box of a product
(C) Included with an order of fabric
(D) Posted inside a repair shop

197. In the first Web page, the word "suit" in paragraph 1, line 5, is closest in meaning to

(A) appeal to
(B) qualify
(C) dress up
(D) accommodate

198. What criticism does Ms. Roberts make about the product?

(A) It is complicated.
(B) It is loud.
(C) It is heavy.
(D) It is pricey.

199. What feature does Ms. Roberts like that is NOT mentioned in the product description?

(A) Its various settings
(B) Its metal interior
(C) Its large load capacity
(D) Its decorative appearance

200. What feature does Mr. Calmont not like about his product?

(A) The Anti-vibration Technology
(B) The Blue Shift Technology
(C) The LED display lights
(D) The alert signal

Stop! This is the end of the test. If you finish before time is called, you may go back to Parts 5, 6, and 7 and check your work.

READING TEST

In the Reading test, you will read a variety of texts and answer several different types of reading comprehension questions. The entire Reading test will last 75 minutes. There are three parts, and directions are given for each part. You are encouraged to answer as many questions as possible within the time allowed.

You must mark your answers on the separate answer sheet. Do not write your answers in your test book.

PART 5

Directions: A word or phrase is missing in each of the sentences below. Four answer choices are given below each sentence. Select the best answer to complete the sentence. Then mark the letter (A), (B), (C), or (D) on your answer sheet.

101. The customer canceled his order ------- the computer monitor he requested was sold out.

(A) therefore
(B) for instance
(C) despite that
(D) because

102. Passengers are advised to keep their luggage tag stubs to prove that claimed suitcases are indeed -------.

(A) them
(B) they
(C) themselves
(D) theirs

103. An executive suite has been ------- for the contract negotiations with Cortel Corp next Friday.

(A) notified
(B) reserved
(C) postponed
(D) determined

104. The enhanced account management software helps Dewey Financial associates to respond to customer inquiries more -------.

(A) quick
(B) quickly
(C) quicker
(D) quickness

105. To ensure ------- with safety standards, random batches of light bulbs are selected for testing before they are packaged.

(A) compliance
(B) cooperation
(C) operation
(D) expiration

106. We appreciate you updating us ------- the progress of the landscaping work on our gardens.

(A) without
(B) near
(C) through
(D) regarding

107. To attach the insulation to the window frames, ------- small nails spaced about 20 centimeters apart.

(A) use
(B) useful
(C) using
(D) used

108. When you are arranging your client meetings, remember to keep your schedule ------- of any conflicts.

(A) freeing
(B) freedom
(C) free
(D) frees

109. The Lagos Resort advises booking rooms two months ------- to secure your reservation.

(A) in advance
(B) at last
(C) then
(D) so as

110. The yearly corporate picnic is held to give employees an opportunity to meet ------- in other teams.

(A) colleagues
(B) tenants
(C) positions
(D) businesses

111. This device allows researchers to get a ------- reading than the previous model.

(A) accurately
(B) more accurate
(C) more accurately
(D) accurate

112. All technicians at Gelco Pharmaceuticals ------- to wash their hands before entering the laboratories.

(A) expects
(B) expecting
(C) are expected
(D) to be expecting

113. It is just the first week of winter, but the airport ------- had to cancel flights due to a heavy snowstorm.

(A) best
(B) rather
(C) thoroughly
(D) already

114. Heber Industries' best-selling crane can lift ------- of up to 10 tons.

(A) loader
(B) loads
(C) load
(D) loaded

115. Ms. Kusanagi was ------- retire when she was invited to manage the Security Team at the Asian headquarters.

(A) close to
(B) about to
(C) ahead of
(D) aside from

116. Before starting a new project, it is the team manager's ------- to assign work to each project member.

(A) precision
(B) functioning
(C) condition
(D) responsibility

117. While the information gathered in this survey will enable us to improve our customer service, your participation is completely -------.

(A) volunteers
(B) voluntary
(C) volunteering
(D) voluntarily

118. Various goods and services are provided by the Healthy Living Society, a non-profit organization that ------- a balanced lifestyle.

(A) dispenses
(B) deserves
(C) encourages
(D) expects

119. Members of the Trainlink board of directors argued ------- for a high speed line at the last shareholders meeting.

(A) forcefully
(B) routinely
(C) infrequently
(D) lastingly

120. Ceylon Corporation's ------- Customer Service personnel provide callers with any kind of assistance they require.

(A) inevitable
(B) continuous
(C) dedicated
(D) established

GO ON TO THE NEXT PAGE

121. The goal of this portfolio review is to figure out ------- the allocation of Providential Investment's funds matches client objectives.

(A) although
(B) whether
(C) because
(D) either

122. Greenville consistently enjoys a 10 percent annual property value -------.

(A) payment
(B) census
(C) statistic
(D) increase

123. Ayoub Publications has ------- of the most devoted readerships in Lebanese news media.

(A) one
(B) still
(C) those
(D) instead

124. Babylon Real Estate has seen ------- sales over the last three quarters.

(A) complete
(B) refillable
(C) steady
(D) specific

125. The Web site created by Ceylon Tech Solutions has been ------- to meet your customers' needs.

(A) customize
(B) customized
(C) customizes
(D) customizing

126. Programming on the Educational Broadcasting Network is made ------- thanks to financial support from companies like Broadmoor Investing.

(A) recognized
(B) clear
(C) thoughtful
(D) possible

127. Since its first international contract was signed last quarter, the Yutani Corporation has received record-high -------.

(A) earnings
(B) earns
(C) earn
(D) earner

128. The popular documentary series, *The Blue World*, ------- a well-known narrator.

(A) realizes
(B) marks
(C) features
(D) applies

129. We expect to receive many more online orders next month, so it is crucial that our server be functioning -------.

(A) relying
(B) reliable
(C) relies
(D) reliably

130. Dessous la Table's steadfast devotion to quality is consistent ------- its entire menu of authentic French wines and cheeses.

(A) near
(B) between
(C) into
(D) across

PART 6

Directions: Read the texts that follow. A word, phrase, or sentence is missing in parts of each text. Four answer choices for each question are given below the text. Select the best answer to complete the text. Then mark the letter (A), (B), (C), or (D) on your answer sheet.

Questions 131-134 refer to the following article.

Airport Forecast

January 22

According to figures from the National Airport Authority, cargo shipments through Ontario Airport have once again increased. -------, this marks the fifth straight year of
131.
significant growth. Ontario is a point of transit for a wide array of merchandise, with ------- like clothing, medicine, and construction equipment topping the list. -------.
132.   **133.**
Because of this, hiring at the airport has also continued. Analysts ------- the increase in
134.
cargo as a sign that economic activity will continue to grow in this area.

131. (A) Even though
(B) However
(C) Still
(D) In fact

132. (A) goods
(B) advantages
(C) facilities
(D) costs

133. (A) About half of this cargo will be sent overseas.
(B) Deliveries of other products decreased this year.
(C) The airport recently released updated figures.
(D) More staff is required to handle the shipments.

134. (A) seeing
(B) see
(C) were seen
(D) sees

GO ON TO THE NEXT PAGE

Questions 135-138 refer to the following e-mail.

To: Danielle Bandy <dbandy@benmail.com>
From: Eric Calhoun <e.calhoun@terryvalechildrenszoo.org>
Date: June 20
Subject: Your membership

Dear Ms. Bandy,

Thank you for your support over the past year. Please remember that your Terryvale Children's Zoo membership ------- on July 31. If you renew now, you will receive a $50
135.
gift certificate to our gift shop. This offer is available only ------- June 30. Just mention
136.
the code, TCZFAN3, to one of our Customer Service representatives. We appreciate all of our members, and we hope that you will decide to renew and continue to enjoy all the advantages of membership without -------. Also, keep in mind that zoo members will be
137.
receiving guest passes to our new exhibit, *the African Safari Trail*. The exhibit will be available to the public on August 15. -------.
138.

Warmest regards,

Eric Calhoun
Director of Member Services

---

135. (A) should have expired
(B) to be expiring
(C) will expire
(D) has expired

136. (A) through
(B) except
(C) including
(D) among

137. (A) interruption
(B) interrupt
(C) interrupting
(D) interrupted

138. (A) The construction should be completed by the end of the month.
(B) We apologize in advance for any inconvenience this may cause.
(C) Please let us know what type of exhibit you would like us to create in this area.
(D) Our members, however, will be invited to a special preview of it on August 11.

Questions 139-142 refer to the following information.

Setting Up Appointments at Istanbul Dissiz Hospital

We at Istanbul Dissiz Hospital make our best effort to meet with patients at their booked times. ------- is possible due to our efficient reservation system. To help us ------- it,
139.   140.
make sure to arrive on time for your appointment. Even though we do all we can to stick to the schedule, sudden delays can occur because of unexpected situations. -------. In
141.
these cases, we ask for your -------.
142.

We encourage you to give us a call on the day of your appointment to confirm the expected wait time.

139. (A) Here
(B) Other
(C) Some
(D) This

140. (A) enter
(B) consider
(C) adjust
(D) maintain

141. (A) There are times when our doctors have to perform urgent surgeries.
(B) It is important to make a note of this in your file.
(C) You can reschedule your appointment at any time.
(D) To ensure this does not happen, you should follow your physician's advice carefully.

142. (A) preparation
(B) cooperation
(C) participation
(D) anticipation

GO ON TO THE NEXT PAGE

UBV Financial: Company Vehicle Policy

Company vehicles are for the ------- use of the Sales Department staff. Members of other
             143.
departments should use their own vehicles or public transportation. Sales Department

members can each drive a company car a maximum of 200 kilometers a week without

prior approval. Sales staff should obtain their branch manager's authorization before

driving ------- distances.
   144.

Remember that company vehicles ------- for business activities only. -------. UBV
                145.   **146.**
Financial automobiles can only be driven by employees with a valid driver's license and

proper insurance coverage.

We appreciate your cooperation in this matter.

---

143. (A) unique
(B) delicate
(C) exclusive
(D) traditional

144. (A) further
(B) those
(C) any
(D) limited

145. (A) provides
(B) providing
(C) should provide
(D) are provided

146. (A) Currently, only the economy sized
vehicle is available.
(B) Personal use of the vehicle is not
allowed.
(C) This vehicle has recently been
inspected and repaired.
(D) The company plans on upgrading all
of its vehicles.

PART 7

Directions: In this part you will read a selection of texts, such as magazine and newspaper articles, emails, and instant messages. Each text or set of texts is followed by several questions. Select the best answer for each question and mark the letter (A), (B), (C), or (D) on your answer sheet.

Questions 147-148 refer to the following voucher.

Hyacinth Bistro

Hyacinth Thank-you Voucher

To receive a free medium-sized drink of your choice, present this voucher with the order of any soup, pasta, or steak entrée. This voucher may be used during regular business hours, Tuesdays through Sundays (closed Mondays).

Let us hear from you!

Check our events board, next to entrance, to see what's going on at Hyacinth! While you're there, fill out a customer questionnaire and give it to any staff member for a chance to win a free dinner.

147. What complimentary item can be obtained by using a voucher?

(A) A beverage
(B) A steak
(C) Some soup
(D) Some pasta

148. How can a customer win a prize?

(A) By completing a questionnaire
(B) By participating in an event
(C) By visiting the restaurant on a Sunday
(D) By making a reservation on a Monday

GO ON TO THE NEXT PAGE

To: sjacobs@sjacobsfashion.co.uk
From: orders@fleurdelis.co.fr
Date: November 7
Subject: Purchase #09345A

Dear Mr. Jacobs,

We regret to inform you that the red and pink sunglasses you purchased from our Web site in November (70 pairs in all) are not currently available. Right now, we have no way to complete and ship your order, and therefore, cannot provide you with an exact arrival date. However, we have similar models that we think you might like. One has red and white striped frames, and another has solid purple frames. To make modifications to your order, just log on to our Web site and click on the shopping cart at the top of your screen. Once again, we'd like to apologize for this situation and look forward to earning your continued business.

Sincerely,
Brenda Chang
Customer Support

149. What is the purpose of the e-mail?

(A) To check a shipping date
(B) To announce a change in prices
(C) To explain an issue with a purchase
(D) To describe a refund process

150. What is Mr. Jacobs asked to do?

(A) Visit a Web site
(B) Call for more details
(C) Pay an additional fee
(D) Update some billing information

Questions 151-152 refer to the following text message chain.

Edward Spencer

Hi, Kathy. Do you still have the extra printer ink cartridges? They used to be under your desk. 4:47 P.M.

Katherine Greene

4:48 P.M. No, I moved them to the new storage cabinets.

Katherine Greene

4:50 P.M. You know, the white ones by the break room.

Edward Spencer

Oh, right. I still don't have a key for those. 4:50 P.M.

Edward Spencer

Can I borrow yours? 4:51 P.M.

Katherine Greene

4:54 P.M. Of course. Drop by my office anytime.

Edward Spencer

See you in a few minutes. 4:55 P.M.

151. Why did Mr. Spencer contact Ms. Greene?

(A) To discuss a furniture order
(B) To confirm the location of some supplies
(C) To submit a complaint about a process
(D) To inquire about a meeting room reservation

152. At 4:54 P.M., what does Ms. Greene mean when she writes, "Drop by my office anytime"?

(A) She will lend an item to Mr. Spencer.
(B) She encourages Mr. Spencer to use her printer.
(C) She would like Mr. Spencer to bring a document.
(D) She is only available to meet for a limited time.

GO ON TO THE NEXT PAGE

February 10
RLA Parts & Supplies

Dear Mr. Estrada,

I am writing to inform you of my interest in the recently posted International Marketing Director position at RLA. I was referred to your company by Haewon Choi, with whom I closely worked with at Kelson Metal Manufacturers. She believes I would be a good fit for RLA and urged me to contact you.

With my 10 years of experience as the Global Advertising Manager for Kelson in Asia and Europe, I have no doubt that I can contribute to RLA's goal of increasing its international sales. My history at Kelson will show that I have not only established a large client base, but also increased revenue each year in my assigned regions. Moreover, I have developed an extensive understanding of all of the metal parts and products sold in the industry.

Please review the enclosed résumé for more detailed information regarding my background and experience. Contact me at 682-555-4352 or abrea@clpemail.com at your convenience. Thank you, and I look forward to hearing from you.

Sincerely,

Abby Brea
Abby Brea
Enclosure

153. Why did Ms. Brea write the letter?

(A) To follow up on a recent interview
(B) To communicate her desire to work at RLA
(C) To ask about some driving directions
(D) To recommend a colleague for a position at RLA

154. What did Ms. Brea do while at Kelson Metal Manufacturers?

(A) She hired new marketing staff members.
(B) She proposed alternative means of revenue.
(C) She created several new designs for metal parts.
(D) She secured many clients from different countries.

155. According to Ms. Brea, what has she been able to develop?

(A) Effective management abilities
(B) Innovative advertising campaigns
(C) Relevant industry knowledge
(D) Sophisticated metal making skills

Workplace Solutions – Monthly Tips

Inspire your team!

Cornelia Hulbert

Although increasing salaries and offering more benefits are probably the best ways to recognize employees with outstanding performance records, managers usually are not in a position to give out these kinds of rewards. However, there are other effective, low-cost ways of showing appreciation to raise morale and encourage even better performance. Here are a few tips to do that.

- Make use of the company's newsletter to announce any awards received or goals that staff members have achieved. Employees can also be acknowledged for doing volunteer work in the community.
- Allow workers to have a flexible work schedule when possible.
- Bring in treats such as cakes and donuts to celebrate the end of a project.
- Organize luncheons to celebrate employees' birthdays; each person can bring food to share.
- Offer staff members further development opportunities through additional training.

Cornelia Hulbert is the CEO of Hulbert Management Consultations.

156. Why was the article written?

(A) To describe the benefits of working as a management consultant
(B) To outline methods for hiring volunteers to help out with projects
(C) To explain the best ways to evaluate employee performance
(D) To give supervisors ideas for motivating staff members

157. What activity is NOT mentioned in the article?

(A) Mentioning employees' achievements in a newsletter
(B) Providing learning opportunities
(C) Giving free tickets to a community event
(D) Recognizing special occasions

GO ON TO THE NEXT PAGE

Gonzalez Glass Makers

Gonzalez Glass Makers is a medium-sized glass producer based in Barcelona, Spain. The company manufactures high-quality, heavy-duty glass for use in skyscrapers and other high-rise commercial buildings. The company's products are mainly distributed in Southwestern Europe–approximately 50 percent of the products are used in buildings in Spain. Currently, the company has almost 900 employees throughout the world (600 of whom work in Barcelona), a 25 percent increase from the year before. In addition to its headquarters and manufacturing facilities in Spain, the company has shipping centers in Lisbon, Rome, Athens, and Sofia. CEO Lauren Torres joined Gonzalez Glass last year, and under Ms. Torres' direction, the company has greatly expanded its Research Department with the aim of developing products that are more environmentally-friendly and energy-efficient. To facilitate this effort, earlier this year, Gonzalez acquired Leon Systems, a small research company located in Sevilla.

158. Who most likely are customers of Gonzalez Glass Makers?

(A) Research centers
(B) Construction companies
(C) Pharmaceutical firms
(D) Eyeglasses manufacturers

159. What did Gonzalez Glass Makers do last year?

(A) It purchased another company.
(B) It hired a new CEO.
(C) It built a shipping center.
(D) It moved its headquarters.

160. What is mentioned about Gonzalez Glass Makers?

(A) It increased the size of its research division.
(B) It was featured in a magazine article.
(C) It reduced its energy use by 25 percent.
(D) It participated in a conference in Sevilla.

Questions 161-163 refer to the following e-mail.

To: Tech Support team
From: HR team
Date: November 12
Subject: Arabic courses

Hello all,

Due to our firm's upcoming expansion to Lebanon, there will be more projects that require familiarity with Arabic to work with our regional partners and clients. In preparation for this move, Arabic courses will be offered to all tech support employees who will be interacting with Arabic speakers online. There is no obligation to take the courses, but we believe that this chance to improve your language abilities is a valuable one.

We will be bringing in the Polyglobe Language Academy, a leader in the field of language learning here in Busan. The courses will be held in the downstairs conference rooms, to save on travel time, and free drinks will be offered. Three levels of Arabic will be offered (intermediate, advanced, and high-advanced). Participating employees will be given a test to place them in the appropriate class. The courses will be offered Mondays and Fridays at 7:00 P.M.

Please consider signing up for this valuable professional development opportunity. Reply to this e-mail by Friday to be put on a list for next week's test.

Sincerely,

Mina Shin
HR team
Arcturus Software, Inc.

161. Why is the firm offering Arabic courses?

(A) It will be doing business in Lebanon.
(B) It is planning to hire more Arabic speakers.
(C) Some staff members will move to Lebanon.
(D) A language academy is offering free courses.

162. What is implied about some tech support team members?

(A) They travel frequently to meet partner companies.
(B) They have moved to a new office in Busan.
(C) They are currently attending courses at Polyglobe Academy.
(D) They already know how to speak some Arabic.

163. What is NOT suggested about the courses?

(A) Beverages will be provided.
(B) They will be held twice a week.
(C) There is a one-time fee.
(D) There are three available levels.

GO ON TO THE NEXT PAGE

Questions 164-167 refer to the following e-mail.

To: Addy Lukin <a.lukin@emorymedical.org>
From: Mark Hinton <hinton@arwn.org>
Date: October 3
Subject: Conference

Dear Ms. Lukin,

The Appalachian Rural Wellness Network (ARWN) is hosting a conference on the subject of "Digitizing Medical Records to Boost Patient Care" on Friday, November 10, and Saturday, November 11, in Washington D.C. —[1]—. Medical professionals who, like you, have devoted their lives to serving rural areas will discuss the challenges they have faced over the years. These speakers will also share ways to raise money to invest in technology that can drastically reduce your paperwork and improve the overall quality of the patient experience. —[2]—.

Featured presenters will be Dr. Miranda Tam, Director of Charlottesville Regional Clinics; Dr. Jun-seo Park, CEO of Appalachian Insurance Cooperative; and Allison Bryce, MD, President of the Organization of Clinical Medical Education. —[3]—. All are knowledgeable experts whose work has appeared in a variety of publications.

To register, visit www.arwnconference.org/register by Friday, November 3. To watch the presentations on that day, you must have a media player installed on your Internet-enabled device. —[4]—. The entire conference will be recorded and uploaded to our Web site on November 20.

Regards,

Mark Hinton
ARWN Members Coordinator

---

164. What is the subject of the conference?

(A) Improving healthcare in rural communities with technology
(B) Promoting medical education in rural communities
(C) New medical treatments for patients in rural communities
(D) Research findings of insurance options in rural communities

165. Who most likely is Ms. Lukin?

(A) A rural real estate agent
(B) A rural healthcare professional
(C) An insurance salesperson
(D) A medical journalist

166. What will happen on November 20?

(A) Presentation slides will be emailed.
(B) An article on rural health will be published.
(C) A professional gathering will begin.
(D) A video will become available.

167. In which of the positions marked [1], [2], [3], and [4] does the following sentence best belong?

"As an alternative, you can tune into the event via radio."

(A) [1]
(B) [2]
(C) [3]
(D) [4]

Questions 168-171 refer to the following online chat discussion.

Andy Palas [7:43 A.M.]
Good morning, Kim and Ari. Can anyone help me out? I'm heading to Gavin Industries to go over their R&D supply requirements, but I forgot the glassware samples for their laboratory experiments.

Kimberly Lee [7:45 A.M.]
Our product catalog is available online. Can't you just use your laptop?

Andy Palas [7:46 A.M.]
Those images won't do. It is impossible to emphasize the clarity and strength of our glass on a computer screen.

Kimberly Lee [7:48 A.M.]
You'll probably have to drive back and get them from the office then.

Arianna Noskov [7:51 A.M.]
Well, I might be able to help. I still have a kit containing our glassware with me from a meeting yesterday. I'm stopped at 3rd Avenue right now.

Andy Palas [7:55 A.M.]
That's great news! I'm parked on 10th Avenue and Laurel Street. Could we meet nearby?

Arianna Noskov [7:56 A.M.]
OK. Let's meet at the coffee shop on 5th Avenue.

Kimberly Lee [7:57 A.M.]
Ari, you could just make the exchange at the client's office.

Arianna Noskov [7:58 A.M.]
I have to get into the office early to prepare for a 9:30 A.M. conference call.

Andy Palas [7:59 A.M.]
The coffee shop sounds good. It'll take me about 10 minutes to get there. Can you be there by then?

Arianna Noskov [8:02 A.M.]
Sure. I'll see you soon.

SEND

168. Who most likely is Mr. Palas?

(A) A sales associate
(B) A computer technician
(C) A Gavin Industries staff member
(D) A client of Ms. Lee

169. At 7:46 A.M., what does Mr. Palas most likely mean when he writes, "Those images won't do"?

(A) He will provide a Web site address.
(B) He plans to offer the client a catalog subscription.
(C) He prefers to show a client some product samples.
(D) He will purchase some glassware for a lab.

170. Where is Mr. Palas?

(A) In a conference room
(B) In a laboratory
(C) In a vehicle
(D) In a coffee shop

171. What does Ms. Noskov offer to do?

(A) Prepare a presentation for a client
(B) Purchase coffee for her colleagues
(C) Arrive at a meeting early
(D) Deliver some merchandise to Mr. Palas

GO ON TO THE NEXT PAGE

ACTUAL TEST 08 PART 7

From	Calleigh Stokes <callstokes@evergreenmail.com>
To	Jonathon Bauer <jonbauer@tenymail.com>
Date	November 13, 3:47 P.M.
Subject	Evergreen TFP
Attach	TFP

Dear Mr. Bauer,

Thank you for expressing interest in Evergreen Solutions' Tailored Fertilizing Program (TFP). We are sorry that you were unable to access this information directly via our Web site, but the page featuring the program is currently undergoing routine maintenance. Attached to this message you will find a thorough and detailed explanation of the program, but I would like to take the time to give you a basic outline here.

Fertilizing is an integral part of agriculture and has been for thousands of years. —[1]— Methods and materials have changed over time, but the advent of inorganic fertilizers in the 19th century has arguably had the greatest effect on the farming industry. Their use dramatically raised crop yields and supported population growth. —[2]—

When properly managed, organic fertilizers have far less environmental impact and can be just as effective, if not more so. Our trained experts examine the soil properties of individual fields and develop fertilizer blends that will provide the desired crop with its ideal nutrition. Our ingredients are 100 percent natural, and they all have Environmental Security Agency approval for use. —[3]—

However, the benefits of our products are not limited to environmental concerns and sustainability. —[4]— In a survey we conducted with the customers we have had since our founding 20 years ago, all of them reported savings when they used chemical fertilizers; some as much as 30 percent. We currently have contracts with some of the largest agricultural collectives in the country, as well as hundreds of smaller family-owned farms. These clients include a wide variety of farming types from rice paddies to corn fields to apple orchards. Therefore, we are confident that we can help you produce more, with less impact on the environment and on your wallet.

Sincerely,

Calleigh Stokes
Customer Service Director
Evergreen Solutions

172. What is indicated about Evergreen Solutions?

(A) It is a division of the Environmental Security Agency.
(B) It is currently updating a part of its Web site.
(C) It was established by a single individual.
(D) It owns several large farm collectives.

173. The word "integral" in paragraph 2, line 1, is the closest in meaning to

(A) collected
(B) critical
(C) regulated
(D) productive

174. What is NOT mentioned about TFP?

(A) It was developed 20 years ago.
(B) It reduces a farm's pollution output.
(C) It was designed for smaller farms.
(D) It uses only organic ingredients.

175. In which of the positions marked [1], [2], [3], and [4] does the following sentence best belong?

"Unfortunately, their use has also led to incredible amounts of pollution and soil toxicity."

(A) [1]
(B) [2]
(C) [3]
(D) [4]

GO ON TO THE NEXT PAGE

The Sweet Life

How would you like to get paid to eat ice cream all day? If this sounds too good to be true, then you should know that there are people who work as ice cream tasters.

Marianna Duncan works as an ice cream taster for Tommen Frozen Delights, a New Zealand-based company that produces handmade ice cream and sorbet. Contrary to popular belief, many years of study and training are required for this position. After studying for five years and receiving her food science degree at Purnett University, she interned at Huggins Ice Cream Factory in Canada for one year. Ms. Duncan then returned to New Zealand and was recruited by Tommen, where she has been tasting ice cream for the last decade.

One of the perks of her job is that she gets to travel around the world in search of rare and exotic ingredients for the company's new ice cream varieties. One year, she spent a summer tasting curry in India and the next season savoring basil in Thailand. She explains, "I bring the ingredients to our lab in New Zealand, where our production staff and food chemists use them to create amazing tasting ice cream."

As for the actual tasting, she carefully inspects the ice cream with her eyes before sampling it. "I look at the product as if a consumer would. If the ice cream doesn't look appealing, they're not going to buy it." Even though she tastes up to 30 different flavors of ice cream daily, she never gets tired of her work. She enthusiastically claims, "No life could be sweeter."

Hector Mendoza
Staff Writer, *Gourmet Flavors Magazine*

From	Kazuki Hachiro <k.hachiro@huggins.com>
To	Marianna Duncan <m.duncan@tommendelights.co.nz>
Date	10 November
Subject	*Gourmet Flavors Magazine* Article

Dear Marianna,

I saw the article about you in *Gourmet Flavors Magazine* and got your e-mail address from your company's Web site. We used to work together at an ice cream company as interns. I'm sure you remember me. Anyway, I'm going to be visiting Auckland in three weeks for the Food Science Symposium, and I thought it would be great to see each other again! If you have time, maybe we could have lunch and catch up. I'll look forward to your reply.

Best regards,

Kazuki

176. What is the purpose of the article?

(A) To explain a manufacturing process at a factory
(B) To compare different brands of ice cream
(C) To preview a company's products
(D) To describe a professional's career

177. What is suggested about Tommen Frozen Delights?

(A) It creates ice cream with unusual flavors.
(B) It is the most successful company in its industry.
(C) It was founded five years ago.
(D) It has laboratories in several countries.

178. What is suggested about Ms. Duncan?

(A) She has limited work experience.
(B) She enjoys her job.
(C) She trains interns at Tommen Frozen Delights.
(D) She is business partners with Mr. Hachiro.

179. Why did Mr. Hachiro send the e-mail to Ms. Duncan?

(A) To inquire about a job position
(B) To share information for a presentation
(C) To arrange a meeting
(D) To request feedback on an article

180. Where did Mr. Hachiro and Ms. Duncan first meet?

(A) At Huggins Ice Cream Factory
(B) At *Gourmet Flavors Magazine*
(C) At the Food Science Symposium
(D) At Purnett University

GO ON TO THE NEXT PAGE

Rascat Jazz Trio
For Immediate Release

Topeka, Kansas, April 5 – The Rascat Jazz Trio, the country's leading jazz group, has just announced the dates of their June tour. This six-day tour includes a performance at the popular Toro Theater, where the trio first made their concert appearance 10 years ago. Scheduled performances are listed below.

DATE	LOCATION	VENUE
JUNE 5	Topeka	Blaine Concert Hall
JUNE 8	Wichita	Versa Theater
JUNE 11	Lawrence	Toro Theater
JUNE 14	Derby	Rolla Performing Arts Center
JUNE 17	Overland Park	Dirkwood Stadium
JUNE 20	Pittsburg	Kurtis Stadium

Tickets range from $30 for balcony level seats to $100 for front-row seats in the center section at all tour stops, and they can be purchased at participating venue box offices and Blimp Music Stores. Members of the newly formed Rascat Jazz Trio Fan Club can order tickets at 20 percent off by logging in to the Member's Only section at www.rascatjazz.com. A complete list of fan club benefits and a detailed explanation of annual dues are available at www.rascatjazz.com/membership_fanclub.

Contact: Hershel Delotte, 785-555-4936, hdelotte@rascatjazz.com

---

Dirkwood Stadium

Immediate Release

Canceled and Postponed Performances

Overland Park, Kansas, May 20 – Nearly all performances scheduled for June at Dirkwood Stadium have been postponed due to emergency repairs being made to the building. Concert goers are asked to keep their tickets as all performances, with the exception of the Rascat Jazz Trio concert, will be held at a later date, and tickets for the June performances will be honored.

For the most up-to-date information on the rescheduled performances, please visit the Dirkwood Stadium Web site, www.dirkwoodstadium.com. If you wish to receive a refund for the canceled Rascat Jazz Trio concert, call 913-555-3042.

Contact: Janice Riker, 913-555-3020, jriker@dirkwoodstadium.com

181. Where did the Rascat Jazz Trio play its first concert a decade ago?

(A) In Topeka
(B) In Lawrence
(C) In Overland Park
(D) In Pittsburg

182. What is stated about the tickets for the Rascat Jazz Trio's concert?

(A) Their costs have increased from last year's tour.
(B) They are cheaper for students who present their school identification card.
(C) Their prices are the same for balcony seating at each concert venue.
(D) They are sold only through online ticketing vendors.

183. What is suggested about the Rascat Jazz Trio Fan Club?

(A) Its members have to pay a fee every year.
(B) It meets annually in the month of June.
(C) Its members receive discounts through Blimp Music Stores.
(D) It was founded over 10 years ago.

184. When will the Rascat Jazz Trio be unable to play a scheduled performance?

(A) On June 5
(B) On June 8
(C) On June 17
(D) On June 20

185. According to the second press release, what will be posted on Dirkwood Stadium's Web site?

(A) New venue locations
(B) A revised list of dates
(C) Details about building repairs
(D) A refund request form

GO ON TO THE NEXT PAGE

Questions 186-190 refer to the following e-mails and advertisement.

To: Aster Valley Ski & Resort Staff
From: Lisa Rose
Date: October 7
Subject: Seasonal Offerings

Greetings Sales Representatives,

As most of you are aware, a lot of Aster University students remain in town over their winter break. As usual, our annual 40 percent student holiday discount applies to anyone signing up during the last two weeks of November. Management is also debating two other potential deals that we could offer to all resort members for the upcoming winter season (December 1-February 1).

We are soliciting your feedback to help choose between the two potential promotions. One option is a discount extended to the families of existing Aster Valley Ski & Resort members. Members would be able to put any member (at least 17 years old) of their immediate family under their current membership plan for 20 percent off the regular rate.

The other option is that Blue-level members would receive a complimentary one-day pass for a friend that is good between Mondays and Fridays. This would provide access to all resort areas, including the ski slopes. However, the spa would be excluded from this offer as our members already wait quite a long time to use it.

We ask that you respond to this e-mail with what you believe would best please our members.

We appreciate your help in this matter.

Sincerely,
Lisa Rose
Vice President, Marketing Department
Aster Valley Ski & Resort

Winter Promotions

Aster University Students Welcome!
Register between November 15 and December 15 and get 40% off a resort membership—and your first ski or snowboard rental will be on us!

Ski with a friend for a day!
Starting December 1, all Blue- and Black-level resort members are eligible to bring a friend for a day of skiing fun, at no additional charge. Members' friends must present a photo ID upon arrival to receive a guest pass.

Aster Valley Ski & Resort

To: Sam Hermann
From: Seong-hee Lim
Date: February 2
Subject: Re: Results are in

Hi Sam,

Thank you for emailing the charts from the latest report. I'm really excited by the 18 percent increase in sales of Blue-level memberships due to the winter promotions.

The boost in our numbers mostly came from Aster University, with the majority of students registering for our Blue-level membership. I think we should offer the same promotion again next winter. Also, the university's athletic facilities will be remodeled next year, which means that students will need somewhere else to engage in physical activities. As we're the closest location to the university that offers extensive recreational facilities, we should look into partnering with the school to provide transportation services to their students. This would certainly increase our membership numbers.

I'll keep you updated.

Seong-hee Lim
Manager, Marketing Department
Aster Valley Ski & Resort

186. What is the purpose of the notice?

(A) To congratulate some workers on a completed project
(B) To announce a scheduled closure
(C) To inform resort members of a new service
(D) To request comments from staff

187. What is implied about the spa?

(A) It will have new equipment soon.
(B) It will charge an extra fee.
(C) It is closed for repairs.
(D) It is a popular facility.

188. How did the special for the students change since October?

(A) The sign-up period was extended.
(B) The discount rate was reduced.
(C) Students can make monthly payments.
(D) Students can visit the resort only once a week.

189. What is indicated about Aster Valley Sky & Resort?

(A) Many students brought their friends during the winter season.
(B) It opens earlier between Monday and Friday.
(C) All relatives of current members can receive a discount.
(D) Black-level members receive free ski accessories.

190. What will happen at Aster University?

(A) The school year will start in the winter.
(B) Sales courses will be added.
(C) Its athletic facilities will undergo renovations.
(D) Skiing lessons will be offered to its faculty.

GO ON TO THE NEXT PAGE

https://www.kitchendesignco.com/catalog

| Home | **Catalog** | Feedback | Contact |

Item: Kotka 90 island cart

The Kitchen Design Company proudly announces the Kotka 90, our first kitchen storage product. We've merged our attractive modern designs with the futuristic functionality we apply to all of our electronic kitchen utensils to bring the Kitchen Design Company's signature style to your culinary workspace. This island cart is built with light, durable materials, and features a stainless steel countertop and wheels for mobility. The countertop can be pulled out to create a spacious but stable surface for all sorts of kitchen tasks. Its sleek look will also complement any cooking area.

Catalog No.: #8345A
Price: $579.00*
Comes in white, black, or brown.

*Coupon codes are not valid for the purchase of this item. We ship anywhere in the world, but shipping charges vary according to the destination.

From	Bernard O'Rourke <borourke@infovision.com>
To	Customer Support <cs@kitchendesignco.com>
Date	June 28
Subject	Kotka 90

Hello,

I have several questions about the Kotka 90 island cart, which I am thinking about purchasing. Could I get a granite countertop, rather than a stainless steel one? Additionally, I've heard some reviewers discussing their difficulties in assembling the island cart, which is an issue I would prefer to avoid.

Is it possible to get one that has been put together beforehand? Please let me know how much extra that would cost.

Sincerely,

Bernard O'Rourke

Bernard O'Rourke, July 19

I was worried about putting the island cart together, so I spoke with a company representative. It was definitely time well spent! The Kitchen Design Company did a great job of answering all my questions. They directed me to a Web page where I could look at the instructions before making a purchase. They also gave me a number to call for if I needed further assistance. But I never called that number, as it didn't even take me even 20 minutes to put the island cart together.

The island cart is very sturdy and easy to push around. But I should mention that there are a few things that could be improved. First of all, this product is more expensive than many similar ones. And it's heavy, so depending on where you are, shipping expenses can add quite a bit to the final cost. Second, although the expanded countertop provides an impressive amount of space, it just wouldn't be stable enough if you were doing very detailed work. Lastly, repackaging this product would be challenging, should you need to return it. But that's fine— I have no intention of sending it back.

191. What does the product description suggest about the Kitchen Design Company?

(A) It has more than one location.
(B) It mainly sells kitchen equipment.
(C) It plans to manufacture kitchen counters.
(D) It offers reduced prices for first-time customers.

192. According to the e-mail, what is probably true about Mr. O'Rourke?

(A) He checks customer feedback when shopping for items.
(B) He regularly purchases from the Kitchen Design Company.
(C) He is ordering an island cart for his restaurant.
(D) He recently learned an item is out of stock.

193. What is one reason Mr. O'Rourke wrote the review?

(A) To suggest a step be added to some instructions
(B) To recommend a better kitchen accessory
(C) To compliment a company's customer service
(D) To complain about the lack of delivery options

194. What is suggested about the Kotka 90?

(A) It is not sold in certain countries.
(B) It is available in different sizes.
(C) It has a one-year warranty.
(D) It cannot be purchased preassembled.

195. According to the review, what aspect of the product description is inaccurate?

(A) The company's shipping costs
(B) The island cart's price
(C) The company's refund policy
(D) The island cart's stability

GO ON TO THE NEXT PAGE

The Auckland branch of Superior Distribution is looking for a motivated individual to lead our warehouse team. Superior Distribution is one of the leading companies in the transportation and distribution of high-quality fruits and vegetables in New Zealand.

The warehouse manager must monitor work conditions and processes in the warehouse to ensure the employees' safety. Candidates must have a minimum of five years of relevant experience in the same industry. Evening and weekend hours are occasionally necessary to make sure that shipments are sent out on schedule. Applicants should be knowledgeable in warehousing and shipping. Familiarity with SWP inventory tracking software is required.

Applicants should email their cover letter and résumé to Ms. Tricia Helfor at thelfor@superiordist.co.nz. Three recommendation letters are also required and must be sent directly from the person writing the letter.

To	Tricia Helfor <thelfor@superiordist.co.nz>
From	Mao Lai <mlai@kalexperts.com>
Date	18 September
Subject	Owen Recommendation

Dear Ms. Helfor,

I am writing on behalf of Owen Carter for the warehouse manager position at Superior Distribution. I have been Owen's manager for six of his nine years at KAL Experts, since he was promoted from a part-time position to a full-time employee here. As the current shift manager, he has proven more than capable of handling his tasks.

Owen possesses all the required qualifications, including the necessary work experience and technical background. Our company also uses the SWP program, which Owen has worked with extensively, and he has trained many staff members to use it.

I am confident that Owen will adapt to the demands of any new work setting quickly and successfully. Should you have any questions, feel free to contact me.

Sincerely,

Mao Lai
KAL Experts, Shipping Director

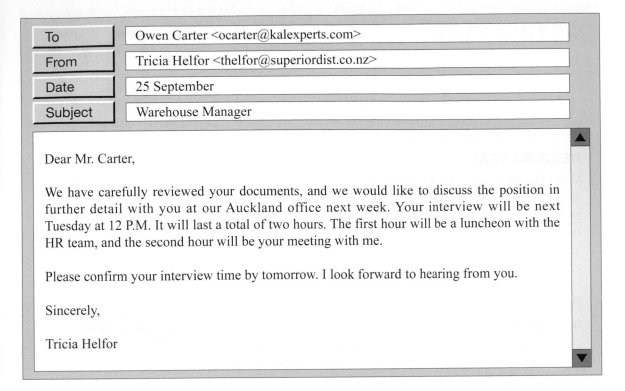

To	Owen Carter <ocarter@kalexperts.com>
From	Tricia Helfor <thelfor@superiordist.co.nz>
Date	25 September
Subject	Warehouse Manager

Dear Mr. Carter,

We have carefully reviewed your documents, and we would like to discuss the position in further detail with you at our Auckland office next week. Your interview will be next Tuesday at 12 P.M. It will last a total of two hours. The first hour will be a luncheon with the HR team, and the second hour will be your meeting with me.

Please confirm your interview time by tomorrow. I look forward to hearing from you.

Sincerely,

Tricia Helfor

196. What is suggested about Superior Distribution?

(A) It owns a large chain of supermarkets.
(B) It specializes in handling food items.
(C) It is headquartered in Auckland.
(D) It offers a wide selection of software products.

197. According to the job advertisement, what must the warehouse manager be willing to do?

(A) Lift heavy items
(B) Take safety training classes
(C) Sign a three-year contract
(D) Work some weekend hours

198. Why does Mr. Lai write the e-mail?

(A) To explain a schedule change
(B) To welcome a new warehouse manager
(C) To express a positive opinion of an employee
(D) To learn more about a job applicant

199. What is indicated about Mr. Carter?

(A) He is skilled in the use of inventory tracking software.
(B) He is seeking a part-time position at Superior Distribution.
(C) He has recently moved to New Zealand.
(D) He has experience developing new software programs.

200. According to the second e-mail, what is mentioned about the interview?

(A) A meal will be provided.
(B) It will last one hour.
(C) A CEO will make a speech.
(D) It has been moved.

Stop! This is the end of the test. If you finish before time is called, you may go back to Parts 5, 6, and 7 and check your work.

233

ACTUAL TEST

09

READING TEST

In the Reading test, you will read a variety of texts and answer several different types of reading comprehension questions. The entire Reading test will last 75 minutes. There are three parts, and directions are given for each part. You are encouraged to answer as many questions as possible within the time allowed.

You must mark your answers on the separate answer sheet. Do not write your answers in your test book.

PART 5

Directions: A word or phrase is missing in each of the sentences below. Four answer choices are given below each sentence. Select the best answer to complete the sentence. Then mark the letter (A), (B), (C), or (D) on your answer sheet.

101. The causes of the increase in car ownership throughout the area are not ------- clear.

(A) entirely
(B) steadily
(C) firmly
(D) justly

102. Laurentine Corporation received many applications for the management position but few were -------.

(A) qualifies
(B) qualify
(C) qualified
(D) qualification

103. The company will be making new business cards, ------- contact Mr. Lebeau if you need to change any of your information.

(A) so
(B) than
(C) to
(D) ahead

104. Critics of Bradford Seaside Resort ------- the claim that it has attracted more visitors to the city.

(A) depend
(B) suggest
(C) reject
(D) extend

105. Takata Solutions helps companies apply innovative management techniques to greatly increase team -------.

(A) productivity
(B) produce
(C) productively
(D) produced

106. The Web site is programmed to send a confirmation e-mail within five minutes to customers ------- place an order.

(A) once
(B) theirs
(C) they
(D) who

107. Building construction that requires street space can start only ------- a street use permit is obtained from the Public Works Department.

(A) through
(B) from
(C) after
(D) on

108. Carrie Mendoza has been acting ------- since her first role at age 10.

(A) professionals
(B) professionalism
(C) profession
(D) professionally

109. Readers showed so much ------- for the novels that the publisher asked to turn them into a movie trilogy.

(A) indication
(B) enthusiasm
(C) belief
(D) knowledge

110. Overland Hotel has 75 rooms, ------- with a terrace facing the mountains.

(A) most
(B) highly
(C) much
(D) nearly

111. Although Albert Lain was going to retire from Meadows Tech, he ------- has a seat on the board of directors.

(A) once
(B) besides
(C) especially
(D) still

112. After merging with Ramshead Savings and Loan, Milton Ltd. ------- a broad selection of financial services.

(A) to offer
(B) offered
(C) offer
(D) offering

113. Osnabruck University students have to file a renewal ------- for a dormitory room each semester.

(A) application
(B) specification
(C) formation
(D) contribution

114. The abandoned Willowcrest textile factory and the ------- properties are being renovated into an upscale apartment complex.

(A) surrounds
(B) surround
(C) surroundings
(D) surrounding

115. The Costa Rojo Resort and Hotel is always searching for methods to ------- the visitor experience.

(A) gain
(B) notify
(C) cure
(D) enhance

116. Reliant Electric's new Web site lets company representatives contact repair specialists who are ------- service calls.

(A) here
(B) going
(C) within
(D) on

117. Lancer Sporting Goods signed contracts with several famous athletes, and ------- it will begin advertising its products more widely.

(A) for that reason
(B) since
(C) once
(D) on account of

118. The winter clothes collection was featured on Outdoor Wear's Web site, leading to a ------- increase in sales.

(A) considerably
(B) considerable
(C) consider
(D) considering

119. Dr. Engstrom's gentle ------- to explaining diagnoses has aided him in putting many patients at ease.

(A) example
(B) approach
(C) meeting
(D) appearance

120. When visiting Smarter Kitchen's booth at the convention, remember to help ------- to a free sample.

(A) yourself
(B) you
(C) yours
(D) your

GO ON TO THE NEXT PAGE

121. You must enter a ------- of passwords every time you access your personal account on the company database.

(A) comprehension
(B) specification
(C) series
(D) proof

122. ------- Friday is a factory inspection day, shipments this week will be sent out a day later than usual.

(A) Yet
(B) When
(C) But
(D) As

123. Passengers should have their ticket and passport ------- to present to the Immigration Control officer at the counter.

(A) whether
(B) openly
(C) ready
(D) since

124. The IT team was able to find out exactly ------- made the company's Web site go offline this morning.

(A) this
(B) these
(C) whose
(D) what

125. Lowering prices on products made of recyclable materials ------- consumers to purchase them more and reduce waste.

(A) encourage
(B) encouraging
(C) is encouraged
(D) would encourage

126. Many businesses ------- overprice their products so that their sale discounts seem like bargains.

(A) strategize
(B) strategy
(C) strategically
(D) strategic

127. Since the complete financial report would take too much time to explain, Machiko will present a ------- version at the meeting.

(A) duplicate
(B) condensed
(C) steady
(D) fulfilled

128. A competent supervisor usually ------- authority to other personnel in order to improve employee morale and performance.

(A) delegates
(B) organizes
(C) introduces
(D) initiates

129. ------- low first quarter sales, the Marketing team remains positive about the product line's potential.

(A) In spite of
(B) Relying on
(C) According to
(D) Because of

130. If a staff member ------- to transfer to another branch, the employee must first speak to his or her supervisor.

(A) wish
(B) wishes
(C) will wish
(D) was wishing

236

PART 6

Directions: Read the texts that follow. A word, phrase, or sentence is missing in parts of each text. Four answer choices for each question are given below the text. Select the best answer to complete the text. Then mark the letter (A), (B), (C), or (D) on your answer sheet.

Questions 131-134 refer to the notice.

Richard Boyce Web Marketing Lecture

Richard Boyce is a nationally recognized ------- in online advertising and promotion. Mr.
131.
Boyce ------- as Creative Director for Media Zero for 17 years. With the experience from
132.
his time spent at Media Zero, Mr. Boyce now gives lectures that use real world

techniques. -------. As a result, Mr. Boyce's audiences receive invaluable practice
133.
applying theory to actual marketing endeavors. Please be aware that the lectures on

January 24 and 27 are now full. -------, a small number of seats remain for the February
134.
12 and 15 sessions.

---

131. (A) authorization
(B) authorized
(C) authority
(D) authorizing

132. (A) is working
(B) will work
(C) had been working
(D) has worked

133. (A) One is to involve the audience in a social networking campaign.
(B) During his time at Media Zero, he conducted several employee events.
(C) Audience members are requested to provide workplace recommendations.
(D) He received a degree from the Seattle School of Journalism.

134. (A) However
(B) Therefore
(C) Particularly
(D) Lastly

GO ON TO THE NEXT PAGE ➡

Safety Regulations: Emergency Fire Doors

Emergency fire doors are located on every floor of the building and must be kept -------
                                                                                                    135.
of any obstacles. Every door must be checked annually by the local Fire Department.

-------. However, staff should also examine the doors on a weekly basis. ------- for any
136.   **137.**
electronic malfunctions, damage, or obstructions. Make sure that the signs above the

doors are ------- lit and visible from all angles.
                   138.

---

135. (A) ovious
(B) broken
(C) clear
(D) distinct

136. (A) Management plans on revising these
procedures within the coming weeks.
(B) You should see an up-to-date
inspection sticker in the upper left-
hand corner of each exit.
(C) At this time, we are not sure who will
take over the responsibilities.
(D) We hope to extend this period by one
month.

137. (A) Look
(B) Arrange
(C) Take
(D) Sign

138. (A) full
(B) fuller
(C) fully
(D) fullness

Questions 139-142 refer to the following e-mail.

To: Natherman employees
From: Personnel Department
Date: November 20
Subject: Corporate party

The end-of-the-year corporate party will take place on Thursday, December 9, from 1 P.M. to 5 P.M. at the Shamforth Banquet Hall. All staff are invited to join and have a great time with their coworkers in this wonderful -------. All of our branches will close at 1 P.M.
139.
on that day so that employees -------.
140.

To obtain tickets to the party, please drop by the personnel office. Staff will still be paid for their time (a total of four hours) at the event. Alternatively, staff can opt to go home early instead of participating. -------, these employees will need to use half a day from
141.
their remaining vacation days.

-------.
142.

---

139. (A) demonstration
(B) town
(C) exhibition
(D) setting

140. (A) can attend
(B) attendance
(C) who attended
(D) attending

141. (A) Moreover
(B) Nevertheless
(C) However
(D) Consequently

142. (A) Most employees agreed that they had a good time at the party.
(B) Please direct any questions you might have to your manager.
(C) The banquet hall now features a much larger dining area.
(D) We anticipate that sales for the fourth quarter will be high.

GO ON TO THE NEXT PAGE

Questions 143-146 refer to the following e-mail.

To: All Staff
From: richard.haber@locatrans.com
Date: 15 October
Subject: Payment Procedure
Attachment: paymentform.rtf

Dear Translators,

We ------- our procedure for paying our freelance translators for their work. Instead of
   143.
sending a payment for each assignment, we will make just one payment on the 10th of
every month. I realize this could be a -------. But, it has become a big hassle to process
       144.
an invoice for each completed assignment. From now on, there is no need to fill out an
online invoice every time you finish a project. -------, just send one invoice at the end of
       145.
the month for all work completed in that month. Please print out the document attached
to this e-mail and return a signed copy to me by next Monday. -------.
       146.

Thank you in advance for your understanding on this matter.

Sincerely,

Richard Haber
Manager, Accounting and Payroll
Locatrans Translation

---

143. (A) should revise
(B) would have revised
(C) are revising
(D) may be revising

144. (A) burden
(B) chance
(C) cancelation
(D) priority

145. (A) Depending on that
(B) Similarly
(C) In light of this
(D) Instead

146. (A) Translations must meet the
previously detailed standards.
(B) This will serve as confirmation that
you have read and agreed to the new
system.
(C) Contact us immediately if your
payment appears incorrect.
(D) Some sections of the document
require changes.

240

PART 7

Directions: In this part you will read a selection of texts, such as magazine and newspaper articles, emails, and instant messages. Each text or set of texts is followed by several questions. Select the best answer for each question and mark the letter (A), (B), (C), or (D) on your answer sheet.

Questions 147-148 refer to the following text message.

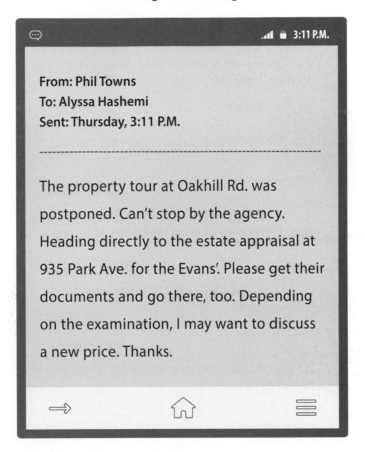

From: Phil Towns
To: Alyssa Hashemi
Sent: Thursday, 3:11 P.M.

The property tour at Oakhill Rd. was postponed. Can't stop by the agency. Heading directly to the estate appraisal at 935 Park Ave. for the Evans'. Please get their documents and go there, too. Depending on the examination, I may want to discuss a new price. Thanks.

147. In what industry does Mr. Towns most likely work?

(A) Insurance
(B) Housing
(C) Transportation
(D) Banking

148. What does Mr. Towns ask Ms. Hashemi to do?

(A) Discuss an agreement
(B) Bring some paperwork
(C) Analyze some examination results
(D) Arrange a conference

GO ON TO THE NEXT PAGE

Bernard Gallagher

Do you have time to meet with me about the Pickens' wedding? The groom's family is asking for some major changes to the menu.

11:34 A.M.

Valerie Timmermans

I have a lunch meeting with a client, but I'll be back in my office after 1 o'clock. Why don't you stop by then?

11:40 A.M.

Bernard Gallagher

Wonderful. I'll bring their request, along with my plans for handling it.

11:43 A.M.

Valerie Timmermans

And try to relax. I know this is the first wedding you're arranging catering for, but it will be fine.

11:46 A.M.

Bernard Gallagher

Thank you. I'm grateful that you're guiding me through the process.

11:48 A.M.

Valerie Timmermans

It's my pleasure. OK, I am taking off. I'll see you in the afternoon.

11:52 A.M.

149. What is most likely true about Mr. Gallagher?

(A) He is learning from Ms. Timmermans.
(B) He is going to purchase a gift for Ms. Timmermans.
(C) He has a job interview at 1 P.M.
(D) He recently attended a relative's wedding celebration.

150. At 11:52 A.M., what does Ms. Timmermans mean when she writes, "I am taking off "?

(A) She must leave to attend a meeting.
(B) She removed some items from a list.
(C) She will schedule a vacation day.
(D) She agreed to handle another task.

Questions 151-153 refer to the following e-mail.

From: Joel Admunsen
To: Madison Lee, Sam O'Caroll
Date: July 14
Subject: Plans for the restaurant

Good afternoon Madison and Sam,

I've got great news. I went to City Hall this morning and received the business license for our bistro. Now the hard work begins. To be ready by our grand opening date of November 10, I've planned out our monthly tasks.

August: Plan the interior and contract with a renovation company. Contact suppliers and choose dinnerware. Set up a Web site and print business cards.

September: Schedule building safety inspections. Supply the kitchen with cookware and utensils. Advertise job openings online and in local newspapers.

October: Finalize the hiring decisions and begin training. Print ads and contact food critics.

If this plan doesn't seem realistic, please let me know what changes you think are needed. But don't forget that our doors open in less than four months, so everything needs to get done within that time frame.

Joel

151. What is indicated about Mr. Admunsen?

(A) He is looking for business investors.
(B) He will sell his restaurant to Ms. Lee.
(C) He is attending a convention with colleagues in November.
(D) He recently registered a business.

152. What goal is proposed for September?

(A) Printing promotional materials
(B) Arranging necessary inspections
(C) Training new staff
(D) Ordering kitchen supplies

153. Why does Mr. Admunsen ask for feedback?

(A) He is concerned a timeline may not be feasible.
(B) He would like suggestions for a recruiting program.
(C) He would like input on some design options.
(D) He is revising a newspaper advertisement.

GO ON TO THE NEXT PAGE

To: sponsor_list@weststart.org
From: aweiser@weststart.org
Date: Wednesday, September 16
Subject: Charity Race on Saturday

Dear Sponsors,

It is with regret that I must write to tell you that this Saturday's charity race in Westfall State Park has been canceled. Due to unfinished renovation work, in addition to the weekend's forecast of unseasonable heavy snowfall, we must postpone the event.

Westfall State Park representatives alerted me on Monday that the covered picnic area where we planned to set up is still being renovated and will not be done by the end of the week. Instead, it was suggested that we use the parking area for the start and finish lines and set up booths. However, the parking area is not paved, making it impossible to access in this type of weather.

While the event was going to be held even if the weather was cold, the safety of all participants must come first. I apologize for this situation, but please understand that it is not up to the Planning Committee. This move was ultimately made by Westfall State Park management.

We hope to hold the event in late October and ask that you offer your support then. For the time being, please note that your sponsor fees will be refunded to you via wire transfer by the end of the business day on Friday. If you would prefer to have the fee returned by check, reply to this e-mail with your current address and a contact number where we can reach you.

Regretfully,

Andrew Weiser

154. Who most likely is Mr. Weiser?

(A) A government official
(B) A professional athlete
(C) A local reporter
(D) An event planner

155. What is suggested about the unpaved parking area at Westfall State Park?

(A) It is frequently full on weekends.
(B) It is currently under construction.
(C) It can be used only by Westfall residents.
(D) It cannot be accessed during snowy weather.

156. The word "move" in paragraph 3, line 3, is the closest in meaning to

(A) relocation
(B) shift
(C) decision
(D) transfer

157. What will the charity race sponsors receive?

(A) An updated contract
(B) A gift certificate
(C) A reimbursement
(D) A brochure

Questions 158-160 refer to the following Web page.

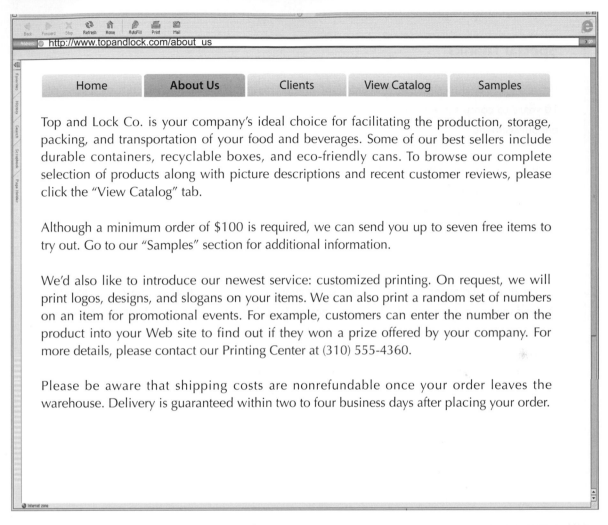

Top and Lock Co. is your company's ideal choice for facilitating the production, storage, packing, and transportation of your food and beverages. Some of our best sellers include durable containers, recyclable boxes, and eco-friendly cans. To browse our complete selection of products along with picture descriptions and recent customer reviews, please click the "View Catalog" tab.

Although a minimum order of $100 is required, we can send you up to seven free items to try out. Go to our "Samples" section for additional information.

We'd also like to introduce our newest service: customized printing. On request, we will print logos, designs, and slogans on your items. We can also print a random set of numbers on an item for promotional events. For example, customers can enter the number on the product into your Web site to find out if they won a prize offered by your company. For more details, please contact our Printing Center at (310) 555-4360.

Please be aware that shipping costs are nonrefundable once your order leaves the warehouse. Delivery is guaranteed within two to four business days after placing your order.

158. For whom is the Web page most likely intended?

(A) Transportation services
(B) Local recycling centers
(C) Publishing firms
(D) Food preparation companies

159. What is NOT stated as a service offered by Top and Lock Co.?

(A) Giving a discount to first-time customers
(B) Providing a limited number of sample items
(C) Writing messages on products at the customer's request
(D) Displaying the latest opinions of customers

160. What is indicated about orders placed through Top and Lock Co.?

(A) They can be shipped at no cost with a minimum purchase of $100.
(B) They can be delivered within four working days.
(C) They can be paid for in installments.
(D) They can be exchanged within one month of the purchase date.

GO ON TO THE NEXT PAGE

Questions 161-164 refer to the following information.

Special Thanks

I owe a great deal to all those who aided me in the creation of this book, which took a total of 10 years to complete. *A Geological Study of Wyoming* would not exist without your support and encouragement.

A lot of people were involved in the development of this work. In particular, I would like to thank Dr. Patrick Flynn for going over my drafts, in spite of his full-time teaching schedule, and providing ideas that simplified several concepts discussed in sections regarding crystals and gemstones. Also, I would like to extend my heartfelt gratitude to Ms. Ha Yang, whose elaborate illustrations introduce each chapter.

Above all, I would especially like to express my appreciation for Ms. Evelyn Ionesco. Ms. Ionesco showed me around important rock layers located far off the main Wyoming highways, drawing upon her extensive knowledge of regional geologic formations. A long-time resident of the state, she knew exactly the right places to go to see the best samples of rocks from different geological eras. Without her expertise, this project would have been nearly impossible to complete.

Anna Kilday

161. What is NOT indicated about *A Geological Study of Wyoming*?

(A) It contains detailed drawings.
(B) It took 10 years to finish.
(C) It includes maps of different states.
(D) It was written by Ms. Kilday.

162. What is mentioned about Dr. Flynn?

(A) He often traveled to Wyoming.
(B) He helped revise some content.
(C) He recently changed occupations.
(D) He recommended an artist.

163. The word "formations" in paragraph 3, line 3, is closest in meaning to

(A) establishments
(B) compilations
(C) structures
(D) layouts

164. For what is Ms. Ionesco acknowledged?

(A) Doing research
(B) Being a guide
(C) Teaching classes
(D) Reviewing a draft

Questions 165-168 refer to the following online chat session.

Xiwei Wong [2:34 P.M.]
Good afternoon, all. I hope everyone is getting ready for our upcoming marketing meeting on Wednesday. We didn't see an increase in sales at all last quarter. We should think about a new course of action.

Kylie Losse [2:35 P.M.]
What would you like us to do?

Xiwei Wong [2:37 P.M.]
The demand for leather wallets and purses is dropping, so we should look into increasing Galloway's product offerings.

Angela Kim [2:38 P.M.]
We could try mobile phone cases. It seems like everyone has one these days.

Caleb Steuter [2:40 P.M.]
That's a pretty good idea. Or we could consider making special cases for tablets and laptops.

Kylie Losse [2:41 P.M.]
Right. We might even try airplane carry-on luggage for business travelers who have all of those devices.

Xiwei Wong [2:44 P.M.]
Excellent ideas, everyone. For the meeting, please look up some suppliers online and find out price quotes to include in your presentation to the team. With that information, I will then make a budget estimate for our department head to go along with the proposals.

Caleb Steuter [2:45 P.M.]
Got it.

Xiwei Wong [2:46 P.M.]
If you run into any problems, send me an e-mail, and we'll talk them over.

SEND

---

165. What kind of product does Galloway currently sell?

(A) Leather accessories
(B) Metal luggage
(C) Fitness watches
(D) Mobile phones

166. At 2:34 P.M., what does Mr. Wong mean when he writes, "We should think about a new course of action"?

(A) Each presentation should focus on a different topic.
(B) The company should provide more training workshops.
(C) Each presentation should last for at least 10 minutes.
(D) The company should expand its line of merchandise.

167. What will Mr. Steuter most likely do next?

(A) Draft a proposal
(B) Email a supervisor
(C) Conduct some research
(D) Book a conference room

168. What will Mr. Wong submit to the department head?

(A) Data on product vendors
(B) A monthly sales report
(C) Results of a customer survey
(D) An event calendar

GO ON TO THE NEXT PAGE ➡

Questions 169-171 refer to the following Web page.

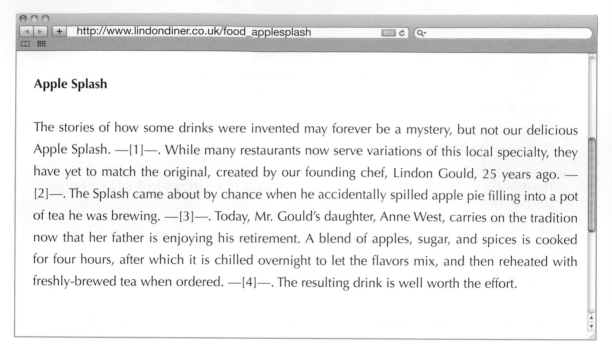

http://www.lindondiner.co.uk/food_applesplash

Apple Splash

The stories of how some drinks were invented may forever be a mystery, but not our delicious Apple Splash. —[1]—. While many restaurants now serve variations of this local specialty, they have yet to match the original, created by our founding chef, Lindon Gould, 25 years ago. —[2]—. The Splash came about by chance when he accidentally spilled apple pie filling into a pot of tea he was brewing. —[3]—. Today, Mr. Gould's daughter, Anne West, carries on the tradition now that her father is enjoying his retirement. A blend of apples, sugar, and spices is cooked for four hours, after which it is chilled overnight to let the flavors mix, and then reheated with freshly-brewed tea when ordered. —[4]—. The resulting drink is well worth the effort.

169. What is suggested about the beverage?

(A) It does not contain artificial ingredients.
(B) It is only served in the winter.
(C) It comes with a side of dessert.
(D) It is always served hot.

170. What is implied about Chef Gould?

(A) His mentor was Ms. West.
(B) He enjoys reading mystery novels.
(C) His diner has relocated several times.
(D) He no longer works in a restaurant.

171. In which of the positions marked [1], [2], [3], and [4] does the following sentence best belong?

"This mishap resulted in Lindon Diner's signature beverage."

(A) [1]
(B) [2]
(C) [3]
(D) [4]

Questions 172-175 refer to the following letter.

May 15

Erin Sanders
1022 W. Wesleyan Dr.
Santa Cruz, CA 95060

Dear Ms. Sanders,

Thank you for your support of *Iden Global Journal* over the years. This letter is to inform you of some changes to our annual subscription package. —[1]—. Starting June 1, annual subscription prices are going up from $114 to $138. The new rate ($11.50 per month) is still much cheaper (40 percent less) than purchasing it at the regular store price of $18.40 for one issue. —[2]—.

Be sure to take advantage of your special access to the *Iden Global Journal* Web site. Not only does it provide everything contained in the print journal, but as a subscriber, you can go online and access the Members-only section for additional content, including member-submitted reviews of recipes and comment forums on a variety of culinary topics, such as ingredient substitutions, special kitchen equipment, and tips for artful meal presentation. —[3]—.

Take advantage of the feedback section of the Web site to send a letter to our knowledgeable editorial staff. Selected letters will get published in the Journal Correspondence section.

Your subscription ends with next month's issue. Take advantage of this short window to re-subscribe at the lower rate before prices go up either by filling out the included subscription order form and mailing it back or by contacting our subscription hotline. —[4]—.

We look forward to hearing from you!

Caley Bowen
Caley Bowen
Subscription Services Representative

Subscription Hotline: (831) 555-2941

Enclosure

172. What is implied about Ms. Sanders?

(A) She has long been interested in cooking.
(B) She is relocating to Santa Cruz in June.
(C) She wrote a letter that was published in *Iden Global Journal*.
(D) She is a frequent commenter on Iden Global Journal's forums.

173. How much will an issue of *Iden Global Journal* cost next month if purchased through a subscription?

(A) $11.50
(B) $18.40
(C) $22.50
(D) $25.00

174. In which of the positions marked [1], [2], [3], and [4] does the following sentence best belong?

"Our staff is standing by for your call from 9 A.M. to 6 P.M. every day."

(A) [1]
(B) [2]
(C) [3]
(D) [4]

175. According to Ms. Bowen, what is available only on the journal's Web site?

(A) Advertising for business subscribers
(B) Recipe submissions by members
(C) Restaurant reviews
(D) Special discounts

GO ON TO THE NEXT PAGE →

Questions 176-180 refer to the following e-mail and bus ticket.

From:	Cian Rousseau <c.rousseau@eurofox.fr>
To:	Milla Grzesik <milla.g@maplage.fr>
Date:	December 6
Subject:	Bus 749

The holiday season is always a busy one for travelers, and your scheduled bus trip (EFX 749) from Marseille to Vienna is certainly an example. Due to the large number of bookings, EuroFox Express will be putting additional vehicles into service for those who are willing to switch to a different bus. In exchange, we will provide a travel coupon good for future savings on any EuroFox Express route in France and throughout Europe, valued at €120.00, good for six months from the date of issuance.

Below are two alternative routes that might interest you. The first leaves on the same day, but stops in Milan along the way.

EFX 430	Marseille	Dec 20 7:20 P.M.	Milan	Dec 21 3:40 A.M.
EFX 430	Milan	Dec 21 4:50 A.M.	Vienna	Dec 21 2:10 P.M.

The second, a direct route, leaves early in the morning the day after you were originally scheduled to depart.

EFX 789	Marseille	Dec 21 6:25 A.M.	Vienna	Dec 21 11:50 P.M.

To volunteer your seat, please call the EuroFox Express ticketing office at 0800-4-91-01-39-21. Because of high passenger volume, we suggest arriving at least an hour before your scheduled departure. For general information, please visit our Web site at www.eurofox.fr.

On behalf of EuroFox Express, we hope you have a wonderful holiday season.

Sincerely,

Cian Rousseau
Ticketing
EuroFox Express

Passenger Name: Milla Grzesik

Route	Date	Boarding	Departing
EFX 789	Dec 21	6:10 A.M.	6:25 A.M.
To	**From**	**Gate**	**Seat**
Vienna	Marseille	5	10B

Please board with GROUP 3 passengers. Be aware that all wheeled baggage must be stored underneath the carriage to comply with European safety regulations.

176. Why was the e-mail written?

(A) To promote a new destination for holiday vacations
(B) To warn passengers about long wait times
(C) To update a traveler on new routes to Vienna
(D) To encourage a traveler to change buses

177. What is indicated about the coupon?

(A) It must be used within a certain period.
(B) It is valid for multiple bus companies.
(C) It was given to Ms. Grzesik as a gift.
(D) It can only be used in France.

178. What did Ms. Grzesik most likely do after receiving the e-mail?

(A) Downloaded a booking application
(B) Contacted a ticketing office
(C) Sent an e-mail response
(D) Left for the bus station

179. What does the bus ticket indicate about Ms. Grzesik's new bus route?

(A) Passengers must not use wheeled suitcases.
(B) It passes through Milan.
(C) It departs in the evening.
(D) Passengers must board according to their group number.

180. When is Ms. Grzesik scheduled to arrive at her final destination?

(A) At 4:50 A.M.
(B) At 6:25 A.M.
(C) At 2:10 P.M.
(D) At 11:50 P.M.

GO ON TO THE NEXT PAGE

Global Corporation Philanthropy Association (GCPA)
Business Education

The GCPA welcomes you to take part in a live, online lecture titled "How to Receive Corporate Grants." The lecture focuses on important information to be included in a grant proposal which will increase your organization's chances of receiving financial or other types of support from various local and international companies.

Dimitri Rio, Director of Development at the Baltar Foundation, will present this event. The lecture, which will be on 23 March from 4:15 P.M. to 6:15 P.M. EST, will be hosted by Janice Lacherman from the television news program, *International Business Relations*. Registration must be completed by 28 February; please visit www.gcpa.org/1512_lecture for more information on fees and other details. While filling out the registration form, you will have the option of including a question for Mr. Rio. During the lecture, he will answer as many as he can. In addition, all answers to questions submitted by those participating will be posted online by 1 April.

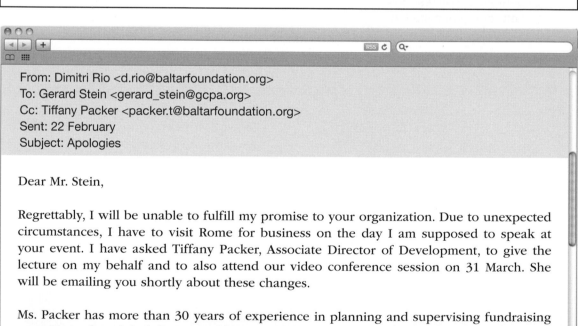

From: Dimitri Rio <d.rio@baltarfoundation.org>
To: Gerard Stein <gerard_stein@gcpa.org>
Cc: Tiffany Packer <packer.t@baltarfoundation.org>
Sent: 22 February
Subject: Apologies

Dear Mr. Stein,

Regrettably, I will be unable to fulfill my promise to your organization. Due to unexpected circumstances, I have to visit Rome for business on the day I am supposed to speak at your event. I have asked Tiffany Packer, Associate Director of Development, to give the lecture on my behalf and to also attend our video conference session on 31 March. She will be emailing you shortly about these changes.

Ms. Packer has more than 30 years of experience in planning and supervising fundraising campaigns for global firms. Furthermore, she is currently in charge of running our company's ongoing online and in-person training seminars, so please be assured that the lecture participants are in good hands.

Again, I sincerely apologize for any inconvenience this cancellation may cause.

Regards,

Dimitri Rio

181. What is suggested about the lecture?

(A) It has been paid for by corporate grants.
(B) It is intended for news reporters.
(C) It will be broadcasted live on a television network.
(D) It will provide fundraising advice.

182. What is indicated about lecture participants?

(A) They will receive a professional certificate.
(B) They should send any questions to Ms. Lacherman.
(C) They must sign up for the event in advance.
(D) They must be GCPA members.

183. When will Mr. Rio go on a business trip?

(A) On February 22
(B) On March 23
(C) On March 31
(D) On April 1

184. What has Mr. Rio has arranged?

(A) To send a financial contribution to the GCPA
(B) To meet with Mr. Stein in Rome
(C) To have a colleague take his place at an event
(D) To have his presentation made available on a Web site

185. What is suggested about the Baltar Foundation?

(A) It is looking for a new Director of Development.
(B) It offers online training opportunities.
(C) It has been in business for 30 years.
(D) It is regularly featured on *International Business Relations*.

GO ON TO THE NEXT PAGE

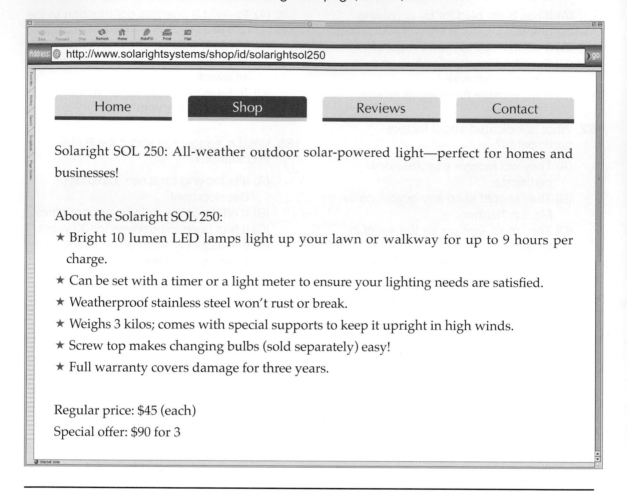

Address: http://www.solarightsystems/shop/id/solarightsol250

| Home | Shop | Reviews | Contact |

Solaright SOL 250: All-weather outdoor solar-powered light—perfect for homes and businesses!

About the Solaright SOL 250:

★ Bright 10 lumen LED lamps light up your lawn or walkway for up to 9 hours per charge.
★ Can be set with a timer or a light meter to ensure your lighting needs are satisfied.
★ Weatherproof stainless steel won't rust or break.
★ Weighs 3 kilos; comes with special supports to keep it upright in high winds.
★ Screw top makes changing bulbs (sold separately) easy!
★ Full warranty covers damage for three years.

Regular price: $45 (each)
Special offer: $90 for 3

Notice to Solaright Owners

OAKDALE (Jan 23) – The popular Solaright SOL 250, an outdoor light that charges during the daytime, has a problem.

A public relations coordinator for Solaright Systems issued a notice earlier today stating that, "Some SOL 250 units have been found to have an issue with the charging panel. Solaright Systems guarantees customer satisfaction. Businesses with large installations can request a service technician to come and repair faulty units. Residential owners can return any faulty units and get a replacement, free of charge."

Questions about any of Solaright's products can be directed to their 24-hour helpdesk at info@solarightsystems.com.

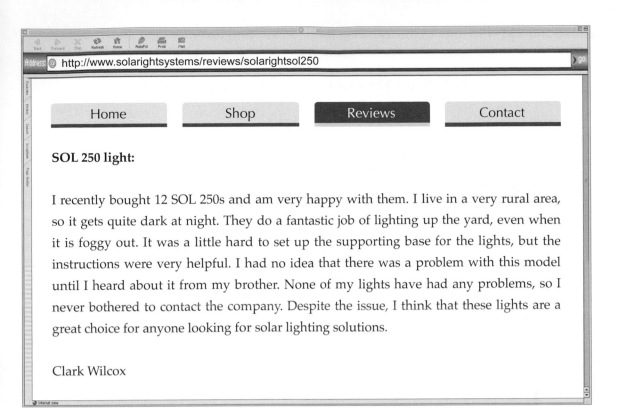

186. What is included in the price of the SOL 250?

(A) A three-year warranty
(B) Free delivery
(C) Replacement components
(D) Protective covers

187. Why was the article written?

(A) To announce a new home appliance
(B) To correct inaccurate pricing information
(C) To compare several products
(D) To alert readers to a product defect

188. In the article, the word "issued" in paragraph 2, line 1, is the closest in meaning to

(A) made public
(B) brought out
(C) assigned
(D) appeared

189. What does Mr. Wilcox confirm about the SOL 250's product description?

(A) The light is difficult to charge.
(B) The light is easy to clean.
(C) The light is very bright.
(D) The light is simple to set up.

190. What does Mr. Wilcox suggest about his lights?

(A) Their warranty was unable to cover everything.
(B) Their maintenance costs are much more expensive than expected.
(C) Their materials are not very strong.
(D) Their charging panels work well.

GO ON TO THE NEXT PAGE

VISITOR ACCESS CODE (VAC) APPLICATION FORM

Send this form to Ms. Jacqueline Yakazuki, fax number 410-555-6953.

VAC recipient's information:
Name: Sally Paige   **Department:** IT
Staff/Company ID number: 8027
__ **Basic access:** Monday to Friday, 8:00 A.M. – 8:00 P.M.
X **Extended access:** Monday to Friday, 8:00 A.M. – 10:30 P.M.
X **Special access** (Fill in relevant days and times): Saturdays, 10:30 A.M. – 5:30 P.M.
Building(s): __ Benford X Pine
Start date: February 8   **End date:** March 5

Requestor's information (Requestor must be either a manager or director of the recipient's department)
Name: Donnie Shaw
E-mail: dshaw@epsen.gov
Signature and date: *Donnie Shaw* January 28

Note:
After we receive your VAC request, it will take a minimum of four working days to process. Once access has been granted, an e-mail containing a 5-digit VAC will be sent to the recipient.

To	Sally Paige <s_paige@epsen.gov>
From	Jacqueline Yakazuki <j_yakazuki@epsen.gov>
Date	February 3
Subject	VAC

Dear Ms. Paige,

Your request for special and extended access to the Pine Building has been approved. To gain entry, you must use the provided visitor access code (VAC) along with your employee card. Your VAC is 27795. To enter the building after normal business hours, please follow these steps:

• Place your card to the card reader. An orange light on the reader will begin to flash.
• Next, enter your VAC using the touch screen.
• The flashing orange light will then turn green, allowing you to enter the building.

If you input your VAC incorrectly, the light will turn red, and you will hear a loud beep for five seconds. You will then have three more chances to input the correct code before you are completely locked out. Should you have any issues accessing the building, or once you are inside, please contact me at 410-555-4033.

Sincerely,

Jacqueline Yakazuki, Security Management

From: Sally Paige, 351-555-7240
Received: Monday, February 8, 8:02 A.M.

Hello Ms. Yakazuki,

I tried calling, but I couldn't reach you. I entered the VAC (27795) you emailed me, but the light keeps flashing red. Could you please contact me as soon as you receive this message? I have been shut out of the building.

---

191. What is suggested about Mr. Shaw?

(A) He has a leadership role in the IT Department.
(B) He submitted the application in February.
(C) He works in a different office than Ms. Paige.
(D) He will have a meeting with Ms. Paige regarding her project.

192. What is indicated about the VAC application form?

(A) It must be emailed to the security management office.
(B) It must provide a reason for the access request.
(C) It must include a copy of the employee's card.
(D) It must be filed at least four days in advance of the code being used.

193. How will Ms. Paige know that the VAC she enters is valid?

(A) The color of a light will change.
(B) A sound will ring for five seconds.
(C) A light will repeatedly flash.
(D) The volume of a sound will increase.

194. What is NOT indicated about the Security Management Office?

(A) It has a fax machine.
(B) It provides after-hours access.
(C) It issues access codes to employees.
(D) It has introduced new security policies.

195. What is suggested about Ms. Paige?

(A) She interviewed with Ms. Yakazuki.
(B) She will be promoted to a manager.
(C) She entered her VAC more than three times.
(D) She would like an extension to her access period.

GO ON TO THE NEXT PAGE

Questions 196-200 refer to the following advertisement, e-mail, and online review.

QiTech Electronics

32 Westpark Road, Charleston, WV 25302
(304) 555-0722
Seven Days a Week, 10 A.M. to 7 P.M.

Get Great Deals at Our Weeklong New Year's Sale!

Saturday, January 1, to Sunday, January 9

Desktop and laptop computers, monitors, and accessories - 30% Off
Cameras, A/V equipment, and portable storage - 10% Off
Mobile phones and tablets - 20% Off
Software - 25% Off

Note: To get ready for the sale, QiTech will close its doors at 5 P.M. on December 31. Refunds for products sold during the sale will be made in in-store credit only.

QiClub members will receive an additional 5% discount and extended warranties on all products. Sign up today on our Web site! Questions? Ask any of our helpful staff members at any time.

To:	All Staff
From:	Michael Chan <m.chan@qitech.com>
Date:	November 26
Subject:	Availability

Hello all,

In order to move stock to the shelves and clean the store, a crew will be needed to work through the night of December 31. I have organized a late-night meal from Icarus so that everyone who works that day will be able to enjoy dinner as well as receive overtime pay. Contact Rebekah Johnson by December 20 if you are able to work that shift.

Sincerely,
Michael Chan, General Manager

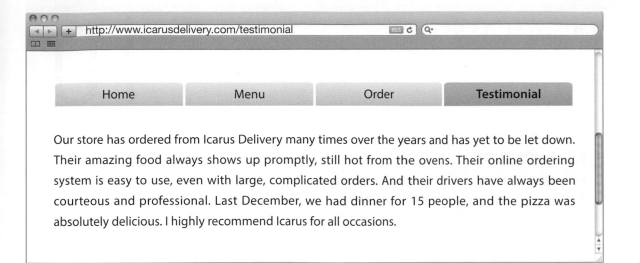

Our store has ordered from Icarus Delivery many times over the years and has yet to be let down. Their amazing food always shows up promptly, still hot from the ovens. Their online ordering system is easy to use, even with large, complicated orders. And their drivers have always been courteous and professional. Last December, we had dinner for 15 people, and the pizza was absolutely delicious. I highly recommend Icarus for all occasions.

196. According to the advertisement, what will happen on December 31?

(A) An electronics sale will begin.
(B) A Web site will be updated.
(C) A business will close early.
(D) A delivery of merchandise will arrive.

197. What does Mr. Chan ask employees to do?

(A) Join a quarterly meeting
(B) Prepare for a weeklong event
(C) Explain a scheduling process
(D) Add additional staff to help customers

198. In the e-mail, the word "organized" in paragraph 1, line 2 is closest in meaning to

(A) classified
(B) arranged
(C) adjusted
(D) straightened

199. How many employees responded to Mr. Chan's request?

(A) 10
(B) 15
(C) 25
(D) 30

200. What is NOT mentioned in Icarus's online testimonial?

(A) The performance of its employees
(B) The simplicity of its Web site
(C) The low prices of its dishes
(D) The speed of its service

Stop! This is the end of the test. If you finish before time is called, you may go back to Parts 5, 6, and 7 and check your work.

READING TEST

In the Reading test, you will read a variety of texts and answer several different types of reading comprehension questions. The entire Reading test will last 75 minutes. There are three parts, and directions are given for each part. You are encouraged to answer as many questions as possible within the time allowed.

You must mark your answers on the separate answer sheet. Do not write your answers in your test book.

PART 5

Directions: A word or phrase is missing in each of the sentences below. Four answer choices are given below each sentence. Select the best answer to complete the sentence. Then mark the letter (A), (B), (C), or (D) on your answer sheet.

101. Mr. Kang asked some coworkers to help ------- with the staff training workshop.

(A) he
(B) him
(C) his
(D) himself

102. Prager Engineering's staff members have thorough ------- of the latest drafting software.

(A) known
(B) knowledgeable
(C) know
(D) knowledge

103. ------- 50,000 people are anticipated to visit the amusement park over the holiday weekend.

(A) Considerably
(B) Fairly
(C) Roughly
(D) Heavily

104. Masie Stark's newest article is a ------- and revealing analysis of stock market trends.

(A) wisest
(B) wisdom
(C) wise
(D) wisely

105. ------- the end of the convention, company representatives are requested to fill out an exhibitor opinion survey.

(A) When
(B) While
(C) Toward
(D) Since

106. Before opening the access panel, make sure that the power cord has not been ------- connected.

(A) accident
(B) accidental
(C) accidents
(D) accidentally

107. Dartmoor Clinical College is committed to keeping costs ------- for its medical students.

(A) necessary
(B) trimming
(C) affordable
(D) allowed

108. Ms. Hatcher ------- posts in many parts of the organization before she retired.

(A) occupied
(B) occupation
(C) occupational
(D) occupying

109. To publish the book on time, designers must send all ------- to the illustrations to the editor by Monday.

(A) articles
(B) proposals
(C) suggestions
(D) revisions

110. Full-scale production of the selected design will not be ------- before the new year.

(A) checked in
(B) carried out
(C) turned away
(D) packed up

111. Refurbishing the Merseyside Assembly Plant is the ------- of the four relocation proposals.

(A) costly
(B) costing
(C) cost
(D) costliest

112. Luigi Produce provides the freshest fruits and vegetables to stores thanks to advanced ------- and delivery methods.

(A) preservation
(B) preserve
(C) preserved
(D) preserves

113. ------- the demand for the PFS-2x model smart phone, production will be tripled next quarter.

(A) Even if
(B) Just as
(C) As a result of
(D) Moreover

114. Depending on the results of your interview, we ------- you to take a written test.

(A) are asking
(B) must be asking
(C) have been asked
(D) may ask

115. A red tag means that a shipment must be inspected, ------- a green tag means that it can be sent out.

(A) almost
(B) whereas
(C) both
(D) whether

116. Always mention the reference number of your transaction in any ------- with our client service associates.

(A) correspondence
(B) corresponds
(C) correspondent
(D) correspondingly

117. The editorial team at the *Calumet Gazette* ------- prefers articles with short headlines.

(A) generally
(B) finally
(C) originally
(D) annually

118. Lerner Associates focuses on ------- promotional campaigns to help businesses market their services.

(A) personally
(B) personality
(C) personalizes
(D) personalized

119. ------- the subscription fee is less than 150 dollars, Kwak Financial Services will continue to receive the publication.

(A) Otherwise
(B) In addition
(C) As long as
(D) Together with

120. Tipton Freight's union leaders meet monthly with staff to make sure that labor laws ------- properly.

(A) would have followed
(B) are being followed
(C) to be followed
(D) had been followed

GO ON TO THE NEXT PAGE

121. Inquiries about our new products should be directed to the ------- sales representative.

(A) appropriate
(B) subsequent
(C) traceable
(D) critical

122. Dr. Akihara normally ------- only with patients who made appointments, but she decided to make an exception today.

(A) appears
(B) suits
(C) meets
(D) comments

123. Company stakeholders are carefully examining the monthly budget ------- proposed to them by the contracting firm.

(A) attributes
(B) planners
(C) requirements
(D) transmissions

124. The designer admitted that the popularity of his new line of clothing was ------- the result of opportune timing.

(A) parting
(B) partly
(C) parted
(D) parts

125. Ms. Patel kept records of ------- the employee training program covered in the last quarter.

(A) several
(B) everything
(C) other
(D) any

126. Initially manufacturing only computer software, Dyno Tech ------- produces wireless audio devices as well.

(A) thereby
(B) soon
(C) much
(D) now

127. The research shows that television commercials have a more ------- impact than either internet or radio advertisements.

(A) lasted
(B) last
(C) lasting
(D) lastly

128. Mr. Chen finished his ------- of his client's accounts this Tuesday.

(A) submission
(B) renovation
(C) audit
(D) comment

129. ------- events in the fourth quarter of last year caused Wisdan Publishing's production schedule to be delayed.

(A) Characteristic
(B) Unforeseen
(C) Entire
(D) Marginal

130. Ms. Koike accessed the online database ------- the progress reports from the last two quarters.

(A) to analyze
(B) will analyze
(C) analyzed
(D) analyzes

PART 6

Directions: Read the texts that follow. A word, phrase, or sentence is missing in parts of each text. Four answer choices for each question are given below the text. Select the best answer to complete the text. Then mark the letter (A), (B), (C), or (D) on your answer sheet.

Questions 131-134 refer to the following letter.

Pamela Stone
8920 Alderman Drive
San Jose, CA 94088

Dear Ms. Stone,

This letter is to confirm your reservation for the Executive Suite at the Gaze Sky Hotel from October 12 to October 14. You can check in ------- at 1 P.M. on Thursday. -------.
                                                                    131.   **132.**
You will be charged extra if you check out later.

We are confident that you and your husband will like the ------- designed facilities. The
                                                         133.
hotel has both an indoor and outdoor pool. We also have a state-of-the-art fitness center for your exercise needs. If you need to print something, stop by our advanced media room. Information on other ------- can be found on our Web site.
                              134.

We look forward to welcoming you to the Gaze Sky Hotel.

Sincerely,

Bernard Witson

Bernard Witson
Head of Guest Services

131. (A) starts
(B) started
(C) start
(D) starting

132. (A) You must leave your room before 12 P.M. on the last day.
(B) We have applied the family discount to your invoice.
(C) Fortunately, our hotel is conveniently located in the downtown area.
(D) Thank you for filling out the guest satisfaction survey.

133. (A) possibly
(B) tastefully
(C) initially
(D) nearly

134. (A) utilities
(B) costs
(C) amenities
(D) visits

GO ON TO THE NEXT PAGE →

Questions 135-138 refer to the following brochure.

Kensoi Transport operates the biggest public parking lot in Jeffmont. Commuters who wish to reserve a parking spot can do so by registering online or in person. A range of contract ------- are offered to interested individuals. There are occasions when all 3,000
135.
spots in the parking lot are -------. In this case, commuters without a designated spot
136.
may park their vehicles in the overflow garage ------- the street. Those with a reserved
137.
spot can rent a spot for three months at a time. -------. Please review the agreement and
138.
submit it to Kensoi's main office. To receive more details, send an e-mail to info@kensoitp.com.

135. (A) typing
(B) types
(C) type
(D) typed

136. (A) constructed
(B) filled
(C) tight
(D) accessible

137. (A) through
(B) within
(C) beyond
(D) across

138. (A) The terms and conditions of use can be found online.
(B) Kensoi operates another lot in a neighboring city.
(C) Jeffmont has recently increased its public parking fees.
(D) Commuters should download a mobile traffic application.

November 30

Tasteful Eats Magazine
8000 Duferford Road
Pittsburgh, PA 15106

Dear *Tasteful Eats Magazine* readers,

We are sending you this letter to inform you that starting January 1, the annual subscription price for *Tasteful Eats Magazine* will be ------- . **139.** The usual fee of $35.99 will increase to $37.85. Rest assured that this ------- **140.** does come with advantages. Seven new sections ------- **141.** in the magazine, including a coupon page and a restaurant review column. To terminate your subscription, please call our customer service center. ------- . **142.**

139. (A) refunded
(B) raised
(C) exchanged
(D) stopped

140. (A) obstacle
(B) association
(C) team
(D) adjustment

141. (A) features
(B) will be featured
(C) a feature
(D) have featured

142. (A) Several local restaurants will be participating in the program.
(B) A discount coupon will be sent to you as a sign of appreciation.
(C) *Tasteful Eats Magazine* is celebrating its 50 year anniversary in December.
(D) If we don't hear anything from you, your contract will be automatically renewed.

GO ON TO THE NEXT PAGE

Questions 143-146 refer to the following review.

Theater Performance Wows Spectators

By Ashraf Iftikhar

Karachi (May 22) – The critically-acclaimed new production, *Zindabad!*, had its opening night last Saturday at the Sindh Theater.

Presented by members of Karachi's Acting Wheel Drama Club, this play ------- the
143.
cultural and spiritual traditions that have deeply influenced the values of modern Pakistan.

------- are seen from the perspective of Ali Bhagat, who finds a new home in Karachi
144.
after leaving behind his home in India.

This play is powerful and moving, and the acting is amazing, especially knowing that it is an amateur production. -------. The performance takes just an hour to cover the story of
145.
a lifetime. A story like this requires more time to fully develop, and that is my only complaint about ------- was otherwise a superb performance.
146.

---

143. (A) will examine
(B) had examined
(C) examines
(D) to examine

144. (A) Attendees
(B) Stages
(C) Events
(D) Directions

145. (A) The actors really bring their characters to life.
(B) However, there will be no opportunity to rehearse for a while.
(C) Theater management will have to be careful about expenses.
(D) It is clear that professional assistance is necessary.

146. (A) what
(B) which
(C) one
(D) some

PART 7

Directions: In this part you will read a selection of texts, such as magazine and newspaper articles, emails, and instant messages. Each text or set of texts is followed by several questions. Select the best answer for each question and mark the letter (A), (B), (C), or (D) on your answer sheet.

Questions 147-148 refer to the following e-mail.

From:	Wishsong Ceramics <cs@wishsongceramics.com>
To:	Da-eun Kang <dkang@bindlestiffscafe.com>
Date:	March 19
Subject:	Order 335401

Dear Ms. Kang,

This is to verify that your order has been canceled. Please keep the following order summary for your records:

Order 335401:
120 white 20oz coffee mugs (payment processed on March 18)
Current status: canceled

The amount billed to your credit card will be refunded within three business days.

Thank you for your interest in Wishsong Ceramics.

Affordable, attractive dishware for every culinary need!

147. Why was the e-mail sent?

(A) To confirm an original order quantity
(B) To provide notice of a changed order
(C) To update a customer about a shipping delay
(D) To offer details about a store policy

148. What information does Ms. Kang receive about a payment?

(A) She will be sent a receipt in three days.
(B) She will receive a discount on her next purchase.
(C) She will not get a full refund.
(D) She will not pay for the items.

GO ON TO THE NEXT PAGE

To: staff_list@theomarketing.com

From: ctheobald@theomarketing.com

Date: March 8

Subject: Personnel Update

Good afternoon everyone,

I'm pleased to introduce our latest addition to the Marketing Department, Andrew Hendriksson. He will be taking over many of Blake Hirano's responsibilities, including creating online advertising and promotions. Ian Young and Kasim Aksoy are also going to take care of some of Blake's daily tasks. Ian will now be in charge of writing press releases, and Kasim will manage our social media accounts, including our own Web site. On behalf of everyone in the department, I would like to wish Blake a happy retirement and also congratulate Andrew on joining our team!

Regards,

Cory Theobald

149. What is one purpose of the e-mail?

(A) To discuss a recent press release
(B) To announce a job vacancy
(C) To welcome a new employee
(D) To request staff feedback

150. Who used to create online promotions?

(A) Blake Hirano
(B) Ian Young
(C) Kasim Aksoy
(D) Cory Theobald

Questions 151-152 refer to the following text message chain.

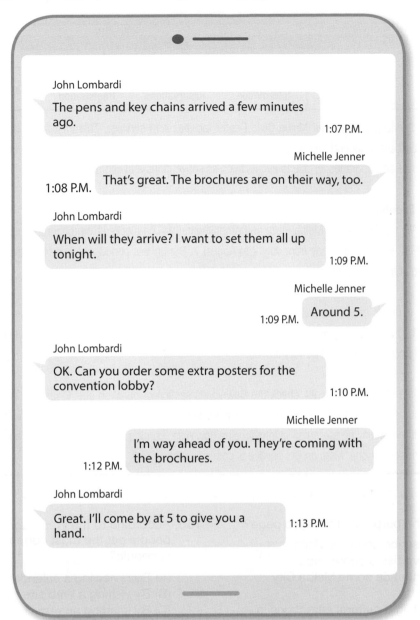

John Lombardi

The pens and key chains arrived a few minutes ago.

1:07 P.M.

Michelle Jenner

1:08 P.M. That's great. The brochures are on their way, too.

John Lombardi

When will they arrive? I want to set them all up tonight.

1:09 P.M.

Michelle Jenner

1:09 P.M. Around 5.

John Lombardi

OK. Can you order some extra posters for the convention lobby?

1:10 P.M.

Michelle Jenner

I'm way ahead of you. They're coming with the brochures.

1:12 P.M.

John Lombardi

Great. I'll come by at 5 to give you a hand.

1:13 P.M.

151. What does Mr. Lombardi plan to do?

(A) Redesign a convention poster
(B) Organize some promotional materials
(C) Pick up more brochures for the booth
(D) Leave the office at five o'clock

152. At 1:12 P.M., what does Ms. Jenner mean when she writes, "I'm way ahead of you"?

(A) She has arrived at an event early.
(B) She made a payment in advance.
(C) She has already requested additional supplies.
(D) She would like directions to a venue.

GO ON TO THE NEXT PAGE

Questions 153-155 refer to the following information on a Web page.

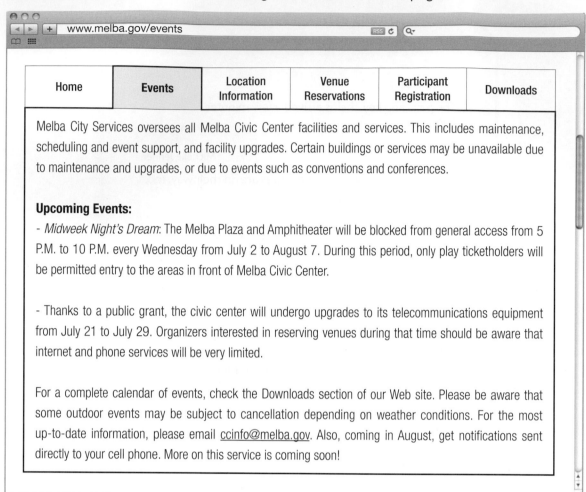

| Home | Events | Location Information | Venue Reservations | Participant Registration | Downloads |

Melba City Services oversees all Melba Civic Center facilities and services. This includes maintenance, scheduling and event support, and facility upgrades. Certain buildings or services may be unavailable due to maintenance and upgrades, or due to events such as conventions and conferences.

Upcoming Events:

- *Midweek Night's Dream*: The Melba Plaza and Amphitheater will be blocked from general access from 5 P.M. to 10 P.M. every Wednesday from July 2 to August 7. During this period, only play ticketholders will be permitted entry to the areas in front of Melba Civic Center.

- Thanks to a public grant, the civic center will undergo upgrades to its telecommunications equipment from July 21 to July 29. Organizers interested in reserving venues during that time should be aware that internet and phone services will be very limited.

For a complete calendar of events, check the Downloads section of our Web site. Please be aware that some outdoor events may be subject to cancellation depending on weather conditions. For the most up-to-date information, please email ccinfo@melba.gov. Also, coming in August, get notifications sent directly to your cell phone. More on this service is coming soon!

153. What is the purpose of the Web page?

(A) To describe some services
(B) To advertise a conference
(C) To announce some Melba City projects
(D) To highlight cultural attractions in Melba City

154. Why will some areas of the Melba Civic Center be closed to the public on Wednesdays?

(A) They will be undergoing renovation work.
(B) They will host a performance.
(C) They were affected by inclement weather.
(D) They will be part of a local race route.

155. According to the Web page, how can people get the most current event schedule?

(A) By reviewing a calendar
(B) By visiting a Web site
(C) By sending an e-mail
(D) By signing up for text message alerts

Metro Business Update

MAPLE CITY (Aug. 12) – DGC Industries will be acquired by Peyton Automation, according to an announcement yesterday. That's good news for city residents as Peyton affirmed that it would resume the expansion of DGC's manufacturing plant.

DGC's local plant handles the bulk of its manufacturing needs, providing work for thousands in Maple City. However, due to decreasing sales over the past five years, the expansion on the facility was put on hold. Peyton spokesperson Jesse Jarvi confirmed plans to begin hiring after the work on the plant is completed.

"Final job interviews will be conducted in November, and the new fabrication areas are expected to come online in December," said Jarvi.

The plant will continue to make DGC's main line of industrial products, as well as become the main production site for Peyton's new, six-axis assembly robots.

Peyton Automation has been the leader in the automation equipment market for three years in a row, according to industry experts. It is based in Singapore.

156. What is the purpose of the article?

(A) To report on the relocation of a business
(B) To confirm the opening of a new store
(C) To give an update on a halted project
(D) To review changing trends in manufacturing.

157. According to Mr. Jarvi, what will happen in November?

(A) A business will hire more staff.
(B) A new product line will be announced.
(C) A plant will undergo repairs.
(D) A building will be demolished.

158. What is indicated about Peyton Automation?

(A) It is closing its Singapore office.
(B) It has its headquarters in Maple City.
(C) It manufactures assembly robots.
(D) It has recently lost important clients.

GO ON TO THE NEXT PAGE

Questions 159-162 refer to the following online chat discussion.

Frank Carver [2:07 P.M.]
Hello, everyone. Do we have any updates on the Lawson Building bid?

Kiyoma Aditya [2:08 P.M.]
I spoke with Ms. Rasan over the phone on Tuesday. She said the executives were still looking over the proposals and that a decision would be made within the week.

Frank Carver [2:09 P.M.]
I'm concerned. We need to order the custom lighting we included in our estimate by tomorrow. Otherwise, even if we complete the flooring ahead of schedule, we won't be able to finish on time.

Anna Kang [2:10 P.M.]
Oh, I put in that order yesterday afternoon.

Frank Carver [2:11 P.M.]
That might be problematic. If we don't win the bid, we'll be stuck with those lighting fixtures. We don't have any other current projects that need them. When do we have to cancel the order by before needing to pay a fee?

Anna Kang [2:14 P.M.]
I assumed that we'd be selected again this time as we've done business with them for many years now. I'll look into it.

Frank Carver [2:15 P.M.]
Kiyoma, would you please contact Ms. Rasan to see if she has any news for us?

Anna Kang [2:21 P.M.]
We're able to back out before 6 P.M. today without incurring a fine.

Kiyoma Aditya [2:22 P.M.]
Actually, Frank, I've just spoken with Ms. Rasan, and Lawson has selected Mangrove Co. to do the work.

Frank Carver [2:24 P.M.]
That's unfortunate. But this wasn't the only pending contract we have, so let's not get too disappointed.

SEND

---

159. What industry do the writers most likely work in?

(A) Gardening
(B) Interior design
(C) Photography
(D) Real estate

160. At 2:14 P.M. what does Ms. Kang indicate she will do when she says, "I'll look into it"?

(A) Check the quantity of an item
(B) Inquire about a deadline
(C) Reschedule a shipment
(D) Calculate the price of a service

161. What information does Ms. Rasan give?

(A) How to provide a product refund
(B) Who will renovate the Lawson Building
(C) Where to locate affordable flooring
(D) Why Mr. Lawson did not call back

162. What will Ms. Kang most likely do next?

(A) Try to persuade Ms. Rasan
(B) Draft a new proposal
(C) Cancel a purchase
(D) Plan a work schedule

Questions 163-165 refer to the following e-mail.

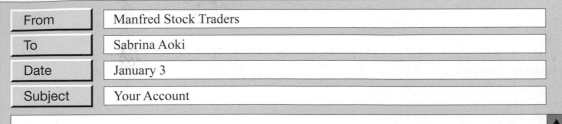

From	Manfred Stock Traders
To	Sabrina Aoki
Date	January 3
Subject	Your Account

Dear Ms. Aoki,

Please note that the password to your account has been successfully updated. If you did not make this change, please contact us at (800) 555-1212 within 48 hours. —[1]—. This is an automated e-mail, so please do not reply or send it to another address. —[2]—.

If you requested to change your information, no further action is required on your part. —[3]—.

This alert has been sent as part of our effort to keep your account safe. —[4]—.

Sincerely,
Daniel Pasqualetti
Manfred Stock Traders

Make strategic stock purchases with our revolutionary trading software, available at www.mstrade.com!

163. Why was the e-mail sent to Ms. Aoki?

(A) To announce a promotional event
(B) To ask for a payment
(C) To notify her of some account activity
(D) To inform her of a new security program

164. What is Ms. Aoki advised to do?

(A) Call if she did not request a change
(B) Check a monthly billing statement
(C) Download a program
(D) Change her account settings

165. In which of the positions marked [1], [2], [3], and [4] does the following sentence best belong?

"An Operations Support representative will help you to resolve the situation."

(A) [1]
(B) [2]
(C) [3]
(D) [4]

GO ON TO THE NEXT PAGE

From: info@towercontrolvid.com
To: registered-user list
Date: August 23
Subject: Version 4.5

Hello,

We are happy to announce that Towercontrol 4.5, the latest version of the video editing software you have purchased is available for download.

Visual and Sound Effects: An additional 50 effects are included in the updated effects library. All effects feature several options which can be turned on and off. To get them, access your online account and select the "updates" tab. A manual that explains how to use these new effects will be delivered by express shipping soon.

Introducing Stock Video: You can now take advantage of free video clips; use them for transitions between your clips whenever you want to add extra content to your project. There are many stock videos to choose from, so be sure to set aside some time to become familiar with them.

Manage Online Distribution Quickly: Share quickly, whether with a movie studio or with friends on social media! Download the file sharing manual at www.towercontrolvid.com/sharing to find step-by-step instructions to bridge your various network accounts to your video masterpiece.

Your support is important to us. We welcome the opportunity to help you make your video editing experience a pleasure!

Regards,

Towercontrol Video Customer Support Team

166. What is the purpose of the e-mail?

(A) To offer long-time customers a reward
(B) To promote a new software product
(C) To ask for additional information
(D) To provide details about a computer program

167. What is being mailed to the customers?

(A) A magazine about the latest electronic devices
(B) A tutorial on installing an update
(C) A large gallery of stock videos
(D) A guide on using some new effects

168. In the e-mail, the word "bridge" in paragraph 4, line 3, is closest meaning to

(A) link
(B) extend
(C) reach
(D) cross

Questions 169-171 refer to the following letter.

To the Editor:

This letter is in regard to the hospitality review, "Timeless Vacation Destinations: Hatheh Resort," that was printed in the September issue of *Comfy Traveler*. The pictures of the resort were beautiful, and it was wonderful to see the business get some much-deserved attention. But I noticed something that should be mentioned. —[1]—.

The reviewer says Arthur Taylor originally designed the resort's unique buildings. However, while he was certainly an important contributor, his role was mainly to provide funding. —[2]—. Instead, Kyle Silva was in charge of Hatheh's planning and construction. The reason why I know this is that I was the main person that Hatheh Resort hired to design the gardens and outdoor areas of the facility, so I interacted with Mr. Silva frequently. —[3]—.

The building design only gets a short mention in the review, but I feel that it's important to the history of Hatheh Resort. Thanks to Mr. Silva, tourism to our island has greatly increased and helped local businesses thrive, though he rarely gets credited for it. —[4]—. I feel it is important to set the record straight.

Sincerely,

Afa Faiz
Afa Faiz

169. Why was the letter written?

(A) To highlight a CEO's accomplishments
(B) To describe a vacation
(C) To correct some information
(D) To review some accommodations

170. Who most likely is Mr. Faiz?

(A) A facility custodian
(B) A travel writer
(C) A landscape architect
(D) A hotel manager

171. In which of the positions marked [1], [2], [3], and [4] does the following sentence best belong?

"He had little to no role in the decision-making process at that stage of the resort's development."

(A) [1]
(B) [2]
(C) [3]
(D) [4]

GO ON TO THE NEXT PAGE

Beach Tree Enterprises
92 E. Chadwell Ct., Pennington, NJ

October 27

Dear Ms. Sirko,

It is my pleasure to inform you that you have been selected for the position of Senior Marketing Manager, starting Tuesday, November 15, at a base salary of $76,000 per year. Per company policy, you will start with a 6-month introductory period. After that time, your performance will be reviewed to determine your eligibility for continued employment.

Please verify your intention to accept this offer no later than Tuesday, November 8. You may do this by either texting or calling (609) 555-0058. If you must start on a date other than the one indicated, be sure to include that information when you contact us. However, due to ongoing projects and the need to actively support our current client accounts, we will not be able to postpone your starting date beyond Thursday, November 24.

On your first day, please visit the Personnel Office before reporting to your department. Please bring this letter, since you will have to sign and date it in front of a Personnel employee (be sure to keep a copy for your own records). Also, during this time, you will need to turn in a copy of your driver's license or passport.

To make your training experience as smooth as possible, we always try to place new hires with a mentor who works in the same role. For this reason, you will work closely with Mr. Kyle Wesleyan, who has held this position for many years. If you have any questions before your first day about our company culture or special requirements, please feel free to get in touch with him by e-mail at kwesleyan@beachtree.com. You are scheduled for the standard staff orientation on Wednesday, November 16, to review company guidelines and procedures, although this can be rescheduled depending on your availability.

We are pleased to welcome you to Beach Tree Enterprises and look forward to working with you.

Sincerely,
Janet Roper
Personnel Director

Acknowledgement of Initial Terms and Conditions
I hereby agree to the terms and conditions as given to me by Beach Tree Enterprises.

Employee signature: *Dasha Sirko*
Employee name: Dasha Sirko
Signed on: November 15

172. What is NOT a requirement for new staff?

(A) Submitting the job offer letter
(B) Training under an experienced employee
(C) Providing a form of identification
(D) Showing proof of address

173. What is true about Mr. Wesleyan?

(A) He is a client of Beach Tree.
(B) He will lead a staff orientation.
(C) He will evaluate Ms. Sirko in six months.
(D) He is a Senior Marketing Manager.

174. When will Ms. Sirko learn more about the company's rules?

(A) On Tuesday
(B) On Wednesday
(C) On Thursday
(D) On Friday

175. What is suggested about Ms. Sirko?

(A) She did not reschedule her first working day.
(B) She did not contact anyone about the company culture.
(C) She will not get a pay raise after six months.
(D) She will not work directly with clients during the introductory period.

GO ON TO THE NEXT PAGE

Seaside Escape

Rudy Paula

October 2 – Autumn is officially here, so I set out to check out Maine's countryside. I was anticipating a peaceful, but perhaps somewhat dull, drive along the back roads. Instead, it was gorgeous, with trees bursting with color around every curve. I arrived in Bar Harbor, a quaint seaside town, which can be reached by bus from nearby Portland four times a day. It has a history dating back to 1796 and is bordered by an incredible national park.

I stayed in an inn run by Mr. Bartholomew Dagney called the Critter Lodge. Once I entered, I felt like I was in another era—it was wonderful. Not only is the interior the same as it was more than 100 years ago, some of the food is the same as well! Mr. Dagney specializes in lobster chowder, a dish that the town is famous for. If you happen to be in the area, you should definitely consider visiting this lodge.

Take a look at my Web site for more information:
www.rudygetsout.com
or visit the lodge's site for room availability and bookings:
www.critterlodge.com

From	Anish Khan <akhan@springertech.com>
To	Blaze Larson <blaze.l@takefive.com>
Date	October 8
Subject	Convention schedule

Good morning Mr. Larson,

I appreciate you organizing my trip for the convention I will be attending. However, I just found out that the Critter Lodge, www.critterlodge.com, is just a short way outside of the city hosting the convention. I'd like to be able to end each day with a drive through the beautiful countryside, followed by a relaxing evening by the sea. Would you please find out if they can accommodate my schedule for the same dates? If so, you will also need to cancel the reservations at the Hardport Hotel. According to the confirmation document you emailed to me, they need two days' notice (i.e., by October 13) to avoid a penalty.

Sincerely,

Anish Khan
Vice President, Springertech, Inc.

176. What is the purpose of the article?

(A) To recommend accommodations
(B) To describe a new menu
(C) To promote a car rental service
(D) To review an online magazine

177. What is stated about the lobster chowder?

(A) It is a regional dish.
(B) It contains many ingredients.
(C) It is affordable.
(D) It is only available in the fall.

178. Who most likely is Mr. Larson?

(A) A hotel clerk
(B) A waiter
(C) A programmer
(D) A travel agent

179. What is suggested about the convention?

(A) Its lead organizer is Mr. Khan.
(B) Its early registration deadline is October 13.
(C) It offers lunch for participants.
(D) It is taking place in Portland.

180. Why does Mr. Khan mention about the Hardport Hotel?

(A) A Web site gave it positive reviews.
(B) It provides transportation to Bar Harbor.
(C) A booking has been made there.
(D) It has no vacancies in October.

GO ON TO THE NEXT PAGE

Holderfield Parks

Event Permits

Any party that wishes to hold an event of 30 people or more at any of the community parks within the Holderfield city limits must obtain an event permit from Holderfield's Parks and Recreation Department.

Things to Note Before Applying

* All event permits require a $30.00 processing fee, which is nonrefundable. Checks should be made out to the Holderfield Parks and Recreation Department.

* A request for a permit must be submitted to the Holderfield Parks and Recreation Department at least one month prior to the date of the event.

* Applications for event permits must be made in person at the Holderfield Parks and Recreation Department office between 9:00 A.M. and 6:00 P.M., Monday to Friday. Applications will not be accepted online or by postal mail. A completed application form and the application fee must be submitted at the time of processing.

* Applications will be reviewed on a first-come, first-served basis. Please view our event calendar at www.holderfieldparksrecdept.com to see the available dates for each of the parks.

Other Fees

Most events do not require an additional fee aside from the permit fee. For considerably larger events that involve multiple outside food vendors or live music equipment, other fees will be added. Applicants should include all relevant information on the permit application.

Holderfield Parks
Event Permit Application

Requester: Carissa Kosko

Organizations and Number: Markos Greek Cultural Association, 555-3937

Event Name: Flavors of the Mediterranean

Event Description: The purpose of the event is to promote different types of Mediterranean foods. Participants can enjoy cooking demonstrations, meet with local chefs, and try authentic Mediterranean cuisine from various food vendors.

Event Start Time / Date: 11:00 A.M. / Sunday, August 25

Event End Time / Date: 5:00 P.M. / Sunday, August 25

Location: Oak Creek Park

Anticipated Attendance: 400-700 people

This portion is to be completed by a Holderfield Parks and Recreation Department staff member only: **APPROVED**

---

181. For whom is the information sheet intended?

(A) Job candidates
(B) Park employees
(C) Event planners
(D) Travel agents

182. What is indicated about the Holderfield Parks and Recreation Department?

(A) It oversees space in several parks.
(B) It accepts online applications.
(C) It issues only 30 permits per year.
(D) It is open seven days a week.

183. What is implied about Ms. Kosko?

(A) She gives cooking demonstrations every Sunday.
(B) She recently moved to Holderfield.
(C) She works at a popular local restaurant.
(D) She submitted the application before July 25.

184. What is indicated about Flavors of the Mediterranean?

(A) It will feature a music performance.
(B) It is expected to attract over 400 people.
(C) It will require an entrance fee.
(D) It is scheduled to run for two days.

185. What will Ms. Kosko probably need to do?

(A) Renew her current permit
(B) Reserve space in another park
(C) Sell tickets at a discount
(D) Pay more than one fee

GO ON TO THE NEXT PAGE

K.A. Roth's Archives on Display

The treasured archives of historian and writer K.A. Roth are now open for research at the Wayfield Center, a history research library located at 50 Grove Avenue. "K.A. Roth is one of the most respected writers in the country," said Wayfield Center staff member Clarice Royce. The documents, which contain all of his notable writings as well as a few handwritten copies of his first books, trace Roth's successful career. Also, the archives include interviews, biographies, public speeches, as well as the documentary film based on his life.

The Wayfield Center allows access to rare books, manuscripts, audio materials, and other texts for research purposes only. Patrons must read the Wayfield Center regulations and sign an agreement at the front desk. They also have to go to the third floor, where they must watch a brief video about using the library's materials and facilities. The Wayfield Center is open Monday-Saturday, 10:00 A.M. - 6:00 P.M.

Wayfield Center

Membership Registration Agreement

Welcome to the Wayfield Center. To ensure that all documents are used for research and to preserve the quality of the collections, patrons must adhere to the regulations regarding the usage of library materials. Please read over the attached document and confirm your understanding of the Wayfield Center's regulations by providing your signature at the bottom. Submit this form at the front desk along with a copy of your photo identification to receive a two-year membership card. Please note that you are not allowed to take any materials from the center.

I have read and accept the terms and conditions of the Wayfield Center.

Date: <u>February 26</u>

Name: <u>Bernard Porter</u>

Signature: <u>*Bernard Porter*</u>

General Rules for Wayfield Center

- Food and drinks are not permitted inside the library.
- All bags may be subject to search when patrons leave the library.
- Cellular phones must be silenced in the library.
- Wayfield is not responsible for your personal property.
- Pets are not allowed in the library.

186. In the article, the word "treasured" in paragraph 1, line 1, is closest in meaning to

(A) cherished
(B) hidden
(C) perished
(D) conserved

187. Who is Ms. Royce?

(A) A researcher
(B) A novelist
(C) A library employee
(D) A film producer

188. What is indicated about the Wayfield Center?

(A) It is available for research only.
(B) It is looking for new materials.
(C) It is revising its policies.
(D) It is adding more storage space.

189. What is Mr. Porter required to do?

(A) Return some materials he signed out
(B) Submit a sample of his writing
(C) Pay a fee for membership
(D) Watch an informational video

190. What rule in the agreement is NOT mentioned in the information?

(A) Patrons should not bring snacks into the library.
(B) Patrons may not take any library documents.
(C) Patrons may have their bags searched.
(D) Patrons should take care of their personal belongings.

GO ON TO THE NEXT PAGE ➡

To	Katherine Ahn
From	Jessica Estes
Date	3 July
Subject	New space

Dear Katherine,

I appreciate the time you took to meet with me yesterday. Like I said, I am in search of a new commercial space for my cosmetics shop. My current lease ends in November. I am interested in downtown locations, in or around Aspen Plaza, which cost £3500 or less per month. It's important that the size be close to what we have now, but I'm flexible on the interior design and layout.

In consideration of my employees' financial situations, I need to open at the start of December. So, I am primarily interested in newer spaces that will need less work. The current building we are located in is adequate, but both my workers and I believe moving will help grow the business even further.

Thank you,
Jessica Estes

To	Jessica Estes
From	Katherine Ahn
Date	6 July
Subject	RE: New space

I have found several available locations that I believe may suit your needs. Call me at your convenience, and let me know when you will have time to look at them. I can book visitations around your schedule.

A. 1029 W. Southern Ave.
£3430/mo.
Previously occupied by a bakery. Metered street parking available for customers in front. Kitchen area can be converted into a stockroom or office. Limited area for merchandise displays.

B. 78 Myrtle Pl.
£3180/mo.
Prime spot opposite First City Bank's headquarters. Underground parking garage located next door. Wheelchair ramp in front of the entrance is damaged. Will need renovations.

C. 839 S. 10th Dr.
£3240/mo.
Second floor of Flatpine Mall in the Riverfront neighborhood. Well served by public transportation. Many opportunities for advertising throughout the facility.

Sincerely,
Katherine Ahn

The Glamour Cat Finds New Spot

By Yvonne Garner

BAYPORT (9 Dec) — The Glamour Cat, a mainstay at 17 Sayer Drive for more than a decade, has been the community's go-to shop for beauty products. Last Saturday, it reopened for business at 78 Myrtle Place, next to the Muon Building.

You can still expect the Glamour Cat to offer you high-quality products and great customer service. If you stop by, I highly recommend treating yourself to a manicure or face massage. Our employees are talented artists in their own right!

Long-time patrons should be aware that the seating area for massages and manicures is slightly smaller than it used to be. It can fill up quickly on weekend afternoons, but the reward for your wait will be great products and the amazing service that has kept the store going all these years.

The new downtown storefront is conveniently located near the Federal Street Commercial Center. The shop itself is wheelchair-friendly. It is open every day, from 10 A.M. to 7 P.M.

191. Who most likely is Ms. Ahn?

(A) A building owner
(B) A loan officer
(C) A real estate agent
(D) A cosmetics designer

192. What is implied about Ms. Estes?

(A) She created a new beauty product line.
(B) She was able to reopen her business on time.
(C) She could not afford higher rent.
(D) She did not want to renovate some displays.

193. What is indicated about The Glamour Cat?

(A) It closes early on weekends.
(B) Its services have improved.
(C) It repaired a ramp.
(D) Its stockroom can store more items.

194. How is the new cosmetics shop different from the original?

(A) It holds fewer customers.
(B) It is located in a shopping mall.
(C) It provides more manicure services.
(D) It no longer offers face massages.

195. In the article, the word "going" in paragraph 3, line 6, is closest in meaning to

(A) operating
(B) passing
(C) departing
(D) traveling

GO ON TO THE NEXT PAGE

Intern Needed

Bluefly, an award-winning marketing firm, is looking for an intern to join our team in its downtown Atlanta office. The successful applicant will have previous experience in office work, preferably with extensive knowledge of social media services. Duties will include responding to online inquiries, tracking subscriber data, posting announcements on social media Web sites, and other administrative tasks. This part-time internship is 15 hours a week and may involve some evening and weekend work to be done at home. Students and recent graduates interested in the position should send their résumés to internship@bluefly.com.

To	: internship@bluefly.com
From	: wrasmussen@esuarts.edu
Date	: May 19
Subject	: Internship
Attachments	: Rasmussen-résumé; Rasmussen-slides

Dear Bluefly HR,

I hope that you will consider my interest in applying for the internship at Bluefly. While I am currently in school studying design, I already have two years of experience in positions related to social media. I have maintained Web pages for several university clubs, and I am also very active on my personal social media accounts. In addition, I am familiar with most of the necessary software for creating great online content.

Right now, I am working as a museum guide four mornings a week. I'm looking for an internship that allows me to maintain this schedule. Although I have not worked in marketing before, I am eager to learn and believe that my skills would benefit your agency. Attached to this e-mail are my résumé and a set of slides highlighting my artistic abilities. They show my skill at creating attractive, interesting content, and my meticulous attention to quality.

Thank you for your time, and I hope to hear from you soon.

Sincerely,
Wendy Rasmussen

To: Bluefly HR Team
From: Adam Ivanovich
Date: May 26
Subject: Regarding the internship position

Good afternoon,

The last interview for the intern position, with Ms. Rasmussen, will begin tomorrow morning at 10 A.M. Be sure to review the submitted materials before the interview to familiarize yourself with her qualifications, as they might be an issue for some. I'm sure she'll learn the routine social media tasks we require quickly. But I think she has the potential to do much more. The materials she emailed to us show a level of quality that our online audience will really like. If you would like to discuss this further before tomorrow's meeting, please get in touch.

Adam

196. According to the advertisement, what is a duty of the internship?

(A) Holding client meetings
(B) Updating Web sites
(C) Contacting new subscribers
(D) Sorting office bills

197. What aspect of the position is likely the most appealing to Ms. Rasmussen?

(A) The salary figure
(B) The work schedule
(C) The company's reputation
(D) The company's location

198. What is indicated about Ms. Rasmussen?

(A) She plans to move to Atlanta.
(B) She has recently graduated from university.
(C) She regularly showcases her work at a museum.
(D) She has no experience in marketing.

199. What is the purpose of the second e-mail?

(A) To request that interviewers review a candidate's documents
(B) To inform employees why an interview has been delayed
(C) To alert employees to a company policy
(D) To ask that interviewers reach a decision soon

200. Why does Mr. Ivanovich think Ms. Rasmussen is a good candidate for the position?

(A) Her willingness to travel
(B) Her experience in advertising
(C) Her knowledge of computers
(D) Her skills as an artist

Stop! This is the end of the test. If you finish before time is called, you may go back to Parts 5, 6, and 7 and check your work.

TRANSLATION

ACTUAL TEST ①

101. 帕克維爾公司有三成事業，均沿著百老匯大道營運。
(A) 有效地
(B) 沿著
(C) 傾向側邊
(D) 分開地

102. 網路問卷的多數回覆者均熟知「冰炫優格」，且其中 65% 的人至少購買過一次此產品。
(A) 其中……的人／他們
(B) 他們的
(C) 他們自己
(D) 他們

103. 拓展至新市場的公司，常因不瞭解當地文化而遭遇困境。
(A) 市場
(B) 市場
(C) 已上市的
(D) 暢銷的

104. 採購部門打算下個月搬遷至較大的辦公室。
(A) 預測
(B) 報告
(C) 打算
(D) 認為

105. 營建主管期許克雷斯特韋圖書館對外開放的時間，最晚不能超過下週四。
(A) 最近
(B) 最新
(C) 遲到
(D) 最晚不能超過……

106. 濾水專家將把調查結果上呈評委小組。
(A) 決議
(B) 資格
(C) 見解
(D) 調查

107. 伊米立亞航太公司上週聘請到一名出色的年輕工程專家。
(A) 極端的
(B) 準確的
(C) 整體的
(D) 出色的

108. 該名技師檢查過克雷文先生的電腦處理器後，建議他更換處理器。
(A) 檢查
(B) 檢查
(C) 檢查
(D) 檢查

109. 準備所有必要品項所需的人員數量，均取決於訂單大小。
(A) 取決於
(B) 仰賴
(C) 取決於
(D) 取決於

110. 如果週日的天氣炎熱到令人不適，我們就會延期陵線公園健行之旅。
(A) 令人不適地
(B) 基本上
(C) 小心地
(D) 幾乎

111. 為了從事專業電工的工作，阮甘納桑先生有義務每五年更新一次職業證照。
(A) 仍然
(B) 較少的
(C) 每……
(D) 無論到哪裡

112. 為了因應學生的需求，賽維爾大學將舉辦一系列的職業發展講座。
(A) 許可證
(B) 平衡
(C) 入學
(D) 需求

113. 研習會後，出席者均有充分時間提出簡報相關問題。
(A) 充分的
(B) 慷慨
(C) 慷慨地
(D) 慷慨大方

114. 布魯德爾公司在廚具展覽上的操作示範，讓不少人產生興趣。
(A) 興趣
(B) 興趣
(C) 有趣的
(D) 感興趣的

115. 副總昨天在尼斯舉辦的早午餐會上會見法國的投資人。
(A) 猶如
(B) 當……時
(C) 在……
(D) 吃

116. 為了顧及董事會的意見，每月預算報告的截止日已延期。
(A) 把……變成
(B) 耗盡
(C) 顧及，考慮到
(D) 仰賴

117. 乘客必須在班機起飛前提早至少一小時抵達機場。
(A) 屆時
(B) 為了……
(C) 很少
(D) 至少

118. 化學工程師團隊正在實驗一種可以承受極端條件的面板塗層。
(A) 彼時
(B) 什麼
(C) 進入
(D) ……的（事物）

119. 銀驛汽車零件公司製造的機油濾芯品質，比對手的還要更好。
(A) 如此
(B) 比……更……
(C) 何處
(D) 這些

120. 由於布維納維斯塔戶外用品公司即將遷至新地點，因此正在舉行盛大的出清特賣會。
(A) 可清除的
(B) 出清
(C) 正在出清
(D) 已出清

121. 「商業頻道」將播出一個專門討論產品開發和創新設計的新節目。
(A) 介紹
(B) 許可
(C) 安排
(D) 專門以……為主

122. 明女士客氣地婉拒維拉薩諾進口有限公司主動提出的職位。
(A) 轉換
(B) 婉拒
(C) 減少
(D) 限制

123. 雖然相當有難度，但大師健身房的攀岩牆還是非常受到會員歡迎。
(A) 基本上
(B) 雖然
(C) 整體
(D) 推論

124. 亞莫女士先在店面工作了三天，才正式被引見給分店經理。
(A) 目前
(B) 正式地
(C) 非常可觀地
(D) 主要地

125. 銀行的新政策能讓你根據可負擔的 10 年期方案，來進行房貸轉貸。
(A) 管理
(B) 管理
(C) 可應付的
(D) 可應付地

126. 李先生已經要求，維護工人最好在兩小時內到場。
(A) 偏好
(B) 更合適的
(C) 最好
(D) 偏好

127. 「赫克賽爾工業」雖然降低了營運成本，但對公司未來更重要的卻是強化了自己的競爭優勢。
    (A) 多元的
    (B) 競爭的
    (C) 敏銳的
    (D) 謹慎的

128. 費茲派翠克女士認為，「可靠」是她所有員工均應具備的重要特質。
    (A) 版本
    (B) 特質
    (C) 儀器
    (D) 作為

129. 我們必須取得最終批准，才能處理這批貨物。
    (A) 正在被處理
    (B) 處理
    (C) 已處理
    (D) （被）處理

130. 系統安裝費已包含了教育訓練講師的費用。
    (A) 含括進去
    (B) 來自……
    (C) 一起
    (D) 到……上面

PART 6   P. 13–16

131–134 公告

6 月 22 日星期五，公共工程部門 (DPW) 將針對穿越市立大學校區的主要道路，進行養護工程。這段道路是介於馬龍大道和胡佛街之間的棕櫚路部分路段。工程小組將於 8 月 1 日前，完成所有必要的維修事務。此工程案將於大學暑假期間執行，因為學生於此期間通行棕櫚路的機率最低。DPW 亦將保留單線車道，讓該道路於施工期間仍能保持開放。儘管如此，用路人仍應考慮替代路線。

131. **(A) 介於……之間**
    (B) 來自……
    (C) 在……之上
    (D) 在……之中

132. (A) 地鐵仍開放通車。
    (B) 此工程案將於大學暑假期間執行。
    (C) 他們最初希望能提早六個月完工。
    (D) 確切的工程時間仍在討論中。

133. (A) 開放
    (B) 開放中
    (C) 開放
    (D) 開瓶器

134. (A) 考慮中
    (B) 將考慮好
    (C) 已考慮
    (D) 應考慮

135–138 公告

保護環境是「爾尼馬特公司」所注重的價值。我們在乎的是為後代建立一個健康的世界。秉持這樣的信念，我們即將推出「綠色十一月」活動。在 11 月整個月期間，我們會從客人購買特定商品的利潤中撥出四分之一，捐給提倡清淨空氣與乾淨水源的機構組織。

爾尼馬特公司農產品、烘焙品項與多數的包裝食品，均為符合此條件的商品。糖果類、個人保養品和飲料均不符資格。爾尼馬特公司的首頁將列出其他排除在本次活動之外的產品，以便您參考。

去年的「綠色十一月」活動募得近一百萬元，並用於各種環保善舉。我們期望今年能達到去年金額的三倍。如需了解更多訊息，請至 www.erniemart.com/erniecares，或到我們的任何據點索取說明冊。

135. (A) 穿過
    (B) 像……一樣
    (C) ……的
    (D) 透過

136. (A) 將捐獻
    (B) 捐獻中
    (C) 被捐獻
    (D) 將被捐獻

137. (A) 未開放的
(B) 受損的
(C) 排除在外的
(D) 停產的

138. (A) 我們期望今年能達到去年金額的三倍。
(B) 對本協會而言,這段時期一直很難熬。
(C) 每一家參與的公司將付費入場。
(D) 這將是我們最後一年舉辦此活動。

139–142 電子郵件

寄件人:倫狄‧福馬歐羅
收件人:屈克健身中心 (TFC) 全體會員
日期:4 月 25 日
主旨:健身房直付中心

親愛的 TFC 會員:

您應已收到我們新配合的結帳公司「健身房直付中心」所傳送的訊息。訊息裡包含一個會員網站連結,提供會員使用所有的繳費功能。請您儲存此網址以便使用。自下個月起,您所有的帳單均透過該網站處理,之後您將不再收到帳單通知的相關訊息。

此外,健身房直付中心的訊息應有一組臨時帳號和密碼,供您登入新的網站。請務必於本週結束之前完成登入。您的臨時帳密將在登入後失效。

如您於此過程中需要協助,請撥打 1-800-555-1212 與我聯絡。

敬祝 安康

TFC 會員服務部經理
倫狄‧福馬歐羅

139. (A) 可能收到
(B) 已經在收到
(C) 應已收到
(D) 即將收到

140. (A) 請您儲存此網址以便使用。
(B) 此網頁目前無法使用。
(C) 我們有幾項新設施可供您使用。
(D) 不巧的是,您的帳號結帳錯誤。

141. (A) 其他
(B) 這樣
(C) 再次
(D) 兩者

142. (A) 與此同時
(B) 然而
(C) 任何時間
(D) 在那之後

143–146 信函

3 月 15 日

賈維斯‧麥馬宏
46806 印第安那州韋恩堡市東加州路
1211 號

親愛的麥馬宏先生:

此信為回應您近期拜訪我們的投資人服務中心一事。當時我們討論過,將您的退休儲蓄移至凱博利斯金融中心的可能性。我們很高興能協助您處理此項事務。信封內附上應您要求的說明手冊,內有各種服務與投資選擇的詳細介紹。您將發現,我們擁有各式各樣的出色理財選擇。

您如需了解額外的資訊或協助,我們的投資人服務專員隨時能為您服務。您準備好的時候,我們會負責將您的帳戶從目前的機構移至凱博利斯金融中心。

我想再次感謝您有興趣了解凱博利斯金融中心。期待未來與您合作。

敬祝 安康

凱博利斯金融中心
投資人服務專員

詹姆斯‧克爾瑞
219-555-1212

143. (A) 更多的
(B) 最近的
(C) 下一個的
(D) 延誤的

144. (A) 附上
(B) 附上的
(C) 附上
(D) 附件

145. (A) 我們將免收您第一年的維護費。
(B) 您的反饋將協助我們未來提供更優質的服務。
(C) 您已選定並購入所有投資項目。
(D) 您將發現，我們擁有各式各樣的出色理財選擇。

146. (A) 建議
(B) 版次
(C) 帳戶
(D) 偏好

PART 7　P. 17–37

147–148 指示

使用方法

1. 投入現金。〔147〕

2. 開門放入衣物。〔147〕 請勿超過機器的最大洗衣容量。

3. 放入洗衣精，並選擇適當溫度。〔147〕

4. 關門並按下啟動按鈕以開始清洗程序。〔147〕

5. 如果聽到警示音，請重新整理機器內的衣物，平衡衣物分布的重量。〔148〕

6. 完成時，請在五分鐘內將衣物放入乾衣機內，以便他人使用機器。

147. 此指示最有可能出現在什麼場所？
(A) 洗車廠
(B) 洗衣店
(C) 家電商店
(D) 服飾店

148. 根據指示，何時為非必要的步驟？
(A) 步驟 2
(B) 步驟 4
(C) 步驟 5
(D) 步驟 6

149–150 表格

亞弧資訊科技基礎建設
安裝申請表

客戶：玫瑰木診所
聯絡人：linda.richards@rosewoodmc.com
地址：22030 維吉尼亞州費爾法克斯市亞旭小巷 35 號
日期：7 月 26 日
技師：羅貝塔・科埃
訂單編號：8233
設備：700 公尺的第五類網路傳輸線
預估工時：4.5 小時
工作地點：東側廳 〔150〕

工作說明：將所有職員區的電腦和印表機，全部連接至牆面的網路插孔，並測試連線品質。診所進行手術時，請勿進入。請於非看診時段（晚上 8 點至凌晨 4 點 30 分）完工。〔149〕 撥打分機 457，與大廳警衛聯繫。

149. 文中提到關於玫瑰木診所施工的哪些事？
(A) 將於晚間完工。
(B) 已於 7 月 26 日付款。
(C) 需要若干工人。
(D) 為此專案的第一階段。

150. 文中提到玫瑰木診所的哪些事？
(A) 診所位於亞弧資訊科技基礎建設公司的附近。
(B) 已延長看診時間。
(C) 正在僱用新警衛。
(D) 建築物有許多分區。

151–152 廣告

傑佛森公寓公司 (JAC)：
位於法蘭西斯街的嶄新公寓

JAC 今年秋季即將開放嶄新的公寓大樓。此公寓大樓僅開放給不想住學校宿舍、卻又希望在校園生活圈中的麥德威大學學生承租。151 本大樓位置便利，距離巴雷特學生宿舍僅三個街區，152 穿越桑安傑斯公園的美麗自然步道僅需步行五分鐘，即可方便搭乘大眾運輸工具。大家可享受我們先進的健身中心，參加各種娛樂活動。152 所有公寓均包含私人廚房與客廳。大樓亦設有 24 小時開放的洗衣設施，配備全新的洗衣機與乾衣機。我們還有廣大的停車場，均為每位租客提供一個停車位。152 欲租從速，以免向隅。

151. 此廣告在推銷什麼？
(A) 大學的研習會系列活動
(B) 新事業的開幕訊息
(C) 為特定族群提供的住所
(D) 新增的健行步道

152. 廣告裡未提及什麼內容？
(A) 價格
(B) 地點
(C) 活動
(D) 停車位

153–154 簡訊串

安德魯・阮〔下午 2:34〕
帕拉狄恩文化館您好。我可以幫您什麼忙呢？

克羅伊・羅倫斯〔下午 2:35〕
我買了戲劇《伊利亞德家族》前排座位的票，但不巧的是我必須處理一些緊急事務。我在想是否能取消訂票並退款。153

安德魯・阮〔下午 2:36〕
很抱歉，開演前七天內無法退票。不過，在某些情況下，我們可以幫您把票換到其他日期。

克羅伊・羅倫斯〔下午 2:38〕
我的票適用這個規定嗎？

安德魯・阮〔下午 2:39〕
可以的。您想換到其他日期嗎？154

克羅伊・羅倫斯〔下午 2:41〕
那就太好了。154 我需要看一下我的行程表，然後再和你聯絡。

安德魯・阮〔下午 2:44〕
當然沒問題。

153. 羅倫斯女士為什麼要聯絡帕拉狄恩文化館？
(A) 想提出反饋
(B) 想升級座位
(C) 想詢問某表演者的資訊
(D) 想要求退款

154. 下午 2:41 的時候，羅倫斯女士的訊息「那就太好了」，最有可能是什麼意思？
(A) 她可以立即購買新票券
(B) 她會依照阮先生的建議去做
(C) 她下週可以去看一場表演
(D) 她將在線上觀賞表演

155–157 公告

致巴雷特咖啡廳 (BCH) 的所有顧客：

這是關於如何正確使用我們告示欄的公告。155

由於空間有限，告示欄上張貼的任何傳單，僅會保留 14 天。為了實施此項規定，我們要求所有張貼資料均須有 BCH 的日期貼紙，標示張貼日期。（請注意：我們會移除沒有貼上此貼紙的任何資料。）156 此外，不可張貼任何過大的傳單，或重複張貼相同活動的傳單。

若您有意在我們的告示欄張貼傳單，請和我們預約時間，一起討論資料內容。您至少要在預計張貼日的五天前，給我們看一下您的資料。157 傳單資料一經批准，我們會以電話通知您。

敬祝　安康

店長 提傑・詹森

155. 此公告的目的為何？
- **(A) 說明政策**
- (B) 通知顧客某項拓店計畫
- (C) 解釋部分資料被移除的原因
- (D) 廣告新店面

156. 告示欄出現哪一種資料會被徹下？
- (A) 推廣社交活動的資料
- (B) 張貼超過七天的資料
- **(C) 沒有日期貼紙的資料**
- (D) 包含公司標誌的資料

157. 關於張貼於 BCH 的資料，文中提及什麼注意事項？
- (A) 不能推廣產品。
- **(B) 必須提前五天出示資料。**
- (C) 必須事先付款。
- (D) 必須電郵給 BCH 辦公室。

158–160 報導

CityBeat.com/local

埃肯‧迪亞羅　撰
5 月 30 日

塔芭瑟‧林自 15 年前，開始在「吐溫＆羅斯」擔任記錄員。她因為該公司對當地社群的付出而受到激勵，因此就讀法學院。現在她不僅是知名法律事務所的合夥人之一，還負責領導在緬因大道開立法律事務所新分處，專門處理財產法的相關事務。 **158**

現今林女士經常是第一個抵達公司、又最晚下班的人。她就算不在公司，也是在搜尋資料或會見新客戶。不過，她表示自己很開心能長時間投入工作。她說道：「我們正在積累特殊的經驗，我很榮幸能參與其中。」

林女士表示，她在事務所各階層的經歷，造就了她現今的工作模式。 **159** 她平易近人、思慮周到，願意花時間傾聽他人，上至頂尖訴訟律師、下至新進實習生的想法。她表示：「每一個人的見解和經驗都很重要。每個人都需要他人的協助，才能盡力表現出色。」

林女士認為，雖然**事務所因僱用國內頂尖法學院的畢業生而受惠， 160 但「團隊合作與溝通能力，一直是成功的最大關鍵。」**

158. 此文章的主要目的為何？
- **(A) 簡介某律師**
- (B) 公布法律助理職缺
- (C) 討論近期的審判
- (D) 解釋法學院的新政策

159. 第三段第二行的「informs」，意思最接近何者？
- (A) 指示
- (B) 投資
- **(C) 影響**
- (D) 互動

160. 文中提及「吐溫＆羅斯」的哪些資訊？
- **(A) 會從有聲望的大學徵人。**
- (B) 近期遷至新辦公室。
- (C) 打贏幾件大宗財產官司。
- (D) 已僱用一些新實習生。

161–163 信函

卡瑪拉‧威廉斯
埃姆斯工業
84104 猶他州鹽湖城玫瑰木路 32 號

親愛的威廉斯女士：

您最後一期的《米卡莎雜誌》已於兩週前送達，但我們尚未收到您的續訂要求。 **163** 我們只想提醒您一下，以防您遺忘而發生此事。過去十年來，《米卡莎雜誌》總是能辨別室內空間的流行趨勢，含括地板建材圖樣、照明設計，以及有效的室內空間管理。 **161** 這種對貴公司生意有用的資源，其價值遠超於 55 美元的訂閱年費。不過，本通知內含續訂優惠，相當於一般訂閱年費的七折。 **162** 於 4 月 30 日前回函，便享有此項優惠。別錯過此寶貴的商業資源，馬上行動！

敬祝　安康

客服部人員
邁爾斯．史丹佛

附件

161. 威廉斯女士最有可能是什麼身分？
(A) 廣電業主管
(B) 雜誌編輯
(C) 企業會計
(D) 室內設計師

162. 威廉斯女士可獲得什麼優惠？
(A) 訂閱費折扣
(B) 免費廣告版面
(C) 個人諮詢服務
(D) 一些商品樣品

163. 「我們只想提醒您一下，以防您遺忘而發生此事。」最適合放在 [1]、[2]、[3]、[4] 的哪個位置？
(A) [1]
(B) [2]
(C) [3]
(D) [4]

164–167　網路聊天室

雪倫．威斯特〔下午 1:02 〕
希望大家午餐用餐愉快。公司打算在下週二或下週三召開與近期合併案有關的說明會。我想了解一下，各團隊哪天可以出席。公司強制要求所有員工都要參加。164

葛羅莉亞．福崎〔下午 1:04 〕
人事部週二全天排滿了職缺面試。165 不過，我們週三的行程很彈性。說明會何時召開呢？

雪倫．威斯特〔下午 1:06 〕
我們還沒訂定確切時間。所有經理必須先讓我們知道自己偏好的時間。奧利佛，哪個時間對你來說比較好？

奧利佛．費格森〔下午 1:08 〕
資訊科技部的員工通常下午比較忙，所以週二上午會比較理想。167

雪倫．威斯特〔下午 1:09 〕
如果會議廳在這幾天都有開放，我們或許可以分別召開兩場說明會。葛羅莉亞，可以請妳確認一下，會議廳是否可以使用嗎？

葛羅莉亞．福崎〔下午 1:12 〕
根據系統顯示，會議廳週二上午和週三下午已有活動佔用。

雪倫．威斯特〔下午 1:14 〕
是否能請妳聯絡已預訂週二上午使用會議廳的部門呢？請查看他們是否願意更改活動時間。如果他們同意的話，就請預訂這兩天上午 10 點到上午 11 點的會議廳。166

葛羅莉亞．福崎〔下午 1:18 〕
聯絡好了。166 我剛和卡特曼女士講完電話。我們現在這兩天都能使用會議廳。我會要求我的團隊參加週三上午的說明會。

奧利佛．費格森〔下午 1:19 〕
我們還是維持週二上午參加。167

164. 此討論內容的主題為何？
(A) 會見潛在客戶
(B) 更新電腦系統
(C) 分析一些問卷結果
(D) 安排說明會的時間

165. 文中提到關於福崎女士的哪些資訊？
(A) 她這週不會有空。
(B) 她是人事部的員工。
(C) 她將延後她的預約事務。
(D) 她是卡特曼女士的經理。

166. 下午 1:18，福崎女士的訊息「聯絡好了」意指什麼？
(A) 她已經交出申請表。
(B) 她已設法完成場地預約。
(C) 她已提早完成某專案。
(D) 她已修訂某文件。

167. 資訊科技團隊何時會參加説明會？

   (A) 週二上午

   (B) 週二下午

   (C) 週三上午

   (D) 週三下午

168–171 資訊

俄亥俄州代頓市，中西部室內設計博覽會 (MIDF)

使用條款

A. 合約： 所有批准參展的廠商，務必最晚於活動開始前兩週，填妥所有相關文件並簽章。MIDF 針對適切的參展內容制定嚴格的規範，**若參展廠商無法配合，將不提供攤位。** 168

B. 費用： 會議廳攤位空間開放給參展廠商使用的時段為上午 9 點至晚上 7 點，包括對外開放前後的一小時。**攤位單日費用為 435 美元，或兩日 800 美元。** 169 攤位的使用可能會產生額外費用（請參閱條款 C 和 D）。

C. 攤位： 會議廳為參展廠商提供的攤位空間為 14 英尺 ×14 英尺。一個地板式插座具有 4 個插孔 (120V)。關於擺設布置、網路連線或招牌輸出等服務，請洽 vendor_info@midf.org。請注意，上述服務會產生額外費用。此外，攤位舉辦抽獎、競賽或其他活動，可能導致群眾聚集，請務必事先取得 MIDF 的批准，以確保這些活動不會給同行帶來過多的負擔。 170 而所有供應茶點的參展廠商，將被額外收取 10 美元的垃圾清理費。

D. 資料分發： 參展廠商可分發傳單類資料、樣品和推廣物品。不過，基於安全限制，觀展者僅能攜帶會議廳所提供的提袋。因此，我們強烈建議，任何欲分發的物品必須符合 5 英吋 ×15 英吋的提袋開口大小。 171

168. 根據此份資訊內容，申請攤位遭拒的原因可能為何？

   (A) 參展廠商的產品不適合該活動。

   (B) 公司未準時付款。

   (C) 未提供公司聯絡資訊。

   (D) 參展廠商要求更大的攤位。

169. 文中提到關於中西部室內設計博覽會的哪些訊息？

   (A) 為期兩天。

   (B) 為參觀者提供免費上網的服務。

   (C) 每年都在代頓市舉辦。

   (D) 入場費 10 美元。

170. 根據此份資訊內容，MIDF 員工的工作目標最有可能是什麼？

   (A) 吸引大量參展廠商

   (B) 確保所有參展廠商均能公平使用空間

   (C) 為國外參觀者安排交通事宜

   (D) 將相似產品的參展公司歸類為同一組

171. 關於 MIDF 參展廠商的描述，何者正確？

   (A) 僅能帶來特定人數的員工。

   (B) 必須隨時佩戴識別證。

   (C) 博覽會開放前的一小時，攤位將接受視察。

   (D) 推廣物品不可超過特定尺寸。

172–175 網頁

倫敦 訊（8 月 8 日）——熱門手機應用程式「美食報報」的創辦者「伊利提公司」，於週二晚間宣布了新一波的投資計畫。該投資計畫將此公司的企業價值提升到五千萬美元。該應用程式的使用量攀升後，即促成了此投資計畫。該應用程式向已註冊的本地用戶徵求用餐建議，而非由匿名用戶推薦。 172

伊利提公司執行長安琪拉・莫斯表示：「我們的想法很單純。我們想引導大家根據自己的飲食喜好，前往合適的用餐地點。用戶能透過此應用程式閱讀關於餐廳菜單、地點和環境的深入評價。『美食報報』讓大家能輕鬆選擇最佳的嘗鮮去處。」 173

雖然應用程式以消費者為主要的使用對象，但受歡迎的程度，已經不再侷限於原本的目標受眾。**175** 店家一樣會使用此應用程式。經營倫敦餐酒館老店之一的丹尼爾·米勒認為，「美食報報」幫助他改善下滑的業績。**175** 米勒表示：「我們剛開始不知道哪裡出錯，因為大家都說我們的食物很好吃。然而，查看一些評價之後，我們發現原來是員工人數不足，導致無法及時送餐。而我們已在一個月內改善。」**174**

您可至各大應用程式商店平台，或網站 ElliptiCorp.com/insider，下載「美食報報」。

---

172. 可從文中得知「美食報報」的哪些訊息？
(A) 任命了新的執行長。
(B) 六個月前上線。
(C) 貼文均來自當地居民。
(D) 用戶均不具名。

173. 根據此網頁內容，應用程式「美食報報」有何功能？
(A) 安排食物外送
(B) 找到合適的餐飲店
(C) 餐廳訂位
(D) 購買廚房用品

174. 米勒先生很有可能改變了什麼？
(A) 某些產品的價格
(B) 員工人數
(C) 職訓的日期
(D) 商店的營業時間

175.「店家一樣會使用此應用程式。」最適合放在 [1]、[2]、[3]、[4] 的哪一個位置？
(A) [1]
(B) [2]
(C) [3]
(D) [4]

176–180 文章和電子郵件

卡佛頓共和國
商業聚焦

由尚·克里斯多夫·阿由布所自營管理的「貝魯特咖啡廳」，於十年前開幕，**180** 至今仍然屹立不搖，這得歸功於他的商業知識。他於餐飲業服務多年，深知每家餐廳需要花上一段時間，才能累積可靠的客群和獲得利潤。不過，連阿由布先生都料想不到，當地的經濟衰退情況會持續這麼久。

阿由布先生上週二接受「卡佛頓商會」的訪問，為事業才剛起步的餐廳老闆提供一些建議。他強調，一個事業能否長期生存，均取決於周圍的社區。他表示：「很多消費者一個月只會外出用餐幾次，所以你必須具備獨特的賣點，來吸引他們光顧你的餐廳。」**176**

他接著解釋：「卡佛頓是一個多元化的地區，很多人都習慣吃黎巴嫩料理。這對我早期的經營是一大幫助。還有一些提供優質新鮮食材的特產市場。」

在談話中，阿由布先生大多強調及早準備好重大開銷的重要性，尤其是刊登廣告的部分。他表示：「先預估你所認為的有效廣告會需要多少費用，然後往上加至三倍。」早期投入廣播和報紙促銷廣告的做法，讓貝魯特咖啡廳有辦法繼續營業，並在熬過辛苦的頭四年後，開始轉虧為盈。**177**

如今，阿由布先生的餐廳已有一群忠實粉絲，而他留住顧客的建議很簡單。他表示：「我們試著以每週特餐和提供常客優惠的方式，讓客人迫不及待再度光臨。**178** 此外，如果客人對於餐點有特殊要求，我的廚師們也會盡力完成。畢竟，讓顧客感到開心才是重點。」

收件人：米娜‧薩拉札
<msalazar@dfu.edu>
寄件人：瑞薩‧寇十
<rezak@carvertoncc.org>
日期：11 月 18 日
主旨：新訊

親愛的米娜：

我很開心得知妳從餐飲學校畢業。我想妳已經開始在找工作了，所以我想寫信告訴妳，卡佛頓這邊有個職缺。**179** 這是早班的廚房助理工作，必須幫忙備料、烘烤食物與處理外送事宜。妳可以到 www.beirutcafe.com/recruit 查看徵人啟事。老闆是我念蘇利文大學時的同學。**180** 別忘了提到妳在梅爾夏令營的烹飪經驗。

祝　好

瑞薩

---

176. 文章中第二段第四行的「pull」，意思最接近何者？
(A) 伸展
(B) 吸引
(C) 移除
(D) 撕除

177. 阿由布先生如何幫助自己的餐廳挺過經濟衰退的時期？
(A) 他向卡佛頓商會貸款。
(B) 他只和當地的農場做生意。
(C) 他搬到較小的大樓裡。
(D) 他已先預估初期的高額費用。

178. 貝魯特咖啡廳最近創下佳績的成功因素為何？
(A) 精選有機食材
(B) 擁有知名主廚
(C) 豐富的餐點選擇
(D) 致力於服務常客

179. 寇十先生寫這封電子郵件的原因為何？
(A) 要求更換網站
(B) 推廣新餐廳的地點
(C) 說明準備某菜餚的方法
(D) 通知一項職缺

180. 可從文中得知關於寇十先生的哪些訊息？
(A) 他和阿由布先生就讀同一所學校。
(B) 他正要為自己的新餐廳僱用職員。
(C) 貝魯特咖啡廳的某項餐點是他設計的。
(D) 薩拉札小姐是他在餐飲學校的學生。

181–185 廣告和表格

艾杜林學園的海外數位行銷課程

您是否曾考慮過提升國際業績的方法？您是否考慮在國外網站投放廣告？如果您有以上考量，歡迎至網站 www.eduline.org 建立帳號，報名專為海外視聽眾所設計的一系列網路行銷互動課程。**181** 將有行銷資深團隊，與大家探討如何運用簡單的電腦工具，來吸引全球市場中的企業。**183** 此系列課程將於 10 月 17 日星期四下午 3:20 至晚上 6:30（夏威夷標準時間）進行現場直播 **181** 。

總共有三場簡報會：

「以照片達到推銷目的：中國的病毒式影像分享技巧」——馬瑞‧波克 主講

「善用自動翻譯功能」——索拉‧韓 主講

「在越南運用社群網絡服務」——瑞尼‧托瑞斯 主講 **184**

如果您線上報名時遇到問題，請於 10 月 15 日前，隨時撥打 1-800-555-3627 聯絡拉斯‧歐洛夫即可。**182**

您在課程直播時段忙得無法分身嗎？可至我們網站的串流區觀看影片。現場直播後的 12 小時內，均可觀賞每場簡報會的內容。

www.eduline.org/feedback_survey/1017

親愛的喬許・科提茲：

感謝您報名艾杜林學園的海外數位行銷課程。我們想邀請您提供反饋，以便我們精進往後的課程。

請評分課程（1 = 沒有幫助 5 = 很有幫助）

課程主題的實用性	5
主講人的資訊和講解清晰度	5
課程主題的相關範例	5

您最喜歡哪個部分？

托瑞斯先生的簡報幫我對如何更有效推銷我的產品有了更多的了解。**184** 簡報內容真的很有深度，主講方式亦充滿熱忱。我很感謝他撥出滿多時間來回答所有學員的問題。

您希望往後的課程能有哪些改進？ **185**

我目前住在倫敦，我必須等到凌晨 1:20 才能參加現場直播課程。我想如果有更多課程時段的選擇，許多學員應該都會很感激。**185**

181. 可從文中得知課程的哪些訊息？
(A) 僅開放夏威夷的商界老闆參加。
(B) 課程將開放整整一個月的時間。
(C) 專為研究生所設計。
(D) 將以線上教學的方式進行。

182. 根據廣告內容，讀者為何要聯絡歐洛夫先生？
(A) 取得上課方式
(B) 要求影片檔
(C) 提出新活動的主題
(D) 詢問主講人問題

183. 可從文中得知主講人的哪些訊息？
(A) 他們是會議籌辦人。
(B) 他們是行銷科系教授。
(C) 他們均曾在艾杜林工作。
(D) 他們在海外廣告方面擁有豐富經驗。

184. 可從文中得知科提茲先生的哪些訊息？
(A) 他會在十月底搬到倫敦。
(B) 他打算在越南推銷自己的商品。
(C) 他常超時工作。
(D) 他常參加專業研習會。

185. 科提茲先生建議課程的哪個方面做出改變？
(A) 舉辦場所
(B) 報名程序
(C) 價格
(D) 時間安排

186–190 電子郵件、公告和報導

收件人：akatrakis@ecodress.org **186**
寄件人：bmunoz@texcycle.com
日期：2 月 12 日
主旨：三月預定行程

親愛的卡崔琪斯女士：

此訊息的目的是要向您確認，紡織品回收公司的卡車將於 3 月 26 日下午抵達您的公司。**188** 所捐贈的衣物如已分類，將有利於加快我們的收取程序，我們不勝感激。**186** 請注意，您需簽名才能收到款項。

「紡織品回收公司」為回收的二手衣物和織物，提供每天浮動的市場費率。目前亞麻布料的價格比上個月略減。雪紡紗和皮革的價格，則因為用量變少的關係而創新低。不過，由於冬季快結束，我們目前在尋找聚酯纖維，此布料的價格從去年 11 月就漲了三倍。**188** 某家越南公司在未來幾個月內，會向我們盡數收購此布料。**189**

很感謝能與您做生意。

敬祝　安康

紡織品回收公司
顧客關係專員　邦妮・木諾茲

環保服飾公司 186

本公司自 1986 年起就開始在都會區服務，絕對是您首選的二手服飾衣物商店。186 我們也永遠歡迎大家捐贈衣物！請將捐贈衣物置於以下地點：187

A 籃：大衣、夾克和毛衣

B 籃：長褲、襯衫和短褲

置物架：手套、披肩和其他配件 187

目前特定絕緣布料的需求量很高。因此，我們暫且從現在到 3 月 25 日為止，歡迎大家捐贈保溫物品，例如冷藏箱、冬季床組和鞋墊。188

環保服飾公司透過衣物回收計畫來保護地球。如果您有任何需求，只要詢問結帳櫃檯的人員即可。

海防市　訊（10 月 3 日）—— 博卡特公司宣布新推出健行專用靴系列「疾走 DX」。此新系列鞋款非常適合極端的氣候條件，包括溫度會驟降至攝氏零下 55 度（華氏零下 67 度）的高海拔長途徒步運動。此鞋款以全新開發的客製化織法，運用合成絕緣材質來保護足部。「疾走 DX」亦為採用超過 70% 的回收材質所製的第一款高效能鞋款，多數材質均來自回收的舊衣。「疾走 DX」將於下週開賣，由河內市的博卡特總店獨家販售。189 國際通路將於 10 月 31 日開賣，190 而博卡特將於 10 月 15 日前開始將新鞋款配送至全越南的零售商。

---

186. 卡崔琪斯女士最有可能從事什麼工作？
- (A) 設計女性服飾
- (B) 為時尚雜誌寫稿
- **(C) 經營二手服飾店**
- (D) 經營紡織工廠

187. 根據公告內容，圍巾這類物品應置於哪裡？
- (A) A 籃
- (B) B 籃
- (C) 結帳櫃檯
- **(D) 置物架**

188. 環保服飾公司為什麼要求大家在 3 月 25 日前捐贈保溫物品？
- **(A) 因為買家隔天會來取貨**
- (B) 因為冬季很快就要結束
- (C) 因為即將開始促銷
- (D) 因為即將進新貨

189. 博卡特公司的新款健行靴，最有可能使用何種材質？
- (A) 亞麻布
- (B) 雪紡紗
- (C) 皮革
- **(D) 聚酯纖維**

190. 越南以外的地區，何時可購得新鞋款？
- (A) 10 月 3 日
- (B) 10 月 10 日
- (C) 10 月 15 日
- **(D) 10 月 31 日**

191–195 手冊、行程表和報導

納斯威爾商業發展委員會
為應屆畢業生設計的特殊講座

納斯威爾商業發展委員會 (KCDC) 將於 1 月 4 日至 7 日，在納斯威爾河岸會議中心，為有意募資創立網路公司的應屆畢業生，舉辦一系列研習會。191

每年與無數新公司合作的獨立顧問大衛·麥克斯，將與學員聊聊撰寫商業策略提案摘要的基本技巧。 **192** 克里斯·歐卡羅爾則會探討，以網路廣告來吸引投資人注意力的方法。奧莉維亞·亞瑞塔將解說群眾募資或從網路捐款獲得小額資金，能對創業初期帶來什麼樣的良好幫助。而最後一天的課程將幫助學員做好準備，學會向實際投資人解說自己的願景和目標。

多數課程均為免費，但投資人簡報會的部分，需要繳交 25 美元的講義費。 **194**

如需報名，請傳送電子郵件至 courses@kcdc.org。

KCDC 課程時間表
為應屆畢業生設計的特殊課程

日期、星期與課程名稱	場地	時間
1月4日星期三 **192**		
● 研擬銷售話術	會議室 B	上午 9:30
● 商業計畫基礎課程 **192**	會議室 C	上午 10:30
● 個別諮詢 **193**	714 室	上午 11:30
1月5日星期四		
● 網路推銷	會議室 B	上午 10:30
● 個別諮詢 **193**	714 室	上午 11:30
1月6日星期五		
● 公開募資	會議室 B	上午 10:30
● 個別諮詢 **193**	714 室	上午 11:30
1月7日星期六		
● 投資人簡報練習	會議廳 A	上午 10:30

KCDC 研習會　圓滿成功

納斯威爾　訊（1月10日）——滿懷希望的各行各業老闆，參加了專為協助經營其新創公司而安排的四天研習會與課程，而這全得歸功於納斯威爾商業發展委員會 (KCDC)。

打算設立餐廳評價網站的大衛·魏斯納表示：「研習會提供的豐富資訊，與透過網路來推廣我的事業有關。」

另一位學員是希望開設數位教育公司的瑪莉·金。她特別開心能有機會練習向投資人做簡報。 **194** 因為在此練習課程中，講師能幫她評估公司的主要賣點。她表示：「多虧課程所提供的資訊，讓我能夠更有效的向投資人傳達訊息。」

由於大家的反饋十分正面且出席率高，因此 KCDC 會長桑鐸克·塔賓，預計於七月再舉辦一次此類活動。 **195**

191. 根據手冊內容，此計畫的目的為何？
(A) 聘僱系列課程的講師
(B) 提升 KCDC 的聲望
(C) 教導畢業生如何取得開公司的資金
(D) 幫助專業從商人士拓展網絡

192. 可從文中得知麥克斯先生的哪些訊息？
(A) 他已於週三演講。
(B) 他深諳網路促銷手法。
(C) 他負責管理 KCDC 的會計團隊。
(D) 他負責分析學員的反饋。

193. 課程時間表透露出哪些訊息？
(A) 所有活動均於相同的會議室舉辦。
(B) 簡報練習開始的時間比其他課程早。
(C) 學員會有數次私人諮詢的機會。
(D) 每天只有一堂課。

194. 可從文中得知金小姐的哪些訊息？
(A) 她針對簡短演說方面給予建議。
(B) 她想聽塔賓先生的演講。
(C) 她很感謝亞瑞塔女士的反饋。
(D) 她有向 KCDC 繳費。

195. 文中提及 KCDC 的哪些資訊？
(A) 已由塔賓先生經營多年。
(B) 已向魏斯納先生提供投資資金。
(C) 在納斯威爾並不有名。
(D) 將於夏季提供相似課程。

寄件人：e.hassan@typeflow.com
收件人：m.lim@kare.edu
日期：6 月 30 日
主旨：會計課程

親愛的林女士：

我剛報名參加您的專業會計訓練證照課程，並將於今年秋季開始上第一期。您網站上的常見問題頁面寫著「AC113：會計遵循準則」是此證照的必修課，但我已經在奧克拉荷馬州立大學上過卡洛琳·史密斯教授的類似課程。 199 因此，我想問問看是否能退選此必修課。 196 此外，我不太確定什麼樣的上課順序最合適。希望您能給我一些建議，感激不盡。 198

艾略特·哈珊　敬上

寄件人：m.lim@kare.edu
收件人：e.hassan@typeflow.com
日期：7 月 1 日
主旨：關於：會計課程

親愛的哈珊先生：

我想先恭喜您想取得會計證照的決定。不巧的是，我們無法讓您退選 AC113 課程。此課程提供了最新適用的「財務通報法」基礎知識，而在其他課程裡，也會經常以此知識為參考資料。

在秋季學期中，您的必修課包括「AC102：會計基本知識」，我們將於某間電腦教室上課。

由於您是新學生，因此您可在課程指南裡，查找與本教學機構規定政策有關的詳細說明。以下單元的內容與您的課程有關：

專業會計訓練證照概述：第 1-5 頁
必修會計課：第 6-10 頁
選修會計課：第 11-12 頁

建議的上課順序：第 22-23 頁 198

您應該會於本週收到我們郵寄的指南手冊。 197 您翻閱後，如有任何疑問，可與我聯絡。

敬祝　安康

卡爾教學機構
梅·林

卡爾教學機構電腦教室

卡爾教職員和學生均可使用配備完善的電腦教室（以下列出更多資訊），以滿足其需求。

一般用途：200 教室
具備會計和文書處理軟體的 50 台電腦；200 具有卡爾教職員證或學生識別證的人均可使用。

會計用途：210 教室
具備現行一般會計軟體的 15 台電腦；200 只有報名第一年課程的學生可使用。 199

專業用途：212 教室
具備薪資與稅務會計軟體、以及銀行金融模擬應用程式的 21 台電腦，200 報名以下課程的學生可使用：「AC203：企業報稅」與「AC215：職員專款」，或經教職員許可，即可使用。

考試用途：315 教室
具備模擬各種會計情境 200 的證照考試電腦，僅供證照考試期間使用。

各教室的公告均列出上課時段，以及可供個人自由使用的時段。一樓的休息區則有學生和大眾均可使用的其他電腦，並且全年開放。

196. 哈珊先生為何提及「會計遵循準則」課程？

(A) 了解看看他是不是一定要修此課
(B) 詢問教授的相關資訊
(C) 了解看看是不是能透過網路上課
(D) 詢問教科書的價格

197. 可從文中得知指南手冊的哪些訊息？
(A) 有提供教職員的聯絡資料。
(B) 內含有聲 CD。
(C) 哈珊先生很快就會收到。
(D) 林女士有協助編輯此手冊。

198. 指南裡的哪幾頁最能回答哈珊先生的
疑問？
(A) 第 1-5 頁
(B) 第 6-10 頁
(C) 第 11-12 頁
(D) 第 22-23 頁

199.「會計遵循準則」課最有可能在哪間
教室上課？
(A) 一般用途教室
(B) 會計用途教室
(C) 專業用途教室
(D) 考試用途教室

200. 關於電腦教室的描述，何者正確？
(A) 都有會計軟體。
(B) 都有預約使用的時間表。
(C) 都有技術支援人員。
(D) 都 24 小時開放使用。

ACTUAL TEST ②

101. 莫寧特貨運公司現在已和 32 家主流服飾零售商簽約。
(A) 合約
(B) 合約
(C) 承包商
(D) 承包中

102. 在使用桑尼亞股份有限公司的商標前，務必取得官方授權。
(A) 取得
(B) 被取得
(C) 取得中
(D) 取得中

103. 既然客戶帳戶已增加了 45%，客服部門應僱用更多人員。
(A) 因此
(B) 由於
(C) 儘管
(D) 既然

104. 費特里股份有限公司流失到普藍特企業的客戶比例最大。
(A) 最遠的
(B) 最深的
(C) 最大的
(D) 最淺的

105. 鹿島女士的會計職務，包括整理和計算近期合作客戶的資產。
(A) 應負責任的
(B) 會計
(C) 視為
(D) 帳戶

106. 醫師建議每天將冰塊敷於腫脹部位約二十至三十分鐘。
(A) 藉由……
(B) 像……一樣
(C) 至
(D) 上方

107. 伯瑞恩股份有限公司的人資部，主動給付獎金來促進員工產能。
(A) 促進中
(B) 促進
(C) 促進
(D) 將促進

108. 我已經加入我的設計作品集範本供您考量。
(A) 考量
(B) 預期
(C) 解釋
(D) 參與

109. 儘管該任務僅花了五小時就完成，但員工仍可獲得全日薪的報酬。
(A) 之前
(B) 為了……
(C) 只要
(D) 正確

110. 電視機在包裝之前，會先經過徹底檢查，以確保是否運作正常。
(A) 指派
(B) 選定
(C) 管理
(D) 檢查

111. 主辦委員會的每個人，都對成功舉辦工作坊一事有所貢獻。
(A) 無論是誰
(B) 每個人
(C) 彼此
(D) 互相

112. 克雷文金融機構已簽下契約，準備承租空間較大的辦公室。
(A) 已簽名
(B) 已定義
(C) 已從事
(D) 已涉及

113. 史坎創個人理財軟體能幫您追蹤帳戶、建立預算和處理付款。
(A) 您自己
(B) 您的（持有物）
(C) 您的
(D) 您

114. 為許多公司供應客製化玻璃製品的普瑞茲·格雷斯爾公司，剛慶祝於伯恩開業150年的成就。
(A) 加寬
(B) 寬廣的
(C) 寬度
(D) 廣大地

115. 所有公告內容在對外公布以前，務必先取得公關部經理的批准。
(A) 大幅地
(B) 完全地
(C) 絕對地
(D) 對外地

116. 國際裝訂聯盟代表了全球書籍出版社的利益。
(A) 重現
(B) 代表
(C) 運作
(D) 貢獻

117. 在您前往面試前，請先填妥信封內隨附的應徵者資料表。
(A) 隨附中
(B) 隨附
(C) 隨附的
(D) 附件

118. 我們已發出曼徹斯特營造股份有限公司，收購西斯造景公司的提案備忘錄。
(A) 遵循
(B) 收購
(C) 附件
(D) 文件

119. 許多理財應用程式僅能匯款至國內銀行，而「金時」應用程式還能匯款至海外銀行。
(A) 在那之前
(B) 目前
(C) 全程
(D) 還能……

120. 副總已強調明年獲得新客戶的重要性。
(A) 治理
(B) 下令
(C) 強調
(D) 要求

121. 帕克女士已證實自己是研發團隊裡忠誠又具創新思維的一員。
(A) 她自己
(B) 它自己
(C) 它
(D) 她

122. 奎特梅因解決方案公司的代表人塔莉亞·古拉樂女士，強調該公司支持較嚴格的品質標準。
(A) 意識
(B) 放置
(C) 公平性
(D) 支持

123. 該商店大量展示了此熱門科幻作家的最新小説。
(A) 有天賦的
(B) 預設
(C) 大量的
(D) 感恩的

124. 迪米特科技公司打算在下個月的可再生能源博覽會之前，升級可攜式裝置。
(A) 與……相反
(B) 儘管
(C) 除了……之外
(D) 在……之前

125. 鬥牛犬拳擊公司的儲藏室既堅固又安全，而且空間也大到足夠容納車輛。
(A) 好
(B) 完全地
(C) 親近地
(D) 足夠

126. 根據金先生的計算，需要300平方公尺的大理石磁磚，才能完成大廳地板的鋪設。
(A) 計算
(B) 已計算
(C) 計算
(D) 計算

127. 無論您何時在法蘭克林家具公司購買辦公桌，均可享任何一款椅子的六折優惠。

(A) 無論何時
(B) 雖然
(C) 畢竟
(D) 諸如……

128. 患者一直都很感激我們努力減少候診時間。

(A) 感激的
(B) 感謝
(C) 感激
(D) 欣賞中

129. 拋光作業完工後，大廳地板上的刮痕就幾乎看不見了。

(A) 不真實地
(B) 幾乎沒有
(C) 正確地
(D) 精準地

130. 股東已要求特朗先生調查能降低曼谷廠營運開支的所有可行辦法。

(A) 調查
(B) 調查中
(C) 調查
(D) 已調查

PART 6 P. 41-44

131-134 文章

關西公園主管機關於今天上午，延後做出是否要在關西國家森林新增健行步道的決定。公園負責人麗莎·長谷川在今天的記者會上表示，公園主管機關在繼續執行此專案之前，必須針對環境進行更多研究。目前僅對遊客開放三條步道。然而，自從關西森林度假村開幕後，此森林已吸引非常多的觀光客。分析師將健行活動增加的情況，歸因於該度假村。根據長谷川女士的說法，公園主管機關將於四個月後，再討論此議題。

131. (A) 質疑
(B) 確認
(C) 批准
(D) 延後

132. (A) 一旦
(B) 在……之後
(C) 在……之前
(D) 在……期間

133. (A) 長谷川女士建議，所有健行者均需攜帶護具。
(B) 公園主管機關希望聘僱資深導遊。
(C) 目前僅對遊客開放三條步道。
(D) 關西最近制定全新的環境法。

134. (A) 增加
(B) 廣告
(C) 失望
(D) 停滯

135-138 電子郵件

寄件人：雪莉·渡邊
收件人：全體員工
日期：8月12日
主旨：系統更新

今天所有員工電腦的資安軟體，將會升級至最新版本。下午1點就會自動執行升級程序。安裝程序執行的時候，雖然大家還是能夠存取程式，但是你們可能會注意到系統運行的速度沒有往常快速。一旦完成安裝，電腦需要重開機。不過，如果大家正在處理某些事務，可以在自己比較方便的時間完成此重開機程序。我們先針對任何干擾情況，提前向大家道歉。

135. (A) 我們正在修訂資安規範。
(B) 我們的警衛室會開到今天晚上8點為止。
(C) 下午1點就會自動執行升級程序。
(D) 此升級僅能在特定電腦型號運行。

136. (A) 記得
(B) 注意到
(C) 説服
(D) 批評

137. (A) 事實上
(B) 尤其是
(C) 因而
(D) 不過

138. (A) 干擾的
(B) 干擾
(C) 干擾
(D) 被干擾

139–142 文章

過去四十年來，恩尼斯特・方一直在赫茲菲爾德市設計與販售桌子和櫃子。這個月底，他終將要向忠誠的顧客道別，並在當地的社區大學就任新職位。方先生將會同時教課與指導接班人。他表示：「我花了多年時間，讓自己的工藝更加完美，現在我想向年輕同仁分享這份熱忱與技藝。」方先生的商店永久歇業之前，他打算為剩下的商品舉辦特賣會。幾款獨特的家具將降價出售。部分自有桌子和櫃子，一樣可供購買。該活動將於下週六的下午 2 點開始。

139. (A) 把……定下
(B) 終於
(C) 最後的
(D) 完結篇

140. (A) 方先生將會同時教課與指導接班人。
(B) 方先生在大學就讀時，一邊在亞洲的一間家飾公司兼職。
(C) 他的產品每年都會在會展中展出。
(D) 他的商店提供全市最優惠的價格。

141. (A) 畫作
(B) 電子產品
(C) 服飾
(D) 家具

142. (A) 反而
(B) 鮮少
(C) 也
(D) 簡單地

143–146 備忘錄

寄件人：TW 電子公司董事長 凱文・紐頓
收件人：TW 電子公司全體員工
日期：3 月 12 日
主旨：收購案的最新進展

大家可能都有留意到我們收購威瑟曼科技公司一事，將於 5 月 2 日進入結案階段。從那天開始，我們將更名為「TWW 電子企業」。此收購案將使我們成為國內規模最大的消費類電子產品供應商。

大家可能會想知道，此收購案會對大家產生的影響。幸好，大家的職稱、職務與薪資，仍將維持目前與 TW 電子公司簽訂勞動契約時所指明的內容。其實，公司正在考慮設立更多職位。

儘管如此，大家在未來幾個月內，還是會看到許多異動。我們將於 4 月 3 日上午 9 點，在大禮堂舉辦的下一季度會議中討論這些異動。我們會確保屆時解答大家所有的疑問。

143. (A) 在一旁
(B) 之後；晚一點
(C) 直到
(D) 往後

144. (A) 供應商
(B) 供應
(C) 供應中
(D) 已供應

145. (A) 我們將開始徵求能取代現任董事長的合適人選。
(B) 大家具體的職務可能會有某程度的差別。
(C) 我們將會傳送確認異動的新契約給大家。
(D) 其實，公司正在考慮設立更多職位。

146. (A) 我們。
(B) ……也不。
(C) 這些。
(D) 它。

PART 7   P. 45-65

147-148 徵才廣告

艾斯本格洛夫

「艾斯本格洛夫」將為 5 月 31 日在蘭諾克斯會議中心對面新開幕的據點，**147** 徵求櫃台人員、房務人員、禮賓接待員和維修人員。櫃台人員必須具備兩年以上的顧客關係工作經驗，而禮賓接待員則需一年或以上的工作經驗。房務人員和維修人員的部分，如有相關工作經驗者尤佳，不過我們會針對基層人員進行訓練。**148** 下週 5 月 22 日和 23 日將進行面試。求職者請攜帶履歷表和其他相關文件。如需了解更多資訊，請至 www.aspengrove.com 查詢。

147. 艾斯本格洛夫是什麼樣的事業體？

(A) 連鎖飯店
(B) 製造廠
(C) 造景公司
(D) 會議設施

148. 可從文中得知徵才職位的哪些訊息？

(A) 多數職位均需要有過往的工作經驗。
(B) 所有職位必須在 5 月 23 日前找到人選。
(C) 求職者可在任何公司據點應徵。
(D) 所有職位均提供支薪的職訓。

149-150 簡訊串

米契爾‧宋〔下午 2:07〕
嗨，我在校園裡看到徵人傳單，內容是想找有興趣的學生到野生動物保育協會，當會員募款活動的志工。傳單說傳簡訊到此號碼，以便了解提供協助的方式。**149**

艾琳‧門多薩〔下午 2:08〕
謝謝您的洽詢！我們目前正準備舉辦藝術品拍賣會來募款。我們需要有人幫忙聯絡藝術家，並安排他們捐獻作品的相關事宜。我們需仰賴此次拍賣會，來資助今年的活動，因此我們需要他們的支持。

米契爾‧宋〔下午 2:11〕
沒問題！我很樂意幫忙。可以請你告訴我你們的地點，還有可以拜訪的時間嗎？我下午 5 點就結束教課了。**150**

艾琳‧門多薩〔下午 2:13〕
好的，可以請您給我您的電話號碼嗎？我一旦接到更多人的響應，就能排定最終的時間表。屆時我會再傳送更多資訊給您。

米契爾‧宋〔下午 2:14〕
當然沒問題。我的電話是 555-9423。我很高興能幫上忙。

149. 宋先生為什麼要聯絡門多薩女士？
(A) 他要捐款
(B) 他要針對某課程提出反饋
(C) 想詢問某志工職位的資訊
(D) 他想預約展覽攤位

150. 下午 2:11，宋先生的訊息「我下午 5 點就結束教課了」，最有可能是什麼意思？
(A) 他擔心自己開會會遲到。
(B) 他打算晚一點再打給門多薩女士。
(C) 他傍晚有時間去幫忙。
(D) 他希望門多薩女士能載他一程。

151–153 資訊

國立博物館館長協會

8 月 15 日 –17 日，康乃爾大學
紐約州伊薩卡市
第十屆年度會議

用餐選擇

歡迎參加國立博物館館長協會第十屆年度會議。 151 我們鼓勵與會者於奧利弗・查登廳登記處報到時，購買預付餐卡。餐卡含括早、午、晚餐，一天的餐卡是 20 美元，三天的餐卡是 55 美元。報到時會一起發送會議通行證，請務必隨時佩戴。雖然餐卡可自由選購，但如果未購買餐卡，與會者每餐將需要支付全額 10 美元。請注意，餐卡僅能用於大學校園的範圍內。153

校園裡的餐館於上午 6 點開始營業，晚上 9 點打烊。瑞斯里廳與愛佩爾餐廳均供應自助餐，152 亦設有咖啡廳。威勒德・史崔特廳則供應亞洲、中東與拉丁美洲料理等國際美食選擇。152 請參閱會議行程表裡的校園地圖，以便得知符合您口味的餐飲店位置。

會議場地附近亦有許多位於校園外的用餐選擇，包括「澤西麥克燒烤」、「克里斯賓餐酒館」以及「帝國披薩」。

---

151. 可從文中得知國立博物館館長協會的哪些訊息？
(A) 與會者均於網路報名參加。
(B) 協會正為賓客舉辦特殊晚宴。
(C) 第一場專業聚會是在十年前舉辦。
(D) 由國際館長參加。

152. 哪一廳不會為會議出席者供應午餐？
(A) 奧利弗・查登廳
(B) 瑞斯里廳
(C) 威勒德・史崔特廳
(D) 愛佩爾餐廳

153. 關於會議場地以外的用餐地點，以下敘述何者正確？
(A) 此類餐廳不會接受會議發行的餐卡。
(B) 午餐收取 10 美元。
(C) 會議行程表裡的地圖亦有顯示此類餐廳。
(D) 均於晚上 9 點關門。

154–155 信函

洛克黑德實驗室

4 月 2 日

親愛的瑞丁頓先生：

我們已經看過您 3 月 31 日詢問洛克黑德實驗室研究助理職位的電子郵件。如我們徵才廣告所述，我們無法受理 3 月 14 日之後應徵的求職信函。之前已有許多符合資格的求職者，我們亦錄取其中一名人員。155 不過，您的履歷十分亮眼，我會把您的資料存檔。我對於您目前擔任漢柏勒科學機構研究助理的職位特別感到興趣，156 因為他們的工作性質與我們相似。

感謝您有意任職於洛克黑德實驗室。本公司如有其他研究助理職缺，我將與您聯絡。

敬祝　安康

實驗室經理

伊莉莎白・梵・宏倫斯

---

154. 寫這封信的目的為何？
(A) 確認面試日期
(B) 詳細說明某職務內容
(C) 要求作品樣本
(D) 說明某職缺已有人錄取

155. 可從文中得知瑞丁頓先生的哪些訊息？
(A) 他目前有在上班。
(B) 他的應徵資料是在截止日前交出。
(C) 他要應徵實驗室經理的職位。
(D) 他的工作經驗有限。

收件人：m.luciano@californiacatering.com

寄件人：r.hall@fshie.org

日期：6 月 27 日

主旨：餐飲飯店業博覽會

親愛的盧西亞諾女士：

我們很開心您去年有參加餐飲飯店業博覽會。不過，到目前為止，我們尚未收到您報名今年活動的音訊。及早報名可享折價後的 225 歐元優惠，僅到這個月底。 **156** 6 月 30 日以後，報名費將調漲至 300 歐元。

會議費用包含以下項目： **157**

- 10 月 7 日星期二的迎賓自助餐會預約席
- 可進出所有博覽會活動
- 10 月 9 日星期四的閉幕典禮入場券

報名費未含以下項目： **157**

- 10 月 8 日星期三協會會員的晚宴。 **157** （我們將提供前往活動地點的交通工具。如果您想參加此活動，請務必直接透過餐飲業協會網站來另外付費。 **157** ）

我們期待今年再次與您見面。

羅伯塔‧霍爾　謹啟

---

156. 霍爾先生為什麼要傳電子郵件給盧西亞諾女士？

(A) 告知她即將到來的截止日

(B) 鼓勵她在展覽會上演講

(C) 要求她修改行程表

(D) 確認已收到某款項

157. 可從文中得知 10 月 8 日所舉辦活動的哪些訊息？

(A) 會有重要的來賓參加。

(B) 可額外付費參加此活動。

(C) 會在博覽會的場地舉辦。

(D) 沒剩多少位子了。

---

http://www.parliamentarylibrary.co.uk/archivesdatabase

國會圖書館檔案館資料庫

此資料庫旨在幫助您查找國會的歷史紀錄，包括可追溯至 17 世紀的數十萬筆立法文件，其中許多文件至今已絕無僅有。 **160** 許多文件由於歷史悠久而十分脆弱，因此僅供網路瀏覽。可依照文件的作者或創建日期來搜尋檔案清單。每筆清單均含有內容提要。今年春季，我們即將推出可透過地點搜尋檔案的新版本。而在某些情況下，標示「離線觀看」的資料，可於檔案館辦公室觀看。如需存取此類資料，您必須先取得我們員工的批准。 **158**

[記錄範本]

羅蘭森 — 洛伊德書信

此為彼得‧羅蘭森與保羅‧喬治於一百年前書信往來的館藏。 **159** 往來的八封書信當中，已保存七封，包括討論稅率提案，以及羅蘭森的個人省思。此外，還含有喬治於 4 月 29 日在下議院發表演說時的部分草稿，還可看見許多手寫修改的痕跡。

---

158. 關於國會圖書館檔案館資料庫的資料，可從文中得知哪些訊息？

(A) 均按照字母順序來編排。

(B) 均有電子檔。

(C) 某些資料需要批准才能存取。

(D) 某些資料可帶回家看。

159. 關於羅蘭森 — 洛伊德往來書信的描述，何者正確？

(A) 書信是一世紀以前寫的。

(B) 含有舊稅務文件的影像。

(C) 由圖書館員工修復。

(D) 即將上傳至網站。

160. 「許多文件由於歷史悠久而十分脆弱，因此僅供網路瀏覽。」 最適合放在 [1]、[2]、[3]、[4] 的哪一個位置？

(A) [1]
(B) [2]
(C) [3]
(D) [4]

161–164 信函

麥克艾利斯特高中
33125 佛羅里達州邁阿密市南第 18 台地
3455 號
786-555-6623

10 月 10 日
潔芮·庫柏女士
90638 加州米拉達市海德威道 1452 號
庫柏府

親愛的庫柏女士：

我想讓您知道，麥克艾利斯特高中音樂科十分感激您慷慨解囊。 **161** 您的協會所捐贈的二十支銅管樂器以及樂譜和唱片，對我們的幫助極大。我們學校目前已擁有足夠的樂器，能夠一次教導 32 名學生。我們上次談話的時候，您很好奇學生是如何共用設備。我們目前是在平日的時候，讓三個學生共用一支樂器。 **163** 學生如果需要吹嘴，僅需付 25 美元。學年剛開始的時候，每個人會收到選用樂器的登記表。

此外，您的捐款讓我們得以聘用兩名兼職老師，來指導課後的音樂活動。 **162** 音樂教室開放練習的時間是週一至週五的晚上 6 點前。家長有在上班的學生，也因此踴躍參加課後活動。 **還有，平日無法上音樂課的同學，儘管行程排得很滿，也能因此有機會學音樂。** 有些學生甚至和其中一名新老師組成樂團。 **164** 如果您有時間，請前來參加我們的活動，欣賞他們的表演！

未來我們希望在麥克艾利斯特禮堂增設管弦樂團的座位，就能在我們的戲劇演出搭配現場演奏的音樂。如果您對此提案感興趣，我們將對您的支持感激涕零。我會繼續告知您此計畫的進度。

再次感謝您支持麥克艾利斯特高中胸懷大志的音樂人。

麥克艾利斯特高中校長

丹尼爾·歐麥利　謹啟

161. 寫這封信的目的為何？
(A) 邀請庫柏女士參加音樂甄選會
(B) 感謝庫柏女士的貢獻
(C) 簡介新老師
(D) 要求協助表演

162. 可從文中得知麥克艾利斯特高中的哪些訊息？
(A) 已招募更多職員。
(B) 正在考慮增設音樂廳。
(C) 將調漲學費。
(D) 將開設新劇院。

163. 可從文中得知麥克艾利斯特高中樂器的哪些訊息？
(A) 是由歐麥利先生訂購。
(B) 必須維修。
(C) 幾個學生一起共用。
(D) 僅能用於課後活動。

164. 「還有，平日無法上音樂課的同學，儘管行程排得很滿，也能因此有機會學音樂。」最適合放在 [1]、[2]、[3]、[4] 的哪一個位置？
(A) [1]
(B) [2]
(C) [3]
(D) [4]

愛莉・阮〔上午 8:43〕
早安,海克特和克里斯。我星期三沒辦法值班。我知道你們兩人都曾問過加班的事。你們中有誰感興趣嗎? 165

海克特・拉米雷茲〔上午 8:44〕
好啊,不過要看時段。你的上班時間是什麼時候?

愛莉・阮〔上午 8:46〕
上午 6 點到下午 2 點。

克里斯・特勞斯霍德〔上午 8:47〕
我的班表是下午 2 點到晚上 10 點,不過我可以早點進公司幫你代班,愛莉。

海克特・拉米雷茲〔上午 8:48〕
我有預約牙科門診,到上午 10 點才會結束,而且開車到公司要 40 分鐘,所以我想我時間會來不及。 167

愛莉・阮〔上午 8:52〕
啊,原來如此,我了解。 167 那麼克里斯,你確定你可以代班嗎?

克里斯・特勞斯霍德〔上午 8:53〕
當然可以。我會跟金女士說,我星期三會提早到公司。 168

愛莉・阮〔上午 8:55〕
好的。我會傳訊息請她確認。星期天公司見,克里斯。 166 太感謝你了!

---

165. 阮女士為什麼要聯絡她的同事?
(A) 查看他們的工作狀態。
(B) 指導他們輸入加班時數。
(C) 指導他們提出休假要求。
(D) 看看他們能不能幫她代班。

166. 可從文中得知特勞斯霍德先生的哪些訊息?
(A) 他最近訓練阮女士執行某些事務。
(B) 他被排在週末時段和阮女士一起工作。
(C) 他通常會加班。
(D) 他值班常提早上班。

167. 上午 8:52,阮女士的訊息「我了解」最有可能是什麼意思?
(A) 她接受拉米雷茲先生的解釋。
(B) 她相信特勞斯霍德先生很可靠。
(C) 她事先聽說過拉米雷茲先生預約門診的事。
(D) 她很熟悉交通狀況。

168. 關於金女士的敘述,下列何者最有可能是真的?
(A) 她開車上班。
(B) 她試著加班。
(C) 她被排定於星期天上班。
(D) 她負責管理員工的班表。

亞伯達報

親愛的沈女士:

感謝您繼續支持《亞伯達報》。您一定會開心得知,我們現在開始推出週報, 169 其中含有列出亞伯達省未來節慶與表演活動的行事曆, 170 還有電影與戲劇評論的單元, 170 也會附上可在娛樂場所、餐廳和其他當地事業體使用的折價券。 170

為了特別感謝長期支持我們的顧客,我們將免費為您提供一個月的週報。您的免費試閱時間將從 9 月 1 日星期一開始,到 9 月 30 日星期二結束。如果在試閱期之後,您希望繼續收到週報,每個月僅需多付 7.5 美元。 171

我們亦想邀請您參加試用推薦計畫,只要向您的親朋好友介紹我們的報紙即可。若您的任何親朋好友訂閱《亞伯達報》,您將可免費收到一整個月的本報!

如您有任何疑問,請聯繫
customerservice@albertanews.com。

客服代表
莎夏・林瓦爾德 謹啟

169. 此封信函的目的為何？

(A) 要求顧客付款

(B) 提供娛樂場所的折扣

(C) 向當地事業體宣傳投放報紙廣告

(D) 向既有顧客說明新服務

170.《亞伯達報》的週報不包含以下哪個內容？

(A) 傳統料理的食譜

(B) 未來活動清單

(C) 電影和戲劇的評論

(D) 當地餐廳的折價券

171. 沈女士如果選擇九月之後繼續收到週報，會發生什麼事？

(A) 將降低廣告費。

(B) 她的親朋好友可享折扣。

(C) 週報費用會新增至每月帳單。

(D) 她會獲得觀賞表演的免費門票。

172–175 公告

白貓頭鷹工業

所有職員請注意

我們正在進行「企業環保計畫」！以下是最新進度的細節：`172`

董事會已投票決定要提高資金，來減少辦公室內部產生的垃圾。

管理高層很開心許多人決定參加「騎單車上班」的提案活動。超過半數的員工一週至少騎車上班三次。

我們的辦公室切換為節能照明設備後，亦收到很棒的成果。我們雖然現在的用電量減少了45%，但仍需要提醒員工在不使用的時候，關掉電器、燈具和電腦的電源。`173`

每個部門的辦公區都放有待丟棄物品的垃圾桶。

- 一般垃圾應丟入藍色垃圾桶。`174`
- 可回收的物品應按照材質放入正確的垃圾桶。`174` 請將金屬電鍍物品放入紅色垃圾桶（包括任何尺寸的金屬瓶罐、迴紋針和鋁箔紙）。紙類需放入綠色垃圾桶。`175` 請確保所有敏感文件在丟棄前，已進行碎紙處理。
- 藍色垃圾桶需每天淨空。其他垃圾桶可每隔一天，於傍晚清空。`174`

公司最近的調查結果顯示，員工亦希望回收塑膠製品。`175` 我們正在研究，週五開會時再向大家更新。

讓我們齊心協力，一起帶來影響力！

維修部門總監

安華・阿法拉希　謹啟

172. 阿法拉希先生為什麼要寫這份公告？

(A) 更新某計畫的進度

(B) 宣布即將到來的視察程序

(C) 討論大家對某調查結果的反應

(D) 要求擴大預算

173. 文中提到節約資源的其他方法是什麼？

(A) 一週騎腳踏車上班兩次

(B) 關掉未使用電器的電源

(C) 確保碎紙處理要丟棄的文件

(D) 將可回收產品帶到辦公室

174. 可回收物需多久清倒一次？

(A) 每天

(B) 每隔一天

(C) 一週一次

(D) 一個月一次

175. 該公司目前尚未回收什麼物品？

(A) 塑膠瓶

(B) 紙類

(C) 迴紋針

(D) 金屬小瓶罐

www.adoradocc.org_location_contact **177**

關於我們	我們的服務	據點與聯絡方式	課程與外展服務

商業行銷研習會 **176**
由班頓廣告公司與阿多拉多商會贊助

班頓廣告公司與阿多拉多商會 (ACC) 很高興能推出全新系列的行銷研習會。**177** 我們的會員可免費參加，**177** 講師均為行銷領域的專家，屆時將為大家指導一系列的議題。**176** 請注意，每場研習會的報名人數僅限 100 個名額，**177** 且必須在 ACC 位於百赫斯特大道的市中心據點辦理。與會者將收到印有 ACC 標誌的旅行馬克杯。

主題	時間	日期	地點	講師
社群媒體廣告的價值	下午 1:00-下午 5:00	6 月 3 日	ACC 禮堂	艾莉莎·瓦茲奎茲
幫新公司打廣告的正確方式 **178**	上午 10:00-下午 1:00	6 月 8 日	ACC 禮堂	安立奎·培瑞茲 **178**
小型企業適用的大數據	下午 3:30-晚上 6:00	6 月 15 日	ACC 禮堂	安德瑞亞·費南德茲
布告欄已過時，彈出式廣告正夯	晚上 6:00-晚上 7:30	6 月 29 日	ACC 禮堂	荷西·馬丁

寄件人：info@adoradocc.org
收件人：ajohns@ihat.com
日期：6 月 2 日
主旨：研習會報名事宜
附件：Johns.rtf

親愛的瓊斯女士：**178**

我們為您決定參加商業行銷研習會而感到開心。我們相信您將能獲得寶貴的知識，了解宣傳您商店開業的方法。**178** 您將能馬上學以致用。**179**

我們於此電子郵件附上您報名研習會的確認信。**180** 請至我們的網站查看前往活動場地的地圖。請您務必到櫃檯報到，以領取訪客識別證。從櫃檯開始，會有標示指引您前往禮堂。

感謝您身為阿多拉多商會會員所做的貢獻。

阿多拉多商會
亞歷山大·德雷斯托瑞斯

176. 根據網頁內容，有哪些活動項目？
(A) 與專家私下一對一的會談
(B) 能分析資料的電腦程式
(C) 增進行銷知識的機會
(D) 在當地商學院教課的機會

177. 關於研習會的敘述，下列何者為非？
(A) 由班頓廣告公司和 ACC 舉辦。
(B) 每年都在不同地點舉辦。
(C) 僅供 ACC 會員參加。
(D) 研習會僅能容納特定名額。

178. 何人將主講瓊斯女士即將參加的研習活動？
(A) 瓦茲奎茲女士
(B) 培瑞茲先生
(C) 費南德茲女士
(D) 馬丁先生

179. 在電子郵件中，第一段第二行的
「apply」，意思最接近何者？
(A) 詢問
(B) 使用
(C) 散播
(D) 放置

180. 電子郵件裡的附件是什麼檔案？
(A) 出席者報名成功的確認信
(B) 結業證書
(C) 研習會主題的清單
(D) 前往某場地的交通資訊

181–185 備忘錄和電子郵件

收件人：全體職員
寄件人：人資部門
日期：2月3日
主旨：公告

今年年初，西諾科技公司已新增政策「第
31-4 規定」，內容說明了公司的服裝儀容
規範。**181** **183** 請避免上班穿著運動相關
服飾（例如連帽運動外套或緊身內搭褲），
以及具有圖像元素的服飾（例如大型的品牌
標誌或圖片）。並請避免戴帽子或穿球鞋上
班。

我們感謝大家遵守更新後的政策。**181** 第
31-4 規定能幫助我們維持專業的辦公環境。

寄件人：人資部門
收件人：職員名單
日期：2月12日
主旨：調查：適當的上班穿著

職員請注意：

格拉斯公司的研究員史丹・強森，將於週
五造訪西諾科技公司，來和自願者聊聊他
們對於休閒的上班穿著以及禁止休閒穿著
的規定，有何看法與經驗。他將提出休閒
穿著標準會降低士氣的研究內容，因為職
員越來越常向人資部投訴。**182** **183**

強森先生亦將透過向我們的職員提供網路
問卷，來將此結果新增至他的研究。問卷
僅需五分鐘的時間即可完成，且可自由決
定是否填寫。而選擇填寫問卷的西諾科技
公司職員，不需提供可識別其身分的任何
資料，且公開出版的研究結果將去除所有
姓名。**184**

大家可至網站 https://www.glassoffice.
com/questionnaire 填寫問卷。

我們十分重視大家的意見。**185**

181. 傳送此備忘錄的原因為何？
(A) 更新某新品即將上市的進度
(B) 解說修改過的員工福利待遇
(C) 提醒職員某項公司規定
(D) 宣布新的企業標誌

182. 強森先生造訪的目的為何？
(A) 討論行銷技巧
(B) 示範操作某裝置
(C) 介紹新款布料
(D) 分享服裝規定的研究

183. 根據強森先生的研究，第 31-4 規定最有
可能減少什麼情況？
(A) 職員曠班
(B) 員工投訴
(C) 出貨錯誤
(D) 服飾業績

184. 可從文中得知問卷的哪些訊息？
(A) 可透過西諾科技公司的網站來讀取
問卷。
(B) 只有五道題目。
(C) 將由西諾科技公司的廣告團隊主導。
(D) 不會出示問卷作答者的身分。

185. 在電子郵件中，第四段第一行的
「value」，意思最接近何者？
(A) 重視
(B) 評估
(C) 利潤
(D) 收費

收件人：wjenkins@photoshoot.biz
寄件人：esmythe@aspentree.com
日期：5月3日
主旨：艾斯朋特里鄉村俱樂部的社群感謝日

親愛的詹金斯先生： 186

由於您是艾斯朋特里鄉村俱樂部的長期會員，如果您能光臨5月31日星期日的社群感謝日活動，我們將深感榮幸。 186 我們很興奮能歡迎您到場，因屆時會有許多不同的活動，來推廣參與各種運動的好處。如果您在5月10日前回覆此電子郵件，我們將寄送可獲得特殊禮品的兌換券給您。 187

艾斯朋特里鄉村俱樂部的外展服務總監
艾瑞克·史密斯 187

艾斯朋特里鄉村俱樂部的社群感謝日，5月31日

職務與負責事項：

- 外展活動統籌：艾瑞克·史密斯

- 贊助商接洽人員：麗娜·歌德斯坦

- 主講人：李智慧（游泳）、史考特·麥克艾利斯特（網球）

- 兒童羽毛球賽：安東尼奧·委拉斯貴茲 190

- 運動和藝術指導老師／教練：希拉蕊·梵·戴斯德、米歇爾·約克、雪莉·隆里夫特

艾斯朋特里鄉村俱樂部的感謝會
6月2日，艾琳·克里斯通 撰

艾斯朋特里鄉村俱樂部於上週日舉辦令人興奮的「社群感謝日」活動。除了慶祝營運35週年，俱樂部亦以此活動表達對社區支持的謝意。此高朋滿座的活動，俱樂部均開放會員與同好大眾參加。

參加者能聽到頂尖運動好手的演講，贊助公司亦於現場發送T恤、筆記本和原子筆。持有特殊兌換券的出席者，能與專業指導老師免費打一輪高爾夫球。 187

一整天下來，為一睹米歇爾·約克風采的人群十分可觀。瓦利·詹金斯表示：「我原本是想深入了解網球課和游泳課，但沒想到約克先生示範隨著拉丁音樂的節奏踩踏舞步如此有趣。」 188

無庸置疑，吸引最多人群的活動，就是奧運冠軍李智慧分享她成長過程中，在此俱樂部的泳池上課的經驗。觀眾（包括七十多名學生）明顯深受她游泳生涯故事的吸引。 189 她停留在現場的時間比原本預計的久，同時回答大家的問題與親筆簽名。

而羽球的單打與雙打比賽，則讓所有的孩子感到非常開心。監督比賽的職員還頒予獎勵和勳帶。 190 艾斯朋特里鄉村俱樂部對於此次活動的參與人數感到開心，因此可能會考慮將此轉變為年度活動。

---

186. 詹金斯先生被鼓勵做什麼事情？
(A) 參加某活動
(B) 填寫問卷
(C) 與史密斯先生見面
(D) 規劃某活動

187. 某些出席者要如何獲得參加免費上高爾夫球課的機會？
(A) 回覆電子郵件給史密斯先生
(B) 參加某比賽
(C) 聽隆里夫特女士演講
(D) 提早抵達活動現場

188. 約克先生最有可能專攻什麼領域？

(A) 網球

(B) 舞蹈

(C) 游泳

(D) 羽毛球

189. 可從文中得知游泳演講的哪些訊息？

(A) 吸引很多人的注意。

(B) 被取消了。

(C) 有在電視上播出。

(D) 由鄉村俱樂部主任主講。

190. 哪一個人最有可能負責分發動帶？

(A) 艾瑞克·史密斯

(B) 希拉蕊·梵·戴斯德

(C) 安東尼奧·委拉斯貴茲

(D) 史考特·麥克艾利斯特

191–195 網頁、電子郵件和公告

www.pinelakecabins.co.ca/
accommodations

房型介紹	訂房	交通資訊	聯絡我們

歡迎您直接與「松木湖度假村」預訂度假小木屋，即可享有其他旅行社未提供的優惠。我們知識豐富的工作人員能提供最新資訊，並回答您對特殊服務的任何疑問。**由於我們自營度假村，因此可接受於清晨或深夜入住與退房、額外寢具需求以及延長住房時間等要求。191**

此外，為了慶祝營運 20 週年，在七月預訂任意天數的房客，均能自動享有贏得前往松木湖參加「克里斯釣魚之旅」的機會。193 馬上點選「訂房」頁籤或撥打 204-555-4587，預訂我們的小木屋。

收件人：
Marcia_Weissblum@friendlymail.com 192

寄件人：
cabins@pinelakecabins.co.ca

日期：6 月 12 日

主旨：訂房成功

親愛的魏斯布魯姆女士：

感謝您透過松木湖度假村的網站預訂小木屋。以下列出您的住宿資訊：

V0L1C0 加拿大卑詩省松木湖
松木湖度假村

小木屋房型	粉紅色小木屋
每晚房價	215 美元
額外費用	3 個充氣式皮艇（每個皮艇一天租金為 30 美元）
入住時間	7 月 20 日星期四 192 193 195
退房時間	7 月 22 日星期六 193 195
確認碼	#759J34

請您入住時，務必出示有效證件，以及 **20% 的押金。192** 我們將於退房時收取剩餘的房款。如需我們推薦當地活動或各式活動票券，請洽詢值班經理。

希望您能在松木湖度假村玩得開心。

松木湖度假村

安娜·胡伯　謹啟

房客請注意

住宿期間請注意以下事項：

- 我們度假村內的「傑莫爾餐酒館」正在進行養護工程，關閉期間為 7 月 20 日至 7 月 24 日。請洽詢接待人員，了解市區裡的其他絕佳用餐選擇。 194 195

- 我們的碼頭因為近期的暴風雨而受損，因此會在 7 月 23 日當週重建。我們的鄰居「松木湖公寓」將提供您停泊船隻的地方，並且適用平常的 25 美元每日停泊費。

我們先在此為可能造成的任何不便致歉。

松木湖度假村租賃管理部門

---

191. 根據網頁內容，關於松木湖度假村的敘述何者正確？
(A) 當地居民可享折扣。
(B) 常被旅行社預訂。
(C) 顧客可以提出特殊要求。
(D) 目前正在招聘額外的員工。

192. 根據電子郵件的內容，魏斯布魯姆女士必須在 7 月 20 日做什麼事？
(A) 回覆某電子郵件
(B) 支付押金
(C) 攜帶優惠券
(D) 歸還某設備

193. 可從文中得知松木湖度假村的哪些訊息？
(A) 七月已無空房。
(B) 房客主要是家庭族群。
(C) 已透過電話處理魏斯布魯姆女士的訂房。
(D) 魏斯布魯姆女士已獲得抽獎資格。

194. 根據公告的內容，房客可從接待人員那裡獲得什麼資訊？
(A) 附近的餐飲店
(B) 聯絡清潔人員的方式
(C) 舉辦社區活動的時間
(D) 觀光景點的地點

195. 可從文中得知魏斯布魯姆女士的哪些訊息？
(A) 她將無法預訂額外的皮艇。
(B) 她偏好當天提早入住。
(C) 她偏好升級小木屋。
(D) 她無法在度假村內的餐廳用餐。

196–200 信函和電子郵件

10 月 6 日

德西蕾・西諾
法連特製造有限公司
衛克漢大樓
行銷部門

西諾女士您好：

請您於 11 月 11 日參加安全教育訓練課程。課程內容包括職場健康安全方面的公司政策與程序，並且將分發當地緊急救護服務單位的聯絡名單。 200

請注意，所有全職人員均須參加此活動。課程將於諾斯拉普大樓的活動廳舉辦，時間是上午 9 點至中午 12 點。課程結束後，我們將於對面的卡姆蘭大樓餐廳提供外燴餐點。

為了做好進行教育訓練的準備，請詳讀公司發給您的手冊， 196 其中含有課程會討論到的內容。假使您無法參加，請務必立刻提醒組長以及所屬部門指定的人事部助理大衛・西蒙斯。您可透過 dsymonds@valiantltd.co.uk 或撥打公司分機 432，聯繫西蒙斯先生。

希望您能參加訓練課程。

法連特製造有限公司
人事部主管 197
布萊恩・亞瑟　謹啟

寄件人：德西蕾‧西諾
收件人：大衛‧西蒙斯
日期：11 月 12 日
主旨：安全教育訓練課程

西蒙斯先生您好：

我參加安全教育訓練課程的時間被排在 11 月 11 日。不巧的是，我那天清晨得了重感冒而去看醫生。我的醫師寫了一張就醫證明，如有必要，我可以提供此文件。⟨199⟩ 如果需要我採取其他措施來解決此狀況的話，再請告訴我。⟨198⟩

敬祝　安康

德西蕾‧西諾

寄件人：大衛‧西蒙斯
收件人：德西蕾‧西諾
日期：11 月 12 日
主旨：關於：安全教育訓練課程

哈囉，西諾女士：

很遺憾聽到妳身體不舒服的消息。請妳拿就醫證明影本給我，我會新增至妳的檔案。我在夏洛特大樓 407 室的人事部工作。⟨197⟩ ⟨199⟩ 妳也可以用公司的電子信箱傳給我。我們僅需要這份資料，因為妳的主管已經告訴過我們他知道這個情況。

另一場教育訓練課程已排在 12 月 2 日。⟨200⟩ 由於當天稍早將召開其他會議，所以課程時間會是下午 3 點至 6 點。屆時不會提供餐點，但會供應咖啡和輕食。如果需要了解更多細節，請參考妳原本收到的邀請函。⟨200⟩

法連特製造有限公司
人事部助理
大衛‧西蒙斯　謹啟

---

196. 根據信函內容，關於教育訓練課程的敘述，以下何者正確？
(A) 每兩週舉行一次。
(B) 僅開放人事部員工參加。
(C) 不會要求全職員工參加。
(D) 員工需預習講義內容。

197. 亞瑟先生的辦公室位於何處？
(A) 衛克漢大樓
(B) 諾斯拉普大樓
(C) 卡姆蘭大樓
(D) 夏洛特大樓

198. 西諾女士為何向西蒙斯先生傳送電子郵件？
(A) 要求提供研討會的詳細時間表
(B) 想知道該如何補上缺席的課程
(C) 提議修訂某些安全規範
(D) 了解如何前往人事部辦公室

199. 西諾女士接下來大概會怎麼做？
(A) 向人事部提供文件
(B) 要求新的邀請函
(C) 完成與上傳某檔案至公司的網站
(D) 與主管討論她的問題

200. 可從文中得知 12 月 2 日所舉辦活動的哪些訊息？
(A) 出席者將收到餐券。
(B) 將由西蒙斯先生主持。
(C) 將提供緊急救護聯絡資料。
(D) 將於上午舉行。

ACTUAL TEST ③

101. 他們尚未預訂每月會議的會議室。
(A) 很快
(B) 很多
(C) 尚未
(D) 較少

102. 為了申請汽車保險理賠，投保人務必提供至少兩家修車廠提出的估價單。
(A) 預約
(B) 協會
(C) 組成
(D) 估價單

103. 自從與「NW 卡契」公司合併之後，我們在北美鮭魚產業市場的佔有率擴大了。
(A) 它
(B) 我們
(C) 它的
(D) 我們

104. 上個月日產出超過 40 萬桶石油的「麥克桂格油田」，已被一家挪威公司買下。
(A) 朝……方向
(B) 穿越
(C) 附近
(D) 超過

105. 過去六個月以來，瑞達公司一直著重於為其全新設計的「R40」機車款式進行廣告宣傳活動。
(A) 已著重於
(B) 被著重於
(C) 正在著重
(D) 著重

106. 儘管第三季的產量增加，但單位生產商品數量仍低於進度表上預計的每月目標。
(A) 曾增加
(B) 增加
(C) 欲增加中
(D) 增加中

107. 黑薔薇非政府組織的代表必須對董事會負責。
(A) 會計
(B) 帳戶
(C) 對……負責
(D) 責任

108. 由於停車場目前正在整修，賓客搭公車抵達普倫提斯商務中心會更方便。
(A) 明顯地
(B) 準確地
(C) 廣泛地
(D) 方便地

109. 人資部的張女士會致電被選定的應徵者，安排面試。
(A) 被選定的
(B) 選定
(C) 選擇中
(D) 選項

110. 近期的公司合併意味著 SW 企業與 DC 公司的幾個部門，將以合併的方式來降低成本。
(A) 若干，幾個
(B) 哪個
(C) 範圍
(D) 另一個

111. 佔地 150 萬平方公尺的格魯恩植物園，曾經是巴特頓最大的公園。
(A) 都不是
(B) 曾經是
(C) 相隔
(D) 那個

112. 經營 GMS 有限公司網站的職責，已委派給瑞斯先生。
(A) 更新
(B) 提供
(C) 委派
(D) 回應

113. 有人近期在該房產中找到十本書，其中五本書均擁有百年以上的歷史。
(A) 什麼
(B) 那些
(C) 他們
(D) 這些

114. 柯比廚房用品公司在面臨破產後不到一年的時間，其股票的交易狀態良好。
(A) 面臨
(B) 面臨
(C) 正在面臨
(D) 面臨

115. 《實際投資策略》中，含有專為股票交易新手而寫的實用建議。
(A) 建議的
(B) 顧問
(C) 建議
(D) 建議

116. 儘管進行了徹底的分析，工程師仍無法判斷導致新太陽能板出問題的原因。
(A) 排氣
(B) 疲勞的
(C) 疲勞地
(D) 徹底的

117. 此研究會的主辦單位，將洽詢來自國內的各大專院校。
(A) 在……（某處）
(B) 來自……
(C) 在……裡面
(D) 然後

118. 教科書通常由我們主倉庫的助理運送到校園。
(A) 大幅地
(B) 及時的
(C) 嚴厲地
(D) 通常

119. 從今天早上開始，所有的決賽入圍者均會收到通知成績的電子郵件和簡訊。
(A) 曾通知
(B) 已被通知
(C) 將通知
(D) 正在通知

120. 在接待主管請假的期間，她的助理將暫時升職來替補她的職位。
(A) 而不是
(B) 反而
(C) 在……期間
(D) 尚未

121. 「評價時尚」公司接受人家不需要的衣服，轉而捐贈給當地慈善機構。
(A) 願意的
(B) 粗心的
(C) 已宣布的
(D) 不被需要的

122. 選擇參加自助徒步之旅的威爾瑪奇國家公園遊客，可以依照自己的步調來探索步道。
(A) 穩定度
(B) 風格
(C) 行動
(D) 步調

123. 此出版公司想徵求能夠一次處理多種事務的編輯助理。
(A) 管理
(B) 經理
(C) 管理
(D) 處理

124. 柏林斯超市的經理指示大家，所有的展示架必須在週五晚上之前整理好，為週末的促銷活動做好準備。
(A) 退貨
(B) 準備
(C) 結果
(D) 補償

125. 為了確保充足的編輯時間，我們建議至少在出版日的一週前，以電子郵件寄出文章。
(A) 傳輸
(B) 認可
(C) 建議
(D) 確保

126. 根據莫里斯頓市議會的說法，該市的購屋率比前一年增加了 20%。
- (A) 關於
- (B) 而不是
- (C) 在……期間
- **(D) 根據……**

127. 紀錄檔案經過相當大的重整後，工作人員能輕鬆地找到顧客資料。
- (A) 常見地
- **(B) 相當地**
- (C) 粗心地
- (D) 連續地

128. 由於杭茲維爾缺乏租車公司，因此計程車司機在博覽會期間，賺取了龐大的利潤。
- (A) 最短的
- **(B) 缺乏**
- (C) 短的
- (D) 縮短

129. 最新發行的指南裡面，常有相關術語的詞彙說明表，方便不熟悉指南主題的讀者查找。
- **(A) 相關的**
- (B) 受損的
- (C) 最終的
- (D) 固定的

130. 陳女士將為所有參加研習會的員工預訂火車票。
- **(A) 預訂**
- (B) 受理
- (C) 授權
- (D) 販賣

PART 6 P. 69–72

131–134 文章

售屋率攀升

房屋委員會預測，新屋成交數到年底將超過 2,000 筆。此數目比前一年的數據高出 20%，且超越了兩年前創下新高的紀錄。房屋委員會認為，造成此攀升率的因素很多，尤其是銀行釋出了專為首購族設計的特別貸款方案。與住宅需求相反的是，儘管本市努力吸引新事業體進駐此區，但過去十年間的商業房地產市場，幾乎沒有起色。事實上，一些辦公大樓將於明年拆除。

131. **(A) 之前的**
- (B) 現在的
- (C) 接下來的
- (D) 整體的

132. (A) 特別的
- **(B) 特別，尤其**
- (C) 詳情
- (D) 特殊性

133. (A) 競爭
- (B) 優勢
- (C) 成本
- **(D) 起色；改善**

134. **(A) 事實上，一些辦公大樓將於明年拆除。**
- (B) 另一個因素是當地校區的聲譽。
- (C) 多虧社區的支持，才能讓這份心血嘗到成功的果實。
- (D) 各公司行號受到低稅率和優秀基礎建設的吸引，而進駐本市。

135–138 資訊

您的丹尼茲利飲料機將會為您的店家大大加分。因此，確保飲料機是否正常運作，絕對是您日常營運不可或缺的一部分。請切記以下幾個重點，即可讓您的飲料機維持良好狀態。首先，請使用通過丹尼茲利公司認證的零組件，尤其是丹尼茲利濾水器。第二，請小心更換水箱和軟管線。請查閱使用指南，有助您避免外漏溢灑問題。第三，請遵循我們建議的定期清洗時間表，確保您僅使用丹尼茲利公司所核准的已消毒設備和清潔溶液。最後，如果您的飲料機需要保養維修，我們建議您選擇合格的維修人員。若您謹記上述四項重點，飲料機絕對能維持相當長的使用壽命。

135. (A) 因此
    (B) 儘管如此
    (C) 基本上
    (D) 在此情況下

136. (A) 連接
    (B) 電源
    (C) 工人
    (D) 零組件

137. (A) 飲料機可持續運作。
    (B) 確保您僅使用丹尼茲利公司所核准的已消毒設備和清潔溶液。
    (C) 如果需要緊急維修的服務，請撥打飲料機背面的電話號碼。
    (D) 特定飲品的容量比其他飲品大。

138. (A) 合格
    (B) 合格的
    (C) 合格
    (D) 資格

139–142 備忘錄

寄件人：動物園園長 S．伯斯
收件人：全體職員
日期：8 月 15 日
主旨：動物秀的政策

此份備忘錄的目的，在於讓全體員工了解動物秀座位安排政策的更新狀態，且該政策即日生效。我們在同一天內，接獲許多持票人因為有額外空間的緣故，而要求希望能坐在靠走道的位置。即日起，我們僅允許預訂座位的當日適用此異動。往後如有觀眾要求更多伸腿空間，請鼓勵他們坐在常有空位的後排。雖然無法擁有最好的視野，但能坐得更舒適。此異動應能減少民眾於動物秀進行期間分心的情況。

139. (A) 座位
    (B) 停車
    (C) 相機
    (D) 付款

140. (A) 更多
    (B) 僅有
    (C) 遲到
    (D) 良好

141. (A) 他們要求
    (B) 所需的
    (C) 已要求
    (D) 要求

142. (A) 雖然無法擁有最好的視野，但能坐得更舒適。
    (B) 海豚秀目前是最受歡迎的亮點之一。
    (C) 對我們而言，週末是格外忙碌的日子。
    (D) 我們會提醒遊客，任何時候都不能碰觸或餵食動物。

位在堪薩斯州雷內克薩市的塑膠生產公司「科西亞製造廠」，已獲得堪薩斯保育協會（KCO）的資助金。KCO 根據所審核的發展計畫，來核發此筆資助金。此類計畫要求將科西亞公司的總廠重新設計為環境友善的設施。

其中一項重大改造，就是設置為機器發電的太陽能板。此外，資助金亦將用來升級空氣濾淨和廢料回收系統等廠內設備。完成上述改善事項後，任何剩餘的資助金，均將投入開發更能生物降解的產品等研究。

此製造公司的副董事長丹・史特契爾，將與 KCO 的凱特琳・華倫廷合作監督此專案。

143. (A) 在塑料產業中，環境問題已獲得許多關注。
   (B) 據報史特契爾先生曾在前任公司執行過相似的專案。
   (C) 其中一項重大改造，就是設置為機器發電的太陽能板。
   (D) 製造公司的共同目標，就是尋得替代的物料來源。

144. **(A) 諸如**
   (B) 然而
   (C) 儘管
   (D) 以便於

145. (A) 預約
   (B) 改正
   (C) 進展
   (D) 改善

146. (A) 監督
   (B) 監督中
   (C) 將監督
   (D) 曾監督中

分類廣告的詳細說明

《吉列姆週報》刊登分類廣告的截止日，為週四早上的 11 點半，並於週五刊出。**147** 提交廣告文字後，我們將不再受理後續更動要求。而《吉列姆週報》保有編輯文字的權力。

請事先支付廣告費。已付費刊登一個月的廣告，可於刊登一週後取消廣告，並獲得等值的抵用金，供往後刊登廣告之用。**148** 請將您的廣告文字傳送至 adv@gilliamweekly.com。刊登多則廣告，可享折扣優惠。

請撥打 413-9598 以了解價格。

147. 如果某廣告業主於週五早上提交廣告文字，會發生什麼情況？
   (A) 廣告費會更昂貴。
   (B) 報社將拒收該廣告。
   (C) 該廣告會於下週五刊出。
   (D) 該廣告會在當天下午刊出。

148. 根據公告內容，廣告業主何時會收到抵用金？
   (A) 報社編輯文字的時候
   (B) 刊登半版廣告的時候
   (C) 報社誤植文字的時候
   (D) 廣告業主取消廣告的時候

瑪莉・瑞克斯〔上午 10:09〕
普瑞斯頓先生您好。今早我能為您提供什麼服務呢？

歐利・普瑞斯頓〔上午 10:12〕
早安。我有收到柯爾萊特辦公用品訂單的確認簡訊，但郵務室尚未收到任何包裹。

瑪莉・瑞克斯〔上午 10:14〕

好的，我看一下是什麼狀況。可以請您給我結帳時的訂單編號嗎？

歐利・普瑞斯頓〔上午 10:15〕

好的，是 0223913。

瑪莉・瑞克斯〔上午 10:21〕

我在系統上看得出來，「英勝公司」是常客，**149** 我們非常重視貴公司與我們的業務往來。我們的紀錄似乎出了問題，不小心誤傳了該則簡訊。您訂的商品其實今天下午才會出貨，所以應該下週一就會送達。**150**

歐利・普瑞斯頓〔上午 10:27〕

<u>這樣就說得通了。</u> **150** 我本來很驚訝，怎麼會這麼快送達。謝謝妳撥冗處理。

149. 可從文中得知「英勝公司」的哪些訊息？
- (A) 下週將面試普瑞斯頓先生。
- (B) 是一家大規模的貨運行。
- (C) 剛更新了部分的顧客記錄。
- **(D) 以前曾向柯爾萊特購買商品。**

150. 上午 10:27，普瑞斯頓先生表示「這樣就說得通了」，最有可能是什麼意思？
- **(A) 他了解商品還沒到貨的原因。**
- (B) 他忘了回覆簡訊。
- (C) 他發現有一筆款項尚未處理。
- (D) 他走錯郵務室。

151–152 廣告

北美伐木商會議〔NALC〕

十多年來，NALC 已吸引了各大產業巨擘和上千名與會者。今年絕對又是另一大盛事。開場的主題演講由「西瀑伐木公司」的執行長艾倫・盧西安諾所主講。**152** 爾後一週會舉辦由業界各大公司領導人所主持的工作坊、研習會與講座。**151** 今年的主題是「林業打造永續未來的責任感」，以及「無紙化辦公室對未來業務成長的影響」。**152**

參加 NALC，保證讓您獲知現今競爭激烈市場的內幕消息。請於 4 月 15 日前至 www.nalc.org 報名，即可獲得促銷折扣。**152**

151. 可從文中得知 NALC 的哪些訊息？
- **(A) 有業界領袖主講的演講活動。**
- (B) 是由國際公司所贊助。
- (C) 有產品操作示範會。
- (D) 由西瀑布伐木公司所主辦。

152. 廣告裡未提及什麼細節？
- (A) 會議主題
- (B) 促銷折扣的截止日
- **(C) 會議地點**
- (D) 演講嘉賓的職稱

153–154 網頁

https://www.whittakerarts.co.sg/about

首頁	關於我們	作品集	委員會	聯絡我們

加入惠特克的行列

惠特克藝術公司的職場文化，在於培養藝術創意。我們想徵求專業藝術家，在為商業客戶設計獨特作品之時，進而找到改變世界的契機。

惠特克藝術公司的員工結構十分多元，呼應了我們馬來西亞與新加坡客群的特性。 **153** 這樣的多元化，是讓我們的智庫團隊能夠拓展知識與經驗的關鍵。這些團隊是由公司裡各部門的職員所組成，以最大限度提高生產率和分享技術為目標而頻繁召開會議。 **154**

惠特克藝術公司提供了提升專業藝術能力與保障薪資的機會。

153. 可從文中得知惠特克藝術公司職員的哪些訊息？
- (A) 是由人力仲介公司所僱用。
- (B) 喜歡與其他藝術家合作。
- (C) 曾在許多公司任職。
- **(D) 來自各種背景。**

154. 惠特克藝術公司智庫團隊成立的目的為何？
- **(A) 討論可能的解決辦法**
- (B) 招募新員工
- (C) 聯絡潛在客戶
- (D) 提供財務建議

155–157 電子郵件

收件人：salesteam@kino.com
寄件人：LMiller@kino.com
日期：7 月 10 日
主旨：各位的餐點選擇

大家好：

我要打電話向羅瑞義大利餐酒館預訂明天業務會議的午餐套餐。義大利麵的選擇有波隆那肉醬義大利麵、白醬雞肉義大利麵、香蒜蝦仁義大利麵或奶油青醬義大利麵。飲料方面，大家可選汽水、冰茶或礦泉水。 155 每份午餐還附有一小份沙拉、一顆橘子和一片餅乾。 156 請大家在今天下午 5 點前，用電子郵件回傳喜歡的餐點口味。我會請餐酒館於早上 11 點 45 分，將套餐送至第二會議室，這樣就不會打擾會議進行。無論大家決定何時休息吃午餐， 157 均可直接到第二會議室用餐，或是將午餐帶到會議室或屋頂露臺享用。由於會議要到傍晚 6 點才會結束，因此大家應該考慮一下到外面透透氣、曬曬太陽。

敬祝　安康

人資部
琳賽・米勒

155. 此電子郵件的用意為何？
- (A) 告知職員開會地點
- **(B) 安排用餐細節**
- (C) 宣布新餐廳開幕的消息
- (D) 要求報銷餐費

156. 可從文中得知午餐套餐的哪些訊息？
- **(A) 含有一份水果。**
- (B) 有打折。
- (C) 會在 7 月 10 日送餐。
- (D) 會在戶外上菜。

157. 可從文中得知會議的哪些訊息？
- (A) 一年舉行一次。
- **(B) 不會因為要在特定時間吃午餐而中斷會議。**
- (C) 將會討論食品和飲料的業績。
- (D) 將於第二會議室開會。

158–160 電子郵件

寄件人：艾琳・隋
收件人：全體職員
日期：3 月 29 日
主旨：須知

大家好：

從星期三開始，桑坎普電子公司將開始要求使用全新的身分驗證系統。付現或刷卡的顧客，結帳時不會發現異樣。但以支票付款的顧客，則會感受到程序有所改變。 158

顧客仍能使用支票結帳。不過，收銀員將須使用位於每台收銀機旁的新掃描器，來掃描顧客的身分證， 159 它會將身分證和支票上所示的資料進行比對，然後在每張收據蓋上「核准購貨」的戳章。 160

全國門市均將實施此項新的預防措施。不過，使用國內銀行核發之現金券的顧客，則不在此限。大家如有任何疑問，請參閱員工手冊的第十章。

桑坎普電子公司

財務長
艾琳・隋　謹啟

158. 寫這封電子郵件的目的為何？
- (A) 說明某問卷調查的結果
- (B) 後續追蹤近期某筆訂單的狀態
- (C) 建議提升業績的計畫
- **(D) 說明新程序**

159. 隋女士說明了桑坎普電子公司的何種事務？
- **(A) 公司需要針對部分購貨程序進行身分驗證。**
- (B) 公司正在銷售新的掃描器系列。
- (C) 公司計劃更新員工手冊。
- (D) 公司每週三都會提早關門。

160. 何者付款時會收到核准戳章？

(A) 付現的顧客

(B) 刷卡的顧客

(C) 以支票付款的顧客

(D) 以現金券付款的顧客

161–164 文章

「趙＆曹廣告公司」計劃擴增職員。公司發言人喬治·趙已證實，至少會多僱用 150 名員工，來迎頭趕上產業多變的現況。

趙表示：「廣播的廣告量一直穩定下滑，而數位廣告量卻疾速攀升。因此，我們對於兼具創意與編輯技能、還有科技知識方面的專業人才需求與日俱增。」 161 164 公司想特別徵求平面設計師、審稿編輯、技術顧問與業務人員。

為了擴增應徵者的人數，「趙＆曹廣告公司」將參加當地的就業博覽會。而下一次的香港就業博覽會， 162 定於 11 月 28 日在濱水會議中心舉行，12 月 9 日則在香港城市大學舉行。想求職卻又無法參加就業博覽會的人，可用電子郵件聯絡金有哪（YKim@chaotzaoad.com），以了解更多資訊。 163

161. 趙先生說明了數位廣告方面的哪些資訊？

(A) 價格比傳統廣告方法低廉。

(B) 公司需要尋找具備多重技能的員工。

(C) 屬於大學的熱門科目。

(D) 將取代傳統的廣告形式。

162. 根據文章內容，「趙＆曹廣告公司」打算怎麼做？

(A) 提高員工的薪資

(B) 另開新據點

(C) 參加在香港舉辦的活動

(D) 修改教育訓練的流程

163. 金小姐最有可能是什麼身分？

(A) 人資部專員

(B) 公司的業務代表

(C) 大學教授

(D) 大樓經理

164. 「公司想特別徵求平面設計師、審稿編輯、技術顧問與業務人員。」最適合放在 [1]、[2]、[3]、[4] 的哪一個位置？

(A) [1]

(B) [2]

(C) [3]

(D) [4]

165–167 網頁

https://www.sierratheater.org

席亞拉劇院

呈現本地與國內製作作品的表演藝術劇院
我們很高興為大家介紹音樂劇
《邊境的吶喊》

屬於本劇院《美國名人》系列的本齣音樂劇，將於 9 月 15 日開演。劇院會員可於音樂劇開演前，先預訂門票。本劇的特色是結合了經典與現代歌曲，唱出西部邊境的生活樣貌。 165

此音樂劇的導演艾莉森·林迪製作本劇碼時，發揮了她超過二十年的執導經驗。本劇上演時間為七週。林迪女士於今年一月加入劇院管理團隊之前，曾任波士頓 SRO 劇院的製片總監 166 達七年之久；亦曾於芝加哥的法蘭克林藝術學院，任教表演藝術課程達四年的時間。

《邊境的吶喊》運用先進的燈光變化、特效與煙火藝術，搭配還原當年美國拓荒時代的考究服裝、髮型與道具。表演人員將於十月舉行數次演戲研習會。此研習課程的價格，是一般票價加 20 美元，亦含括免費的戲服租借。 167

165. 可從文中得知《邊境的吶喊》的哪些訊息？
- **(A) 劇中結合新舊音樂。**
- (B) 將於九月底上演。
- (C) 改編自近期時事。
- (D) 是《美國名人》系列的第一場表演。

166. 林迪女士的身分為何？
- **(A) 劇院員工**
- (B) 知名的表演人員
- (C) 藝術評論家
- (D) 歷史教授

167. 根據網頁的內容，劇院觀眾若額外付費便可進行什麼活動？
- (A) 獲得紀念品
- **(B) 加入演戲研討課程**
- (C) 參觀劇院設施
- (D) 觀賞獨家的表演節目

168–171 網路聊天室

> **裴宇靜〔下午 1:09〕**
> 希望大家午餐都用餐愉快。我想了解一下，週四要跟客戶開會所準備的行銷簡報進度到哪裡了。 168
>
> **康妮・朱利斯〔下午 1:10〕**
> 快完成了，但我們仍需要加入公司簡介的影片。 168
>
> **裴宇靜〔下午 1:11〕**
> 我想應該是傑負責製作影片。
>
> **傑・柏金斯〔下午 1:12〕**
> 嗯，我已經拍完所有內容。不過我的影片編輯軟體有點問題，似乎無法儲存我的檔案。
>
> **裴宇靜〔下午 1:14〕**
> 這可不妙。你問過資訊科技部的人嗎？ 169
>
> **傑・柏金斯〔下午 1:15〕**
> 有的，我昨天和提姆・史托談過， 169 但他不太熟悉這個軟體程式。
>
> **康妮・朱利斯〔下午 1:17〕**
> 那你問過軟體製造商嗎？ 170 他們也許能幫你解決。

> **傑・柏金斯〔下午 1:18〕**
> 我怎麼沒想到？ 170 好，我現在就問。
>
> **裴宇靜〔下午 1:20〕**
> 傑，問題解決後，請馬上通知我。對了康妮，妳確定過我們週四有會議室可用嗎？ 171
>
> **傑・柏金斯〔下午 1:21〕**
> 當然沒問題。
>
> **康妮・朱利斯〔下午 1:22〕**
> 我會聯絡人資部經理，跟他確認一下。 171

168. 可從文中得知簡報的哪些訊息？
- (A) 已延後截止日。
- **(B) 尚缺某些資料。**
- (C) 需要修改內容。
- (D) 將含有產品操作示範的內容。

169. 史托先生最有可能任職於什麼部門？
- (A) 行銷部
- **(B) 資訊科技部**
- (C) 編輯部
- (D) 人資部

170. 下午 1:18，柏金斯先生表示「我怎麼沒想到？」是什麼意思？
- (A) 他不清楚技術問題。
- (B) 他希望自己已提出較好的解決辦法。
- **(C) 他早該聯絡某公司。**
- (D) 他將考慮與史托先生會面。

171. 朱利斯女士被要求接下來做什麼事情？
- **(A) 確認某預約行程**
- (B) 面試應徵者
- (C) 提交某申請表
- (D) 審核文件

柯基提斯開設大型廠點

韋柳港市 訊〔10 月 10 日〕——於本市設置總部的巴西咖啡生產公司「柯基提斯農業」，開始在瓜地馬拉的米斯科市建造全新的加工處理廠，預計於 1 月 7 日正式啟用。**172** **173** 該廠即將成為全國規模最大的其中一座工廠，完全由當地員工管理營運。

此廠將能幫助該公司打入北美市場。**172** 柯基提斯執行長馬席拉·蘇沙表示：「在米斯科烘焙我們咖啡農的咖啡，可讓我們產出更新鮮、品質更好的產品。」<u>而此廠的生產目標為每年產出 9,000 噸咖啡，實屬雄心壯志。</u>蘇沙女士表示：「此目標應能讓我們在這個競爭激烈的產業中，成為佼佼者之一。」**175** 蘇沙女士與其他董事會成員，將主導米斯科廠的落成典禮。**173**

柯基提斯公司三年前已開始向北美廠商供應產品。**172** 北美亦為首次推出最新調和咖啡的市場。不過，地區銷售數據已動搖，從第一年的 510 萬美元佳績，驟降至今年的 340 萬美元。該公司認為，較靠近目標市場的新廠點，將能改善產品品質，進而提高業績。

柯基提斯另外三座烘焙廠位於巴西的雅魯市、索羅卡巴市，以及玻利維亞的科洽班巴。蘇沙女士亦表示，目前正與墨西哥的洽帕斯州政府官員，協商開設新廠事宜。**174** 她認為雙方將很快達成協議共識。

172. 可從文中得知「柯基提斯農業」公司的哪些訊息？
(A) 打算拓展北美的業務。
(B) 將與原為競爭對手的北美公司合併。
(C) 打算搬遷總公司。
(D) 三年前開始營運。

173. 可從文中得知蘇沙女士的哪些訊息？
(A) 她將於一月造訪瓜地馬拉。
(B) 她經常前往北美地區。
(C) 她將成為米斯科廠的首位廠長。
(D) 她對於最新推出的調和咖啡利潤感到滿意。

174. 「柯基提斯農業」公司最有可能將下一座烘焙廠建於何處？
(A) 巴西
(B) 瓜地馬拉
(C) 墨西哥
(D) 玻利維亞

175. 「而此廠的生產目標為每年產出 9,000 噸咖啡，實屬雄心壯志。」 最適合放在 [1]、[2]、[3]、[4] 的哪一個位置？
(A) [1]
(B) [2]
(C) [3]
(D) [4]

松橡健行俱樂部 **176**

九月行程說明 **176**

● **9 月 9 日**——紅鹿步道 **178**

導遊：諾拉·布里森
難度：輕鬆 **178**
總長度：5 公里
步道狀況：障礙物鮮少；開闊區域可能會有強風。

請於早上 11 點在松橡中心門口集合。請自行攜帶飲用水和點心，確保穿著保暖衣物。

● **9 月 16 日**——紅杉自然步道 **178**

導遊：柴克瑞·昆恩 **177**
難度：適中 **178**
總長度：7.5 公里 **180**
步道狀況：有部分路面不平的情況與碎石路徑。

請攜帶飲用水和點心。亦建議攜帶健行手杖。

TEST
3

PART
7

• **9 月 23 日**——未安排健行行程

• **9 月 30 日**——阿帕拉契火焰步道 **178**

導遊：庫柏・海登

難度：適中至艱難 **178**

總長度：11 公里

步道狀況：步道坡度剛開始很陡峭。接下來的路徑為適中難度。必須穿越兩條小溪。

請自備午餐和飲用水。建議攜帶相機，以便捕捉歎為觀止的美景。請穿著防水鞋。

除非另行說明，否則所有健行行程均需於早上 9 點在松橡中心門口集合。如需報名或了解更多資訊，請以電子郵件聯絡心妮・布蘭儂（sbrennan@pineoakhike.com）。

如有任何疑問，或想自願帶隊健行，亦請洽詢心妮。 177

寄件人：心妮・布蘭儂
<sbrennan@pineoakhike.com>
收件人：朱利安・葛里芬
<jgriffin@lac.net>
日期：9 月 14 日星期三
主旨：星期五的健行行程

朱利安您好：

您已報名原本是由柴克瑞・昆恩帶隊的健行行程。不巧的是，柴克瑞臨時被調去出差，因此這次無法帶隊。所以，我們會將此行程重新安排到十月中旬， **179** 並且將步道更換為廣受歡迎的高原美景步道。此步道的長度和難度均與紅杉自然步道相似。 **178 180** 我將親自帶隊。我們將於費爾溪飯店的主要停車場集合，然後一起走到步道口。如果您想參加此健行行程，請於明天早上 8 點前以電子郵件回覆我。

敬祝　安康

心妮

---

176. 此公告的目的為何？
(A) 宣布俱樂部政策的異動
(B) 比較相似的步道種類
(C) 要求大家協助接下來的俱樂部活動
(D) 通知大家參加健行活動的機會

177. 昆恩先生最有可能是什麼身分？
(A) 俱樂部志工
(B) 飯店接待人員
(C) 俱樂部會長
(D) 專業攝影師

178. 哪一條步道可能最具挑戰性？
(A) 紅鹿步道
(B) 紅杉自然步道
(C) 阿帕拉契火焰步道
(D) 高原美景步道

179. 關於 9 月 16 日的健行行程，以下敘述何者正確？
(A) 需要穿著防水鞋。
(B) 已經延期。
(C) 原本應該由布蘭儂女士帶隊。
(D) 非常適合新手。

180. 可從文中得知高原美景步道的哪些訊息？
(A) 步道會與幾條小溪交會。
(B) 步道會颳強風。
(C) 該團隊沒有走過此健行路線。
(D) 約 7.5 公里長。

寄件人：
lfernandes@musemarketers.com
收件人：
customersupport@officepoint.com
日期：1月11日
主旨：貨物
附件：帳單

敬啟者：

我從 OfficePoint 購買了各式各樣的產品，且昨天已到貨。雖然網路型錄說訂單出貨的時間需要七到十天，但這次四天內就到貨了。**181** 不過，我很訝異，產品的品質竟如此差勁。文件孔夾無法正常闔上；三個內圈未準確對齊，導致塑膠活頁資料袋掉出來。電動釘書機很難啟動電源。我用亮面影印紙印了一些手冊，但是塗布沒有我預想的明亮。**184** 雖然我沒有開箱霧面影印紙，但我想我會直接另買其他牌子。**183**

我打算退回所附帳單上列的第1、2、4和5的品項。**184** 如果方便，希望您能儘快將包裹標籤寄來，我將不勝感激。我們公司上次透過你們的型錄所購買的商品，並沒有出狀況，**182** 而且我們也在貴公司網站留下正面評價。可惜的是，這次的經驗讓我們相當不滿意。

萊諾·佛南迪斯　謹啟

OfficePoint
www.officepoint.com
專業辦公用品首選

品項	數量	金額
1. 亮面影印紙（5令一箱）**184**	2 箱 * $40.25	$80.50
2. 霧面影印紙（5令一箱）	3 箱 * $29.50	$88.50
3. 迴紋針（100支一盒）	50 盒 * $2.99	$149.50
4. 透明內頁袋的文件孔夾（3件一組）	25 組 * $1.99	$49.75
5. 釘書機（電動）	5 支 * $14.99	$74.95

小計：$443.20

促銷碼：OFFICE10 – $15.00

稅金（7.5%）：$32.12

運費和手續費：
（標準 7-10 個工作天）$20.00

總計：$480.32

退貨方式： 多數未開封或未使用的產品，均可於到貨的三個月內退貨，我們會以抵用金的方式，將等值的購貨金額退款至您的帳號。**185** 已開封或使用的產品，則不受此政策的保障，且在任何情況下均無法退貨。**184** 若經確認為瑕疵品，則可再訂購等值商品。

181. 可從文中得知佛南迪斯先生的訂單發生什麼事？
(A) 到貨的時間比預期的早。
(B) 含有十支電動訂書機。
(C) 含有受損的商品。
(D) 含有額外品項。

182. 佛南迪斯先生在電子郵件裡提及什麼事？
(A) 他的公司已經幫 OfficePoint 公司完成行銷廣告。
(B) 他已經打電話給 OfficePoint 的客服部。
(C) 他已收到 OfficePoint 的包裹標籤。
(D) 他的公司以前曾向 OfficePoint 訂貨。

183. 在電子郵件中，第一段第六行的「go for」，意思最接近何者？
(A) 移動
(B) 趕緊做（某事）
(C) 抵達
(D) 選擇

184. 佛南迪斯先生最有可能必須保留哪一項產品？

(A) 亮面影印紙

(B) 霧面影印紙

(C) 文件孔夾

(D) 釘書機

185. OfficePoint 主動向顧客提供什麼服務？

(A) 退回的商品可以抵用金的形式退款

(B) 大筆訂單可享折扣

(C) 辦公設備可享資訊科技售後服務

(D) 瑕疵品可免運費

186–190 電子郵件和新聞稿

寄件人：尚恩・金

收件人：丹妮卡・托馬希

日期：6 月 7 日，星期五，上午 10:48

主旨：廣告

親愛的托馬希女士：

總公司向妳說聲早安！ **190**

我們北京的行銷經理于冠云表示，「動起來計畫」廣告的中文翻譯版本，可如期在星期二前完成，以便將其發送至我們往來業務的中文地區。

不過，于先生建議圖片的說明能再精簡一點。 **187** 他表示，多數中文媒體通訊社均要求廣告不能超過 200 字。 **186** 他還說，如果廣告篇幅短一點，刊登的機率會更高。（我等一下就把他的簡訊傳給妳。）因此，更改一下可能會比較好。妳和團隊決定好改法之後，請回覆我。

敬祝　安康

斯佩卓諾華股份有限公司

社群外展部主管

尚恩・金

寄件人：丹妮卡・托馬希

收件人：尚恩・金

日期：6 月 7 日，星期五，下午 3:25

主旨：關於：廣告

附件：New_program.doc

尚恩午安：

很高興收到你的來信。我已經根據于先生的建議做了調整。 **187** 請你瀏覽確認一切無誤後，傳給他進行翻譯和後續廣告發布的流程。除了我們的媒體聯絡窗口之外，亦請提醒他，有些廣告務必在印刷後提供給計畫參與者。

斯佩卓諾華股份有限公司

媒體關係部經理

丹妮卡・托馬希　謹啟

斯佩卓諾華公司推出援助新計畫

斯佩卓諾華股份有限公司開始執行「動起來計畫」。該公司針對有生意往來的國家，致力為其學校投入四千萬美元於運動服飾和設備，目的在於讓更多學童接觸各類運動，並扮演著在年輕族群之間推廣健康活動的重要角色。藉由和各校區與教育外展單位合作的方式，專業教育人員和學校行政人員，都會接受各種體適能技巧的指導。 **188** 教育機構將運用自己的場地設施來舉辦各項活動，教師則需指導各組學生，來幫學生建立更高的榮譽感與成就感。您可至 www.spectranova.co.au/eep 網站查找此計畫的更多資訊。

斯佩卓諾華股份有限公司是一間專賣運動用品的公司，總部位於雪梨， **189** **190** 並於新加坡、北京、台北和洛杉磯設有分公司。

186. 關於于先生的敘述，以下何者最正確？

(A) 他深諳中國的新聞報導格式。

(B) 他曾住在洛杉磯。

(C) 他負責執行「動起來計畫」。

(D) 他下週要和金先生會面。

187. 托馬希女士最近做了什麼事？
　　(A) 她去雪梨出差。
　　(B) 她造訪了幾所學校。
　　(C) 她更新了部分內容。
　　(D) 她翻譯了廣告內容。

188. 推出此計畫的原因之一為何？
　　(A) 投資生產運動用品的工廠
　　(B) 訓練教師學會體適能活動
　　(C) 開設新的教育機構
　　(D) 幫助學生了解國內運動團隊

189. 文中提及新聞稿的哪些資訊？
　　(A) 斯佩卓諾華舉辦的運動活動類型
　　(B) 斯佩卓諾華每年產生的利潤
　　(C) 斯佩卓諾華計畫的申請條件
　　(D) 斯佩卓諾華專攻的市場

190. 金先生最有可能在哪個地點工作？
　　(A) 雪梨
　　(B) 新加坡
　　(C) 台北
　　(D) 洛杉磯

191–195　網頁、表格和論壇貼文

> **全球蝴蝶論壇板規**
>
> ● 僅限辨識蝴蝶種類的相關討論。貼文雖然沒有長度限制，但是與採集和育種蝴蝶有關、或販售設備等離題貼文，均會被刪文。
>
> ● 請遵循以下的標題寫法格式：「地點，蝴蝶外觀」。 **194** 請大家謹記，由於貼文來自世界各地的會員，因此這樣的下標資訊十分重要。 **191** 可接受的標題如下：「加告茲，橘色、茶色、黑點」。然而，版規不會接受「我需要協助」這類的標題。
>
> ● 請附上高解析度的蝴蝶影像，以及賞蝶的日期、時間與氣溫等相關資訊。您提供的資料越少，大家越難準確辨識蝴蝶的種類。

> ● 由於本網站十分受歡迎，因此管理員需要將近三到五天的時間，才會在貼文留言。因此，我們懇請會員自律，每天發一篇文章即可。

> **全球蝴蝶論壇板規**
> **馬上加入會員！**
>
> 全名：威廉‧赫曼 **195**
>
> 電子郵件信箱：whermann@openmail.net
>
> * **昆蟲相關領域的背景**：植物學碩士學位，以開花類灌木的研究為主。 **195**
>
> * **最近期的雇主**：梅立克特學院 **195**
>
> * 雖然非必填資料，但可協助會員在貼文留言裡，分辨資料來源的專業度。
>
> **您願意訂閱並在收件匣中收到我們每月出刊的電子報嗎？**
>
> 願意 ☑　　不願意 ☐
>
> **會員同意書：**
>
> 我同意全球蝴蝶論壇將會員的發文內容，作為推廣或廣告用途。**會員的私人資料絕不會售予他人。** **192**
>
> 我同意 ☑　　我不同意 ☐

> **新主題貼文**
>
> 會員：威廉‧赫曼
>
> 標題：需要種類識別的協助 **194**
>
> 時間：7 月 24 日下午 2:35
>
> 我目前正在羅馬尼亞出差，進行為期一年的研究。 **195** 我在考察地點附近的田野裡，看見這隻古銅色與藍色相間的蝴蝶。雖然我認為這是長尾藍蝶，但我仍想再確認一下。 **193** 我的前任研究助理說，這種

蝴蝶對於金雀花植物相當具有破壞性，**195** 這也是我來此研究的目的。在我試著驅離牠們之前，我想得到肯定的答案。**193** 附上的是我昨天所拍的照片。

copper_blue_0723.jpg

191. 可從網頁內容得知此論壇的哪些訊息？
(A) 需要會員費才能檢視內容。
(B) 24 小時後會刪文。
(C) 能讓使用者推廣自己的商品。
(D) 有許多國際會員使用。

192. 全球蝴蝶論壇承諾會員哪些事項？
(A) 提供每週電子報。
(B) 會查核新會員的工作推薦信。
(C) 會保密私人資料。
(D) 會在一天內回覆貼文。

193. 赫曼先生為什麼在論壇上發文？
(A) 針對某主題提供專業建議
(B) 確認某項假設
(C) 回覆另一名會員發的文章
(D) 尋求育種蝴蝶的協助

194. 赫曼先生何以違反版規？
(A) 標題不夠詳細。
(B) 貼文沒有包含影像。
(C) 為販售某物而打廣告。
(D) 貼文內容太長。

195. 關於赫曼先生的敘述，以下何者最正確？
(A) 他是某網站的管理員。
(B) 他正在申請研究經費。
(C) 他近期在科學期刊刊登文章。
(D) 他曾在某學院做研究。

196–200 網頁、網路評論和電子郵件

https://pinehollowcc.com/inductees/

本月新加入的店家——松谷商會（PHCC）特此介紹

本月將有四家新店於熱鬧的格洛夫廣場大道開幕：**196**

→ 位於此街南端的 1320 號的「亞維中心」，擁有來自世界各地的咖啡。**196** 且「藍鐘四重奏」會在每週五晚上的 6 點到 9 點進行現場演出。

→ 位於 1345 號的「松谷汽車公司」，是一家為各種車款提供全套服務的汽車公司，由卡拉‧詹克斯自營。**199**

→ 位於 1365 號的「未來科技電腦商場」，擁有專業人士和業餘電腦愛好者所喜歡的各種商品。

→ 位於 1380 號的「老虎印刷行」是一家專為本地服務的印刷設計公司。**198** 由專業平面設計師所經營的老虎印刷行，目前為所有當地公司提供服務全打九折的優惠，時間只到本月底。

如需了解本地最新加入的店家，請至 https://pinehollowcc.com。

松谷電子報——商業類

在寧靜城鎮裡新開幕的亞維中心

潭美‧史密斯　撰

昨天新開幕的亞維中心，喚醒了昏昏欲睡的松谷居民。老闆蓋瑞‧傑佛斯在開幕後的短短數小時內，就服務了鎮裡半數以上的人口。當天的活動亮點，就是傑佛斯先生在店裡為每位顧客送上免費的卡布奇諾。**197** 如果不熟悉「肉桂摩卡雙重奏」等咖啡飲品也沒關係，牆上均展示每款飲品的彩色裱框圖片。傑佛斯先生下個月還會在亞維中心旁邊增設小型烘焙坊，為咖啡店錦上添花。**196**

亞維中心想特此感謝艾德‧布朗，幫店裡不同的飲品製作精美圖片。布朗先生的店址位於格洛夫廣場大道 1380 號。 **198**

收件人：艾德‧布朗
<edbrown@sendanemail.com>
寄件人：卡拉‧詹克斯
<c.jenks@phauto.com>
日期：4 月 13 日，星期三
主旨：不情之請

嗨，艾德：

我是「松谷汽車公司」的卡拉。我們在兩週前的商會典禮上有過一面之緣。我在《松谷電子報》讀到關於亞維中心的文章，看到了精美的圖片。我想請教一下，你是否能幫我製作 500 張海報。 **198** 麻煩再告訴我，需要多久時間可完成我這筆訂單。可以的話，我希望海報能在下週五前送到我的店裡。 **199** 我之所以要在此日期前拿到海報，是因為我正在準備參加柏根夏爾即將舉辦的貿易展覽會。該活動的時間是 4 月 25 日至 4 月 27 日。 **200** 噢、我還想知道，我是否可以使用你們提供的優惠折扣。非常感謝你。

卡拉

---

196. 可從文中得知格洛夫廣場大道的哪些訊息？
(A) 租金已上漲。
(B) 各店家將為當地居民提供折扣。
(C) 靠近南端的地方，將有新店開幕。
(D) PHCC 的總公司位於此地。

197. 在網路評論中第一段第二行的「highlight」，意思最接近以下何者？
(A) 地點
(B) 特色
(C) 最精彩的部分
(D) 重點

198. 關於詹克斯女士的敘述，以下何者最正確？
(A) 她是松谷市議會的成員。
(B) 她下個月要將她的辦公室賣給傑佛斯先生。
(C) 她打算在開幕典禮上和布朗先生會面。
(D) 她希望老虎印刷公司能設計一些宣傳資料。

199. 詹克斯女士希望她的訂單能在下週五送達何處？
(A) 格洛夫廣場大道 1320 號
(B) 格洛夫廣場大道 1345 號
(C) 格洛夫廣場大道 1365 號
(D) 格洛夫廣場大道 1380 號

200. 根據電子郵件的內容，4 月 25 日會有什麼活動？
(A) 布朗先生將舉辦特賣會。
(B) 詹克斯女士的商店將遷址。
(C) 柏根夏爾會舉行某貿易展覽會。
(D) 格洛夫廣場大道會有新烘焙坊開幕。

ACTUAL TEST ④

PART 5 P. 94-96

101. 維也納烘焙坊使用經過認證的有機食材，來提升酥皮類點心的品質。
(A) 使用
(B) 設定
(C) 花費
(D) 允許

102. 你身為市場研究人員的職責，基本上和他的職責相同。
(A) 他的（職責）
(B) 他自己
(C) 他
(D) 他

103. 所有的遊客將能在我們位於水晶沙洲所全新翻修的度假村，體驗出色的服務。
(A) 隨時地
(B) 廣泛地
(C) 新近
(D) 每年地

104. 阿伯汀鞋業提供專為各種室內及戶外環境，所量身訂製的完整靴子系列。
(A) 種類
(B) 系列；範圍
(C) 時尚
(D) 方法

105. 請告知房客，所有商務套房家具齊全，並有無線網路連接。
(A) 各個
(B) 所有
(C) 每個
(D) 整體

106. 請在下週五前，支付水電帳單上的款項。
(A) 已付款
(B) 付款
(C) 正付款
(D) 款項

107. 如果你無法找到所需的資訊，請隨時寄電子郵件至 notfaqs@dgmail.com 給我們。
(A) 如果
(B) 由於
(C) 所以
(D) 或者

108. 三松建築師大賞委員會引進了一個新獎項類別，是專為採用環保建材來營建的設計所創。
(A) 優越感
(B) 招募
(C) 類別
(D) 從事

109. 自信的演講人，通常會在台上四處走動或站在講桌旁邊，而不是講桌後面。
(A) 靠著
(B) 在……之後
(C) 在……的旁邊
(D) 進入

110. 馬丁妮茲女士雖然猜想到迎新會可能會持續三小時，但演講時間比預計的久。
(A) 持續
(B) 可能會持續
(C) 持續中
(D) 已持續

111. 接待人員會向你提供報名此課程所需的文件清單。
(A) 提供
(B) 建議
(C) 解釋
(D) 概述

112. 提供運動員穿著此服飾的圖片，能讓任何運動服飾的系列廣告活動更有效果。
(A) 成效
(B) 有效地
(C) 有效果的
(D) 效果

113. 科幻圖像小說《搗蛋鬼的季節》正被改編成由瑞秋・史東沃爾與賽琳娜・維斯克茲主演的迷你影集。
(A) 主演
(B) 主演
(C) 曾主演
(D) 主演

114. 經過漫長的辯論後，建造第二座橫越莫希干河橋樑的提案，終於被駁回。
(A) 以前地
(B) 終於
(C) 密集地
(D) 幾乎不

115. 此合併案要到下個月才能正式生效，因為合約無法在國定假日送達。
(A) 在……之間
(B) 儘管
(C) 接下來的
(D) 直到……

116. 股票經紀人卡莉・迪佛雷納將自己進行獲利交易的能力，歸功於從母親那裡學到的技能。
(A) 已獲利
(B) 獲利中
(C) 獲利的
(D) 利潤

117. 新上任的人資部總監黃女士，剛解決了造成上一季許多複雜情況的排程衝突問題。
(A) 解決
(B) 提醒
(C) 完成
(D) 主動示意

118. 帕克先生從在大學實習以來，一直是霍克羅夫特事務所的可靠成員。
(A) 在……的同時
(B) 自從
(C) 在……上方
(D) 是

119. 加田愛羅女士覺得在大阪科技大會上做簡報，其實相對輕鬆。
(A) 相對地
(B) 相較下
(C) 可相比的
(D) 比較的

120. 代爾頓企業被要求在熱浪襲擊期間，嚴格限制用電量。
(A) 可使用的
(B) 用量
(C) 使用者
(D) 有用的

121. 科技會議的預算已經敲定，沒有討論的可能性。
(A) 建立中
(B) 已建立
(C) 建立
(D) 建立

122. 哈特福德市議會所收取的假日捐款，將會分發至全市的慈善機構。
(A) 收取
(B) 曾收取
(C) 已收取
(D) 收取中

123. 「月光之旅」船隊所推出的最新郵輪，擁有專為長時間航海與應對暴風雨海象，所設計的舒適船艙。
(A) 立即地
(B) 極度地
(C) 大約地
(D) 刻意地

124. 由於艾可碩爾報稅公司推出吸引人的會員套裝服務，因此幾乎沒有流失客戶。
(A) 支持……
(B) 在……內部
(C) 由於
(D) 關於

125. 筆記型電腦製造商「便利波特」，今天早上證實 ZPC-2050 已進入生產階段，並將於年底前到店販售。
(A) 衰退
(B) 見解
(C) 生產
(D) 管理

126. 會計部門要求所有職員在星期四傍晚六點以前，提交付款單。
(A) 提交中
(B) 已提交
(C) 提交
(D) 曾提交

127. 賀瑪士律師事務所鮮少允許律師，在案件審判期間對媒體發言。
(A) 難以
(B) 高高地
(C) 有距離的
(D) 鮮少

128. 只要塔特斯先生能盡其所能改善手機應用程式，我們都很歡迎。
(A) 很多
(B) 這件事
(C) 任何事
(D) 幾乎

129. 柯提斯醫療集團定期更新會員檔案的做法十分安全，且能確保患者的資安與保密性。
(A) 安全的
(B) 真實的
(C) 絕對的
(D) 專門以……為主的

130. 過去十年以來，園區的設施養護工作，一直由紐澤西休閒遊憩局處理。
(A) 曾被處理
(B) 一直（被）處理
(C) 過去曾處理
(D) 可能已處理

PART 6　P. 97–100

131–134 新聞稿

由東尼‧加勒布里斯和喬瑟芬‧加岡諾所主持的《市場追蹤快訊》，是播報最新經濟概況以及投資相關新聞的當地電視節目。《市場追蹤快訊》於十年前首播，當時只有加勒布里斯負責播報新訊。

加勒布里斯於五年後開始僱用加岡諾，隨即成為新英格蘭最受推崇的節目。經年累月下來，合夥人同意將節目主題的範圍，拓展至投資事務的相關建議。節目亦常邀請成功的理財專員來分享看法。

《市場追蹤快訊》於每週五下午股市休市後播出一集。

131. (A) 因此
(B) 以及；伴隨著
(C) 此外
(D) 關於

132. (A) 參考
(B) 調職
(C) 加入
(D) 僱用

133. (A) 同意中
(B) 協議書
(C) 已同意
(D) 可接受的

134. **(A) 節目亦常邀請成功的理財專員來分享看法。**
(B) 過去十年來，金融新聞業已成為競爭激烈的領域。
(C) 投資人可透過上網，自行做相關功課。
(D) 多數顧問均建議持有各種投資商品，以便降低風險。

格林普羅斯飯店
常見問題

我該如何確認,貴飯店已處理我的訂房資料?

您應於訂房的 24 小時內,收到載明客房資訊的電子郵件。若您未收到此通知,請聯絡您的金融機構。如果我們度假村沒有收到該款項的紀錄,表示此筆交易很有可能尚未完成。

假如有此情況,請您撥打 800-555-1212 與我們聯絡,以便我們協助您解決此問題。此號碼為國內可用的免付費電話。切記,若您從國外撥打此號碼,可能需要付費。

135. (A) 請注意,我們從來不會以電子郵件與您聯絡付款事宜。
(B) 我們為海外房客提供多種便利的網路訂房選擇。
(C) 未訂房而直接光臨的房客,我們會盡可能安排住房。
(D) 您應於訂房的 24 小時內,收到載明客房資訊的電子郵件。

136. (A) 有可能的
(B) 簡單的
(C) 必要的
(D) 適當的

137. (A) 然而
(B) 此外
(C) 假如有此情況
(D) 總之

138. (A) 切記
(B) 切記
(C) 曾記得
(D) 記得

收文者:馬利用品公司的全體職員
發文者:艾德加‧馬利
日期:12 月 3 日
主旨:問卷調查的結果

今天的董事會會議,做了一項將增加公司利潤與提高公司聲譽的決定。

策略部門已於會議上,分享問卷調查的結果。他們亦展示了採購當地生產的農產品來支持該地區經濟的做法,會降低我們的運輸費用。

問卷結果顯示,顧客會更願意從投資當地經濟的公司購買產品。因此,我們會以附近的生產業者取代現有的海外合作廠商。

此外,出貨部門將開始與鎮上一些提供倉儲和宅配服務的公司合作,以便為此地的居民創造工作機會。我們亦將從緊鄰的周遭地區僱用司機、倉管人員和其他寶貴的員工。

我們的網站會發布公告,通知大眾此令人振奮的計畫。長期來看,上述改變應能為我們在此地的獲利與形象的建立產生有利的影響。

139. (A) 將已分享
(B) 將分享
(C) 已分享
(D) 分享中

140. (A) 我們
(B) 它
(C) 你的;你們的
(D) 她的

141. (A) 純粹是因為這一領域符合資格的應徵者太少。
(B) 現有的員工應擁有率先申請此類職缺的機會。
(C) 我們的網站會發布公告,通知大眾此令人振奮的計畫。
(D) 某些董事會人員因為先前所承諾的事項,而無法參加。

TEST 4

PART 6

339

142. (A) 互補的
(B) 降低的
(C) 有利的
(D) 國外的

143–146 信函

喬瑟芬 · 盧切斯
特魯希略系統公司
66212 堪薩斯州奧佛蘭帕克市
西九十五街 9822 號

親愛的盧切斯女士：

我很樂意以艾格碩工業業務代表的身分，向您提供使用心得感想。我們安裝特魯希略系統公司的產品分類機六個月以來，為我們帶來極大的幫助。我們的工廠曾缺乏可靠又準確的方法，來檢查與分類大量的農作物資。如今，使用特魯希略系統公司的產品後，我們已能在廠內更有效評估農產品的品質與快速分類。也因為其客製化的特色，讓我們的員工能夠將機器設置成自己所需的設定。由於此機器減少了我們處理專案的時間，因此大幅改善了我們的工作效率。我們一直對特魯希略系統公司的產品印象深刻，希望將來能因長期使用特魯希略系統而讓我們公司更上一層樓。

敬祝　安康

艾格碩工業公司
副總　大衛 · 班納維斯　謹啟

143. (A) 感謝您考慮應徵艾格碩工業公司。
(B) 貴公司一直是艾格碩工業公司的忠實客戶。
(C) 艾格碩工業公司需要儘快購買新的產品分類機。
(D) 我很樂意以艾格碩工業業務代表的身分，向您提供使用心得感想。

144. (A) 將缺乏
(B) 缺乏中
(C) 缺乏
(D) 曾缺乏

145. (A) 最後的
(B) 所需的
(C) 額外的
(D) 有用的

146. (A) 指示
(B) 分離
(C) 改善
(D) 答案

PART 7　P. 101–121

147–148 資訊

「全市跑透」資訊

您沒有時間前往郵局嗎？本公司保證旗下自行車快遞員，能不分晝夜在一小時內，完成市內任何一處的急件快遞任務。

只要登入我們的網站，就可知道需要支付多少快遞費。**147** 我們會根據包裹重量來報價。

快遞員向您收取包裹後，您會收到一組特殊代碼，可即時追蹤配送進度與了解持續更新的到貨時間。**148**

147. 可從文中得知哪些資訊？
(A) 短距離配送可享折扣。
(B) 大型包裹務必以平信的方式郵寄。
(C) 顧客能在線上計算價格。
(D) 自行車快遞員會在出發前聯絡收件人。

148. 此特殊代碼的目的為何？
(A) 更改訂單的送達地點
(B) 查看配送進度
(C) 接收成本估算
(D) 預估包裹的尺寸

149–150 電子郵件

收件人：黎恩姆·丹尼爾斯
寄件人：伊蓮娜·格德斯
日期：5 月 29 日
主旨：雷默頓分店

親愛的丹尼爾斯先生：

你去年 11 月想申請調職到雷默頓分店卻未被批准，原因在於當時並無空缺。不過，雷默頓分店負責人今天聯繫我，表示他正想徵求資深的副店長。此外，他想先考慮公司內部的應徵者，所以我想讓你優先考慮。如果你仍對此機會感興趣，**149** 請於本週四之前告訴我。如果你想留在目前的分店，我會直接將職缺消息發在公司的公告欄。我會等待你的回覆。**150**

伊蓮娜·格德斯　謹啟

149. 寫這封電子郵件的目的為何？
(A) 要求對方提出某電腦程式的反饋
(B) 介紹新副店長
(C) 將指示轉寄給某辦事處
(D) 宣布某職缺

150. 格德斯女士將等著做什麼事？
(A) 和分店負責人談話
(B) 舉辦教育訓練課程
(C) 回覆某電子郵件
(D) 公告某廣告

151–152 簡訊串

克勞德·勒巴德〔上午 7:06〕
抱歉在上班前聯繫你。我有些商展相關問題還沒問你。**151**

馬文·陳〔上午 7:07〕
沒關係。**151** 我能幫你什麼忙？

克勞德·勒巴德〔上午 7:09〕
我剛抵達菲爾費斯會議廳，他們在詢問我們的「活動保險」。我來公司只有一個月的時間，**152** 還不太熟悉所有的政策。這項保險是必要的嗎？

馬文·陳〔上午 7:11〕
我們在任何地點設置活動攤位之前，一定要先買保險。

克勞德·勒巴德〔上午 7:12〕
公司允許我刷公司信用卡嗎？還是我要自己付費？

馬文·陳〔上午 7:15〕
刷公司的卡可以讓會計比較好處理。只要確保收好收據即可。

克勞德·勒巴德〔上午 7:16〕
他們提供電子收據，所以不難查找。

151. 上午 7:07，陳先生回覆「沒關係」，是什麼意思？
(A) 他認為勒巴德先生不應購買額外的保險。
(B) 他很歡迎勒巴德先生問問題。
(C) 勒巴德先生可以提交電子收據。
(D) 勒巴德先生能輕鬆找到攤位設置的相關資訊。

152. 可從文中得知關於勒巴德先生的哪些訊息？
(A) 他要求報銷餐費。
(B) 他已經申請新信用卡。
(C) 他需要準備簡報的協助。
(D) 他最近剛加入新公司。

153–154 備忘錄

備忘錄
發文者：加勒特·亞柯提
收文者：「巧當」全體員工
日期：6 月 3 日
主旨：看板的進度更新

關於餐廳老闆說要將我們最近購入的電子看板放在大門口一事，最新消息如下。**153**

新螢幕會顯示巧當餐廳每日特餐和常態餐點的影像，**154** 但我們還要敲定平面設計圖的部分。我們未來幾天內會做好決定，以便敲定看板樣式。希望能在七月初就裝設好看板。

大家如果對此事件有任何疑問，請與我聯絡。

加勒特・亞柯提

153. 可從文中得知看板的哪些訊息？
(A) **會有數位顯示器。**
(B) 會顯示每週的新菜色。
(C) 最近剛裝設好。
(D) 需要額外的資訊。

154. 此看板將呈現哪些資訊？
(A) 員工通訊錄
(B) 座位表
(C) 餐廳老闆的簡介
(D) **菜單內容**

155–157 報導

6 月 5 日——狄蘭尼灣文化協會（DBCA）昨天宣布，珍妮絲・蘇利文贏得第八屆年度業餘攝影比賽。DBCA 的藝術中心將於 8 月 1 日至 8 月 10 日展出她名為《和平》的得獎作品，以及其他 12 名決賽入圍者的參賽作品。**155** **157** 8 月 11 日則會舉辦頒獎典禮，由 DBCA 會長菲利浦・岡薩雷斯向蘇利文女士頒發現金 2,000 美元的獎金，以表揚她的成就。**156** 雖然可免費入場觀展，**155** 不過我們仍歡迎各界以捐款方式支持 DBCA 所做的努力。

今年 DBCA 將首次在網站展出所有競賽者的作品。岡薩雷斯先生表示：「線上藝廊能讓更多人瀏覽與欣賞本市最才華洋溢的攝影師的精選作品。」

請注意，由於暑假即將到來，因此藝術中心在 8 月 12 日至 8 月 31 日均不會開放。**157** 本中心會在 9 月 1 日星期一再次開放秋季展，**157** 屆時會由當地音樂學家米瑞安姆・交野博士，就不同類型的爵士樂進行特別講座。

155. 關於展覽的敘述，下列何者不正確？
(A) 將於 8 月 10 日閉展。
(B) **僅開放專業攝影師參加。**
(C) 不收取入場費。
(D) 會展出蘇利文女士的作品。

156. 可從文中得知蘇利文女士的哪些訊息？
(A) 她將擔任六月分某攝影比賽的評審。
(B) 她是文化協會的會員。
(C) 她是某大學的音樂系教授。
(D) **她會在 8 月 11 日參加某活動。**

157. 可從文中得知藝術中心的哪些訊息？
(A) 為大眾提供藝術課程。
(B) 最近吸引了更多觀展人。
(C) 去年的得獎作品亦於線上展出。
(D) **攝影展將是本季的最後一場展覽。**

158–160 廣告

多隆金融公司

多隆金融公司提供卓越的投資和財富管理服務。艾倫・多隆在哈特福德擔任成功的銀行家多年後，於 25 年前來到紐黑文創辦本公司。**159**

公司的業務原本著重在希望準備退休或投資股票的個人客戶，**160** 而在當地建立了良好聲譽。**158** 也因此讓公司接觸到不只有基本投資需求的中小型企業客戶。**160** 艾倫的女兒在六年前成為公司的執行長，**159** **160** 開始與州內許多知名企業合作，包括德塔悠製藥公司與艾維科技電子公司，**160** 並於哈特福德和橋港設立新據點。**160**

雖然市場時有高低起伏，競爭亦非常激烈，該公司提供長期策略的聲譽，經得起時間的考驗，亦協助企業與個人客戶達成其目的。

您如需值得依賴的理財協助，請立刻洽詢多隆金融公司。**158** 我們的網站 www.doironfinancial.com 均詳列各項服務與資訊。

158. 此廣告最有可能出現在什麼場所？
    (A) 在電子產品會展上
    (B) 在市內報紙上
    (C) 在就業博覽會上
    (D) 在旅遊雜誌上

159. 關於多隆金融公司的敘述，以下何者最正確？
    (A) 預計買下對手的公司。
    (B) 屬於家族企業。
    (C) 客戶多已退休。
    (D) 總公司位於哈特福德。

160. 文中未提及多隆金融公司經歷過何種變遷？
    (A) 資安政策更新
    (B) 指派新任主管
    (C) 拓點至他市
    (D) 客群擴大

161–164 網路聊天室

> **茱莉亞・卡塞爾〔下午 2:09〕**
> 索拉和凱文，午安。我在想是否已有包裹送達。我今天應該要收到一些文件，但我擔心可能被送到另一棟大樓。寄件人是奧特利本行銷公司，包裹上應貼有「優先處理」的標籤。 **161**

> **索拉・強森〔下午 2:10〕**
> 我們接待櫃檯沒有收到任何物品。我想妳應該要去主大廳的警衛室看看。 **162**

> **凱文・李〔下午 2:12〕**
> 我在人資部這邊看到奧特利本行銷公司寄來的大信封袋，但我找不到收件人的姓名。

> **茱莉亞・卡塞爾〔下午 2:13〕**
> 那可能是我的。可以請你再幫我看一下包裹上的標籤嗎？ **163**

> **凱文・李〔下午 2:14〕**
> 不好意思。我現在看到妳的名字了，是寫在地址下面。 **163**

> **茱莉亞・卡塞爾〔下午 2:16〕**
> 太好了。我需要有人馬上將包裹送到我辦公室，拜託了。 **164**

> **凱文・李〔下午 2:17〕**
> 沒問題。反正我正要去三樓。 **164**

> **茱莉亞・卡塞爾〔下午 2:20〕**
> 非常感謝你。

161. 卡塞爾女士為什麼會開始此網路聊天內容？
    (A) 她正在準備業務報告。
    (B) 她正在等一些重要的文件。
    (C) 她寄出的包裹地址錯誤。
    (D) 她期待一些客戶很快到來。

162. 強森女士建議做什麼事？
    (A) 聯絡奧特利本行銷公司
    (B) 前往另一區
    (C) 檢查接待櫃檯
    (D) 遷移會議地點

163. 下午 2:14，李先生說「不好意思」，最有可能是什麼意思？
    (A) 他沒看清楚標籤內容。
    (B) 他需要卡塞爾女士指示再清楚一點。
    (C) 他無法準時抵達該辦公室。
    (D) 他無法找到貨物裝運單。

164. 李先生大概會怎麼處理此包裹？
    (A) 檢視內容物
    (B) 拿給接待人員
    (C) 拿去郵局
    (D) 拿給卡塞爾女士

歡迎安德莉亞・薩切特回歸

營運監督部門很開心歡迎資深企業法律顧問安德莉亞・薩切特回歸本公司。**165** 安德莉亞這六週以來，一直在紐約市參加「企業法規」的專業研討會。**166** 法務政策教育訓練能讓公司行號確保自己遵守最新法規。**166** 參加此訓練的主管人數不斷增加，而安德莉亞已完成此極具挑戰性的課程。**166** 有若干學員均為知名企業的執行長。身為全國企業法務顧問委員會（NCCLC）的一員，安德莉亞在編寫一套指南方面扮演重要角色，也因此舉讓公司行號免於訴訟而獲得肯定。安德莉亞真的表現得太棒了！

165. 可從文中得知安德莉亞・薩切特的哪些訊息？
(A) 她最近升官。
(B) 她是律師。
(C) 她常出差。
(D) 她住在紐約市。

166. 關於研討會的敘述，下列何者不正確？
(A) 為期六週。
(B) 提供企業法規方面的教育訓練。
(C) 由 NCCLC 主辦。
(D) 已持續吸引更多主管參加。

167. 「有若干學員均為知名企業的執行長。」最適合放在 [1]、[2]、[3]、[4] 的哪一個位置？
(A) [1]
(B) [2]
(C) [3]
(D) [4]

當地公園持續進行工程

密德頓　訊（9 月 6 日 **169**）——密德頓鎮目前正在擴建與翻新 15 座公園（共有 30 座）。上述改善工程目前已耗資 410 萬歐元公帑，等於密德頓公園部門（MPD）每年經營和養護公園設施的開銷。**168** 下個月完成所有翻修工程之前，還會再花費 150 萬歐元，**169** 因此總開銷將近 560 萬歐元。

不過，此翻修專案不會對本鎮的預算帶來負擔，因為是由 MPD 所資助進行。過去幾年來，當地公園已吸引越來越多的外地遊客。

停車費、設備租金、零食小店的銷售額以及公園舉辦的活動，均讓收益大幅成長。事實上，去年的數據顯示 MPD 收益 660 萬歐元，算是國內少數經濟獨立的公園部門之一。**170**

MPD 去年六月針對鎮內公園狀態進行廣泛研究後，決定執行此翻修專案。研究內容包括向當地常去鎮內公園的 2,000 名居民分發問卷。作答者被問的主要事項之一，就是評估設施的品質以及提出建議。**171** 然後將彙整的資料與提案送交鎮議會。經過謹慎審核，鎮議會決定批准 MPD 的翻修案。

168. 密德頓公園部門每年經營鎮內公園的費用有多少？
(A) 150 萬歐元
(B) 410 萬歐元
(C) 560 萬歐元
(D) 660 萬歐元

169. 十月預計會發生什麼事？
(A) 翻修工程將完工。
(B) 某公園將關閉。
(C) 將分發問卷調查表。
(D) 將指派新任的官員。

170. 密德頓公園部門與其他相似的機關單位有何不同？

    (A) 提供各種活動。

    (B) 經營國內規模最大的公園系統。

    (C) 大多依賴捐款。

    (D) 能靠收益自給自足。

171. 執行目前的專案之前，有向何者諮詢建議？

    (A) 密德頓居民

    (B) 外國遊客

    (C) 經濟學教授

    (D) 景觀建築師

172–175 電子郵件

寄件人：盧佩・坎圖

收件人：狄倫・天野；史蒂芬・門多薩；
          琦拉・歌德斯坦；梅莉莎・安

日期：9 月 19 日

主旨：公司計畫

附件：Class_Goals;
      Policies_Code_of_Conduct;
      Press_Release_Template

大家好：

感謝大家都同意制定新進員工培訓計畫，以迎接我們 12 月 3 日即將在卡加立開設的第二間分部。<u>分部開始營運前，還有很多事要做。</u>如我們上週在企劃會議所討論的內容，我們必須設計出五種課程。**175**我會將以下職務分配給你們每個人；請注意每項任務的完成日期。

狄倫・天野：請於 10 月 21 日前，提出每種課程所涵括內容的詳細摘要。**172**（請參閱所附的課程目標。）**173**

史蒂芬・門多薩：請根據指導方針與政策的教學內容，來建立簡報投影片。（請參閱所附的人資部文件。）**173**

狄倫・天野：請將教育訓練講義上傳到員工網頁。（請將此資訊傳給資訊部的賽斯・阿德加。）

琦拉・歌德斯坦：請聯絡所有新錄取人員，告知教育訓練課程的時間表。（我們下個月會以電子郵件寄出人員名單。）**173**

梅莉莎・安：請製作一份新聞稿，宣布我們開設第二間分部與推出新教育訓練課程的消息。（請完成所附的新聞稿，並於 11 月 19 日前傳給行銷部的瑞恩・托利亞。）**173**

下次的企劃會議將於 10 月 18 日舉行，以便檢視進度。在那之前，大家如有任何問題或疑問，請告訴我。**174**

人事部經理
盧佩・坎圖

172. 課程說明的截止日是什麼時候？

    (A) 10 月 18 日

    (B) 10 月 21 日

    (C) 11 月 19 日

    (D) 12 月 3 日

173. 誰不需要使用電子郵件的附件？

    (A) 天野先生

    (B) 門多薩先生

    (C) 歌德斯坦女士

    (D) 安女士

174. 坎圖先生要求收件人在下次會議前做什麼事？

    (A) 視察新職場環境

    (B) 將完成的任務交給他

    (C) 兩人一組完成所有任務

    (D) 有任何問題就告訴他

175.「分部開始營運前，還有很多事要做。」最適合放在 [1]、[2]、[3]、[4] 的哪一個位置？

    (A) [1]

    (B) [2]

    (C) [3]

    (D) [4]

http://www.everyoffice.co.uk/orderinfo

首頁	用品區	家具區	訂購資訊

艾維瑞辦公用品股份有限公司
每家公司的辦公用品首選！

透過網路或電話訂購的標準訂單，將馬上進行配送處理。不過請注意，特殊要求的訂單，處理時間會比標準訂單久。若您有任何問題或疑慮，請聯絡 customersupport@everyoffice.co.uk 的客服代表人員。 **177**

總訂購金額	優先急件（24 小時內）	限時（2 天）**179**	平信（5-7 天）**176**
50 美元以下	12 美元	8 美元	5 美元
50-150 美元	15 美元	10 美元	不收費
150 美元以上 **179**	27 美元	20 美元 **179**	不收費

收件人：
customersupport@everyoffice.co.uk
寄件人：
mkline@supermail.co.uk
日期：9 月 6 日
主旨：#4508-1E 的配送

敝公司已訂購共 165 美元的名牌和識別證帶，準備要在星期五的會議使用。 **179** **180** 根據我下訂後所收到的電子郵件內容，昨天應該就要到貨了。儘管我已經多付了限時的郵費，但目前仍在等商品到貨，**178** 所以我希望貴公司能將限時郵費退還至我們公司的帳戶。如果明天早上仍未到貨，我希望你們能取消訂單，因為我們必須到當地店家購買此類產品了。 **180**

謝謝。

馬克・克萊

176. 可從網頁裡得知艾維瑞辦公用品股份有限公司的哪些配送資訊？
(A) 50 美元以下的訂單，平信郵費為免費。
(B) 運費需視商品重量而定。
(C) 當地訂單可享折扣。
(D) 某些訂單可能需要七天的配送時間。

177. 網頁中第一段第三行的「forward」，意思最接近以下何者？
(A) 運送
(B) 迫使
(C) 加快
(D) 提交

178. 此電子郵件的用意為何？
(A) 通報某些受損的商品
(B) 表明配送問題
(C) 詢問客製化訂單
(D) 獲得前往當地供應商的交通資訊

179. 克萊先生支付了多少運費？
(A) 5 美元
(B) 12 美元
(C) 20 美元
(D) 27 美元

180. 根據電子郵件的內容，克萊先生為何考慮前往當地店家？
(A) 他必須在特定日期前拿到所需品項。
(B) 他想擁有更多的產品選擇。
(C) 他偏好與當地零售商做生意。
(D) 他希望購得便宜一點的品項。

181–185 網頁與電子郵件

http://www.flavorsofberkeville.com/advertising_order

首頁	聯絡資訊	**訂單**	評價

《波克維爾的風味》是熱門的電子雜誌，訂閱人數超過一千名。大家訂閱的目的，就是要了解波克維爾地區食品採買與外食的最新資訊。⑱ 如有店家有意自我宣傳，可任選以下四種版面的其中一種來刊登廣告：

版面 A	版面 B
此橫幅廣告位於網頁頂部，會率先吸引讀者的目光。⑱ 此版面不含任何音訊檔或圖像。	此直式橫幅廣告會擺放在專題文章的旁邊。此版面不含任何音訊檔或圖像。
版面 C	版面 D
此小版面會出現在專題文章的中間。含有音訊檔和伴隨文字的一張圖像。	屬於篇幅最大的半版版面，⑱ 含有音訊檔與伴隨文字的多張圖像。

如需購買廣告版面，請洽詢泰瑞莎‧拉波特（t.laparte@flavorsbville.com）。⑱

寄件人：班傑明‧凱恩
<b.kane@bruebistro.com>
收件人：泰瑞莎‧拉波特
<t.laparte@flavorsbville.com>
日期：10 月 24 日
主旨：布魯餐酒館的廣告

親愛的拉波特女士：

我希望在《波克維爾的風味》刊登另一則廣告。我想再次刊登大的廣告版面。⑱
⑱ 請直接使用和以往相同的音訊檔與文字，不過我這次會把餐廳重新裝潢後的三張新照片傳給妳。至於照片該放在廣告的何處，我就留待妳的設計師自行決定。可否請妳告訴我繳交圖像的尺寸規定呢？⑱

布魯餐酒館老闆
班傑明‧凱恩　謹啟 ⑱

TEST 4

PART 7

181. 拉波特女士在哪裡上班？
(A) 在當地的餐廳
(B) 在美食相關的出版社
(C) 在網頁設計公司
(D) 在食品製造公司

182. 可從文中得知版面 A 的哪些訊息？
(A) 易於受到注意。
(B) 平價。
(C) 可快速完成廣告內容。
(D) 可容納最多文字。

183. 凱恩先生對哪一種廣告版面最感興趣？
(A) 版面 A
(B) 版面 B
(C) 版面 C
(D) 版面 D

184. 可從文中得知布魯餐酒館的哪些訊息？
(A) 翻修期間將不營業。
(B) 由知名的設計師重新裝潢。
(C) 曾在《波克維爾的風味》刊登廣告。
(D) 最近入圍某獎項。

185. 凱恩先生詢問了關於照片的哪些問題？
(A) 印刷的費用
(B) 照片要多大
(C) 照片應傳送至何處
(D) 可放多少張照片

186–190 報導、網頁和電子郵件

多倫多　訊（11 月 23 日）——從下週開始，榮獲獎項肯定的記者兼擁有十年歷史的《安大略在線》創辦人——偉恩‧邁阿利斯特，⑱ 即將針對新聞業目前面臨的議題，舉辦一連串的研習會。

邁阿利斯特先生將於 12 月 1 日和 2 日，在溫哥華的緬因街禮堂開講。12 月 4 日的演講地點是魁北克市的瓦索會議中心。12 月 6 日的演講地點是溫尼伯的市中心禮堂。⑱ 12 月 8 日在多倫多的大都會會議中心。而 12 月 9 日則在蒙特婁的公共圖書館，進行最後一場演講。

門票很快售罄。如需了解更多資訊與購票，請至 www.ontarioonline.co.ca。

首頁	新訊	十二月的 研習會	訂票	訂閱

偉恩・邁阿利斯特的十二月研習會時間表

日期	時間	主題	地點
12月1日	下午 4:30	網路聯絡窗口：在網上查找線索	溫哥華
12月2日	下午 4:00	行動新聞業的崛起	溫哥華
12月4日	下午 4:30	如何運用社群媒體來獲得報導的曝光率	魁北克市
12月6日 **187**	下午 5:30	減法概念：頭條標題即連結 **187**	溫尼伯 **187**
12月8日 **189**	下午 5:00	如何運用社群媒體來獲得報導的曝光率	多倫多 **189**
12月9日	下午 4:30	創造獨立平台的內容	蒙特婁

請點選訂票頁籤，以了解場地和票價的更多資訊。

收件人：klovett@mediaminder.co.ca
寄件人：dslater@ontarioonline.co.ca
日期：11月28日
主旨：邁阿利斯特先生的研習會

親愛的勒福特女士：

很開心得知您有意參加偉恩・邁阿利斯特先生的研習會。不過，您詢問的多倫多場次，門票恐怕已經售罄。 **188** **189** 請注意，同樣的主題將在12月4日於魁北克市舉行，該場次目前尚有門票。

如果您想要跟邁阿利斯特先生預約親自見面或以視訊會議的方式，在您的公司進行私人講座活動的話，我可以幫您安排。 **190**

《安大略在線》
丹尼爾・史萊特　謹啟 **190**

186. 可從文中得知關於邁阿利斯特先生的哪些訊息？
(A) 他於十年前創業。
(B) 他住在魁北克市。
(C) 他定期在會議中心舉辦免費研習會。
(D) 他每年十二月都會到加拿大旅遊。

187. 與頭條標題有關的講座，將於何處舉辦？
(A) 緬因街禮堂
(B) 市中心禮堂
(C) 瓦索會議中心
(D) 公共圖書館

188. 此電子郵件的用意為何？
(A) 宣布某行程的時間需延後
(B) 接受某項邀請
(C) 預約私人演講活動
(D) 回覆某詢問事項

189. 勒福特女士原本有意參加哪一天的活動？
(A) 12月2日
(B) 12月4日
(C) 12月6日
(D) 12月8日

190. 史萊特先生最有可能從事何種職業？
(A) 公司執行長
(B) 網站開發人員
(C) 行政專員
(D) 新聞記者

《商業合夥人》：第 34 期

10 個提升盈餘的手機程式

1.「差旅達人」提供了一種簡單的方式來追蹤所有出差車馬費開銷。它非常適合經常開車奔波的職員，能將所有開支儲存在便利的單一程式中，並以方便使用的介面加以整理。

當您一邊開車、一邊使用「差旅達人」的行動裝置，程式就會以裝置的導航功能追蹤您的去處，**192** 並上傳資料。每一趟路程都會輸入虛擬記錄檔，建立您的路線確切紀錄。**191** 您可存取該紀錄，來新增油費等細節，或註記交通概況。

您可使用顯示交通概況、可用停車位或節省時間的捷徑等新功能。其中一項熱門功能，就是最佳化定期往返的路程，例如配送路線、每週客戶會議與機場接駁路線。

每條路線均會備份於應用程式的伺服器。**191** 本程式的價格已涵蓋使用、儲存和持續開發的費用。個人方案每個月的價格是 5 美元，當月可儲存 20 個虛擬記錄檔。**195** 價格越高的方案，虛擬記錄檔的數量越多。

感謝您下載「差旅達人」手機應用程式！

開始使用前，請先填妥以下資料。完成後，即可使用第一筆虛擬記錄檔。別忘了升級訂閱的功能。若您需要更多筆記錄檔，請至 www.tripfolioapp.com/accounts。祝您行車平安！

使用者詳細資料：
姓名：威廉・柏克 **193**
電子郵件信箱：williamb@sunkitsales.com
手機號碼：702-555-6813
您多常開車往返各地？每週 11-14 次

您是否前往其他城市：是
常去的目的地：洛杉磯、鳳凰城、聖塔菲、阿布奎基

請選擇方案：
個人方案：每月 5 美元 □
小型企業：每月 15 美元 □
中型企業：每月 30 美元 ☑ **193**
大型企業：每月 50 美元 □

收件人：williamb@sunkitsales.com
寄件人：support@tripfolioapp.com
日期：11 月 27 日
主旨：使用者須知

「差旅達人」使用者您好：

我們的訂閱套裝價格，將於明年開始異動。此舉能讓我們提供重要的服務更新，如包括更多筆費用記錄功能，**194** 以及多兩種語言的選擇。**194** 此外，中型和大型企業的訂閱者，將能購買新的特殊套裝方案，**194** 其中包括無法使用手機服務時，可列印記錄檔和路線圖的功能。而修訂後的定價將於 1 月 1 日生效，具體內容如下：

方案	月費	虛擬記錄檔容量
個人方案 **195**	5 美元	30 筆記錄檔 **195**
小型企業	15 美元	50 筆記錄檔
中型企業	30 美元	100 筆記錄檔
大型企業	60 美元	300 筆記錄檔

中型和大型企業的訂閱者，將可獲贈一個旅行袋。**193** 如果您有任何疑問，歡迎與我們聯絡！

support@tripfolioapp.com

191. 根據文章節錄的內容，「差旅達人」手機應用程式能讓使用者做什麼事情？
(A) 記錄顧客的購物情況
(B) 預訂國際班機
(C) 預約租車服務
(D) 儲存詳細的路線資訊

192. 可從文中得知關於「差旅達人」手機應用程式的哪些訊息？
(A) 設計榮獲多種獎項的肯定。
(B) 需要存取行動裝置的某功能。
(C) 僅能與最新的智慧型裝置相容。
(D) 比競爭對手的應用程式更昂貴。

193. 柏克先生為何符合獲得旅行袋的資格？
(A) 他以付費訂閱「差旅達人」的方式作為贈禮。
(B) 他參加某社區比賽。
(C) 他去過當地許多景點。
(D) 他是中型企業方案的訂閱者。

194. 關於價格異動的原因，電子郵件裡未提及什麼事？
(A) 提供新的特殊套裝方案
(B) 提供更多記錄花費的方式
(C) 能讓更多國家使用該應用程式
(D) 增加新的語言選項

195. 個人方案有何種特定異動？
(A) 更新駕駛交通資訊。
(B) 改善了付款方法。
(C) 已刪除部分非必要的資安功能。
(D) 將增加虛擬記錄檔的容量。

196-200 廣告、表格和信函

徵求全職網站程式設計師

獲得獎項肯定的資訊科技公司「媒體馬克」，自 1992 年開始服務芝加哥的公司行號。我們想徵求網站程式設計師，在軟體開發主管的指示下，為我們的線上付款程式設計特定內容。196 應徵資格是具備電腦科學的碩士學位或一年的程式設計工作經驗。應徵者需要展現架設高科技網站與維護網站資安的能力。197

請至 www.mediamark.com/jobs 應徵。

www.mediamark.com/jobs/web_programmer/

姓名：丹妮卡‧柯維克
電話號碼：650-555-7835
電子郵件信箱：dkovac@lightningmail.com

教育程度：西港大學電腦科學系學士學位

目前任職公司：數據鎖資安公司
職位：網站程式設計師
工作時間：三個月

前任雇主：蘭斯特程式設計公司
職位：程式設計師
工作時間：十二個月 197

前任雇主：iNet 網路公司
職位：初階軟體開發人員
工作時間：兩個月 200

附件：
履歷
推薦信

求職信：我希望應徵媒體馬克公司的全職網站程式設計師職位。我已經在一家資安公司裡擔任網站程式設計師一段時間，此公司的業務是維護受到保護的資料庫。197 由於該公司剛成立，我需要負責幾乎所有專案的程式設計工作。我曾受僱於國際軟體公司「蘭斯特程式設計公司」，我的上司是世界知名的大衛‧摩斯。197 此外，我的老師兼論文指導教授吉娜‧羅曼諾，能證實我會使用最新科技來架設網站。197 198 事實上，我在大學期間，曾因為架設網路商店的專案而贏得現金 200 美元的獎勵。此專案目前則成為其他大學學生的範本教材。199

提交表格

西港大學

電腦科學系 198

黎恩姆・艾伯頓
媒體馬克
94025 加州門洛帕克市
柏克利大道 2992 號

親愛的艾伯頓先生：

此封信函與丹妮卡・柯維克應徵貴公司職務有關。由於羅曼諾女士在本學期均休假，因此她要求我代她撰寫此信。198 柯維克小姐強大的程式設計技能，以及迅速解決艱難問題的能力，使她在班上名列前茅。她在實習兩個月後，主管暨知名的產業領導人飛利浦・周，向她提出繼續兼職工作的機會。200 我相信柯維克小姐將會成為貴公司的重要一員。

敬祝　安康

西港工程學系系主任
喬許華・羅迪斯

196. 可從文中得知關於網站程式設計師職位的哪些訊息？
(A) 可前往不同國家出差。
(B) 只需任職一年。
(C) 需設計限定數量的應用程式功能。
(D) 需要在週末上班。

197. 關於柯維克小姐的敘述，以下何者正確？
(A) 她和摩斯先生的恩師是同一人。
(B) 她在零售商店工作。
(C) 她已向許多公司傳送應徵資料。
(D) 她符合某職缺的資格。

198. 羅曼諾女士的身分為何？
(A) 商務軟體開發人員
(B) 電腦科學系講師
(C) 大學行政人員
(D) 工程學系學生

199. 可從文中得知關於西港大學的哪些訊息？
(A) 會邀請產業領導人來演講。
(B) 提供軟體操作展示會。
(C) 提供獎金。
(D) 正要聘僱新教授。

200. 周先生最有可能任職於哪家公司？
(A) 媒體馬克
(B) 數據鎖資安公司
(C) 蘭斯特程式設計公司
(D) iNet 網路公司

ACTUAL TEST ⑤

PART 5 P. 122–124

101. 如要參加比賽，我們必須在 6 月 10 日之前收到您的報名資料。
- **(A) 提交物**
- (B) 提交
- (C) 已提交
- (D) 繳交人

102. 新租戶通常會在支付押金後，拿到公寓鑰匙。
- **(A) 通常**
- (B) 之前
- (C) 持續地
- (D) 每年地

103. 北歐垂釣公司會僱用對釣魚充滿熱忱的銷售人員，才能讓顧客對購買商品感到躍躍欲試。
- (A) 愉快的
- (B) 有禮的
- **(C) 熱忱的**
- (D) 有邏輯的

104. 柏克福德辦公用品商店為了酬謝我們公司持續不斷的惠顧，而寄給我們價值 100 美元的禮券。
- (A) 餘額
- **(B) 禮券**
- (C) 方式
- (D) 收據

105. 索登咖啡廳邀請顧客試喝含有當地出產食材的各種飲品。
- (A) 含有
- (B) 含有
- (C) 曾含有
- **(D) 含有**

106. 如果你的計畫改變了，你可以更改預約日期，或是要求部分退款。
- (A) 無論是
- **(B) 或者……或者……**
- (C) 除非
- (D) 在……期間

107. 不管會有多少來賓出席，我們已經印出足夠分送的資料袋。
- (A) 反而
- (B) 很多
- **(C) 不管**
- (D) 在……之內

108. T&G 事務所很高興能向大家宣布，「李健身中心」即將搬遷至布萊爾街上一處更寬敞的場所。
- (A) 組裝
- (B) 宣傳
- **(C) 報告**
- (D) 監督

109. 金先生任職部門經理才短短兩個月的時間，就已參加將近 12 場會議。
- (A) 比較靠近的
- (B) 接近的
- (C) 靠近中
- **(D) 將近，幾乎**

110. 執行長授權與「塔斯貝克企業」合併。
- (A) 層面
- **(B) 授權**
- (C) 愉快
- (D) 影響

111. 狄肯大學法律圖書館以往僅向就讀本校的學生開放，如今一般民眾亦可入館使用。
- (A) 廣泛地
- (B) 突然地
- **(C) 以往**
- (D) 很快地

112. 今天下午的劇院來賓請注意，《靜謐之湖》表演將因禮堂維修工程而延後。
- (A) 已訂票
- (B) 已組成
- **(C) 被延後**
- (D) 預期的

113. 由於馬丁尼先生成了新的部門主管，因此他將監督新技師的教育訓練課程。
(A) 他自己
(B) 他的
(C) 他
(D) 他

114. 雖然卡特女士錯過了轉機航班，但她仍在預計時間內抵達了科技博覽會。
(A) 既然
(B) 雖然
(C) 由於
(D) 儘快

115. 投影機在湯普森女士介紹產品時當機，她便現場發揮，即興演說。
(A) 即興做……
(B) 授權
(C) 主持
(D) 到達

116. 由於下雨的緣故，工人還沒有完成屋頂的工程。
(A) ……的
(B) 來自……
(C) 在……裡面
(D) 處理……與……

117. 來店購物者應使用購物中心後門附近的廁所，因為大門附近的那些廁所正在重新粉刷。
(A) 每個
(B) 那些
(C) 那個
(D) 另一個

118. HD 百貨公司今年在全國銷售業績中總排名第二。
(A) 整體地
(B) 聯合地
(C) 寬廣地
(D) 連續地

119. 要想買到優質又平價的產品，一定要到威明頓的「櫻桃溪暢貨中心」購物。
(A) 曾負擔
(B) 平價的
(C) 負擔
(D) 負擔中

120. 導演森千惠子很開心得知，一些影評家將她的影片和井桁金太郎的熱門作品《橫濱的一天》相提並論做了一番比較。
(A) 差異
(B) 比較
(C) 要求
(D) 關係

121. 新的包裹追蹤應用程式，不僅能顯示包裹目前的位置，還可顯示預計配送的日期和時間。
(A) 何時
(B) 不但……而且……
(C) 為了……
(D) 此外

122. 克拉克森有限公司正在徵求能夠管理其東南亞分公司的資深管理人員。
(A) 治理中
(B) 管理的
(C) 管理者
(D) 掌管

123. 「火湖輪胎公司」的先進胎紋科技，能讓輪胎行經雪地或結冰路面時，提供最紮實牢固的抓地力。
(A) 穩固地
(B) 最穩固的
(C) 穩固的
(D) 比較穩固的

124. 在首頁納入客戶見證的做法，能讓公司提升在大眾心目中的信賴度。
(A) 預期
(B) 許可
(C) 目的
(D) 可信度

125. 開幕典禮的地點改到喬迪體育場舉行，以確保所有觀眾都有足夠的座位可坐。
(A) 持續的
(B) 足夠的
(C) 整體的
(D) 現代化的

126. 居民將於下週，在蒂埃里宴會廳公開表揚黑李·卡特數十年來為地方服務的貢獻。
- (A) 曾公開表揚
- (B) 已公開表揚
- (C) 將已公開表揚
- **(D) 即將公開表揚**

127. PDL 生物科技公司要求工作人員在偵測到實驗室出現任何外洩或故障情況時，應馬上打電話聯絡警衛室。
- (A) 而不是
- **(B) 馬上**
- (C) 像……一樣
- (D) 不是很多……

128. 誰最後一個離開辦公室，誰就要負責關燈。
- **(A) 無論是誰**
- (B) 任何人
- (C) 所有人
- (D) 某人

129. 威爾股份有限公司與戴維森企業近期合作進行了一項清理都市街道的環保活動。
- **(A) 合作**
- (B) 建立
- (C) 平息
- (D) 委派

130. 兒童科博館今年暑假比去年同期，多吸引了 20% 的遊客。
- **(A) 吸引了**
- (B) 吸引
- (C) 將吸引
- (D) 已吸引

PART 6 P. 125-128

131–134 廣告

報名「都會高爾夫」為期兩週的會員體驗期，您將可享有試用我們高爾夫設施、課程與其他便利設施的機會。試用期間不需付款或簽約，完全不需履行任何承諾。若要開始試用，您只需要準備信用卡和有效的身分證件。除非您保留會員身分超過 15 天的時間，否則我們不會向您的帳戶扣款。在此期間，若您覺得「都會高爾夫」不適合您，只要撥打 1-800-555-1212 聯絡客服中心即可。您與客服代表聯絡時，請在確認身分後，要求取消會籍即可。那麼，您還在等什麼？心動不如馬上行動！

131.
- (A) 本次不會提供私人高爾夫課程。
- (B) 我們的客服專員隨時可協助您。
- **(C) 試用期間不需付款或簽約。**
- (D) 您註冊成為會員時，請務必繳交小額押金。

132. (A) 超過
- (B) 低於
- (C) 將近
- (D) 不完全是……

133. (A) 只要……即可
- (B) 公正地
- (C) 持續地
- (D) 正常地

134. (A) 啟動
- (B) 更新
- (C) 延長
- **(D) 取消**

135–138 信函

與所有法瑞斯公司的員工一樣，公司允許你可因就醫申請一定天數的帶薪病假。為了收到請假日的全薪薪資，公司會要求你提交一份正式的醫師證明，確認你有健康上的問題。醫師證明必須清楚顯示就醫日期、醫師建議你不適合工作的事實，以及能恢復工作的日期。此資料會由分公司經理存留在你的人事檔案中。而法瑞斯公司會嚴格保密你的個人資料。只有你的直屬主管和人資部可存取職員的就醫檔案，我們不會向其他人、部門或外部機構共享此資料。

135. (A) 資格
(B) 保險
(C) 設備
(D) 原因

136. (A) 要求
(B) 正要求
(C) 曾要求
(D) 被要求

137. (A) 它
(B) 我
(C) 這些
(D) 他們

138. (A) 你請假的時間長短，取決於很多情況。
(B) 而法瑞斯公司會嚴格保密你的個人資料。
(C) 你會收到人資部的年度考核報告。
(D) 如果你的工作對健康產生負面影響，你應和分公司經理談一談。

139–142 電子郵件

收件人：ericnakagawa@xrmail.com
寄件人：JohnKim@hartleylaboratories.com
日期：10 月 2 日
主旨：開始到哈特利實驗室上班

親愛的中川先生：

歡迎加入哈特利實驗室。感謝您接任全職的研究助理一職。10 月 9 日是您第一天到加州雷德蘭茲廠上班，我們都很興奮。屆時請前來主實驗室，並告知接待人員，您要找凱倫·包蒂斯塔。她會指引您前往您的工作區。您會在自己的工作區，看到實驗袍以及工作所需的所有設備。如您所知，由於我們需處理各種危險物質，因此需要遵守許多安全規定。請仔細查看流程手冊，以便清楚處理不同物質的規定。您的電子信箱應該已收到此手冊。

如果您對手冊任何內容有疑問，歡迎隨時告訴我。

感謝您。

廠長
約翰·金

139. (A) 申請
(B) 考慮
(C) 刊登
(D) 接受

140. (A) 指引
(B) 將指引
(C) 確實指引
(D) 指引

141. (A) 以及
(B) 此外
(C) 也
(D) 也

142. (A) 今年不久後，我們將改變規定。
(B) 您的電子信箱應該已收到此手冊。
(C) 如果某物質看似危險，應聯絡主管。
(D) 務必每天檢查所有設備。

7 月 21 日──全國規模最大的恆溫器供應商「ARF 溫控股份有限公司」，預計明年的訂單即將大幅增加。之所以有此預測，在於有消息指出發電廠法規變嚴格後，必須依法安裝更多恆溫器。執行長巴特·皮爾森預測，本季 ARF 公司的銷售量將達到驚人的 75 萬組。這是該公司成立以來，第一次創下如此新高的紀錄。

ARF 會向規模較小的公司購買許多產品，然後為各種大小的廠房客製化產品。皮爾森先生表示：「業界的製造量需求增加，使 ARF 公司得以迅速拓展業務。我們認為未來的潛力無可限量。」

143. (A) 取消
(B) **預測**
(C) 價格
(D) 選擇

144. (A) 皮爾森先生在業界的資歷已超過 35 年。
(B) ARF 的前五大客戶均為主流的發電廠製造商。
(C) **這是該公司成立以來，第一次創下如此新高的紀錄。**
(D) 如今，工廠恆溫器已經十分先進。

145. (A) 在……期間
(B) **為了……**
(C) 像……一樣
(D) 在……上方

146. (A) 製造
(B) 製造商
(C) 曾製造
(D) **正在製造**

147–148 公告

歡迎光臨捷爾森飯店

我們會盡力讓您在此度過愉快的時光。147 若您基於任何因素而對住宿品質不滿意，請撥打分機 200 聯絡房務組。

我們位於一樓接待大廳右側的餐廳，會在每天早上 7 點至 11 點供應早餐。請於進入餐廳時，向服務人員出示房卡即可。

我們一直在努力改善服務品質，若您有任何建議或疑問，請撥打分機 202 與我聯絡。148

敬祝　安康

捷爾森飯店
經理 147
艾力克斯·科明塔

147. 此公告的目的為何？
(A) **與飯店房客溝通**
(B) 歡迎新職員加入
(C) 推廣某菜單
(D) 僱用房務人員

148. 房客應以何種方式提出反饋？
(A) 寫電子郵件
(B) **找飯店經理談談**
(C) 打電話聯絡櫃台人員
(D) 填寫問卷

149–150 廣告

寇奇專賣店

我們的海灘用品專賣店即將大清倉！ 150

寇奇專賣店現正出清上一季的各種商品庫存！從大品牌的泳鏡到涼鞋，全都降價到低於零售價格。全面打 6 折到 2.5 折！

此清倉大拍賣時間為 9 月 25 日至 10 月 3 日。千萬別錯過！

營業時間：每天早上 9:30 至晚上 8:00。我們的店址就在緬因街和高瑞斯大道的東北角，或可至 www.corkysemporium.co.ca 線上購物。

149. 此公告最有可能是誰發布的？

    (A) 鞋款設計師

    (B) 倉庫主管

    (C) 行銷總監

    (D) 店家老闆

150. 可從文中得知關於寇奇專賣店的什麼訊息？

    (A) 最近剛開幕。

    (B) 經常提供折價券。

    (C) 位於靠近某水域的地方。

    (D) 每週都有促銷活動。

151–152 簡訊串

> **卡麥隆・席維斯特〔下午 3:12〕**
> 妮可，午安。我昨天早上寄出廠商合約後，至今還沒收到你們部門的回音。你們審核完了嗎？ 151
>
> **妮可・門多薩〔下午 3:13〕**
> 合約交給了我的助理。她今天下班前應該能改完條款內容。 151
>
> **卡麥隆・席維斯特〔下午 3:14〕**
> 太好了！我明天早上和業務處長與執行長開會時要交出。
>
> **妮可・門多薩〔下午 3:16〕**
> 我們幾小時後就會將註記修改建議的合約傳給你。如果你還有其他建議，打給我就可以了。 152
>
> **卡麥隆・席維斯特〔下午 3:17〕**
> <u>沒問題</u>。感激不盡。

151. 門多薩女士最有可能任職於哪一個部門？

    (A) 財務部門

    (B) 法務部門

    (C) 業務部門

    (D) 人事部門

152. 下午 3:17，席維斯特先生說：「沒問題」，最有可能是什麼意思？

    (A) 他會透過電話做筆記。

    (B) 他會將最後定稿的合約，以電子郵件的方式傳給廠商。

    (C) 他會將某些文件交給執行長。

    (D) 他會讓門多薩女士知曉任何異動。

153–154 備忘錄

> 收文者：全體職員
> 發文者：史蒂芬・蒙特羅伊
> 日期：5 月 17 日
> 主旨：加班事宜
>
> 早安：
>
> 傳統上，六月和七月是計程車司機最忙碌的月分。因此，**我們預計會比平常多出 30% 的工時。** 153 在刊登徵才廣告前，我想先了解一下，有沒有現任員工有意加班。 153 154 司機每加班一小時，可獲得比平常時薪多 10% 的工資。如果有人感興趣，請在 5 月 17 日的下午 4 點前通知我。 154 此外，如果有人在六月和七月休假，亦請在上述日期前通知我，我才能在規劃僱用臨時司機的時候，將大家請假的情況納入考量。
>
> 史蒂芬・蒙特羅伊　謹啟

153. 此備忘錄的目的為何？

    (A) 建議職員在七月休假

    (B) 通報計程車車資異動

    (C) 要求大家提供過去兩個月的公帳開銷

    (D) 宣布員工適用的工作機會

154. 根據備忘錄的內容，蒙特羅伊先生 5 月 17 日以後，大概很快會執行什麼計畫？

    (A) 修訂現行的休假政策

    (B) 辭去職務

    (C) 招募更多正式員工

    (D) 張貼招募季節性臨時工的廣告

歡迎捐獻

威洛瀑布博物館（WFM）的使命，在於讓大眾免費入場觀展。**156** WFM 十分仰賴捐款，才能設立與維護大家現在看到的各項展覽。**155** 請考慮至櫃檯或至我們的網站 www.willowfallsmuseum.org/support 填寫捐款表。

若您有興趣成為 WFM 之友俱樂部的會員，請至服務台或此網址 www.willowfallsmuseum.org/sponsor 註冊會員。贊助人將收到我們博物館的收藏家指南，裡面詳述了至今最知名的歷史展覽，**155** **157** 以及每月一封電子郵件，告知博物館所有活動，**157** 還有展現您支持我們博物館的時尚 WFM T 恤。**157** 贊助人每年至少須捐助 180 美元。

155. 此傳單最有可能在什麼場所發送？
(A) 歷史博物館
(B) 學校的辦公室
(C) 書店
(D) 政府辦公大樓

156. 可從文中得知關於博物館展覽的什麼資訊？
(A) 每個月會更換一次。
(B) 由知名館長管理。
(C) 不需入場費。
(D) 最近剛整修過。

157. 文中並未提到哪一項成為贊助人的福利？
(A) 贊助人會收到一件衣物。
(B) 贊助人會收到活動行事曆。
(C) 會在線上公布贊助人的名字。
(D) 贊助人會得到一本介紹某些展品的書。

寄件人：蘭斯・普拉特
收件人：內森・佛瑞斯特
日期：10 月 4 日星期一
主旨：洛許山莊度假村

親愛的佛瑞斯特先生：

根據我們的紀錄，您與家人將於下下週末抵達洛許山莊度假村。很開心您選擇在我們這裡度假。

我們想特此告知，兩週後這裡將舉行沃特福德自行車錦標賽。**158** 為期兩天的自行車賽，從沃特福德出發至布倫特夏爾。**159** 雖然觀賽很有趣，但請注意，數個觀光景點將於比賽期間關閉，包括沃特福德博物館。**160** 由於您已預訂住宿五個晚上，您還是有機會前往上述景點參觀。

穿越城鎮的公路仍維持開放，因此您仍可安心抵達我們的地點。由於屆時會有許多觀賽民眾，而且度假村非常靠近比賽的起點，如果您打算進城，請做好會嚴重塞車的心理準備。由於遊客數量增加的緣故，沃特福德的餐廳可能會一位難求。**159**

我不希望等到您抵達時才驚覺有此活動，因此想提早告知您。若您希望了解更多資訊，請打電話聯絡我們。

洛許山莊度假村總經理
蘭斯・普拉特　謹啟

158. 普拉特先生為何寄電子郵件給佛瑞斯特先生？
(A) 針對訂房錯誤的情況道歉
(B) 回應對方所詢問的度假村服務
(C) 說明獲得家庭折扣的流程
(D) 提供某排定活動的資訊

159. 可從文中得知關於洛許山莊度假村的什麼資訊？
(A) 無法從公路開到度假村。
(B) 位於沃特福德市。
(C) 為房客安排自行車觀光行程。
(D) 比賽期間將不營業。

160. 「由於您已預訂住宿五個晚上，您還是有機會前往上述景點參觀。」最適合放在 [1]、[2]、[3]、[4] 的哪一個位置？
(A) [1]
(B) [2]
(C) [3]
(D) [4]

161–163 信函

亨利・拉巴斯
5451 法國波爾多市拉羅特街 911 號

親愛的拉巴斯先生：

由於當前的全球商業環境發展極為相互依存且相互聯繫，因此與世界各地的同仁建立專業關係變得比以往更加重要。這就是為何「聯合醫事中心」針對遍布 60 個國家、超過五萬多名醫學實驗室研究人員，建立完善詳細名錄的原因。162 163 今天就加入聯合醫事中心來拓展您的同儕圈。161 162

若您訂閱我們的「銀等商務名錄」，即可存取我們資料庫裡所列每位人士的姓名與聯絡資料，以及如護士、醫師與核磁共振造影技師等其他醫學專業人士的資料。163 若您決定訂閱「金等商務名錄」，您不僅能存取上述所有資料，還能存取目前醫學專案與進展的詳細資訊。

為了讓您有機會探究此項服務，我們將提供您免費試用一個月。如果您想註冊使用此免費服務，或是成為定期訂閱會員，請前往我們的網站 www.mcunited.com.bg/subscription。

行銷總監
伊蘭諾・雷納　謹啟

161. 此信函的目的為何？
(A) 吸引新顧客
(B) 要求對方提供更多資料
(C) 安排檢查的時間
(D) 推薦醫學專家

162. 拉巴斯先生最有可能是什麼身分？
(A) 實驗室研究人員
(B) 醫師
(C) 護士
(D) 核磁共振造影技師

163. 聯合醫事中心提供何種服務？
(A) 救回遺失的資料檔案
(B) 促使專業人士交流
(C) 提供醫療保健課程
(D) 開發網站

164–167 簡訊串

艾美・費雪〔上午 10:09〕
大家早，我在找金柏莉。

荷西・那華若〔上午 10:11〕
我幾分鐘前才看到她。一切都還好嗎？

艾美・費雪〔上午 10:12〕
不巧的是投影機似乎無法運作，164 165 我試過各種方法了。

荷西・那華若〔上午 10:13〕
糟糕！165 今天的教育訓練課幾點開始？164

艾美・費雪〔上午 10:15〕
10:30 準時上課。已經大約有 20 人到場，我們預計會有 44 人來參加。

金柏莉・明〔上午 10:16〕
我剛去儲藏室，想找看看有沒有額外的投影機，166 但運氣不好。艾美和我還得設置喇叭與整理資料袋，我們只剩幾分鐘的時間而已。

荷西・那華若〔上午 10:17〕
也沒有足夠的時間去別家分公司借投影機了。我現在就去麥斯電子買一部新的投影機。167 就在我們這條街上而已。

164. 費雪女士最有可能身在何處？
(A) 音樂廳
(B) 會議室
(C) 倉庫
(D) 電子產品商店

165. 上午 10:13 的時候，那華若先生說：「糟糕」，最有可能代表什麼意思？

  (A) 機器無法運作。
  (B) 主講人會晚到。
  (C) 某職員太忙碌。
  (D) 已延後某場會議。

166. 可從文中得知關於明女士的什麼資訊？

  (A) 她主動想辦法。
  (B) 她是那華若先生的主管。
  (C) 她制定了教育訓練計畫。
  (D) 她是新進員工。

167. 那華若先生接下來最有可能做什麼事？

  (A) 加入費雪女士和明女士
  (B) 聯絡別家分公司
  (C) 告知經理
  (D) 購買某物品

168–171 電子郵件

寄件人：瑪莎·瑞華
<mriva@employprospects.com>
收件人：莎曼珊·普萊斯
<sprice@tmail.com>
日期：3 月 17 日
主旨：下一步

親愛的莎曼珊：

謝謝您傳履歷和大學成績單給我。**169** 我已經將您的資料新增至「就業前景公司」的資料庫。

我們已經媒合到適合您學經歷的幾個短期職位，其中包括兩個行政職位、一個律師事務所的辦公助理職位，還有一個牙科診所的櫃台職位。**170** 此外，我們還有媒合到一個全職正式員工的職位。此份全職工作需要先實習三個月，但之後就可轉正成為廣電公司的製作助理。由於您具備媒體傳播方面的學位，因此此職位對您而言，可說是十分理想。不過，您的履歷裡提及目前居住於史特拉瀑布市，**170** 距離位於巴爾的摩的廣電公司滿遠的。如果您願意通勤，請告訴我。**168** **171** 雖然其他短期職缺的上班地點，均在您所處區域範圍內，**170** 但如果您能彈性些，不排斥遠距離上班，我們會再向您提供更多工作機會。

在我們聯絡任何雇主之前，要請您提供兩封推薦信。**168** **171** 必須是前雇主或大學教授所撰寫的專業推薦函。請您在明天之前，以電子郵件告訴我推薦人的姓名和電話。**168** 您完成上述步驟後，我們將安排您與我們的專業徵才顧問面試。**171** 屆時請聯繫我的辦公室，以便安排您方便面試的時間。**168**

就業前景公司

瑪莎·瑞華　謹啟

168. 此電子郵件的用意為何？

  (A) 確認某預約行程
  (B) 要求對方提供更多資料
  (C) 宣布面試結果
  (D) 提供行車交通資訊

169. 可從文中得知關於普萊斯小姐的什麼資訊？

  (A) 她任職於就業前景公司。
  (B) 她已寄出一些文件給瑞華女士。
  (C) 她是資深的製作人。
  (D) 她最近剛拿到學位。

170. 關於櫃台職位的描述，何者正確？
   (A) 工作時間彈性。
   (B) 隸屬於法律事務所。
   (C) 屬於正職。
   (D) 上班地點靠近史特拉瀑布市。

171. 瑞華女士並未要求普萊斯小姐做什麼事情？
   (A) 填寫並回傳某表格
   (B) 確認通勤意願
   (C) 提供推薦信
   (D) 安排會面時間

172–175 活動時間表

墨西哥市全球行銷會議

11 月 15 日至 18 日 172 ★內卡哈商務中心★
墨西哥，墨西哥市

活動行程
11 月 15 日星期一 172

搜尋引擎大補帖
上午 7:45 至上午 8:30 172　C 演講廳

《今日行銷》的專欄作家伊莉莎白·李，將探討產業變化、回答問題與推廣她的新書《搜尋引擎大補帖》。

網站設計入門
上午 8:45 至上午 9:30 172　阿納瓦克館 173

網站設計師瑪莉·艾倫·托瑞斯與瑞克·賈西亞，將透過許多易於實際操作的課程，來引導學員創建具有成效的網頁。 173

線上廣告研習會
上午 9:45 至上午 10:30 172　藍花楹劇院

針對網路客戶所做的行銷策略。

主講人：「i 推廣公司」廣告總監——荷西·埃爾南德茲，以及「真實市場公司」社群媒體活動經理——蘇珊·凱爾。我們會在研習會當天，於劇院入口處特價販售此課程的教材講義。 174

21 世紀的消費者
上午 10:45 至上午 11:30 172　403 會議室

主講人羅伊·辛能與伯納德·狄亞茲，將帶領大家探討如何從現今消費模式，看出未來的行銷趨勢。

- 可至我們的網站 www.gmconf.mx 預訂靠近商務中心的住宿地點。商務中心的美食街均有供餐，或可至附近許多餐廳用餐。

- 可上網或現場購買適用於上述活動或其他會議活動的一日票券，票價為 1,100 比索。

- 為了確保有座位可坐，請儘早到場，因為我們的活動無法預先保留座位。 175 請注意，雖然會場允許拍照，但禁止任何錄影和錄音行為。

172. 可從文中得知關於墨西哥市全球行銷會議開幕當天的什麼資訊？
   (A) 預計當天的出席率較低。
   (B) 李女士將討論新書裡的看法。
   (C) 下午沒有安排任何活動。
   (D) 是由行銷出版社所規劃。

173. 行銷會議參加者能在何處參加互動活動？
   (A) C 演講廳
   (B) 阿納瓦克館
   (C) 藍花楹劇院
   (D) 403 會議室

174. 文中提到關於研習會講義的什麼資訊？
   (A) 應於最後一天訂購。
   (B) 必須向主講人索取。
   (C) 可在會場購得。
   (D) 票價已包括教材費。

175. 行銷會議鼓勵出席者採取什麼行動？
(A) 有問題可聯絡主辦單位
(B) 搭接駁車至商務中心
(C) 提早到場參加活動
(D) 課程結束後拍照

176–180 時間表與信函

「一A」企業

位於羅斯戴爾社區中心的早晨研習會
6 月 30 日 星 期 五，上 午 8:30 到 中 午 12:15

時程表

上午 8:15：一A 公司職員簽到並領取名牌

上午 8:30 課程：「擔任會計部經理的頭一年」 176

上午 9:15 課程：「如何管理需要協助的客服部員工」 176

上午 10:00 課程：「激勵業務人員取得優異業績」 178

上午 10:30：與主講人會面寒暄；茶點時間

上午 11:00 課程：「讓資訊工程管理事業更上一層樓」 176 177

上午 11:30：閉幕致詞

---

7 月 14 日

大衛·雪帕德先生
克雷企業
CB2 3ND 英國 劍橋市席尼街 88 號

親愛的雪帕德先生：

您也許還記得，我與一A 公司同事參加兩週前的研習會時，有和您見過一面。 177 您與主講夥伴進行的課程，內容豐富實用，很有幫助。我很欣賞艾拉·拉森探討督導客服部員工的方法，以及安德魯·吉安諾傳授激勵團隊成員取得優異業績。 178

不過，您的課程格外有趣，因為我很快就要擔任公司的管理職。聽您訴說管理一大群專業人士的經驗，真的讓我在管理這條路上獲益良多。我希望您可以再多分享，您在擔任技術長時所有效運用的技巧、資源等更多資訊。 177 若您能在我實踐未來目標方面指引我，我將不勝感激。 179

真摯感謝您撥冗回覆。 180 希望很快能在您方便的時候，與您聊一聊。

麗莎·武田　謹啟

176. 舉辦此研習會的目的為何？
(A) 邀請員工到社區中心當志工
(B) 教導職員管理技能
(C) 鼓勵員工取得行銷學位
(D) 訓練新進人員了解資安政策

177. 雪帕德先生最有可能任職於什麼部門？
(A) 會計部
(B) 行銷部
(C) 客服部
(D) 資訊科技部

178. 吉安諾先生最有可能在幾點演講？
(A) 上午 8:30
(B) 上午 9:15
(C) 上午 10:00
(D) 上午 11:00

179. 信函中第二段第六行的「realize」，意思最接近何者？
(A) 贏得；獲得
(B) 欣賞；感激
(C) 分辨；區分
(D) 達成；實現

180. 武田女士寫信給雪帕德先生時，採取了何種行動？
(A) 要求對方寫推薦信
(B) 感謝對方的建議
(C) 更動某議程
(D) 要求簽新合約

181–185 電子郵件

寄件人：victoriaf@brightpecan.com
收件人：all-employees@brightpecan.com
日期：1 月 27 日
主旨：系統更新

大家好：

我們將於 1 月 31 日星期五，更新所有辦公室電腦的系統。 `181` `182` 每一部公司名下的電腦都會進行更新。特別是人事部、會計部與客服部的同仁，請務必做好更新準備，因為更新作業可能會對上述部門目前使用的一些程式造成不良影響。 `181`

請大家謹記以下重點，一定要儲存與備份所有重要的檔案。因為一旦完成更新，我們就會重新開啟電腦。同仁使用的軟體如果屬於持續運作的類型，請小心更新作業可能會不慎刪除部分檔案。 `183` 因此我們強烈建議，系統轉換當天的例行事務，請提早或延後進行。星期五當天休假或出差外出的員工，必須在星期五前確保自己的檔案已妥善備份。

維多莉亞・佛羅瑞 `182`

寄件人：mjarvi@brightpecan.com
收件人：klao@brightpecan.com
日期：1 月 28 日 `184`
主旨：款項

劉女士妳好：

這封電子郵件與處理員工薪資可能會碰到的問題有關。我的電腦程式目前已設定在星期五下午，將薪資資料傳給銀行。然而，根據佛羅瑞女士昨天的電子郵件內容所言，這個月的付款日可能需要因應更新異動而有所調整。 `183` 我明天和星期四要參加會計法規的研習會。 `185` 我今天下午可以先處理此程序， `184` 但這表示我們可能需要將匯給某些廠商的應付款項，延期到下週。或者我們可以將發薪日後推到下週一（2 月 3 日）。某些員工可能會難以

接受，尤其是有些人必須在 2 月 1 日星期六繳款。無論如何，我需要妳的許可，再採取適當的應對措施。

馬丁・賈維　謹啟

181. 第一封電子郵件的用意為何？
(A) 讓職員做好軟體可能會有問題的心理準備
(B) 說明安裝新程式的過程
(C) 要求出差時提前通知
(D) 針對某付款問題提出可能的解決辦法

182. 佛羅瑞女士最有可能任職於什麼部門？
(A) 資訊科技部
(B) 會計部
(C) 人事部
(D) 客服部

183. 賈維先生為什麼很有可能要重新安排某事務的處理時間？
(A) 他的電腦壞了。
(B) 某專案的截止日已變動。
(C) 他想避免遺失資料。
(D) 他尚未支付信用卡費。

184. 根據賈維先生的說法，此事務最有可能被重新安排到哪一個日期進行？
(A) 1 月 27 日
(B) 1 月 28 日
(C) 1 月 31 日
(D) 2 月 1 日

185. 賈維先生預計 1 月 29 日要做什麼事情？
(A) 存入額外的薪資
(B) 去度假
(C) 與主管見面
(D) 參加專業會議

讓您的餐廳生意變得更成功

您的餐廳是否供應優質菜色與服務，卻仍苦惱於獲利的問題？加入「餐廳管理資源協會」（RMRA），即可接受監督與管理您餐廳財務的全面訓練！關鍵是，專業人士的協助已是時下必備條件。過去十多年來，我們已協助全國許多餐廳業者實現他們的財務目標。以下簡介 RMRA 提供的服務內容。

取得豐富資源——由業界專家以協助餐廳業者實現持續獲利能力為目標，撰寫各種豐富文章、評論與報告。**186** 此類資源會每週更新，為會員提供最新資訊。

客製化的範本——可免費下載的各類表格、工作表和報告範本，能讓您因應生意的特定需求而自訂內容。

與社群交流——加入我們的線上論壇「RMRA 網絡」，即可與深知業界挑戰與需求的上千名會員，分享見解與看法。

專業課程——可參加各種線上課程，內容從控管食物成本、菜單定價到管理整體開支等策略皆涵蓋在內。
請注意：此功能僅適用於金等會員。**187**

馬上加入 RMRA，僅需一次性的註冊費 80 美元，加上每年 100 美元（基本等級）或 150 美元（金等）的會員費。**188**

RMRA 入會者資料

名字：蓋瑞

姓氏：韓森

公司名稱：韓森披薩店

電話號碼：206-318-4336

街名：花園巷 18744 號

城市：西雅圖

州別：華盛頓

郵遞區號：98102

電子郵件信箱地址：
ghansen@hansenpizzeria.com

請建立使用者名稱：ghansen99

請建立密碼：*******

請確認密碼：*******

請選擇會員類型：☑ **基本等級** ☐ 金等
187 **188**

RMRA 承諾提供可成功維持長期財務目標的必要技能與知識。若您加入 RMRA 會員一年後，餐廳財務狀況沒有改善，我們將退還一半的 RMRA 會員費。請注意：此功能僅適用於金等會員。**189**

蓋瑞·韓森
韓森披薩店
98102 華盛頓州西雅圖市花園巷 18744 號

親愛的韓森先生：

很遺憾得知您成為會員後，餐廳生意仍未見起色。可惜我們無法核發您的退款。

我們的退款政策已清楚說明，退款僅適用於金等會員。由於您註冊的是基本等級會員，因此無法享有退款的資格。不過，**我可以幫您爭取延長六個月的免費會員服務**。**190** 如果您有興趣，請告訴我。

敬祝　安康

RMRA 客服部經理
班傑明·金

---

186. 廣告中第二段第三行的「sustained」，意思最接近何者？
(A) 讚許
(B) 支持
(C) 持續
(D) 節省

187. 可從文中得知關於韓森先生的什麼訊息？

(A) 他沒有興趣上網路課程。

(B) 他打算到其他城市拓店。

(C) 他最近剛翻修店面。

(D) 他以前回覆過金先生的來信。

188. 韓森先生為成為 RMRA 會員付了多少美元？

(A) 100 美元

(B) 150 美元

(C) 180 美元

(D) 230 美元

189. RMRA 在什麼情況下會退款？

(A) 公司收到受損產品時

(B) 課程被取消時

(C) 客戶對於課程品質不滿時

(D) 服務未能創造出正面成效時

190. 金先生主動提出什麼做法？

(A) 追蹤宅配進度

(B) 延長服務時間

(C) 郵寄產品型錄

(D) 審核訂單

191–195 報導、信函和電子郵件

增加安全稽核次數

聖地牙哥 訊〔2 月 27 日〕——市議會已通過一項與所有學校安全稽核有關的新法規。即日在學期期間，所有私立學校必須每兩個月稽核一次，而非每個季度一次；**192** 公立學校則必須每個月稽核一次，而非一年一次。稽核項目包括緊急整備與安全程序。去年當選的市議員狄恩·柳是「保持警覺」的提案者。**191** 柳先生表示：「確保學童的福祉對我們所有人都很重要。」市政府會直接聯絡學校行政人員，說明更新後的規定，與安排稽核時間。民眾可撥打（858）555-9823 聯絡公共安全部門的班·麥克斯。

---

3 月 21 日

卡洛琳·基爾戴

賽維爾私立中學

親愛的基爾戴女士：

由於市府法規更新的緣故，私立學校的稽核次數即將增加。**192** 本部的檢視紀錄指出，貴校最近一次通過安全稽核的時間是 11 月 10 日。**193** **195** 根據新規定，貴校的稽核時間已過期。我們已經安排稽核人員於 3 月 28 日上午 9 點抵達貴校。若您因任何原因而需更改此預約時間，請您以電子郵件**194**（b.michaels@sandiego-dps.gov）或撥打電話（858）555-9823 聯絡公共安全部的班·麥克斯先生。

公共安全部門

伊芳·葛林姆

收件人：班·麥克斯
<b.michaels@sandiego-dps.gov>

寄件人：卡洛琳·基爾戴
<c.kilday@xavierprep.edu>

日期：3 月 23 日

主旨：安全稽核

親愛的麥克斯先生：

我收到一封通知信，提醒我賽維爾私立中學仍有待進行安全稽核一事。我必須延後稽核程序。**194** 因為本校已購入全新的煙霧偵測器，好換掉那些老舊故障的偵測器。**195** 負責更新偵測器的裝設專員表示，這需要大約五個工作天完成，外加一天來進行全面測試。我希望能將稽核時間，重新安排到原日期的下一週。期待您的回覆。

賽維爾私立中學校長

卡洛琳·基爾戴 謹啟

191. 柳先生的身分為何？
- (A) 當地新聞記者
- (B) 學校行政人員
- (C) 維修技師
- **(D) 市政官員**

192. 賽維爾私立中學將來會多久接受視察一次？
- (A) 每個月
- **(B) 每隔一個月**
- (C) 每三個月一次
- (D) 一年一次

193. 信函中第一段第一行的「check」，意思最接近何者？
- (A) 標記
- (B) 控制
- **(C) 審核**
- (D) 停止

194. 基爾戴女士傳送電子郵件的原因為何？
- (A) 想投訴新法規
- **(B) 想延後市府員工訪視的時間**
- (C) 想確認預約的服務
- (D) 想要求翻修專案的帳單

195. 可從文中得知關於賽維爾私立中學煙霧偵測器的哪些訊息？
- (A) 以平價購得。
- **(B) 11 月 10 日以後就故障了。**
- (C) 設置於不對的地方。
- (D) 由基爾戴女士所裝設。

196–200 電子郵件和報價單

寄件人：羅倫斯・麥吉爾 <lmcgill@createadate.com>
收件人：溫蒂・宋 <wsong@minnesota.edu>
日期：6 月 2 日星期四
主旨：場地報價
附件：quote.rtf

親愛的宋女士：

感謝您來電討論，即將於明尼亞波利斯舉辦「明尼蘇達州教育協會頒獎早午餐會」的活動。 196 我已經附上符合您需求的各種場地細節資料。

我有根據您的要求，納入某家義大利餐廳。 197 雖然我們從未在該餐廳舉辦過活動，但有同仁大力推薦。

為了保有報價費率，請您於 6 月 10 日星期五前，繳交全額款項。我期待進一步與您合作，為您安排活動事宜。 196

敬祝　安康

羅倫斯・麥吉爾

用餐場地的報價

客戶：明尼蘇達州教育協會

嘉賓人數：36 人

餐點類型：自助早午餐

預定日期：8 月 8 日

餐廳	料理類型	額外特色	每人收費 *	總費用
河彎餐廳	墨西哥菜	可應要求提供現場音樂表演	25 美元	900 美元

吉美里餐酒館 197	義大利菜 197	設有庭院區	30 美元	1,080 美元
許願樹餐廳 198	越南菜	可提供外燴用的客製化菜單 198	35 美元	1,260 美元
新鮮事餐廳	肯瓊菜	步行 3 分鐘即可抵達最近的地鐵站 199	40 美元	1,440 美元 199
生蠔拼盤餐廳	海鮮	可容納至多 50 人的團體座位	45 美元	1,620 美元

* 價格內含所有服務，不過若於場地以外的範圍停車，可能會衍生額外費用。

寄件人：溫蒂・宋
<wsong@minnesota.edu>
收件人：羅倫斯・麥吉爾
<lmcgill@createadate.com>
日期：6 月 7 日星期二
主旨：已存入押金

親愛的麥吉爾先生：

很感謝你為了安排早午餐會所做的一切努力。我已經透過你們的線上付款系統，繳交全額款項。雖然音樂表演服務很吸引人，但我們的會員首重可以方便搭乘大眾運輸工具的場地。 199

既然我們已經選定活動地點，我現在需要你幫忙推薦訂購獎牌的商店。 200 我也希望能在餐會舉行期間，播放簡短的投影片。不過我們就等到 6 月 23 日，再一起當面討論此事。此外，我們見面的時候，我會需要請你幫忙決定邀請函的設計樣式，以及選出印刷行。

溫蒂・宋　謹啟

196. 可從文中得知關於麥吉爾先生的什麼資訊？
(A) 他是餐廳評論專家。
(B) 他擁有一間外燴公司。
(C) 他在一間義大利餐廳附近上班。
(D) 他正在規劃餐點。

197. 麥吉爾先生根據宋女士的要求，納入了哪一家餐廳？
(A) 河彎餐廳
(B) 吉美里餐酒館
(C) 許願樹餐廳
(D) 新鮮事餐廳

198. 可從文中得知關於許願樹餐廳的什麼資訊？
(A) 是最便宜的餐廳。
(B) 提供戶外用餐區。
(C) 可更改菜單內容。
(D) 晚上可享免費停車優惠。

199. 宋女士最有可能付了多少錢？
(A) 1,080 美元
(B) 1,260 美元
(C) 1,440 美元
(D) 1,620 美元

200. 根據第二封電子郵件的內容，宋女士接下來會做什麼事情？
(A) 寄出邀請函
(B) 訂購獎牌
(C) 彩排簡報
(D) 預訂會議室

ACTUAL TEST ⑥

PART 5 P. 150–152

101. 現今快速發展的全球經濟下，能說多種外語是項重要技能。
- (A) 發展者
- (B) 發展
- **(C) 正在發展**
- (D) 發展

102. 等到我們抵達會議中心時，全體講者可能都發表完研討會的演講了。
- (A) 以相似方式
- (B) 只有在
- **(C) 等到……時**
- (D) 早在……時

103. 尼莫國際的貨櫃最大重量是 30 公噸。
- (A) 正在秤重
- **(B) 重量**
- (C) 秤重
- (D) 加權的

104. 林女士休假期間，若有任何緊急情況發生，請聯絡莫侯先生。
- **(A) 緊急的**
- (B) 正確的
- (C) 代替的
- (D) 已刪除的

105. 九繆斯學院的導師幫卡羅琳‧麥克默菲改善了她的歌聲，效果顯著。
- (A) 她的（東西）
- (B) 她本人
- (C) 她
- **(D) 她的**

106. 訂單處理因季節性需求，可能會比平常多花上一天時間。
- **(A) 更長的**
- (B) 最久的
- (C) 長度
- (D) 長的

107. 寄藍圖給公司客戶時，請用此快遞服務來確保文件安全。
- (A) 牢固地
- (B) 正在弄牢
- **(C) 使安全**
- (D) 安全

108. CPS 汽車聲稱，其最新款電動車行駛得比市面上其他車輛都來得安靜且燃油效率更高。
- (A) 目前
- (B) 主要地
- (C) 突然地
- **(D) 效率高地**

109. 雖然經銷商保證會找到貨件，但帕克女士仍在考慮終止合約。
- (A) 一定地
- **(B) 保證**
- (C) 保證
- (D) 被保證的

110. 業務代表須經常出差拜訪客戶，對他們來說，一個耐用的公事包是不可或缺的物品。
- (A) 精力充沛的
- (B) 比得上的
- (C) 一絲不苟的
- **(D) 耐用的**

111. 葛里芬保全公司將在一天內，回覆所有透過公司網站提出的客訴。
- **(A) 提出的**
- (B) 提出
- (C) 提出
- (D) 正在提出

112. 拉米雷茲先生仔細測量辦公室的大小，好決定房間內能擺幾張桌子。
- (A) 但也
- **(B) 在……之前**
- (C) 事實上
- (D) 反而

113. 梅森先生的信用紀錄和積欠的抵押貸款數額，都將是影響他申請轉貸能否通過的因素。
(A) 佔用的
(B) 租借的
(C) 被包含的
(D) 欠的

114. 工業法規規定，所有員工在廠區均須穿戴適當的防護裝備。
(A) 支出
(B) 主題
(C) 意見
(D) 法規

115. 租車的押金將在車輛歸還並經檢查後立即退還。
(A) 只
(B) 一⋯⋯就⋯⋯
(C) 兩者皆非
(D) 雖然

116. 為確保公正性，帕勒梅先生將隨機選出一名員工讓他使用大樓前的停車位。
(A) 大幅地
(B) 隨機地
(C) 完全地
(D) 成比例地

117. 松田廚房家電公司仍被視為亞洲市場的龍頭。
(A) 將持續被視為
(B) 將持續看到
(C) 以持續看到
(D) 持續被視為

118. 尚·雷諾將從 6 月 6 日起處理奧特曼實驗室現有專案相關的所有問題。
(A) 獻出
(B) 遵從
(C) 回覆
(D) 處理

119. 阮先生是位足智多謀的員工，其設計引人注目的廣告能力令人印象深刻。
(A) 充實的
(B) 足智多謀的
(C) 機智地
(D) 足智多謀

120. 電腦程式設計是南亞地區薪資最高的行業之一。
(A) 裝置
(B) 產業
(C) 來源
(D) 情況

121. 接駁巴士進行例行性維修時不會行駛。
(A) 已進行
(B) 正在進行的
(C) 正在進行
(D) 進行了

122. 這名歷史學者證實這幅畫是 15 世紀文藝復興時期的真跡。
(A) 真正的
(B) 描述的
(C) 正確的
(D) 暫時的

123. 副總裁對重整架構後兩個部門合併的順利進展感到滿意。
(A) 鞏固
(B) 鞏固
(C) 合併
(D) 被鞏固的

124. 深受好評的紀錄片《保海騙局》，提倡人們關注與水和能源節約有關的環境問題。
(A) 在
(B) ⋯⋯的
(C) 藉由
(D) 到

125. 金德科技公司據稱以大約四億美元的價格被收購。
(A) 正在報導的
(B) 據稱
(C) 報導
(D) 記者

126. 研發部的季度時間表列出六個目標，要在未來三個月內完成。
(A) 競爭對手
(B) 目標
(C) 結論
(D) 客戶

127. 有時，高層允許員工在特殊的日子穿便服來辦公室。

(A) 偶爾，有時
(B) 此刻
(C) 到這時
(D) 立刻

128. 該手冊的完整標題為《修訂版實驗室實驗規則》，但通常稱之為《規則》。

(A) 組裝好的
(B) 被提到
(C) 被擴張
(D) 被比較

129. 雖然本地絕大多數的餐廳都提供外燴服務，但很少餐廳和我們一樣提供品項多樣的菜單菜色。

(A) 任何
(B) 全部
(C) 皆非
(D) 很少

130. 增加更多的航線可能會對航程預訂造成重大影響。

(A) 重大的
(B) 多樣的
(C) 最大的
(D) 合作的

PART 6 P. 153–156

131–134 電子郵件

寄件者：service@campersdepot.co.uk
收件者：hendricks1577@mugremail.co.uk
日期：4 月 22 日
主旨：關於：露營者補給站登入資訊

親愛的貴客：

我們因收到您要求重設您的露營者補給站帳號的密碼，而寄出這封信。根據要求，我們更新了您的帳號，並發出一組臨時密碼：I23bon18。請注意，密碼僅在 4 月 23 日午夜之前有效。在此之前，請使用您的密碼登入我們網站的會員專用頁面。請依頁面提示輸入必要資訊，完成重設密碼的程序。

我們露營者補給站將盡力保護您的個資。如果您並非提出重設密碼者，請立即和我們的技術支援部門聯絡。

敬祝　安康

露營者補給站網路服務部

131. (A) 可能要求
(B) 正在要求
(C) 已要求
(D) 要求

132. (A) 被獲得的
(B) 可使用的
(C) 打開的
(D) 有效的

133. (A) 從
(B) 在……期間
(C) 當
(D) 在……後立即

134. (A) 註冊我們網路服務的客戶將獲得第一年九折的購物優惠。
(B) 您將在我們官網會員專屬頁面上找到許多升級內容。
(C) 如果您並非提出重設密碼者，請立即和我們的技術支援部門聯絡。
(D) 我們為您的任何戶外探險活動，提供最優質的露營用品和安全設備。

135–138 廣告

招募房客

校園塔公寓大樓將在 7 月 15、16 日兩天舉行年度泳池派對和開放參觀日。你也能擁有如此舒適的生活方式！我們公寓到格蘭菲爾德大學校園的交通非常便利。房間家具一應俱全、廚房設施先進，你一定會喜歡。每位租戶還可使用健身房和閱覽室。不過，你也許會想常常出門走走！

校園塔公寓大樓位於市都心，家門外就有各式餐廳和玩樂的好去處。我們租屋顧問的服務時段為上午 7 點到下午 6 點，一週七天均可洽詢。下班時間也可事先通知安排預約。立即來電預約看房！

卡爾‧尼曼（858）555-5512

135. (A) 最多的
(B) 他們的（東西）
(C) 你的（東西）
(D) 我的（東西）

136. (A) 提供
(B) 正在提供
(C) 已提供
(D) 提供了

137. (A) 同樣地
(B) 相應地
(C) 顯然
(D) 但，不過

138. (A) 下班時間也可事先通知安排預約。
(B) 我們將在夏天延長工作時間。
(C) 我們正在考慮要為這個案子雇用更多的維修人員。
(D) 下個月將有一些店面開放出租。

139–142 意見卡

我真的很喜歡 Ekmekci 500。它能快速、均勻地烤出美味食物。它比傳統烤箱快多了，3 分鐘內就能烤好披薩。Ekmekci 500 有許多好用的功能，而且操作簡單。例如只需按幾個機器上的按鈕，就能一次烘烤三種不同的食物。特殊感應器可防止食物烤過頭或燒焦。更棒的是它節省空間的巧妙設計，方便使用後收納。

139. (A) 更便宜的
(B) 更快的
(C) 更強的
(D) 更整齊的

140. (A) 操作
(B) 複製
(C) 擴充
(D) 安裝

141. (A) 我現在幾乎每天都烤甜點。
(B) 特殊感應器可防止食物烤過頭或燒焦。
(C) 我發現用這個設備烹調沒有比較容易。
(D) 埃克梅奇公司也製造做麵包的特殊設備。

142. (A) 在……之後
(B) 在……的時候
(C) 一旦
(D) 和

143–146 報導

去年，蘭喬潘納斯吉多斯區的公司行號數量急遽增加。近期調查指出，數量攀升了 20％，增加速度是鄰近地區的四倍以上。目前該地區的辦公空間不足以因應此成長。因此，已通過了三個新商業園區的建設提案。動工所需的建築許可證也已取得。目前，蘭喬潘納斯吉多斯區僅有北郡綜合辦公大樓這麼一個商業園區。新的商業園區將增加 1,500 間辦公地點。

143. (A) 攀升
(B) 正在攀升
(C) 攀升了
(D) 將攀升

144. (A) 促銷
(B) 結果
(C) 需求
(D) 條件

145. (A) 當地公司已要求新增多間大型會議設施。
(B) 確保遵守所有安全和環境法規是很重要的。
(C) 將定期進行市調以確保當地商家滿意。
(D) 動工所需的建築許可證也已取得。

146. (A) 初步的
(B) 暫時的
(C) 更多的
(D) 拋棄式的

PART 7　P. 157–177

147–148 信函

9 月 30 日

親愛的摩瑟先生：

恭喜！您的旅程獎勵帳戶已累積足夠的積分來兌換一張免費機票。隨信附上積分的使用說明、預訂時所需的特殊代碼。此外還包括合作航空公司的航班時刻表。147
該優惠效期至 12 月 31 日。

帳戶持有者每賺取 3,000 點積分，即可獲得一張免費機票。只要您透過旅程獎勵旅行社購票，均可賺取積分。

您可在 www.travelrewards.co.nz 登入您的帳號，查看您的積分紀錄。148

敬祝　安康

旅程獎勵

附件

147. 摩瑟先生收到了什麼？
(A) 航班時刻表
(B) 獎勵卡
(C) 餐券
(D) 旅行配件禮券

148. 摩瑟先生可在網路上做什麼事情？
(A) 續訂帳號
(B) 在官網發表意見
(C) 搜尋鄰近地區的旅程獎勵旅行社
(D) 查看他已積累的積分數

149–150 簡訊串

哈維爾‧羅茲〔下午 1:22〕
蘇珊，妳快到了嗎？工廠代表剛到。149

蘇珊‧寇〔下午 1:24〕
我很抱歉。高速公路正在施工。我得下別的交流道。我大約 20 分鐘後到。可以請你在沒有我的情況下先開始嗎？149

哈維爾‧羅茲〔下午 1:25〕
當然可以。我會先跟他們談談拉頓堡廠的產能。

蘇珊‧寇〔下午 1:27〕
好！我知道他們以前生產的腕錶和我們的很類似。

哈維爾‧羅茲〔下午 1:29〕
對。我很驚訝的是我們的業務成長得這麼快，快到我們需要和其他工廠合作才能滿足需求。150

蘇珊‧寇〔下午 1:30〕
我也是！150 幾分鐘後見。

149. 寇女士想要羅茲先生做什麼？
(A) 發放產品樣品
(B) 和幾名公司代表見面
(C) 敲定製造合約
(D) 延後預約

150. 下午 1:30，寇女士說「我也是」，意思為何？
(A) 她以前曾去過拉頓堡。
(B) 業務擴張也讓她印象深刻。
(C) 她認為工廠應整修。
(D) 她認為高速公路交流道將於 20 分鐘後重新開放。

151–152 邀請函

苔絲大學醫院

4C6 9FD 都柏林市伯靈頓路 204 號

7 月 13 日

22G 6NM 都柏林市果園街 403 號
藤岡芳野 醫師

親愛的藤岡醫師：

我誠摯邀請您和我們一起慶祝韋恩·布萊德雷醫師在苔絲大學醫院服務屆滿 30 年。 **151** 布萊德雷醫師不只為病人提供優質的醫療照護，更投入大量心力，為當地宣導保健意識的慈善基金會「改善生活」募款。

作為該慈善機構的創辦人，布萊德雷醫師退休後將出任董事。 **151** 我們希望您能出席我們為向他表示敬意而舉辦的晚宴，地點在博福德飯店。晚宴訂於 9 月 10 日晚間 6 點，在該飯店的大宴會廳舉行。 **151** 請在 8 月 30 日之前傳送電子郵件至 jsteele@tessunihospital.ie 給我的助理潔西卡·斯蒂爾，確認您是否出席。 **152**

祝　一切順心

苔絲大學醫院主任

凱蒂·霍金斯

151. 將舉行什麼活動？
(A) 公司週年慶
(B) 退休晚宴
(C) 醫院開業
(D) 慈善活動

152. 受邀者被要求做什麼事？
(A) 在特定日期之前回覆
(B) 提前 30 分鐘到場
(C) 在飯店訂房間
(D) 捐款

153–154 電子郵件

寄件者：卡爾·布歐宏
收件者：蘇西·鮑
日期：10 月 29 日
主旨：請求

蘇西妳好：

我的課表有點變動，所以想請妳修改網路上的課表。 **153** 我星期一下午的課因選課學生不足將停開。但我這週忙著教其他四門課，因此請把該時段保留為學生諮詢時間。

另外，蘿拉·霍華德須取消下個月（11月 18 日至 20 日）在奧馬哈教育會議的演講，而我答應要代替她。所以，我需要 11 月 17 日飛往奧馬哈的機票，最好是晚上 8 點以後出發，回程機票則是 11 月 20 日下午。 **154** 妳如果有任何疑問，請直接聯絡我。

卡爾

153. 布歐宏先生為何寄出這封電子郵件？
(A) 索取某班的資訊
(B) 安排教員聚會
(C) 安排接機服務
(D) 更新網站

154. 鮑女士被要求做什麼？
(A) 預約會議室
(B) 安排出差
(C) 預約諮詢時間
(D) 寄電子郵件給霍華德女士

155–157 資訊

感謝您購買市面上最強大的可攜式空氣清淨機 Speedspin。 **155** 為確保性能持久，請每天以濕布和溫水清潔濾網。請按照用戶說明書所示，每週拆卸機器一次，並使用消毒液擦拭所有的表面。 **156** 另外，請注意須每年更換濾網。

Speedspin 使用鎳鎘電池供電，電池壽命長達數年。機器接上電源時，電池會自動充電，因此無須關機進行充電。**157** 請務必只使用產品附贈的連接傳輸線。使用其他傳輸線可能造成機器損壞。想了解更多相關資訊，請查看我們官網 http://www.speedspin.co.uk。

Speedspin：空氣就清淨！

155. 此資訊最有可能位於何處？
(A) 在產品的盒子上
(B) 在家電型錄上
(C) 在報紙廣告中
(D) 在當地報紙上

156. 可從文中得知關於 Speedspin 的哪些訊息？
(A) 每年須清潔一次。
(B) 含保固。
(C) 由環保材料製成。
(D) 可拆卸。

157. 可從文中得知關於電池的什麼資訊？
(A) 很重。
(B) 很持久耐用。
(C) 很小巧。
(D) 很平價。

158–160 電子郵件

寄件者：塞西莉亞・強森
<c.johnson@caicorp.co.uk>
收件者：漢娜・沃爾
<h.wall@caicorp.co.uk>
日期：12 月 9 日
主旨：通知
附件：運籌管理資訊

親愛的沃爾女士：

我很高興與 Caicorp 全體員工，恭賀您晉升為資深經理。倫敦分公司是所有資訊技術相關的主要支援據點，因此是 Caicorp 國際網絡裡非常重要的地方。**158** **159**

您將於 1 月 3 日上午 8 點，開始接受人事部米契・李的培訓。屆時李先生將提供您關於部門法規、未來發展規畫的資料，以及與您職位相關的詳細資訊。另外，由於我們目前正在更新安全系統，您須到設備辦公室登記報到。因此，請準備最晚在上午 7:50 之前抵達這裡。**158** **160**

附檔的文件包含從都柏林調動至此的細節，並說明訂購用品與設置公司筆電及手機的方法。如果 1 月 3 日前有我能提供的任何其他協助，請用電話或電子郵件和我聯絡。

Caicorp 總部 人資部 159

塞西莉亞・強森　謹啟

158. 強森女士聯絡沃爾女士的原因為何？
(A) 確認一些行程安排
(B) 討論新職位相關資訊
(C) 詢問遺失的身分證件
(D) 宣布即將到來的公司合併案

159. 可從文中得知關於 Caicorp 的什麼資訊？
(A) 將增聘資訊技術人員。
(B) 最近才更新網絡。
(C) 將總部遷至倫敦。
(D) 有不只一個辦公地點。

160. 沃爾女士被指示做什麼？
(A) 簽下公寓租約
(B) 和李先生在安檢門會合
(C) 為某部門購買用品
(D) 為了培訓課程提早到達

161–164 新聞報導

〈紐約上州的成功故事〉

2 月 16 日——餐廳業者喬治・帕帕斯奠基於第一家餐廳「希臘塔」的成功經驗，將在紐約州其他地方展店。**161** 帕帕斯表示：「我去過州內的許多城市，也找到幾個很適合我開餐廳的絕佳地點。我的菜單已獲得大家好評也有幫助。」

15 年前他的第一家餐廳在猶蒂卡地區開幕，至今依然生意興隆。帕帕斯先生計劃在奧本尼和傑納西兩地開設餐廳，未來將忙得不可開交。「我想要我們的新餐廳擁有與本店相同的氛圍。我與許多顧客就像家人一樣，而這正是我想為新餐廳打造的——家庭感和希臘美食。」

帕帕斯先生一開始都是自己親自掌廚。**164** 他從未受過正規的廚師培訓，而是仿效母親和祖母的廚藝、學習做菜。近來，他大多將時間投入宣傳與管理自家餐廳，以確保品質穩定、讓顧客有家的感覺。「我媽媽總跟我說『如果你好好餵飽別人，他將成為你一生的朋友』。我也一直向廚房的所有員工灌輸同樣的態度。我們希望讓人吃得飽，就能有許多畢生的好友，而他們會再度光臨、享受我們的菜餚和款待。」

希臘塔被評選為猶蒂卡最佳餐廳，帕帕斯先生也希望能在奧本尼和傑納西獲得同樣的殊榮。**162** 他打算在兩家分店投入大量時間，直到它們茁壯到可以獨立經營為止。他將派他的弟弟管理奧本尼店，**163** 傑納西店則由堂弟管理。

兩家餐廳預計六個月後開張。新店將供應與本店相同的菜色，同時推出一些新餐點。「新餐廳將持續供應讓希臘塔大受歡迎的熱門菜色，同時也提供我嘗試食譜的機會。」

薩布麗娜·洛文斯坦

161. 本文的目的為何？
(A) 描述一名業者的新店
(B) 討論公司之間的合併計畫
(C) 提供一家新餐飲學校的相關資訊
(D) 總結一家新餐廳的表現

162. 第四段第二行的「earn」，意思最接近何者？
(A) 輸
(B) 增加
(C) 稱讚
(D) 獲得

163. 可從文中得知關於帕帕斯先生的弟弟的哪些資訊？
(A) 他 15 年前上過烹飪課。
(B) 他將管理其中一家餐廳。
(C) 他將幫忙整修餐廳。
(D) 他從銀行借錢。

164. 「他從未受過正規的廚師培訓，而是仿效母親和祖母的廚藝、學習做菜。」最適合放在 [1]、[2]、[3]、[4] 的哪一個位置？
(A) [1]
(B) [2]
(C) [3]
(D) [4]

165–167 小冊子

達許企業服務公司
89101 拉斯維加斯市北十七大道 1881 號
www.dashycorproviders.com
702-555-6374

我們協助貴公司搬進新址，輕鬆搬遷免煩惱。**165** 為此，我們將考量您的具體需求，提出專業計畫。我們提供的一些服務如下。

- 辦公室搬遷：打包、運送與拆箱服務
- 短、長期倉儲保管
- 易碎物品特殊處理：客製包裝及溫控倉儲保管
- 安全處理不需要的公司資產
- 新舊辦公室空間清潔 **165**

免費估價：專家將拜訪您的工作場所，調查辦公空間和物流需求，並於 24 小時內提供所需服務的估價。**166** 之後，只要您準備好了，我們就能立即服務。初次拜訪將不收費，即使您決定不進行後續委託，也無須負擔其他責任。如欲預約，請寄電子郵件至 info@dashycorproviders.com。**166**

引領潮流的經營實踐：達許企業服務公司兼具卓越的服務與負責任的經營方式。舉凡可重複使用的包材至電動運輸系統，我們皆極力降低對環境的影響，同時兼顧和同業相比毫不遜色的價格。 167

想了解更多關於公司及服務的資訊，請洽702-555-6374 或查看我們的官網 www.dashycorproviders.com。

165. 達許是什麼類型的公司？
(A) 清潔公司
(B) 包裝廠
(C) 辦公用品店
(D) 搬家服務公司

166. 潛在客戶如何收到費用估算？
(A) 聯絡客服
(B) 查看達許的官網
(C) 填寫表格
(D) 安排達許到府服務

167. 達許提供的服務與它的競爭對手有何不同？
(A) 更便宜。
(B) 專精於小型企業。
(C) 受到安全保證。
(D) 對環境更好。

168–171 網路聊天室

艾拉・艾弗森〔上午 10:03〕
大家好。關於六月開會宣布公司要搬到陸上企業園區一事，我想了解你們部門同仁的看法。 168

松家次郎〔上午 10:04〕
大家都很驚訝。但我的同事們對於搬遷似乎都很興奮。

米許卡・佩特羅夫〔上午 10:05〕
有幾名員工好奇，需要帶多少現有設備過去。什麼時候會有更多資訊？ 169

漢娜・林〔上午 10:07〕
這邊大多數員工都在問我，搬遷將如何影響他們的排程表。 169 但目前我不知道該如何向他們解釋。

艾拉・艾弗森〔上午 10:10〕
一切仍在規劃中。這個月內高層會釋出更多訊息。 169 我會在七月的經理會議上給你們完整細節。 170

米許卡・佩特羅夫〔上午 10:11〕
我聽到傳言說，新地點將沒有個人辦公室，而是開放式座位。是真的嗎？

艾拉・艾弗森〔上午 10:13〕
我認為有可能。八月初，運籌管理部將規劃各部門的地點，以及工作站的安置方式，以充分利用新空間。 171

168. 艾弗森女士聯絡部門主管的原因為何？
(A) 解釋新流程
(B) 徵求員工意見
(C) 提供政策細節
(D) 告知確定的搬遷日期

169. 上午 10:10，艾弗森女士寫道：「一切仍在規劃中」，最有可能是什麼意思？
(A) 將很快做出決定。
(B) 須修改建築平面圖。
(C) 建築工程正在進行。
(D) 正在重新分配專案。

170. 部門主管何時會收到更新資訊？
(A) 六月
(B) 七月
(C) 八月
(D) 九月

171. 運籌管理團隊預期做什麼事情？
(A) 管理員工的排程表
(B) 訂購新設備
(C) 維護購入貨品
(D) 分配辦公室

打造胡蘿蔔？

〔1月22日〕——胡蘿蔔多年來一直都是重要食材。它的出口國分布廣泛，包括土耳其、南非、美國和俄羅斯，出口量高達數百萬磅。近期的農業改良讓農民將採收期延長為 11 個月，**173** 也使得胡蘿蔔能長得更大、口感更脆，顏色也更豐富。

然而，胡蘿蔔的味道卻不太受關注。**172** 這讓美國研究員賽巴斯汀·康很擔憂。他認為，如今更大、形狀更制式化的胡蘿蔔在幾十年前可能會讓消費者失望。「在我小時候，我們吃的胡蘿蔔，比現在市面上的好吃多了。」**175**

這項變化並非突如其來。康先生解釋，每一次對胡蘿蔔品種的改良，都會些微削減蔬菜的原味，**172** 這也是消費者並未感受到味道逐年改變的原因。**175** 這導致許多人根本不記得胡蘿蔔最初令人喜歡的微甜滋味。

康先生的首要目標是恢復胡蘿蔔原有的味道，同時保持目前已改善的口感與外觀等品質。**172** **174** 他補充道：「我認為，如果味道變得更好，消費者並不介意蔬菜長得小一點。」康先生與他的同事有信心，能以標準化的育種方式，種出預期的品質，而他們的初步成果也前景看好。**174**

172. 本文聚焦於胡蘿蔔的哪個面向？
(A) 重量
(B) 味道
(C) 顏色
(D) 口感

173. 胡蘿蔔的生產有何變化？
(A) 所有胡蘿蔔的採收方式皆相同。
(B) 全年都能採收胡蘿蔔。
(C) 種植胡蘿蔔的用水減少了。
(D) 現在可在實驗室種植胡蘿蔔。

174. 可從文中得知關於康先生的什麼資訊？
(A) 他持續從事植物育種的實驗。
(B) 他因創新蔬食料理而聞名。
(C) 他在農業地區長大。
(D) 他已在多國進行研究。

175. 「這項變化並非突如其來。」最適合放在 [1]、[2]、[3]、[4] 的哪一個位置？
(A) [1]
(B) [2]
(C) [3]
(D) [4]

176–180 資訊和電子郵件

澳洲度假小屋

• **6735 號度假屋：綠野** —溫馨二房公寓 —至少住宿兩晚 點擊這裡 了解詳細資訊	• **2500 號度假屋：康沃 180** —連住四晚，加贈第五晚住宿 **176** —適合想放下一切、盡情享受放鬆假期的人 —湖景 點擊這裡 了解詳細資訊
• **3038 號度假屋：墨爾本** —三房公寓 —近市中心，適合喜歡熱鬧城市生活的人 點擊這裡 了解詳細資訊	• **8220 號度假屋：漢密爾頓島 179** —每週 1,000 美元的私人海灘 點擊這裡 了解詳細資訊

TEST **6**

PART **7**

收件者：羅倫‧卡盧索
<lcaluso@auvacationrentals.co.au>
寄件者：惠妮‧強森
<wjohnson@bermaninc.co.au>
日期：6 月 25 日
主旨：關於：休假規畫

羅倫您好：

您去年協助安排我們一家暑假在墨爾本的住宿，租屋處和您的服務品質讓我很滿意。話雖如此，我不是很喜歡周圍地區的環境。繁忙的城市生活不太適合我。**178** 這次，我想住在能夠較為放鬆的地方，至少有三間臥室，方便前往湖泊或海灘。我一週能負擔的上限是 750 到 800 美金。**179** 2500 號度假屋似乎最吸引我。**180** 能請您告訴我它的可入住日嗎？**177** 它似乎最適合我的需求。

希望能儘快收到您的答覆。

惠妮‧強森　謹啟

176. 哪間度假屋提供一晚免費住宿？
(A) 6735 號度假屋
(B) 2500 號度假屋
(C) 3038 號度假屋
(D) 8220 號度假屋

177. 強森女士為何寄這封電子郵件？
(A) 確認付款
(B) 要求指示
(C) 修改預約
(D) 索取資訊

178. 強森女士不滿意上次假期中的哪個部分？
(A) 附近地區的生活步調
(B) 租屋處與她家的距離
(C) 一位員工提供的客戶服務
(D) 她住宿地點的狀況

179. 為何 8220 號度假屋可能不適合強森女士？
(A) 她寧可租公寓。
(B) 她不喜歡沙灘。
(C) 她在找比較便宜的地方。
(D) 她不需要兩間以上的臥室。

180. 強森女士對哪個地點感興趣？
(A) 綠野
(B) 康沃
(C) 墨爾本
(D) 漢密爾頓島

181–185 行程表和電子郵件

國際救援行動理事會（CIRA）

「社群媒體在救援行動中的作用」

西恩納大學伯恩分校，6 月 5–8 日 **181**

◆ 6 月 5 日 週一 預定議程表 **181**

上午 7:00 至 8:30	與會者簽到
上午 8:45 至 9:00	歡迎致詞：艾拉‧寶拉，大會主席
上午 9:00 至 9:30	專題演講：盧卡‧鮑爾，CIRA 主任 **181**
上午 9:45 至 11:00 **182**	抓住你的目標觀眾：馬丁‧卡斯帕里，e-Hoy 行銷研究中心（西班牙）**182**
上午 11:10 至下午 12:05	了解慈善機構線上募款：講者：待宣布，歐洲募款協會（法國）
下午 12:05 至下午 1:30	午餐：桂冠餐廳

下午 1:40 至 2:45	以贊助獲得可見度： 馬可・利提亞：病毒式工作室（斯洛維尼亞）（184）
下午 3:00 至 4:15	演講主題待定： 講者：待宣布，緊急救護專業人員協會（英國布萊頓）
下午 4:20 至 5:30	按讚：提高網頁瀏覽數： 米拉利・華森，NetMetrix 企業（美國）

收件者： 艾拉・寶拉 <epaula@aidfirst.org>
寄件者： 盧卡・鮑爾 <lborer@cira.or.it>
日期： 4 月 11 日
主旨： 關於：週一預定議程表

艾拉早安：

我已根據您上週四網路討論的意見，將週一預定議程表上的空缺補上了。（183）法國的安雅・萊納正在準備關於網路募款的演講，畢竟網路募款是由她國家的慈善機構所承辦。我也打給了布萊頓的聯絡人，據轉達，麥可・羅賓遜醫生很高興能代表當地醫療社群出席。

不過，遺憾的是，馬可・利提亞退出會議了。（184）將由他的同事薩拉・科斯接手，她會儘快將演講題目寄給我們。（185）

順帶一提，我從維也納出發的火車會在週一早上 5:40 到達。我已買票，所以有相當充裕的時間準備當天早上的演講。

盧卡・鮑爾　謹啟

181. 可從文中得知關於鮑爾先生的什麼資訊？
(A) 他將在服務台工作。
(B) 他將在午餐時間後發表演說。
(C) 他最近接管 CIRA。
(D) 他將在大會首日發表演講。

182. 行銷研究的專家將於何時發表演講？
(A) 上午 9:00
(B) 上午 9:45
(C) 下午 1:40
(D) 下午 4:20

183. 在電子郵件中，第一段第一行的「spaces」，意思最接近何者？
(A) 空缺
(B) 地點
(C) 距離
(D) 能力

184. 可從文中得知，必須取消哪一個演講？
(A) 抓住你的目標觀眾
(B) 了解慈善機構線上募款
(C) 以贊助獲得可見度
(D) 按讚：提高網頁瀏覽數

185. 根據電子郵件的內容，鮑爾先生正在等待接收什麼資訊？
(A) 一名講者的簡歷
(B) 演講主題
(C) 週二的議程表
(D) 羅賓森先生的電話號碼

186-190 租約、檢查表和電子郵件

諾福克會議中心租賃契約

23504 維吉尼亞州諾福克市
楓石大道 262 號

條款

本契約有效期限為 6 月 4 日至 11 日，總計一週，租金為每日 3,500 美元，應於最後一天全額支付。（189）逾期付款將收取每日 700 美元的罰款。提前終止租賃契約將處 350 美元罰款。（189）水電及特許販售攤位免收費。不提供餐點，且必須與當地商家洽談供餐。（186）另可投保每日 500 美元的保險。會議中心可容納最多 800 輛車。街尾的諾福克棒球場停車區也有提供額外的停車位。（187）

義務

4 月 12 日已收到 2,000 美元保證金,將於全額付款後 15 天內退還。諾福克會議中心員工將在活動舉辦前後檢查設施。活動前的必要維修工作將由設施管理部負責處理。租賃期結束後,若場地遭受任何毀損,將以保證金支付。 **188**

諾福克會議中心設施檢查表

檢查員:艾倫 · 弗林特

日期:5 月 31 日

檢查員紀錄:

裝卸貨區、會議廳和販售區狀況非常良好。前廳地毯需修復。 **190** 此外,東翼的暖氣設備也需維修。諾福克會議中心的維修人員將在 6 月 2 日之前完成這項工作。

諾佛克設施管理部　　內克瑟企業代表

安卓 · 拉蒙特　　　納塞夫 · 阿梅德

寄件者:alamont@nccenter.com
收件者:nasefa@nexo.com
日期:6 月 10 日
主旨:保證金
附件:檢查__表格

親愛的拉蒙特女士:

敝公司內克瑟企業本週在諾福克會議中心舉辦一場活動, **189** 之後取回部分保證金。我寫這封信是想詢問關於其中扣除 900 美元的事。我們預料要支付 350 美元的罰款, **189** 但無法接受另外 550 美元的罰款。請款單把它列作更換地毯的費用,但在我們舉辦活動之前,地毯已損壞(請參閱附檔)。 **190** 您先前曾表示貴公司的維護人員將更換地毯,但在我們活

動開始前,並沒有足夠的時間完成作業。因此,請退還 550 美元的款項。

納塞夫 · 阿梅德　謹啟

---

186. 租賃契約中指出什麼資訊?
(A) 會議中心提供免費接駁服務。
(B) 承租人須自行安排餐點。
(C) 會議中心正在進行電氣維修。
(D) 承租人可隨時修改合約條款。

187. 關於諾福克會議中心的描述,何者為真?
(A) 有私人用餐區。
(B) 提供演講者技術支援。
(C) 正在興建新的展覽廳。
(D) 離體育館很近。

188. 在租賃契約中,第二段第四行的「provide for」,意思最接近何者?
(A) 貢獻
(B) 提供
(C) 足以支付
(D) 安排

189. 內克瑟企業為什麼必須付 350 美元的罰款?
(A) 未決定購買保險。
(B) 使用另一處停車場。
(C) 提前終止租約。
(D) 逾期付款。

190. 阿梅德先生的主張為何?
(A) 地毯交貨逾期。
(B) 場館的暖氣不正常。
(C) 暖氣設備不需維修。
(D) 大廳內的損壞並非內克瑟企業的錯。

http://www.localpages.org

本月活動

夏季瘋衝浪賽
地點：斐濟，卡皮海灘
日期：7 月 20 日至 21 日
歡迎業餘及專業人士參加！
聯絡窗口：蘿拉·范迪克
<lvd@wavesurfer.com>

一年一度的「夏季瘋衝浪賽」吸引世界各地的頂尖衝浪選手、其贊助商以及業餘好手前來。 **191** 他們都希望能衝出名聲並抱回獎金。比賽每年吸引將近 8,000 名遊客， **193** 是斐濟諸島上單場最有人氣的活動。卡皮海灘為世界著名的衝浪勝地，八公尺高的大浪屢見不鮮。除了衝浪賽外，贊助商也為了各種年齡層的遊客，沿著沙灘設置遊戲和活動攤位。無需入場費，但務必帶 7 美元付停車費。 **193**

夏季瘋衝浪賽得獎者

國際組

名次	國家	姓名		贊助商
1	巴西	西爾維歐·德·索札		剛貝瑞
2	日本	新井加努阿		札路斯
3	美國	西蒙·寇爾		耐卡
4	澳洲	蓋·雅各布斯 **195**	**195**	阿拉拉
5	法國	馬紹·杜飛		波挪亞

卡皮衝浪去！

法蘭克·加尼勞　撰

今年的「夏季瘋衝浪賽」為旅遊旺季帶來絕佳的開始。部分原因是，活動多少受到難得好天氣的影響，輕鬆吸引比往年多了一倍的觀眾。

在為期兩天的比賽中，國際知名的衝浪好手及業餘愛好者都面臨著挑戰，即卡皮出了名的惡劣衝浪條件。 **192** 選手們乘著近十公尺高的海浪，使衝浪看來輕鬆又享受。幾波巨浪讓救生員很緊張，不過選手們都成功征服了排山倒海的浪濤，並沒有傳出任何人受傷。

西爾維歐·德·索札勇奪冠軍，打敗受到粉絲熱愛、連續三屆衛冕「夏季瘋衝浪賽」的新井加努阿。 **194** 雖然一直到最後都是險象環生，新井選手還是於傍晚的最後一波海浪中落水。今年的參賽者有不少出色的表現，但澳洲的代表選手特別讓我驚艷。 **195** 我看過許多來自北美洲與南美洲的衝浪者，但從未見過這樣的動作。

遊客同樣玩得很愉快。這裡不只能見到衝浪名人，還有許多美食、購物去處與活動。日落之時，踏上歸途的眾人都知道美好的夏季才正要開始。

191. 文中提到關於衝浪者的什麼資訊？
(A) 他們都是專業衝浪選手。
(B) 他們先前見過范迪克女士。
(C) 他們來自不同的國家。
(D) 其中一些選手會攜帶自己的設備。

192. 在報導中，第二段第二行的「faced」，意思最接近何者？
(A) 面對
(B) 看
(C) 穿越
(D) 冒險

193. 文中提到關於今年活動的什麼資訊？
(A) 首次在卡皮海灘舉辦。
(B) 有超過 8,000 名觀眾。
(C) 收取 7 美元的入場費。
(D) 活動時間比去年短。

194. 文中提到關於新井先生的什麼資訊？
(A) 他住在澳大利亞。
(B) 他比賽中差點落水。
(C) 他教授衝浪課程。
(D) 他以前曾參加過比賽。

195. 哪位選手最讓加尼勞先生感到印象深刻？
(A) 西爾維歐・德・索札
(B) 新井加努阿
(C) 西蒙・寇爾
(D) 蓋・雅各布斯

196-200 電子郵件和簡訊

收件者：菲莉西亞・哈克
<fharker@gateways.com>
寄件者：巴瑞・艾薩克森
<bisaacson@havenvh.com>
日期：5 月 18 日
主旨：您預訂的住宿

親愛的哈克女士：

我們已在 5 月 2 日收到您在網路上預訂三房公寓的要求。您的預訂已經過「避風港」的專員審核，並確認 6 月 5 日至 6 月 11 日可供住宿。⑱

根據「避風港」的房價表，您將支付 1,694.88 美元。⑱ 請您留意，付款後即完成訂房，取消訂房將不予退款。⑱ 我們寄了另一封電子郵件給您，信中附上具體的入住和退房說明。⑲ 如您有任何疑問，請致電（310）555-8221，或以電子郵件聯絡我們。**請務必於聯絡時提供您的四位數訂房號碼。**⑯ 期待您蒞臨「避風港」！

避風港度假住宿
禮賓服務經理
巴瑞・艾薩克森　謹啟

收件者：巴瑞・艾薩克森
<bisaacson@havenvh.com>
寄件者：菲莉西亞・哈克
<fharker@gateways.com>
日期：6 月 2 日
主旨：關於：您預訂的住宿

親愛的艾薩克森先生：

我寫信給您，想詢問關於我在「避風港度假住宿」預訂 6 月 5 日至 6 月 11 日的住宿（代碼 4502）。您在信中提到，將在五月底前寄其他資訊給我。但我並未收到您另外的任何電子郵件。由於我想在前往休假前收到這項資訊，⑲ 請儘快以電子郵件寄給我。我好幾次試著用電話聯絡您，但都在忙線中。如果您無法聯絡到我，我會在抵達住宿地點時，拜訪您的辦公室。⑲

我希望能儘快收到您的答覆。

菲莉西亞・哈克　謹啟
（562）555-4839

至：菲莉西亞・哈克，562-555-4839

從：6 月 5 日，下午 3:00 ⑳

菲莉西亞您好：

我是「避風港度假住宿」的柴克・艾薩克森。由於您並未接聽電話，我改用簡訊通知您。因為目前已超過您登記入住時間一小時了，⑳ 我想知道您是否已在前來的路上。請您收到這封簡訊後回電給我。謝謝。

196. 哈克女士被告知在聯絡「避風港度假住宿」時，須提供什麼？
(A) 她的房間號碼
(B) 她的聯絡資訊
(C) 她的訂房號碼
(D) 她的信用卡資訊

197. 第二封電子郵件中,第一段第六行的
「property」,意思最接近何者?
(A) 地點
(B) 溝通
(C) 持有
(D) 特徵

198. 艾薩克森先生的電子郵件中,未附上
哪一項資訊?
(A) 取消訂房規定
(B) 前往某地的交通路線
(C) 住宿費
(D) 預訂日期

199. 哈克女士要求艾薩克森先生提供什麼?
(A) 入住與退房的詳細資訊
(B) 客房服務費
(C) 當地嚮導
(D) 信用卡請款明細

200. 可從簡訊中得知關於哈克女士的什麼
資訊?
(A) 她應該要在下午 2 點抵達。
(B) 她想升級房間。
(C) 她尚未付款。
(D) 她將於 6 月 12 日退房。

ACTUAL TEST ⑦

PART 5 P. 178–180

101. 「探路者旅遊」正在招聘有海外工作經驗的合適人才。
(A) 曾體驗
(B) 已體驗
(C) 經驗
(D) 正在經歷

102. 持有烹飪證照可提高應徵者被新喀里多尼亞度假村錄取的機會。
(A) 提高
(B) 運作
(C) 達到
(D) 使結束

103. 拉德先生對瓦杜茲美術館進行的創新改建值得肯定。
(A) 稱讚
(B) 值得讚許的
(C) 稱讚
(D) 正在稱讚

104. 馮魯汶女士要求修復在水災中損毀的招牌。
(A) 也
(B) 很像
(C) 包含
(D) 在……期間

105. 出於安全考量，進出伺服器機房受到嚴格限制。
(A) 嚴格地
(B) 僅僅，幾乎不
(C) 輕微地
(D) 隨意地

106. 和客戶互動時，期望所有員工都能維持適當的專業水準。
(A) 專業地
(B) 專業水準
(C) 專業的；專家
(D) 職業

107. 人資主任康堤女士將會把求職者分為兩類。
(A) 提供
(B) 劃分
(C) 考慮
(D) 建議

108. 由於乳製品非常容易腐敗，運送過程中應儘可能冷藏保存。
(A) 更高地
(B) 最高地
(C) 非常
(D) 高的

109. 會計部表示，要是下一季度的收益沒增加，公司將被迫關閉一些服務據點。
(A) 如果……不……；除非
(B) 反而
(C) 但是
(D) 那

110. 崔蘭特企業於過去九個月內一直集中資源建造更多的工廠。
(A) 持續的
(B) 持續了
(C) 過去的
(D) 最終地

111. 市場測試結果顯示，冷卻機 X100 無法精確控制營業用冷凍系統的溫度。
(A) 精確性
(B) 精準地
(C) 精密度
(D) 精準的

112. 艾蜜莉亞・卡波雷托接受了一家公司開出的管理職，該公司提供的福利待遇符合她的期待。
(A) 使用
(B) 遺失
(C) 符合；達到
(D) 給予

113. 垂直裝潢公司因為能用合理的價格完成工程，而獲選為整修大廳的廠商。
(A) 嚴重的
(B) 提升的
(C) 濃縮的
(D) 合理的

114. 儘管已多次延後期限，馬勒堆焊公司還是遲遲未給出報價。
(A) 其實
(B) 儘管
(C) 雖然
(D) 仍然

115. 機場提供接駁服務，幾乎可抵達這座島上所有的飯店和度假村。
(A) 在裡面
(B) 更遠地
(C) 幾乎
(D) 恰當地

116. 最新的消費者調查結果顯示，RW 新上市汽車的缺點大於它的優點。
(A) 稱讚
(B) 打擾
(C) 成就
(D) 缺點

117. 康納博士在年會上因對應用科學領域的貢獻而獲獎。
(A) 稱讚
(B) 接受；獲得
(C) 希望
(D) 提名

118. 在許默汽車工廠工作的 30 年中，歐德里斯科女士在工廠現場操作過好幾種機具。
(A) 操作
(B) 正在操作
(C) 操作過
(D) 營運

119. 在抵達時間前 48 小時內不得修改預訂。
(A) 相當
(B) 在……之前
(C) 因為
(D) 除……外

120. 由於實體店面顧客是我們的主要收入來源，所以強制所有店內員工參加銷售培訓。
(A) 卓越的
(B) 有法律責任的
(C) 強制的
(D) 模糊不清的

121. 有傑出資歷的朴晉浩先生被選為經理，讓資訊科技部很高興。
(A) （哪裡）……的
(B) 某人的……
(C) ……的東西
(D) ……的原因

122. 因潘女士四月將轉調東京分公司，希利維坦先生已開始接替她的工作。
(A) 互動
(B) 識別
(C) 前進
(D) 接替

123. 透過與各行各業及各地的企業合作，P.L. 霍華德股份有限公司將擴大它在中亞的市占率。
(A) 已擴展
(B) 要去擴展
(C) 擴展了
(D) 將擴展

124. 「初階時尚」設計出創新服飾系列，有助於提高產品銷量。
(A) 關心的
(B) 各色具備的
(C) 創新的
(D) 緊急的

125. 行銷部一獲准，主任就開始分派實習生。
(A) 開始
(B) 過去正在啟動
(C) 開始
(D) 已開始

126. 請確保您的研習會最後有充裕的時間讓聽眾提問。
(A) 充裕的
(B) 困難的
(C) 精確的
(D) 可靠的

127. 金柏先生不斷嘗試聯絡村田公司的公關團隊，但是都沒有得到回應。

(A) 重複的

(B) 不斷地

(C) 重複過

(D) 重複

128. 艾哲頓女士將因其在醫學研究領域的終身成就而獲獎。

(A) 正在取得

(B) 取得

(C) 可取得的

(D) 成就

129. 市場趨勢如果持續下去，波圖斯程式公司不僅可完全恢復，甚至可能成為軟體業的龍頭。

(A) 此外

(B) 也

(C) 例如

(D) 不只

130. 這款較便宜的洗面乳經證實能作為知名廠牌的有效替代品。

(A) 可能性

(B) 替代品

(C) 選擇

(D) 選項

PART 6 P. 181–184

131–134 資訊

季度績效考核

員工考核程序的最後步驟是口頭與書面考核。它是針對三個月期間工作績效的正式評估。總成績將根據部門主管訂定的標準而定。考核的主要目的是給予員工有意義的意見回饋，亦能幫助設定下個季度的目標。而與績效相關的定期討論對提升工作效能依然有其必要，季度考核並不能取代它。

131. (A) 版本

(B) 情況

(C) 編輯

(D) 步驟

132. (A) 不少公司最近開始實施每月評鑑。

(B) 考核的主要目的是給予員工有意義的意見回饋。

(C) 根據公司政策，員工評鑑紀錄將會存檔。

(D) 主管有權決定部門的工作時數。

133. (A) 推出

(B) 嘗試

(C) 決定

(D) 感謝

134. (A) 必需的

(B) 必需品

(C) 必要地

(D) 使成為必需的

135–138 信函

2 月 22 日

埃里卡・馬許

攝政法院

46805 印第安納州韋恩堡市

東加州路 1423 號

敬愛的馬許女士：

這封信和克林頓大街 1822 號的租約有關，該合約將於 2 月 28 日到期。我想和您續約。我在三月之前還無法住進新房子。因此，我希望能在目前的公寓住到 3 月 31 日。請告訴我該準備什麼。

如果您有空，我們就約明天早上的時間通個電話討論一下。如果您偏好面對面談的話，我也很樂意配合。

敬祝　安康

德瑞克・拉格曼

135. (A) 將……的（東西）

(B) 該正在

(C) 它是

(D) ……之一

136. (A) 要求
(B) 否定
(C) 購買
(D) 投資

137. (A) 他們的
(B) 任何的
(C) 我的
(D) 它的

138. (A) 我已經快搬完了。
(B) 請告訴我該準備什麼。
(C) 我想看看符合這些要求的公寓。
(D) 我目前住在韋恩堡。

139–142 電子郵件

寄件者：renaldpark87@mycos.net
收件者：info@sleekformalwear.com
日期：4 月 24 日
主旨：帳單單號 89827

您好：

我兩個月前在「時髦禮服」的官網上買了一件夾克。我一收到，便試穿檢查是否合身。然而，我今早第一次穿，卻發現夾克內裡有個小裂縫。我了解所有的瑕疵品須在一週內換貨或退貨，而此商品已不在上述期限內。

然而，我仍希望您這次能破例。如果它已經完售，我不介意換為等價商品。

麻煩再告訴我能怎麼做。

謝謝您。

雷納德・帕克

139. (A) 否則
(B) 然而
(C) 因此
(D) 而且

140. (A) 瑕疵的
(B) 錯誤的
(C) 不合身的
(D) 確認過的

141. (A) 我在到貨三週後將商品退貨。
(B) 請把錢匯到我提供的銀行帳戶。
(C) 然而，我仍希望您這次能破例。
(D) 還好申請期間延長到下個月了。

142. (A) 正在出售
(B) 已出售
(C) 持續被出售
(D) 將出售

143–146 電子郵件

收件者：簡・朗
<jlong@pwc.co.jp>
寄件者：羅伯特・弗格森
<ferg@gspec.co.jp>
日期：3 月 5 日
主旨：產品問題

敬愛的朗女士：

感謝您最近購買了 G-spec Slim-X 筆記型電腦。我們想通知最近和我們購買這台筆電的客戶：有極少數的型號需維修。

我們某些筆電中，作為指向裝置的觸控板有時運作會失靈。這問題會持續干擾您電腦的操作。為確認您的筆電是否為受影響的型號，請您查看位於筆電底部的產品序號。序號開頭如果為「SXRE」即需要維修。我們將承擔您退回 Slim-X 的運費，且 G-spec 將提供免費維修。

143. (A) 推薦
(B) 購買
(C) 測試
(D) 捐獻

144. (A) 這問題會持續干擾您電腦的操作。
(B) 我們相信您會喜歡這款筆記型電腦。
(C) 該型號被認為是同類產品中最值得信賴的。
(D) 欲知更多資訊，請參考我們的「常見問答」頁面。

145. (A) 確認
　　　(B) 被確認的
　　　(C) 確認
　　　(D) 確認

146. (A) 他們的（東西）
　　　(B) 我的（東西）
　　　(C) 這些
　　　(D) 它

PART 7　P. 185–205

147–148 簡訊

> **法蘭克・里奇〔下午 1:45〕**
>
> 卡羅好。我和市議會議員的電話會議剛結束，他們很喜歡我們的市鎮公園設計案。147 傑森・希克斯議員要求提供其他的客戶參考資料，但我手邊沒有這些檔案。我正在前往施工現場，所以可否請妳聯絡一家快遞公司，把鋸谷廣場檔案夾的副本寄給他？148 也請記得附上我們的小手冊。謝謝妳。

147. 里奇先生最有可能在哪裡工作？
　　　(A) 政府部門
　　　(B) 郵局
　　　(C) 保險公司
　　　(D) 造景公司

148. 法蘭克被要求做什麼？
　　　(A) 寄出一些客戶參考資料
　　　(B) 回覆訊息
　　　(C) 製作電子郵件列表
　　　(D) 安排會面約定

149–150 電子郵件

> 寄件者：帕特・梅里克
> 收件者：卡特飯店全體員工
> 日期：2 月 21 日
> 主旨：公告
>
> ---
>
> 自 3 月 1 日起，卡特飯店的房客須提前至少一週取消訂房，才能獲得全額退款。149

我們將在本週結束前，在我們的官網和櫃檯公告這項資訊。也將寄電子郵件給所有登記在冊的房客，説明這項新規定。如果有房客在不到一週的時間內通知我們要取消入住，請向有關的經理尋求協助。150 感謝您的配合。

卡特飯店總經理

帕特・梅里克

149. 此電子郵件的目的為何？
　　　(A) 公告員工訓練相關事宜
　　　(B) 説明升級後的飯店設施
　　　(C) 介紹新政策
　　　(D) 報告近期銷售數據

150. 根據電子郵件的內容，經理將做什麼事情？
　　　(A) 選擇可修改班表的員工
　　　(B) 教客戶網路訂房的方法
　　　(C) 決定新家具的擺設方式
　　　(D) 協助有特殊需求的客戶

151–152 簡訊串

> **妮可・梅爾斯〔12:52〕**
> 你離開馬丁宴會廳了嗎？
>
> **雨果・維斯利〔12:55〕**
> 還沒。最後一位講者才剛上台。
>
> **妮可・梅爾斯〔12:56〕**
> 你打算去 BR 科技公司的虛擬實境展示嗎？在 A 廳。152
>
> **雨果・維斯利〔12:57〕**
> 我一定會過去。他們的展示一向都很有趣。151
>
> **妮可・梅爾斯〔12:58〕**
> <u>確實如此。</u>151 也很有教育意義。
>
> **雨果・維斯利〔12:59〕**
> 我會坐在靠舞台的位置。要我幫妳留位子嗎？152
>
> **妮可・梅爾斯〔13:01〕**
> 要，拜託了！

151. 在 12:58 的時候,梅爾斯女士寫道:「確實如此」,她的意思最接近何者?
(A) 馬丁宴會廳的講者很有趣。
(B) 她同意維斯利先生對 BR 科技公司展示的看法。
(C) 她知道維斯利先生將參與展示會。
(D) 她打算採訪 BR 科技公司。

152. 關於維斯利先生的描述,何者最有可能為真?
(A) 他希望梅爾斯女士能進行展示。
(B) 他是虛擬實境軟體的開發者。
(C) 他將是馬丁宴會廳的最後一位講者。
(D) 他將比梅爾斯女士更早到 A 廳。

153–154 備忘錄

發文者:馬克・格洛弗
收文者:恰客餐廳員工
日期:7 月 21 日
主旨:要求

我們最近收到很多換班的要求。恰客餐廳高層想提醒大家,應儘早提出換班要求,且每班都需要 12 名員工。153

請至少提前兩週以公司系統提出申請,以確保您排到想要的班組。但很遺憾的是,並不是每一個人的要求都能得到滿足。為了維持我們優質服務的地方商譽,我們必須讓餐廳人手充足,而這有賴各位的合作。

如有任何疑問,請和您的經理洽詢。154

153. 此備忘錄的目的為何?
(A) 詢問對新菜色的回饋意見
(B) 指出訂餐系統的問題
(C) 說明新流程
(D) 提醒員工排班事宜

154. 如果員工有問題,應該怎麼做?
(A) 和他們的經理談
(B) 寫電子郵件給格洛弗先生
(C) 參閱手冊
(D) 填寫問卷

155–157 報導

《經濟月刊》

商貿快報

索萊里吉 訊,11 月 20 日——開發商肯尼・李特爾已開始獵鷹中央綜合大樓預定地的施工工程。155 這棟於西爾斯街 7863 號的大樓,先前為索萊里吉家具公司所在地。李特爾先生的獵鷹投資公司於六月買下該棟大樓。157 前工廠改建後,將成為 400 間公寓和約 8 千平方公尺的商業空間。155 156

這項耗資兩億歐元的建案將分為兩階段。第一階段預計將花一年半的時間,完成 300 間公寓的建設。其餘公寓及一棟三層樓高的百貨公司則在第二階段興建,156 約需七個月的時間完成。獵鷹投資公司最近也買下了湖景街的雷諾大樓。157 雖然其開發計畫尚未宣布,但獵鷹投資公司的一位發言人表示,將在下個月擇日釋出更多消息。

155. 本文的主要目的為何?
(A) 宣布公寓大樓竣工
(B) 刊載知名建築開發商的介紹
(C) 宣傳新整修的商店
(D) 說明建案的細節

156. 文中提到關於獵鷹中央綜合大樓的什麼資訊?
(A) 它將包含公寓和零售店面。
(B) 它將在七個月內完工。
(C) 它位在湖的附近。
(D) 它是李特爾先生開發的首棟建築。

157. 文中提到什麼與李特爾先生的公司有關的資訊?
(A) 將在下個月搬遷。
(B) 不只買下一棟建築。
(C) 公司離索萊里吉家具公司很近。
(D) 專門從事老屋翻新。

158–161 電子郵件

寄件者：薩布麗娜·桑盧西亞諾
收件者：各部門主管
日期：7月5日
主旨：提高員工效率

各部門主管您好：

人事部在接下來幾週將和各部門主管召開一系列會議，針對員工的工作習慣和效率進行討論。

開放式辦公空間，即員工辦公桌彼此相鄰、中間沒有隔板相隔的設計，因為能使工作時的溝通和合作變得更輕鬆，近來有愈來愈多的公司採用。**159** 由於我們辦公室安排12月下旬進行重新配置，**160** 我們正在考慮，開放式辦公空間的設計是否對我們公司更有益。對於此提案，我們將在考量利弊後做出決議。

我寫這封電子郵件是想徵詢您的意見。**158** 請留意，我們還沒決定開放式辦公空間是否適合我們。人事部現階段仍在蒐集資料。**159** 請您填寫公司內部網頁的開放式辦公空間意見調查。**158** 連結就在您登錄頁面的右側。

感謝您的協助。如您有任何疑問，請寫電子郵件給我。

聞聲響科技
人事經理
薩布麗娜·桑盧西亞諾

---

158. 寫這封電子郵件的目的為何？
(A) 宣布會議時間安排
(B) 宣傳公司年度聚會
(C) 通知政策異動
(D) 要求填寫問卷

159. 關於開放式辦公空間的好處，文中提到什麼資訊？
(A) 能讓公司僱用更多員工。
(B) 能幫助員工的專案合作更順利。
(C) 能減低營運成本。
(D) 能改善辦公室的空氣品質。

160. 該公司計劃年底要做什麼事情？
(A) 籌備主管研習營
(B) 改變辦公室設計
(C) 建立網站
(D) 招募新的人事主任

161. 「請留意，我們還沒決定開放式辦公空間是否適合我們。」最適合放在[1]、[2]、[3]、[4]的哪一個位置？
(A) [1]
(B) [2]
(C) [3]
(D) [4]

162–164 說明書

恭喜您購買新的伊斯特芬深眠床墊。

為確保您有效使用床墊，請遵守以下簡單的準則。

- 為保持床墊清潔，請務必使用床墊套。絕大多數床墊套可以機洗。

- 搬運或收納時，切勿折疊床墊。

- 請使用無水乾洗的襯墊清潔劑去除污漬。**如需用水清潔床墊，請務必謹慎，因大量水分恐導致黴菌滋生。163** **162** 使用床墊前，請確保它完全乾燥。

- **為避免床墊磨損不均，每年請將床墊翻轉數次（使上側朝下，反之亦然）。** **163**

- 每七至九年、或您感覺睡得不舒服時，請更換床墊。

- 請勿拆除床墊的資訊標籤。如您需要保固，它將作為保固識別之用。**164**

---

162. 說明書中提到什麼情況可能會損壞床墊？
(A) 不能機洗的床墊套
(B) 太濕
(C) 使用清潔產品
(D) 搬到室外

163. 床墊持有人應定期做什麼事情？
- (A) 熨燙床墊
- (B) 晾床墊
- (C) 換床墊套
- **(D) 翻轉床墊**

164. 根據說明，床墊持有人為何需要保留床墊的標籤？
- **(A) 作為申請保固時用。**
- (B) 它提供產品安全使用的準則。
- (C) 它說明了床墊所使用的材料種類。
- (D) 它有店家位置的資訊。

165–168 網路聊天室

羅傑・朱〔上午 10:27〕
我是人資部的羅傑。金女士和碰上女士，您們兩位下個月都排定參加主管研習營，對嗎？

勞拉・金〔上午 10:29〕
對。我們訂了 7 月 24 日下午 6:35 的機票。怎麼了嗎？

羅傑・朱〔上午 10:30〕
結果顯示艾柏麗塔度假村的網路系統弄丟了我們的訂房紀錄。所以**我們計劃把研習營改到七月的第二週。** 165 166

愛波・碰上〔上午 10:32〕
真的嗎？我已經花錢在那個禮拜把小孩送去夏令營了。如果小孩在，我就沒辦法參加。 166

羅傑・朱〔上午 10:33〕
嗯，就是這樣我才會聯絡您，了解您可能會有任何特殊需求。我們當然不會再住艾柏麗塔，所以我們團隊正在找舉辦研習營的替代地點。

勞拉・金〔上午 10:35〕
愛波，如果度假村有託兒中心的話，妳能來嗎？

愛波・碰上〔上午 10:36〕
嗯……那應該就可以。但我要先看過他們的服務內容，才能給出明確答案。

羅傑・朱〔上午 10:37〕
那金女士您呢？您有什麼需求，好讓行程更改更順暢的嗎？ 168

勞拉・金〔上午 10:39〕
我這邊沒有。我會讓我的助理去處理。 168

愛波・碰上〔上午 10:40〕
朱先生，感謝您通知。新地點決定好之後，請把小冊子給我們。 167

羅傑・朱〔上午 10:42〕
我會的，碰上女士。謝謝。

165. 此討論的目的為何？
- (A) 為錯誤表示歉意
- **(B) 說明行程異動**
- (C) 要求提供航班資訊
- (D) 推廣近期活動

166. 文中提到關於主管研習營的什麼資訊？
- (A) 它提供托兒服務。
- (B) 它每月舉行一次。
- **(C) 它和夏令營在同一週舉行。**
- (D) 它的場地向來都是艾柏麗塔度假村。

167. 碰上女士請朱先生做什麼事情？
- **(A) 提供場地的相關資訊**
- (B) 寄送活動日程的詳細資訊
- (C) 增加專案預算
- (D) 解釋付款流程

168. 上午 10:39，金女士說：「我這邊沒有」，其意思為何？
- (A) 她沒交報告。
- (B) 她還沒有收到某份文件。
- **(C) 她不需要更多協助。**
- (D) 她不會參加研習營。

169–171 電子郵件

寄件者：m.simmons@razmail.com
收件者：jcrowder@antioch.edu
日期：8月8日
主旨：安蒂奧克文學會議

敬愛的西蒙斯先生：

儘管通知得很突然，您仍同意在8月20日，於年度安蒂奧克文學會議上發表演講，非常感謝。克里斯・強森取消演講後，像您這樣有才華的作者能應邀前來，著實讓人鬆了一口氣。**169**

無論如何，我們很期待您關於印度生活的演講。我們的學生覺得現代文學很有吸引力，從去年夏天前來觀看強森博士的人數可見一斑。**170** 我們預期下個月將有類似的人潮，所以已將莫頓講堂預留給您。

如果您打算販售您的小說，我們能幫您在講堂外設置書攤，並請志工管理。另外，如果您需要投影機，請在下週二之前告訴我。**171** 我可以應您要求設置視聽設備。最後，能否請您給我一份簡歷，好讓我們的開幕講者在她介紹時使用呢？

謝謝您。

活動統籌
珍娜・克勞德

---

169. 克勞德女士為何寫這封電子郵件？
(A) 宣布有本書出版
(B) 修改講座時間
(C) 確認西蒙斯先生將參與活動
(D) 詳細討論西蒙斯先生的志工職責

170. 可從文中得知關於克里斯・強森的什麼資訊？
(A) 他寫了一本關於印度的大眾小說。
(B) 他於去年演講。
(C) 他先前和西蒙斯先生共事。
(D) 他在安蒂奧克的一所大學教書。

171. 「我可以應您要求設置視聽設備。」
最適合放在 [1]、[2]、[3]、[4] 的哪一個位置？
(A) [1]
(B) [2]
(C) [3]
(D) [4]

172–175 文章

準備貴店開幕式

開店後的頭幾天，是激起潛在客戶的興趣與獲得他們關注的絕佳機會，**172** **173** 但是您需要做很多規劃，才能成功。以下是在開幕前，您應考量的幾個重要問題：

● 您打算設置什麼樣的招牌或海報？
裝飾品在展示不同種類的商品時，相當有效果。

● 裝飾品將陳列多久？
如果只有開幕日擺出裝飾品，許多當天要上班的客人極有可能無法看見。**174**

● 您將使用哪種廣告？
有些研究指出，比起聽到的訊息，人們更容易記住視覺接收的資訊。在討論是否使用印刷品、電視或廣播做廣告時，請考量到這一點。**175**

● 您如何鼓勵員工？
員工是滿足客人的關鍵角色，因此您應考慮獎勵最優秀的員工。

---

172. 這篇文章的目標讀者是誰？
(A) 計劃開業的企業家
(B) 計劃展店到海外的店主
(C) 想要擔任管理職的員工
(D) 尋找新型產品的客戶

173. 第一段第二行的「gain」，意思最接近何者？
(A) 建立
(B) 改進
(C) 取得
(D) 成長

174. 根據文章的內容，人們在工作日不太可能做什麼事？

(A) 收聽廣播

(B) 查看工作機會列表

(C) 比較不同的產品

(D) 逛商店

175. 根據文章的內容，平面媒體廣告的好處為何？

(A) 比較有可能被當地人看到。

(B) 比其他形式的廣告便宜。

(C) 能在單一空間內提供較多資訊。

(D) 比其他形式的廣告更令人難忘。

176–180 備忘錄和表格

備忘錄

日期：5 月 25 日

收文者：拉斯塔汽車公司員工

發文者：行政部，莎拉·克洛維斯

主旨：與 GMNS 的合作關係

作為公司員工福利專案的一部分，拉斯塔汽車公司與全球行動網路系統（GMNS）合作，提供同仁優惠的手機服務方案。**176** 同仁選擇申辦 GMNS 的家庭或個人服務方案，將於申辦後的前兩個月分別省下 20% 或 15% 的費用。**179** 此外，也將扣除開通費，可再省下 25 美元。**177** 所有方案為期 12 個月，若不續約，租約將於期滿時自動終止。

同仁如欲使用此優惠，須撥打 914-555-4029 聯絡 GMNS 客戶支援中心。或透過網路，在 www.gmns.com/promotion 提出申請。申辦時，同仁須提供員工編號，**178** 以及公司的電子郵件信箱地址。**178** 另外，也須提交信用卡號碼**178** 及附有照片的有效身分證件，如駕照或護照。

GMNS 客訴表

客戶資料

姓名：<u>謝伊·萊恩斯</u>

帳號：<u>85948310</u>

日期：<u>7 月 30 日</u>

電子信箱地址：<u>sryans@rastamotors.com</u>

客訴詳情

我在六月看過拉斯塔汽車公司員工的專案後，開設了 GMNS 手機帳號。根據我的公司發放的促銷廣告，開通服務無須支付開通費。而且，申辦時和我通話的 GMNS 代表人員也確認過了。然而，我第一個月、日期為 7 月 28 日的帳單，仍收取了開通費。請從我的帳單扣除這筆費用，並將修改後的帳單寄給我。**180** 以防萬一，提醒一下，新版帳單也需包含 15% 的電話費折扣。**179** 謝謝。

176. 為何會簽發備忘錄？

(A) 提醒員工不要用公司電話打私人電話

(B) 告知員工特殊福利

(C) 鼓勵員工將現有的電話租約續約

(D) 通知員工申辦 GMNS 為強制命令

177. 文中提到開通費的什麼資訊？

(A) 價格為 25 美元。

(B) 可分期付款。

(C) 將於一年後退款。

(D) 將加到前兩期的帳單上。

178. 申辦 GMNS 不需要什麼東西？

(A) 促銷碼

(B) 員工編號

(C) 電子郵件信箱地址

(D) 信用卡卡號

179. 關於萊恩斯女士，下列何者最可能為真？

(A) 她在拉斯塔汽車網站申請了。

(B) 她以前曾用過 GMNS 的服務。

(C) 她申辦了個人服務方案。

(D) 她在克洛維斯女士的部門工作。

180. 萊恩斯女士要求 GMNS 做什麼事情？

(A) 寄給她更正後的帳單
(B) 取消她的一年期方案
(C) 多提供兩個月的折扣
(D) 修改該公司的續約政策

181–185 資訊和表格

歡迎蒞臨尚納雷特工程圖書館

蘇爾根大學的尚納雷特工程圖書館向有意參觀的學生與訪客，開放了我們位於一、二樓的公共閱覽區，以及位於地下室、有溫溼度控管的舊文獻區。館藏有文本、電影、攝影作品，還有大量的建築設計原稿和草稿。

為保護館藏，訪客與學生須了解以下圖書館規定：

- 所有訪客入館前須出示有效身分證件，並填寫必要的表格，成為圖書館讀者。 **181**

- 讀者可自由使用公共閱覽區的資料。為確保所有資料整理得宜，請將無需使用的資料放回全館任一還書區；讀者請勿自行上架書刊。 **182**

- 若發現讀者造成資料毀損，如劃記、刮痕、撕毀和污損，或上述以外之情況，將處以罰款。

- 二樓的電腦工作站旁有兩台大型掃描機可供使用。

- 尚納雷特圖書館於下午 6 點閉館。書刊均須於下午 5 點 45 分之前歸還。

舊文獻區要求遵守以下附加規定：

- 禁止攜帶私人物品進入舊文獻區。請在圖書館服務台使用臨時置物服務。如您須筆記或繪製草稿，館員將提供您筆或鉛筆。 **183**

- 須在舊文獻區的櫃檯以書面形式提出借閱資料。

- 舊文獻區的資料不可帶到圖書館的其他區域，且一次借閱的上限為三件。其餘資料將保留於櫃檯。 **185**

- 舊文獻區的資料將於下午 5 點 15 分收回，沒有例外。

尚納雷特工程圖書館
舊文獻區資料申請表

會員編號：84323-45
全名：詹姆士・海耶斯
日期：10 月 15 日
申請原因：研究

請在兩欄內填寫資訊，以利館員找到您所需的資料。

	書名	目錄編碼
資料 1	《西奧・馮・托恩之居家設計總史》 **184**	720.22VF
資料 2	《西奧・馮・托恩之1929 芝加哥藍圖》 **184**	728JJ
資料 3	《西奧・馮・托恩之私人日誌》 **184**	720.9AR
資料 4 **185**	《都市工程週刊》（12/08/1946） **185**	PP325-A **185**
資料 5		

181. 可從文中得知尚納雷特圖書館的什麼資訊？

(A) 訪客須註冊為會員。
(B) 向當地居民提供折扣。
(C) 有大學生專區。
(D) 週末提早閉館。

182. 根據規定，訪客禁止做什麼事？
(A) 閱讀機密文件
(B) 攜入飲料
(C) 提前預約資料
(D) 將使用過的資料重新上架

183. 舊文獻區的訪客能以何種方式記錄他們的研究內容？
(A) 讓專家幫忙記錄
(B) 向圖書館租借筆記型電腦
(C) 向圖書館館員索取書寫工具
(D) 使用個人的數位相機

184. 海耶斯先生的研究主題最有可能為何？
(A) 某位建築師的作品
(B) 工程刊物的歷史
(C) 歷史手稿的修復
(D) 歐洲知名的工程學校

185. 可從海耶斯先生要求的資料得知什麼資訊？
(A) 他將無法一次查看他所請求的所有資料。
(B) 他是蘇爾根大學工程系的學生。
(C) 他將在下午 5 點 45 分前歸還資料。
(D) 他將付費索取其他資料。

186–190 小冊子和電子郵件

格哈特窗框

格哈特窗框公司 30 多年來，一直為建築專業人士與承包商提供因應各種天氣的窗框。我們最暢銷的產品如下。

超級陽光：節能耐久，且有 20 多種顏色。 188

多重靠山：僅有白色、棕紅與黑色，其他方面則與超級陽光類似。 188 但框架較厚，隔熱效果更佳。

強化抗曬：此窗框適合大量陽光直射的房屋，其框架角度能阻擋刺眼強光，並維持舒適的室內溫度。

超絕緊緻：提供極端溫度下的大樓或住宅使用。安裝此產品時，須聯絡有執照的專業人員，以確保其所需的精確性。

價格和確切規格請參考我們的型錄。如有疑問或需求，請寫電子郵件至 info@gerhartwindowframes.co.uk，或致電 020-7946-0924。

挑選窗框時，請務必考慮各種因素。請至 www.gerhartwindowframes.co.uk/calc 使用我們的網路計算機，查詢您需要的窗框尺寸。 186 只需輸入窗戶的高度和寬度即可。

寄件者：
m.sheppard@rightbuild.co.uk
收件者：
info@gerhartwindowframes.co.uk
日期：4 月 7 日
主旨：近期訂單

格哈特窗框客服您好：

我寫這封信是想詢問訂單號碼 55-234A 的茄紫色窗框的事。我的客戶擔心框色會讓他的房子變得太熱。我已解釋窗框不太可能影響室內溫度，但我想知道這到底會不會成為問題。 187 188 他很喜歡這個顏色，可能的話，希望能不用改單。

我上次訂購貴公司產品時，可在官網上參考安裝影片。 190 我想再參考這些影片，畢竟近期都沒使用這項特定產品。我記得，安裝時有需要特別注意的地方。可否請您把該頁面的連結寄給我呢？ 190

瑪麗亞・薛佛　謹啟 187

寄件者：
freede@gerhartwindowframes.co.uk
收件者：
m.sheppard@rightbuild.co.uk
日期：4 月 7 日 189
主旨：關於：近期訂單

敬愛的薛佛女士：

感謝您與格哈特窗框聯絡。該窗框使用的材料並不會吸收陽光。另外，根據您訂單上的地址，鄰近地區的其他建築物均未反映過深色窗框的問題，包括深藍或灰黑色。如果貴客戶仍想更改訂單，請在今天營業時間結束前跟我說。 189

至於我們的官網，我們現在是請客戶參考特定製造商的網站，因為他們才有特定窗框的最新資訊。**190** 感謝您的選購。

法蘭西斯‧里德　謹啟

186. 根據小冊子的內容，客戶如何決定購買的窗框尺寸？
(A) 諮詢專家
(B) 使用網路服務
(C) 訂購產品樣品
(D) 下載一些圖片

187. 薛佛女士需要窗框哪一方面的更多資訊？
(A) 防潮性
(B) 褪色的容易度
(C) 與同類產品相比的厚度
(D) 吸收熱能的可能性

188. 薛佛女士最有可能為客戶訂購哪種窗框？
(A) 超級陽光
(B) 多重靠山
(C) 強化抗曬
(D) 超絕緊緻

189. 根據里德先生的說法，薛佛女士為什麼要在 4 月 7 日再次與他聯繫？
(A) 拿到報銷的費用
(B) 索取請款單
(C) 追蹤貨運
(D) 修改訂單

190. 文中提到關於安裝影片的什麼資訊？
(A) 薛佛女士不小心把檔案刪了。
(B) 現在無法在格哈特窗框的官網上收看。
(C) 格哈特窗框會用電子郵件寄給薛佛女士。
(D) 影片主要介紹當地承包商。

191–195　小冊子、評論和電子郵件

在巴黎學新聞

巴黎新聞學院（PJI）位於巴黎市中心，提供各類課程給計劃到研究所學程進修的學生。**191** 這裡有許多全球性媒體的駐地辦公室，是在學時就能建立寶貴人脈的好地方。我們的課程涵蓋錄音、攝影、資料探勘，以及一般常見的專題和報導寫作。課程中也提供撰寫自傳、製作履歷和彙編作品集的建議，為學生申請研究所作準備。迄今我們已有數百名學生到全球知名學院就讀。為協助學生成功，我們聘請備受業界尊崇的講師，如《國際晚報》總編輯戴倫‧安德森 **194** 和《倫敦新聞社》的伯大尼‧基爾派翠克。如欲申請入學、了解學校及課程詳情、或安排與學術顧問進行諮詢，請瀏覽我們的官網 www.pji.ed.fr。

http://www.pji.ed.fr/feedback

首頁	課程	回饋意見	聯絡

凱利‧羅德里格斯 **194**

12 月 4 日

我春天時將到加拿大的米勒德新聞學院就讀。我大學快畢業時，仍缺少幾門轉換到加拿大學術體制的必修課程。這就是我選擇就讀 PJI 的原因。

在巴黎求學時，我負擔不起學校附近的公寓租金，只好每天開車上學。通勤的狀況很糟糕，主要是因為學校周遭地區的車流量很大。**192** 我希望校方能在校園內提供住宿。**195**

課程本身非常棒。我的教授戴倫‧安德森博士 **194** 備課太充分了，上課經常超過規定的課堂時間。**193** 在為期十週的暑期課程中，我覺得我學到了該課程兩倍的內容。

安德森教授提供的教材和其他推薦讀本幫我趕上學習進度。他在諮詢時間提供的額外協助也對我準備研究所有關鍵性的影響。

收件者：krodriguez@multimail.co.br
寄件者：mdubois@pji.ed.fr
日期：12 月 7 日
主旨：謝謝您的意見回饋

羅德里格斯小姐：

我們一向都很感謝聽到學生回來分享心得。其他 PJI 學生也反映過與您類似的困擾，我們目前正在處理當中。從 2 月 1 日起，和您狀況類似的學生就能利用蓋好的建築。**195** 我們希望您能和未來 PJI 的學生分享這項消息。

馬克斯・杜波伊斯　謹啟

191. 這本小冊子的目標讀者是誰？
(A) 想申請研究所的大學生
(B) 電視製作人
(C) 求職的教授
(D) 財經記者

192. 文中提到關於 PJI 的什麼資訊？
(A) 提供大學生獎學金。
(B) 協助學生求職。
(C) 有實習計畫。
(D) 所在地點很擁擠。

193. 羅德里格斯小姐提到什麼與她的教授有關的事？
(A) 他要求學生參加很多互動活動。
(B) 他幾乎沒時間讓學生去辦公室諮詢。
(C) 他花了額外時間講課程內容。
(D) 他每個星期會分派案子。

194. 羅德里格斯小姐的指導老師沒有教課時，在哪裡工作？
(A) PJI
(B) 《國際晚報》
(C) 《倫敦新聞社》
(D) 巴黎的一家新聞社

195. PJI 如何處理羅德里格斯小姐抱怨的事情？
(A) 擴大教室空間
(B) 提供學生住宿
(C) 增加公共運輸的選項
(D) 縮短上課時間

196–200 特色列表和網頁

濕威樂 JS-4425 型 12 公斤噴流式洗衣機 **196**

特色： 196

——超大洗衣槽能比一般洗衣機裝更多的衣物，**199** 幫您省時。

——內部為不銹鋼材質，**199** 可防異味及生鏽。

——洗衣行程結束後，若洗衣機內遺留衣物，將有信號提醒您。LED 面板也會顯示您的洗衣行程狀態。

——新的藍移光學技術可測量衣物量，並設定合適的搖動幅度，減少耗電。

——針對水量、溫度、洗滌行程與不同纖維種類，有多種設定可供選擇。**199**

——抗震技術讓您的洗衣機比一般洗衣機運轉更加安靜，**200** 讓您在任何時間都能使用洗衣機洗滌衣物。

www.swirler.com/testimonials

| 評價 | 產品 | 常見問題 | 據點 |

「物超所值」

發表人：索尼婭‧羅伯茨 198

發表日期：2 月 23 日

所在地：蘇格蘭亞伯丁市

我用過的是別間公司生產的洗衣機，但它只撐了五年，所以我很樂見濕威樂推出一款價格非常實惠的產品。我很驚訝，因為它比我的舊洗衣機強大得多。該機型甚至能洗淨各類衣服上的頑強污漬。它適用於各種織物，有四種行程（輕量、一般、抗皺與精緻衣物）與三種溫度（冷、溫、熱）的設定。 197 它的外觀顏色也有多種選擇，我很喜歡。 199 我唯一遇到的問題是我花了一個多月才習慣這台洗衣機，因為很難掌握它所有的功能。 198

www.swirler.com/testimonials

| 評價 | 產品 | 常見問題 | 據點 |

「非常失望」

發表人：布萊恩‧卡爾蒙特

發表日期：2 月 24 日

所在地：愛爾蘭都柏林市

看到濕威樂洗衣機的評價這麼好，讓我購買時非常期待。但買了還不到一週，我就發現**這台洗衣機太吵了。** 200 有一次它晃得太大力，我甚至擔心會解體。濕威樂的客服人員提議換貨給我，但我還是決定退款就好。

196. 最有可能在哪裡看到這個特色列表？
(A) 印在服裝型錄上
(B) 在產品包裝上
(C) 布料的訂單裡
(D) 張貼於維修店內

197. 在第一個網頁中，第一段第五行的「suit」，意思最接近何者？
(A) 上訴
(B) 合格
(C) 穿衣
(D) 適應

198. 關於該產品，羅伯茨女士有何批評？
(A) 很複雜。
(B) 很吵。
(C) 很重。
(D) 很昂貴。

199. 在產品描述中，並未提及羅伯茨女士喜歡的哪一項特色？
(A) 各類設定
(B) 金屬內部
(C) 大容量
(D) 裝飾性的外觀

200. 卡爾蒙特先生不喜歡他買的產品的哪項特色？
(A) 抗震技術
(B) 藍移技術
(C) LED 指示燈
(D) 通知信號

ACTUAL TEST ⑧

101. 因為客戶想買的電腦螢幕賣完了，便取消了訂單。
(A) 因此
(B) 例如
(C) 儘管
(D) 因為

102. 建議乘客保留行李標籤的存根，以便證明領取的行李確實是他們的。
(A) 他們
(B) 他們
(C) 他們自己
(D) 他們的（東西）

103. 已預約好行政套房，留待下週五與寇特爾公司磋商合約時用。
(A) 已通知
(B) 已預約
(C) 已延後
(D) 已決定

104. 加強版的帳戶管理軟體，使杜威金融公司的員工能夠迅速答覆客戶的諮詢。
(A) 快的
(B) 快速地
(C) 更快的
(D) 敏捷

105. 為確保符合安全標準，包裝前將隨機選取幾批燈泡進行測試。
(A) 符合
(B) 合作
(C) 運作
(D) 到期

106. 我們很感謝您向我們報告花園造景工程的最新進度。
(A) 沒有
(B) 鄰近
(C) 經由
(D) 關於

107. 大概每隔 20 公分釘根小釘子，來固定窗框的隔熱條。
(A) 使用
(B) 有用的
(C) 正在使用
(D) 被使用的

108. 你安排和客戶開會時，切記不要讓時間重疊到。
(A) 正在解除
(B) 自由
(C) 沒有
(D) 解除

109. 拉苟斯度假村建議提前兩個月訂房，以確保您有訂到房。
(A) 提前
(B) 最後
(C) 然後
(D) 只要

110. 每年舉辦公司野餐，是為了讓員工有機會認識其他部門的同事。
(A) 同事
(B) 住戶
(C) 職位
(D) 生意

111. 比起以前的型號，這台設備能讓研究人員獲得更精準的讀數。
(A) 精準地
(B) 更精準的
(C) 更精準地
(D) 精準的

112. 蓋爾科藥廠的所有技術人員，在進入實驗室前都要先洗手。
(A) 期待
(B) 正在期待
(C) 被預期
(D) 將要期待

113. 冬季才剛開始第一週，機場已經因為一場強烈暴風雪而不得不取消航班。
(A) 最好的
(B) 相當
(C) 全面地
(D) 已經

114. 「赫伯工業」銷路最好的起重機，能吊起高達 10 公噸的貨物。
(A) 裝貨機
(B) （裝載的）貨物
(C) 裝載
(D) 被裝載的

115. 草薙女士即將退休時，受邀管理亞洲總部的資安團隊。
(A) 鄰近
(B) 即將
(C) 在……之前
(D) 除……外

116. 新專案開始前，將工作指派給專案裡的每一位成員是部門經理的職責。
(A) 準確性
(B) 正常運作
(C) 情況
(D) 責任

117. 雖然問卷收集而來的資訊將有助於改善我們對客戶的服務，但您的參與是完全志願的。
(A) 志工
(B) 志願的；無償的
(C) 志願做
(D) 志願地

118. 提倡均衡發展生活型態的非營利組織「健康生活協會」，提供各種產品和服務。
(A) 分配
(B) 值得
(C) 提倡
(D) 預期

119. 鐵路連線公司的董事會成員在上一次的股東大會上，針對一條高速鐵路路線爭論得很激烈。
(A) 激烈地
(B) 例行地
(C) 不常；很少
(D) 持續地

120. 錫蘭公司盡責的客服人員能為來電者提供任何所需的協助。
(A) 不可避免的
(B) 持續的
(C) 盡責的
(D) 已制定的

121. 投資組合的審查目的是為了弄清楚天意投資公司的基金配置是否符合客戶的目標。
(A) 雖然
(B) 是否
(C) 因為
(D) 兩者之中任一的

122. 格林維爾的房地產價值每年維持著 10% 的增值。
(A) 付款
(B) 普查
(C) 統計數據
(D) 增值

123. 艾育比出版社是黎巴嫩其中一家擁有很忠實讀者群的新聞媒體。
(A) 其一
(B) 仍然
(C) 那些
(D) 反而

124. 巴比倫房地產公司在近三季中維持穩定的銷售量。
(A) 完全的
(B) 可重新填裝的
(C) 穩定的
(D) 具體的

125. 錫蘭技術諮詢公司架設的網站已為了滿足客戶的需求，量身打造完成。
(A) 客製化
(B) 已被量身打造
(C) 客製化
(D) 正在客製化

126. 多虧「布羅德莫投資」等公司的資金支持，教育廣播網的節目才得以播出。
(A) 被認可的
(B) 清楚的
(C) 思慮周全的
(D) 可能的

127. 湯谷企業自從上一季簽下第一份國際合約後，其收益便創新高。

(A) 利潤；收益

(B) 賺得

(C) 賺得

(D) 賺錢的人

128. 請到知名旁白，是廣受好評的系列紀錄片《藍色世界》的一大特色。

(A) 領悟

(B) 表示

(C) 以……為特色

(D) 應用

129. 我們預計下個月會收到更多網路訂單，所以確保我們的伺服器穩定運作非常重要。

(A) 正在仰賴

(B) 可信賴的

(C) 仰賴

(D) 穩定地

130. 「Dessous la Table」對品質的堅定承諾，反映在它整份道地法國葡萄酒和乳酪菜單裡的每一處。

(A) 鄰近

(B) 在……之間

(C) 到……裡

(D) 遍及……各處

PART 6　P. 209–212

131–134 報導

機場預報

1 月 22 日

根據國家機場管理局的數據顯示，安大略機場的貨運吞吐量再度增加。事實上，這已寫下連續第五年的顯著成長。安大略省是各類商品的轉運站，榜上最主要的貨品有服飾、藥物和建築設備等。處理貨物需要更多人員。因此，機場也持續徵才。分析師認為，貨運量成長表示該地區經濟活動將繼續蓬勃發展。

131. (A) 儘管

(B) 然而

(C) 依然

(D) 事實上

132. (A) 貨物

(B) 優點

(C) 設施

(D) 成本

133. (A) 約一半的貨物將運往海外。

(B) 今年其他產品的配送量下滑了。

(C) 機場最近公布最新數據。

(D) 處理貨物需要更多人員。

134. (A) 正在看

(B) 認為

(C) 被看見

(D) 認為

135–138 電子郵件

收件者：丹尼爾・班迪 <dbandy@benmail.com>

寄件者：艾瑞克・卡爾宏 <e.calhoun@terryvalechildrenszoo.org>

日期：6 月 20 日

主旨：會員資格

敬愛的班迪女士：

感謝您過去一年的支持。請留意，您的泰瑞維爾兒童動物園會員資格將於 7 月 31 日到期。若您現在續約，將獲得一張價值 50 美元的禮券，可在我們的禮品店使用。該優惠僅至 6 月 30 日以前有效。請您向我們的客服人員報上代碼 TCZFAN3 即可。我們感謝全體會員，並希望您願意續約、享受會員所有的福利。也請您記得，動物園會員將收到新展覽《非洲遊獵步道》的賓客通行證。展覽將於 8 月 15 日開放民眾入園，但我們的會員將受邀參加 8 月 11 日的特別預展。

祝　平安順心

會員服務部主任　艾瑞克・卡爾宏

135. (A) 應已過期
(B) 將要到期
(C) 將要到期
(D) 已經過期

136. **(A) 直到**
(B) 除……之外
(C) 包括
(D) 在……之中

137. **(A) 中斷**
(B) 打斷
(C) 正在打斷
(D) 被打斷的

138. (A) 工程應在月底之前完成。
(B) 我們對於可能造成的任何不便提前表示歉意。
(C) 請讓我們知道,您希望我們在這個區域辦哪一種展覽。
(D) 但我們的會員將受邀參加 8 月 11 日的特別預展。

139–142 資訊

> **到伊斯坦堡迪西茲醫院務必約診**
>
> 伊斯坦堡迪西茲醫院盡力在病患預約的時間為他們看診。這是由於我們有高效率的預約掛號系統的關係。為了協助我們維持下去,務必準時到診。儘管我們盡全力配合門診時間,但仍有可能因意外情況造成延誤。我們的醫生有時須執行緊急手術。遇到上述情況,我們需要您的配合。
>
> 我們建議您於門診當天聯絡我們,以確認預估的候診時間。

139. (A) 這裡
(B) 其他
(C) 有些
(D) 這

140. (A) 進入
(B) 考慮
(C) 調整
(D) 維持

141. **(A) 我們的醫生有時須執行緊急手術。**
(B) 在您的文件中記下這點很重要。
(C) 您可隨時重新預約掛號。
(D) 為確保這種情況不會發生,您應該仔細聽從醫師的建議。

142. (A) 準備
(B) 配合
(C) 參與
(D) 期待

143–146 公告

> **「UBV 金融公司」:公司車輛使用政策**
>
> 公司車為業務部門員工專用。其他部門員工應使用自家車或公共運輸。業務人員無需事先批准,每人均可使用公司車,每週至多行駛 200 公里。超出此距離,業務人員則需事先取得分公司經理的批准。
>
> 請謹記,公司車僅供業務活動使用,車輛禁止私用。僅持有有效駕照和投保相關保險的員工,才能駕駛「UBV 金融公司」的車輛。
>
> 感謝您配合此一事項。

143. (A) 獨特的
(B) 細緻的
(C) 專用的
(D) 傳統的

144. **(A) 更遠的**
(B) 那些的
(C) 任何的
(D) 有限的

145. (A) 提供
(B) 正在提供
(C) 應提供
(D) 供作

146. (A) 目前只有經濟型車種可用。
(B) 車輛禁止私用。
(C) 這輛車最近已檢查並維修過。
(D) 公司計劃升級所有車輛。

147–148　優惠券

風信子餐酒館

風信子感謝券

點任何湯、義大利麵或排餐時，出示此優惠券，將可免費任選一杯中杯飲料。 147 此優惠券可於週二至週日正常營業時間使用（週一公休）。

告訴我們您的想法！

歡迎查看我們入口旁的活動布告欄，了解風信子舉辦的活動！您也可在布告欄填寫顧客意見調查表並轉交給任一餐廳人員，就有機會抽中一份免費晚餐。 148

147. 使用優惠券可獲得哪項免費贈品？
(A) 一杯飲料
(B) 一份牛排
(C) 一些湯
(D) 一些義大利麵

148. 顧客如何能得到獎品？
(A) 填寫問卷
(B) 參加活動
(C) 在週日造訪餐廳
(D) 在週一訂位

149–150　電子郵件

收件者：sjacobs@sjacobsfashion.co.uk
寄件者：orders@fleurdelis.co.fr
日期：11 月 7 日
主旨：訂單 #09345A

敬愛的雅各布斯先生：

我們很遺憾通知您，您 11 月在我們網站購買的紅色及粉紅色太陽眼鏡（總計 70 件），目前沒有存貨。 149 現在我們無法完成您的訂單並出貨，也因此無法給您確切的到貨日期。不過，我們有些您可能會喜歡的類似款式。一款是有紅白條紋的鏡框，另一款則為純紫色鏡框。如欲修改訂單，只需登入我們的官網，並點擊螢幕上

方的購物車。 150 我們再次對此情形向您致歉，並期待您再度光臨。

客戶支援部
布蘭達・張　謹啟

149. 此電子郵件的目的為何？
(A) 確認送貨日期
(B) 通知價格異動
(C) 解釋購物問題
(D) 解釋退款流程

150. 雅各布斯先生被要求做什麼事情？
(A) 瀏覽官網
(B) 致電了解詳情
(C) 支付額外費用
(D) 更新部分帳單資訊

151–152　簡訊串

愛德華・斯賓塞〔下午 4:47〕
凱西好。妳還有多的印表機墨水匣嗎？它們通常放在妳的桌子底下。 151

凱薩琳・格林〔下午 4:48〕
沒有喔。我把它們移到新的儲物櫃了。 151

凱薩琳・格林〔下午 4:50〕
你也知道，就休息室旁邊的白色櫃子。

愛德華・斯賓塞〔下午 4:50〕
喔，對。但我還沒拿到那些櫃子的鑰匙。 152

愛德華・斯賓塞〔下午 4:51〕
我可以借妳的嗎？ 152

凱薩琳・格林〔下午 4:54〕
當然可以。隨時可以順路過來我的辦公室。 152

愛德華・斯賓塞〔下午 4:55〕
幾分鐘後見。

151. 斯賓塞先生為何聯絡格林女士？
(A) 討論家具訂單
(B) 確定某些物品的位置
(C) 投訴某個流程
(D) 詢問會議室預訂情形

152. 下午 4:54，格林女士說：「隨時可以順路過來我的辦公室」，其意思為何？

    (A) 她會借某個東西給斯賓塞先生。
    (B) 她建議斯賓塞先生使用她的印表機。
    (C) 她想請斯賓塞先生帶某份文件過來。
    (D) 她能會面的時間有限。

153–155 信函

2 月 10 日
RLA 零件和用品公司

敬愛的艾斯特拉達先生：

我寫這封信給您，是想表示我對 RLA 日前開出的國際行銷總監一職很感興趣。 **153** 介紹貴公司給我的人是崔海媛，她和我在柯生金屬工業曾密切合作。她認為我很適合 RLA，並建議我聯絡您。

憑藉我在柯生工業亞洲與歐洲區擔任全球廣告經理的十年經驗，我很有信心能幫 RLA 達成其擴展國際業務的目標。從我在柯生的經歷可證明，我不僅建立了廣大基本客戶群， **154** 而且我負責地區的收益逐年成長。此外，我對於業界的金屬零件及產品也有更加廣泛的了解。 **155**

關於我更詳細的背景和經歷，請您參考附件的履歷。您方便時可打 682-555-4352 或經由 abrea@clpemail.com 聯絡我。謝謝您，我很期待收到您的答覆。

艾比·布雷亞　謹啟

附件

153. 布雷亞女士為何寫這封信？

    (A) 追蹤近日面試的後續
    (B) 轉達她想在 RLA 工作的意願
    (C) 詢問幾條駕駛路線
    (D) 推薦同事一個 RLA 的職位

154. 布雷亞女士在柯生金屬工業時做了什麼事情？

    (A) 她僱用了新的行銷人員。
    (B) 她提出另外的獲利手段。
    (C) 她完成很多金屬零件的新設計。
    (D) 她留住許多來自不同國家的客戶。

155. 根據布雷亞女士的說法，她能發展出什麼？

    (A) 有效的管理能力
    (B) 創新的廣告活動
    (C) 相關的產業知識
    (D) 精密金屬的加工技術

156–157 文章

職場諮詢——每月建議 156

激勵你的團隊！ **156**

柯妮莉亞·赫伯特　撰

為獎勵員工的卓越績效，加薪或多提供福利可能是最佳辦法，但是經理通常無權給予上述的獎勵。然而，還有其他有效、低成本的作法，能夠感謝員工、提振士氣或提升績效。以下有幾點建議： **156**

- 利用公司刊物，公布同仁得獎或達成目標的消息。 **157** 同仁在社區的志願服務也能予以認可。

- 可能的話，讓同仁能有彈性的工作時間表。

- 專案完成時，可帶如蛋糕或甜甜圈之類的點心來慶祝。

- 舉辦午餐聚餐來慶祝同仁生日； **157** 每人可自備食物和大家分享。

- 提供額外培訓，讓員工有進一步發展的機會。 **157**

柯妮莉亞·赫伯特為赫伯特管理顧問公司的執行長。

156. 撰寫這篇文章的原因為何？

    (A) 說明從事管理顧問的好處
    (B) 概述僱用志願者幫忙做專案的方法
    (C) 解釋評估員工表現的最佳方法
    (D) 為主管提供激勵員工的建議

157. 文中未提及哪一項活動？

    (A) 在公司刊物內提及員工的成就
    (B) 提供學習機會
    (C) 免費贈送社區活動的門票
    (D) 對特定活動的認可

岡薩雷茲玻璃製造商

岡薩雷茲玻璃製造商總部位於西班牙的巴塞隆納，是一間中型玻璃生產商。該公司**生產摩天大樓及其他高層商辦大樓用的高品質強力玻璃。** 158 公司產品主要銷往歐洲西南部，其中約 50% 用於西班牙的建築。該公司目前在全球擁有將近 900 名員工（其中 600 名在巴塞隆納），比前一年增長了 25%。該公司除了在西班牙設立總部和廠房，在里斯本、羅馬、雅典和索非亞亦設有航運中心。**執行長勞倫・托雷斯去年加入岡薩雷茲玻璃，** 159 **該公司在她的領導下大幅擴展研究部門，** 160 目標是開發更環保節能的產品。為此，岡薩雷茲於今年初收購了「里昂系統」，這是一家位於塞維亞的小型研究公司。

158. 誰最有可能是岡薩雷茲玻璃製造商的客戶？
(A) 研究中心
(B) 建築公司
(C) 藥廠
(D) 眼鏡製造商

159. 岡薩雷茲玻璃製造商去年做了什麼事情？
(A) 買下另一家公司。
(B) 僱用新的執行長。
(C) 蓋了航運中心。
(D) 搬遷總部。

160. 文中提到關於岡薩雷茲玻璃製造商的什麼事情？
(A) 擴大了研究部門的規模。
(B) 曾出現在雜誌的專題報導中。
(C) 能源使用減少了 25%。
(D) 參與了在塞維亞舉行的會議。

收件者：技術支援部
寄件者：人力資源部
日期：11 月 12 日
主旨：阿拉伯語課程

各位好：

由於我們公司即將進軍黎巴嫩，未來有更多專案需要熟悉阿拉伯語的同仁，方便與當地合夥對象及客戶合作。 161 為因應此一進展，公司將提供阿拉伯語課程，給所有會和阿語人士有線上互動的技術支援部員工。課程非義務參加，但我們認為這是一個珍貴的機會，讓各位精進語言能力。 162

我們將引進釜山當地語言學習的龍頭業者——多語寰球語言學院。為節省通勤時間，課程將於樓下的會議室舉行，並提供免費飲料。 163 一共提供三種等級（中級、高級和特高級）的阿拉伯語課程。 163 參與課程的同仁將在測驗之後分發到適合的班級。上課時間為週一及週五晚間 7 點。 163

這次發展職能的機會很寶貴，請各位認真考慮報名。欲參加下週的測驗，請於週五之前回覆此電子郵件。

大角星軟體有限公司

人力資源部
米娜・申　謹啟

161. 該公司為何提供阿拉伯語課程？
(A) 將在黎巴嫩做生意。
(B) 計劃僱用更多阿語人士。
(C) 有些員工將轉調至黎巴嫩。
(D) 語言學校正提供免費課程。

162. 關於某些技術支援部的員工，文中指出什麼？
(A) 他們經常出差拜訪合夥公司。
(B) 他們已搬到釜山的新辦公室。
(C) 他們目前正在上多語寰球語言學院的課程。
(D) 他們已經會說一點阿拉伯語。

163. 文中沒有提及關於課程的什麼事？
(A) 將提供飲料。
(B) 一週上課兩次。
(C) 有一次性收費。
(D) 有三個等級可供選擇。

164–167 電子郵件

收件者：艾迪·盧欽
<a.lukin@emorymedical.org>
寄件者：馬克·辛頓
<hinton@arwn.org>
日期：10 月 3 日
主旨：會議

親愛的盧欽女士：

阿帕拉契鄉村健康網絡（ARWN）將於 11 月 10 日週五至 11 日週六在華盛頓特區舉辦會議，主題為「數位化病歷如何改善病患照護」。與您一樣在鄉村畢生奉獻的醫療專業人員，將與會討論多年來面對的挑戰。 165 這些講者還會分享如何募款投入科技研發，以大幅簡化文書作業，並提升病患就醫經驗的整體品質。 164

特邀講者包括夏洛茨維爾地區診所的主任米蘭達·譚博士、阿帕拉契保險合作社執行長朴俊書博士，與臨床醫學教育研究組織董事長暨醫學博士埃里森·布萊斯。他們皆為學識豐富的專家，於各大期刊發表過研究論文。

請於 11 月 3 日週五之前至 www.arwn conference.org/register 報名。如需觀看活動當日的演講，您須在可上網的裝置上安裝媒體播放器軟體。 167 <u>或者改以收音機收聽。</u>會議將全程錄影，並於 11 月 20 日上傳至我們官網。 166

祝 好

ARWN 會員專員
馬克·辛頓

164. 該會議的主題為何？
(A) 以科技改善鄉村地區的醫療保健服務
(B) 在鄉村地區推廣醫學教育
(C) 為鄉村地區的病患提供新療法
(D) 農村地區投保選項的研究發現

165. 盧欽女士最有可能的職業為何？
(A) 鄉村房地產仲介
(B) 鄉村醫療保健專業人員
(C) 保險業務員
(D) 醫學線新聞記者

166. 11 月 20 日將發生什麼事？
(A) 會用電子郵件寄出演講投影片。
(B) 將出版鄉村公衛相關的文章。
(C) 將開始專業從業人員的聚會。
(D) 將可以觀看影片。

167. 「或者改以收音機收聽。」最適合放在
[1]、[2]、[3]、[4] 的哪一個位置？
(A) [1]
(B) [2]
(C) [3]
(D) [4]

168–171 網路聊天室

安迪·帕拉斯〔上午 7:43〕
阿金、亞莉早。有誰能幫我個忙嗎？ 171 我在前往「蓋文工業」的路上，要去了解他們研發部對實驗用品的要求，但我忘了帶要給他們實驗室看的玻璃樣品。 168 171

金柏利·李〔上午 7:45〕
我們的產品型錄網路上都看得到。不能用你自己的筆電嗎？ 169

安迪·帕拉斯〔上午 7:46〕
<u>那些照片不行。</u>電腦螢幕是絕對沒辦法強調我們玻璃的透明度和強度的。 169

金柏利·李〔上午 7:48〕
這樣你可能得開車回辦公室拿。 170

亞莉安娜・諾斯科夫〔上午 7:51〕

嗯，我應該能幫上忙。我還帶著昨天開會用的工具箱，裡面有我們的玻璃器皿。我的車現在塞在第三大道。 171

安迪・帕拉斯〔上午 7:55〕

這消息太棒了！我正停在第十大道和月桂街的路口。 170 我們能在附近碰頭嗎？ 171

亞莉安娜・諾斯科夫〔上午 7:56〕

好。就在第五大道的咖啡廳碰面吧。

金柏利・李〔上午 7:57〕

亞莉，妳可以把樣品直接送去客戶公司。

亞莉安娜・諾斯科夫〔上午 7:58〕

我必須早點到公司準備上午 9:30 的電話會議。

安迪・帕拉斯〔上午 7:59〕

咖啡廳就好。我大概需要 10 分鐘才能到那裡。妳能在那之前趕到嗎？

亞莉安娜・諾斯科夫〔上午 8:02〕

當然可以。等會見。

---

168. 帕拉斯先生最有可能的職業為何？

(A) 業務員
(B) 電腦技術員
(C) 「蓋文工業」員工
(D) 李女士的客戶

169. 上午 7:46，帕拉斯先生寫道：「那些照片不行」，最有可能是什麼意思？

(A) 他會提供網址。
(B) 他打算請客戶訂閱型錄。
(C) 他傾向給客戶看產品的樣品。
(D) 他將為實驗室購買玻璃器皿。

170. 帕拉斯先生在哪裡？

(A) 會議室
(B) 實驗室
(C) 車上
(D) 咖啡廳

171. 諾斯科夫女士主動提議做什麼事情？

(A) 為客戶準備簡報
(B) 幫同事買咖啡
(C) 提前去開會
(D) 把產品送去給帕拉斯先生

172–175 電子郵件

寄件者：凱萊・斯托克斯
<callstokes@evergreenmail.com>
收件者：強納森・鮑爾
<jonbauer@tenymail.com>
日期：11 月 13 日，下午 3:47
主旨：長榮 TFP
附件：TFP

敬愛的鮑爾先生：

感謝您對長榮顧問公司的訂製肥料計畫（TFP）表達興趣。我們很抱歉，您無法直接透過我們官網取得相關資訊，但該計畫的專頁目前仍在進行定期維護。 172 這封信的附件為這項計畫完整詳盡的說明，請您參閱，但我也想花些篇幅在此向您簡要介紹。

施肥是農業不可或缺的一部分，數千年來一向如此。 173 農法和原料隨著時間而發生變化，但 19 世紀無機肥料的出現無疑對農業造成莫大的影響。使用無機肥料大幅提高了作物的產量，並促使了人口成長。遺憾的是，這也導致難以想像的大量污染和土壤毒物污染。

若妥善管理，有機肥料對環境的影響遠小於無機肥料，且效果若不是更有效，可能也相去不遠。 174 175 我們受過訓練的專家會檢驗各個田地的土壤屬性，並針對欲栽培作物研發所需的混和養分肥料。我們使用純天然的原料，且皆獲環境安全局許可使用。 174

我們產品的優點並不只是對環境的關注和永續性。**我們曾針對公司成立 20 多年以來的用戶進行調查，**⟨174⟩ 所有用戶都表示比使用化肥時更節省成本，有些人甚至減省高達 30%。我們目前不只和國內幾大農業合作社簽約，也與數百間家族經營的小型農場合作。這些客戶擁有各式各樣的農業型態，從稻田、玉米田到蘋果園都有。因此，我們有信心能幫您提高生產量、同時減少對環境的影響，以及節省您的成本。

長榮顧問公司

客戶服務部主任
凱萊‧斯托克斯　謹啟

---

172. 文中提到關於長榮顧問公司的什麼資訊？
- (A) 它是環境安全局下的一個部門。
- **(B) 目前部分官網正在更新中。**
- (C) 由個人創立。
- (D) 擁有幾個大型農業合作社。

173. 第二段第一行的「integral」，意思最接近何者？
- (A) 被收集的
- **(B) 至關重要的**
- (C) 受規範的
- (D) 有生產力的

174. 文中沒有提到關於 TFP 的什麼資訊？
- (A) 開發於 20 年前。
- (B) 減少某座農場排放的污染物。
- **(C) 專為小農所設計。**
- (D) 僅用有機材料製作。

175. 「遺憾的是，這也導致難以想像的大量污染和土壤毒物污染。」最適合放在 [1]、[2]、[3]、[4] 的哪一個位置？
- (A) [1]
- **(B) [2]**
- (C) [3]
- (D) [4]

甜蜜生活

你想不想吃一整天的冰淇淋，同時還可賺錢？如果這聽起來好得令人難以置信，那麼你得知道，有些人的工作就是冰淇淋試吃員。

瑪麗安娜‧鄧肯在總部設於紐西蘭的手工冰淇淋和雪酪製造商「糖漫冰品」裡⟨177⟩擔任冰淇淋試吃員。⟨176⟩ 這份工作和一般認知很不一樣，其實需要經過多年學習和培訓。鄧肯在普納特大學讀了五年書取得食品科學學位後，就去加拿大的哈金斯冰淇淋工廠實習一年。⟨180⟩ 隨後她回到紐西蘭並被延攬到糖漫，⟨177⟩ 這十年來她都在那裡試吃冰淇淋。

有機會環遊世界是她這份工作額外的福利之一，好為公司的新款冰淇淋尋找稀有奇特的食材。⟨177⟩ 有一年，她整個夏天都在印度試吃咖哩，秋天則在泰國試羅勒。她解釋：「我把食材帶到我們在紐西蘭的實驗室，在那裡生產人員和食品化學家用它們創造驚人口味的冰淇淋。」⟨177⟩

至於實際試吃的時候，鄧肯在品嚐前會先用眼睛仔細檢查冰淇淋。「我會像消費者一樣看著產品。如果冰淇淋看起來不吸引人，他們就不會買單。」雖然她每天要品嚐多達 30 種不同口味的冰淇淋，但從未對工作感到厭倦。她熱情地說：「這是最甜蜜的生活。」⟨178⟩

《美食家風味雜誌》獨立撰稿人
赫克托‧門多薩

寄件者：和樹八郎
<k.hachiro@huggins.com>
收件者：瑪麗安娜・鄧肯
<m.duncan@tommendelights.co.nz>
日期：11 月 10 日
主旨：《美食家風味雜誌》報導

親愛的瑪麗安娜：

我在《美食家風味雜誌》上讀到關於妳的報導，並在妳公司網站上找到了妳的電子郵件信箱地址。**我們曾一起在冰淇淋公司實習。** 180 我相信妳記得我。無論如何，我三週後將前往奧克蘭參加食品科學研討會，我想如果能再見面應該會很棒！如果妳有空，也許我們可以共進午餐敘敘舊。179 我期待妳的答覆。

祝　好

和樹

176. 該篇報導的目的為何？
(A) 解釋工廠裡的製造過程
(B) 比較不同品牌的冰淇淋
(C) 預告某間公司的產品
(D) 描述一份專業工作

177. 文中提到「糖漫冰品」的什麼資訊？
(A) 它開發獨特口味的冰淇淋。
(B) 是業界最成功的公司。
(C) 成立於五年前。
(D) 在多國設有實驗室。

178. 關於鄧肯女士，文中指出什麼？
(A) 她的工作經驗有限。
(B) 她熱愛她的工作。
(C) 她在「糖漫冰品」負責訓練實習生。
(D) 她是八郎先生的商業合夥人。

179. 八郎先生為何寄電子郵件給鄧肯女士？
(A) 詢問工作職位
(B) 分享一場演講的資訊
(C) 安排會面
(D) 要求對於一篇報導的意見回饋

180. 八郎先生和鄧肯女士初次見面是在哪裡？
(A) 哈金斯冰淇淋工廠
(B) 《美食家風味》雜誌
(C) 食品科學研討會
(D) 普納特大學

181–185 新聞稿

拉斯卡特爵士三重奏
快報

4 月 5 日，堪薩斯州托彼卡市——我國首屈一指的爵士樂團「拉斯卡特爵士三重奏」剛剛宣布六月的巡演日期。為期六天的表演行程包括於知名的**托羅劇院**進行演出，即該樂團 10 年前首次登台舉行音樂會的地點。181 預定的演出時間如下。

日期	地點	場館
6 月 5 日	托彼卡	布蘭演奏廳
6 月 8 日	威契塔	維爾莎劇院
6 月 11 日	**勞倫斯** 181	**托羅劇院** 181
6 月 14 日	德比	蘿勒拉表演藝術中心
6 月 17 日 184	奧弗蘭帕克	**德克伍德體育館** 184
6 月 20 日	匹茲堡	柯提斯體育館

各巡迴站的票價範圍從樓座座位的 30 美元，到中央區前排座位的 100 美元不等，182 可於活動場館售票口或至飛船音樂商店購票。新成立的「拉斯卡特爵士三重奏粉絲俱樂部」會員可在 www.rascatjazz.com 登入會員專區以八折的優惠價格訂票。粉絲俱樂部福利的完整清單與年費的詳細說明，可上 www.rascatjazz.com/membership_fanclub 查詢。183

聯絡人：哈薛勒・德洛特
（電話：785-555-4936 ／電子郵件信箱地址：hdelotte@rascatjazz.com）

德克伍德體育館

快報

演出取消與延期

5 月 20 日，堪薩斯州奧弗蘭帕克市——德克伍德體育館因進行緊急維修，原定於六月舉行的演出幾乎全數延期。請參加音樂會的觀眾保留門票，因為除了「拉斯卡特爵士三重奏」的演出外，其他場次全都將延後舉辦，屆時則可持六月音樂會的門票入場。

音樂會改期的最新資訊，請瀏覽德克伍德體育館官網 www.dirkwoodstadium.com 查詢。**185** 若您需要「拉斯卡特爵士三重奏」演奏會取消的退款，**184** 請致電 913-555-3042。

聯絡人：珍妮斯・李克爾
（電話：913-555-3020／電子郵件信箱地址：jriker@dirkwoodstadium.com）

181. 「拉斯卡特爵士三重奏」十年前在哪裡進行首演？
(A) 托彼卡
(B) 勞倫斯
(C) 奧弗蘭帕克
(D) 匹茲堡

182. 文中提到關於「拉斯卡特爵士三重奏」演奏會門票的什麼資訊？
(A) 與去年的巡演相比，售價上漲了。
(B) 持學生證的學生可享更便宜的價格。
(C) 所有演出場地的樓座座位價格相同。
(D) 只透過網路售票。

183. 文中提到關於「拉斯卡特爵士三重奏粉絲俱樂部」的什麼資訊？
(A) 會員須繳年費。
(B) 每年六月見面。
(C) 會員可於飛船音樂商店獲得折扣。
(D) 它成立於十幾年前。

184. 「拉斯卡特爵士三重奏」哪天無法按既定行程演出？
(A) 6 月 5 日　　　**(C) 6 月 17 日**
(B) 6 月 8 日　　　(D) 6 月 20 日

185. 根據第二篇新聞稿的內容，什麼將公告在德克伍德體育館的官網？
(A) 新的舉辦地點
(B) 更改後的日期清單
(C) 建物維修細節
(D) 退款申請表

186-190 電子郵件和廣告

收件者：紫苑谷滑雪度假村員工
寄件者：麗莎・羅斯
日期：10 月 7 日 **188**
主旨：季節性優惠

各位銷售人員好：

誠如大家所知，很多紫苑大學學生放寒假時會留在鎮上。**我們將如常提供學生假期打六折的優惠，所有 11 月下半月註冊成為會員的人均適用。188** 高層也正在討論兩種可能的優惠方案，擬於即將到來的冬季（12 月 1 日至 2 月 1 日）提供給度假村全體會員。

我們正在徵詢各位的意見，以便從兩個可能的促銷活動中擇一。186 其一是把折扣適用範圍擴大至紫苑谷滑雪度假村現有會員的親人。會員將可將任一直系親屬（17 歲以上）掛在他現有的會員方案下，親屬可享平常價格的八折折扣。

另一個選項則是免費贈送一日通行券給藍色等級會員，可供他們的友人於週一至週五使用。該券可進入度假村的所有區域，包括滑雪場在內。**不過，水療中心例外，畢竟目前我們的會員都要等上好一陣子才能使用。187**

請選擇您認為我們的會員將會感到最滿意的方案，並回覆此電子郵件。

感謝您在此事上的協助。

紫苑谷滑雪度假村
行銷部副總經理
麗莎・羅斯　謹啟

冬季促銷

歡迎紫菀大學學生！

於 11 月 15 日至 12 月 15 日期間註冊成為會員，即可享度假村會員費打六折的優惠，**188** 及首次租用滑雪板（雙板或單板）免費！

與朋友滑雪一天！

12 月 1 日起，度假村的藍色及黑色等級會員均可招待一名友人同行，享受一日滑雪樂趣，而無需額外收費。**189** 會員友人入場時須出示有照片的身分證件，以便領取來賓證。

紫菀谷滑雪度假村

收件者：山姆・赫曼
寄件者：林承熙
日期：2 月 2 日
主旨：關於：結果已經出來了

山姆你好：

謝謝你用電子郵件把最新報告的圖表寄給我。我真的很高興，冬季促銷讓藍色會員的業績成長了 18%。

會員數增加主要仰賴紫菀大學，大多數學生都加入藍色等級會員。我認為下個冬天應該再推同樣的促銷活動。189 另外，該大學的運動設施將於明年整修，**190** 這表示學生會需要尋找其他地點進行體育活動。有鑑於我們是最靠近學校、且提供許多休閒設施的地點，我們應考慮和校方合作，提供學生接駁服務。這肯定還能增加我們的會員數。

後續有任何新消息，我會再通知你。

紫菀谷滑雪度假村

行銷部經理
林承熙

---

186. 此通知的目的為何？
- (A) 恭喜一些員工完成專案
- (B) 宣布排定的休業消息
- (C) 告知度假村會員有新的服務
- **(D) 詢問同仁的意見**

187. 文中提到關於水療中心的什麼資訊？
- (A) 很快就會有新設備。
- (B) 將收取額外費用。
- (C) 目前關閉維修中。
- **(D) 是很受歡迎的設施。**

188. 十月起，學生優惠有何異動？
- **(A) 會員註冊期限延長了。**
- (B) 折現率減少。
- (C) 學生可按月付會員費。
- (D) 學生一週只能去度假村一次。

189. 文中提到關於紫菀谷滑雪度假村的什麼資訊？
- **(A) 這個冬季有許多學生攜友人同行。**
- (B) 週一至週五較早開始營業。
- (C) 目前會員的所有親屬均享折扣。
- (D) 黑色等級會員可免費獲贈滑雪配件。

190. 紫菀大學將發生什麼事情？
- (A) 將在冬天開始新學年。
- (B) 將增加銷售課程。
- **(C) 將翻修其運動設施。**
- (D) 將有滑雪課程提供給該校教職人員。

191–195 產品介紹、電子郵件和網路評論

https://www.kitchendesignco.com/catalog

首頁	型錄	評論	聯絡

商品：Kotka 90 中島推車

「廚具設計公司」自豪地宣布，首款廚房收納產品 Kotka 90 上市。結合迷人的現代設計，與旗下品牌廚房家電皆有的新潮功能性，為您的料理空間帶來「廚具設計」鮮明的獨特風格。**191** 這款中島推車採用輕量耐用的材料製成，具不銹鋼檯面及輪子，便於移動。檯面可拉伸成為寬敞、穩固的平面，適合各種廚房作業。**195** 優美的外型也能為任何廚房空間增色不少。

型號：#8345A
價格：579.00 美元 *
有白、黑或棕色可供選擇。

* 優惠碼不適用於此產品。我們提供全球
配送服務，但運費則依寄達地區而異。

寄件者：伯納德・奧羅克
<borourke@infovision.com>
收件者：客戶支援中心
<cs@kitchendesignco.com>
日期：6 月 28 日
主旨：Kotka 90

您好：

關於我想購買的 Kotka 90 中島推車，我有
幾個問題想請教一下。 **194** 我可以購買花
崗岩的檯面，而非不銹鋼的嗎？另外，我
聽到一些評論人在討論組裝這台中島推車
時遇到的困難，而我希望能夠避免遇到這
個問題。 **192**

請問可以購買已事先組裝好的產品嗎？ **194**
還請告訴我額外的組裝費需要多少錢。

伯納德・奧羅克　謹啟

---

https://www.kitchendesignco.com/
catalog/kotka90islandcart

伯納德・奧羅克

7 月 19 日

組裝這台中島推車讓我很擔心，因此我和
一位公司業務談過。時間真的花得很值
得！「廚具設計公司」妥善回答了我所有
的問題。他們指引我參考一個網頁，讓我
購買前可以先查看說明。另外也提供我
電話號碼，供我尋求進一步的協助。 **193**
194 不過我沒有用到那支電話，因為組
裝這台中島推車根本花不到我 20 分鐘。
194

這台中島推車非常堅固又好推。但我還是
要提出一些需改進的小地方。首先，該產
品比其他類似產品貴。而且很重，因此
根據寄達地點，運費可能會讓總額增加不
少。再者，雖然延伸的檯面提供了大得驚
人的空間，但在進行非常精細的工作時，
它不夠穩定。 **195** 最後，萬一需要退貨，
重新包裝產品將會非常困難。但我不打算
退貨，所以這不成問題。

191. 產品介紹中提到「廚具設計公司」的
什麼資訊？
(A) 有不只一間店面。
(B) 主要販售廚房設備。
(C) 計劃生產廚房流理檯。
(D) 首購客戶可享折扣價。

192. 根據電子郵件的內容，關於奧羅克先生
的資訊何者可能為真？
**(A) 他購買產品時，有查看客戶意見
回饋。**
(B) 他定期購買「廚具設計公司」的
產品。
(C) 他為自己的餐廳訂購中島推車。
(D) 他最近得知某項產品缺貨。

193. 奧羅克先生撰寫評論的其中一項原因
為何？
(A) 建議在某些說明新增一個步驟
(B) 推薦更好的廚房配件
(C) 稱讚公司的客戶服務
(D) 抱怨貨運選擇太少

194. 文中提到關於 Kotka 90 的什麼資訊？
(A) 沒有在特定國家販售。
(B) 可選購不同尺寸。
(C) 保固一年。
(D) 不能購買事先組裝好的產品。

195. 根據評論的內容，產品介紹的哪一方面
不準確？
(A) 該公司的運費
(B) 中島推車的價格
(C) 公司的退款政策
(D) 中島推車的穩固性

196–200 徵才廣告和電子郵件

「超群配送」的奧克蘭分公司正在招募積極進取的人來領導我們的倉儲部。「**超群配送」是紐西蘭運輸配送優質蔬果的龍頭企業之一。** 196

倉儲經理須監控倉庫內的工作環境與流程，以確保同仁安全。應徵者須具備至少五年的同業相關工作經驗。**晚上或週末有時須加班，** 197 以確保貨物如期運送。應徵者須具備倉儲及貨運的豐富知識。**須熟悉 SWP 庫存追蹤軟體。** 199

應徵者應將求職信及履歷以電子郵件寄給崔西亞・赫爾佛女士（thelfor@superiordist.co.nz）。另需三封推薦信，須由寫信的推薦者直接寄來。

收件者：崔西亞・赫爾佛
<thelfor@superiordist.co.nz>
寄件者：賴貿
<mlai@kalexperts.com>
日期：9 月 18 日
主旨：歐文的推薦信

敬愛的赫爾佛女士：

我寫這封信推薦歐文・卡特，他正在應徵「超群配送」的倉儲經理一職。 198 歐文在「KAL 專家」服務九年了；他從兼職轉為全職員工後的六年來，我一直都是歐文的主管。歐文目前作為輪班經理，他已證明有能力處理他的任務。

歐文完全符合貴公司的需求，包括必要的工作經驗和技術背景。**我們公司也是使用 SWP 程式，歐文工作時很多方面都會用到它，並且已培訓許多同仁操作使用。** 199

我相信歐文將能迅速完美地適應任何新職場環境的需求。 198 如果您有任何疑問，隨時可跟我聯絡。

KAL 專家
貨運主任
賴貿　謹啟

收件者：歐文・卡特
<ocarter@kalexperts.com>
寄件者：崔西亞・赫爾佛
<thelfor@superiordist.co.nz>
日期：9 月 25 日
主旨：倉儲經理

親愛的卡特先生：

我們仔細審查了您的文件，希望下週在奧克蘭辦公室與您進一步詳細討論該職位。您的面試將於下週二正午 12 點舉行，共將持續兩小時。**前一小時是和人力資源部共進午餐，** 200 後一小時則是與我面談。

請在明天之前確認您的面試時間。我期待您的答覆。

崔西亞・赫爾佛　謹啟

---

196. 文中提到關於「超群配送」的什麼資訊？
(A) 擁有許多連鎖超市。
(B) 專門處理食品。
(C) 總部位於奧克蘭。
(D) 提供各種軟體產品。

197. 根據徵才廣告的內容，倉儲經理應願意做什麼事情？
(A) 舉起重物
(B) 參加安全培訓課程
(C) 簽下三年的合約
(D) 週末加班

198. 賴先生為何撰寫電子郵件？
(A) 解釋行程異動
(B) 歡迎新的倉儲經理
(C) 對一名員工表示正面評價
(D) 深入了解某位應徵者

199. 文中提到關於卡特先生的什麼資訊？
(A) 他善於使用庫存追蹤軟體。
(B) 他正在應徵「超群配送」的兼職工作。
(C) 他剛搬到紐西蘭。
(D) 他有開發新軟體程式的經驗。

200. 第二封電子郵件中提到關於面試的什麼
資訊？

(A) **將提供一餐。**

(B) 將持續一小時。

(C) 執行長將發表演講。

(D) 時間已異動。

ACTUAL TEST ⑨

PART 5 P. 234–236

101. 還不完全清楚該地區整體汽車持有率成長的原因。
(A) **完全地**
(B) 穩定地
(C) 堅固地
(D) 公正地

102. 勞倫汀企業收到很多應徵管理職的資料，但符合條件的卻寥寥無幾。
(A) 使合格
(B) 使合格
(C) **符合條件的**
(D) 資格條件

103. 公司將製作新名片，所以您要是有任何資訊需要更改，請聯絡勒柏先生。
(A) **所以**
(B) 比
(C) 向
(D) 在前

104. 批評者不接受布拉德福海濱度假村，吸引更多遊客造訪該市的說法。
(A) 仰賴
(B) 建議
(C) **拒絕**
(D) 延伸

105. 高田顧問公司協助其他公司運用創新管理技術，來大幅提高部門的生產力。
(A) **生產力**
(B) 生產
(C) 有效地
(D) 生產的

106. 該網站預設在客戶下單的 5 分鐘內，寄出一封電子郵件確認信。
(A) 一旦
(B) 他們的（東西）
(C) 他們
(D) **……的人**

107. 需要佔用道路空間的建築工程，只有在取得公共工程局的道路使用許可證後，才能動工。
(A) 穿越
(B) 從
(C) **在……之後**
(D) 在……上

108. 凱莉‧門多薩自十歲演出第一個角色以來，就一直從事專業表演工作。
(A) 專家
(B) 專業水準
(C) 職業
(D) **專業地**

109. 讀者對這幾本小說反應很熱烈，以至於出版商要求將它們改編成電影三部曲。
(A) 指示
(B) **熱情**
(C) 信念
(D) 知識

110. 陸上飯店有 75 間客房，大多都有山景陽臺。
(A) **大多數**
(B) 非常
(C) 很
(D) 幾乎

111. 雖然亞伯特‧萊恩將從草地科技公司退休，但他在董事會仍有席次。
(A) 一旦
(B) 此外
(C) 尤其
(D) **仍然**

112. 米爾頓有限公司與公羊首儲蓄借貸公司合併後，提供了多種金融服務。
(A) 提供
(B) **提供了**
(C) 提供
(D) 正在提供

113. 奧斯納布呂克大學的學生，每學期須重新申請宿舍房間。

(A) 申請
(B) 規格
(C) 形成
(D) 貢獻

114. 廢棄的柳頂紡織廠與周圍建築，正在改建成高級公寓大樓。

(A) 環繞
(B) 環繞
(C) 周遭環境
(D) 周圍的

115. 哥斯大羅赫度假飯店總是想方設法改善房客的體驗。

(A) 得到
(B) 通知
(C) 治療
(D) 改善

116. 信賴電力公司的新網站讓公司員工能聯絡正在值班的維修專家。

(A) 這裡
(B) 將去
(C) 在……內
(D) 正在

117. 蘭瑟體育用品公司已和多位知名運動員簽約，因此將更廣泛地宣傳自家產品。

(A) 因此
(B) 自從
(C) 一旦
(D) 由於

118. 「戶外穿搭」的網站主打了冬季服裝系列，使銷量大增。

(A) 相當大地
(B) 相當大的
(C) 考慮
(D) 正在考慮

119. 恩斯特隆醫生說明診斷結果的溫和方式，有助於他安撫病患。

(A) 例子
(B) 方法
(C) 會議
(D) 外表

120. 在會展上參觀「聰明廚房」的攤位時，請記得自行取用免費試用品。

(A) 你自己
(B) 你
(C) 你的（東西）
(D) 你的

121. 每次使用公司資料庫的個人帳戶時，您都必須輸入一串密碼。

(A) 理解
(B) 規格
(C) 串；系列
(D) 證明

122. 由於週五是工廠檢查日，這週將比平常晚一天出貨。

(A) 可是
(B) 當
(C) 但是
(D) 由於

123. 乘客應備妥機票和護照，於查驗櫃台向出入境管理局官員出示。

(A) 是否
(B) 公開地
(C) 準備好的
(D) 自從

124. 資訊科技部找到了公司網站今早斷線的確切原因。

(A) 這個
(B) 這些
(C) 有……的人）
(D) ……的東西

125. 降低回收再製產品的價格能鼓勵消費者購買更多這種產品，從而減少垃圾。

(A) 鼓勵
(B) 正在鼓勵
(C) 被鼓勵
(D) 能鼓勵

126. 不少店家策略性地把產品價格定得很高，好讓特價時似乎很便宜。

(A) 制定策略
(B) 策略
(C) 策略性地
(D) 策略的

127. 由於完整説明財務報告將佔用太多時間，所以真知子開會時將以濃縮版來報告。
(A) 複製的
(B) 扼要的；濃縮的
(C) 穩固的
(D) 感到滿足的

128. 一個稱職的主管常將權力下放給其他人，以此提升員工士氣和績效。
(A) 將……委派……
(B) 組織
(C) 介紹
(D) 開始

129. 儘管第一季銷量不佳，但行銷部對於這系列產品的潛力依舊保持樂觀態度。
(A) 儘管
(B) 仰賴
(C) 根據
(D) 由於

130. 同仁若想轉調至其他分店，得先與其主管談談。
(A) 想
(B) 想
(C) 將想
(D) 曾在想

PART 6   P.237-240

131-134 告示

理查・博伊斯網站行銷講座

理查・博伊斯是全國公認的網路廣告與推銷領域權威。博伊斯先生已在「零媒體」擔任了 17 年的創意總監。有了在「零媒體」工作多年累積下來的經驗，現在他運用現實世界的技術進行講座。其中一種方式是讓參加講座的學生一起參與社群媒體行銷。因此，博伊斯的學生得以將理論應用到行銷實務上，從而得到寶貴的實踐經驗。請留意，1 月 24 日和 27 日的講座已經額滿。但 2 月 12 日和 15 日的演講還有一些名額。

131. (A) 授權
(B) 已授權的
(C) 權威
(D) 正在授權

132. (A) 正在工作
(B) 將工作
(C) 曾在工作
(D) 已工作

133. (A) 其中一種方式是讓參加講座的學生一起參與社群媒體行銷。
(B) 他在「零媒體」工作期間，舉辦過多場員工活動。
(C) 聽眾被要求提供職場建議。
(D) 他取得西雅圖新聞學院的學位。

134. (A) 然而
(B) 因此
(C) 尤其
(D) 最後

135-138 資訊

安全規定：緊急逃生門

此建築每層樓均有緊急逃生門，出口前須保持淨空無任何障礙物。每一道門每年須由當地消防單位進行檢查。在每一道逃生門的左上角，均須有最新的檢查標籤。不過，員工也應每週進行一次檢查。尋找有無任何電子設備故障、毀損或障礙物。確保門上方的指示牌燈完全亮起，且從任何角度均清楚可見。

135. (A) 明顯的
(B) 故障的
(C) 淨空的
(D) 明顯不同的

136. (A) 高層計劃在未來幾週內修改這些程序。
(B) 在每一道逃生門的左上角，均須有最新的檢查標籤。
(C) 我們目前還不確定誰將接下責任。
(D) 我們希望將期限延長一個月。

137. (A) 尋找
(B) 安排
(C) 拿取
(D) 簽名

138. (A) 滿的
(B) 更滿的
(C) 充分地
(D) 充實

139–142　電子郵件

收件者：納瑟曼員工
寄件者：人事部
日期：11 月 20 日
主旨：公司聚會

公司的尾牙將在 12 月 9 日（週四）下午 1 點至 5 點，於舍姆佛斯宴會廳舉行。敬邀全體員工蒞臨，與同仁們在此精心安排的場合共度美好時光。我們所有的分公司將於當日下午 1 點關閉，以便同仁出席。

請至人事部領取尾牙的入場券。員工出席活動的時間（共計四小時）仍將支薪。另外，同仁可選擇提前回家而不出席，但需從剩餘的休假日中扣除半天時間。

若您有任何疑問，請直接詢問您的經理。

139. (A) 展示
(B) 城鎮
(C) 展覽
(D) 場合；地點

140. (A) 可出席
(B) 出席人數
(C) 出席的人
(D) 正在出席

141. (A) 再者
(B) 儘管
(C) 然而
(D) 結果

142. (A) 多數員工都同意尾牙玩得很開心。
(B) 若您有任何疑問，請直接詢問您的經理。
(C) 宴會廳現在設有更大的用餐區。
(D) 我們預計第四季的銷售額會很高。

143–146　電子郵件

收件者：全體同仁
寄件者：richard.haber@locatrans.com
日期：10 月 15 日
主旨：付款流程
附件：paymentform.rtf

親愛的譯者們大家好：

我們正在修改支付自由譯者稿費的付款流程。我們將於每月 10 日只進行一次付款，取代逐案付款的方式。我了解這可能很麻煩，但個別處理每份結案的請款單已成了非常繁瑣的作業。從現在起，您不須在完成單一稿件時，填寫線上請款單；取而代之的是，只須於每個月的月底為當月結案的案件提供一份請款單即可。請印出此電子郵件的附檔，簽名後於下週一之前將檔案回傳給我。它代表您已閱讀並同意新的制度。

我們向您對此事的理解提前致謝。

譯道地翻譯公司
會計與薪資出納部經理
理查・哈伯　謹啟

143. (A) 應修改
(B) 可能已修改
(C) 正在修改
(D) 可能正在修改

144. (A) 負擔
(B) 機會
(C) 取消
(D) 優先事項

145. (A) 根據這一點
(B) 同樣地
(C) 有鑒於此
(D) 作為替代

146. (A) 譯文必須符合以前的詳細標準。
(B) 它代表您已閱讀並同意新的制度。
(C) 若您的款項有錯誤之虞，請立即與我們聯繫。
(D) 文件的某些部分須修改。

PART 7　P. 241-259

147-148 簡訊

來自：菲爾·湯斯
至：阿麗莎·哈薛米
發送時間：週四，下午 3:11

———————————————

延後去橡丘路看房了。無法順路回公司。
147 直接前往公園大道 935 號幫埃文斯家的房產估價。**請妳也帶著他們的文件過去。148** 看鑑價結果怎麼樣，我可能要討論一下新價格。謝謝。

147. 湯斯先生最有可能從事哪一個行業？
(A) 保險業
(B) 房產業
(C) 運輸業
(D) 銀行業

148. 湯斯先生要求哈薛米女士做什麼事情？
(A) 討論合約
(B) 帶某些文件
(C) 分析鑑價結果
(D) 安排會議

149-150 簡訊串

柏納·蓋拉格〔上午 11:34〕
妳有空和我談皮根家的婚禮嗎？新郎家要求要在菜單上做幾個大變動。

維列麗·提摩曼斯〔上午 11:40〕
我得和客戶開午餐會議，**150** 但一點後會回辦公室。不如你到時過來？

柏納·蓋拉格〔上午 11:43〕
太好了。我會帶上他們的要求，還有我的解決方案。

維列麗·提摩曼斯〔上午 11:46〕
也要試著放輕鬆。我知道這是你第一次籌備婚宴，但一切都會順利的。

柏納·蓋拉格〔上午 11:48〕
謝謝。我很感謝妳帶我走完整個流程。
149

維列麗·提摩曼斯〔上午 11:52〕
這是我的榮幸。好，我要走了。我們下午見。**150**

149. 文中提到關於蓋拉格先生的資訊，何者最有可能為真？
(A) 他正在和提摩曼斯女士學習。
(B) 他要買送提摩曼斯女士的禮物。
(C) 他在下午一點有場面試。
(D) 他最近參加了一場親戚的婚宴。

150. 上午 11:52，提摩曼斯女士說「我要走了」，意思為何？
(A) 她得出發去開會。
(B) 她刪除了清單上的一些項目。
(C) 她將安排一天休假。
(D) 她同意接手其他工作。

151-153 電子郵件

寄件者：喬艾爾·阿德蒙森
收件者：麥迪遜·李，山姆·奧卡羅爾
日期：7 月 14 日
主旨：餐廳規畫

———————————————

麥迪遜和山姆午安：

我有個好消息。我今早去了趟市政廳，拿到了我們餐酒館的營業執照。**151** 接下來要開始忙了。為了趕在 11 月 10 日盛大開幕前做好準備，我規劃了每個月的待辦事項。

八月：規劃室內並與裝修公司簽約。聯絡廠商挑選餐具。架設網站與印名片。

九月：安排建築安全檢查的時間。**152** 備好廚房的廚具和用品。在網路與地方報紙上刊登徵才廣告。

十月：決定好錄取員工並開始培訓。印傳單、聯絡美食評論家。

如果覺得這規畫不太實際，請再跟我說你們認為需要修改的地方。 **153** 但別忘了我們的餐廳還不到四個月就要開張了，所以得在這段時間內搞定所有事情。

喬艾爾

---

151. 文中提到關於阿德蒙森先生的什麼資訊？
(A) 他正在找生意的投資者。
(B) 他將把餐廳賣給李女士。
(C) 他 11 月要和同事參加會議。
(D) 他最近登記了一家企業。

152. 九月的預定目標為何？
(A) 印製宣傳資料
(B) 安排必要的檢查
(C) 培訓新員工
(D) 訂購廚房用品

153. 阿德蒙森先生為何徵詢意見？
(A) 他擔心時間表可能不可行。
(B) 他想徵詢關於招聘計畫的建議。
(C) 他想徵詢關於一些設計方案的意見。
(D) 他正在修改報紙廣告。

154–157 電子郵件

收件者：sponsor_list@weststart.org
寄件者：aweiser@weststart.org
日期：9 月 16 日，週三
主旨：週六公益賽跑

敬愛的贊助商：

很遺憾通知您，我們已取消原定本週六於西瀑布州立公園舉辦的公益賽跑。**154** 由於整修工程尚未完成，再加上天氣預報表示本週末有季節反常的大雪，我們不得不將活動延期。**155**

西瀑布州立公園的人員週一提醒我，我們打算使用的棚架野餐區仍在整修中，本週結束前仍無法完工。**154** 有人建議我們改在停車場架設起點與終點線並設置攤位。然而，停車場並未鋪設路面，在這種天氣下無法進入使用。**155**

雖然天氣再冷，原定活動仍要舉行，但必須優先考量所有參賽者的安全。我對這種情況深感歉意，但請諒解此非籌備委員會所能決定的。**這是由西瀑布州立公園高層做出的最終決定。** **156**

我們希望在十月下旬舉辦比賽，屆時還請您提供贊助。目前則**請您留意，您的贊助費將以電匯方式於週五銀行營業時間結束前退還給您。** **157** 若您偏好以支票取得退款，請回覆此電子郵件，並附上您的現址與可聯絡的電話號碼。

非常抱歉。

安德魯・韋瑟 **154**

---

154. 韋瑟先生最有可能是什麼身分？
(A) 公職人員
(B) 職業運動員
(C) 地方記者
(D) 活動策劃

155. 關於西瀑布州立公園未鋪設路面的停車場，文中提到什麼資訊？
(A) 週末經常爆滿。
(B) 目前正在施工。
(C) 僅供西瀑布的居民使用。
(D) 下雪時無法進出。

156. 第三段第三行的「move」，意思最接近何者？
(A) 搬遷
(B) 移動
(C) 決定
(D) 轉移

157. 公益賽跑的贊助商將收到什麼東西？
(A) 更新版合約
(B) 禮券
(C) 退款
(D) 宣傳手冊

158-160 網頁

http://www.topandlock.com/about_us

| 首頁 | **關於我們** | 客戶 | 查看型錄 | 樣品 |

「頂上鎖藏公司」是貴公司旗下食品飲料便於生產、儲存、包裝和運輸的理想選擇。**158** 我們最暢銷的產品有耐用容器、可回收再利用的盒子與環保罐頭。**請點擊「查看型錄」頁籤，查看我們的全系列產品，159** 以及圖片說明和最新的消費者評論。

單筆訂單需達 100 美元或以上金額，儘管如此，**我們可免費寄發最多七項產品供您試用。159** 請點選「樣品」頁面了解更多資訊。

我們也想向您介紹我們最新的服務「客製化印刷」。可依您要求在產品上印製商標、設計與標語；**159** 也能為促銷活動於產品上印製隨機序號。例如，該序號可供客戶在貴公司網站登錄以確認是否中獎。更多資訊，請撥打（310）555-4360 與我們的印刷中心聯繫。

請留意，一旦您訂購的產品離開倉庫，將不退還運費。**我們保證在您訂購後的 2 至 4 個工作日內到貨。160**

158. 誰最有可能是該網頁的目標客群？
(A) 運輸服務業者
(B) 地方回收站
(C) 出版公司
(D) 食品製備公司

159. 文中並未提及「頂上鎖藏公司」的哪一項服務？
(A) 提供首購客戶折扣
(B) 提供限量的樣品
(C) 應客戶要求在產品上寫下訊息
(D) 列出客戶的最新意見

160. 文中提到關於在「頂上鎖藏公司」下訂單的什麼資訊？
(A) 購物滿 100 美元可享免運費。
(B) 可在 4 個工作日內到貨。
(C) 可分期付款。
(D) 可於購買日後一個月內換貨。

161-164 資訊

致謝辭

這本書花了我整整十年寫成，非常感謝所有在創作過程中協助我的人。**161** 沒有各位的支持與鼓勵，《懷俄明州地質研究》不可能問世。

有許多人參與了這本書的寫作。其中，我特別要感謝派翠克・佛林博士，儘管他全職的教學工作繁忙，仍撥冗檢查本書草稿，並提供了一些想法簡化了水晶和寶石原石章節中討論的幾個概念。**162** 另外，我也由衷感謝楊夏女士，她精心繪製了每一章開頭的插圖。**161**

最重要的是，我也想特別向伊芙琳・尤涅斯科致上謝意。尤涅斯科女士利用她對當地地質構造的豐富知識，帶我到離懷俄明州主要公路很遠的重要岩石層考察。**163** **164** 她在懷俄明州住了很久，清楚知道應該去哪裡看不同地質年代的最佳岩石樣本。若缺少她的專業知識，這本書恐怕無法完成。

安娜・基爾迪 **161**

161. 文中並未提到關於《懷俄明州地質研究》的什麼資訊？
(A) 內含詳細圖片。
(B) 花費十年寫成。
(C) 內含不同州的地圖。
(D) 由基爾迪女士撰寫。

162. 文中提到關於佛林博士的什麼資訊？
(A) 他經常去懷俄明州。
(B) 他幫助修改了某些內容。
(C) 他最近換了工作。
(D) 他推薦了一位藝術家。

163. 第三段第三行的「formations」，意思最接近何者？
(A) 機構，設施
(B) 彙編
(C) 結構
(D) 布局

164. 為何感謝尤涅斯科女士？
(A) 做研究
(B) 擔任導遊
(C) 教課
(D) 審草稿

165–168 網路聊天室

翁希瑋〔下午 2:34〕
大家午安。我希望大家都準備好即將到來的週三行銷會議了。我們上一季的銷售量完全沒有起色。<u>我們得考慮新的方案。</u>
166

凱莉·洛斯〔下午 2:35〕
你想要我們怎麼做？166

翁希瑋〔下午 2:37〕
對於皮夾和皮包的需求逐漸下降，我們得想辦法增加「蓋洛威」的產品供應。165 166

安潔拉·金〔下午 2:38〕
我們可以試試手機殼。現在幾乎人人都在用。

迦勒·斯圖特〔下午 2:40〕
這主意不錯。我們也可以考慮為平板或筆電製作特別的保護套。

凱莉·洛斯〔下午 2:41〕
對。我們甚至可以針對擁有這些裝置的商務人士，試著推出手提行李登機箱。

翁希瑋〔下午 2:44〕
大家的想法都很棒。請為開會做準備，上網找一些供應商，並取得報價，放進你要向團隊做的報告裡。167 我可以根據這些資訊估算預算，一起向部門經理提案。168

迦勒·斯圖特〔下午 2:45〕
了解。167

翁希瑋〔下午 2:46〕
大家如果遇到任何問題，再寫電子郵件給我，我們一起討論。

165. 「蓋洛威」目前銷售的是哪一類產品？
(A) 皮革配件
(B) 金屬行李箱
(C) 健身手錶
(D) 手機

166. 下午 2:34，翁先生寫道：「我們得考慮新的方案」，最有可能是什麼意思？
(A) 各簡報應聚焦於不同的主題。
(B) 公司應提供更多的培訓工作坊。
(C) 每場簡報須持續至少 10 分鐘。
(D) 公司應擴大產品線。

167. 斯圖特先生接下來最有可能做什麼事情？
(A) 草擬一項提案
(B) 寄電子郵件給主管
(C) 進行一些調查
(D) 預約會議室

168. 翁先生將交給部門經理什麼東西？
(A) 產品供應商的資料
(B) 月度銷售報告
(C) 消費者意見調查結果
(D) 活動日程表

http://www.lindondiner.co.uk/food_applesplash

蘋果飛濺

有些飲料誕生的故事可能永遠成謎，但絕不會是我們美味的「蘋果飛濺」。目前不少餐廳都有販售這種地方特色飲料，口味各異，但都比不上我們創始人林頓·古爾德主廚於 25 年前發明的原創口味。「蘋果飛濺」的誕生可謂偶然，主廚正在煮茶時，不小心把蘋果派的餡料灑了進去。**171** 這場小意外造就了林頓餐館的招牌飲料。古爾德先生目前已退休，由女兒安妮·威斯特繼承傳統。**170** 蘋果、糖與香料混合烹煮 4 小時後，再冷藏一晚，使風味融合，然後在顧客點餐時以現沖現泡的茶重新加熱。**169** 成品滋味值得這般講究。

169. 文中提到關於該飲料的什麼資訊？
- (A) 不含人工添加物。
- (B) 冬季限定販售。
- (C) 與甜點搭配。
- **(D) 只有熱飲。**

170. 文中提到關於古爾德主廚的什麼資訊？
- (A) 威斯特女士是他的師傅。
- (B) 他喜歡看懸疑小說。
- (C) 他的餐館搬遷了好幾次。
- **(D) 他已不在餐廳工作。**

171. 「這場小意外造就了林頓餐館的招牌飲料。」最適合放在 [1]、[2]、[3]、[4] 的哪一個位置？
- (A) [1]
- (B) [2]
- **(C) [3]**
- (D) [4]

5 月 15 日 **173**
艾琳·桑德斯
95060 加利福尼亞州聖塔克魯茲市
西衛斯理道 1022 號

敬愛的桑德斯女士： **172**

感謝您長年支持《艾登全球雜誌》。**172** 此信旨在通知您，一年期訂閱方案有部分異動。一年訂閱費用將從 6 月 1 日起，自 114 美元調漲為 138 美元。新的價格（每月 11.50 美元）仍比在一般零售店買的價格（18.40 美元一期）便宜許多（省下 40%）。**173**

請務必利用《艾登全球雜誌》網站的特殊瀏覽權限。您不僅能看到紙本雜誌的全部內容，訂閱用戶還可使用「會員限定」專區閱讀額外內容，包括會員上傳的食譜評論與各種料理主題的論壇，如替代食材、特殊廚房設備及創意擺盤小技巧。**172** **175**

請多加利用網站的意見回饋專區，寄信給我們見多識廣的編輯同仁。獲選信件將刊登在讀者投書專區。

您的訂閱方案將在下一期終止。請在價格調漲前，把握短暫機會以較低價格續訂，可填寫隨信附上的訂閱申請表格後寄回，或撥打我們的訂閱專線。**174** 我們同仁每日上午 9 點至下午 6 點隨時恭候您的來電。

我們期待您的回音！

訂閱服務專員
凱莉·鮑恩

訂閱熱線：（831）555-2941

附件

172. 文中提到關於桑德斯女士的什麼資訊？
- **(A) 她長期對料理感興趣。**
- (B) 她六月搬到聖塔克魯茲市。
- (C) 她寫的信被刊登在《艾登全球雜誌》上。
- (D) 她經常在《艾登全球雜誌》的論壇發表意見。

173. 如果透過訂閱方式購買，下個月一期《艾登全球雜誌》的價格是多少？

(A) 11.50 美元
(B) 18.40 美元
(C) 22.50 美元
(D) 25.00 美元

174.「我們同仁每日上午 9 點至下午 6 點隨時恭候您的來電。」最適合放在 [1]、[2]、[3]、[4] 的哪一個位置？

(A) [1]
(B) [2]
(C) [3]
(D) [4]

175. 根據鮑恩女士的說法，何者為該雜誌網站的限定內容？

(A) 企業訂閱用戶的廣告
(B) 會員上傳的食譜
(C) 餐廳評價
(D) 特別折扣

176–180 電子郵件和客運車票

寄件者：席昂‧盧梭
<c.rousseau@eurofox.fr>
收件者：米拉‧格瑞席克
<milla.g@maplage.fr> 178
日期：12 月 6 日
主旨：749 號客運

聖誕節假期向來是乘客旅遊往返的旺季，而您預定由馬賽開往維也納的客運班次（EFX 749）無疑就是如此。由於訂票人數眾多，歐狐快線將為願意改乘其他班次的乘客加開車輛。176 178 我們將提供價值 120 歐元的旅遊券作為補償，可用於歐狐快線在法國與歐洲全境的任何路線，效期為發行日後的六個月內。177

以下是您可能感興趣的兩種替代路線。178 第一條路線於同一天出發，但中途會在米蘭停靠。

EFX 430	馬賽	12 月 20 日 下午 7:20	米蘭	12 月 21 日 上午 3:40
EFX 430	米蘭	12 月 21 日 上午 4:50	維也納	12 月 21 日 下午 2:10

第二條為直達路線，於您原定出發日的隔天早上出發。

EFX 789 178 180	馬賽	12 月 21 日 上午 6:25 178	維也納	12 月 21 日 下午 11:50 180

若您想主動更換車次，請撥打歐狐快線票務部電話 0800-4-91-01-39-21。178 由於乘客客流量大，我們建議您在預定發車前，至少提早一小時抵達。一般資訊請上官網 www.eurofox.fr 查詢。

僅代表歐狐快線，祝您假期愉快。

歐狐快線
票務部
席昂‧盧梭　謹啟

乘客姓名：米拉‧格瑞席克 178

路線	日期	乘車	發車 178
EFX 789 178 180	12 月 21 日	上午 6:10	上午 6:25 180
目的地	**出發地**	**閘門**	**座位**
維也納	馬賽	5	10B

請隨第三組乘客上車。179 請留意，為遵守歐洲安全規定，滾輪式行李均須放置於車廂下方。

176. 撰寫這封電子郵件的原因為何？
- (A) 推廣聖誕假期度假的新去處
- (B) 提醒旅客漫長的等待時間
- (C) 告知旅客往維也納的新路線
- **(D) 鼓勵旅客改搭其他班次**

177. 文中提到關於優惠券的什麼事情？
- **(A) 須在特定期限內使用。**
- (B) 可用於多家客運業者。
- (C) 是致贈給格瑞席克女士的。
- (D) 僅限在法國使用。

178. 格瑞席克女士收到電子郵件後，最有可能做什麼事情？
- (A) 下載訂票應用程式
- **(B) 聯絡票務部**
- (C) 回覆電子郵件
- (D) 動身前往客運車站

179. 關於格瑞席克女士的新客運路線，可從車票得知什麼資訊？
- (A) 乘客不得使用滾輪式行李箱。
- (B) 行經米蘭。
- (C) 於晚間出發。
- **(D) 乘客須按照組別編號上車。**

180. 格瑞席克女士預定何時抵達目的地？
- (A) 凌晨 4:50
- (B) 上午 6:25
- (C) 下午 2:10
- **(D) 晚上 11:50**

181–185 公告和電子郵件

全球企業慈善協會（GCPA）

商業教育

GCPA 歡迎您參加主題為「如何爭取企業補助」的線上直播講座。課程著重於申請補助提案所需的重要資訊，有助貴組織爭取到國內外各企業的資金或其他類型資助的機會。**181**

該課程將由巴爾塔基金會發展部經理迪米崔·里約主講，**185** 訂於 3 月 23 日美東時間下午 4:15 至 6:15 舉行，**182** **183** 主持人則是來自電視新聞節目《國際商業關係》的珍妮絲·拉徹曼。請於 2 月 28 日之前完成報名；**182** 可瀏覽 www.gcpa.org/1512_lecture 了解費用及其他詳細資訊。您填寫報名表時，可選擇向里約先生提問。講課時他將儘可能回答所有問題。此外，與會者的提問與解答均會於 4 月 1 日之前上網公布。

寄件者：迪米崔·里約
<d.rio@baltarfoundation.org>
收件者：傑拉德·許坦
<gerard_stein@gcpa.org>
副本：蒂芬尼·帕克
<packer.t@baltarfoundation.org>
日期：2 月 22 日
主旨：致歉

敬愛的許坦先生：

我很遺憾無法兌現對貴協會的承諾。因為突發狀況，我在貴協會原定講座活動當天，必須到羅馬出差。**183** 我已委託開發部副理蒂芬尼·帕克代為演講，並請她參加 3 月 31 日的視訊會議。關於這些異動，**184** 她應該很快也會用電子郵件通知您。

帕克女士在針對跨國公司募款活動的規劃與管理上，已有 30 多年經驗。不僅如此，她目前也負責辦理敝公司正在進行的網路和實體培訓課程，**185** 保證能讓講座聽眾滿意，還請您放心。

對於取消可能造成的任何不便，我想再次向您由衷致歉。

祝　好

迪米崔·里約

181. 文中提到關於講座的什麼資訊？
    (A) 費用由公司補助款支付。
    (B) 專門為新聞記者舉辦。
    (C) 將在電視聯播網上直播。
    (D) 提供募款建議。

182. 文中提到關於講座聽眾的什麼資訊？
    (A) 他們將取得專業證書。
    (B) 他們應該將問題寄給拉徹曼女士。
    (C) 他們須提前報名參加活動。
    (D) 他們必須是 GCPA 的會員。

183. 里約先生將於何時出差？
    (A) 2 月 22 日
    (B) 3 月 23 日
    (C) 3 月 31 日
    (D) 4 月 1 日

184. 里約先生已安排什麼事情？
    (A) 將捐款給 GCPA
    (B) 將在羅馬與許坦先生見面
    (C) 讓同事代替他出席活動
    (D) 讓他的演講可在網站上觀看

185. 文中提到關於巴爾塔基金會的什麼事情？
    (A) 正在尋覓新的開發部經理。
    (B) 提供網路培訓的機會。
    (C) 已經營 30 年了。
    (D) 經常被《國際商業關係》專題報導。

186–190 網頁、報導和評論

http://www.solarightsystems/shop/id/solarightsol250

| 首頁 | 店家 | 評論 | 聯絡 |

日光 SOL 250：全天候戶外太陽能照明，最適合家用或營業用！

關於日光 SOL 250：

- 明亮的 10 流明 LED 燈，能照亮您的草坪或走廊，單次充電後可使用長達 9 小時。**189**

- 可配置定時器或測光表，以滿足您的照明需求。

- 防風防雨的不銹鋼材質，不會生鏽或碎裂。

- 重達三公斤，附有特製支架，強風中也挺得住。

- 螺旋燈座，換燈泡（另售）好簡單！

- 三年保固含維修。**186**

原價：45 美元／一組

特價：90 美元／三組

給日光產品用戶的公告

歐克岱（1 月 23 日）──暢銷的戶外燈具、可在白天充電的日光 SOL 250 有瑕疵。

日光系統的公關專員今天稍早發布公告，表示「有些 SOL 250 的充電面板發現有問題。186 188 190『日光系統』保證會讓客戶滿意。 店家如有大量安裝，可要求技術服務人員前往修理瑕疵產品。住宅用戶則可退回瑕疵品並免費更換。」

任何與「日光系統」產品有關的疑問，都可寫電子郵件至 24 小時服務信箱：info@solarightsystems.com 諮詢。

http://www.solarightsystems/reviews/solarightsol250

| 首頁 | 店家 | 評論 | 聯絡 |

SOL 250 燈具：

我最近購買了 12 組 SOL 250，對產品非常滿意。我住的地方很偏僻，晚上真的很暗。但即便外面有霧，SOL 250 燈具也能將院子照得通明。**189** 安裝燈具的支架有點困難，但說明書寫得很清楚。我聽我弟說才得知這個型號有瑕疵。但我的燈全都沒有問題，所以我沒有聯絡廠商。**190** 如果有人正在找太陽能照明的產品，我認為雖然它有瑕疵問題仍是非常棒的選擇。

克拉克・魏考克斯

186. SOL 250 的價格中包含了什麼？
(A) 三年保固
(B) 免費運送
(C) 替換零件
(D) 保護罩

187. 撰寫這篇報導的原因為何？
(A) 宣布新家電上市
(B) 更正不正確的標價
(C) 比較幾項產品
(D) 警告讀者產品有缺陷

188. 報導中第二段第一行的「issued」，意思最接近何者？
(A) 公布，公開
(B) 帶出
(C) 分配
(D) 出現

189. 關於 SOL 250 的產品說明，魏考克斯先生對什麼表示肯定？
(A) 燈具很難充電。
(B) 燈具很容易清潔。
(C) 燈具很明亮。
(D) 安裝燈具很簡單。

190. 關於他的燈具，魏考克斯先生指出什麼事情？
(A) 保固不能涵蓋所有範圍。
(B) 維修費用比預期的貴很多。
(C) 材質不是很堅固。
(D) 充電面板運作正常。

191–195 表格、電子郵件和簡訊

訪客門禁代碼（VAC）申請表

請將此表傳至賈桂琳 · 谷和樹女士，傳真號碼 410-555-6953。 **194**

VAC 使用者資訊：
姓名：莎莉 · 佩姬　**部門：**資訊科技部 **191**
員工／公司識別證號：8027
☐ **基本權限：**週一至週五，上午 8:00 至晚間 8:00

☒ **擴充權限：**週一至週五，上午 8:00 至晚間 10:30
☒ **特殊權限**（請填入指定日期與時間）：週六，上午 10:30 至下午 5:30
大樓：☐ 班佛　☒ 潘恩
開始日期：2 月 8 日
結束日期：3 月 5 日
申請人資訊（申請人須為使用者所屬部門經理或主任） **191**
姓名：唐尼 · 蕭 **191**
電子郵件：dshaw@epsen.gov
簽名與日期：Donnie Shaw 1 月 28 日

備註：
我們收到您的 VAC 申請後，至少需四個工作日處理。 **192** 門禁的權限一經獲准後，將寄給使用者一封內含五位數 VAC 的電子郵件。 **194**

收件者：莎莉 · 佩姬
<s_paige@epsen.gov>
寄件者：賈桂琳 · 谷和樹
<j_yakazuki@epsen.gov>
日期：2 月 3 日
主旨：VAC

親愛的佩姬女士：

您申請進出潘恩大樓的擴充及特殊權限已經獲准。您進入大樓時，須使用訪客門禁代碼（VAC）以及您的員工識別證。您的 VAC 為 27795。若於正常上班時間後進入大樓，請遵循以下步驟： **194**

● 將您的卡片靠近讀卡器。讀卡器上的橘色燈將開始閃爍。
● 接著在觸控螢幕上輸入您的 VAC。
● 橙色燈轉為綠色時，您即可進入大樓。 **193**

若您輸入不正確的 VAC，燈號會變成紅色，並發出 5 秒大聲的嗶嗶聲，此後您還有三次輸入正確代碼的機會，若錯誤，您將完全被拒絕入內。 **195** 如果您進入大樓時有任何問題或一進入大樓，請撥打 410-555-4033 聯絡我。

安全管理部　賈桂琳 · 谷和樹　謹啟

來自：莎莉‧佩姬，351-555-7240

收到時間：2月8日，週一，上午 8:02

谷和樹女士您好：

我試著撥了電話，但無法聯絡您。我輸入了您以電子郵件寄給我的 VAC（27795），但它一直閃紅燈。可以請您收到訊息後盡快聯絡我嗎？我被擋在大樓外了。 195

191. 文中提到關於蕭先生的什麼資訊？
(A) 他是資訊科技部的主管。
(B) 他二月時提出申請表。
(C) 他和佩姬女士工作的辦公室不同。
(D) 他將和佩姬女士開會討論她的專案。

192. 文中提到關於 VAC 申請表的什麼資訊？
(A) 須用電子郵件寄到安全管理辦公室。
(B) 須說明要求進出的原因。
(C) 須提供員工證的影本。
(D) 須在代碼使用前至少四天提出申請。

193. 佩姬女士該如何得知她所輸入的 VAC 是有效的？
(A) 燈光顏色會改變。
(B) 會發出 5 秒鐘的聲響。
(C) 會反覆閃燈。
(D) 聲音的音量會增大。

194. 文中並未提到關於安全管理辦公室的什麼資訊？
(A) 那裡有台傳真機。
(B) 下班後允許進入。
(C) 負責核發門禁代碼給員工。
(D) 實施新的安全政策。

195. 文中提到關於佩姬女士的什麼資訊？
(A) 她和谷和樹女士進行了面試。
(B) 她將升為經理。
(C) 她輸入她的 VAC 超過三次。
(D) 她想延長門禁期限。

196–200 廣告、電子郵件和網路評論

奇特電子

25302 西維吉尼亞州查爾斯頓市西園路 32 號
（304）555-0722

一週七天，上午 10 點至下午 7 點 196

為期一週的新年大促銷，買到賺到！ 197

1 月 1 日週六至 1 月 9 日週日 197

桌上型與筆記型電腦、顯示器及配件 —— 7 折

相機、影音設備和隨身硬碟 —— 9 折

手機與平板電腦 —— 8 折

軟體 —— 75 折

註： 奇特電子將在 12 月 31 日下午 5 點關門，準備促銷活動。 196 促銷期間售出商品的退款金額僅會轉為店內抵用金。

奇特電子會員可享全部商品 95 折的額外折扣及延長保固。請馬上到官網申辦會員！有問題嗎？請隨時詢問我們熱心的店員。

收件者：全體員工
寄件者：麥可‧陳 <mchan@qitech.com>
日期：11 月 26 日
主旨：誰有空

大家好：

12 月 31 日需要一組員工通宵將庫存上架並打掃店面。 197 我已安排好伊卡洛斯的宵夜， 198 所以當天工作不只有加班費，還附晚餐。 199 請可加班的同仁於 12 月 20 日之前聯絡蕾貝卡‧強森。

總經理　麥可‧陳　謹啟

http://www.icarusdelivery.com/testimonial

| 首頁 | 菜單 | 訂購 | **顧客推薦** |

我們店長期以來一直訂購伊卡洛斯外賣，買過好幾次了從未失望過。它的美食總是準時送到，**200** 還是熱騰騰剛出爐的。網路訂餐系統很容易操作，複雜的大單也沒問題。**200** 而且送貨員向來是專業又有禮貌。**200** 我們去年 12 月叫了 15 人份的晚餐，披薩只能用美味來形容。**199** 我強烈推薦伊卡洛斯，任何場合都很適合。

196. 根據廣告的內容，12 月 31 日將發生什麼事情？
(A) 電子產品的特賣會開跑。
(B) 將會更新網站。
(C) 店家會提前關門。
(D) 商品會到貨。

197. 陳先生請員工做什麼事情？
(A) 參加季度會議
(B) 替為期一週的活動做準備
(C) 解釋排定行程的過程
(D) 增加額外協助客戶的員工

198. 電子郵件中第一段第二行的
「organized」，意思最接近何者？
(A) 分類
(B) 安排
(C) 調整
(D) 拉直

199. 多少名員工答應陳先生的要求？
(A) 10
(B) 15
(C) 25
(D) 30

200. 伊卡洛斯的線上顧客推薦中沒有提到什麼資訊？
(A) 其員工表現
(B) 其網站簡約
(C) 其餐點價格便宜
(D) 其服務速度

ACTUAL TEST ⑩

101. 康先生請幾名同事協助他進行員工培訓工作坊。
- (A) 他
- **(B) 他**
- (C) 他的
- (D) 他自己

102.「普拉格工程」的員工對最新款的製圖軟體有透徹的理解。
- (A) 知名的
- (B) 知識淵博的
- (C) 知道
- **(D) 理解**

103. 連假週末預計將有大約五萬人到這間遊樂園玩。
- (A) 非常
- (B) 相當地
- **(C) 大約**
- (D) 沈重地

104. 馬西·史塔克的最新報導文章是篇股市趨勢的分析,明智且發人深省。
- (A) 最明智的
- (B) 智慧
- **(C) 明智的**
- (D) 機智地

105. 會議接近尾聲時,公司代表們被要求填寫一份參展意見調查表。
- (A) 當
- (B) 當
- **(C) 接近**
- (D) 自從

106. 打開檢修門之前,請確保沒有意外接上電源線。
- (A) 意外
- (B) 意外的
- (C) 意外
- **(D) 意外地**

107. 達特穆爾臨床醫學院致力於讓醫學院學生負擔得起學費。
- (A) 必需的
- (B) 修剪的
- **(C) 可負擔的**
- (D) 獲准的

108. 哈契爾女士退休前曾在該組織的許多部門任職。
- **(A) 任職**
- (B) 職業
- (C) 職業的
- (D) 正在佔用

109. 為了讓這本書準時出版,設計師須在週一之前將插圖全部改完寄給編輯。
- (A) 文章
- (B) 提案
- (C) 建議
- **(D) 修改**

110. 選定的設計在新年之前,不會進行全面生產。
- (A) 報到
- **(B) 執行**
- (C) 離開
- (D) 收拾

111. 麥西塞德裝配廠的整修,是四個遷廠提案中成本最高的。
- (A) 昂貴的
- (B) 成本核算
- (C) 成本
- **(D) 最昂貴的**

112. 多虧了先進的保存和運輸方法,「路易吉農產」供應最新鮮的蔬果給商家。
- **(A) 保存**
- (B) 保存
- (C) 保存的
- (D) 保存

113. 因受到智慧型手機型號 PFS-2x 的需求帶動，下一季的產量將增加到三倍。
(A) 即使
(B) 正如
(C) 因為
(D) 此外

114. 根據您的面試結果，我們可能會要求您參加筆試。
(A) 正在要求
(B) 必會要求
(C) 已被要求
(D) 可能要求

115. 紅色標籤代表貨物須經檢查，而綠色標籤則代表可出貨。
(A) 幾乎
(B) 然而
(C) 兩者皆
(D) 是否

116. 在與我們的客服專員通信時，請務必提供您的交易編號。
(A) 通信
(B) 對應
(C) 特派記者
(D) 相應地

117. 《卡盧梅特報》的編輯部，通常偏好標題簡短的報導。
(A) 通常
(B) 終於
(C) 本來
(D) 年度地

118. 「勒納協會」著重客製化的廣告宣傳活動，協助商家行銷他們的服務。
(A) 個人地
(B) 個性
(C) 使個人化
(D) 客製化的

119. 只要訂閱費低於 150 美金，郭氏金融服務公司將繼續訂閱這份刊物。
(A) 否則
(B) 此外
(C) 只要
(D) 伴隨

120. 提普頓貨運公司的工會領袖每月與員工開會，以確保公司確實遵守勞動法。
(A) 可能有遵守
(B) 正在被遵守
(C) 將被遵守
(D) 曾被遵守過

121. 關於我們新產品的諮詢，應直接聯繫適當的銷售代表。
(A) 適當的
(B) 後來的
(C) 可追蹤的
(D) 重大的

122. 秋原醫師通常只看約診的病患，但她今天決定破例。
(A) 出現
(B) 適合
(C) 會面
(D) 評論

123. 公司股東正在仔細審查承包商，向他們提出的每月預算需求。
(A) 屬性
(B) 規劃師
(C) 需求
(D) 傳送

124. 設計師坦言，其新服裝系列大受歡迎，部分原因是由於時機還不錯。
(A) 正在分離
(B) 部分地
(C) 已分離的
(D) 零件

125. 上一季員工培訓計畫的一切事務，帕特爾女士都有記錄下來。
(A) 一些
(B) 一切
(C) 其他
(D) 任何

126. 最初只生產電腦軟體的「戴諾科技」現在也製造無線音訊裝置。
(A) 因此
(B) 不久
(C) 多
(D) 現在

127. 研究顯示，電視廣告比網路廣告或廣播廣告具有更持久的影響力。
- (A) 已持續
- (B) 持續
- **(C) 持久的**
- (D) 最終

128. 陳先生這週二完成了他對客戶帳戶的稽核。
- (A) 提交
- (B) 整修
- **(C) 稽核**
- (D) 評論

129. 去年第四季的突發事件導致維斯丹出版社的出版進度延誤。
- (A) 獨特的
- **(B) 未預料到的**
- (C) 全部的
- (D) 微小的

130. 小池女士使用了網路資料庫來分析過去兩季的進度報告。
- **(A) 來分析**
- (B) 將分析
- (C) 分析了
- (D) 分析

PART 6 P. 263–266

131–134 信函

帕梅拉・斯通
94088 加利福尼亞州聖荷西市
阿德曼道 8920 號

敬愛的斯通女士：

這封信旨在確認您預訂了仰望天空飯店的行政套房，住宿日期為 10 月 12 日至 10 月 14 日。您可於週四下午 1:00 起辦理登記入住。您須在最後一天的中午 12 點之前退房。若超過此時間，將收取額外費用。

我們的設施設計高雅，相信您和您的先生一定會喜歡。飯店設有室內與戶外游泳池。另有最先進的健身中心，來滿足您的運動需求。若您有什麼要列印的，請至高科技媒體室。其他設施資訊請上我們官網查詢。

期待您蒞臨仰望天空飯店。

賓客服務主任
伯納德・惠特森　謹啟

131. (A) 開始
- (B) 開始了
- (C) 開始
- **(D) （時間）……起**

132. (A) 您須在最後一天的中午 12 點之前退房。
- (B) 我們已在您的帳單上使用家庭折扣。
- (C) 幸運的是，我們的飯店位於市區，交通便利。
- (D) 感謝您填寫來賓滿意度調查表。

133. (A) 可能地
- **(B) 高雅地**
- (C) 起先
- (D) 幾乎

134. (A) 水電等公用事業
- (B) 花費
- **(C) 設施**
- (D) 參觀

135–138 小冊子

肯歲運輸公司經營傑夫蒙特市最大的公用停車場。欲預訂停車位的上班族可上網或親自前往登記。有多種合約類型提供給有意的個人客戶。停車場共計 3,000 個車位，有時可能客滿。在此情況下，無指定車位的上班族可將汽車停放於對街的滿場分流停車場。有指定車位的車主單次可租用三個月。使用條款與條件可於網路查詢。請仔細閱讀同意書並交給肯歲運輸總公司。請寄電子郵件至 info@kensoitp.com 取得更多資訊。

135. (A) 打字
(B) 類型
(C) 打字
(D) 被輸入的

136. (A) 蓋好的
(B) 滿的
(C) 緊的
(D) 易達的

137. (A) 穿越
(B) 在……範圍內
(C) 超過
(D) 在……對面

138. (A) 使用條款與條件可於網路查詢。
(B) 肯歲在鄰近城市經營另一座停車場。
(C) 傑夫蒙特市最近提高了公共停車費。
(D) 上班族應下載有關交通狀況的手機應用程式。

139–142 信函

11 月 30 日
《品味美食雜誌》
15106 賓夕法尼亞州匹茲堡市
杜法佛特街 8000 號

親愛的《品味美食雜誌》讀者：

我們寫這封信是想通知您，自 1 月 1 日起，《品味美食雜誌》的年訂閱費將調漲。一般費用從 35.99 美金調漲為 37.85 美金。請您放心，本次調整將帶來好處。特色為雜誌內將新增七個新版面，包括優惠券與餐廳評論專欄。如欲取消訂閱，請聯絡我們的客服中心。若未接獲您的任何消息，合約期滿將自動續訂。

139. (A) 退款
(B) 調漲
(C) 交換
(D) 停止

140. (A) 阻礙
(B) 協會
(C) 隊伍
(D) 調整

141. (A) 以……作特色
(B) 將以……作為特色
(C) 功能
(D) 已用……為特色

142. (A) 多家當地餐館將參與該計畫。
(B) 將寄折扣券給您以示感謝。
(C) 《品味美食雜誌》將於十二月慶祝成立 50 週年。
(D) 若未接獲您的任何消息，合約期滿將自動續訂。

143–146 評論

劇場表演令觀眾驚呼連連
阿許拉夫・伊夫提喀爾／撰稿

喀拉蚩（5 月 22 日）——受到劇評盛讚的新作《萬歲！》上週六晚間在辛德劇院首演。

該劇由喀拉蚩表演車輪戲劇俱樂部的成員演出，探討了深切影響當代巴基斯坦價值觀的文化和宗教傳統。

劇中事件由阿里・巴格特的觀點詮釋。他離開家鄉印度後，在喀拉蚩落腳建立新家園。

本劇震撼且感人，表演令人驚嘆，特別是考量到其為業餘製作。演員確實讓角色栩栩如生。演出僅花了一小時時間來述說一生的故事。像這樣的故事需要更多時間充分發展，我除了對這點不滿外，這是一場精彩絕倫的表演。

143. (A) 將檢視
(B) 已檢視
(C) 檢視
(D) 去檢視

144. (A) 出席者
(B) 舞台
(C) 事件
(D) 方向

145. (A) 演員確實讓角色栩栩如生。
(B) 不過，暫時沒有機會排練了。
(C) 劇院高層須注意支出。
(D) 很明顯地，專業協助有其必要。

146. (A) ……的事物
(B) ……的東西
(C) 其一
(D) 一些

PART 7 P. 267–287

147–148 電子郵件

寄件者：許願歌陶瓷
<cs@wishsongceramics.com>
收件者：姜多恩
<dkang@bindlestiffscafe.com>
日期：3 月 19 日
主旨：訂單編號 335401

敬愛的姜女士：

此信確認您已取消訂單。**147** 請保留下列的訂單摘要，以備不時之需：

訂單編號 335401：
120 個 20 盎司的白色咖啡馬克杯（已於 3 月 18 日付款）
目前狀態：已取消

您信用卡扣除的款項將在三個工作日內退還。**148**

感謝您選購許願歌陶瓷。

價格實惠且迷人的餐具，滿足您每一種料理的需求！

147. 寄出此封電子郵件的原因為何？
(A) 確認原始訂單數量
(B) 通知訂單異動
(C) 向客戶更新延遲出貨的資訊
(D) 提供商店政策的詳細資訊

148. 姜女士收到關於付款的哪一項資訊？
(A) 她將在三天後收到收據。
(B) 她下次購買時將獲得折扣優惠。
(C) 她不會獲得全額退款。
(D) 她不會為商品付款。

149–150 電子郵件

收件者：staff_list@theomarketing.com
寄件者：ctheobald@theomarketing.com
日期：3 月 8 日
主旨：最新人事異動

各位午安：

我很高興介紹行銷部的新同仁安德魯·韓德里克森。**149** 他將接管布雷克·平野的許多職務，包括網路廣告和促銷活動企劃。**150** 伊恩·楊恩和卡西姆·阿克索伊也將處理布雷克的日常事務，現在將由伊恩負責撰寫新聞稿、卡西姆管理我們的社群媒體帳戶，包括我們的官網。我謹代表部門所有同仁祝賀布雷克退休愉快，並歡迎安德魯加入我們團隊！

祝　好

寇瑞·希爾包德

149. 此電子郵件的目的為何？
(A) 討論最近的新聞稿
(B) 公告職缺
(C) 歡迎新進員工
(D) 徵詢員工意見

150. 之前誰負責企劃網路促銷活動？
(A) 布雷克·平野
(B) 伊恩·楊恩
(C) 卡西姆·阿克索伊
(D) 寇瑞·希爾包德

約翰・隆巴迪〔下午 1:07〕
幾分鐘前筆和鑰匙圈送到了。

米雪・喬納〔下午 1:08〕
太好了。小冊子也在路上了。**151**

約翰・隆巴迪〔下午 1:09〕
什麼時候會到？我想在今晚全部準備好。
151

米雪・喬納〔下午 1:09〕
大約 5 點。

約翰・隆巴迪〔下午 1:10〕
好。妳可以多訂幾張會議廳用的海報嗎？
152

米雪・喬納〔下午 1:12〕
我早料到了。它們會和小冊子一起到。**152**

約翰・隆巴迪〔下午 1:13〕
太好了。我 5 點會過去幫妳。

151. 隆巴迪先生打算做什麼事情？
(A) 重新設計參展海報
(B) 整理一些宣傳資料
(C) 多拿一些小冊子放在展台上
(D) 5 點離開辦公室

152. 下午 1:12，喬納女士說：「我早料到了」，其意思為何？
(A) 她提前抵達活動現場。
(B) 她已提早付款。
(C) 她已要求加訂物品。
(D) 她想知道抵達會場的路線。

153–155 網頁資訊

www.melba.gov/events

首頁	活動	地點資訊	預約場地	報名註冊	下載

梅爾巴市服務處負責監督梅爾巴市政中心的所有設施和服務，其中包括維修保養、日程安排、活動支援與設施升級。部分建築物或服務將因應維修、改善工程或舉辦大型集會或會議等活動，可能無法使用。**153**

近期活動：

—《週間夜夢》：梅爾巴廣場和露天劇場將於 7 月 2 日至 8 月 7 日期間，每週三下午 5 點至晚上 10 點停止對外開放。該時段僅允許持有表演門票的民眾能進入梅爾巴市政中心前方區域。**154**

—梅爾巴市政中心受惠於公共補助，將於 7 月 21 日至 29 日升級中心的電信設備。若有承辦單位想在此期間預約場地，請務必留意，網路和電話服務訊號將非常受限。

有關完整的活動日程，請上我們官網的「下載」頁面查詢。**155** 請注意，部分戶外活動可能因天氣不佳而取消。最新資訊請寫電子郵件至 ccinfo@melba.gov 洽詢。**155** 此外，從八月分起，您將收到直接發送到您手機的通知。服務詳情將於近期公布！

153. 此網頁的目的為何？
(A) 說明幾項服務
(B) 推廣一場會議
(C) 宣布梅爾巴市的一些專案
(D) 強調梅爾巴市的文化景點

154. 梅爾巴市政中心部分區域週三不對外開放的原因為何？
(A) 將進行整修工程。
(B) 將舉辦一場表演。
(C) 受惡劣天氣影響。
(D) 將是當地路跑路線的一部分。

155. 根據網頁的內容，人們如何得知最新的活動日程？
(A) 查看日程表
(B) 瀏覽官網
(C) 發送電子郵件
(D) 註冊簡訊通知

大都會商訊

楓樹市（8月12日）——據昨日公告，「佩頓自動化工業」將收購「DGC工業」。這對市民來說是個好消息，因為佩頓證實，將恢復擴建DGC製造廠。 **156**

DGC在當地的工廠可因應其大多數的產量需求，提供了楓樹市數千個工作機會。然而，過去五年裡，隨著銷售量下滑，導致工廠擴建工程暫時擱置。佩頓發言人傑西·賈爾維證實，將於工廠完工後開始進行徵才。 **157**

賈維表示：「面試最終階段將在十一月進行， **157** 新廠區可望在十二月投入使用。」

該工廠將繼續生產DGC的系列工業產品，並將作為佩頓新型六軸裝配機器人的生產重心。 **158**

多名產業專家表示，「佩頓自動化工業」已連續三年獨佔自動化設備市場的龍頭位置。佩頓總部設於新加坡。

156. 此報導的目的為何？
(A) 報導企業搬遷情況
(B) 確認有一家新店開張
(C) 提供一項擱置計畫的最新資訊
(D) 回顧製造業的變化趨勢

157. 根據賈爾維先生的說法，十一月將發生什麼事情？
(A) 企業將僱用更多員工。
(B) 將公布新產品系列。
(C) 一間工廠將進行維修。
(D) 一棟建築物將被拆除。

158. 文中提到關於「佩頓自動化工業」的什麼資訊？
(A) 將關閉新加坡分部。
(B) 總部位於楓樹市。
(C) 它生產裝配機器人。
(D) 最近失去重要客戶。

法蘭克·卡維〔下午 2:07〕
大家好。我們有任何關於羅森大廈競標的最新消息嗎？

清磨·阿迪亞〔下午 2:08〕
我週二與拉珊女士通過電話。她說高層還在審查提案，這週將決議。

法蘭克·卡維〔下午 2:09〕
我很擔心。我們必須在明天之前訂購估價單上的訂製燈具。 **160** 不然就算提前鋪設好地板，我們也沒辦法準時完工。 **159**

安娜·姜〔下午 2:10〕
喔、我昨天下午已經下單了。 **160**

法蘭克·卡維〔下午 2:11〕
這可能會有問題。如果我們沒有得標，這些照明設備會造成麻煩。 **160** 目前正在進行的專案都不需要它們。我們得在何時取消訂單才不用付違約金？ **160** **162**

安娜·姜〔下午 2:14〕
我們已和他們合作多年，我認為這次我們也會被選上。我會再深入了解。 **160**

法蘭克·卡維〔下午 2:15〕
清磨，能否請你聯絡拉珊女士，問她是否有我們的消息？

安娜·姜〔下午 2:21〕
我們能在今天下午6點之前取消就不會被罰錢。 **162**

清磨·阿迪亞〔下午 2:22〕
事實上，法蘭克，我剛和拉珊女士通話，羅森已選擇讓紅樹林公司施工。 **161** **162**

法蘭克·卡維〔下午 2:24〕
真遺憾。但這也不是第一次流標，我們也不要太失望。

159. 傳訊息的人最有可能從事哪一個行業？
(A) 園藝
(B) 室內設計
(C) 攝影
(D) 房地產

160. 下午 2:14，姜女士説：「我會再深入了
　　　解」，其意思為何？
　　　(A) 確認一項產品的數量
　　　(B) 詢問時限
　　　(C) 重新安排送貨
　　　(D) 計算服務成本

161. 拉珊女士提供了什麼資訊？
　　　(A) 提供產品退款的方式
　　　(B) 負責整修羅森大樓的廠商
　　　(C) 價格實惠的地板的購買地點
　　　(D) 羅森先生不回電的原因

162. 姜女士接下來最有可能做什麼事情？
　　　(A) 試圖説服拉珊女士
　　　(B) 草擬新提案
　　　(C) 取消購買
　　　(D) 安排班表

163–165 電子郵件

寄件者：曼佛瑞德證券交易商
收件者：薩布琳娜·青木
日期：1 月 3 日
主旨：您的帳戶

敬愛的青木女士：

請注意，您的帳戶密碼已更新成功。**163**
若您並未變更，請在 48 小時內致電
（800）555-1212 與我們聯絡。**164** **165**
<u>一名券商後線人員將協助您解決問題</u>。本
封電子郵件為自動發送，請勿回覆或轉寄
至其他地址。

若為您本人要求更改資訊，則無須採取進
一步措施。

此通知係基於保護您的帳戶安全發送。

曼佛瑞德證券交易商
丹尼爾·帕斯夸萊蒂　謹啟

用我們革命創新的交易軟體策略性購買
股票，詳參 www.mstrade.com ！

163. 此封電子郵件寄給青木女士的原因
　　　為何？
　　　(A) 宣布促銷活動
　　　(B) 要求付款
　　　(C) 提醒她帳戶有些活動
　　　(D) 告知新的安全方案

164. 青木女士被建議做什麼事情？
　　　(A) 若她並未要求變更則須打電話
　　　(B) 檢查每月帳單明細
　　　(C) 下載程式
　　　(D) 更改她的帳戶設定

165. 「一名券商後線人員將協助您解決問
　　　題。」最適合放在 [1]、[2]、[3]、[4] 的
　　　哪一個位置？
　　　(A) [1]
　　　(B) [2]
　　　(C) [3]
　　　(D) [4]

166–168 電子郵件

寄件者：info@towercontrolvid.com
收件者：註冊用戶表
日期：8 月 23 日
主旨：4.5 版

您好：

我們很高興宣布，您所購買的最新版影片
剪輯軟體 Towercontrol 4.5 已可供下載。
166

視覺與聲音特效：效果庫更新後新增 50
種特效。特效均有多個可供開關的選項。
下載更新須登入您的網路帳號，並選擇
「更新」標籤。新特效的使用說明書將在
近期內以快遞送達。**167**

添加庫存影片素材：現在可下載免費影像
片段供您使用；若您想在專案裡增添變
化，隨時能將它們插入片段中作為轉場。
有許多庫存影片可供挑選，請務必花點時
間熟悉。

快速管理網路發布內容：快速與電影工作室或社群媒體好友分享您的影片！請至 www.towercontrolvid.com/sharing 下載檔案分享說明書，逐步了解該如何**連結您的多個網絡帳號與您的影音傑作**。168

您的支持對我們至關重要。我們很榮幸有機會幫您將影片剪輯的體驗變得愉快！

Towercontrol 影片客戶支援部　謹啟

166. 此封電子郵件的目的為何？
(A) 獎勵長期老客戶
(B) 廣告新軟體產品
(C) 要求額外資訊
(D) 提供電腦程式的詳細資訊

167. 將郵寄什麼東西給客戶？
(A) 有關最新電子產品的雜誌
(B) 安裝更新的教學
(C) 大量庫存影片的檔案
(D) 新特效的使用手冊

168. 電子郵件中第四段第三行的「bridge」，意思最接近何者？
(A) 連接
(B) 延伸
(C) 達到
(D) 交叉

169–171 信函

致編輯部：

這封信與〈永恆不朽的度假勝地：海瑟度假村〉此篇飯店評論有關，它刊登在 9 月號的《輕鬆旅行家》。度假村的照片很漂亮，飯店能得到應有的關注也是很棒的事。但我注意到一件事必須告知您。169

評論家寫道，亞瑟・泰勒是度假村獨特建築的原創設計師。儘管他的貢獻無疑非常重要，但他主要是位資助者的角色。169 他在度假村開發階段的決策過程幾乎沒有任何作用。反倒是由凱爾・席爾瓦負責海瑟的規畫和建設。171 我知道此事是因為我是海瑟度假村聘請去設計花園與室外區域的負責人，170 因此與席爾瓦先生互動頻繁。

評論中只簡短提及該棟建築的設計，但我想這對海瑟度假村的歷史來說意義重大。多虧席爾瓦先生，我們島上的旅遊業才能快速發展，使當地商家繁榮起來，但這方面卻鮮少提及他的功勞。我認為澄清事實真相很重要。

阿法・法伊茲　謹啟

169. 撰寫這封信的原因為何？
(A) 強調某位執行長的成就
(B) 描述度假情形
(C) 更正一些資訊
(D) 評論幾家旅宿業者

170. 法伊茲先生最有可能的身分為何？
(A) 設施管理員
(B) 旅行作家
(C) 景觀設計師
(D) 飯店經理

171. 「他在度假村開發階段的決策過程幾乎沒有任何作用。」最適合放在 [1]、[2]、[3]、[4] 的哪一個位置？
(A) [1]
(B) [2]
(C) [3]
(D) [4]

172–175 信函

灘樹企業
紐澤西州佩寧頓市東查威爾路 92 號

10 月 27 日

敬愛的瑟可女士：

我很榮幸通知您，自 11 月 15 日週二起，您獲聘為資深行銷經理，基本薪資為年薪 76,000 美元。173 175 根據公司政策，您將從六個月的試用期開始。期滿後將評估您的業績表現，決定您是否有續聘的資格。

請最晚在 11 月 8 日週二以前確認您是否接受此錄取機會。可用簡訊或撥打（609）555-0058 通知。若您須在指定日期以外的日期到職，請您聯絡我們時務必提供可到職日期。然而，我們有正在進行的專案且須積極因應現有客戶業務的需求，因此您的到職日最晚只能延後到 11 月 24 日（週四）。

到職當天，請您先到人力資源辦公室，再前往您的部門報到。請務必攜帶這封通知書，因您須於人資專員見證下在通知書上簽署姓名與日期 **172** **175** （務必自己留存副本）。您到時候也須繳交駕照或護照的影本。 **172**

我們公司為確保培訓順利，將盡力為新進員工安排一位職務相同的導師。 **172** 因此，您工作時將與負責該職務多年的凱爾‧衛斯理安先生密切合作。 **173** 若報到前您對公司文化或特殊需求有任何疑問，可隨時寫電子郵件至 kwesleyan@beachtree.com 與他聯絡。標準的員工職前訓練將協助您了解公司準則與流程，您的場次訂於 11 月 16 日（週三）， **174** 但此日期可根據您的到職時間重新安排。

我們很高興歡迎您加入灘樹企業，並期待與您共事。

人力資源主任
珍娜‧羅帕　謹啟

批准入職合約條款與條件
我在此同意灘樹企業提供之條款與條件。

員工簽名：**達夏‧瑟可**
員工姓名：達夏‧瑟可
簽署日期：11 月 15 日 **175**

172. 新進員工沒有哪一項義務？
(A) 繳交錄取通知
(B) 在有經驗的員工指導下接受培訓
(C) 出示某種形式的身分證件
(D) 出示住所證明

173. 關於衛斯理安先生，何者為真？
(A) 他是「灘樹」的客戶。
(B) 他將主持員工的職前訓練。
(C) 他將在六個月後評估瑟可女士。
(D) 他是資深行銷經理。

174. 瑟可女士將於何時了解有關公司規則的資訊？
(A) 週二
(B) 週三
(C) 週四
(D) 週五

175. 文中提到關於瑟可女士的什麼資訊？
(A) 她並未重新安排到職日。
(B) 她沒有為了詢問公司文化而聯絡任何人。
(C) 她六個月後將不會獲得加薪。
(D) 她在試用期內不會直接與客戶打交道。

176–180 報導和電子郵件

離行海濱
魯迪‧寶拉

10 月 2 日——秋天正式到來，我起心動念想去緬因州鄉間看看。我預想會是平靜地、甚至有些無聊地行駛在偏僻的鄉間小路上，卻意外碰上每個轉彎處顏色繽紛的林木，美得出奇。我到了巴爾港，是一個古樸的濱海小鎮，從鄰近城市波特蘭往來的公車一天有四班。 **179** 它的歷史可追溯到 1796 年，緊鄰秀麗的國家公園。

我在巴塞洛繆‧達涅先生經營的旅社留宿，其名為「毛獸小屋」。 **179** 剛走進去，我彷彿穿越到另一個時代——簡直妙不可言。 **176** 不只內部裝潢設計與百年之前一樣，甚至連部分菜色亦然！達涅先生擅長料理當地名菜龍蝦雜燴濃湯。 **177** 您若剛好在此地區，一定要考慮造訪這家旅社。 **176**

更多資訊請瀏覽我的網站：
www.rudygetsout.com

住房情況與訂房，請瀏覽該旅社的網站：
www.critterlodge.com

關於哈特港飯店，汗先生提到什麼資訊？
(A) 有網站給予該飯店正面評價。
(B) 有提供交通工具前往巴爾港。
(C) 在該處已有訂房。
(D) 十月已客滿。

寄件者：阿尼許・汗
<akhan@springertech.com>
收件者：布萊茲・拉爾森
<blaze.l@takefive.com>
日期：10 月 8 日
主旨：會議行程

拉爾森先生早安：178

我很感謝您安排我參加會議的行程。178 但我方才得知，在主辦大會的城市外路途不遠處有家毛獸小屋，www.critterlodge.com。179 我希望每天都能開著車行經美麗的鄉間小路、接著在海邊度過輕鬆的夜晚，來結束這一天。能否請您幫我查看，同樣的日期那邊有沒有空房可供我入住？178 如果可以，也得請您取消哈特港飯店的訂房。178 180 根據您用電子郵件寄給我的確認文件，提前兩天（即 10 月 13 日之前）告知應可避免罰款。

春人科技公司副總裁　阿尼許・汗　謹啟

176. 此篇報導的目的為何？
(A) 推薦住宿地點
(B) 講解新菜單
(C) 宣傳租車服務
(D) 評論網路雜誌

177. 文中提到關於龍蝦雜燴濃湯的什麼資訊？
(A) 為地方菜。
(B) 使用許多食材。
(C) 價格實惠。
(D) 為秋季限定。

178. 拉爾森先生最有可能的身分為何？
(A) 飯店員工
(B) 服務生
(C) 程式設計師
(D) 旅行社員工

179. 文中提到關於會議的什麼資訊？
(A) 汗先生是領銜主辦人。
(B) 提前報名的截止日期為 10 月 13 日。
(C) 提供與會者午餐。
(D) 它在波特蘭舉行。

181–185 資訊單和表格

霍德菲爾德公園
活動許可證

任何希望在霍德菲爾德市轄下任一社區公園舉辦 30 人或以上的活動者，必須取得霍德菲爾德公園與休閒管理部的活動許可證。181 182

申請須知

＊活動許可證均須支付 30 美元的手續費，該筆費用概不退還。185 支票須開給霍德菲爾德公園與休閒管理部。

＊須於活動日前至少一個月，提交許可證申請書給霍德菲爾德公園與休閒管理部。183

＊須親自前往霍德菲爾德公園與休閒管理部辦公室申請活動許可證，其辦公時間為週一至週五上午 9 點至下午 6 點。不接受網路與郵寄申請。申辦時須繳交填妥的申請表與申請手續費。

＊申請將按照先來後到的順序審核。請上 www.holderfieldparksrecdept.com 查看我們的活動行事曆，以了解各個公園可供使用的日期。

其他費用

除申請許可證的費用外，多數活動均無額外費用。規模較大的活動如需要大量戶外食物攤位或現場演出的音樂設備，將會加收額外費用。185 申請人須於申請許可證時載明所有相關資訊。

霍德菲爾德公園

活動許可證申請書

申請人：<u>卡蕊莎‧科斯科</u> `183`

組織和電話：<u>馬可斯希臘文化協會，555-3937</u>

活動名稱：<u>地中海風味賞</u> `184`

活動概述：<u>活動旨在推廣各種地中海美食。參加民眾可參觀料理示範、見到當地主廚，並在多家小吃攤品嚐道地的地中海美食。</u> `185`

活動開始日期／時間：<u>8月25日，週日，上午 11:00</u> `183`

活動結束日期／時間：<u>8月25日，週日，下午 5:00</u>

地點：<u>橡溪公園</u>

預計參加人數：<u>400-700 人</u> `184` `185`

此區僅限霍德菲爾德公園與休閒管理部人員填寫：**核准**

---

181. 此篇資訊單的目標對象是誰？
(A) 求職者
(B) 園區人員
(C) 活動企劃
(D) 旅行社員工

182. 文中提到關於霍德菲爾德公園與休閒管理部的什麼資訊？
(A) 管理多個公園的空間。
(B) 接受網路申請。
(C) 每年僅發放 30 張許可證。
(D) 一週七天都營業。

183. 文中提到關於科斯科女士的什麼資訊？
(A) 她每週日都會進行料理示範。
(B) 她最近搬到霍德菲爾德。
(C) 她在當地受歡迎的餐廳工作。
(D) 她在 7 月 25 日之前提交申請書。

184. 文中提到關於「地中海風味賞」的什麼資訊？
(A) 標榜有音樂表演。
(B) 預計將吸引超過 400 人。
(C) 需要入場費。
(D) 安排進行兩天。

185. 科斯科女士可能需要做什麼事情？
(A) 更新她現有的許可證
(B) 預約另一個公園的空間
(C) 以折扣價格賣票
(D) 支付不只一項費用

186–190 報導、同意書和資訊

K.A.羅斯文獻展

歷史學者兼作家 K.A.羅斯的珍藏文獻 `186` 已開放供研究使用，目前於格羅夫大道 50 號的歷史研究圖書館「威菲爾德中心」 `187` 展出。該中心員工克拉萊斯‧羅伊斯 `187` 表示：「K.A.羅斯是國內備受推崇的作家之一。」這些文件回顧了羅斯的成功生涯，收錄他的全套知名著作與早期著作的少數手稿。此外，文獻還包括訪談、傳記、公開演講及根據其生平拍攝的紀錄片。

威菲爾德中心館藏之稀有書籍、手稿、聲音資料和其他文獻僅供研究目的使用。 `188` 讀者須閱讀威菲爾德中心規定並於櫃台簽署一份同意書，並到三樓觀看有關使用圖書館資料和設施的短片。 `189` 中心開放時間為週一至週六上午 10 點至下午 6 點。

威菲爾德中心

會員註冊同意書

歡迎來到威菲爾德中心。為了確保所有文件僅供研究之用與維護館藏品質，請讀者必須遵守圖書館資料的使用規定。請閱讀所附文件並於底部簽名，以示您已了解威菲爾德中心的規定。請於櫃台繳交此表並附上有照片的身分證件影本，以取得兩年的會員卡。請注意，本中心的資料均不得攜出。 `190`

我已閱讀並同意威菲爾德中心的條款與規定。

日期：2 月 26 日

姓名：柏納·波特 **189**

簽名：*柏納·波特*

威菲爾德中心一般規定

- 圖書館內禁止飲食。**190**

- 讀者離開圖書館時，館方有權檢查其所有的包包或袋子。**190**

- 手機於館內須維持靜音。

- 威菲爾德中心對於您的個人財產概不負責。**190**

- 不允許寵物進入館內。

---

186. 報導文章中第一段第一行的「treasured」，意思最接近何者？

(A) 珍貴的
(B) 隱藏的
(C) 脆裂的
(D) 保存的

187. 羅伊斯女士的身分為何？

(A) 研究員
(B) 小說家
(C) 圖書館工作人員
(D) 電影製片

188. 文中提到關於威菲爾德中心的什麼資訊？

(A) 僅供研究使用。
(B) 正在尋找新資料。
(C) 正在修訂政策。
(D) 正在擴充收藏空間。

189. 波特先生被要求做什麼事情？

(A) 歸還其借閱的資料
(B) 繳交他的試寫作品
(C) 繳納會員費
(D) 觀看資訊影片

190. 一般規定中並未提及同意書的哪一項規則？

(A) 不允許讀者將零食帶進圖書館。
(B) 不允許讀者攜帶任何館藏文件外出。
(C) 讀者可能需要將包包提供檢查。
(D) 讀者應妥善保管私人物品。

191–195 電子郵件和報導

收件者：凱薩琳·安
寄件者：潔西卡·埃斯茨
日期：7 月 3 日
主旨：新店面

親愛的凱薩琳：

感謝您昨天撥冗與我見面。如我所說，我正在為我的化妝品店尋找新店面。**191** 我目前的租約將在十一月到期。我偏好市區的地點，在阿斯彭廣場或者附近，月租在 3,500 英鎊或以下。重要的是坪數要和現在的店面差不多，但內部裝潢和格局可以比較彈性。

考量到我員工的經濟狀況，我必須在十二月初開業。**192** 因此，我優先考量不太需要施工處理的新店面。我們目前所在的大樓很合適，但員工和我都認為換個位置能讓業績還要更好。

感謝您。

潔西卡·埃斯茨

收件者：潔西卡·埃斯茨
寄件者：凱薩琳·安
日期：7 月 6 日
主旨：關於：新店面

我找到了幾個地點，相信能符合您的需求。請您方便時打給我，告訴我您方便看房的時間。我會根據您的時間來安排看房。

A. 西南大街 1029 號
3,430 英鎊／月
先前為麵包店，店面前的路邊有計時收費停車格可供顧客使用。廚房區可改為倉庫或辦公室。商品展示空間有限。

B. 默特爾廣場 78 號

3,180 英鎊／月 193

位於第一城市銀行總部對面的黃金地點。隔壁棟有地下停車場。大門前的無障礙坡道損毀。193 需整修。

C. 南十道 839 號

3,240 英鎊／月

於河堤社區淺松購物中心 2 樓。有完善的公共交通服務。該大樓內有不少刊登廣告的機會。

凱薩琳‧安　謹啟

魅貓找到新址

伊馮‧加納／報導

港灣（12 月 9 日）192 ──魅貓，這家位於沙耶爾道 17 號的名店，十幾年來都是當地美容產品的首選商店。它上週六於默恩大樓旁的默特爾廣場 78 號重新開張。192 193

您在魅貓依然可見高品質商品和絕佳服務。如您來店裡，我強烈建議您嘗試美甲與臉部按摩。我們店員都是自學出師的藝術家！

老顧客應該有注意到，按摩和美甲的座位區比以前略小。194 週末午後可能很快就會滿座，但貴賓等待後將獲得最棒的產品和超讚的服務，而它們正是魅貓多年經營的堅持。195

新店面位於聯邦街商業中心附近，交通十分便利。店面有針對輪椅人士的友善設計，193 營業時間為每天上午 10 點至晚上 7 點。

191. 安女士最有可能的身分為何？
- (A) 屋主
- (B) 信貸人員
- **(C) 房仲業者**
- (D) 化妝品設計師

192. 文中提到關於埃斯茨女士的什麼資訊？
- (A) 她開發了新的美容產品系列。
- **(B) 她的店能夠準時重新開業。**
- (C) 她無力支付更高的租金。
- (D) 她並不想翻新某些陳列展示。

193. 文中提到關於魅貓的什麼資訊？
- (A) 週末提早關門。
- (B) 服務已改善。
- **(C) 整修了坡道。**
- (D) 倉庫可容納更多物品。

194. 新的美妝店與之前的有何不同？
- **(A) 能容納的顧客數較少。**
- (B) 位於購物中心內。
- (C) 提供更多的美甲服務。
- (D) 不再提供臉部按摩。

195. 報導文章中第三段第六行的「going」，意思最接近何者？
- **(A) 營運**
- (B) 通過
- (C) 離開
- (D) 旅行

196–200 廣告和電子郵件

實習生招募中

屢獲殊榮的「藍飛行銷公司」位於亞特蘭大商業區的分公司正在招募實習生。合適的應徵者須有辦公室文書作業經驗，有廣泛社群媒體服務知識為佳。工作內容包括回答線上諮詢、追蹤訂閱數據、發布社群網站公告196 及其他行政管理任務。該兼職實習工時為每週 15 個小時，晚間和週末有時須在家工作。197 學生或應屆畢業生若對該職位感興趣，請將履歷寄至 internship@bluefly.com。

收件者：internship@bluefly.com
寄件者：wrasmussen@esuarts.edu
日期：5 月 19 日
主旨：實習生的職位
附件：拉斯穆森—簡歷；拉斯穆森—簡報

敬愛的藍飛人資部：

我對貴公司的實習生一職很感興趣，希望貴公司能考慮我的申請。我目前還在學校讀設計，但已有兩年社群媒體職務相關的經驗。我管理多個大學社團的網頁，在我個人社群媒體帳號上也非常活躍。此外，我非常熟悉製作出色網路文案所需的絕大多數軟體。

我目前每週有四天早上在美術館擔任導覽員。我希望找的實習工作能維持這份工作的排班。 **197** 我從未從事過行銷， **198** 但我求知若渴，也相信我的能力對貴公司能有所幫助。我在此信附上履歷和一份充分應用我藝術才能的簡報。它們能夠說明我創作吸引人、有趣文案的能力，以及我對品質的執著。 **200**

感謝您的寶貴時間，我希望很快能收到您的答覆。 **200**

溫迪・拉斯穆森　敬上

收件者：藍飛人力資源部
寄件者：亞當・伊凡諾維奇
日期：5 月 26 日
主旨：關於實習生職缺

午安：

明早 10 點將開始最後一場實習生面試，對象為拉斯穆森小姐。請在面試前詳閱她繳交的資料，讓自己更了解她具備的資格條件， **199** 畢竟有一些人可能對此有疑慮。我相信她很快就能學會我們要求的社群媒體例行性任務。但我認為她有潛力能做得更多。她以電子郵件寄來的資料表現出的水準確實是我們網路客群會喜歡的。 **200** 若您想在明天見面前深入討論此事，請與我聯絡。

亞當

196. 根據廣告的內容，此實習生的職責為何？
   (A) 主持客戶會議
   (B) 更新網站內容
   (C) 聯絡新訂戶
   (D) 整理辦公室帳單

197. 此職位的哪個方面最吸引拉斯穆森小姐？
   (A) 薪資數字
   (B) 排班時間
   (C) 公司聲譽
   (D) 公司地點

198. 文中提到關於拉斯穆森小姐的什麼資訊？
   (A) 她打算搬到亞特蘭大。
   (B) 她剛從大學畢業。
   (C) 她定期在美術館展出自己的作品。
   (D) 她沒有行銷方面的工作經驗。

199. 第二封電子郵件的目的為何？
   (A) 要求面試官審查應徵者的文件
   (B) 告知員工某場面試延後的原因
   (C) 使員工了解公司政策
   (D) 要求面試官儘快得出結論

200. 伊凡諾維奇先生認為拉斯穆森小姐很適合該職位的原因為何？
   (A) 她有出差意願
   (B) 她在廣告方面的經驗
   (C) 她的電腦知識
   (D) 她的藝術家才能

答案紙

ACTUAL TEST 01

READING SECTION

101	Ⓐ Ⓑ Ⓒ Ⓓ	111	Ⓐ Ⓑ Ⓒ Ⓓ	121	Ⓐ Ⓑ Ⓒ Ⓓ	131	Ⓐ Ⓑ Ⓒ Ⓓ	141	Ⓐ Ⓑ Ⓒ Ⓓ	151	Ⓐ Ⓑ Ⓒ Ⓓ	161	Ⓐ Ⓑ Ⓒ Ⓓ	171	Ⓐ Ⓑ Ⓒ Ⓓ	181	Ⓐ Ⓑ Ⓒ Ⓓ	191	Ⓐ Ⓑ Ⓒ Ⓓ
102	Ⓐ Ⓑ Ⓒ Ⓓ	112	Ⓐ Ⓑ Ⓒ Ⓓ	122	Ⓐ Ⓑ Ⓒ Ⓓ	132	Ⓐ Ⓑ Ⓒ Ⓓ	142	Ⓐ Ⓑ Ⓒ Ⓓ	152	Ⓐ Ⓑ Ⓒ Ⓓ	162	Ⓐ Ⓑ Ⓒ Ⓓ	172	Ⓐ Ⓑ Ⓒ Ⓓ	182	Ⓐ Ⓑ Ⓒ Ⓓ	192	Ⓐ Ⓑ Ⓒ Ⓓ
103	Ⓐ Ⓑ Ⓒ Ⓓ	113	Ⓐ Ⓑ Ⓒ Ⓓ	123	Ⓐ Ⓑ Ⓒ Ⓓ	133	Ⓐ Ⓑ Ⓒ Ⓓ	143	Ⓐ Ⓑ Ⓒ Ⓓ	153	Ⓐ Ⓑ Ⓒ Ⓓ	163	Ⓐ Ⓑ Ⓒ Ⓓ	173	Ⓐ Ⓑ Ⓒ Ⓓ	183	Ⓐ Ⓑ Ⓒ Ⓓ	193	Ⓐ Ⓑ Ⓒ Ⓓ
104	Ⓐ Ⓑ Ⓒ Ⓓ	114	Ⓐ Ⓑ Ⓒ Ⓓ	124	Ⓐ Ⓑ Ⓒ Ⓓ	134	Ⓐ Ⓑ Ⓒ Ⓓ	144	Ⓐ Ⓑ Ⓒ Ⓓ	154	Ⓐ Ⓑ Ⓒ Ⓓ	164	Ⓐ Ⓑ Ⓒ Ⓓ	174	Ⓐ Ⓑ Ⓒ Ⓓ	184	Ⓐ Ⓑ Ⓒ Ⓓ	194	Ⓐ Ⓑ Ⓒ Ⓓ
105	Ⓐ Ⓑ Ⓒ Ⓓ	115	Ⓐ Ⓑ Ⓒ Ⓓ	125	Ⓐ Ⓑ Ⓒ Ⓓ	135	Ⓐ Ⓑ Ⓒ Ⓓ	145	Ⓐ Ⓑ Ⓒ Ⓓ	155	Ⓐ Ⓑ Ⓒ Ⓓ	165	Ⓐ Ⓑ Ⓒ Ⓓ	175	Ⓐ Ⓑ Ⓒ Ⓓ	185	Ⓐ Ⓑ Ⓒ Ⓓ	195	Ⓐ Ⓑ Ⓒ Ⓓ
106	Ⓐ Ⓑ Ⓒ Ⓓ	116	Ⓐ Ⓑ Ⓒ Ⓓ	126	Ⓐ Ⓑ Ⓒ Ⓓ	136	Ⓐ Ⓑ Ⓒ Ⓓ	146	Ⓐ Ⓑ Ⓒ Ⓓ	156	Ⓐ Ⓑ Ⓒ Ⓓ	166	Ⓐ Ⓑ Ⓒ Ⓓ	176	Ⓐ Ⓑ Ⓒ Ⓓ	186	Ⓐ Ⓑ Ⓒ Ⓓ	196	Ⓐ Ⓑ Ⓒ Ⓓ
107	Ⓐ Ⓑ Ⓒ Ⓓ	117	Ⓐ Ⓑ Ⓒ Ⓓ	127	Ⓐ Ⓑ Ⓒ Ⓓ	137	Ⓐ Ⓑ Ⓒ Ⓓ	147	Ⓐ Ⓑ Ⓒ Ⓓ	157	Ⓐ Ⓑ Ⓒ Ⓓ	167	Ⓐ Ⓑ Ⓒ Ⓓ	177	Ⓐ Ⓑ Ⓒ Ⓓ	187	Ⓐ Ⓑ Ⓒ Ⓓ	197	Ⓐ Ⓑ Ⓒ Ⓓ
108	Ⓐ Ⓑ Ⓒ Ⓓ	118	Ⓐ Ⓑ Ⓒ Ⓓ	128	Ⓐ Ⓑ Ⓒ Ⓓ	138	Ⓐ Ⓑ Ⓒ Ⓓ	148	Ⓐ Ⓑ Ⓒ Ⓓ	158	Ⓐ Ⓑ Ⓒ Ⓓ	168	Ⓐ Ⓑ Ⓒ Ⓓ	178	Ⓐ Ⓑ Ⓒ Ⓓ	188	Ⓐ Ⓑ Ⓒ Ⓓ	198	Ⓐ Ⓑ Ⓒ Ⓓ
109	Ⓐ Ⓑ Ⓒ Ⓓ	119	Ⓐ Ⓑ Ⓒ Ⓓ	129	Ⓐ Ⓑ Ⓒ Ⓓ	139	Ⓐ Ⓑ Ⓒ Ⓓ	149	Ⓐ Ⓑ Ⓒ Ⓓ	159	Ⓐ Ⓑ Ⓒ Ⓓ	169	Ⓐ Ⓑ Ⓒ Ⓓ	179	Ⓐ Ⓑ Ⓒ Ⓓ	189	Ⓐ Ⓑ Ⓒ Ⓓ	199	Ⓐ Ⓑ Ⓒ Ⓓ
110	Ⓐ Ⓑ Ⓒ Ⓓ	120	Ⓐ Ⓑ Ⓒ Ⓓ	130	Ⓐ Ⓑ Ⓒ Ⓓ	140	Ⓐ Ⓑ Ⓒ Ⓓ	150	Ⓐ Ⓑ Ⓒ Ⓓ	160	Ⓐ Ⓑ Ⓒ Ⓓ	170	Ⓐ Ⓑ Ⓒ Ⓓ	180	Ⓐ Ⓑ Ⓒ Ⓓ	190	Ⓐ Ⓑ Ⓒ Ⓓ	200	Ⓐ Ⓑ Ⓒ Ⓓ

ACTUAL TEST 02

READING SECTION

101	Ⓐ Ⓑ Ⓒ Ⓓ	111	Ⓐ Ⓑ Ⓒ Ⓓ	121	Ⓐ Ⓑ Ⓒ Ⓓ	131	Ⓐ Ⓑ Ⓒ Ⓓ	141	Ⓐ Ⓑ Ⓒ Ⓓ	151	Ⓐ Ⓑ Ⓒ Ⓓ	161	Ⓐ Ⓑ Ⓒ Ⓓ	171	Ⓐ Ⓑ Ⓒ Ⓓ	181	Ⓐ Ⓑ Ⓒ Ⓓ	191	Ⓐ Ⓑ Ⓒ Ⓓ
102	Ⓐ Ⓑ Ⓒ Ⓓ	112	Ⓐ Ⓑ Ⓒ Ⓓ	122	Ⓐ Ⓑ Ⓒ Ⓓ	132	Ⓐ Ⓑ Ⓒ Ⓓ	142	Ⓐ Ⓑ Ⓒ Ⓓ	152	Ⓐ Ⓑ Ⓒ Ⓓ	162	Ⓐ Ⓑ Ⓒ Ⓓ	172	Ⓐ Ⓑ Ⓒ Ⓓ	182	Ⓐ Ⓑ Ⓒ Ⓓ	192	Ⓐ Ⓑ Ⓒ Ⓓ
103	Ⓐ Ⓑ Ⓒ Ⓓ	113	Ⓐ Ⓑ Ⓒ Ⓓ	123	Ⓐ Ⓑ Ⓒ Ⓓ	133	Ⓐ Ⓑ Ⓒ Ⓓ	143	Ⓐ Ⓑ Ⓒ Ⓓ	153	Ⓐ Ⓑ Ⓒ Ⓓ	163	Ⓐ Ⓑ Ⓒ Ⓓ	173	Ⓐ Ⓑ Ⓒ Ⓓ	183	Ⓐ Ⓑ Ⓒ Ⓓ	193	Ⓐ Ⓑ Ⓒ Ⓓ
104	Ⓐ Ⓑ Ⓒ Ⓓ	114	Ⓐ Ⓑ Ⓒ Ⓓ	124	Ⓐ Ⓑ Ⓒ Ⓓ	134	Ⓐ Ⓑ Ⓒ Ⓓ	144	Ⓐ Ⓑ Ⓒ Ⓓ	154	Ⓐ Ⓑ Ⓒ Ⓓ	164	Ⓐ Ⓑ Ⓒ Ⓓ	174	Ⓐ Ⓑ Ⓒ Ⓓ	184	Ⓐ Ⓑ Ⓒ Ⓓ	194	Ⓐ Ⓑ Ⓒ Ⓓ
105	Ⓐ Ⓑ Ⓒ Ⓓ	115	Ⓐ Ⓑ Ⓒ Ⓓ	125	Ⓐ Ⓑ Ⓒ Ⓓ	135	Ⓐ Ⓑ Ⓒ Ⓓ	145	Ⓐ Ⓑ Ⓒ Ⓓ	155	Ⓐ Ⓑ Ⓒ Ⓓ	165	Ⓐ Ⓑ Ⓒ Ⓓ	175	Ⓐ Ⓑ Ⓒ Ⓓ	185	Ⓐ Ⓑ Ⓒ Ⓓ	195	Ⓐ Ⓑ Ⓒ Ⓓ
106	Ⓐ Ⓑ Ⓒ Ⓓ	116	Ⓐ Ⓑ Ⓒ Ⓓ	126	Ⓐ Ⓑ Ⓒ Ⓓ	136	Ⓐ Ⓑ Ⓒ Ⓓ	146	Ⓐ Ⓑ Ⓒ Ⓓ	156	Ⓐ Ⓑ Ⓒ Ⓓ	166	Ⓐ Ⓑ Ⓒ Ⓓ	176	Ⓐ Ⓑ Ⓒ Ⓓ	186	Ⓐ Ⓑ Ⓒ Ⓓ	196	Ⓐ Ⓑ Ⓒ Ⓓ
107	Ⓐ Ⓑ Ⓒ Ⓓ	117	Ⓐ Ⓑ Ⓒ Ⓓ	127	Ⓐ Ⓑ Ⓒ Ⓓ	137	Ⓐ Ⓑ Ⓒ Ⓓ	147	Ⓐ Ⓑ Ⓒ Ⓓ	157	Ⓐ Ⓑ Ⓒ Ⓓ	167	Ⓐ Ⓑ Ⓒ Ⓓ	177	Ⓐ Ⓑ Ⓒ Ⓓ	187	Ⓐ Ⓑ Ⓒ Ⓓ	197	Ⓐ Ⓑ Ⓒ Ⓓ
108	Ⓐ Ⓑ Ⓒ Ⓓ	118	Ⓐ Ⓑ Ⓒ Ⓓ	128	Ⓐ Ⓑ Ⓒ Ⓓ	138	Ⓐ Ⓑ Ⓒ Ⓓ	148	Ⓐ Ⓑ Ⓒ Ⓓ	158	Ⓐ Ⓑ Ⓒ Ⓓ	168	Ⓐ Ⓑ Ⓒ Ⓓ	178	Ⓐ Ⓑ Ⓒ Ⓓ	188	Ⓐ Ⓑ Ⓒ Ⓓ	198	Ⓐ Ⓑ Ⓒ Ⓓ
109	Ⓐ Ⓑ Ⓒ Ⓓ	119	Ⓐ Ⓑ Ⓒ Ⓓ	129	Ⓐ Ⓑ Ⓒ Ⓓ	139	Ⓐ Ⓑ Ⓒ Ⓓ	149	Ⓐ Ⓑ Ⓒ Ⓓ	159	Ⓐ Ⓑ Ⓒ Ⓓ	169	Ⓐ Ⓑ Ⓒ Ⓓ	179	Ⓐ Ⓑ Ⓒ Ⓓ	189	Ⓐ Ⓑ Ⓒ Ⓓ	199	Ⓐ Ⓑ Ⓒ Ⓓ
110	Ⓐ Ⓑ Ⓒ Ⓓ	120	Ⓐ Ⓑ Ⓒ Ⓓ	130	Ⓐ Ⓑ Ⓒ Ⓓ	140	Ⓐ Ⓑ Ⓒ Ⓓ	150	Ⓐ Ⓑ Ⓒ Ⓓ	160	Ⓐ Ⓑ Ⓒ Ⓓ	170	Ⓐ Ⓑ Ⓒ Ⓓ	180	Ⓐ Ⓑ Ⓒ Ⓓ	190	Ⓐ Ⓑ Ⓒ Ⓓ	200	Ⓐ Ⓑ Ⓒ Ⓓ

答案紙

ACTUAL TEST 03

READING SECTION

	A	B	C	D
101	Ⓐ	Ⓑ	Ⓒ	Ⓓ
102	Ⓐ	Ⓑ	Ⓒ	Ⓓ
103	Ⓐ	Ⓑ	Ⓒ	Ⓓ
104	Ⓐ	Ⓑ	Ⓒ	Ⓓ
105	Ⓐ	Ⓑ	Ⓒ	Ⓓ
106	Ⓐ	Ⓑ	Ⓒ	Ⓓ
107	Ⓐ	Ⓑ	Ⓒ	Ⓓ
108	Ⓐ	Ⓑ	Ⓒ	Ⓓ
109	Ⓐ	Ⓑ	Ⓒ	Ⓓ
110	Ⓐ	Ⓑ	Ⓒ	Ⓓ
111	Ⓐ	Ⓑ	Ⓒ	Ⓓ
112	Ⓐ	Ⓑ	Ⓒ	Ⓓ
113	Ⓐ	Ⓑ	Ⓒ	Ⓓ
114	Ⓐ	Ⓑ	Ⓒ	Ⓓ
115	Ⓐ	Ⓑ	Ⓒ	Ⓓ
116	Ⓐ	Ⓑ	Ⓒ	Ⓓ
117	Ⓐ	Ⓑ	Ⓒ	Ⓓ
118	Ⓐ	Ⓑ	Ⓒ	Ⓓ
119	Ⓐ	Ⓑ	Ⓒ	Ⓓ
120	Ⓐ	Ⓑ	Ⓒ	Ⓓ
121	Ⓐ	Ⓑ	Ⓒ	Ⓓ
122	Ⓐ	Ⓑ	Ⓒ	Ⓓ
123	Ⓐ	Ⓑ	Ⓒ	Ⓓ
124	Ⓐ	Ⓑ	Ⓒ	Ⓓ
125	Ⓐ	Ⓑ	Ⓒ	Ⓓ
126	Ⓐ	Ⓑ	Ⓒ	Ⓓ
127	Ⓐ	Ⓑ	Ⓒ	Ⓓ
128	Ⓐ	Ⓑ	Ⓒ	Ⓓ
129	Ⓐ	Ⓑ	Ⓒ	Ⓓ
130	Ⓐ	Ⓑ	Ⓒ	Ⓓ
131	Ⓐ	Ⓑ	Ⓒ	Ⓓ
132	Ⓐ	Ⓑ	Ⓒ	Ⓓ
133	Ⓐ	Ⓑ	Ⓒ	Ⓓ
134	Ⓐ	Ⓑ	Ⓒ	Ⓓ
135	Ⓐ	Ⓑ	Ⓒ	Ⓓ
136	Ⓐ	Ⓑ	Ⓒ	Ⓓ
137	Ⓐ	Ⓑ	Ⓒ	Ⓓ
138	Ⓐ	Ⓑ	Ⓒ	Ⓓ
139	Ⓐ	Ⓑ	Ⓒ	Ⓓ
140	Ⓐ	Ⓑ	Ⓒ	Ⓓ
141	Ⓐ	Ⓑ	Ⓒ	Ⓓ
142	Ⓐ	Ⓑ	Ⓒ	Ⓓ
143	Ⓐ	Ⓑ	Ⓒ	Ⓓ
144	Ⓐ	Ⓑ	Ⓒ	Ⓓ
145	Ⓐ	Ⓑ	Ⓒ	Ⓓ
146	Ⓐ	Ⓑ	Ⓒ	Ⓓ
147	Ⓐ	Ⓑ	Ⓒ	Ⓓ
148	Ⓐ	Ⓑ	Ⓒ	Ⓓ
149	Ⓐ	Ⓑ	Ⓒ	Ⓓ
150	Ⓐ	Ⓑ	Ⓒ	Ⓓ
151	Ⓐ	Ⓑ	Ⓒ	Ⓓ
152	Ⓐ	Ⓑ	Ⓒ	Ⓓ
153	Ⓐ	Ⓑ	Ⓒ	Ⓓ
154	Ⓐ	Ⓑ	Ⓒ	Ⓓ
155	Ⓐ	Ⓑ	Ⓒ	Ⓓ
156	Ⓐ	Ⓑ	Ⓒ	Ⓓ
157	Ⓐ	Ⓑ	Ⓒ	Ⓓ
158	Ⓐ	Ⓑ	Ⓒ	Ⓓ
159	Ⓐ	Ⓑ	Ⓒ	Ⓓ
160	Ⓐ	Ⓑ	Ⓒ	Ⓓ
161	Ⓐ	Ⓑ	Ⓒ	Ⓓ
162	Ⓐ	Ⓑ	Ⓒ	Ⓓ
163	Ⓐ	Ⓑ	Ⓒ	Ⓓ
164	Ⓐ	Ⓑ	Ⓒ	Ⓓ
165	Ⓐ	Ⓑ	Ⓒ	Ⓓ
166	Ⓐ	Ⓑ	Ⓒ	Ⓓ
167	Ⓐ	Ⓑ	Ⓒ	Ⓓ
168	Ⓐ	Ⓑ	Ⓒ	Ⓓ
169	Ⓐ	Ⓑ	Ⓒ	Ⓓ
170	Ⓐ	Ⓑ	Ⓒ	Ⓓ
171	Ⓐ	Ⓑ	Ⓒ	Ⓓ
172	Ⓐ	Ⓑ	Ⓒ	Ⓓ
173	Ⓐ	Ⓑ	Ⓒ	Ⓓ
174	Ⓐ	Ⓑ	Ⓒ	Ⓓ
175	Ⓐ	Ⓑ	Ⓒ	Ⓓ
176	Ⓐ	Ⓑ	Ⓒ	Ⓓ
177	Ⓐ	Ⓑ	Ⓒ	Ⓓ
178	Ⓐ	Ⓑ	Ⓒ	Ⓓ
179	Ⓐ	Ⓑ	Ⓒ	Ⓓ
180	Ⓐ	Ⓑ	Ⓒ	Ⓓ
181	Ⓐ	Ⓑ	Ⓒ	Ⓓ
182	Ⓐ	Ⓑ	Ⓒ	Ⓓ
183	Ⓐ	Ⓑ	Ⓒ	Ⓓ
184	Ⓐ	Ⓑ	Ⓒ	Ⓓ
185	Ⓐ	Ⓑ	Ⓒ	Ⓓ
186	Ⓐ	Ⓑ	Ⓒ	Ⓓ
187	Ⓐ	Ⓑ	Ⓒ	Ⓓ
188	Ⓐ	Ⓑ	Ⓒ	Ⓓ
189	Ⓐ	Ⓑ	Ⓒ	Ⓓ
190	Ⓐ	Ⓑ	Ⓒ	Ⓓ
191	Ⓐ	Ⓑ	Ⓒ	Ⓓ
192	Ⓐ	Ⓑ	Ⓒ	Ⓓ
193	Ⓐ	Ⓑ	Ⓒ	Ⓓ
194	Ⓐ	Ⓑ	Ⓒ	Ⓓ
195	Ⓐ	Ⓑ	Ⓒ	Ⓓ
196	Ⓐ	Ⓑ	Ⓒ	Ⓓ
197	Ⓐ	Ⓑ	Ⓒ	Ⓓ
198	Ⓐ	Ⓑ	Ⓒ	Ⓓ
199	Ⓐ	Ⓑ	Ⓒ	Ⓓ
200	Ⓐ	Ⓑ	Ⓒ	Ⓓ

ACTUAL TEST 04

READING SECTION

	A	B	C	D
101	Ⓐ	Ⓑ	Ⓒ	Ⓓ
102	Ⓐ	Ⓑ	Ⓒ	Ⓓ
103	Ⓐ	Ⓑ	Ⓒ	Ⓓ
104	Ⓐ	Ⓑ	Ⓒ	Ⓓ
105	Ⓐ	Ⓑ	Ⓒ	Ⓓ
106	Ⓐ	Ⓑ	Ⓒ	Ⓓ
107	Ⓐ	Ⓑ	Ⓒ	Ⓓ
108	Ⓐ	Ⓑ	Ⓒ	Ⓓ
109	Ⓐ	Ⓑ	Ⓒ	Ⓓ
110	Ⓐ	Ⓑ	Ⓒ	Ⓓ
111	Ⓐ	Ⓑ	Ⓒ	Ⓓ
112	Ⓐ	Ⓑ	Ⓒ	Ⓓ
113	Ⓐ	Ⓑ	Ⓒ	Ⓓ
114	Ⓐ	Ⓑ	Ⓒ	Ⓓ
115	Ⓐ	Ⓑ	Ⓒ	Ⓓ
116	Ⓐ	Ⓑ	Ⓒ	Ⓓ
117	Ⓐ	Ⓑ	Ⓒ	Ⓓ
118	Ⓐ	Ⓑ	Ⓒ	Ⓓ
119	Ⓐ	Ⓑ	Ⓒ	Ⓓ
120	Ⓐ	Ⓑ	Ⓒ	Ⓓ
121	Ⓐ	Ⓑ	Ⓒ	Ⓓ
122	Ⓐ	Ⓑ	Ⓒ	Ⓓ
123	Ⓐ	Ⓑ	Ⓒ	Ⓓ
124	Ⓐ	Ⓑ	Ⓒ	Ⓓ
125	Ⓐ	Ⓑ	Ⓒ	Ⓓ
126	Ⓐ	Ⓑ	Ⓒ	Ⓓ
127	Ⓐ	Ⓑ	Ⓒ	Ⓓ
128	Ⓐ	Ⓑ	Ⓒ	Ⓓ
129	Ⓐ	Ⓑ	Ⓒ	Ⓓ
130	Ⓐ	Ⓑ	Ⓒ	Ⓓ
131	Ⓐ	Ⓑ	Ⓒ	Ⓓ
132	Ⓐ	Ⓑ	Ⓒ	Ⓓ
133	Ⓐ	Ⓑ	Ⓒ	Ⓓ
134	Ⓐ	Ⓑ	Ⓒ	Ⓓ
135	Ⓐ	Ⓑ	Ⓒ	Ⓓ
136	Ⓐ	Ⓑ	Ⓒ	Ⓓ
137	Ⓐ	Ⓑ	Ⓒ	Ⓓ
138	Ⓐ	Ⓑ	Ⓒ	Ⓓ
139	Ⓐ	Ⓑ	Ⓒ	Ⓓ
140	Ⓐ	Ⓑ	Ⓒ	Ⓓ
141	Ⓐ	Ⓑ	Ⓒ	Ⓓ
142	Ⓐ	Ⓑ	Ⓒ	Ⓓ
143	Ⓐ	Ⓑ	Ⓒ	Ⓓ
144	Ⓐ	Ⓑ	Ⓒ	Ⓓ
145	Ⓐ	Ⓑ	Ⓒ	Ⓓ
146	Ⓐ	Ⓑ	Ⓒ	Ⓓ
147	Ⓐ	Ⓑ	Ⓒ	Ⓓ
148	Ⓐ	Ⓑ	Ⓒ	Ⓓ
149	Ⓐ	Ⓑ	Ⓒ	Ⓓ
150	Ⓐ	Ⓑ	Ⓒ	Ⓓ
151	Ⓐ	Ⓑ	Ⓒ	Ⓓ
152	Ⓐ	Ⓑ	Ⓒ	Ⓓ
153	Ⓐ	Ⓑ	Ⓒ	Ⓓ
154	Ⓐ	Ⓑ	Ⓒ	Ⓓ
155	Ⓐ	Ⓑ	Ⓒ	Ⓓ
156	Ⓐ	Ⓑ	Ⓒ	Ⓓ
157	Ⓐ	Ⓑ	Ⓒ	Ⓓ
158	Ⓐ	Ⓑ	Ⓒ	Ⓓ
159	Ⓐ	Ⓑ	Ⓒ	Ⓓ
160	Ⓐ	Ⓑ	Ⓒ	Ⓓ
161	Ⓐ	Ⓑ	Ⓒ	Ⓓ
162	Ⓐ	Ⓑ	Ⓒ	Ⓓ
163	Ⓐ	Ⓑ	Ⓒ	Ⓓ
164	Ⓐ	Ⓑ	Ⓒ	Ⓓ
165	Ⓐ	Ⓑ	Ⓒ	Ⓓ
166	Ⓐ	Ⓑ	Ⓒ	Ⓓ
167	Ⓐ	Ⓑ	Ⓒ	Ⓓ
168	Ⓐ	Ⓑ	Ⓒ	Ⓓ
169	Ⓐ	Ⓑ	Ⓒ	Ⓓ
170	Ⓐ	Ⓑ	Ⓒ	Ⓓ
171	Ⓐ	Ⓑ	Ⓒ	Ⓓ
172	Ⓐ	Ⓑ	Ⓒ	Ⓓ
173	Ⓐ	Ⓑ	Ⓒ	Ⓓ
174	Ⓐ	Ⓑ	Ⓒ	Ⓓ
175	Ⓐ	Ⓑ	Ⓒ	Ⓓ
176	Ⓐ	Ⓑ	Ⓒ	Ⓓ
177	Ⓐ	Ⓑ	Ⓒ	Ⓓ
178	Ⓐ	Ⓑ	Ⓒ	Ⓓ
179	Ⓐ	Ⓑ	Ⓒ	Ⓓ
180	Ⓐ	Ⓑ	Ⓒ	Ⓓ
181	Ⓐ	Ⓑ	Ⓒ	Ⓓ
182	Ⓐ	Ⓑ	Ⓒ	Ⓓ
183	Ⓐ	Ⓑ	Ⓒ	Ⓓ
184	Ⓐ	Ⓑ	Ⓒ	Ⓓ
185	Ⓐ	Ⓑ	Ⓒ	Ⓓ
186	Ⓐ	Ⓑ	Ⓒ	Ⓓ
187	Ⓐ	Ⓑ	Ⓒ	Ⓓ
188	Ⓐ	Ⓑ	Ⓒ	Ⓓ
189	Ⓐ	Ⓑ	Ⓒ	Ⓓ
190	Ⓐ	Ⓑ	Ⓒ	Ⓓ
191	Ⓐ	Ⓑ	Ⓒ	Ⓓ
192	Ⓐ	Ⓑ	Ⓒ	Ⓓ
193	Ⓐ	Ⓑ	Ⓒ	Ⓓ
194	Ⓐ	Ⓑ	Ⓒ	Ⓓ
195	Ⓐ	Ⓑ	Ⓒ	Ⓓ
196	Ⓐ	Ⓑ	Ⓒ	Ⓓ
197	Ⓐ	Ⓑ	Ⓒ	Ⓓ
198	Ⓐ	Ⓑ	Ⓒ	Ⓓ
199	Ⓐ	Ⓑ	Ⓒ	Ⓓ
200	Ⓐ	Ⓑ	Ⓒ	Ⓓ

ACTUAL TEST 05

READING SECTION

#		#		#		#		#		#		#		#		#		#	
101	Ⓐ Ⓑ Ⓒ Ⓓ	111	Ⓐ Ⓑ Ⓒ Ⓓ	121	Ⓐ Ⓑ Ⓒ Ⓓ	131	Ⓐ Ⓑ Ⓒ Ⓓ	141	Ⓐ Ⓑ Ⓒ Ⓓ	151	Ⓐ Ⓑ Ⓒ Ⓓ	161	Ⓐ Ⓑ Ⓒ Ⓓ	171	Ⓐ Ⓑ Ⓒ Ⓓ	181	Ⓐ Ⓑ Ⓒ Ⓓ	191	Ⓐ Ⓑ Ⓒ Ⓓ
102	Ⓐ Ⓑ Ⓒ Ⓓ	112	Ⓐ Ⓑ Ⓒ Ⓓ	122	Ⓐ Ⓑ Ⓒ Ⓓ	132	Ⓐ Ⓑ Ⓒ Ⓓ	142	Ⓐ Ⓑ Ⓒ Ⓓ	152	Ⓐ Ⓑ Ⓒ Ⓓ	162	Ⓐ Ⓑ Ⓒ Ⓓ	172	Ⓐ Ⓑ Ⓒ Ⓓ	182	Ⓐ Ⓑ Ⓒ Ⓓ	192	Ⓐ Ⓑ Ⓒ Ⓓ
103	Ⓐ Ⓑ Ⓒ Ⓓ	113	Ⓐ Ⓑ Ⓒ Ⓓ	123	Ⓐ Ⓑ Ⓒ Ⓓ	133	Ⓐ Ⓑ Ⓒ Ⓓ	143	Ⓐ Ⓑ Ⓒ Ⓓ	153	Ⓐ Ⓑ Ⓒ Ⓓ	163	Ⓐ Ⓑ Ⓒ Ⓓ	173	Ⓐ Ⓑ Ⓒ Ⓓ	183	Ⓐ Ⓑ Ⓒ Ⓓ	193	Ⓐ Ⓑ Ⓒ Ⓓ
104	Ⓐ Ⓑ Ⓒ Ⓓ	114	Ⓐ Ⓑ Ⓒ Ⓓ	124	Ⓐ Ⓑ Ⓒ Ⓓ	134	Ⓐ Ⓑ Ⓒ Ⓓ	144	Ⓐ Ⓑ Ⓒ Ⓓ	154	Ⓐ Ⓑ Ⓒ Ⓓ	164	Ⓐ Ⓑ Ⓒ Ⓓ	174	Ⓐ Ⓑ Ⓒ Ⓓ	184	Ⓐ Ⓑ Ⓒ Ⓓ	194	Ⓐ Ⓑ Ⓒ Ⓓ
105	Ⓐ Ⓑ Ⓒ Ⓓ	115	Ⓐ Ⓑ Ⓒ Ⓓ	125	Ⓐ Ⓑ Ⓒ Ⓓ	135	Ⓐ Ⓑ Ⓒ Ⓓ	145	Ⓐ Ⓑ Ⓒ Ⓓ	155	Ⓐ Ⓑ Ⓒ Ⓓ	165	Ⓐ Ⓑ Ⓒ Ⓓ	175	Ⓐ Ⓑ Ⓒ Ⓓ	185	Ⓐ Ⓑ Ⓒ Ⓓ	195	Ⓐ Ⓑ Ⓒ Ⓓ
106	Ⓐ Ⓑ Ⓒ Ⓓ	116	Ⓐ Ⓑ Ⓒ Ⓓ	126	Ⓐ Ⓑ Ⓒ Ⓓ	136	Ⓐ Ⓑ Ⓒ Ⓓ	146	Ⓐ Ⓑ Ⓒ Ⓓ	156	Ⓐ Ⓑ Ⓒ Ⓓ	166	Ⓐ Ⓑ Ⓒ Ⓓ	176	Ⓐ Ⓑ Ⓒ Ⓓ	186	Ⓐ Ⓑ Ⓒ Ⓓ	196	Ⓐ Ⓑ Ⓒ Ⓓ
107	Ⓐ Ⓑ Ⓒ Ⓓ	117	Ⓐ Ⓑ Ⓒ Ⓓ	127	Ⓐ Ⓑ Ⓒ Ⓓ	137	Ⓐ Ⓑ Ⓒ Ⓓ	147	Ⓐ Ⓑ Ⓒ Ⓓ	157	Ⓐ Ⓑ Ⓒ Ⓓ	167	Ⓐ Ⓑ Ⓒ Ⓓ	177	Ⓐ Ⓑ Ⓒ Ⓓ	187	Ⓐ Ⓑ Ⓒ Ⓓ	197	Ⓐ Ⓑ Ⓒ Ⓓ
108	Ⓐ Ⓑ Ⓒ Ⓓ	118	Ⓐ Ⓑ Ⓒ Ⓓ	128	Ⓐ Ⓑ Ⓒ Ⓓ	138	Ⓐ Ⓑ Ⓒ Ⓓ	148	Ⓐ Ⓑ Ⓒ Ⓓ	158	Ⓐ Ⓑ Ⓒ Ⓓ	168	Ⓐ Ⓑ Ⓒ Ⓓ	178	Ⓐ Ⓑ Ⓒ Ⓓ	188	Ⓐ Ⓑ Ⓒ Ⓓ	198	Ⓐ Ⓑ Ⓒ Ⓓ
109	Ⓐ Ⓑ Ⓒ Ⓓ	119	Ⓐ Ⓑ Ⓒ Ⓓ	129	Ⓐ Ⓑ Ⓒ Ⓓ	139	Ⓐ Ⓑ Ⓒ Ⓓ	149	Ⓐ Ⓑ Ⓒ Ⓓ	159	Ⓐ Ⓑ Ⓒ Ⓓ	169	Ⓐ Ⓑ Ⓒ Ⓓ	179	Ⓐ Ⓑ Ⓒ Ⓓ	189	Ⓐ Ⓑ Ⓒ Ⓓ	199	Ⓐ Ⓑ Ⓒ Ⓓ
110	Ⓐ Ⓑ Ⓒ Ⓓ	120	Ⓐ Ⓑ Ⓒ Ⓓ	130	Ⓐ Ⓑ Ⓒ Ⓓ	140	Ⓐ Ⓑ Ⓒ Ⓓ	150	Ⓐ Ⓑ Ⓒ Ⓓ	160	Ⓐ Ⓑ Ⓒ Ⓓ	170	Ⓐ Ⓑ Ⓒ Ⓓ	180	Ⓐ Ⓑ Ⓒ Ⓓ	190	Ⓐ Ⓑ Ⓒ Ⓓ	200	Ⓐ Ⓑ Ⓒ Ⓓ

ACTUAL TEST 06

READING SECTION

#		#		#		#		#		#		#		#		#		#	
101	Ⓐ Ⓑ Ⓒ Ⓓ	111	Ⓐ Ⓑ Ⓒ Ⓓ	121	Ⓐ Ⓑ Ⓒ Ⓓ	131	Ⓐ Ⓑ Ⓒ Ⓓ	141	Ⓐ Ⓑ Ⓒ Ⓓ	151	Ⓐ Ⓑ Ⓒ Ⓓ	161	Ⓐ Ⓑ Ⓒ Ⓓ	171	Ⓐ Ⓑ Ⓒ Ⓓ	181	Ⓐ Ⓑ Ⓒ Ⓓ	191	Ⓐ Ⓑ Ⓒ Ⓓ
102	Ⓐ Ⓑ Ⓒ Ⓓ	112	Ⓐ Ⓑ Ⓒ Ⓓ	122	Ⓐ Ⓑ Ⓒ Ⓓ	132	Ⓐ Ⓑ Ⓒ Ⓓ	142	Ⓐ Ⓑ Ⓒ Ⓓ	152	Ⓐ Ⓑ Ⓒ Ⓓ	162	Ⓐ Ⓑ Ⓒ Ⓓ	172	Ⓐ Ⓑ Ⓒ Ⓓ	182	Ⓐ Ⓑ Ⓒ Ⓓ	192	Ⓐ Ⓑ Ⓒ Ⓓ
103	Ⓐ Ⓑ Ⓒ Ⓓ	113	Ⓐ Ⓑ Ⓒ Ⓓ	123	Ⓐ Ⓑ Ⓒ Ⓓ	133	Ⓐ Ⓑ Ⓒ Ⓓ	143	Ⓐ Ⓑ Ⓒ Ⓓ	153	Ⓐ Ⓑ Ⓒ Ⓓ	163	Ⓐ Ⓑ Ⓒ Ⓓ	173	Ⓐ Ⓑ Ⓒ Ⓓ	183	Ⓐ Ⓑ Ⓒ Ⓓ	193	Ⓐ Ⓑ Ⓒ Ⓓ
104	Ⓐ Ⓑ Ⓒ Ⓓ	114	Ⓐ Ⓑ Ⓒ Ⓓ	124	Ⓐ Ⓑ Ⓒ Ⓓ	134	Ⓐ Ⓑ Ⓒ Ⓓ	144	Ⓐ Ⓑ Ⓒ Ⓓ	154	Ⓐ Ⓑ Ⓒ Ⓓ	164	Ⓐ Ⓑ Ⓒ Ⓓ	174	Ⓐ Ⓑ Ⓒ Ⓓ	184	Ⓐ Ⓑ Ⓒ Ⓓ	194	Ⓐ Ⓑ Ⓒ Ⓓ
105	Ⓐ Ⓑ Ⓒ Ⓓ	115	Ⓐ Ⓑ Ⓒ Ⓓ	125	Ⓐ Ⓑ Ⓒ Ⓓ	135	Ⓐ Ⓑ Ⓒ Ⓓ	145	Ⓐ Ⓑ Ⓒ Ⓓ	155	Ⓐ Ⓑ Ⓒ Ⓓ	165	Ⓐ Ⓑ Ⓒ Ⓓ	175	Ⓐ Ⓑ Ⓒ Ⓓ	185	Ⓐ Ⓑ Ⓒ Ⓓ	195	Ⓐ Ⓑ Ⓒ Ⓓ
106	Ⓐ Ⓑ Ⓒ Ⓓ	116	Ⓐ Ⓑ Ⓒ Ⓓ	126	Ⓐ Ⓑ Ⓒ Ⓓ	136	Ⓐ Ⓑ Ⓒ Ⓓ	146	Ⓐ Ⓑ Ⓒ Ⓓ	156	Ⓐ Ⓑ Ⓒ Ⓓ	166	Ⓐ Ⓑ Ⓒ Ⓓ	176	Ⓐ Ⓑ Ⓒ Ⓓ	186	Ⓐ Ⓑ Ⓒ Ⓓ	196	Ⓐ Ⓑ Ⓒ Ⓓ
107	Ⓐ Ⓑ Ⓒ Ⓓ	117	Ⓐ Ⓑ Ⓒ Ⓓ	127	Ⓐ Ⓑ Ⓒ Ⓓ	137	Ⓐ Ⓑ Ⓒ Ⓓ	147	Ⓐ Ⓑ Ⓒ Ⓓ	157	Ⓐ Ⓑ Ⓒ Ⓓ	167	Ⓐ Ⓑ Ⓒ Ⓓ	177	Ⓐ Ⓑ Ⓒ Ⓓ	187	Ⓐ Ⓑ Ⓒ Ⓓ	197	Ⓐ Ⓑ Ⓒ Ⓓ
108	Ⓐ Ⓑ Ⓒ Ⓓ	118	Ⓐ Ⓑ Ⓒ Ⓓ	128	Ⓐ Ⓑ Ⓒ Ⓓ	138	Ⓐ Ⓑ Ⓒ Ⓓ	148	Ⓐ Ⓑ Ⓒ Ⓓ	158	Ⓐ Ⓑ Ⓒ Ⓓ	168	Ⓐ Ⓑ Ⓒ Ⓓ	178	Ⓐ Ⓑ Ⓒ Ⓓ	188	Ⓐ Ⓑ Ⓒ Ⓓ	198	Ⓐ Ⓑ Ⓒ Ⓓ
109	Ⓐ Ⓑ Ⓒ Ⓓ	119	Ⓐ Ⓑ Ⓒ Ⓓ	129	Ⓐ Ⓑ Ⓒ Ⓓ	139	Ⓐ Ⓑ Ⓒ Ⓓ	149	Ⓐ Ⓑ Ⓒ Ⓓ	159	Ⓐ Ⓑ Ⓒ Ⓓ	169	Ⓐ Ⓑ Ⓒ Ⓓ	179	Ⓐ Ⓑ Ⓒ Ⓓ	189	Ⓐ Ⓑ Ⓒ Ⓓ	199	Ⓐ Ⓑ Ⓒ Ⓓ
110	Ⓐ Ⓑ Ⓒ Ⓓ	120	Ⓐ Ⓑ Ⓒ Ⓓ	130	Ⓐ Ⓑ Ⓒ Ⓓ	140	Ⓐ Ⓑ Ⓒ Ⓓ	150	Ⓐ Ⓑ Ⓒ Ⓓ	160	Ⓐ Ⓑ Ⓒ Ⓓ	170	Ⓐ Ⓑ Ⓒ Ⓓ	180	Ⓐ Ⓑ Ⓒ Ⓓ	190	Ⓐ Ⓑ Ⓒ Ⓓ	200	Ⓐ Ⓑ Ⓒ Ⓓ

答案紙

ACTUAL TEST 07

READING SECTION

101 Ⓐ Ⓑ Ⓒ Ⓓ	111 Ⓐ Ⓑ Ⓒ Ⓓ	121 Ⓐ Ⓑ Ⓒ Ⓓ	131 Ⓐ Ⓑ Ⓒ Ⓓ	141 Ⓐ Ⓑ Ⓒ Ⓓ	151 Ⓐ Ⓑ Ⓒ Ⓓ	161 Ⓐ Ⓑ Ⓒ Ⓓ	171 Ⓐ Ⓑ Ⓒ Ⓓ	181 Ⓐ Ⓑ Ⓒ Ⓓ	191 Ⓐ Ⓑ Ⓒ Ⓓ
102 Ⓐ Ⓑ Ⓒ Ⓓ	112 Ⓐ Ⓑ Ⓒ Ⓓ	122 Ⓐ Ⓑ Ⓒ Ⓓ	132 Ⓐ Ⓑ Ⓒ Ⓓ	142 Ⓐ Ⓑ Ⓒ Ⓓ	152 Ⓐ Ⓑ Ⓒ Ⓓ	162 Ⓐ Ⓑ Ⓒ Ⓓ	172 Ⓐ Ⓑ Ⓒ Ⓓ	182 Ⓐ Ⓑ Ⓒ Ⓓ	192 Ⓐ Ⓑ Ⓒ Ⓓ
103 Ⓐ Ⓑ Ⓒ Ⓓ	113 Ⓐ Ⓑ Ⓒ Ⓓ	123 Ⓐ Ⓑ Ⓒ Ⓓ	133 Ⓐ Ⓑ Ⓒ Ⓓ	143 Ⓐ Ⓑ Ⓒ Ⓓ	153 Ⓐ Ⓑ Ⓒ Ⓓ	163 Ⓐ Ⓑ Ⓒ Ⓓ	173 Ⓐ Ⓑ Ⓒ Ⓓ	183 Ⓐ Ⓑ Ⓒ Ⓓ	193 Ⓐ Ⓑ Ⓒ Ⓓ
104 Ⓐ Ⓑ Ⓒ Ⓓ	114 Ⓐ Ⓑ Ⓒ Ⓓ	124 Ⓐ Ⓑ Ⓒ Ⓓ	134 Ⓐ Ⓑ Ⓒ Ⓓ	144 Ⓐ Ⓑ Ⓒ Ⓓ	154 Ⓐ Ⓑ Ⓒ Ⓓ	164 Ⓐ Ⓑ Ⓒ Ⓓ	174 Ⓐ Ⓑ Ⓒ Ⓓ	184 Ⓐ Ⓑ Ⓒ Ⓓ	194 Ⓐ Ⓑ Ⓒ Ⓓ
105 Ⓐ Ⓑ Ⓒ Ⓓ	115 Ⓐ Ⓑ Ⓒ Ⓓ	125 Ⓐ Ⓑ Ⓒ Ⓓ	135 Ⓐ Ⓑ Ⓒ Ⓓ	145 Ⓐ Ⓑ Ⓒ Ⓓ	155 Ⓐ Ⓑ Ⓒ Ⓓ	165 Ⓐ Ⓑ Ⓒ Ⓓ	175 Ⓐ Ⓑ Ⓒ Ⓓ	185 Ⓐ Ⓑ Ⓒ Ⓓ	195 Ⓐ Ⓑ Ⓒ Ⓓ
106 Ⓐ Ⓑ Ⓒ Ⓓ	116 Ⓐ Ⓑ Ⓒ Ⓓ	126 Ⓐ Ⓑ Ⓒ Ⓓ	136 Ⓐ Ⓑ Ⓒ Ⓓ	146 Ⓐ Ⓑ Ⓒ Ⓓ	156 Ⓐ Ⓑ Ⓒ Ⓓ	166 Ⓐ Ⓑ Ⓒ Ⓓ	176 Ⓐ Ⓑ Ⓒ Ⓓ	186 Ⓐ Ⓑ Ⓒ Ⓓ	196 Ⓐ Ⓑ Ⓒ Ⓓ
107 Ⓐ Ⓑ Ⓒ Ⓓ	117 Ⓐ Ⓑ Ⓒ Ⓓ	127 Ⓐ Ⓑ Ⓒ Ⓓ	137 Ⓐ Ⓑ Ⓒ Ⓓ	147 Ⓐ Ⓑ Ⓒ Ⓓ	157 Ⓐ Ⓑ Ⓒ Ⓓ	167 Ⓐ Ⓑ Ⓒ Ⓓ	177 Ⓐ Ⓑ Ⓒ Ⓓ	187 Ⓐ Ⓑ Ⓒ Ⓓ	197 Ⓐ Ⓑ Ⓒ Ⓓ
108 Ⓐ Ⓑ Ⓒ Ⓓ	118 Ⓐ Ⓑ Ⓒ Ⓓ	128 Ⓐ Ⓑ Ⓒ Ⓓ	138 Ⓐ Ⓑ Ⓒ Ⓓ	148 Ⓐ Ⓑ Ⓒ Ⓓ	158 Ⓐ Ⓑ Ⓒ Ⓓ	168 Ⓐ Ⓑ Ⓒ Ⓓ	178 Ⓐ Ⓑ Ⓒ Ⓓ	188 Ⓐ Ⓑ Ⓒ Ⓓ	198 Ⓐ Ⓑ Ⓒ Ⓓ
109 Ⓐ Ⓑ Ⓒ Ⓓ	119 Ⓐ Ⓑ Ⓒ Ⓓ	129 Ⓐ Ⓑ Ⓒ Ⓓ	139 Ⓐ Ⓑ Ⓒ Ⓓ	149 Ⓐ Ⓑ Ⓒ Ⓓ	159 Ⓐ Ⓑ Ⓒ Ⓓ	169 Ⓐ Ⓑ Ⓒ Ⓓ	179 Ⓐ Ⓑ Ⓒ Ⓓ	189 Ⓐ Ⓑ Ⓒ Ⓓ	199 Ⓐ Ⓑ Ⓒ Ⓓ
110 Ⓐ Ⓑ Ⓒ Ⓓ	120 Ⓐ Ⓑ Ⓒ Ⓓ	130 Ⓐ Ⓑ Ⓒ Ⓓ	140 Ⓐ Ⓑ Ⓒ Ⓓ	150 Ⓐ Ⓑ Ⓒ Ⓓ	160 Ⓐ Ⓑ Ⓒ Ⓓ	170 Ⓐ Ⓑ Ⓒ Ⓓ	180 Ⓐ Ⓑ Ⓒ Ⓓ	190 Ⓐ Ⓑ Ⓒ Ⓓ	200 Ⓐ Ⓑ Ⓒ Ⓓ

ACTUAL TEST 08

READING SECTION

101 Ⓐ Ⓑ Ⓒ Ⓓ	111 Ⓐ Ⓑ Ⓒ Ⓓ	121 Ⓐ Ⓑ Ⓒ Ⓓ	131 Ⓐ Ⓑ Ⓒ Ⓓ	141 Ⓐ Ⓑ Ⓒ Ⓓ	151 Ⓐ Ⓑ Ⓒ Ⓓ	161 Ⓐ Ⓑ Ⓒ Ⓓ	171 Ⓐ Ⓑ Ⓒ Ⓓ	181 Ⓐ Ⓑ Ⓒ Ⓓ	191 Ⓐ Ⓑ Ⓒ Ⓓ
102 Ⓐ Ⓑ Ⓒ Ⓓ	112 Ⓐ Ⓑ Ⓒ Ⓓ	122 Ⓐ Ⓑ Ⓒ Ⓓ	132 Ⓐ Ⓑ Ⓒ Ⓓ	142 Ⓐ Ⓑ Ⓒ Ⓓ	152 Ⓐ Ⓑ Ⓒ Ⓓ	162 Ⓐ Ⓑ Ⓒ Ⓓ	172 Ⓐ Ⓑ Ⓒ Ⓓ	182 Ⓐ Ⓑ Ⓒ Ⓓ	192 Ⓐ Ⓑ Ⓒ Ⓓ
103 Ⓐ Ⓑ Ⓒ Ⓓ	113 Ⓐ Ⓑ Ⓒ Ⓓ	123 Ⓐ Ⓑ Ⓒ Ⓓ	133 Ⓐ Ⓑ Ⓒ Ⓓ	143 Ⓐ Ⓑ Ⓒ Ⓓ	153 Ⓐ Ⓑ Ⓒ Ⓓ	163 Ⓐ Ⓑ Ⓒ Ⓓ	173 Ⓐ Ⓑ Ⓒ Ⓓ	183 Ⓐ Ⓑ Ⓒ Ⓓ	193 Ⓐ Ⓑ Ⓒ Ⓓ
104 Ⓐ Ⓑ Ⓒ Ⓓ	114 Ⓐ Ⓑ Ⓒ Ⓓ	124 Ⓐ Ⓑ Ⓒ Ⓓ	134 Ⓐ Ⓑ Ⓒ Ⓓ	144 Ⓐ Ⓑ Ⓒ Ⓓ	154 Ⓐ Ⓑ Ⓒ Ⓓ	164 Ⓐ Ⓑ Ⓒ Ⓓ	174 Ⓐ Ⓑ Ⓒ Ⓓ	184 Ⓐ Ⓑ Ⓒ Ⓓ	194 Ⓐ Ⓑ Ⓒ Ⓓ
105 Ⓐ Ⓑ Ⓒ Ⓓ	115 Ⓐ Ⓑ Ⓒ Ⓓ	125 Ⓐ Ⓑ Ⓒ Ⓓ	135 Ⓐ Ⓑ Ⓒ Ⓓ	145 Ⓐ Ⓑ Ⓒ Ⓓ	155 Ⓐ Ⓑ Ⓒ Ⓓ	165 Ⓐ Ⓑ Ⓒ Ⓓ	175 Ⓐ Ⓑ Ⓒ Ⓓ	185 Ⓐ Ⓑ Ⓒ Ⓓ	195 Ⓐ Ⓑ Ⓒ Ⓓ
106 Ⓐ Ⓑ Ⓒ Ⓓ	116 Ⓐ Ⓑ Ⓒ Ⓓ	126 Ⓐ Ⓑ Ⓒ Ⓓ	136 Ⓐ Ⓑ Ⓒ Ⓓ	146 Ⓐ Ⓑ Ⓒ Ⓓ	156 Ⓐ Ⓑ Ⓒ Ⓓ	166 Ⓐ Ⓑ Ⓒ Ⓓ	176 Ⓐ Ⓑ Ⓒ Ⓓ	186 Ⓐ Ⓑ Ⓒ Ⓓ	196 Ⓐ Ⓑ Ⓒ Ⓓ
107 Ⓐ Ⓑ Ⓒ Ⓓ	117 Ⓐ Ⓑ Ⓒ Ⓓ	127 Ⓐ Ⓑ Ⓒ Ⓓ	137 Ⓐ Ⓑ Ⓒ Ⓓ	147 Ⓐ Ⓑ Ⓒ Ⓓ	157 Ⓐ Ⓑ Ⓒ Ⓓ	167 Ⓐ Ⓑ Ⓒ Ⓓ	177 Ⓐ Ⓑ Ⓒ Ⓓ	187 Ⓐ Ⓑ Ⓒ Ⓓ	197 Ⓐ Ⓑ Ⓒ Ⓓ
108 Ⓐ Ⓑ Ⓒ Ⓓ	118 Ⓐ Ⓑ Ⓒ Ⓓ	128 Ⓐ Ⓑ Ⓒ Ⓓ	138 Ⓐ Ⓑ Ⓒ Ⓓ	148 Ⓐ Ⓑ Ⓒ Ⓓ	158 Ⓐ Ⓑ Ⓒ Ⓓ	168 Ⓐ Ⓑ Ⓒ Ⓓ	178 Ⓐ Ⓑ Ⓒ Ⓓ	188 Ⓐ Ⓑ Ⓒ Ⓓ	198 Ⓐ Ⓑ Ⓒ Ⓓ
109 Ⓐ Ⓑ Ⓒ Ⓓ	119 Ⓐ Ⓑ Ⓒ Ⓓ	129 Ⓐ Ⓑ Ⓒ Ⓓ	139 Ⓐ Ⓑ Ⓒ Ⓓ	149 Ⓐ Ⓑ Ⓒ Ⓓ	159 Ⓐ Ⓑ Ⓒ Ⓓ	169 Ⓐ Ⓑ Ⓒ Ⓓ	179 Ⓐ Ⓑ Ⓒ Ⓓ	189 Ⓐ Ⓑ Ⓒ Ⓓ	199 Ⓐ Ⓑ Ⓒ Ⓓ
110 Ⓐ Ⓑ Ⓒ Ⓓ	120 Ⓐ Ⓑ Ⓒ Ⓓ	130 Ⓐ Ⓑ Ⓒ Ⓓ	140 Ⓐ Ⓑ Ⓒ Ⓓ	150 Ⓐ Ⓑ Ⓒ Ⓓ	160 Ⓐ Ⓑ Ⓒ Ⓓ	170 Ⓐ Ⓑ Ⓒ Ⓓ	180 Ⓐ Ⓑ Ⓒ Ⓓ	190 Ⓐ Ⓑ Ⓒ Ⓓ	200 Ⓐ Ⓑ Ⓒ Ⓓ

答案紙

ACTUAL TEST 09

READING SECTION

101 Ⓐ Ⓑ Ⓒ Ⓓ	111 Ⓐ Ⓑ Ⓒ Ⓓ	121 Ⓐ Ⓑ Ⓒ Ⓓ	131 Ⓐ Ⓑ Ⓒ Ⓓ	141 Ⓐ Ⓑ Ⓒ Ⓓ	151 Ⓐ Ⓑ Ⓒ Ⓓ	161 Ⓐ Ⓑ Ⓒ Ⓓ	171 Ⓐ Ⓑ Ⓒ Ⓓ	181 Ⓐ Ⓑ Ⓒ Ⓓ	191 Ⓐ Ⓑ Ⓒ Ⓓ
102 Ⓐ Ⓑ Ⓒ Ⓓ	112 Ⓐ Ⓑ Ⓒ Ⓓ	122 Ⓐ Ⓑ Ⓒ Ⓓ	132 Ⓐ Ⓑ Ⓒ Ⓓ	142 Ⓐ Ⓑ Ⓒ Ⓓ	152 Ⓐ Ⓑ Ⓒ Ⓓ	162 Ⓐ Ⓑ Ⓒ Ⓓ	172 Ⓐ Ⓑ Ⓒ Ⓓ	182 Ⓐ Ⓑ Ⓒ Ⓓ	192 Ⓐ Ⓑ Ⓒ Ⓓ
103 Ⓐ Ⓑ Ⓒ Ⓓ	113 Ⓐ Ⓑ Ⓒ Ⓓ	123 Ⓐ Ⓑ Ⓒ Ⓓ	133 Ⓐ Ⓑ Ⓒ Ⓓ	143 Ⓐ Ⓑ Ⓒ Ⓓ	153 Ⓐ Ⓑ Ⓒ Ⓓ	163 Ⓐ Ⓑ Ⓒ Ⓓ	173 Ⓐ Ⓑ Ⓒ Ⓓ	183 Ⓐ Ⓑ Ⓒ Ⓓ	193 Ⓐ Ⓑ Ⓒ Ⓓ
104 Ⓐ Ⓑ Ⓒ Ⓓ	114 Ⓐ Ⓑ Ⓒ Ⓓ	124 Ⓐ Ⓑ Ⓒ Ⓓ	134 Ⓐ Ⓑ Ⓒ Ⓓ	144 Ⓐ Ⓑ Ⓒ Ⓓ	154 Ⓐ Ⓑ Ⓒ Ⓓ	164 Ⓐ Ⓑ Ⓒ Ⓓ	174 Ⓐ Ⓑ Ⓒ Ⓓ	184 Ⓐ Ⓑ Ⓒ Ⓓ	194 Ⓐ Ⓑ Ⓒ Ⓓ
105 Ⓐ Ⓑ Ⓒ Ⓓ	115 Ⓐ Ⓑ Ⓒ Ⓓ	125 Ⓐ Ⓑ Ⓒ Ⓓ	135 Ⓐ Ⓑ Ⓒ Ⓓ	145 Ⓐ Ⓑ Ⓒ Ⓓ	155 Ⓐ Ⓑ Ⓒ Ⓓ	165 Ⓐ Ⓑ Ⓒ Ⓓ	175 Ⓐ Ⓑ Ⓒ Ⓓ	185 Ⓐ Ⓑ Ⓒ Ⓓ	195 Ⓐ Ⓑ Ⓒ Ⓓ
106 Ⓐ Ⓑ Ⓒ Ⓓ	116 Ⓐ Ⓑ Ⓒ Ⓓ	126 Ⓐ Ⓑ Ⓒ Ⓓ	136 Ⓐ Ⓑ Ⓒ Ⓓ	146 Ⓐ Ⓑ Ⓒ Ⓓ	156 Ⓐ Ⓑ Ⓒ Ⓓ	166 Ⓐ Ⓑ Ⓒ Ⓓ	176 Ⓐ Ⓑ Ⓒ Ⓓ	186 Ⓐ Ⓑ Ⓒ Ⓓ	196 Ⓐ Ⓑ Ⓒ Ⓓ
107 Ⓐ Ⓑ Ⓒ Ⓓ	117 Ⓐ Ⓑ Ⓒ Ⓓ	127 Ⓐ Ⓑ Ⓒ Ⓓ	137 Ⓐ Ⓑ Ⓒ Ⓓ	147 Ⓐ Ⓑ Ⓒ Ⓓ	157 Ⓐ Ⓑ Ⓒ Ⓓ	167 Ⓐ Ⓑ Ⓒ Ⓓ	177 Ⓐ Ⓑ Ⓒ Ⓓ	187 Ⓐ Ⓑ Ⓒ Ⓓ	197 Ⓐ Ⓑ Ⓒ Ⓓ
108 Ⓐ Ⓑ Ⓒ Ⓓ	118 Ⓐ Ⓑ Ⓒ Ⓓ	128 Ⓐ Ⓑ Ⓒ Ⓓ	138 Ⓐ Ⓑ Ⓒ Ⓓ	148 Ⓐ Ⓑ Ⓒ Ⓓ	158 Ⓐ Ⓑ Ⓒ Ⓓ	168 Ⓐ Ⓑ Ⓒ Ⓓ	178 Ⓐ Ⓑ Ⓒ Ⓓ	188 Ⓐ Ⓑ Ⓒ Ⓓ	198 Ⓐ Ⓑ Ⓒ Ⓓ
109 Ⓐ Ⓑ Ⓒ Ⓓ	119 Ⓐ Ⓑ Ⓒ Ⓓ	129 Ⓐ Ⓑ Ⓒ Ⓓ	139 Ⓐ Ⓑ Ⓒ Ⓓ	149 Ⓐ Ⓑ Ⓒ Ⓓ	159 Ⓐ Ⓑ Ⓒ Ⓓ	169 Ⓐ Ⓑ Ⓒ Ⓓ	179 Ⓐ Ⓑ Ⓒ Ⓓ	189 Ⓐ Ⓑ Ⓒ Ⓓ	199 Ⓐ Ⓑ Ⓒ Ⓓ
110 Ⓐ Ⓑ Ⓒ Ⓓ	120 Ⓐ Ⓑ Ⓒ Ⓓ	130 Ⓐ Ⓑ Ⓒ Ⓓ	140 Ⓐ Ⓑ Ⓒ Ⓓ	150 Ⓐ Ⓑ Ⓒ Ⓓ	160 Ⓐ Ⓑ Ⓒ Ⓓ	170 Ⓐ Ⓑ Ⓒ Ⓓ	180 Ⓐ Ⓑ Ⓒ Ⓓ	190 Ⓐ Ⓑ Ⓒ Ⓓ	200 Ⓐ Ⓑ Ⓒ Ⓓ

ACTUAL TEST 10

READING SECTION

101 Ⓐ Ⓑ Ⓒ Ⓓ	111 Ⓐ Ⓑ Ⓒ Ⓓ	121 Ⓐ Ⓑ Ⓒ Ⓓ	131 Ⓐ Ⓑ Ⓒ Ⓓ	141 Ⓐ Ⓑ Ⓒ Ⓓ	151 Ⓐ Ⓑ Ⓒ Ⓓ	161 Ⓐ Ⓑ Ⓒ Ⓓ	171 Ⓐ Ⓑ Ⓒ Ⓓ	181 Ⓐ Ⓑ Ⓒ Ⓓ	191 Ⓐ Ⓑ Ⓒ Ⓓ
102 Ⓐ Ⓑ Ⓒ Ⓓ	112 Ⓐ Ⓑ Ⓒ Ⓓ	122 Ⓐ Ⓑ Ⓒ Ⓓ	132 Ⓐ Ⓑ Ⓒ Ⓓ	142 Ⓐ Ⓑ Ⓒ Ⓓ	152 Ⓐ Ⓑ Ⓒ Ⓓ	162 Ⓐ Ⓑ Ⓒ Ⓓ	172 Ⓐ Ⓑ Ⓒ Ⓓ	182 Ⓐ Ⓑ Ⓒ Ⓓ	192 Ⓐ Ⓑ Ⓒ Ⓓ
103 Ⓐ Ⓑ Ⓒ Ⓓ	113 Ⓐ Ⓑ Ⓒ Ⓓ	123 Ⓐ Ⓑ Ⓒ Ⓓ	133 Ⓐ Ⓑ Ⓒ Ⓓ	143 Ⓐ Ⓑ Ⓒ Ⓓ	153 Ⓐ Ⓑ Ⓒ Ⓓ	163 Ⓐ Ⓑ Ⓒ Ⓓ	173 Ⓐ Ⓑ Ⓒ Ⓓ	183 Ⓐ Ⓑ Ⓒ Ⓓ	193 Ⓐ Ⓑ Ⓒ Ⓓ
104 Ⓐ Ⓑ Ⓒ Ⓓ	114 Ⓐ Ⓑ Ⓒ Ⓓ	124 Ⓐ Ⓑ Ⓒ Ⓓ	134 Ⓐ Ⓑ Ⓒ Ⓓ	144 Ⓐ Ⓑ Ⓒ Ⓓ	154 Ⓐ Ⓑ Ⓒ Ⓓ	164 Ⓐ Ⓑ Ⓒ Ⓓ	174 Ⓐ Ⓑ Ⓒ Ⓓ	184 Ⓐ Ⓑ Ⓒ Ⓓ	194 Ⓐ Ⓑ Ⓒ Ⓓ
105 Ⓐ Ⓑ Ⓒ Ⓓ	115 Ⓐ Ⓑ Ⓒ Ⓓ	125 Ⓐ Ⓑ Ⓒ Ⓓ	135 Ⓐ Ⓑ Ⓒ Ⓓ	145 Ⓐ Ⓑ Ⓒ Ⓓ	155 Ⓐ Ⓑ Ⓒ Ⓓ	165 Ⓐ Ⓑ Ⓒ Ⓓ	175 Ⓐ Ⓑ Ⓒ Ⓓ	185 Ⓐ Ⓑ Ⓒ Ⓓ	195 Ⓐ Ⓑ Ⓒ Ⓓ
106 Ⓐ Ⓑ Ⓒ Ⓓ	116 Ⓐ Ⓑ Ⓒ Ⓓ	126 Ⓐ Ⓑ Ⓒ Ⓓ	136 Ⓐ Ⓑ Ⓒ Ⓓ	146 Ⓐ Ⓑ Ⓒ Ⓓ	156 Ⓐ Ⓑ Ⓒ Ⓓ	166 Ⓐ Ⓑ Ⓒ Ⓓ	176 Ⓐ Ⓑ Ⓒ Ⓓ	186 Ⓐ Ⓑ Ⓒ Ⓓ	196 Ⓐ Ⓑ Ⓒ Ⓓ
107 Ⓐ Ⓑ Ⓒ Ⓓ	117 Ⓐ Ⓑ Ⓒ Ⓓ	127 Ⓐ Ⓑ Ⓒ Ⓓ	137 Ⓐ Ⓑ Ⓒ Ⓓ	147 Ⓐ Ⓑ Ⓒ Ⓓ	157 Ⓐ Ⓑ Ⓒ Ⓓ	167 Ⓐ Ⓑ Ⓒ Ⓓ	177 Ⓐ Ⓑ Ⓒ Ⓓ	187 Ⓐ Ⓑ Ⓒ Ⓓ	197 Ⓐ Ⓑ Ⓒ Ⓓ
108 Ⓐ Ⓑ Ⓒ Ⓓ	118 Ⓐ Ⓑ Ⓒ Ⓓ	128 Ⓐ Ⓑ Ⓒ Ⓓ	138 Ⓐ Ⓑ Ⓒ Ⓓ	148 Ⓐ Ⓑ Ⓒ Ⓓ	158 Ⓐ Ⓑ Ⓒ Ⓓ	168 Ⓐ Ⓑ Ⓒ Ⓓ	178 Ⓐ Ⓑ Ⓒ Ⓓ	188 Ⓐ Ⓑ Ⓒ Ⓓ	198 Ⓐ Ⓑ Ⓒ Ⓓ
109 Ⓐ Ⓑ Ⓒ Ⓓ	119 Ⓐ Ⓑ Ⓒ Ⓓ	129 Ⓐ Ⓑ Ⓒ Ⓓ	139 Ⓐ Ⓑ Ⓒ Ⓓ	149 Ⓐ Ⓑ Ⓒ Ⓓ	159 Ⓐ Ⓑ Ⓒ Ⓓ	169 Ⓐ Ⓑ Ⓒ Ⓓ	179 Ⓐ Ⓑ Ⓒ Ⓓ	189 Ⓐ Ⓑ Ⓒ Ⓓ	199 Ⓐ Ⓑ Ⓒ Ⓓ
110 Ⓐ Ⓑ Ⓒ Ⓓ	120 Ⓐ Ⓑ Ⓒ Ⓓ	130 Ⓐ Ⓑ Ⓒ Ⓓ	140 Ⓐ Ⓑ Ⓒ Ⓓ	150 Ⓐ Ⓑ Ⓒ Ⓓ	160 Ⓐ Ⓑ Ⓒ Ⓓ	170 Ⓐ Ⓑ Ⓒ Ⓓ	180 Ⓐ Ⓑ Ⓒ Ⓓ	190 Ⓐ Ⓑ Ⓒ Ⓓ	200 Ⓐ Ⓑ Ⓒ Ⓓ

Answers

Actual Test 01

101 (B)	121 (D)	141 (B)	161 (D)	181 (D)
102 (A)	122 (B)	142 (D)	162 (A)	182 (A)
103 (B)	123 (B)	143 (B)	163 (A)	183 (D)
104 (C)	124 (B)	144 (B)	164 (D)	184 (B)
105 (D)	125 (C)	145 (D)	165 (B)	185 (D)
106 (D)	126 (C)	146 (C)	166 (B)	186 (C)
107 (D)	127 (B)	147 (B)	167 (A)	187 (D)
108 (B)	128 (B)	148 (C)	168 (A)	188 (A)
109 (C)	129 (D)	149 (A)	169 (A)	189 (D)
110 (A)	130 (A)	150 (D)	170 (B)	190 (D)
111 (C)	131 (A)	151 (C)	171 (D)	191 (C)
112 (D)	132 (B)	152 (A)	172 (C)	192 (A)
113 (A)	133 (C)	153 (D)	173 (B)	193 (C)
114 (B)	134 (D)	154 (B)	174 (B)	194 (D)
115 (C)	135 (C)	155 (A)	175 (C)	195 (D)
116 (C)	136 (D)	156 (C)	176 (B)	196 (A)
117 (D)	137 (C)	157 (B)	177 (D)	197 (C)
118 (D)	138 (A)	158 (A)	178 (D)	198 (D)
119 (B)	139 (C)	159 (C)	179 (D)	199 (B)
120 (B)	140 (A)	160 (A)	180 (A)	200 (A)

Actual Test 02

101 (A)	121 (A)	141 (D)	161 (B)	181 (C)
102 (B)	122 (D)	142 (C)	162 (A)	182 (D)
103 (D)	123 (C)	143 (D)	163 (C)	183 (B)
104 (C)	124 (D)	144 (A)	164 (C)	184 (D)
105 (B)	125 (D)	145 (D)	165 (D)	185 (A)
106 (C)	126 (A)	146 (C)	166 (B)	186 (A)
107 (C)	127 (A)	147 (A)	167 (A)	187 (A)
108 (A)	128 (A)	148 (A)	168 (D)	188 (B)
109 (C)	129 (B)	149 (C)	169 (D)	189 (A)
110 (D)	130 (A)	150 (C)	170 (A)	190 (C)
111 (B)	131 (D)	151 (C)	171 (C)	191 (C)
112 (A)	132 (C)	152 (A)	172 (A)	192 (B)
113 (D)	133 (C)	153 (A)	173 (B)	193 (D)
114 (B)	134 (A)	154 (D)	174 (B)	194 (A)
115 (D)	135 (C)	155 (A)	175 (A)	195 (D)
116 (B)	136 (B)	156 (A)	176 (C)	196 (D)
117 (C)	137 (D)	157 (B)	177 (B)	197 (D)
118 (B)	138 (C)	158 (C)	178 (B)	198 (B)
119 (D)	139 (B)	159 (A)	179 (B)	199 (A)
120 (C)	140 (A)	160 (A)	180 (A)	200 (C)

Actual Test 03

101 (C)	121 (D)	141 (D)	161 (B)	181 (A)
102 (D)	122 (D)	142 (A)	162 (C)	182 (D)
103 (B)	123 (D)	143 (C)	163 (A)	183 (D)
104 (D)	124 (B)	144 (A)	164 (B)	184 (A)
105 (A)	125 (C)	145 (D)	165 (A)	185 (A)
106 (B)	126 (D)	146 (C)	166 (A)	186 (A)
107 (C)	127 (B)	147 (B)	167 (B)	187 (C)
108 (D)	128 (B)	148 (D)	168 (B)	188 (B)
109 (A)	129 (A)	149 (D)	169 (B)	189 (D)
110 (A)	130 (A)	150 (A)	170 (C)	190 (A)
111 (B)	131 (A)	151 (A)	171 (A)	191 (D)
112 (C)	132 (B)	152 (C)	172 (A)	192 (C)
113 (B)	133 (D)	153 (D)	173 (A)	193 (B)
114 (A)	134 (A)	154 (A)	174 (C)	194 (A)
115 (D)	135 (A)	155 (B)	175 (A)	195 (D)
116 (D)	136 (D)	156 (A)	176 (D)	196 (C)
117 (B)	137 (B)	157 (B)	177 (A)	197 (C)
118 (D)	138 (B)	158 (D)	178 (C)	198 (D)
119 (B)	139 (A)	159 (A)	179 (B)	199 (B)
120 (C)	140 (B)	160 (C)	180 (D)	200 (C)

Actual Test 04

101 (A)	121 (D)	141 (C)	161 (B)	181 (B)
102 (A)	122 (B)	142 (C)	162 (B)	182 (A)
103 (C)	123 (D)	143 (D)	163 (A)	183 (D)
104 (B)	124 (C)	144 (D)	164 (D)	184 (C)
105 (B)	125 (C)	145 (B)	165 (B)	185 (B)
106 (D)	126 (C)	146 (C)	166 (C)	186 (A)
107 (A)	127 (D)	147 (C)	167 (B)	187 (B)
108 (C)	128 (C)	148 (B)	168 (B)	188 (D)
109 (C)	129 (A)	149 (D)	169 (A)	189 (D)
110 (B)	130 (B)	150 (D)	170 (D)	190 (C)
111 (A)	131 (B)	151 (B)	171 (A)	191 (D)
112 (C)	132 (D)	152 (D)	172 (B)	192 (B)
113 (D)	133 (C)	153 (A)	173 (C)	193 (D)
114 (B)	134 (A)	154 (D)	174 (D)	194 (C)
115 (D)	135 (D)	155 (B)	175 (A)	195 (D)
116 (C)	136 (A)	156 (D)	176 (D)	196 (C)
117 (A)	137 (C)	157 (D)	177 (D)	197 (D)
118 (B)	138 (A)	158 (B)	178 (B)	198 (B)
119 (A)	139 (C)	159 (B)	179 (C)	199 (C)
120 (B)	140 (A)	160 (A)	180 (A)	200 (D)

Actual Test 05

101 (A)	121 (B)	141 (A)	161 (A)	181 (A)
102 (A)	122 (C)	142 (B)	162 (A)	182 (A)
103 (C)	123 (B)	143 (B)	163 (B)	183 (C)
104 (B)	124 (D)	144 (C)	164 (B)	184 (B)
105 (D)	125 (B)	145 (B)	165 (A)	185 (D)
106 (B)	126 (D)	146 (D)	166 (A)	186 (C)
107 (C)	127 (B)	147 (A)	167 (D)	187 (A)
108 (C)	128 (A)	148 (B)	168 (B)	188 (C)
109 (D)	129 (A)	149 (D)	169 (B)	189 (D)
110 (B)	130 (A)	150 (C)	170 (D)	190 (B)
111 (C)	131 (C)	151 (B)	171 (A)	191 (D)
112 (C)	132 (A)	152 (D)	172 (C)	192 (B)
113 (C)	133 (A)	153 (D)	173 (B)	193 (C)
114 (B)	134 (D)	154 (D)	174 (C)	194 (B)
115 (A)	135 (D)	155 (A)	175 (C)	195 (B)
116 (D)	136 (D)	156 (C)	176 (B)	196 (D)
117 (B)	137 (A)	157 (C)	177 (D)	197 (B)
118 (A)	138 (B)	158 (D)	178 (C)	198 (C)
119 (B)	139 (D)	159 (B)	179 (D)	199 (C)
120 (B)	140 (B)	160 (B)	180 (B)	200 (B)

Actual Test 06

101 (C)	121 (C)	141 (B)	161 (A)	181 (D)
102 (C)	122 (A)	142 (A)	162 (D)	182 (B)
103 (B)	123 (C)	143 (C)	163 (B)	183 (A)
104 (A)	124 (B)	144 (B)	164 (C)	184 (C)
105 (D)	125 (B)	145 (D)	165 (D)	185 (B)
106 (A)	126 (B)	146 (C)	166 (D)	186 (B)
107 (C)	127 (A)	147 (A)	167 (D)	187 (D)
108 (D)	128 (B)	148 (D)	168 (B)	188 (C)
109 (B)	129 (D)	149 (B)	169 (A)	189 (C)
110 (D)	130 (A)	150 (B)	170 (D)	190 (D)
111 (A)	131 (C)	151 (B)	171 (D)	191 (C)
112 (A)	132 (D)	152 (A)	172 (B)	192 (A)
113 (D)	133 (C)	153 (D)	173 (B)	193 (B)
114 (D)	134 (C)	154 (B)	174 (A)	194 (D)
115 (B)	135 (C)	155 (A)	175 (C)	195 (D)
116 (B)	136 (A)	156 (D)	176 (B)	196 (C)
117 (D)	137 (D)	157 (B)	177 (D)	197 (A)
118 (D)	138 (A)	158 (B)	178 (A)	198 (B)
119 (B)	139 (B)	159 (D)	179 (C)	199 (A)
120 (B)	140 (A)	160 (D)	180 (B)	200 (A)

Actual Test 07

101 (C)	121 (B)	141 (C)	161 (C)	181 (A)
102 (A)	122 (D)	142 (B)	162 (B)	182 (D)
103 (B)	123 (D)	143 (B)	163 (D)	183 (C)
104 (D)	124 (C)	144 (A)	164 (A)	184 (A)
105 (A)	125 (A)	145 (A)	165 (B)	185 (A)
106 (B)	126 (A)	146 (D)	166 (C)	186 (B)
107 (B)	127 (B)	147 (D)	167 (A)	187 (D)
108 (C)	128 (D)	148 (A)	168 (C)	188 (A)
109 (A)	129 (D)	149 (C)	169 (C)	189 (D)
110 (C)	130 (B)	150 (D)	170 (B)	190 (B)
111 (B)	131 (D)	151 (B)	171 (D)	191 (A)
112 (C)	132 (B)	152 (D)	172 (D)	192 (D)
113 (D)	133 (C)	153 (D)	173 (C)	193 (C)
114 (B)	134 (A)	154 (A)	174 (D)	194 (B)
115 (C)	135 (C)	155 (D)	175 (D)	195 (B)
116 (D)	136 (A)	156 (A)	176 (B)	196 (B)
117 (B)	137 (C)	157 (B)	177 (A)	197 (D)
118 (C)	138 (B)	158 (D)	178 (A)	198 (A)
119 (B)	139 (B)	159 (B)	179 (C)	199 (D)
120 (C)	140 (A)	160 (B)	180 (A)	200 (A)

Actual Test 08

101 (D)	121 (B)	141 (A)	161 (A)	181 (B)
102 (D)	122 (D)	142 (B)	162 (D)	182 (C)
103 (B)	123 (A)	143 (C)	163 (C)	183 (A)
104 (B)	124 (C)	144 (A)	164 (A)	184 (C)
105 (A)	125 (B)	145 (D)	165 (B)	185 (B)
106 (D)	126 (D)	146 (B)	166 (D)	186 (D)
107 (A)	127 (A)	147 (A)	167 (D)	187 (D)
108 (C)	128 (C)	148 (A)	168 (A)	188 (A)
109 (A)	129 (D)	149 (C)	169 (C)	189 (A)
110 (A)	130 (D)	150 (A)	170 (C)	190 (C)
111 (B)	131 (D)	151 (B)	171 (D)	191 (B)
112 (C)	132 (A)	152 (A)	172 (B)	192 (A)
113 (D)	133 (D)	153 (B)	173 (B)	193 (C)
114 (B)	134 (B)	154 (D)	174 (C)	194 (D)
115 (B)	135 (C)	155 (C)	175 (B)	195 (D)
116 (D)	136 (A)	156 (D)	176 (D)	196 (B)
117 (B)	137 (A)	157 (C)	177 (A)	197 (D)
118 (B)	138 (D)	158 (B)	178 (B)	198 (C)
119 (A)	139 (D)	159 (B)	179 (C)	199 (A)
120 (C)	140 (D)	160 (A)	180 (A)	200 (A)

Actual Test 09

101 (A)	121 (C)	141 (C)	161 (C)	181 (D)
102 (C)	122 (D)	142 (B)	162 (B)	182 (C)
103 (A)	123 (C)	143 (C)	163 (C)	183 (B)
104 (C)	124 (D)	144 (A)	164 (B)	184 (C)
105 (A)	125 (D)	145 (D)	165 (A)	185 (B)
106 (D)	126 (C)	146 (B)	166 (D)	186 (A)
107 (C)	127 (B)	147 (B)	167 (C)	187 (D)
108 (D)	128 (A)	148 (B)	168 (A)	188 (A)
109 (B)	129 (A)	149 (A)	169 (D)	189 (C)
110 (A)	130 (B)	150 (A)	170 (D)	190 (D)
111 (D)	131 (C)	151 (D)	171 (C)	191 (A)
112 (B)	132 (D)	152 (B)	172 (A)	192 (D)
113 (A)	133 (A)	153 (A)	173 (A)	193 (A)
114 (D)	134 (A)	154 (D)	174 (D)	194 (D)
115 (D)	135 (C)	155 (D)	175 (B)	195 (C)
116 (D)	136 (B)	156 (C)	176 (D)	196 (C)
117 (A)	137 (A)	157 (C)	177 (A)	197 (B)
118 (B)	138 (C)	158 (D)	178 (B)	198 (B)
119 (B)	139 (D)	159 (A)	179 (D)	199 (B)
120 (A)	140 (A)	160 (B)	180 (D)	200 (C)

Actual Test 10

101 (B)	121 (A)	141 (B)	161 (B)	181 (C)
102 (D)	122 (C)	142 (D)	162 (C)	182 (A)
103 (C)	123 (C)	143 (C)	163 (C)	183 (D)
104 (C)	124 (B)	144 (C)	164 (A)	184 (B)
105 (C)	125 (B)	145 (A)	165 (A)	185 (D)
106 (D)	126 (D)	146 (A)	166 (D)	186 (A)
107 (C)	127 (C)	147 (B)	167 (D)	187 (C)
108 (A)	128 (C)	148 (D)	168 (A)	188 (A)
109 (D)	129 (B)	149 (C)	169 (C)	189 (D)
110 (B)	130 (A)	150 (A)	170 (C)	190 (B)
111 (D)	131 (D)	151 (B)	171 (B)	191 (C)
112 (A)	132 (A)	152 (C)	172 (D)	192 (B)
113 (C)	133 (B)	153 (A)	173 (D)	193 (C)
114 (D)	134 (C)	154 (B)	174 (B)	194 (A)
115 (B)	135 (B)	155 (C)	175 (A)	195 (A)
116 (A)	136 (B)	156 (C)	176 (A)	196 (B)
117 (A)	137 (D)	157 (A)	177 (A)	197 (B)
118 (D)	138 (A)	158 (C)	178 (D)	198 (D)
119 (C)	139 (B)	159 (B)	179 (D)	199 (A)
120 (B)	140 (D)	160 (B)	180 (C)	200 (D)

多益分數換算表

聽力測驗		閱讀測驗	
答對題數	分數	答對題數	分數
96 ~ 100	480 ~ 495	96 ~ 100	450 ~ 495
91 ~ 95	470 ~ 495	91 ~ 95	420 ~ 465
86 ~ 90	440 ~ 490	86 ~ 90	400 ~ 435
81 ~ 85	410 ~ 460	81 ~ 85	370 ~ 410
76 ~ 80	390 ~ 430	76 ~ 80	340 ~ 380
71 ~ 75	360 ~ 400	71 ~ 75	310 ~ 355
66 ~ 70	330 ~ 370	66 ~ 70	280 ~ 325
61 ~ 65	300 ~ 345	61 ~ 65	260 ~ 300
56 ~ 60	270 ~ 315	56 ~ 60	230 ~ 270
51 ~ 55	240 ~ 285	51 ~ 55	200 ~ 245
46 ~ 50	210 ~ 255	46 ~ 50	170 ~ 215
41 ~ 45	180 ~ 225	41 ~ 45	140 ~ 185
36 ~ 40	150 ~ 195	36 ~ 40	120 ~ 160
31 ~ 35	120 ~ 165	31 ~ 35	90 ~ 130
26 ~ 30	90 ~ 135	26 ~ 30	60 ~ 105
21 ~ 25	60 ~ 105	21 ~ 25	30 ~ 75
16 ~ 20	40 ~ 75	16 ~ 20	10 ~ 50
11 ~ 15	10 ~ 45	11 ~ 15	5 ~ 20
6 ~ 10	5 ~ 20	6 ~ 10	5
1 ~ 5	5	1 ~ 5	5
0	0	0	0

註：上述表格僅供參考，實際計分以官方分數為準。

新制多益
閱讀 滿分奪金演練
1000 題練出黃金應試力

作　　者	PAGODA Academy
譯　　者	劉嘉珮／蘇裕承／關亭薇
編　　輯	陳彥臻
主　　編	丁宥暄
校　　對	黃詩韻
內文排版	林書玉／蔡怡柔
封面設計	林書玉
製程管理	洪巧玲
出 版 者	寂天文化事業股份有限公司
發 行 人	黃朝萍
電　　話	+886-(0)2-2365-9739
傳　　真	+886-(0)2-2365-9835
網　　址	www.icosmos.com.tw
讀者服務	onlineservice@icosmos.com.tw
出版日期	2021 年 9 月 初版一刷

國家圖書館出版品預行編目 (CIP) 資料

新制多益閱讀滿分奪金演練：1000 題練出黃金應試力 / PAGODA Academy 著；劉嘉珮, 蘇裕承, 關亭薇譯 . -- 初版 . -- 臺北市：寂天文化事業股份有限公司，2021.09

　面；　公分

ISBN 978-626-300-009-4（平裝）

1. 多益測驗

805.1895　　　　　　　　110006154

파고다 토익 적중 실전 RC Vol. 1

Copyright © 2019 by PAGODA Academy

All rights reserved.

Traditional Chinese Copyright © 2021 by Cosmos Culture Ltd.

This Traditional Chinese edition was published by arrangement with PAGODA SCS, Inc.

(Wit&Wisdom) through Agency Liang